REVELATION SPACE

Alastair Reynolds

An Orion paperback

First published in Great Britain in 2000
by Gollancz
This paperback edition published in 2012
by Orion Books Ltd,
Orion House, 5 Upper St Martin's Lane,
London WC2H 9EA

An Hachette UK company

10 9 8 7 6 5 4 3 2 1

A CIP catalogue record for this book
is available from the British Library

ISBN 978-1-4091-3845-7

Typeset by Deltatype Ltd, Birkenhead, Merseyside

Printed and bound in the UK by
Clays Ltd, St Ives plc

The Orion Publishing Group's policy is to use papers that
are natural, renewable and recyclable products and made
from wood grown in sustainable forests. The logging and
manufacturing processes are expected to conform to the
environmental regulations of the country of origin.

www.orionbooks.co.uk

ONE

There was a razorstorm coming in.

Sylveste stood on the edge of the excavation and wondered if any of his labours would survive the night. The archaeological dig was an array of deep square shafts separated by baulks of sheer-sided soil: the classical Wheeler box-grid. The shafts went down tens of metres, walled by transparent cofferdams spun from hyperdiamond. A million years of stratified geological history pressed against the sheets. But it would take only one good dustfall – one good razorstorm – to fill the shafts almost to the surface.

'Confirmation, sir,' said one of his team, emerging from the crouched form of the first crawler. The man's voice was muffled behind his breather mask. 'Cuvier's just issued a severe weather advisory for the whole North Nekhebet landmass. They're advising all surface teams to return to the nearest base.'

'You're saying we should pack up and drive back to Mantell?'

'It's going to be a hard one, sir.' The man fidgeted, drawing the collar of his jacket tighter around his neck. 'Shall I issue the general evacuation order?'

Sylveste looked down at the excavation grid, the sides of each shaft brightly lit by the banks of floodlights arrayed around the area. Pavonis never got high enough at these latitudes to provide much useful illumination; now, sinking towards the horizon and clotted by great cauls of dust, it was little more than a rusty-red smear, hard for his eyes to focus on. Soon dust devils would come, scurrying across the Ptero Steppes like so many overwound toy gyroscopes. Then the main thrust of the storm, rising like a black anvil.

'No,' he said. 'There's no need for us to leave. We're well sheltered here – there's hardly any erosion pattering on those

1

boulders, in case you hadn't noticed. If the storm becomes too harsh, we'll shelter in the crawlers.'

The man looked at the rocks, shaking his head as if doubting the evidence of his ears. 'Sir, Cuvier only issue an advisory of this severity once every year or two – it's an order of magnitude above anything we've experienced before.'

'Speak for yourself,' Sylveste said, noticing the way the man's gaze snapped involuntarily to his eyes and then off again, embarrassed. 'Listen to me. We cannot afford to abandon this dig. Do you understand?'

The man looked back at the grid. 'We can protect what we've uncovered with sheeting, sir. Then bury transponders. Even if the dust covers every shaft, we'll be able to find the site again and get back to where we are now.' Behind his dust goggles, the man's eyes were wild, beseeching. 'When we return, we can put a dome over the whole grid. Wouldn't that be the best, sir, rather than risk people and equipment out here?'

Sylveste took a step closer to the man, forcing him to step back towards the grid's closest shaft. 'You're to do the following. Inform all dig teams that they carry on working until I say otherwise, and that there is to be no talk of retreating to Mantell. Meanwhile, I want only the most sensitive instruments taken aboard the crawlers. Is that understood?'

'But what about people, sir?'

'People are to do what they came out here to do. Dig.'

Sylveste stared reproachfully at the man, almost inviting him to question the order, but after a long moment of hesitation the man turned on his heels and scurried across the grid, navigating the tops of the baulks with practised ease. Spaced around the grid like down-pointed cannon, the delicate imaging gravitometers swayed slightly as the wind began to increase.

Sylveste waited, then followed a similar path, deviating when he was a few boxes into the grid. Near the centre of the excavation, four boxes had been enlarged into one single slab-sided pit, thirty metres from side to side and nearly as deep. Sylveste stepped onto the ladder which led into the pit and moved quickly down the side. He had made the journey up and down this ladder so many times in the last few weeks that the lack of vertigo was almost more disturbing than the thing itself. Moving down the cofferdam's side, he descended through layers of geological time. Nine hundred thousand years had passed since the Event. Most of that stratification was permafrost – typical in Resurgam's subpolar latitudes; permanent frost-soil which never thawed. Deeper down – close to the Event itself – was a layer of regolith laid down in the impacts which had followed. The Event itself was a single, hair-fine black demarcation – the ash of burning forests.

The floor of the pit was not level, but followed narrowing steps down to a final depth of forty metres below the surface. Extra floods had been brought down to shine light into the gloom. The cramped area was a fantastical hive of activity, and within the shelter of the pit there was no trace of the wind. The dig team was working in near-silence, kneeling on the ground on mats, working away at something with tools so precise they might have served for surgery in another era. Three were young students from Cuvier – born on Resurgam. A servitor skulked beside them awaiting orders. Though machines had their uses during a dig's early phases, the final work could never be entirely trusted to them. Next to the party a woman sat with a compad balanced on her lap, displaying a cladistic map of Amarantin skulls. She saw Sylveste for the first time – he had climbed quietly – and stood up with a start, snapping shut the compad. She wore a greatcoat, her black hair cut in a geometric fringe across her brow.

'Well, you were right,' she said. 'Whatever it is, it's big. And it looks amazingly well-preserved, too.'

'Any theories, Pascale?'

'That's where you come in, isn't it? I'm just here to offer commentary.' Pascale Dubois was a young journalist from Cuvier. She had been covering the dig since its inception, often dirtying her fingers with the real archaeologists, learning their cant. 'The bodies are gruesome, though, aren't they? Even though they're alien, it's almost as if you can feel their pain.'

To one side of the pit, just before the floor stepped down, they had unearthed two stone-lined burial chambers. Despite being buried for nine hundred thousand years – at the very least – the chambers were almost intact, with the bones inside still assuming a rough anatomical relationship to one another. They were typical Amarantin skeletons. At first glance – to anyone who happened not to be a trained anthropologist – they could have passed as human remains, for the creatures had been four-limbed bipeds of roughly human size, with a superficially similar bone-structure.

Skull volume was comparable, and the organs of sense, breathing and communication were situated in analogous positions. But the skulls of both Amarantin were elongated and birdlike, with a prominent cranial ridge which extended forwards between the voluminous eye-sockets, down to the tip of the beaklike upper jaw. The bones were covered here and there by a skein of tanned, desiccated tissue which had served to contort the bodies, drawing them – or so it seemed – into agonised postures. They were not fossils in the usual sense: no mineralisation had taken place, and the burial chambers had remained empty except for the bones and the handful of technomic artefacts with which they had been buried.

'Perhaps,' Sylveste said, reaching down and touching one of the skulls, 'we were meant to think that.'

'No,' Pascale said. 'As the tissue dried, it distorted them.'

'Unless they were buried like this.'

Feeling the skull through his gloves – they transmitted tactile data to his fingertips – he was reminded of a yellow room high in Chasm City, with aquatints of methane icescapes on the walls. There had been liveried servitors moving through the guests with sweetmeats and liqueurs; drapes of coloured crêpe spanning the belvedered ceiling; the air bright with sickly entoptics in the current vogue: seraphim, cherubim, hummingbirds, fairies. He remembered guests: most of them associates of the family; people he either barely recognised or detested, for his friends had been few in number. His father had been late as usual; the party already winding down by the time Calvin deigned to show up. This was normal then; the time of Calvin's last and greatest project, and the realisation of it was in itself a slow death; no less so than the suicide he would bring upon himself at the project's culmination.

He remembered his father producing a box, its sides bearing a marquetry of entwined ribonucleic strands.

'Open it,' Calvin had said.

He remembered taking it; feeling its lightness. He had snatched the top off to reveal a bird's nest of fibrous packing material. Within was a speckled brown dome the same colour as the box. It was the upper part of a skull, obviously human, with the jaw missing.

He remembered a silence falling across the room.

'Is that all?' Sylveste had said, just loud enough so that everyone in the room heard it. 'An old bone? Well, thanks, Dad. I'm humbled.'

'As well you should be,' Calvin said.

And the trouble was, as Sylveste had realised almost immediately, Calvin was right. The skull was incredibly valuable; two hundred thousand years old – a woman from Atapuerca, Spain, he soon learned. Her time of death had been obvious enough from the context in which she was buried, but the scientists who had unearthed her had refined the estimate using the best techniques of their day: potassium-argon dating of the rocks in the cave where she'd been buried, uranium-series dating of travertine deposits on the walls, fission-track dating of volcanic glasses, thermoluminescence dating of burnt flint fragments. They were techniques which – with improvements in calibration and application – remained in use among the dig teams on Resurgam. Physics allowed only so many methods to date objects. Sylveste should have seen all that in an instant and recognised the skull for what it was: the oldest human object on Yellowstone, carried to the Epsilon Eridani system centuries earlier, and then lost during the colony's upheavals. Calvin's unearthing of it was a small miracle in itself.

Yet the flush of shame he felt stemmed less from ingratitude than from the way he had allowed his ignorance to unmask itself, when it could have been so easily concealed. It was a weakness he would never allow himself again. Years later, the skull had travelled with him to Resurgam, to remind him always of that vow.

He could not fail now.

'If what you're implying is the case,' Pascale said, 'then they must have been buried like that for a reason.'

'Maybe as a warning,' Sylveste said, and stepped down towards the three students.

'I was afraid you might say something like that,' Pascale said, following him. 'And what exactly might this terrible warning have concerned?'

Her question was largely rhetorical, as Sylveste well knew. She understood exactly what he believed about the Amarantin. She also seemed to enjoy needling him about those beliefs; as if by forcing him to state them repeatedly, she might eventually cause him to expose some logical error in his own theories; one that even he would have to admit undermined the whole argument.

'The Event,' Sylveste said, fingering the fine black line behind the nearest cofferdam as he spoke.

'The Event happened to the Amarantin,' Pascale said. 'It wasn't anything they had any say in. And it happened quickly, too. They didn't have time to go about burying bodies in dire warning, even if they'd had any idea about what was happening to them.'

'They angered the gods,' Sylveste said.

'Yes,' Pascale said. 'I think we all agree that they would have interpreted the Event as evidence of theistic displeasure, within the constraints of their belief system – but there wouldn't have been time to express that belief in any permanent form before they all died, much less bury bodies for the benefit of future archaeologists from a different species.' She lifted her hood over her head and tightened the drawstring – fine plumes of dust were starting to settle down into the pit, and the air was no longer as still as it had been a few minutes earlier. 'But you don't think so, do you?' Without waiting for an answer, she fixed a large pair of bulky goggles over her eyes, momentarily disturbing the edge of her fringe, and looked down at the object which was slowly being uncovered.

Pascale's goggles accessed data from the imaging gravitometers stationed around the Wheeler grid, overlaying the stereoscopic picture of buried masses on the normal view. Sylveste had only to instruct his eyes to do likewise. The ground on which they were standing turned glassy, insubstantial – a smoky matrix in which something huge lay entombed. It was an obelisk – a single huge block of shaped rock, itself encased in a series of stone sarcophagi. The obelisk was twenty metres tall. The dig had exposed only a few centimetres of the top. There was evidence of writing down one side, in one of the standard late-phase Amarantin graphicforms. But the imaging gravitometers lacked the spatial resolution to reveal the text. The obelisk would have to be dug out before they could learn anything.

Sylveste told his eyes to return to normal vision. 'Work faster,' he told his students. 'I don't care if you incur minor abrasions to the surface. I want at least a metre of it visible by the end of tonight.'

One of the students turned to him, still kneeling. 'Sir, we heard the dig would have to be abandoned.'

'Why on earth would I abandon a dig?'

'The storm, sir.'

'Damn the storm.' He was turning away when Pascale took his arm, a little too roughly.

'They're right to be worried, Dan.' She spoke quietly, for his benefit alone. 'I heard about that advisory, too. We should•be heading back toward Mantell.'

'And lose this?'

'We'll come back again.'

'We might never find it, even if we bury a transponder.' He knew he was right: the position of the dig was uncertain and maps of this area were not particularly detailed; compiled quickly when the *Lorean* had made orbit from Yellowstone forty years earlier. Ever since the comsat girdle had been destroyed in the mutiny, twenty years later – when half the colonists elected to steal the ship and return home – there had been no accurate way of determining position on Resurgam. And many a transponder had simply failed in a razorstorm.

'It's still not worth risking human lives for,' Pascale said.

'It might be worth much more than that.' He snapped a finger at the students. 'Faster. Use the servitor if you must. I want to see the top of that obelisk by dawn.'

Sluka, his senior research student, muttered a word under her breath.

'Something to contribute?' Sylveste asked.

Sluka stood for what must have been the first time in hours. He could see the tension in her eyes. The little spatula she had been using dropped on the ground, beside the mukluks she wore on her feet. She snatched the mask away from her face, breathing Resurgam air for a few seconds while she spoke. 'We need to talk.'

'About what, Sluka?'

Sluka gulped down air from the mask before speaking again. 'You're pushing your luck, Dr Sylveste.'

'You've just pushed yours over the precipice.'

She seemed not to have heard him. 'We care about your work, you know. We share your beliefs. That's why we're here, breaking our backs for you. But you shouldn't take us for granted.' Her eyes flashed white arcs, glancing towards Pascale. 'Right now you need all the allies you can find, Dr Sylveste.'

'That's a threat, is it?'

'A statement of fact. If you paid more attention to what was going on elsewhere in the colony, you'd know that Girardieau's planning to move against you. The word is that move's a hell of a lot closer than you think.'

The back of his neck prickled. 'What are you talking about?'

'What else? A coup.' Sluka pushed past him to ascend the ladder up the side of the pit. When she had a foot on the first rung, she turned back and addressed the other two students, both minding their own business, heads down in concentration as they worked to reveal the obelisk. 'Work for as long as you want, but don't say no one warned you. And if you've any doubts as to what being caught in a razorstorm is like, take a look at Sylveste.'

One of the students looked up, timidly. 'Where are you going, Sluka?'

'To speak to the other dig teams. Not everyone may know about that advisory. When they hear, I don't think many of them will be in any hurry to stay.'

She started climbing, but Sylveste reached up and grabbed the heel of her mukluk. Sluka looked down at him. She was wearing the mask now, but Sylveste could still see the contempt in her expression. 'You're finished, Sluka.'

'No,' she said, climbing. 'I've just begun. It's you I'd worry about.'

Sylveste examined his own state of mind and found – it was the last thing he had expected – total calm. But it was like the calm that existed on the metallic hydrogen oceans of the gas giant planets further out from Pavonis – only maintained by crushing pressures from above and below.

'Well?' Pascale said.

'There's someone I need to talk to,' Sylveste said.

Sylveste climbed the ramp into his crawler. The other was crammed with equipment racks and sample containers, with hammocks for his students pressed into the tiny niches of unoccupied space. They had to sleep aboard the machines because some of the digs in the sector – like this one – were over a day's travel from Mantell itself. Sylveste's crawler was considerably better appointed, with over a third of the interior dedicated to his own stateroom and quarters. The rest of the machine was taken up with additional payload space and a couple of more modest quarters for his senior workers or guests: in this case Sluka and Pascale. Now, however, he had the whole crawler to himself.

The stateroom's décor belied the fact that it was aboard a crawler. It was walled in red velvet, the shelves dotted with facsimile scientific instruments and relics. There were large, elegantly annotated Mercator maps of Resurgam dotted with the sites of major Amarantin finds; other areas of wall were covered in slowly updating texts: academic papers in preparation. His own beta-level was doing most of the scut-work on the papers now; Sylveste had trained the simulation to the point where it could imitate his style more reliably than he could, given the current distractions. Later, if there was time, he would need to proof those texts, but for now he gave them no more than a glance as he moved to the room's escritoire. The ornate writing desk was decorated in marble and malachite, inset with japanwork scenes of early space exploration.

Sylveste opened a drawer and removed a simulation cartridge, an unmarked grey slab, like a ceramic tile. There was a slot in the escritoire's upper surface. He would only have to insert the cartridge to invoke Calvin. He hesitated, nonetheless. It had been some time – months, at least – since he had brought Calvin back from the dead, and that last encounter had gone spectacularly badly. He had promised himself he would only invoke Calvin again in the event of crisis. Now it was a matter of judging whether the crisis had really arrived – and if it was sufficiently troublesome to justify an invocation. The problem with Calvin was that his advice was only reliable about half the time.

Sylveste pressed the cartridge into the escritoire.

Fairies wove a figure out of light in the middle of the room: Calvin seated in a vast seigneurial chair. The apparition was more realistic than any hologram – even down to subtle shadowing effects – since it was being generated by direct manipulation of Sylveste's visual field. The beta-level simulation represented Calvin the way fame best remembered him, as he had been when he was barely fifty years old, in his heyday on Yellowstone. Strangely, he looked older than Sylveste, even though the image of Calvin was twenty years younger in physiological terms. Sylveste was eight years into his third century, but the longevity treatments he had received on Yellowstone had been more advanced than any available in Calvin's time.

Other than that, their features and build were the same, both of them possessing a permanent amused curve to the lips. Calvin wore his hair shorter and was dressed in Demarchist Belle Epoque finery, rather than the relative austerity of Sylveste's expeditionary dress: billowing frock shirt and elegantly chequered trousers hooked into buccaneer-boots, his fingers aglint with jewels and metal. His impeccably shaped beard was little more than a rust-coloured delineation along the line of his jaw. Small entoptics surrounded his seated figure, symbols of Boolean and three-valued logics and long cascades of binary. One hand fingered the bristles beneath his chin, while the other toyed with the carved scroll that ended the seat's armrest.

A wave of animation slithered over the projection, the pale eyes gaining a glisten of interest.

Calvin raised his fingers in lazy acknowledgement. 'So . . .' he said. 'The shit's about to match coordinates with the fan.'

'You presume a lot.'

'No need to presume anything, dear boy. I just tapped into the net and accessed the last few thousand news reports.' He craned his neck to survey the stateroom. 'Nice pad you've got here. How are the eyes, by the way?'

'They're functioning as well as can be expected.'

Calvin nodded. 'Resolution's not up to much, but that was the best I could do with the tools I was forced to work with. I probably only reconnected forty per cent of your optic nerve channels, so putting in better cameras would have been pointless. Now if you had halfway decent surgical equipment lying around on this planet, I could perhaps begin to do something. But you wouldn't give Michelangelo a toothbrush and expect a great Sistine Chapel.'

'Rub it in.'

'I wouldn't dream of it,' Calvin said, all innocence. 'I'm just saying that if you had to let her take the *Lorean*, couldn't you at least have persuaded Alicia to leave us some medical equipment?'

His wife had led the mutiny against him twenty years earlier; a fact Calvin never allowed Sylveste to forget.

'So I made a kind of self-sacrifice.' Sylveste waved an arm to silence the image. 'Sorry, but I didn't invoke you for a fireside chat, Cal.'

'I do wish you'd call me Father.'

Sylveste ignored him. 'Do you know where we are?'

'A dig, I presume.' Calvin closed his eyes briefly and touched his fingers against his temples, affecting concentration. 'Yes. Let me see. Two expeditionary crawlers out of Mantell, near the Ptero Steppes . . . a Wheeler grid . . . how inordinately quaint! Though I suppose it suits your purpose well enough. And what's this? High-res gravitometer sections . . . seismograms . . . you've actually found something, haven't you?'

At that moment the escritoire popped up a status fairy to tell him there was an incoming call from Mantell. Sylveste held a hand up to Calvin while he debated whether or not to accept the call. The person trying to reach him was Henry Janequin, a specialist in avian biology and one of Sylveste's few outright allies. But while Janequin had known the real Calvin, Sylveste was fairly sure he had never seen Calvin's beta-level . . . and most certainly not in the process of being solicited for advice by his son. The admission that he needed Cal's help – that he had even considered invoking the sim for this purpose – could be a crucial sign of weakness.

'What are you waiting for?' Cal said. 'Put him on.'

'He doesn't know about you . . . about us.'

Calvin shook his head, then – shockingly – Janequin appeared in the room. Sylveste fought to maintain his composure, but it was obvious what had just happened. Calvin must have found a way to send commands to the escritoire's private-level functions.

Calvin was and always had been a devious bastard, Sylveste thought. Ultimately that was why he remained of use.

Janequin's full-body projection was slightly less sharp than Calvin's, for Janequin's image was coming over the satellite network – patchy at best – from Mantell. And the cameras imaging him had probably seen better days, Sylveste thought – like much else on Resurgam.

'There you are,' Janequin said, noticing only Sylveste at first. 'I've been trying to reach you for the last hour. Don't you have a way of being alerted to incoming calls when you're down in the pit?'

'I do,' Sylveste said. 'But I turned it off. It was too distracting.'

'Oh,' Janequin said, with only the tiniest hint of annoyance. 'Very shrewd indeed. Especially for a man in your position. You realise what I'm talking about, of course. There's trouble afoot, Dan, perhaps more than you . . .' Then Janequin must have noticed Cal for the first time. He studied the figure in the chair for a moment before speaking. 'My word. It is you, isn't it?'

Cal nodded without saying a word.

'This is his beta-level simulation,' Sylveste said. It was important to clear that up before the conversation proceeded any further; alphas and betas were fundamentally different things and Stoner etiquette was very punctilious indeed about distinguishing between the two. Sylveste would have been guilty of an extreme social gaffe had he allowed Janequin to think that this was the long-lost alpha-level recording.

'I was consulting with him . . . with it,' Sylveste said.

Calvin pulled a face.

'About what?' Janequin said. He was an old man – the oldest person on Resurgam, in fact – and with each passing year his appearance seemed to approach fractionally closer to some simian ideal. His white hair, moustache and beard framed a small pink face in the manner of some rare marmoset. On Yellowstone, there had been no more talented expert in genetics outside of the Mixmasters, and there were some who rated Janequin a good deal cleverer than any in that sect, for all that his genius was of the undemonstrative sort, accumulating not in any flash of brilliance, but through years and years of quietly excellent work. He was well into his fourth century now, and layer upon layer of longevity treatment was beginning to crumble visibly. Sylveste supposed that before very long Janequin would be the first person on Resurgam to die of old age. The thought filled him with sadness. Though there was much upon which Janequin and he disagreed, they had always seen eye to eye on all the important things.

'He's found something,' Cal said.

Janequin's eyes brightened, years lifting off him in the joy of scientific discovery. 'Really?'

'Yes, I . . .' Then something else odd happened. The room was gone now. The three of them were standing on a balcony, high above what Sylveste instantly recognised as Chasm City. Calvin's doing again. The escritoire had followed them like an obedient dog. If Cal could access its private-level functions, Sylveste thought, he could also do this kind of trick, running one of the escritoire's standard environments. It was a good simulation, too: down to the slap of wind against Sylveste's cheek and the city's almost intangible smell, never easy to define but always obvious by its absence in more cheaply done environments.

It was the city from his childhood: the high Belle Epoque.

Awesome gold structures marched into the distance like sculpted clouds, buzzing with aerial traffic. Below, tiered parks and gardens stepped down in a series of dizzying vistas towards a verdant haze of greenery and light, kilometres beneath their feet.

'Isn't it great to see the old place?' Cal said. 'And to think that it was almost ours for the taking; so much within reach of our clan . . . who knows how we might have changed things, if we'd held the city's reins?'

Janequin steadied himself on the railing. 'Very nice, but I didn't come to sight-see, Calvin. Dan, what were you about to tell me before we were so . . .'

'Rudely interrupted?' Sylveste said. 'I was going to tell Cal to pull the gravitometer data from the escritoire, as he obviously has the means to read my private files.'

'There's really nothing to it for a man in my position,' Cal said. There was a moment while he accessed the smoky imagery of the buried thing, the obelisk hanging in front of them beyond the railing, apparently life-size.

'Oh, very interesting,' Janequin said. 'Very interesting indeed!'

'Not bad,' Cal said.

'Not bad?' Sylveste said. 'It's bigger and better preserved than anything we've found to date by an order of magnitude. It's clear evidence of a more advanced phase of Amarantin technology . . . perhaps even a precursor phase to a full industrial revolution.'

'I suppose it could be quite a significant find,' Cal said, grudgingly. 'You – um – are planning to unearth it, I assume?'

'Until a moment ago, yes.' Sylveste paused. 'But something's just come up. I've just been . . . I've just found out for myself that Girardieau may be planning to move against me a lot sooner than I had feared.'

'He can't touch you without a majority in the expeditionary council,' Cal said.

'No, he couldn't,' Janequin said. 'If that was how he was going to do it. But Dan's information is right. It looks as if Girardieau may be planning on more direct action.'

'That would be tantamount to some kind of . . . coup, I suppose.'

'I think that would be the technical term,' Janequin said.

'Are you sure?' Then Calvin did the concentration thing again, dark lines etching his brow. 'Yes . . . you could be right. A lot of media speculation in the last day concerning Girardieau's next move, and the fact that Dan's off on some dig while the colony stumbles through a crisis of leadership . . . and a definite increase in encrypted comms among Girardieau's known sympathisers. I can't break those encryptions, of course, but I can certainly speculate on the reason for the increase in traffic.'

'Something's being planned, isn't it?' Sluka was right, he thought to himself. In which case she had done him a favour, even as she had threatened to abandon the dig. Without her warning he would never have invoked Cal.

'It does look that way,' Janequin said. 'That's why I was trying to reach you. My fears have only been confirmed by what Cal says about Girardieau's sympathisers.' His grip tightened on the railing. The cuff of his jacket – hanging thinly over his skeletal frame – was patterned with peacocks' eyes. 'I don't suppose there's any point my staying here, Dan. I've tried to keep my contact with you below suspicious levels, but there's every reason to think this conversation is being tapped. I shouldn't really say any more.' He turned away from the cityscape and the hanging obelisk, then addressed the seated man. 'Calvin . . . it's been a pleasure to meet you again, after such a long time.'

'Look after yourself,' Cal said, elevating a hand in Janequin's direction. 'And good luck with the peacocks.'

Janequin's surprise was evident. 'You know about my little project?'

Calvin smiled without answering; Janequin's question had been superfluous after all, Sylveste thought.

The old man shook his hand – the environment ran to full tactile interaction – and then stepped out of range of his imaging suite.

The two of them were left alone on the balcony:

'Well?' Cal asked.

'I can't afford to lose control of the colony.' Sylveste had still been in nominal command of the entire Resurgam expedition, even after Alicia's defection. Technically, those who had chosen to stay behind on the planet rather than return home with her should have been his allies, meaning that his position should have been strengthened. But it had not worked like that. Not everyone who was sympathetic to Alicia's side of the argument had managed to get aboard the *Lorean* before it left orbit. And amongst those who had stayed behind, many previously sympathetic to

Sylveste felt he had handled the crisis badly, or even criminally. His enemies said that the things the Pattern Jugglers had done to his head before he met the Shrouders were only now emerging into the light; pathologies that bordered on madness. Research into the Amarantin had carried on, but with slowly lessening momentum, while political differences and enmities widened beyond repair. Those with residual loyalty to Alicia – chief among them Girardieau – had amalgamated into the Inundationists. Sylveste's archaeologists had become steadily embittered, a siege-mentality setting in. There had been deaths on both sides which were not easily explained as accidents. Now things had reached a head, and Sylveste was in nowhere like the right place to resolve the crisis. 'But I can't let go of that, either,' he said, indicating the obelisk. 'I need your advice, Cal. I'll get it because you depend on me absolutely. You're fragile; remember that.'

Calvin stirred uneasily in the chair. 'So basically you're putting the squeeze on your old dad. Charming.'

'No,' Sylveste said, through clenched teeth. 'What I'm saying is that you could fall into the wrong hands unless you give me guidance. In mob terms you're just another member of our illustrious clan.'

'Although you wouldn't necessarily agree, would you? By your reckoning I'm just a program, just evocation. When are you going to let me take over your body again?'

'I wouldn't hold your breath.'

Calvin raised an admonishing finger. 'Don't get stroppy, son. It was you who invoked me, not the other way around. Put me back in the lantern if you want. I'm happy enough.'

'I will. After you've advised me.'

Calvin leaned forward in the seat. 'Tell me what you did with my alpha-level simulation and I might consider it.' He grinned, impishly. 'Hell, I might even tell you a few things about the Eighty you don't know.'

'What happened,' Sylveste said, 'is seventy-nine innocent people died. There's no mystery to it. But I don't hold you responsible. It would be like accusing a tyrant's photograph of war crimes.'

'I gave you sight, you ungrateful little sod.' The seat swivelled so that its high solid back was facing Sylveste. 'I admit your eyes are hardly state of the art, but what could you expect?' The seat spun round. Calvin was dressed like Sylveste now, his hair similarly styled and his face possessing the same smooth cast. 'Tell me about the Shrouders,' he said. 'Tell me about your guilty secrets, son. Tell me what really happened around Lascaille's Shroud, and not the pack of lies you've been spinning since you got back.'

Sylveste moved to the escritoire, ready to flip out the cartridge. 'Wait,' Calvin said, holding up his hands suddenly. 'You want my advice?'

'Finally, we're getting somewhere.'

'You can't let Girardieau win. If a coup's imminent, you need to be back in Cuvier. There you can muster what little support you may have left.'

Sylveste looked through the crawler's window, towards the box grid. Shadows were crossing the baulks – workers deserting the dig, moving silently towards the sanctuary of the other crawler. 'This could be the most important find since we arrived.'

'And you may have to sacrifice it. If you keep Girardieau at bay, you'll at least have the luxury of returning here and looking for it again. But if Girardieau wins, nothing you've found here will matter a damn.'

'I know,' Sylveste said. For a moment there was no animosity between them. Calvin's reasoning was flawless, and it would have been churlish to pretend otherwise.

'Then will you be following my advice?'

He moved his hand to the escritoire, ready to eject the cartridge. 'I'll think about it.'

TWO

Aboard a lighthugger, interstellar space, 2543

The trouble with the dead, Triumvir Ilia Volyova thought, was that they had no real idea when to shut up.

She had just boarded the elevator from the bridge, weary after eighteen hours in consultation with various simulations of once-living figures from the ship's distant past. She had been trying to catch them out, hoping one or more of them would disclose some revealing fact about the origins of the cache. It had been gruelling work, not least because some of the older beta-level personae could not even speak modern Norte, and for some reason the software which ran them was unwilling to do any translating. Volyova had been chain-smoking for the entire session, trying to get her head around the grammatical peculiarities of middle Norte, and she was not about to stop filling her lungs now. In fact, back stiff from the nervous tension of the exchanges, she needed it more than ever. The elevator's air-conditioning was functioning imperfectly, so it took only a few seconds for her to veil the interior with smoke.

Volyova hoisted the cuff of her fleece-lined leather jacket and spoke into the bracelet which wrapped around her bony wrist. 'The Captain's level,' she said, addressing the *Nostalgia for Infinity*, which would in turn assign a microscopic aspect of itself to the primitive task of controlling the elevator. A moment later, the floor plunged away.

'Do you wish musical accompaniment for this transit?'

'No, and as I've had to remind you on approximately one thousand previous occasions, what I wish is silence. Shut up and let me think.'

She rode the spinal trunk, the four-kilometre-long shaft which threaded the entire length of the ship. She had boarded somewhere near the nominal top of the shaft (there were only 1050 levels that she knew of) and was now descending at ten decks a second. The elevator was a glass-walled, field-suspended box, and occasionally the lining of the trackless shaft turned transparent, allowing her to judge her location without reference to the elevator's internal map. She was descending through forests now: tiered gardens of planetary vegetation grown wild with neglect, and dying, for the UV lamps which had once supplied the forest with sunlight were mostly broken now, and no one could be bothered repairing them. Below the forests, she ghosted through the high eight hundreds; vast realms of the ship which had once been at the disposal of the crew, when the crew numbered thousands. Below 800 the elevator passed through the vast and now immobile armature which spaced the ship's rotatable habitat and nonrotatable utility sections, and then dropped through two hundred levels of cryogenic storage bays; sufficient capacity for one hundred thousand sleepers – had there been any.

Volyova was now more than a kilometre below her starting point, but the ship's ambient pressure remained constant, life-support one of the rare systems which still functioned as intended. Nonetheless some residual instinct told her that ears should be popping with the rush of descent.

'Atrium levels,' said the elevator, accessing a long-redundant record of the ship's prior layout. 'For your enjoyment and recreation needs.'

'Very droll.'

'I'm sorry?'

'I mean, you'd need a pretty odd definition of recreation. Unless your idea of relaxation happened to be suiting-up in full vacuum-rated armour and dosing on a bowel-loosening regimen of anti-radiation therapies. Which doesn't strike me as being particularly pleasurable.'

'I'm sorry?'

'Forget it,' Volyova said, sighing.

For another kilometre she passed through only sparsely pressur-ised districts. Volyova felt her weight lessen and knew she was passing the engines – braced beyond the hull on elegant, swept-back spars. Gape-mouthed, they sucked in tiny amounts of interstellar hydrogen and subjected the harvest to some frankly unimaginable physics. No one, not even Volyova, pretended to know how the Conjoiner engines worked. What mattered was that they functioned. What also mattered was that they gave off a steady warm glow of exotic particle radiation, and while most would have been mopped up by the ship's hull shielding, some of it would get through. That was why the elevator sped up momentarily as it dropped past the engines, and then slowed down to its normal descent speed once it had passed out of danger.

Now she was two-thirds of the way down the ship. She knew this district better than any of the other crew members: Sajaki, Hegazi and the others seldom came down this far unless they had excellent reason. And who could blame them? The further down they went, the closer they got to the Captain. She was the only one who was not terrified by the very idea of his proximity.

No; far from fearing this realm of the ship, she had made an empire of it. At level 612 she could have disembarked, navigated to the spider-room and taken it outside the hull, where she could listen to the ghosts which haunted the spaces between the stars. Tempting – always so. But she had work to do – she was on a specific errand – and the ghosts would still be there another time. At level 500, she passed the floor which contained the gunnery, and thought of all the problems which it represented, and had to resist stopping to carry out a few new investigations. Then the gunnery was gone and she was falling through the cache chamber – one of several huge, non-pressurised inclusions within the ship.

The chamber was enormous; the best part of half a kilometre from end to end, but it was dark now and Volyova had to imagine for herself the forty things which it contained. That was never hard. While there were many unanswered questions relating to the functions and origins of the things, Volyova knew their shapes and relative positions perfectly, as if they were the carefully positioned furnishings of a blind person's bedroom. Even in the elevator she felt she could reach out and stroke the alloy husk of the nearest of them, just to reassure herself that it was still there. She had been learning what she could of the things for most of the time since she had joined the Triumvirate, but she would not have claimed to have been at ease with any of them. She approached them with the nervousness of a new lover, knowing that the knowledge she had gleaned to date was entirely skin-deep, and that what lay below might shatter every illusion she had.

She was never entirely sorry to exit the cache.

At 450 she shot through another armature, spacing the utility section from the ship's tapering conic tail, which extended below for another kilometre. Again a surge as the elevator rode through a rad-zone, then the beginning of prolonged deceleration which would eventually bring it to a halt. It was passing through the second set of cryogenic storage decks, two hundred and fifty levels capable of holding one hundred and twenty thousand, though of course there was currently only one sleeper, if one was so generously inclined as to describe the Captain's state as sleep. The elevator was slowing now. Midway through the cryo levels it stopped, cordially announcing that it had reached her destination.

'Passenger cryogenic sleep level concierge,' said the elevator. 'For your in-flight reefersleep requirements. Thank you for using this service.'

The door opened and she stepped across the threshold, glancing down at the converging, illuminated walls of the shaft framed by the gap. She had travelled almost the entire length of the ship (or height – it was difficult not to think of the ship as a tremendously tall building) and yet the shaft seemed to drop down to infinite depths below. The ship was so large – so stupidly large – that even its extremities beggared the mind.

'Yes, yes. Now kindly piss off.'

'I'm sorry?'

'Go away.'

Not that the elevator would, of course – at least not for any real purpose other than placating her. It had nothing else to do but wait for her. Being the sole person awake, Volyova was the only one who had any cause to use the elevators at all.

It was a long hike from the spinal shaft to the place where they kept the Captain. She could not take the most direct route either, since whole sections of the ship were inaccessible, riddled with viruses which were causing widespread malfunction. Some districts were flooded with coolant, while others were infested with rogue janitor-rats. Others were patrolled by defence drogues which had gone berserk and so were best avoided, unless Volyova felt in the mood for sport. Others were filled with toxic gas, or vacuum, or too much high-rad, or were rumoured to be haunted.

Volyova did not believe in hauntings, (though of course she had her own ghosts, accessed via the spider-room), but the rest she took very seriously indeed. Some parts of the ship she would not enter unless armed. But she knew the Captain's surroundings well enough not to take excessive precautions. It was cold, though, and she hiked up the collar of her jacket, tugged the bill of her cap tighter down, its mesh fabric crunching against her scalp stubble. She lit another cigarette, hard sucks perishing the vacuum in her head, replacing it with a frosty military alertness. Being alone suited her. She looked forward to human company, but not with any great fervour. And certainly not if that company also entailed dealing with the Nagorny situation. Perhaps when they reached the Yellowstone system she would consider locating a new Gunnery Officer.

Now, how had that worry escaped from her mental partitioning?

It was not Nagorny that concerned her now, but the Captain. And here he was, or at least the outermost extent of what he had now become. Volyova composed herself. That composure was necessary. What she had to examine always made her sick. It was worse for her than for the others; her repulsion stronger. She was *brezgati*; squeamish.

The miracle was that the reefersleep unit which cased Brannigan was still functional. It was a very old model, Volyova knew – sturdily built. It was still striving to hold the cells of his body in stasis, even though the shell of the reefer had ruptured in great Palaeolithic cracks, fibrous metallic growth spilling out. The growth came from within the reefer, like a fungal invasion. Whatever remained of Brannigan remained at its heart.

It was bitterly cold near the reefer, and Volyova soon found herself shivering. But there was work to do. She fished a curette from her jacket and used it to burn off slivers of the growth for analysis. Back in her lab she would attack them with various viral weapons, hoping to find one which had an edge on the growth. She knew from experience that the routine was largely futile – the growth had a fantastic capacity for corrupting the molecular tools with which she probed it. Not that there was any pressing hurry: the reefer kept Brannigan at only a few hundred millikelvin above absolute zero, and that cold did appear to offer some hindrance to the spread. On the negative side, Volyova knew that no human being had ever survived revival from such a cold, but that seemed oddly irrelevant against the Captain's condition.

She spoke into her bracelet, voice hushed. 'Open my log file on the Captain and append this entry.'

The bracelet chirped to indicate readiness.

'Third check on Captain Brannigan since my revival. Extent of spread of the . . .'

She hesitated, aware that an ill-judged phrase might anger Triumvir Hegazi; not that she particularly cared. Dared she call it the Melding Plague, now that the Yellowstoners had given it a name? Perhaps that would be unwise.

'. . . of the illness, seems unchanged since last entry. No more than a few millimetres of encroachment. Cryogenic functions are still green, miraculously. But I think we should resign ourselves to the inevitability of the unit's failure at some point in the future . . .' Thinking to herself, that when it did fail, if they were not speedy in transferring the Captain to a new reefer (exactly how was an unanswered question), then he would certainly be one less problem for them to worry about. His own problems would be over as well – she sincerely hoped.

She told the bracelet: 'Close log file.' And then added, wishing devoutly that she had spared herself one smoke for this moment: 'Warm Captain's brain core by fifty millikelvins.'

Experience had told her that this was the minimum necessary temperature increase. Short of it, his brain would remain locked in glacial stasis. Above, the plague would begin to transform him too rapidly for her tastes.

'Captain?' she said. 'Can you hear me? It's Ilia.'

Sylveste stepped down from the crawler and walked back towards the grid. During his meeting with Calvin the wind had increased appreciably; he could feel it stinging his cheeks, the scouring dust a witch's caress.

'I hope that little conversation was beneficial,' Pascale said, snatching away her mask to bellow into the wind. She knew all about Calvin, even though she had never spoken to him directly. 'Have you agreed to see sense now?'

'Get Sluka for me.'

Ordinarily she might have rejected an order like that; now she just accepted his mood and returned to the other crawler, emerging shortly afterwards with Sluka and a handful of other workers.

'You're ready to listen to us, I take it?' Sluka stood before him, the wind whipping a loose strand of hair across her goggles. She took periodic inhalations from her mask, cupped in one hand, while the other hand rested on her hip. 'If so, I think you'll find we can be reasonable. We all have your reputation in mind. None of us will speak of this matter once we return to Mantell. We'll say you gave the order to withdraw once the advisory came in. The credit will be yours.'

'And you think any of that matters in the long term?'

Sluka snarled: 'What's so damned important about one obelisk? For that matter, what's so damned important about the Amarantin?'

'You never really saw the big picture, did you?'

Discreetly – but not so discreetly that he missed her doing it – Pascale had begun taping the exchange, standing to one side with her compad's detachable camera in one hand. 'Some people might say there never was one to see,' Sluka said. 'That you inflated the significance of the Amarantin just to keep the archaeologists in business.'

'You'd say that, wouldn't you, Sluka? But then again, you were never exactly one of us to begin with.'

'Meaning what?'

'Meaning that if Girardieau had wanted to plant a dissenter in our midst, you'd have made an excellent candidate.'

Sluka turned back to what Sylveste was increasingly thinking of as her mob. 'Listen to the poor bastard – sinking into conspiracy theories already. Now we're getting a taste of what the rest of the colony has seen for years.' Then her attention snapped back to him. 'There's no point talking to you. We're leaving as soon as we have the equipment packed – sooner, if the storm intensifies. You can come with us.' She caught her breath from the mask, colour returning to her cheeks. 'Or you can take your chances out here. The choice is entirely yours.'

He looked beyond her, to the mob. 'Go on, then. Leave. Don't allow anything as trivial as loyalty to get in your way. Unless one of you has the guts to stay here and finish the job they came to do.' He looked from face to face, meeting only awkwardly averted gazes. He barely knew any of their names. He recognised them, but only from recent experience; certainly none of them had come on the ship from Yellowstone; certainly none had known anything other than Resurgam, with its handful of human settlements strewn like a few rubies across otherwise total desolation. To them he must have seemed monstrously atavistic.

'Sir,' one of them said – possibly the one who had first alerted him to the storm. 'Sir; it's not that we don't respect you. But we have to think of ourselves as well. Can't you understand that? Whatever's buried here, it isn't worth this risk.'

'That's where you're wrong,' Sylveste said. 'It's worth more risk than you can possibly imagine. Don't you understand? The Event didn't happen to the Amarantin. They caused it. They made it happen.'

Sluka shook her head slowly. 'They made their sun flare up? Is that what you actually believe?'

'In a word, yes.'

'Then you're a lot further gone than I feared.' Sluka turned her back to him to address her mob. 'Power up the crawlers. We're leaving now.'

'What about the equipment?' Sylveste said.

'It can stay here and rust for all I care.' The mob began to disperse towards the two hulking machines.

'Wait!' Sylveste shouted. 'Listen to me! You only need to take one crawler – there's enough room for all of you in one, if you leave the equipment behind.'

Sluka faced him again. 'And you?'

'I'll stay here – finish the work myself, along with anyone else who wants to stay.'

She shook her head, snatching off her mask to spit on the ground in disgust. But when she left, she caught up with the rest of her brigade and directed them towards the nearest crawler, leaving the other – the one containing his stateroom – for him alone. Sluka's mob entered the machine, some of them carrying small items of equipment or boxed artefacts and bones recovered from the dig: scholarly instincts prevailing even in rebellion. He watched the crawler's ramps and hatches fold shut, then the machine rose on its legs, shuffled around and moved away from the dig. In less than a minute it had passed out of view completely, and the noise of its engines was no longer audible above the roar of the wind.

He looked around to see who was still with him.

There was Pascale – but that was almost inevitable; he suspected she would dog him to his grave if there was a good story in it. A handful of students who had resisted Sluka; ashamedly he could not place their names. Perhaps half a dozen more still down in the Wheeler grid, if he was lucky.

Composing himself, he snapped his fingers towards two of those who had stayed. 'Start dismantling the imaging gravitometers; we won't need them again.' He addressed another pair. 'Begin at the back of the grid and start collecting all the tools left behind by Sluka's deserters, together with field notes and any boxed artefacts. When you're done, you can meet me at the base of the large pit.'

'What are you planning now?' Pascale said, turning off her camera and allowing it to whisk back into her compad.

'I would have thought it was obvious,' Sylveste said. 'I'm going to see what it says on that obelisk.'

Chasm City, Yellowstone, Epsilon Eridani system, 2524

The suite console chimed as Ana Khouri was brushing her teeth. She came out of the bathroom, foam on her lips.

'Morning, Case.'

The hermetic glided into the apartment, his travelling palanquin decorated in ornate scrollwork, with a tiny, dark window in the front side. When the light was right she could just make out K. C. Ng's deathly pale face bobbing behind an inch of green glass.

'Hey, you look great,' he said, voice rasping through the box's speaker grille. 'Where can I get hold of whatever perks you up?'

'It's coffee, Case. Too much of the damned stuff.'

'I was joking,' Ng said. 'You look like shit warmed over.'

She drew her palm across her mouth, removing the foam. 'I've only just woken up, you bastard.'

'Excuses.' Ng managed to sound as if the act of waking up was an outmoded physical affectation he had long since discarded, like owning an appendix. Which was entirely possible: Khouri had never got a good look at the man inside the box. Hermetics were one of the more peculiar post-plague castes to emerge in the last few years. Reluctant to discard the implants which the plague might have corrupted, and convinced that traces of it still lingered even in the relative cleanliness of the Canopy, they never left their boxes unless the environment itself was hermetically sealed; limiting their mobility to a few orbital carousels.

The voice rasped again, 'Pardon me, but we do have a kill scheduled for this morning, if I'm not very much mistaken. You remember this fellow Taraschi we've been trying to take out for the last two months? Ring any bells in there? It's rather crucial that you do, because you happen to be the individual assigned to put him out of misery.'

'Off my back, Case.'

'Anatomically problematic even if I desired to locate myself thus, dear Khouri. But seriously, we have a probable kill location pegged, and an estimated time of demise. Are you sharpness personified?'

Khouri poured herself a final few sips of coffee and then left the rest of it on the stove for when she got back. Coffee was her only vice, one acquired in her soldiering days on the Edge. The trick was to reach a knife-edge of alertness, but not be so buzzing that she could not point the weapon without shaking.

'I think I've reduced the amount of blood in my caffeine system to an acceptable level, if that's what you mean.'

'Then let us discuss matters of a terminal nature, at least where Taraschi is concerned.'

Ng began to hit her with the final details for the kill. Most of it was already in the plan, or stuff that she had guessed for herself, based on her experience of previous kills. Taraschi was to be her fifth consecutive assassination, so she was beginning to grasp the wider scope of the game. Though they were not always obvious, the game had its own rules, subtly reiterated in the grand movements of each kill. The media attention was even picking up, her name being bandied around Shadowplay circles with increasing frequency, and Case was apparently setting up some juicy, high-profile targets for her next few hunts. She was, she felt, on the way to becoming one of the top hundred or so assassins on the planet; élite company indeed.

'Right,' she said. 'Under the Monument, plaza level eight, west annexe, one hour. Couldn't be easier.'

'Aren't you forgetting one thing?'

'Right. Where's the kill weapon, Case?'

Ng's form nodded behind her. 'Where the tooth fairy left it, dear girl.'

And then he turned his box and retreated from the room, leaving only a faint whiff of lubricant. Khouri, frowning, reached a hand slowly beneath the pillow on her bed. There was something, just as Case had said. There had been nothing there when she went to sleep, but this sort of thing hardly bothered her these days. The company always had moved in mysterious ways.

Soon, she was ready.

She called a cable-car from the roof, the kill weapon snuggling under her coat. The car detected the weapon and the presence of implants in her head, and would have refused to carry her had she not shown it her Omega Point ident, grafted beneath the nail of her right index finger, making a tiny holographic target symbol seem to dance beneath the keratin. 'Monument to the Eighty,' Khouri said.

Sylveste stepped off the ladder and walked across the stepped base of the pit until he reached the pool of light around the obelisk's exposed tip. Sluka and one of the other archaeologists had deserted him, but the one remaining worker – assisted by the servitor – had managed to uncover nearly a metre of the object, peeling away the nested layers of the stone sarcophagi to reach the massive block of obsidian, skilfully carved, on which Amarantin graphicforms had been engraved in precise lines. Most of it was textual: rows of ideopicts. The archaeologists understood the basics of Amarantin language, though there had been no Rosetta Stone to aid them. The Amarantin were the eighth dead alien culture discovered by humanity within fifty light-years of Earth, but there was no evidence that any of those eight species had come into contact with each other. Nor could the Pattern Jugglers or the Shrouders offer assistance: neither had revealed anything remotely resembling a written language. Sylveste, who had come into contact with both the Jugglers and the Shrouders – or at least the latter's technology – appreciated that as well as anyone.

Instead, computers had cracked the Amarantin language. It had taken thirty years – correlating millions of artefacts – but finally a consistent model had been evolved which could determine the broad meaning of most inscriptions. It helped that, at least towards the end of their reign, there had only been one Amarantin tongue, and that it had changed very slowly, so that the same model could interpret inscriptions which had been made tens of thousands of years apart. Of course, nuances of meaning were another thing entirely. That was where human intuition – and theory – came in.

Amarantin writing was not, however, like anything in human experience. All Amarantin texts were stereoscopic – consisting of interlaced lines which had to be merged in the reader's visual cortex. Their ancestors had once been something like birds – flying dinosaurs, but with the intelligence of lemurs. At some point in their past their eyes had been situated on opposite sides of their skulls, leading to a highly bicameral mind, each hemisphere synthesising its own mental model of the world. Later, they had become hunters and evolved binocular vision, but their mental wiring still owed something to that earlier phase of development. Most Amarantin artefacts mirrored their mental duality, with a pronounced symmetry about the vertical axis.

The obelisk was no exception.

Sylveste had no need for the special goggles his co-workers needed to read Amarantin graphicforms: the stereoscopic merging was easily accommodated within his own eyes, employing one of Calvin's more useful algorithms. But the act of reading was still tortuous, requiring strenuous concentration.

'Give me some light here,' he said, and the student unclipped one of the portable floods and held it by hand over the side of the obelisk. From somewhere above lightning strobed: electricity coursing between dust planes in the storm.

'Can you read it, sir?'

'I'm trying,' Sylveste said. 'It isn't the easiest thing in the world, you know. Especially if you don't keep that light steady.'

'Sorry sir. Doing my best. But it is getting windy here.'

He was right: vortices were forming, even in the pit. It would soon get very much windier, and then the dust would begin to thicken, until it formed sheets of grey opacity in the air. They would not be able to work for very long in those conditions.

'I apologise,' Sylveste said. 'I appreciate your help.' Feeling that something more was called for, he added: 'And I'm grateful that you chose to stay with me, rather than Sluka.'

'It wasn't difficult, sir. Not all of us are ready to dismiss your ideas.'

Sylveste looked up from the obelisk. 'All of them?'

'We at least accept they should be investigated. After all, it's in the colony's best interests to understand what happened.'

'The Event, you mean?'

The student nodded. 'If it really was something the Amarantin caused to happen . . . and if it really did coincide with them achieving spaceflight – then it might be of more than academic interest.'

'I despise that phrase. Academic interest – as if any other kind were automatically more worthy. But you're right. We have to know.'

Pascale came closer. 'Know what, exactly?'

'What it was they did that made their sun kill them.' Sylveste turned to face her, pinning her down with the oversized silvery facets of his artificial eyes. 'So that we don't end up making the same mistake.'

'You mean it was an accident?'

'I very much doubt that they did it deliberately, Pascale.'

'I realise that.' He had condescended to her, and she hated that, he knew. He also hated himself for doing it. 'I also know that stone-age aliens just don't have the means to influence the behaviour of their star, accidentally or otherwise.'

'We know they were more advanced than that,' Sylveste said. 'We know they had the wheel and gunpowder; a rudimentary science of optics and an interest in astronomy for agrarian purposes. Humanity went from that level to spaceflight in no more than five centuries. It would be prejudiced to assume another species was not capable of the same, wouldn't it?'

'But where's the evidence?' Pascale stood to shake rivulets of settled dust from her greatcoat. 'Oh, I know what you're going to say – none of the high-tech artefacts survived, because they were intrinsically less durable than earlier ones. But even if there *was* evidence – how does that change things? Even the Conjoiners don't go around tinkering with stars, and they're a lot more advanced than the rest of humanity, us included.'

'I know. That's precisely what bothers me.'

'Then what does the writing say?'

Sylveste sighed and looked back at it again. He had hoped that the distraction would allow his subconscious to work at the piece, and that now the meaning of the inscription would snap into clarity, like the answer to one of the psychological problems they had been posed before the Shrouder mission. But the moment of revelation stubbornly refused to come; the graphicforms were still not yielding meaning. Or perhaps, he thought, it was his expectations that were at fault. He had been hoping for something momentous; something that would confirm his ideas, terrifying as they were.

But instead, the writing seemed only to commemorate something that had happened here – something that might have been of great importance in Amarantin history, but which – set against his expectations – was bound to be parochial in the extreme. It would take a full computer analysis to be sure, and he had only been able to read the top metre or so of the text – but already he could feel the crush of disappointment. Whatever this obelisk represented, it was no longer of interest to him.

'Something happened here,' Sylveste said. 'Maybe a battle, or the appearance of a god. That's all it is – a marker stone. We'll know more when we unearth it and date the context layer. We can run a TE measurement on the artefact itself, too.'

'It's not what you were looking for, is it?'

'I thought it might be, for a while.' Then Sylveste looked down, towards the lowest exposed part of the obelisk. The text ended a few inches above the highest layer of cladding, and something else began, extending downwards out of sight. It was a diagram, of some sort – he could see the topmost arcs of several concentric circles, and that was all. What was it?

Sylveste could not – would not – begin to guess. The storm was growing stronger. No stars at all were visible now, only a single occluding sheet of dust, roaring overhead like a great bat's wing. It would be a kind of hell when they left the pit.

'Give me something to dig with,' he said. And then started scraping away at the permafrost around the topmost layer of the sarcophagus, like a prisoner who had until dawn to tunnel from his cell. Only a few moments passed before Pascale and the student joined him in the work, while the storm howled above.

'I don't remember much,' the Captain said. 'Are we still around Bloater?'

'No,' Volyova said, trying not to make it seem as if she had already explained this to him a dozen times, each time she had warmed his mind. 'We left Kruger 60A some years ago, once Hegazi negotiated us the shield ice we needed.'

'Oh. Then where are we?'

'Heading towards Yellowstone.'

'Why?' The Captain's basso voice rumbled out of speakers

arranged some distance from his corpse. Complex algorithms scanned his brain patterns and translated the results into speech, fleshing out the responses when required. He had no real right to be conscious at all, really – all neural activity should have ended when his core temperature had dropped below freezing. But his brain was webbed by tiny machines, and in a way it was the machines which were thinking now, even though they were doing so at less than half a kelvin above absolute zero.

'That's a good question,' she said. Something was bothering her now and it was more than just this conversation. 'The reason we're going to Yellowstone is . . .'

'Yes?'

'Sajaki thinks there's a man there who can help you.'

The Captain pondered this. On her bracelet she had a map of his brain: she could see colours squirming across it like armies merging on a battlefield. 'That man must be Calvin Sylveste,' the Captain said.

'Calvin Sylveste is dead.'

'The other one, then. Dan Sylveste. Is that the man Sajaki seeks?'

'I can't imagine it's anyone else.'

'He won't come willingly. He didn't last time.' There was a moment of silence; quantum temperature fluctuations pushing the Captain back below consciousness. 'Sajaki must be aware of that,' he said, returning.

'I'm sure Sajaki has considered all the possibilities,' Volyova said, in a manner which made it clear she was sure of anything *but* that. But she would be careful of speaking against the other Triumvir. Sajaki had always been the Captain's closest adjutant – the two of them went back a long way; times long before Volyova had joined the crew. To the best of her knowledge, no one else – including Sajaki – ever spoke to the Captain, or even knew that there was a way to do so. But there was no point taking stupid risks – even given the Captain's erratic memory.

'Something's troubling you, Ilia. You've always been able to confide in me. Is it Sylveste?'

'It's more local than that.'

'Something aboard the ship, then?'

It was not something to which she was ever going to become totally accustomed, Volyova knew, but in recent weeks visiting the Captain had begun to take on definite tones of normality. As if visiting a cryogenically cooled corpse infected with a retarded but potentially all-consuming plague was merely one of life's unpleasant but necessary elements; something that, now and again, everyone had to do. Now, though, she was taking their relationship a step further – about to ignore the same risk which had stopped her expressing her misgivings about Sajaki.

'It's about the gunnery,' she said. 'You remember that, don't you? The room from which the cache-weapons can be controlled?'

'I think so, yes. What about it?'

'I've been training a recruit to become Gunnery Officer; to assume the gunnery seat and interface with the cache-weapons through neural implants.'

'Who was this recruit?'

'Someone called Boris Nagorny. No; you never met him – he came aboard only recently, and I tended to keep him away from the others when I could help it. I would never have brought him down here, for obvious reasons.' Namely that the Captain's contagion might have reached Nagorny's implants if she had allowed the two of them to get too close. Volyova sighed. She was getting to the crux of her confession now. 'Nagorny was always slightly unstable, Captain. In many ways, a borderline psychopath was more useful to me than someone wholly sane – at least, I thought so at the time. But I underestimated the degree of Nagorny's psychosis.'

'He got worse?'

'It started not long after I put the implants in and allowed him to tap into the gunnery. He began to complain of nightmares. Very bad ones.'

'How unfortunate for the poor fellow.'

Volyova understood. What the Captain had undergone – what the Captain was still in the process of undergoing – would make most people's nightmares seem very tame phantasms indeed. Whether or not he experienced pain was a debatable point, but what was pain anyway, compared to the knowledge that one was being eaten alive – and transformed at the same time – by something inexpressibly alien?

'I can't guess what those nightmares were really like,' Volyova said. 'All I know is that for Nagorny – a man who already had enough horrors loose in his head for most of us – they were too much.'

'So what did you do?'

'I changed everything – the whole gunnery interface system, even the implants in his head. None of it worked. The nightmares continued.'

'You're certain they had something to do with the gunnery?'

'I wanted to deny it at first, but there was a clear correlation with the sessions when I had him in the seat.' She lit herself another cigarette, the orange tip the only remotely warm thing anywhere near the Captain. Finding a fresh packet of cigarettes had been one of the few joyful moments of recent weeks. 'So I changed the system again, and still it didn't work. If anything, he just got worse.' She paused. 'That was when I told Sajaki of my problems.'

'And Sajaki's response was?'

'That I should discontinue the experiments, at least until we'd arrived around Yellowstone. Let Nagorny spend a few years in reefersleep, and see if that cured his psychosis. I was welcome to continue tinkering with the gunnery, but I wasn't to put Nagorny in the seat again.'

'Sounds like very reasonable advice to me. Which of course you disregarded.'

She nodded, paradoxically relieved that the Captain had guessed her crime, without her having to spell it out.

'I woke a year ahead of the others,' Volyova said. 'To give me time to oversee the system and keep an eye on how you were doing. That was what I did for a few months, too. Until I decided to wake Nagorny as well.'

'More experiments?'

'Yes. Until a day ago.' She sucked hard on the cigarette.

'This is like drawing teeth, Ilia. What happened yesterday?'

'Nagorny disappeared.' There; she'd said it now. 'He had a particularly bad episode and tried to attack me. I defended myself, but he escaped. He's elsewhere in the ship. I have no idea where.'

The Captain pondered this for long moments. She could tell what he must be thinking. It was a big ship and there were whole regions of it through which nothing could be tracked, where sensors had stopped working. It would be even harder trying to find someone who was actively hiding.

'You're going to have to find him,' the Captain said. 'You can't have him still at large when Sajaki and the others awaken.'

'And then what?'

'You'll probably have to kill him. Do it cleanly, and you can put his body back in the reefersleep unit and then arrange for the unit to fail.'

'Make it look like an accident, you mean?'

'Yes.' There was, as usual, absolutely no expression on the part of the Captain's face she could see through the casket window. He was no more capable of altering his expression than a statue.

It was a good solution – one that, in her preoccupation with the nature of the problem, she had failed to devise herself. Until then, she had feared any confrontation with Nagorny because it might put her in the position of having to kill him. Such an outcome had seemed unacceptable – but as always, no outcome was unacceptable if you looked at it the right way.

'Thank you, Captain,' Volyova said. 'You've been very helpful. Now – with your permission – I'm going to cool you again.'

'You'll be back again, won't you? I do so enjoy our little conversations, Ilia.'

'I wouldn't miss them for the world,' she said, and then told her bracelet to drop his brain temperature by fifty millikelvin; all it would take to send him to dreamless, thoughtless oblivion. Or so she hoped.

Volyova finished her cigarette in silence and then looked away from the Captain, along the dark curve of the corridor. Somewhere out there – somewhere else in the ship – Nagorny was waiting, bearing her what she knew to be the deepest of grudges. He was ill himself now; sick in the head.

Like a dog that had to be put down.

'I think I know what it is,' Sylveste said, when the last obstructing block of stone had been removed from the obelisk's cladding, revealing the upper two metres of the object.

'Well?'

'It's a map of the Pavonis system.'

'Something tells me you'd already guessed that,' Pascale said, squinting through her goggles at the complex motif, which resembled two slightly offset groups of concentric circles. Stereoscopically merged, they fell into one group which seemed to hang some distance above the obsidian. And they were planetary orbits; no doubt of that. The sun Delta Pavonis lay at the centre, marked with the appropriate Amarantin glyph – a very human-looking five-pointed star. Then came correctly sized orbits for all the major bodies in the system, with Resurgam marked with the Amarantin symbol for world. Any doubts that this was just a coincidental arrangement of circles was banished by the carefully marked moons of the major planets.

'I had my suspicions,' Sylveste said. He was fatigued, but the night's work – and the risk – had surely been worthwhile. It had taken them much longer to unearth the second metre of the obelisk than the first, and at times the storm had seemed like a squadron of banshees, only ever a moment away from inflicting shrieking death. But – as had happened before, and would certainly happen again – the storm had never quite reached the fury that Cuvier had predicted. Now the worst of it was done, and though streaks of dust were still rippling in the sky like dark banners, pink dawnlight was beginning to chase away the night. It seemed they had survived after all.

'But it doesn't change anything,' Pascale said. 'We always knew they had astronomy; this just shows that at some point they discovered the heliocentric universe.'

'It means more than that,' Sylveste said, carefully. 'Not all of these planets are visible to the naked eye, even allowing for Amarantin physiology.'

'So they used telescopes.'

'Not long ago you described them as stone-age aliens. Now you're ready to accept that they knew how to make telescopes?'

He thought she might have smiled, but it was hard to tell when she wore the breather mask. Instead, she looked skywards. Something had crossed between the baulks; a bright deltoid moving under the dust.

'I think someone's here,' she said.

They climbed the ladder quickly, out of breath when they reached the top. Though the wind had lessened from its peak of several hours earlier, it was still an ordeal to move around topside. The dig was in disarray, with floods and gravitometers toppled and broken, equipment strewn around.

The aircraft was hovering above them, veering to and fro as it scouted landing sites. Sylveste recognised it immediately as one of Cuvier's; Mantell had nothing as large. Aircraft were in short supply on Resurgam: the only means of crossing distances more than a few hundred kilometres. All the aircraft in existence now had been manufactured during the early days of the colony by servitors working from local raw materials. But the constructional servitors had been destroyed or stolen during the mutiny, and consequently the artefacts they had left behind were of incalculable value to the colony. The aircraft regenerated themselves if they were involved in minor accidents, and never needed maintainance – but they could still be ruined by sabotage or recklessness. Over the years the colony had steadily depleted its supply of flying machines.

The deltoid hurt his eyes. The underside of the plane's wing was sewn with thousands of heat elements which glowed white-hot, generating lift thermally. The contrast was too much for Calvin's algorithms.

'Who are they?' one of his students asked.

'I wish I knew,' Sylveste said. But the fact that this plane had originated in Cuvier entirely failed to cheer him. He watched it lower, casting actinic shadows across the ground before the heat elements slid down the spectrum and the plane settled onto skids. After a moment a ramp folded out and a cluster of figures trooped from the plane. His eyes snapped to infrared – he could see the figures clearly now, even as they moved away from the plane towards him. Clad in dark clothes, they wore breather masks, helmets and what looked like strap-on armour, flashed with the Administration insignia: the closest the colony came to a fully-fledged militia. And they were carrying things – long, evil-looking rifles held in double-grips, with a torch slung under each barrel.

'This doesn't look good,' Pascale said, accurately.

The squad halted a few metres from them. 'Doctor Sylveste?' called a voice, attenuated by the wind, which was still considerable. 'I've got some bad news, I'm afraid, sir.'

He had been expecting nothing else. 'What is it?'

'The other crawler, sir – the one that left earlier tonight?'

'What about it?'

'They never made it back to Mantell, sir. We found them. There'd been a landslide – dust had built up on the ridge. They didn't have a chance, sir.'

'Sluka?'

'They're all dead, sir.' The Administration man's heavy breather mask made him look like an elephantine god. 'I'm sorry. It's lucky not all of you tried to get back at the same time.'

'It's more than luck,' Sylveste said.

'Sir? There's one other thing.' The guard tightened his grip on his rifle, emphasising its presence rather than aiming it. 'You're under arrest, sir.'

K. C. Ng's rasp of a voice filled the cable-car's cockpit like a trapped wasp. 'You developing a taste for it yet? Our fair city, I mean.'

'What would you know?' Khouri said. 'I mean, when was the last time you set foot outside of that damned box, Case? It can't have been in living memory.'

He was not with her, of course – there was nowhere near enough room for a palanquin aboard her cable-car. The car was necessarily small; nothing that would attract attention so close to the conclusion of a hunt. Parked on the roof, the vehicle had looked like a tailless helicopter which had partially furled its rotors. But rather than blades, the cable-car's arms were slender telescopic appendages, each terminating in a hook as viciously curved as a sloth's foreclaw.

Khouri had entered the car, and the door had slumped shut, barriering the rain and the low background noise of the city. She had stated her destination, which was the Monument to the Eighty, down in the deep Mulch. The car had paused momentarily, undoubtedly calculating the optimum route based on current traffic conditions and the generally shifting topology of the cableways which would carry it there. The process took a moment because the car's computer brain was not especially smart.

Then Khouri had felt the car's centre of gravity shift slightly. Through the upper window of the gullwing door, she had seen one of the car's three arms extend to more than twice its previous length, until the clawed end was able to grasp one of the cables which overran the top of the building. Now one of the other arms found a similar grasping point on an adjacent cable, and with a sudden heave they were, in a manner, airborne. For a moment the car slid down the two cables to which it had attached itself, but after a few seconds the latter of the two cables had diverged too far for the car to reach. Smoothly, it released its grasp, but before it could fall the car's third arm swooped out and grabbed another handy cable which happened to cross their approximate path. And then they slid for another second or so, and then fell again, and then rose again, and Khouri began to recognise a too-familiar feeling in her gut. What failed to assist matters was that the car's pendulous progress felt arbitrary, as if it was just making up its trajectory as it proceeded, luckily finding cables when it needed them. To compensate, Khouri ran through breathing exercises, restlessly tightening each finger of her black leather gloves in sequence.

'I admit,' Case said, 'that I haven't exposed myself to the city's native fragrances for some time now. But you shouldn't knock it. The air isn't quite as filthy as it seems. The purifiers were one of the few things still running after the plague.'

Now that the cable-car had lofted itself past the huddle of buildings which defined her neighbourhood, a much greater expanse of Chasm City was coming slowly into view. It was strange to think that this twisted forest of malformed structures had once been the most prosperous city in human history; the place from which – for nearly two centuries – a welter of artistic and scientific innovations had sprung. Now even the locals were admitting that the place had seen better days. With little in the way of irony they were calling it the City That Never Wakes Up, because so many thousands of its one-time rich were now frozen in cryocrypts, skipping centuries in the hope that this period was only an aberration in the city's fortunes.

Chasm City's border was the natural crater which hemmed the city, sixty kilometres from edge to edge. Within the crater the city was ring-shaped, encircling the central maw of the chasm itself. The city sheltered under eighteen domes which spanned the crater wall and reached inwards to the chasm's rim. Linked at their edges, supported here and there by reinforcing towers, the domes resembled sagging drapery covering the furniture of the recently deceased. In local parlance it was the Mosquito Net, though there were at least a dozen other names, in as many languages. The domes were vital to the city's existence. Yellowstone's atmosphere – a cold, chaotic mix of nitrogen and methane, spiced with long-chain hydrocarbons – would have been instantly deadly. Fortunately the crater sheltered the city from the worst of the winds and liquid methane flash-floods, and the broth of hot gases belching from the chasm itself could be cracked for breathable air with relatively cheap and rugged atmospheric processing technology. There were a few other settlements elsewhere on Yellowstone, much smaller than Chasm City, and they all had to go to much more trouble to keep their biospheres running.

Sometimes, in her early days on Yellowstone, Khouri had asked a few of the locals why anyone had ever bothered settling the planet in the first place if it was so inhospitable. Sky's Edge might have its wars, but at least you could live there without domes and atmosphere-cracking systems. She had quickly learned not to expect anything resembling a consistent answer, if the question itself was not deemed an outsider's impudence. Evidently, though, this much was clear: the chasm had drawn the first explorers and around them had accreted a permanent outpost, and then something like a frontier town. Lunatics, chancers and wild-eyed visionaries had come, driven by vague rumours of riches deep within the chasm. Some had gone home disillusioned. Some had died in the chasm's hot, toxic depths. But a few had elected to stay because something about the nascent city's perilous location actually appealed to them. Fast forward two hundred years and that huddle of structures had become . . . this.

The city stretched away infinitely in all directions, it seemed, a dense wood of gnarled interlaced buildings gradually lost in murk. The very oldest structures were still more or less intact: boxlike buildings which had retained their shapes during the plague because they had never contained any systems of self-repair or redesign. The modern structures, by contrast, now resembled odd, up-ended pieces of driftwood or wizened old trees in the last stages of rot. Once those skyscrapers had looked linear and symmetrical, until the plague made them grow madly, sprouting bulbous protrusions and tangled, leprous appendages. The buildings were all dead now, frozen into the shapes which seemed calculated to induce disquiet. Slums adhered to their sides, lower levels lost in a scaffolded maze of shanty towns and ramshackle bazaars, aglow with naked fires. Tiny figures were moving in the slums, walking or rickshawing to business along haphazard roadways laid down over old ruins. There were very few powered vehicles, and most of the contraptions Khouri saw looked like they were steam-driven.

The slums never reached more than ten levels up the sides of the buildings before collapsing under their own weight, so for two or three hundred further metres the buildings rose smoothly, relatively unscathed by plague transformations. There was no evidence of occupation in these mid-city levels. It was only near the very tops that human presence again re-asserted itself: tiered structures perched like cranes' nests among the branches of the malformed buildings. These new additions were aglow with conspicuous wealth and power; bright apartment windows and neon advertise-ments. Searchlights swept down from the eaves, sometimes picking out the tiny forms of other cable-cars, navigating between districts. The cable-cars picked their way through a network of fine branches, lacing the buildings like synaptic threads. The locals had a name for this high-level city-within-a-city: the Canopy.

It was never quite daytime, Khouri had noticed. She could never feel fully awake in this place, not while the city seemed caught in an eternal twilight gloom.

'Case, when are they going to get around to scraping the muck off the Mosquito Net?'

Ng chuckled, a sound like gravel being stirred around in a bucket. 'Never, probably. Unless someone figures a way of making some money out of it.'

'Now who's bad-mouthing the city?'

'We can afford to. When we finish our business we can hightail it back to the carousels with all the other beautiful people.'

'In their boxes. Sorry, Case, count me out of that particular party. The excitement might kill me.' She could see the chasm now, since the car was skirting close to the sloping inner rim of the toroidal dome. The chasm was a deep gully in the bedrock, weathered sides curving lazily over from horizontal before plung-ing vertically down, veined by pipes which reached down into belching vapour, towards the atmospheric cracking station which supplied air and heat to the city. 'Talking of which . . . being killed, I mean – what's the deal with the weapon?'

'Think you can handle it?'

'You pay me to, I'll handle it. But I'd like to know what I'm dealing with.'

'If you have a problem with that you'd better talk to Taraschi.'

'He specified this thing?'

'In excruciating detail.'

The car was over the Monument to the Eighty now. Khouri had never seen it from this precise angle. In truth, without the grandeur that it attained from street level, it looked weatherworn and sad. It was a tetrahedral pyramid, slatted so that it resembled a stepped temple, its lower levels barnacled in slums and reinforcements. Near the apex the marble cladding gave way to stained-glass windows, but portions of glass were shattered or sheeted-over in metal; damage one never saw from the street. This was to be the venue for the kill, apparently. It was unusual to know that in advance, unless it was another thing that Taraschi had actually had written into his contract. Contracting to be hunted by a Shadow-play assassin was only usually done if the client thought that they stood a good chance of evading the pursuer over the period determined by the contract. It was the way the virtually immortal rich kept ennui at bay, forcing their behaviour patterns out of predictable ruts – and ending up with something to brag about when they outlived the contract, as the majority did.

Khouri could date her involvement in Shadowplay very precisely; it was the day she was revived in Yellowstone orbit in a carousel run by an order of Ice Mendicants. Although there had been no Ice Mendicants around Sky's Edge, she had heard stories of them and knew something of their function. They were a voluntary religious organisation who dedicated themselves to assisting those who had suffered some form of trauma while crossing interstellar space, such as the revival amnesia which was a common side-effect of reefersleep.

That in itself was very bad news. Perhaps her amnesia was so bad that it had erased years of her previous life, but Khouri had no recollection even of embarking on an interstellar journey. Her last memories were quite specific, in fact. She had been in a medical tent on the surface of Sky's Edge, lying in a bed next to her husband Fazil. They had both been wounded in a firefight; injuries which – while not actually life-threatening – could best be treated in one of the orbital hospitals. An orderly had come around and prepped them both for a short immersion in reefersleep. They would be cooled, carried to orbit in a shuttle, then stacked up in a cryogenic holding facility until surgical slots were available in the hospital. The process might take months, but – as the orderly smilingly assured them – there was every chance that the war would still be going on when they were again fit for duty. Khouri and Fazil had trusted the orderly. They were both professional soldiers, after all.

Later, she was revived. But instead of coming around in the recuperation ward in the orbital hospital, Khouri was confronted by Ice Mendicants with Yellowstone accents. No, they explained, she was not amnesiac. Nor had she suffered any kind of injury in the reefersleep process. It was considerably worse than that.

There had been what the lead Mendicant chose to call a clerical error. It had happened around Sky's Edge, after the cryogenic holding facility was hit by a missile. Khouri and Fazil had been among the lucky few not to have been killed by the missile, but the attack had still wiped all the data records in the facility. The locals had done their best to identify the frozen, but inevitably they had made mistakes. In Khouri's case they had confused her with a Demarchist observer who had come to Sky's Edge to study the war and who had been ready to return home to Yellowstone when she was caught in the same missile attack. Khouri had been fast-tracked for surgery and then placed aboard a starship scheduled for immediate departure. They had, unfortunately, not made the same mistake in Fazil's case. While Khouri was asleep, winging her way across the light-years to Epsilon Eridani, Fazil was growing older, one year for every year that she flew. Of course, said the Mendicants, the error was discovered quickly – but by then it was much too late. There were no other ships due to follow that route for decades. And even if Khouri had immediately returned to Sky's Edge (which was again impossible given the stated destinations of all the ships now parked around Yellowstone), the best part of forty years would have passed before she met Fazil again. And during most of that time Fazil could have no knowledge that she was coming home; nothing to prevent him picking up the pieces of his life, remarrying, having children and perhaps even grand-children before she returned, a ghost from a part of his life he might have nearly consigned to oblivion by then. Assuming, of course, that he had not died as soon as he returned to combat.

Until that moment when the Ice Mendicant explained the situation to her, Khouri had never really given much thought to the slowness of light. There was nothing in the universe that moved faster . . . but, as she now saw, it was glacial compared to the speed that would be needed to keep their love alive. In one instant of cruel clarity, she understood that it was nothing less than the underlying structure of the universe, its physical laws, which had conspired to bring her to this moment of horror and loss. It would have been so much easier, infinitely easier, if she had known he was dead. Instead, there was this terrible gulf of separation, as much in time as in space. Her anger had become something sharp inside her, something that needed release if it was not going to kill her from within.

Later that day, when the man came to offer her a job as a contract assassin, she found it surprisingly easy to accept.

The man's name was Tanner Mirabel; like her he was an ex-soldier from the Edge. He was a kind of talent scout for potential new assassins. His network taps had flagged her soldiering skills as soon as she was defrosted. Mirabel gave her a business contact: a Mr Ng, a prominent hermetic. An interview with Ng swiftly followed, then a spread of psychometric tests. Assassins, it turned out, had to be among the sanest, most analytic people on the planet. They had to know exactly when a kill would be legal – and when it would cross the sometimes blurred line into murder and send a company's stocks crashing into the Mulch.

She passed all these tests with ease.

There were other kinds of tests, too. The contractees sometimes specified arcane modes of execution for themselves, while secretly assuring themselves that it would never actually come to that, because they imagined themselves clever and resourceful enough to outrun the assassin, even over weeks or months. But Khouri had to learn an easy familiarity with all manner of weapons, and that turned out to be a talent she had never even suspected in herself.

But she had never seen anything quite like the weapon which the tooth fairy had left.

It had only taken her a minute or so to figure out how the gun's precision parts fitted together. Assembled, it had the form of a sniper's rifle with a ridiculously fat perforated barrel. The clip contained a number of dartlike slugs: black swordfishes. Near the snout of each slug was a tiny biohazard symbol. It was that holographic death's head which had set her wondering. She had never used toxins against a target before.

And what was this business with the Monument?

'Case,' Khouri said. 'There's one more thing . . .'

But then the car thumped down on the street, rickshaw drivers peddling furiously to avoid its descent. The toll burst onto her retina. She swiped her little finger through the credit slot, debiting a secure Canopy account which had no traceable links to Omega Point. That was vital, for any well-connected target could have easily traced the movements of their assassin via the ripples they

43

left in the planet's ragged financial systems. Screens and blinds had to be maintained.

Khouri pushed back the gullwing and hopped out. It was, as ever down here, softly raining. Interior rain, they called it. The smell of the Mulch assailed her instantly, a mélange of sewage and sweat, cooking spices, ozone and smoke. The noise was just as inescapable. The constant trundling of rickshaws and the ringing of their bells and horns created a steady clamorous background, spiced with the cries of vendors and caged animals, bursts of song from singers and holograms voicing languages as diverse as Modern Norte and Canasian.

She pulled on a wide-brimmed fedora and closed the raised collar of her kneelength coat. The cable-car rose, grasping high for a dangling cable. It was soon lost among the other specks swinging through the brown depths of the roofed sky.

'Well, Case,' she said. 'It's your show now.'

His voice came through her skull now. 'Trust me. I have a very good feeling about this one.'

The Captain's advice had been excellent, Ilia Volyova thought. Killing Nagorny really had been her only viable option. And Nagorny had made the task that much easier by trying to kill her first, neatly obviating any moral considerations.

All that had happened some months of shiptime ago, and she had delayed attending to the job that now confronted her. But very shortly the ship would arrive around Yellowstone, and the others would emerge from reefersleep. When that happened, her options would be severely limited by the need to maintain the lie that Nagorny had died while sleeping, via some plausible malfunction of his reefersleep casket.

Now she had to steel herself to act. She sat silently in her lab and willed the strength to do what had to be done. Volyova's quarters were not large, by the standards of the *Nostalgia for Infinity*: she could have allocated herself a mansion of rooms, had she wished. But what would have been the point? Her waking hours were consumed with weapon systems, and little else. When she slept, she dreamed of weapon systems. She allowed herself what few luxuries she had time to use – enjoy was too strong a term – and she had sufficient space for her needs. She had a bed and some furniture, utilitarian in design, even though the ship could have outfitted her with any style imaginable. She had a small annexe which contained a laboratory, and it was only here that much in the way of attention to detail had been lavished. In the lab, she worked on putative cures for the Captain; modes of attack too speculative to share with the other crew, for fear of raising their hopes.

It was here, also, that she had kept Nagorny's head since killing him.

It was frozen, of course; entombed within a space helmet of old design which had gone into emergency cryopreservation mode the instant it detected that its occupant was no longer living. Volyova had heard of helmets with razor-sharp irises built into the neck, which quickly and cleanly detached the head from the rest of the body in dire circumstances – but this had not been one of those.

He had died in an interesting manner, though.

Volyova had woken the Captain and explained the whole Nagorny situation to him: how the Gunnery Officer had appeared to have lost his mind as a consequence of her experiments. She had told the Captain about the problems she had encountered in linking Nagorny into the gunnery systems via the implants she had put in his head. She had even mentioned the fact that Nagorny had been somewhat troubled by recurrent nightmares, before getting quickly to the point that the recruit had attacked her and disappeared into the depths of the ship. The Captain had not drawn her on the subject of the nightmares, and at the time Volyova had been glad of that, for she was not entirely comfortable with discussing them herself, much less analysing their content.

Afterwards, however, she had found it much harder to ignore the subject. The problem lay in the fact that these were not simply random nightmares, however disturbing that might have been. No, from what she could gather, Nagorny's nightmares had been highly repetitious and detailed. For the most part they had concerned an entity called Sun Stealer. Sun Stealer was Nagorny's private tormentor, it seemed. It was not at all clear how Sun Stealer had manifested to Nagorny, but what was beyond doubt was the sense of overwhelming evil the apparition had brought. She had glimpsed something of this in sketches she had found in Nagorny's quarters once: feverish pencil marks limning hideous birdlike creatures, skeletal and empty-socketed. If that was a glimpse into

Nagorny's madness, a glimpse was more than adequate. How were these phantasms related to the gunnery sessions? What unsuspected glitch in her neural interface was leaking current into the part of the mind which sparked terrors? With hindsight, it was obvious that she had pushed too hard, too fast. Equally, she had only been following Sajaki's orders to bring the weaponry to a state of full readiness.

So Nagorny had snapped, escaping into the ship's unmonitored warrens. The Captain's recommendation – that she hunt down and kill the man – had tallied with her own instincts. But it had taken many days, Volyova deploying webs of sensor gear through as many corridors as she could manage, listening to her rats for any evidence of Nagorny's whereabouts. It had begun to look hopeless. Nagorny would be still at large when the ship arrived in the Yellowstone system and the other crew were woken . . .

Then, however, Nagorny had made two mistakes: the final flourishes of his madness. The first mistake had been to break into her quarters and leave a message daubed in his own arterial blood on her wall. The message was very simple. She could have guessed in advance the two words Nagorny would choose to leave her.

SUN STEALER.

Afterwards, on the edge of rationality, he had stolen her space helmet, leaving the rest of her suit. The break-in had drawn Volyova to her cabin, and while she had taken precautions, Nagorny had still managed to ambush her. He had relieved her of the gun she was carrying, and then frogmarched her down a long curving corridor to the nearest elevator shaft. Volyova had tried resisting, but Nagorny's strength was that of the psychotic and his hold on her might as well have been steel. Still, she assumed a chance for escape would present itself as Nagorny took her to wherever he had in mind, once the elevator arrived.

But Nagorny had no intention of waiting for the elevator. With her gun, he forced the door, revealing the echoing depths of the shaft. With nothing in the way of ceremony – not even a goodbye – Nagorny pushed Volyova into the hole.

It was a dreadful mistake.

The shaft threaded the ship from top to bottom; she had kilometres to fall before she hit the bottom. And for a few almost heart-stopping moments, she had assumed that was exactly what would happen. She would drop until she hit – and whether it took a few seconds or the better part of a minute was of no consequence at all. The walls of the shaft were sheer and frictionless; there was no way to gain a purchase or arrest her fall in any way whatsoever.

She was going to die.

Then – with a detachment which later shocked her – part of her mind had re-examined the problem. She had seen herself, not falling through the ship, but stationary: floating in absolute rest with respect to the stars. What moved, instead, was the ship: rushing upwards around her. She was not accelerating at all now – and the only thing that made the ship accelerate was its thrust.

Which she could control from her bracelet.

Volyova had not had time to ponder the details. An idea had formed – exploded – in her mind, and she knew that either she executed the idea almost immediately or accepted her fate. She could stop her fall – her apparent fall – by ramping the ship's thrust into reverse for however long it took to achieve the desired effect. Nominal thrust was one gee, which was why Nagorny had found it so easy to mistake the ship for something like a very tall building. She had fallen for perhaps ten seconds while her mind processed things. What was it to be, then? Ten second of reverse thrust at one gee? No – too conservative. She might not have enough shaft to fall through. Better to ramp up to ten gees for a second – she knew the engines were capable of that. The manoeuvre would not harm the other crew, safely cocooned in reefersleep. It would not harm her, either – she would just see the rushing walls of the shaft slow down rather violently.

Nagorny, though, was not so well protected.

It had not been easy – the rush of air had almost drowned out her voice as she screamed the appropriate instructions into the bracelet. Agonising moments had followed before the ship seemed to take any notice of her.

Then – dutifully – it had moved to her whim.

Later, she had found Nagorny. The ten gees of thrust, sustained for a second, would not ordinarily have been fatal. Volyova had, however, not whittled her speed down to zero in one go. She had achieved that through trial and error, and with each impulse Nagorny had been flung between ceiling and floor.

She had been hurt herself; the impacts with the side of the shaft as she fell had broken one leg, but that was healed now and the pain no more than a foggy memory. She remembered using the laser-curette to remove Nagorny's head, knowing that she would need to open it to get at the dedicated implants buried in his brain. They were delicate, those implants, and because they had come into being through laborious processes of mediated molecular growth, she would not be best pleased if they had to be duplicated.

Now it was time to remove them.

She took the head out of the helmet, immersing it in a bath of liquid nitrogen. Then she pushed her hands into two pairs of gauntlets suspended above the workbench within a scaffold of pistons. Tiny, glistening medical instruments whirred into life and descended on the skull, ready to slice it open in pieces which would later lock back together with fiendish precision. Before reassembling the head, Volyova would insert dummy implants so that – if the head were ever examined – it would not seem as if she had removed anything from it. It would have to be re-attached to the body, too – but there was no need to worry herself too much over that. By the time the others found out what had happened to Nagorny – what she was going to convince them had happened – they would not be in a hurry to examine him in any kind of detail. Sudjic might be a problem, of course – she and Nagorny had been lovers, until Nagorny went insane.

Like many others that remained before her, Ilia Volyova would cross that bridge when she came to it.

In the meantime, as she delved deep into Nagorny's head for what was hers, she began to give the first thought to who was going to replace him.

Certainly no one now aboard the ship.

But perhaps around Yellowstone she would find a new recruit.

'Case, are we getting warm?'

The voice came back, blurred and trembly through the mass of the building above her. 'So warm we're incandescent, dear girl. Just hold on and make sure you don't waste those toxin darts.'

'Yes, about those, Case, I—'

Khouri dived aside as three New Komuso trooped past, their heads enveloped in basketlike wicker helmets. Shakuhachi – bamboo flutes – cut the air ahead of them like majorettes' staffs, dispersing a gang of capuchin monkeys into the shadows. 'I mean,' she continued, 'what if we take out a collateral?'

'It can't happen,' Ng said. 'The toxin's keyed directly to

Taraschi's biochemistry. Hit anyone else on the planet and what they'll have to show for it is a nasty puncture wound.'

'Even if I hit Taraschi's clone?'

'You think you might?'

'Just a question.' It struck her that Case was unusually jumpy.

'Anyway, if Taraschi had a clone, and we killed him by mistake, that would be Taraschi's problem, not ours. It's all in the fine print. You should read it sometime.'

'When I'm gripped by existential boredom,' Khouri said, 'I might try it.'

She stiffened, then, because all of a sudden it was different. Ng was silent, and in place of his voice was a clear pulsing tone. It was soft and evil, like the echolocation pulse of a predator. She had heard that tone a dozen times in the last six months, each time signifying her proximity to the target. It meant that Taraschi was no more than five hundred metres away. That fact, coupled with the onset of the pulse, strongly suggested that he was within the Monument itself.

The moves of the game were now public property. Taraschi would know it, for an identical device – implanted in a secure Canopy clinic – was generating similar pulses in his own head. Across Chasm City, the various media networks which concentrated on Shadowplay would even now be sending their field teams across town to the location of the kill. A lucky few would already be in the vicinity.

The tone hastened as they walked further under the Monument's concourse, but not quickly. Taraschi must have been overhead – actually in the Monument – so that the relative distance between them was not changing swiftly.

The concourse beneath was cracked by land subsidence, lying perilously close to the chasm. Originally there had been an underground mall complex beneath the structure, but the Mulch had infiltrated it. The lowest levels were flooded, sunken walkways emerging from water the colour of caramel. The tetrahedron of the Monument was elevated well above the concourse and the flooded plaza by a smaller inverted pyramid abutted deep into rock foundations. There was only one entrance to the structure. That meant that Taraschi was as good as dead already, if she caught him aside. But to reach it she had to cross a bridge across the plaza, and her approach would be obvious to the man inside. She wondered what kind of primal thoughts were slipping through his mind now. In her dreams, she had often found herself in some half-deserted city being chased by some implacable hunter, but Taraschi was experiencing that terror in reality. She remembered that in those dreams the hunter never had to move quickly. That was part of its unpleasantness. She would run desperately, as if through thickened air with weighted-down legs, and the hunter would move with a slowness born of great patience and wisdom.

The pulsing quickened as she crossed the bridge, the ground beneath her feet wet and gritty. Occasionally the pulsing would slow and requicken, evidence that Taraschi was moving around in the structure. But there was no real escape for him now. He could arrange to be met on the roof of the Monument, perhaps, but in utilising aerial transport he would forfeit the terms of the contract. In the parlours of the Canopy, the shame of that might be less desirable than being killed.

She walked through into the atrium within the Monument's supporting pyramid. It was dark inside and it took a few moments for her eyes to adjust. She slipped the toxin gun out of her coat and checked the exit in case Taraschi had planned to sneak out. His absence was unsurprising, the atrium almost empty, ransacked by looters. Rain drummed on metal. She looked up into a suspended cloud of rusted, damaged sculptures hung on copper cables from the ceiling. A few had fallen to the marbled terrazzo, metal birds' wings stabbing into the ground with the impact. They were softly defined in dust, its whiteness like mortar between the primary feathers.

She looked towards the ceiling.

'Taraschi?' she called. 'Can you hear me yet? I'm coming.'

She wondered, briefly, why the television people had not yet arrived. It was strange to be this close to the termination of the kill and not have them baying for blood around her, along with the usual impromptu crowd which they invariably drew.

He had not answered her. But she knew he was above the ceiling, somewhere. She walked across the atrium, towards the spiral staircase that led higher. She climbed quickly, then cast around for large objects she could budge, to obstruct Taraschi's escape route. There were plenty of ruined exhibits and pieces of furniture. She began to assemble an obstructing pile atop the staircase. It would hinder Taraschi more than block his exit completely, but that was all she needed.

By the time it was half done she was sweating and her back was stiff. She took a moment to collect herself and take in her surroundings; the constant arpeggiating note in her head confirming that Taraschi was still nearby.

The upper part of the pyramid had been dedicated to individual shrines to the Eighty. These little memorials were set in recesses within the impressive black marble walls which rose partway to the dizzyingly high ceilings, framed by pillars adorned with suggestively posed caryatids. The walls, pierced by corniced archways, blocked her view for a few tens of metres in any direction. The three triangular sides of the ceiling had been punctured in places; sepia shafts of light entering the chamber. Rain fell in steady streamers from the larger rents. Khouri saw that many of the recesses were empty; evidently, those shrines had either been looted or the families of those members of the Eighty had decided to remove their memorials to some safer place. Perhaps half remained. Of those, roughly two-thirds had been arranged in a similar manner – images, biographies and keepsakes of the dead, placed in a standard fashion. Other exhibits were more elaborate. There were holograms or statues, even, in one or two grisly cases, the embalmed corpses of the actual people being celebrated, doubtless subjected to some skilled taxidermy to offset the worst damage wrought by the procedure which had killed them.

She left the well-tended shrines alone, plundering only those that were obviously derelict, even then uncomfortable with the act of vandalism. The busts were useful – just large enough to move if she got both fingers under the base. Rather than placing them in an ordered pile at the top of the stairs, she just let them drop. Most of them had had their jewelled eyes gouged out already. The full-size statues were much harder to move, and she managed to shift only one of them.

Soon her barricade was done. For the most part it was a rubble-like pile of toppled heads, dignified faces unembarrassed by what she had done to them. The pile was surrounded by smaller, foot-tangling bric-à-brac: vases, Bibles and loyal servitors. Even if Taraschi began to dismantle the pile to reach the stairs, she was sure she would hear him doing it and be able to reach the site long before he was finished. It might even be good to kill him on that pile of heads, since it did slightly resemble Golgotha.

All this time she had been listening to his ponderous footsteps somewhere behind the black dividing walls.

'Taraschi,' she called. 'Make this easy for yourself. There's no escape from here.'

His reply sounded remarkably strong and confident. 'You're so wrong, Ana. The escape's why we're here.'

Shit. He was not supposed to know her name.

'Escape is death, right?'

He sounded amused. 'Something like that.'

It was not the first time she had heard such eleventh-hour bravado. She rather admired them for it. 'You want me to come find you, is that it?'

'Now that we've come this far, why not?'

'I understand. You want your money's worth. A contract with as many clauses in it as this one couldn't have come cheap.'

'Clauses?' – the pulse in her head shifting minutely, rhapsodically.

'This weapon. The fact that we're alone.'

'Ah,' Taraschi said. 'Yes. That did cost. But I wanted this to be a personal matter. When it came to finalities.'

Khouri was getting edgy. She had never had an actual conversation with one of her targets. Usually it would have been impossible, in the roaring bloodlust of the crowd she generally attracted. Readying the toxin gun, she began to walk slowly down the aisle. 'Why the privacy clause?' she asked, unable to sever the contact.

'Dignity. I may have played this game, but I didn't have to dishonour myself in the process.'

'You're very close,' Khouri said.

'Yes, very close.'

'And you're not frightened?'

'Naturally. But of living, not dying. It's taken me months to reach this state.' His footsteps stopped. 'What do you think of this place, Ana?'

'I think it needs a bit of attention.'

'It was well chosen, you must admit.'

She turned the aisle. Her target was standing next to one of the shrines, looking preternaturally calm, almost calmer than one of the statues which watched the encounter. The interior rain had darkened the burgundy fabric of his Canopy finery, his hair was plastered unglamorously to his forehead. In person he looked younger than any of her previous kills, which meant he was either genuinely younger or rich enough to afford the best longevity therapies. Somehow she knew it was the former.

'You do remember why we're here?' he asked.

'I do, but I'm not sure I like it.'

'Do it anyway.'

One of the shafts of light falling from the ceiling shifted magically onto him. It was only an instant, but long enough for her to raise the toxin gun.

She fired.

'You did well,' Taraschi said, no pain showing in his voice. He reached out with one hand to steady himself against the wall. The other touched the swordfish protruding from his chest and prised it free, as if picking a thistle from his clothes. The pointed husk dropped to the floor, serum glistening from the end. Khouri raised the toxin gun again, but Taraschi warded her off with a blood-smeared palm. 'Don't overdo it,' he said. 'One should be sufficient.'

Khouri felt nauseous.

'Shouldn't you be dead?'

'Not for a little while. Months, to be precise. The toxin is very slow-acting. Plenty of time to think it over.'

'Think what over?'

Taraschi raked his wet hair and wiped dust and blood from his hands onto the shins of his trousers.

'Whether I follow her.'

The pulsing stopped and the sudden absence of it was enough to make Khouri dizzy. She fell in a half-faint to the floor. The contract was over, she grasped. She had won – again. But Taraschi was still alive.

'This was my mother,' Taraschi said, gesturing at the nearest shrine. It was one of the few that were well-tended. There was no dust at all on the woman's alabaster bust, as if Taraschi had cleaned it himself just before their meeting. Her skin was uncorrupted and her jewelled eyes were still present, aristocratic features unmarred by dent or blemish. 'Nadine Weng-da Silva Taraschi.'

'What happened to her?'

'She died, of course, in the process of being scanned. The

destructive mapping was so swift that half her brain was still functioning normally while the other half was torn apart.'

'I'm sorry – even though I know she volunteered for it.'

'Don't be. She was actually one of the lucky ones. Do you know the story, Ana?'

'I'm not from around here.'

'No; that was what I heard – that you were a soldier once, and that something terrible happened to you. Well, let me tell you this much. The scannings were all successful. The problem lay in the software which was supposed to execute the scanned information; to allow the alphas to evolve forward in time and experience awareness, emotion, memory – everything that makes us human. It worked well enough until the last of the Eighty had been scanned, a year after the first. But then strange pathologies began to emerge amongst the early volunteers. They crashed irrecoverably, or locked themselves in infinite loops.'

'You said she was lucky?'

'A few of the Eighty are still running,' Taraschi said. 'They've managed to keep doing so for a century and a half. Even the plague didn't hurt them – they'd already migrated to secure computers in what we now call the Rust Belt.' He paused. 'But they've been out of direct contact with the real world for some time now – evolving themselves in increasingly elaborate simulated environments.'

'And your mother?'

'Suggested I join her. Scanning technology's better now; it doesn't even have to kill you.'

'Then what's the problem?'

'It wouldn't be me, would it? Just a copy – and my mother would know it. Whereas now . . .' He fingered the tiny wound again. 'Whereas now, I will definitely die in the real world, and the copy will be all that's left of me. There's time enough for me to be scanned before the toxin leads to any measurable deterioration in my neural structure.'

'Couldn't you just have injected it?'

Taraschi smiled. 'That would have been too clinical. I am killing myself, after all – nothing anyone should take lightly. By involving you, I prolonged the decision and introduced an element of chance. I might decide life was preferable and resist you, and yet you might still win.'

'Russian roulette would have been cheaper.'

'Too quick, too random, and not nearly so stylish.' He stepped towards her and – before she could draw back – reached for her hand and shook it, for all the world like someone concluding an auspicious business deal. 'Thank you, Ana.'

'Thank you?'

Without answering he walked past her, towards noise. The sacrificial mound of heads was tumbling, footsteps clattering on the staircase. A cobalt vase shattered as the barricade gave way. Khouri heard the whisper of floatcams, but when the people emerged, they had none of the faces she expected. They were respectably dressed without being ostentatious, old-money Canopy. Three older men wore ponchos and fedoras and tortoiseshell floatcam glasses, the cameras hovering above them like attendant familiars. Two bronze palanquins rose behind them, one small enough to have held a child. A man with a plum matador's jacket carried a tiny hand-held camera. Two teenage girls carried umbrellas painted with watercolour cranes and Chinese pictograms. Between the girls was an older woman, her face so colourless she might as well have been a lifesize origami toy, infolded, white and easily crushed. She fell to her knees in front of Taraschi, weeping. Khouri had never seen the woman before, but she knew intuitively that this was Taraschi's wife and that the little toxin-filled swordfish had robbed her of him.

She looked at Khouri, her eyes limpid smoke-grey. Her voice, when she spoke, was bleached of anger. 'I hope they paid you well.'

'I just did my job,' Khouri said, but she hardly managed to force the words out. The people were helping Taraschi towards the stairs. She watched them descend out of sight, the wife turning to direct one last reproachful glance at Khouri. She heard the reverberation of their retreat and the sound of footsteps across the terrazzo. Minutes passed, and then she knew that she was completely alone.

Until something moved behind her. Khouri spun round, automatically bringing the toxin gun to bear, another dart in the chamber.

A palanquin emerged from between two shrines.

'Case?' She lowered the gun – it was of little use anyway, with the toxin keyed so precisely to Taraschi's biochemistry.

But this was not Case's palanquin: it was unmarked, unornamented black. And now it opened – she had never seen a palanquin do that – divulging a man who stepped fearlessly towards her. He wore a plum matador's jacket; not the hermetic clothing she might have expected from someone who feared the plague. In one hand he carried a fashion accessory: a tiny camera.

'Case has been taken care of,' the man said. 'He's of no concern to you from now on, Khouri.'

'Who are you – someone connected to Taraschi?'

'No – I just came along to see if you were as efficient as your reputation implied.' The man spoke with a soft accent which was not local – not from this system, nor the Edge. 'And, I'm afraid, you were. Which means – as of now – you're working for the same employer as myself.'

She wondered if she could put a dart in his eye. It would not kill him, but it might take the edge off his cockiness. 'And who would that be?'

'The Mademoiselle,' the man said.

'I've never heard of her.'

He raised the lensed end of the little camera. It split open like a particularly ingenious Fabergé egg, hundreds of elegant jade fragments sliding to new positions. Suddenly she was looking down the barrel of a gun.

'No, but she's heard of you.'

THREE

Cuvier, Resurgam, 2561

He was woken by shouting.

Sylveste checked his tactile bedside clock, feeling the position of the hands. He had an appointment today; in less than hour. The commotion outside had beaten the alarm by a few minutes. Curious, he threw aside the sheets of his bunk and fumbled towards the high, barred window. He was always half-blind first thing in the morning, as his eyes stammered through their wake-up systems check. They threw planar sheets of primary colour across his surroundings, making it seem as if the room had been redecorated overnight by a squad of overenthusiastic cubists.

He pulled aside the curtain. Sylveste was tall, but he could not see through the little window – at least not at a useful angle – unless he stood on a pile of books appropriated from his shelves; old printed facsimile editions. Even then the view was less than inspiring. Cuvier was built in and around a single geodesic dome, most of which was occupied with six- or seven-storey rectangular structures thrown up in the first days of the mission, designed for durability rather than aesthetic appeal. There had been no self-repairing structures, and the need to safeguard against a dome failure had resulted in buildings which were not only able to withstand razorstorms, but which could also be pressurised independently. The grey, small-windowed structures were linked by roadways, along which a few electric vehicles would normally be moving.

Not today, though.

Calvin had given the eyes a zoom/record facility, but it took concentration to use, rather like that needed to invert an optical illusion. Stick figures, foreshortened by the angle, enlarged and became agitated individuals rather than amorphous elements of a swarm. It was not so that he could now read their expressions or even identify their faces, but the people in the street defined their own personalities in the way they moved, and he had become acutely good at reading such nuances. The main mob was moving down Cuvier's central thoroughfare behind a barricade of slogan boards and improvised flagstaffs. Apart from a few daubed storefronts and an uprooted japonica sapling down the mall, the mob had caused little damage, but what they failed to see was the troop of Girardieau militia mobilising at the far end of the mall. They had just disgorged from a van and were buckling on chameleoflage armour, flicking through colour modes until they all wore the same calming shade of chrome-yellow.

He washed with warm water and a sponge, then carefully trimmed his beard and tied back his hair. He dressed, slipping on a velvet shirt and trousers followed by a kimono, decorated with lithographic Amarantin skeletons. Then he breakfasted – the food was always there in a little slot by the time the alarm rang – and checked the time again. She would be here shortly. He made the bed and upended it so that it formed a couch, in dimpled scarlet leather.

Pascale, as always, was accompanied by a human bodyguard and a couple of armed servitors, but they did not follow her into the room. What did was a tiny buzzing blur like a clockwork wasp. It looked harmless, but he knew that if he so much as broke wind in the biographer's direction, what he would have to show for it would be an additional orifice in the centre of his forehead.

'Good morning,' she said.

'I'd say it's anything but,' Sylveste said, nodding towards the window. 'Actually, I'm surprised you made it here at all.'

She sat down on a velvet-cushioned footstool. 'I have connections in security. It wasn't difficult, despite the curfew.'

'It's come to a curfew, now?'

Pascale wore a pillbox hat in Inundationist purple, the geometric line of her blunt black fringe beneath emphasising the pale expressionless cast of her face. Her outfit was tight-fitting, striped purple and black jacket and trousers. Her entoptics were dewdrops, seahorses and flying fish, trailing pink and lilac glitter. She sat with her feet angled together, touching at the toes, her upper body leaning slightly towards him, as his did towards hers.

'Times have changed, Doctor. You of all people should appreciate that.'

He did. He had been in prison, in the heart of Cuvier, for ten years now. The new regime which had succeeded his after the coup had become as fragmentary as the old, in the time-honoured way of all revolutions. Yet while the political landscape was as divided as ever, the underlying topology was quite different. In his time, the schism had been between those who wanted to study the Amarantin and those who wanted to terraform Resurgam, thereby establishing the world as a viable human colony rather than a temporary research outpost. Even the Inundationist terraformers had been prepared to admit that the Amarantin might once have been worthy of study. These days, however, the extant political factions differed only in the rates of terraforming they advocated, ranging from slow schemes spread across centuries to atmospheric alchemies so brutal that humans might have to evacuate the planet's surface while they were being wrought. One thing was clear enough: even the most modest proposals would destroy many Amarantin secrets for eternity. But few people seemed particularly bothered by that – and for the most part those who did care were too scared to raise their voices. Apart from a skeleton staff of bitter, underfunded researchers, hardly anyone admitted to an interest in the Amarantin at all now. In ten years, study of the dead aliens had been relegated to an intellectual backwater.

And things would only get worse.

Five years earlier, a trade ship had passed through the system. The lighthugger had furled its ramscoop fields and moved into orbit around Resurgam; a bright and temporary new star in the heavens. Its commander, Remilliod, had offered a wealth of technological marvels to the colony: new products from other systems, and things which had not been seen since before the mutiny. But the colony could not afford everything Remilliod had to sell. There had been bloody arguments in favour of buying this over that; machines rather than medicine; aircraft rather than terraforming tools. Rumours, too, of underhand deals; trade in weapons and illegal technologies, and while the general standard of living on the colony was higher than in Sylveste's time – witness the servitors, and the implants Pascale now took for granted – unhealable divisions had opened amongst the Inundationists.

'Girardieau must be frightened,' Sylveste said.

'I wouldn't know,' she said, a touch too hastily. 'All that matters to me is that we have a deadline.'

'What is it you want to talk about today?'

Pascale glanced down at the compad she balanced on her knees. In six centuries computers had assumed every shape and architecture imaginable, but something like a simple drawing slate – flat, with a handwritten entry-mode – had seldom been out of fashion for long. 'I'd like to talk about what happened to your father,' Pascale said.

'You mean the Eighty? Isn't the whole thing already sufficiently well documented for your needs?'

'Almost.' Pascale touched the tip of her stylus against her cochineal-dark lips. 'I've examined all the standard accounts, of course. For the most part they've answered my questions. There's just one small matter I haven't been able to resolve to my total satisfaction.'

'Which is?'

He had to hand it to Pascale. The way she answered, without the slightest trace of real interest in her voice, it really was just as if this were a loose end that needed clearing up. It was a skill; one that almost lulled him into carelessness. 'It's about your father's alpha-level recording,' Pascale said.

'Yes?'

'I'd like to know what really happened to it afterwards.'

In the soft interior rain, the man with the trick gun directed Khouri to a waiting cable-car. It was as unmarked and inconspicuous as the palanquin he had abandoned in the Monument.

'Get in.'

'Just a moment—' But as soon as Khouri opened her mouth, he pushed the end of the gun into the small of her back. Not painfully – it was done firmly, not to hurt – but to remind her that it was there. Something in that gentleness told her the man was a professional, and that he was far more likely to use the gun than someone who would have prodded her aggressively. 'All right; I'm moving. Who is this Mademoiselle anyway? Someone behind a rival Shadowplay house?'

'No; I've already told you; stop thinking so parochially.'

He was not going to tell her anything useful; she could see that. Certain it would not get her far, she said: 'Who are you, then?'

'Carlos Manoukhian.'

That worried her more than the way he handled the gun. He said

60

it too truthfully. It was not a cover-name. And now that she knew it – and guessed that this man was at best some kind of criminal, laughable as that category seemed in Chasm City's lawlessness – it meant he planned to kill her later.

The cable-car's door clammed shut. Manoukhian pressed a button on the console which purged the Chasm City air, blasting out in steam jets below the car as it lofted itself via a nearby cable.

'Who are you, Manoukhian?'

'I help the Mademoiselle.' As if that was not blindingly obvious. 'We have a special relationship. We go back a long way.'

'And what does she want with me?'

'I would have thought it was obvious by now,' Manoukhian said. He was still keeping the gun on her, even as he kept one eye on the car's navigation console. 'There's someone she wants you to assassinate.'

'That's what I do for a living.'

'Yeah.' He smiled. 'Difference is, this guy hasn't paid for it.'

The biography, needless to say, had not been Sylveste's idea. Instead, the initiative had come from the one man Sylveste would have least suspected. It had been six months earlier; during one of the very few occasions when he had spoken face to face with his captor. Nils Girardieau had brought up the subject almost casually, mentioning that he was surprised no one had taken on the task. After all, the fifty years on Resurgam virtually amounted to another life, and even though that life was now capped by an ignominious epilogue, it did at least put his earlier life into a perspective it had lacked during the Yellowstone years. 'The problem was,' Girardieau said, 'your previous biographers were too close to the events – too much part of the societal milieu they were attempting to analyse. Everyone was in thrall to either Cal or yourself, and the colony was so claustrophobic there was no room to step back and see the wider perspective.'

'You're saying Resurgam is somehow less claustrophobic?'

'Well, obviously not – but at least we have the benefit of distance, both in time and space.' Girardieau was a squat, muscular man with a shock of red hair. 'Admit it, Dan – when you think back to your life on Yellowstone, doesn't it sometimes seem like it all happened to someone else, in a century very remote from our own?'

Sylveste was about to laugh dismissively, except that – for once – he found himself in complete agreement with Girardieau. It was an unsettling moment, as if a basic rule of the universe had been violated.

'I still don't see why you'd want to encourage this,' Sylveste said, nodding towards the guard who was presiding over the conversation. 'Or are you hoping you can somehow profit from it?'

Girardieau had nodded. 'That's part of it – maybe most of it, if you want the truth. It probably hasn't escaped your attention that you're still a figure of fascination to the populace.'

'Even if most of them would be fascinated to see me hung.'

'You've a point, but they'd probably insist on shaking your hand first – before helping you to the gibbet.'

'And you think you can milk this appetite?'

Girardieau had shrugged. 'Obviously, the new regime determines who gains access to you – and we also own all your records and archival material. That gives us a headstart already. We have access to documents from the Yellowstone years which no one beyond your immediate family even knows exist. We'd exercise a certain discretion in using them, of course – but we'd be fools to ignore them.'

'I understand,' Sylveste said, because suddenly it was all very clear to him. 'You're actually going to use this to discredit me, aren't you.'

'If the facts discredit you . . .' Girardieau left the remark hanging in the air.

'When you deposed me . . . wasn't that good enough for you?'

'That was nine years ago.'

'Meaning what?'

'Meaning long enough for people to forget. Now they need a gentle reminder.'

'Especially as there's a new air of discontent abroad.'

Girardieau winced, as if the remark was in spectacularly poor taste. 'You can forget about True Path – especially if you think they might turn out to be your salvation. They wouldn't have stopped at imprisoning you.'

'All right,' Sylveste said, boring rapidly. 'What's in it for me?'

'You assume there has to be something?'

'Generally, yes. Otherwise, why bother telling me about it?'

'Your co-operation might be in your best interest. Obviously, we could work from the material we've seized – but your insights would be valuable. Especially in the more speculative episodes.'

'Let me get this straight. You want me to authorise a hatchet job? And not just give it my blessing but actually help you assassinate my character?'

'I could make it worth your while.' Girardieau nodded around the confines of the room in which Sylveste was held. 'Look at the freedom I've given Janequin, to continue his peacock hobby. I could be just as flexible in your case, Dan. Access to recent material on the Amarantin; the ability to communicate with your colleagues; share your opinions – perhaps even the occasional excursion beyond the building.'

'Field work?'

'I'd have to consider it. Something of that magnitude . . .' Sylveste was suddenly, acutely aware that Girardieau was acting. 'A period of grace might be advisable. The biography's in development now, but it'll be several months before we need your input. Maybe half a year. What I propose is that we wait until you've begun to give us what we need. You'll be working with the biography's author, of course, and if that relationship is successful – if she considers it successful – then perhaps we'll be ready to enter into discussions about limited field work. Discussions, mind – no promises.'

'I'll try and contain my enthusiasm.'

'Well, you'll be hearing from me again. Is there anything you need to know before I leave?'

'One thing. You mentioned that the biographer would be a woman. Might I ask who it'll be?'

'Someone with illusions waiting to be shattered, I suspect.'

Volyova was working near the cache one day, thinking of weapons, when a janitor-rat dropped gently onto her shoulder and spoke into her ear.

'Company,' said the rat.

The rats were a peculiar quirk of the *Nostalgia for Infinity*; quite possibly unique aboard any lighthugger. They were only fractionally more intelligent than their feral ancestors, but what made them useful – what turned them from pest into utility – was that they were biochemically linked into the ship's command matrix. Every rat had specialised pheromonal receptors and transmitters which allowed it to receive commands and transmit information back to the ship, encoded into complex secreted molecules. They foraged for waste, eating virtually anything organic which was not nailed down or still breathing. Then they ran some rudimentary preprocessing in their guts before going elsewhere in the ship, excreting pellets into larger recycler systems. Some of them had even been equipped with voiceboxes and a small hardwired lexicon of useful phrases, triggered into vocalisation when external stimuli satisfied biochemically programmed conditions.

In Volyova's case, she had programmed the rats to alert her as soon as they began to process human detritus – dead skin cells, and the like – which had not come from her. She would know when the other crew members were awake, even if she was in a completely different district of the ship.

'Company,' the rat squeaked again.

'Yes, I heard first time.' She lowered the little rodent to the deck, and then swore in all the languages at her disposal.

The defensive wasp which had accompanied Pascale buzzed a little nearer to Sylveste as it picked up the stress overtones in his voice. 'You want to know about the Eighty? I'll tell you. I don't feel the slightest hint of remorse for any of them. They all knew the risks. And there were seventy-nine volunteers, not eighty. People conveniently forget that the eightieth was my father.'

'You can hardly blame them.'

'Assuming stupidity is an inherited trait, then no, I can't.' Sylveste tried to relax himself. It was difficult. At some point in the conversation, the militia had begun to dust the domed-in air outside with fear gas. It was staining the reddened daylight to something nearer black. 'Look,' Sylveste said evenly. 'The government appropriated Calvin when I was arrested. He's quite capable of defending his own actions.'

'It isn't his actions I want to ask you about.'

Pascale made an annotation in her compad. 'It's what became of him – his alpha-level simulation – afterwards. Now, each of the alphas comprised in the region of ten to the power eighteen bytes of information,' she said, circling something. 'The records from Yellowstone are patchy, but I was able to learn a little. I found that sixty-six of the alphas resided in orbital data reservoirs around Yellowstone; carousels, chandelier cities and various Skyjack and

Ultra havens. Most had crashed, of course, but no one was going to erase them. Another ten I traced to corrupted surface archives, which leaves four missing. Three of those four are members of the seventy-nine, affiliated to either very poor or very extinct family lines. The other is the alpha recording of Calvin.'

'Is there a point to this?' he asked, trying not to sound as if the issue particularly concerned him.

'I just can't accept that Calvin was lost in the same way as the others. It doesn't add up. The Sylveste Institute didn't need creditors or trustees to safeguard their heirlooms. It was one of the wealthiest organisations on the planet right up until the plague hit. So what became of Calvin?'

'You think I brought it to Resurgam?'

'No; the evidence suggests it was already long lost by then. In fact, the last time it was definitely present in the system was more than a century before the Resurgam expedition departed.'

'I think you're wrong,' Sylveste said. 'Check the records more closely and you'll see that the alpha was moved into an orbital data cache in the late twenty-fourth. The Institute relocated premises thirty years later, so it was certainly moved then. Then in '39 or '40 the Institute was attacked by House Reivich. They wiped the data cores.'

'No,' Pascale said. 'I excluded those instances. I'm well aware that in 2390 around ten to the eighteen bytes of something was moved into orbit by the Sylveste Institute, and the same amount relocated thirty-seven years later. But ten to the eighteen bytes of information doesn't have to be Calvin. It could as easily be ten to the eighteen bytes of metaphysical poetry.'

'Which proves nothing.'

She passed him the compad, her entourage of seahorses and fish scattering like fireflies. 'No, but it certainly looks suspicious. Why would the alpha vanish around the time you went to meet the Shrouders, unless the two events were related?'

'You're saying I had something to do with it?'

'The subsequent data-movements could only have been faked by someone within the Sylveste organisation. You're the obvious suspect.'

'A motive wouldn't go amiss.'

'Oh, don't worry about that,' she said, returning the compad to her lap. 'I'm sure I'll think of one.'

*

Three days after the janitor-rat had warned her of the crew's awakening, Volyova felt sufficiently prepared to meet them. It was never something she particularly looked forward to, for although she did not actively dislike human company, neither had Volyova ever had any difficulty in adjusting to solitude. But things were worse now. Nagorny was dead, and by now the others would be well aware of that fact.

Ignoring the rats, and subtracting Nagorny, the ship now carried six crew members. Five, if one elected not to include the Captain. And why include him, when – as far as the other crew were aware, he was not even capable of consciousness, let alone communication? They carried him only because they hoped to make him well. In all other respects the ship's real centre of power was vested in the Triumvirate. That was Yuuji Sajaki, Abdul Hegazi and – of course – herself. Below the Triumvirate there were currently two more crew, of equal rank. Their names were Kjarval and Sudjic; chimerics who had only recently joined ship. Finally – the lowest rank of all – was the Gunnery Officer, the role Nagorny had filled. Now that he was dead the role had a certain potentiality, like a vacant throne.

During their periods of activity, the other crew tended to stay within certain well-defined districts of the ship, leaving the rest to Volyova and her machines. It was morning now, by shiptime: here up in the crew levels, the lights still followed a diurnal pattern, slaved to a twenty-four hour clock. She went first to the reefersleep room and found it empty, with all but one of the sleep caskets open. The other one, of course, belonged to Nagorny. After reattaching his head Volyova had placed the body in the casket and cooled it down. Later, she had arranged for the unit to malfunction, allowing Nagorny to warm. He had been dead already, but it would take a skilled pathologist to tell that now. Clearly none of the crew had felt much inclined to examine him closely.

She thought about Sudjic again. Sudjic and Nagorny had been close, for a while. It would not pay to underestimate Sudjic.

Volyova left the reefersleep chamber, explored several other likely places of meeting, and then found herself entering one of the forests, navigating through immense thickets of dead vegetation until she neared a pocket where UV lamps were still burning. She approached a glade, making her way unsteadily down the rustic wooden stairs which led to the floor. The glade was quite idyllic – more so now that the rest of the forest was so bereft of life. Shafts of yellow sunlight knifed through a shifting bower of palm trees overhead. There was a waterfall in the distance, feeding a steep-walled lagoon. Parrots and macaws occasionally kited from tree to tree or made ratcheting calls from their perches.

Volyova gritted her teeth, despising the artificiality of the place.

The four living crew were eating breakfast around a long wooden table, piled high with bread, fruit, slices of meat and cheese, jars of orange juice and flasks of coffee. Across the glade, two holographically projected jousting knights were doing their best to disembowel each other.

'Good morning,' she said, stepping from the staircase onto the authentically dewy grass. 'I don't suppose there's any coffee left?'

They looked up, some of them twisting around on their stools to meet her. She registered their reactions as their cutlery clinked discreetly down, three of them murmuring a hushed greeting. Sudjic said nothing at all, while only Sajaki actually raised his voice.

'Glad to see you, Ilia.' He snatched a bowl from the table. 'Care for some grapefruit?'

'Thanks. Perhaps I will.'

She walked towards them and took the plate from Sajaki, the fruit glistening with sugar. Deliberately she sat between the two other women: Sudjic and Kjarval. Both were currently black-skinned and bald, apart from fiery tangles of dreadlocks erupting from their crowns. Dreadlocks were important to Ultras: they symbolised the number of reefersleep stints that each had done; the number of times each had almost kissed the speed of light. The two women had joined after their own ship had been pirated by Volyova's crew. Ultras traded loyalties as easily as the water ice, monopoles and data they used for currency. Both were overt chimerics, although their transformations were modest compared to Hegazi. Sudjic's arms vanished below her elbows into elaborately engraved bronze gauntlets, inlaid with ormoluwork windows which revealed constantly shifting holographics, diamond nails projecting from the too-slender fingers of her mock hands. Most of Kjarval's body was organic, but her eyes were feline cross-hatched red ellipses, and her flat nose exhibited no nostrils; merely sleekly rilled apertures, as if she was partially adapted to aquatic living. She wore no clothes, but apart from eyes, nostrils, mouth and ears, her skin was seamless, like an all-enveloping sheath of ebony neoprene. Her breasts lacked nipples; her fingers were dainty but without nails, and her toes were little more than vague suggestions, as if she had been rendered by a sculptor anxious to begin another commission. As Volyova sat down, Kjarval observed her with indifference that was a little too studied to be genuine.

'It's good to have you with us,' Sajaki said. 'You've been very busy while we were sleeping. Anything much happen?'

'This and that.'

'Intriguing.' Sajaki smiled. 'This and that. I don't suppose that between "this" and "that" you noticed anything which might shed some light on Nagorny's death?'

'I wondered where Nagorny was. Now you've answered my question.'

'But you haven't answered mine.'

Volyova dug into her grapefruit. 'The last time I saw him he was alive. I have no idea . . . how did he die, incidentally?'

'His reefersleep unit warmed him prematurely. Various bacteriological processes ensued. I don't suppose we need to go into the details, do we?'

'Not over breakfast, no.' Evidently they had not examined him closely at all: if they had, they might have noticed the injuries he had sustained during his death, for all that she had tried to disguise them. 'I'm sorry,' she said, flashing a glance towards Sudjic. 'I meant no disrespect.'

'Of course not,' Sajaki said, tearing a hunk of bread in half. He fixed Sudjic with his close-set ellipsoidal eyes, like someone staring down a rabid dog. The tattoos which he had applied during his infiltration of the Bloater Skyjacks were gone now, but there were fine whitish trails where they had been, despite the patient ministrations which had been visited upon him in reefersleep. Perhaps, Volyova thought, Sajaki had instructed his medichines to retain some trace of his exploits among the Bloaterians; a trophy of the economic gains he had wrested from them. 'I'm sure we all absolve Ilia of any responsibility for Nagorny's death – don't we, Sudjic?'

'Why should I blame her for an accident?' Sudjic said.

'Precisely. And there's an end to the matter.'

'Not quite,' Volyova said. 'Now may not be the best time to raise the matter, but . . .' She trailed off. 'I was going to say that I wanted to extract the implants from his head. But even if I was allowed to do so, they'd probably be damaged.'

'Can you make new ones?' Sajaki said.

'Given time, yes.' She said it with a sigh of resignation. 'I'll need a new candidate, too.'

'When we lay over around Yellowstone,' Hegazi said, 'you can search for someone there, can't you?'

The knights were still clashing across the glade, but no one was paying them very much attention now, even though one of them seemed to be having difficulties with an arrow inserted through his faceplate.

'I'm sure someone suitable will turn up,' Volyova said.

The cold air in the Mademoiselle's house was the cleanest Khouri had tasted since arriving on Yellowstone. Which was really saying very little. Clean, but not fragrant. More like the smells she remembered from the hospital tent on Sky's Edge, redolent of iodine and cabbage and chlorine, the last time she had seen Fazil.

Manoukhian's cable-car had carried them across the city, through a partially flooded subsurface aqueduct. They had arrived in an underground cavern. From there, Manoukhian had ushered Khouri into a lift which ascended with ear-popping speed. The lift had brought them to this dark, echoey hallway. More than likely it was just a trick of acoustics, but Khouri felt as if she had just stepped into a huge unlit mausoleum. Filigreed windows floated overhead, but the light which leaked through them was midnight pale. Given that it was still day outside, the effect was subtly disturbing.

'The Mademoiselle has no passion for daylight,' Manoukhian said, leading her on.

'You don't say.' Khouri's eyes were starting to adjust to the gloom. She began to pick out big hulking things standing in the hall. 'You're not from around here, are you, Manoukhian?'

'I guess that makes two of us.'

'Was it a clerical error that brought you to Yellowstone as well?'

'Not quite.' She could tell that Manoukhian was deciding how much he could get away with telling. That was his one weakness, Khouri thought. For a hit-man, or whatever he was, the man liked to talk too much. The trip over had been one long series of brags and boasts about his exploits in Chasm City – stuff, which, if it had been coming from anyone other than this cool customer with the foreign accent and trick gun, she would have dismissed out of hand. But with Manoukhian, the worrying thing was that a lot of it might have been true. 'No,' he said, his urge to spin a story obviously triumphing over his professional instincts towards surliness. 'No; it wasn't a clerical error. But it was a kind of mistake – or an accident, at any rate.'

There were lots of the hulking things. It was difficult to make out their overall shapes, but they all rested on slim poles jutting from black plinths. Some were like sections of smashed eggshell, while others more resembled delicate husks of brain coral. Everything had a metallic sheen, rendered colourless in the sallow light of the hallway.

'You had an accident?'

'No . . . not me. She did. The Mademoiselle. That's how we met each other. She was . . . I shouldn't be telling you any of this, Khouri. She finds out, I'm dead meat. Pretty easy to dispose of bodies in the Mulch. Hey, you know what I found there the other day? You're not going to believe any of this, but I found a whole fucking . . .'

Manoukhian went off on a boast. Khouri brushed her fingers against one of the sculptures, feeling its cool metal texture. The edges were very sharp. It was as if she and Manoukhian were two furtive art lovers who had broken into a museum in the middle of the night. The sculptures seemed to be biding their time. They were waiting for something – but not with infinite reserves of patience.

She was perplexingly glad of the gunman's company.

'Did she make these?' Khouri asked, interrupting Manoukhian's flow.

'Perhaps,' Manoukhian said. 'In which case you could say she suffered for her art.' He stopped, touching her on the shoulder. 'All right. You see those stairs?'

'I guess you want me to use them.'

'You're learning.'

Gently, he stuck the gun in her back – just to remind her it was still there.

*

Through a porthole in the wall next to the dead man's quarters Volyova could see a tangerine-coloured gas giant planet, its shadowed southern pole flickering with auroral storms. They were deep inside the Epsilon Eridani system now; coming in at a shallow angle to the ecliptic. Yellowstone was only a few days away; already they were within light-minutes of local traffic, threading through the web of line-of-sight communications which linked every significant habitat or spacecraft in the system. Their own ship had changed, too. Through the same window Volyova could just see the front of one of the Conjoiner engines. The engines had automatically hauled in their scoop fields as the ship dropped below ramming speed, subtly altering their shapes to in-system mode, the intake maw closing like a flower at dusk. Somehow the engines were still producing thrust, but the source of the reaction mass or the energy to accelerate it was just another mystery of Conjoiner technology. Presumably there was a limit on how long the drives could function like this, or else they would never have needed to trawl space for fuel during interstellar cruise mode . . .

Her mind was wandering, trying to focus on anything but the issue at hand.

'I think she's going to be trouble,' Volyova said. 'Serious trouble.'

'Not if I read her correctly.' Triumvir Sajaki dispensed a smile. 'Sudjic knows me too well. She knows I wouldn't take the trouble of actually reprimanding her if she made a move against a member of the Triumvirate. I wouldn't even give her the luxury of leaving the ship when we get to Yellowstone. I'd simply kill her.'

'That might be a little harsh.'

She sounded weak and despised herself for it, but it was how she felt. 'It's not as if I don't sympathise with her. After all Sudjic had nothing personal against me until I . . . until Nagorny died. If she does anything, couldn't you just discipline her?'

'It's not worth it,' Sajaki said. 'If she has the mind to do something to you, she won't stop at petty aggravation. If I just discipline her she'll find a way to hurt you permanently. Killing her would be the only reasonable option. Anyway – I'm surprised that you see her side of things. Hasn't it occurred to you that some of Nagorny's problems might have rubbed off on her?'

'You're asking me whether I think she's completely sane?'

'It doesn't matter. She won't move against you – you have my

71

word on that.' Sajaki paused. 'Now, can we get this over with? I've had enough of Nagorny for one life.'

'I know exactly how you feel.'

It was several days after her first meeting with the crew. They were standing outside the dead man's quarters, on level 821, preparing to enter his rooms. They had remained sealed since his death – longer, as far as the others were concerned. Even Volyova had not entered them, wary of disturbing something which might place her there.

She spoke into her bracelet. 'Disable security interdict, personal quarters Gunnery Officer Boris Nagorny, authorisation Volyova.'

The door opened before them, emitting a palpable draught of highly chilled air.

'Send them in,' Sajaki said.

The armed servitors took only a few minutes to sweep the interior, certifying that there were no obvious hazards. It would have been unlikely, of course, since Nagorny had probably not planned to die quite when Volyova had arranged it. But with characters like him, one could never be sure.

They stepped in, the servitors having already activated the room lights.

Like most of the psychopaths she had encountered, Nagorny had always seemed perfectly happy with the smallest of personal spaces. His quarters were even more determinedly cramped than her own. A fastidious neatness had been at work there, like a poltergeist in reverse. Most of his belongings – there were not many – had been securely racked down, and so had not been disturbed by the ship's manoeuvres when she killed him.

Sajaki grimaced and held a sleeve up to his nose. 'That smell.'

'It's borscht. Beetroot. I think Nagorny was partial to it.'

'Remind me not to try it.'

Sajaki closed the door behind them.

There was a residual frigidity to the air. The thermometers said that it was now room temperature, but it seemed as if the molecules in the air carried an imprint of the months of cold. The room's overpowering spartanness did not offset this chill. Volyova's quarters seemed opulent and luxurious by comparison. It was not simply a case of Nagorny neglecting to personalise his space. It was just that in so doing he had so miserably failed by normal standards that his efforts actually contradicted themselves and made the room seem even bleaker than had it been empty.

What failed to help matters was the coffin.

The elongated object had been the only thing in the room not lashed down when she killed Nagorny. It was still intact, but Volyova sensed that the thing had once stood upright, dominating the room with a fearful premonitory grandeur. It was huge and probably made of iron. The metal was as ebon and light-sucking as the surface of a Shrouder emboîtement. All its surfaces had been carved in bas-relief, too intricately rendered to give up all their secrets in one glance. Volyova stared in silence. Are you trying to say, she thought, that Boris Nagorny was capable of this?

'Yuuji,' she said. 'I don't like this at all.'

'I don't very much blame you.'

'What kind of madman makes his own coffin?'

'A very dedicated one, I'd say. But it's here, and it's probably the only glimpse into his mind we have. What do you make of the embellishments?'

'Undoubtedly a projection of his psychosis, a concretisation.' Now that Sajaki was forcing calm she was slipping into subservience. 'I should study the imagery. It might give me insight.' She paused, added: 'So that we don't make the same mistake twice, I mean.'

'Prudent,' Sajaki said, kneeling down. He stroked his gloved forefinger over the intagliated rococo surface. 'We were very lucky you were not forced to kill him, in the end.'

'Yes,' she said, giving him an odd look. 'But what are your thoughts on the embellishments, Yuuji-san?'

'I'd like to know who or what Sun Stealer was,' he said, drawing her attention to those words, etched in Cyrillic on the coffin. 'Does that mean anything to you? Within the terms of his psychosis, I mean. What did it mean to Nagorny?'

'I haven't the faintest.'

'Let me hazard a guess, anyway. I'd say that in Nagorny's imagination Sun Stealer represented somebody in his day-to-day experience, and I see two obvious possibilities.'

'Himself or me,' Volyova said, knowing that Sajaki was not to be easily distracted. 'Yes, yes, that much is obvious ... but this doesn't in any way help us.'

'You're quite sure he never mentioned this Sun Stealer?'

'I would remember a thing like that.'

Which was quite true. And of course she did remember: he had written those words on the wall in her quarters, in his own blood. The expression meant nothing to her, but that did not mean she was in any sense unfamiliar with it. Towards the unpleasant termination of their professional relationship, Nagorny had spoken of little else. His dreams were thick with Sun Stealer, and – like all paranoiacs – he saw evidence of Sun Stealer's malignant work in the most humdrum of daily annoyances. When one of the ship's lights failed unaccountably or a lift directed him to the wrong level, this was Sun Stealer's doing. It was never a simple malfunction, but always evidence of the deliberate machinations of a behind-the-scenes entity only Nagorny could detect. Volyova had stupidly ignored the signs. She had hoped – in fact come as close to praying as was possible for her – that his phantom would return to the netherworld of his unconscious. But Sun Stealer had stayed with Nagorny; witness the coffin on the floor.

Yes . . . she would remember a thing like that.

'I'm sure you would,' Sajaki said, knowingly. Then he returned his attention to the engravings. 'I think first we should make a copy of these marks,' he said. 'They may help us, but this damned Braille effect isn't easy to make out with the eye. What do you think these are?' He moved his palm across a kind of radial pattern. 'Birds' wings? Or rays of sunlight shining from above? They look more like birds' wings to me. Now why would he have bird wings on his mind? And what kind of language is this meant to be?'

Volyova looked, but the crawling complexity of the coffin was too much to take in. It was not that she was uninterested – not at all. But what she wanted was the thing to herself, and Sajaki as far away from it as possible. There was too much evidence here of the canyon depths to which Nagorny's mind had plummeted.

'I think it merits more study,' she said carefully. 'You said "first". What do you intend to do after we make a copy of it?'

'I would have thought that was obvious.'

'Destroy the damned thing,' she surmised.

Sajaki smiled. 'Either that or give it to Sudjic. But personally I'd settle for destroying it. Coffins aren't good things to have on a ship, you know. Especially home-made ones.'

The stairs went up for ever. After a while – already in the two hundreds – Khouri lost count. But just when her knees felt as if they were going to buckle, the staircase came to an abrupt end, presenting her with a long, long white corridor whose sides were a series of recessed arches. The effect was like standing in a portico under moonlight. She walked along the corridor's echoey length until she arrived at the double doors which ended it. They were festooned with organic black scrollwork, inset with faintly tinted glass. A lavender light poured through them from the room beyond.

Evidently she had arrived.

It was entirely possible that this was a trap of some kind, and that to enter the room beyond would be a form of suicide. But turning back was not an option either – Manoukhian, for all his charm, had made that abundantly clear. So Khouri grasped the handle and let herself in. Something in the air made her nose tickle pleasantly, a blossomy perfume negating the sterility of the rest of the house. The smell made Khouri feel unwashed, although it was only a few hours since Ng had woken her and told her to go and kill Taraschi. In the meantime she had accumulated a month's worth of dirt from the Chasm City rain, suffused with her own sweat and fear.

'I see Manoukhian managed to get you here in one piece,' said a woman's voice.

'Me or him?'

'Both, dear girl,' the invisible speaker said. 'Your reputations are equally formidable.'

Behind her the double doors clicked shut. Khouri began to take in her surroundings; difficult in the strange pink light of the room. The enclosure was kettle-shaped, with two eyelike shuttered windows set into one concave wall.

'Welcome to my place of residence,' the voice said. 'Make yourself at home, won't you.'

Khouri walked to the shuttered windows. To one side of the windows sat a pair of reefersleep caskets, gleaming like chromed silverfish. One of the units was sealed and running, while the other was open; a chrysalis ready to enfold the butterfly.

'Where am I?'

The shutters whisked open.

'Where you always were,' the Mademoiselle said.

She was looking out across Chasm City. But it was from a higher vantage point than she had ever known. She was actually above the Mosquito Net, perhaps fifty metres from its stained surface. The city lay below the Net like a fantastically spiny sea-creature preserved in formaldehyde. She had no idea where she was; except that this had to be one of the tallest buildings; one that she had probably assumed was uninhabited.

The Mademoiselle said: 'I call this place the Château des Corbeaux; the House of Ravens; by virtue of its blackness. You've undoubtedly seen it.'

'What do you want?' Khouri said, finally.

'I want you to do a job for me.'

'All this for that? I mean, you had to kidnap me at gunpoint just to ask me to do a job? Couldn't you go through the usual channels?'

'It isn't the usual sort of job.'

Khouri nodded towards the open reefersleep unit. 'Where does that come into it?'

'Don't tell me it alarms you. You came to our world in one, after all.'

'I just asked what it meant.'

'All in good time. Turn around, will you?'

Khouri heard a slight bustle of machinery behind her, like the sound of a filing cabinet opening.

A hermetic's palanquin had entered the room. Or had it been here all along, concealed by some artifice? It was as dark and angular as a metronome, lacking ornamentation, and with a roughly welded black exterior. It had no appendages or obvious sensors, and the tiny viewing monocle set into its front was as dark as a shark's eye.

'You are doubtless already familiar with my kind,' said the voice emanating from the palanquin. 'Do not be disturbed.'

'I'm not,' Khouri said.

But she was lying. There was something disturbing about this box; a quality she had never experienced in the presence of Ng or the other hermetics she had known. Perhaps it was the austerity of the palanquin, or the sense – entirely subliminal – that the box was seldom unoccupied. None of this was helped by the smallness of the viewing window, or the feeling that there was something monstrous behind that dark opacity.

'I can't answer all your questions now,' the Mademoiselle said.

'But obviously I didn't bring you here just to see my predicament. Here. Perhaps this will assist matters.'

A figure grew to solidity next to the palanquin, imaged by the room itself.

It was a woman, of course – young, but paradoxically clothed in the kind of finery which no one had worn on Yellowstone since the plague; enrobed in swirling entoptics. The woman's black hair was raked back from a noble forehead, held in a clasp inwoven with lights. Her electric-blue gown left her shoulders bare, cut away in a daring décolletage. Where it reached the floor it blurred into nothingness.

'This is how I was,' the figure spoke. 'Before the foulness.'

'Can't you still be like that?'

'The risk of leaving enclosure is too great – even in the hermetic sanctuaries. I distrust their precautions.'

'Why have you brought me here?'

'Didn't Manoukhian explain things fully?'

'Not exactly, no. Other than explaining how it wouldn't be good for my health not to go along with him.'

'How indelicate of him. But not inaccurate, it must be admitted.' A smile upset the pale composure of the woman's face. 'What do you suppose were my reasons for bringing you here?'

Khouri knew that, whatever else had happened, she had seen too much to return to normal life in the city.

'I'm a professional assassin. Manoukhian saw me at work and told me I was as good as my reputation. Now – maybe I'm jumping to conclusions here – but it occurs to me you might want someone killed.'

'Yes, very good.' The figure nodded. 'But did Manoukhian tell you this would not be the same as your usual contracts?'

'He mentioned an important difference, yes.'

'And would this trouble you?' The Mademoiselle studied her intensely. 'It's an interesting point, isn't it? I'm well aware that your usual targets consent to be assassinated before you go after them. But they do so in the knowledge that they will probably evade you and live to boast about it. When you do catch them, I doubt that many of them go gently.'

She thought of Taraschi. 'Usually not, no. Usually they're begging me not to do it, trying to bribe me, that kind of thing.'

'And?'

Khouri shrugged. 'I kill them anyway.'

'The attitude of a true professional. You were a soldier, Khouri?'

'Once.' She did not really want to think about that now. 'How much do you know about what happened to me?'

'Enough. That your husband was a soldier as well – a man named Fazil – and that you fought together on Sky's Edge. And then something happened. A clerical error. You were put aboard a ship destined for Yellowstone. No one realised the error until you woke up here, twenty years later. Too late by then to return to the Edge – even if you knew Fazil was still alive. He would be forty years older by the time you got back.'

'Now you know why becoming an assassin didn't exactly give me any sleepless nights.'

'No; I can imagine how you felt. That you owed the universe no favours – nor anyone living in it.'

Khouri swallowed. 'But you don't need an ex-soldier for a job like this. You don't even need me: I don't know who you want to take out, but there are better people around than me. I mean, I'm technically good – I only miss one shot in twenty. But I know people who only miss one in fifty.'

'You suit my needs in another manner. I need someone who is more than willing to leave the city.' The figure nodded towards the open reefersleep casket. 'And by that, I mean a long journey.'

'Out of the system?'

'Yes.' Her voice was patient and matronly, as if the rudiments of this conversation had been rehearsed dozens of times. 'Specifically, a distance of twenty light-years. That's how far away Resurgam is.'

'I can't say I've heard of it.'

'I would be troubled if you had.' The Mademoiselle extended her left hand, and a little globe sprang into existence a few inches above her palm. The world was deathly grey – there were no oceans, rivers or greenery. Only a skein of atmosphere – visible as a fine arc near the horizon – and a pair of dirty-white icecaps suggested this was anything other than some airless moon. 'It's not even one of the newer colonies – not what we'd call a colony, anyway. There are only a few tiny research outposts on the whole planet. Until recently Resurgam has been of no significance whatsoever. But all that has changed.' The Mademoiselle paused, seeming to collect her thoughts, perhaps debating how much to reveal at this stage. 'Someone has arrived on Resurgam – a man called Sylveste.'

'That's not a very common name.'

'Then you are aware of his clan's standing in Yellowstone. Good. That simplifies matters enormously. You will have no difficulty finding him.'

'There's more to it than just finding him, isn't there?'

'Oh yes,' the Mademoiselle said. Then she snatched at the globe with her hand, crushing it between her fingers, rivulets of dust pouring between them. 'Very much more.'

FOUR

Carousel New Brazilia, Yellowstone, Epsilon Eridani, 2546

Volyova disembarked from the lighthugger's shuttle and followed Triumvir Hegazi down the exit tunnel. Via twisting gaskets, the tunnel led them into the weightless hub of a spherical transit lounge at the heart of the carousel.

Every fractured strain of humanity was there; a bewildering free-floating riot of colour, like tropical fish in a feeding frenzy. Ultras, Skyjacks, Conjoiners, Demarchists, local traders, intrasystem passengers, freeloaders, mechanics, all following what seemed to be completely random trajectories, but never quite colliding, no matter how perilously close they came. Some – where their bodyplans allowed it – had diaphanous wings sewn under their sleeves, or attached directly to the skin. The less adventurous made do with slim thrust-packs, or allowed themselves to be pulled along by tiny rented tugs. Personal servitors flew through the throng, carrying baggage and folded spacesuits, while liveried, winged capuchin monkeys foraged for litter, tucking what they found into marsupial pouches under their chests. Chinese music tinkled pervasively through the air, sounding to Volyova's untutored ear like windchimes stirred by a breeze with a particular taste for dissonance. Yellowstone, thousands of kilometres below, was an ominous yellow-brown backdrop to all this activity.

Volyova and Hegazi reached the far side of the transit sphere and moved through a matter-permeable membrane into a customs area. It was another free-fall sphere, wall festooned with autonomic weapons which tracked each arrival. Transparent bubbles filled the central volume, each three metres wide and split open along an equatorial bisector. Sensing the newcomers, two bubbles drifted through the airspace and clamped themselves around them.

A small servitor hung inside Volyova's bubble, shaped like a

Japanese Kabuto helmet, with various sensors and readout devices projecting from beneath the rim. She felt a neural tingle as the thing trawled her, like someone daintily rearranging flowers in her head.

'I detect residual Russish linguistic structures but determine that Modern Norte is your standard tongue. Will this suffice for bureaucratic processing?'

'It'll do,' Volyova said, miffed that the thing had detected the rustiness of her native language.

'Then I shall continue in Norte. Apart from reefersleep mediation systems, I detect no cerebral implants or exosomatic perceptual modification devices. Do you require the loan of an implant before the continuation of this interview?'

'Just give me screen and a face.'

'Very well.'

A face resolved beneath the rim. The face was female and white, with just a hint of Mongolism, hair as short as Volyova's own. She guessed that Hegazi's interviewer would appear male, moustached, dark-skinned and heavily chimeric, just like the man himself.

'State your identity,' the woman said.

Volyova introduced herself.

'You last visited this system in . . . let me see.' The face looked down for a moment. 'Eighty-five years ago; '461. Am I correct?'

Against her best instincts, Volyova leaned nearer the screen. 'Of course you're correct. You're a gamma-level simulation. Now dispense with the theatrics and just get on with it. I've wares to trade and every second you detain me is a second more we have to pay to park our ship around your useless dog-turd of a planet.'

'Truculence noted,' the woman said, seeming to jot a remark in a notebook just out of sight. 'For your information, Yellowstone records are incomplete in many areas owing to the data corruption of the plague. When I asked you the question I did so because I wanted to confirm an unverified record.' She paused. 'And by the way; my name is Vavilov. I'm sitting with a rancid cup of coffee and my last cigarette in a draughty office eight hours into a ten-hour shift. My boss will assume I was dozing if I don't turn back ten people today and so far I've only notched up five. With two hours to go I'm looking at ways to fill my quota, so please, think very carefully before your next outburst.' The woman took a drag and blew the smoke in Volyova's direction. 'Now. Shall we continue?'

'I'm sorry, I thought—' Volyova trailed off. 'Your people don't use simulations for this kind of work?'

'We used to,' Vavilov said, with a long-suffering sigh. 'But the trouble with simulations is that they put up with far too much shit.'

From the carousel's hub Volyova and Hegazi rode a house-sized elevator down one of the wheel's four radial spokes, their weight mounting until they reached the circumference. Gravity there was Yellowstone normal, not perceptibly different to the standard Earth gravity adopted by Ultras.

Carousel New Brazilia orbited Yellowstone every four hours, in an orbit which meandered to avoid the 'Rust Belt' – the debris rings which had come into existence since the plague. It had a wheel configuration: one of the commonest carousel designs. This one was ten kilometres in diameter and eleven hundred metres wide, all human activity wound on the thirty-kilometre strip around the wheel. It was sufficient size for a scattering of towns, small hamlets and bonsai landscape features, even a few carefully horticultured forests, with azure snowcapped mountains carved into the rising valley sides of the strip to give the illusion of distance. The curved roof around the concave part of the wheel was transparent, rising half a kilometre above the strip. Metal rails were fretted across its surface, from which hung billowing artificial clouds, choreographed by computer. Apart from simulating planetary weather, the clouds served to break up the upsetting perspectives of the curved world. Volyova supposed they were realistic, but having never seen real clouds with her own eyes, at least not from below, she could not be wholly sure.

They had emerged from the elevator onto a terrace above the carousel's main community, a collision of buildings piled between stepped valley sides. Rimtown, they called it. It was an eyesore of architectural styles reflecting the succession of different tenants which the carousel had enjoyed throughout its history. A line of rickshaws waited at ground level, the driver of the closest quenching his thirst from a can of banana juice which sat in a holder rigged to the taxi's handlebars. Hegazi passed the driver a piece of paper marked with their destination. The driver held it closely to his black, close-set eyes, then grunted acknowledgement. Soon they were trundling through the traffic, electric and pedal vehicles barging recklessly around each other, pedestrians diving bravely between openings in the seemingly random flow. At least half the people Volyova saw were Ultranauts, evidenced by their tendency towards paleness, spindly build, flaunted body augmentations, swathes of black leather and acres of glinting jewellery, tattoos and trade-trophies. None of the Ultras she saw were extreme chimerics, with the possible exception of Hegazi, who probably qualified as one of the half-dozen most augmented people in the carousel. But the majority wore their hair in the customary Ultra manner, fashioned in thick braids to indicate the number of reefersleep stretches they had done, and many of them had their clothes slashed to expose their prosthetic parts. Looking at these specimens, Volyova had to remind herself that she was part of the same culture.

Ultras, of course, were not the only spacegoing faction spawned by humanity. Skyjacks – at least here – made up a significant portion of the others she saw. They were spacedwellers to be sure, but they did not crew interstellar ships and so their outlook was very different to the wraithlike Ultras, with their dreadlocks and old-fashioned expressions. There were others still. Icecombers were a Skyjack offshoot; psychomodified for the extreme solitude which came from working the Kuiper belt zones, and they kept themselves to themselves with ferocious dedication. Gillies were aquatically modified humans who breathed liquid air; capable of crewing short-range, high-gee ships: they constituted a sizeable fraction of the system's police force. Some gillies were so incapable of normal respiration and locomotion that they had to move around in huge robotic fishtanks when not on duty.

And then there were Conjoiners: descendants of an experimental clique on Mars who had systematically upgraded their minds, swapping cells for machines, until something sudden and drastic had happened. In one moment, they had escalated to a new mode of consciousness – what they called the Transenlightenment – precipitating a brief but nasty war in the process. Conjoiners were easy to pick out in crowds: recently they had bio-engineered huge and beautiful cranial crests for themselves, veined to dissipate the excess heat produced by the furious machines in their heads. There were fewer of them these days, so they tended to draw attention.

Other human factions – like the Demarchists, who had long allied themselves with the Conjoiners – were acutely aware that only Conjoiners knew how to build the engines which powered lighthuggers.

'Stop here,' Hegazi said. The rickshaw darted to the streetside, where wizened old men sat at folding tables playing card games and mah-jong. Hegazi slapped payment into the driver's fleshy palm and then followed Volyova onto the streetside. They had arrived at a bar.

'The Juggler and the Shrouder,' Volyova said, reading the holographic sign above the door. It showed a naked man emerging from the sea, backdropped by strange, phantasmagoric shapes among the surf. Above him, a black sphere hung in the sky. 'This doesn't look right.'

'It's where all the Ultras hang out. You'd better get used to it.'

'All right, point made. I suppose I wouldn't feel at home in any Ultra bar, come to think of it.'

'You wouldn't feel at home in anything that didn't have a navigational system and a lot of nasty firepower, Ilia.'

'Sounds like a reasonable definition of common sense to me.'

Youths barged out into the street, plastered in sweat and what Volyova hoped was spilt beer. They had been arm wrestling: one of their number was nursing a prosthetic which had ripped off at the shoulder, another was riffling a wad of notes he must have won inside. They had the regulation sleep-stretch locks and the standard-issue star-effect tattoos, making Volyova feel simultaneously ancient and envious. She doubted that their anxieties extended much beyond the troubling question of where their next drink or bed was coming from. Hegazi gave them a look – he must have seemed intimidating to them, even given their chimeric aspirations, since it was difficult to tell which parts of Hegazi were not mechanical.

'Come on,' he said, pushing through the disturbance. 'Grin and bear it, Ilia.'

It was dark and smoky inside, and with the combined synergistic effects of the noise from the music – pulsing Burundi rhythms overlaid with something that might have been human singing – and the perfumed, mild hallucinogens in the smoke, it took Volyova a few moments to get her bearings. Then Hegazi pointed to a miraculously spare table in the corner and she followed him to it with the minimum of enthusiasm.

'You're going to sit down, aren't you?'

'I don't suppose I have much choice. We have to look as if we at least tolerate each other's company or people will get suspicious.'

Hegazi shook his head, grinning. 'I must like something about you, Ilia, otherwise I'd have killed you ages ago.'

She sat down.

'Don't let Sajaki hear you talking like that. He doesn't take kindly to threats being made against Triumvir members.'

'I'm not the one who has a problem with Sajaki, in case you forgot. Now, what are you drinking?'

'Something my digestive system can process.'

Hegazi ordered some drinks – his physiology allowed that – waiting until the overhead delivery system brought them.

'You're still annoyed by that business with Sudjic, aren't you?'

'Don't worry,' Volyova said, crossing her arms. 'Sudjic isn't anything I can't handle. Besides, I'd be lucky to lay a finger on her before Sajaki finished her off.'

'He might let you have second pickings.' The drinks arrived in a little perspex cloud with a flip-top, the cloud suspended from a trolley which ran along rails mounted on the ceiling. 'You think he'd actually kill her?'

Volyova attacked her drink, glad of something to wash away the dust of the rickshaw ride. 'I wouldn't trust Sajaki not to kill any of us, if it came to that.'

'You used to trust him. What made you change your mind?'

'Sajaki hasn't been the same since the Captain fell ill again.' She looked around nervously, well aware that Sajaki might not be very far from earshot. 'Before that happened, they both visited the Jugglers, did you know that?'

'You're saying the Jugglers did something to Sajaki's mind?'

She thought back to the naked man stepping from the Juggler ocean. 'That's what they do, Hegazi.'

'Yes, voluntarily. Are you saying Sajaki chose to become crueller?'

'Not just cruel. Single-minded. This business with the Captain . . .' She shook her head. 'It's emblematic.'

'Have you spoken to him recently?'

She read his question. 'No; I don't think he's found who he's looking for, though doubtless we'll find out shortly.'

'And your own quest?'

'I'm not looking for a specific individual. My only constraint is that whoever I find should be saner than Boris Nagorny. That ought not to pose any great difficulties.' She let her gaze drift around the drinkers in the bar. Although none of the people looked definitely psychotic, neither was there anyone who exactly looked stable and well-adjusted. 'At least I hope not.'

Hegazi lit a cigarette and offered Volyova a second. She took it gratefully and smoked it solidly for five minutes, until it resembled a glowing speck of fissile material wrapped in glowing embers. She made a mental note to replenish her supply of cigarettes during this stopover. 'But my search is only just beginning,' she said. 'And I have to handle it delicately.'

'You mean,' Hegazi said with a knowing smile, 'that you're not actually going to tell people what the job is before you recruit them.'

Volyova smirked. 'Of course not.'

The sapphire-hulled shuttle he was riding had not come far: only a short inter-orbital hop from the Sylvestes' familial habitat. Even so, it had been difficult to arrange. Calvin strongly disapproved of his son having any contact with the thing which now resided in the Institute, as if the thing's state of mind might infect Sylveste by some mysterious process of sympathetic resonance. Yet Sylveste was twenty-one. He chose his own associations now. Calvin could go hang, or burn his neurons to ash in the madness he was about to inflict on himself and his seventy-nine disciples . . . but he was not going to dictate who Sylveste could see.

He saw SISS looming ahead, and thought, none of this is real; just a narrative strand from his biography. Pascale had given him the rough-cut and asked for his comments. Now he was experiencing it, still walled in his prison in Cuvier, but moving like a ghost through his own past, haunting his younger self. Memories, long buried, were welling up unbidden. The biography, still far from complete, would be capable of being accessed in many ways, from many viewpoints, and with varying degrees of interactivity. It would be an intricately faceted thing, detailed enough that one could easily spend more than a lifetime exploring only a segment of his past.

SISS looked as real as he remembered. The Sylveste Institute for Shrouder Studies had its organisational centre in a wheel-shaped structure dating from the Amerikano days, although there was not a single cubic nanometre which had not been reprocessed many times over the intervening centuries. The wheel's hub sprouted two grey, mushroom-shaped hemispheres, pocked with docking interfaces and the modest defence systems permitted by Demarchist ethics. The wheel's edge was a hectic accretion of living modules, labs and offices, embedded in a matrix of bulk chitin polymer, linked by a tangle of access tunnels and supply pipes walled in shark-collagen.

'It's good.'

'You think so?' Pascale's voice was distant.

'That's how it was,' Sylveste said. 'How it felt when I visited him.'

'Thanks, I . . . well, this was nothing – the easy part. Fully documented. We had blueprints for SISS, and there are even some people in Cuvier who knew your father, like Janequin. The hard part's what happened afterwards – where we have so little to go on except what you told them on your return.'

'I'm sure you've done an excellent job of it.'

'Well, you'll see – sooner rather than later.'

The shuttle coupled with the docking interface. Institute security servitors were waiting beyond the lock, validating his identity.

'Calvin won't be thrilled,' said Gregori, the Institute's housekeeper. 'But I suppose it's too late to send you home now.'

They had been through this ritual two or three times in the last few months, Gregori always washing his hands of the consequences. It was no longer necessary to have someone escort Sylveste through the shark-collagen tunnels to the place where they kept him; the thing.

'You've nothing to worry about, Gregori. If Father gives you any trouble, just tell him I ordered you to show me around.'

Gregori arched his eyebrows, the emotionally attuned entoptics around him registering amusement.

'Isn't that just what you're doing, Dan?'

'I was trying to keep things amicable.'

'Utterly futile, dear boy. We'd all be much happier if you just

87

followed your father's lead. You know where you are with a good totalitarian regime.'

It took twenty minutes to navigate the tunnels, moving radially outwards to the rim, passing through scientific sections where teams of thinkers – human and machine – grappled endlessly with the central enigma of the Shrouds. Although SISS had established monitoring stations around all the Shrouds so far discovered, most of the information-processing and collating took place around Yellowstone. Here elaborate theories were assembled and tested against the facts, which were scant, but unignorable. No theory had lasted more than a few years.

The place where they kept him, the thing Sylveste had come to see, was a guarded annexe on the rim; a generously large allocation of volume given the lack of evidence that the thing within was actually capable of appreciating the gift. The thing's name – his name – was Philip Lascaille.

He did not have many visitors now. There had been lots in the early days, shortly after his return. But interest had dwindled when it became clear that Lascaille could tell his inquisitors nothing, useful or otherwise. But, as Sylveste had quickly appreciated, the fact that no one paid Lascaille much attention these days could actually work to his advantage. Even Sylveste's relatively infrequent visits – once or twice a month – had been sufficiently far from the norm to enable a kind of rapport to form between the two of them ... between himself and the thing Lascaille had become.

Lascaille's annexe contained a garden, under an artificial sky glazed the deep blue of cobalt. A breeze had been created, sufficient to finger the windchimes suspended from the bower of over-arching trees which fringed the garden.

The garden had been landscaped with paths, rockeries, knolls, trellises and goldfish ponds, the effect being of a rustic maze, so that it always took a minute or so to find Lascaille. When Sylveste did find him the man was usually in the same state: naked or half-naked, filthy to some degree, his fingers smeared with the rainbow shades of crayons and chalks. Sylveste would always know he was getting warm when he saw something scrawled on the stone path; either a complex symmetrical pattern, or what looked like an attempt at mimicking Chinese or Sanskrit calligraphy, without actually knowing any real letters. At other times the things which

Lascaille marked on the path looked like Boolean algebra or semaphore.

Then – it was always only a question of time – he would round a corner and Lascaille would be there, working on another marking, or carefully erasing one he had worked on previously. His face would be frozen in a rictus of total concentration, and every muscle in his body would be rigid with the exertion of the drawing, and the process would take place in complete silence, except for the stirring of the windchimes, the quiet whisper of the water or the scraping of his crayons and chalks against stone.

Sylveste would often have to wait hours for Lascaille to even register his presence, which would generally amount to nothing more than the man turning his face to him for an instant, before continuing. Yet the same thing always happened in that instant. The rictus would soften, and in its place would be – if only for a moment – a smile; one of pride or amusement or something utterly beyond Sylveste's fathoming.

And then Lascaille would return to his chalks. And there would be nothing to suggest that this was a man – the only man – the only human being – to ever touch the surface of a Shroud and return alive.

'Anyway,' Volyova said, quenching what remained of her thirst, 'I'm not expecting it to be easy, but I have no doubts that I will find a recruit sooner or later. I've begun to advertise, stating our planned destination. As far as the work is concerned, I say only that it requires someone with implants.'

'But you're not going to take the first one that comes along,' Hegazi said. 'Surely?'

'Of course not. Though they won't know it, I'll be vetting my candidates for some kind of military experience in their backgrounds. I don't want someone who's going to crack up at the first hint of trouble, or someone unwilling to submit to discipline.' She was beginning to relax now, after all her difficulties with Nagorny. A girl was playing on stage, working a gold teeconax through endlessly spiralling ragas. Volyova did not greatly care for music; never had done. But there was something mathematically beguiling about the music which for a moment worked against her prejudices. She said: 'I'm confident of success. We need only concern ourselves with Sajaki.'

At that moment Hegazi nodded towards the door, where bright daylight forced Volyova to squint. A figure stood there, majestically silhouetted in the glare. The man was garbed in a black anklelength cloak and a vaguely defined helmet, the light making it resemble a halo cast around his head. His profile was split diagonally by a long smooth stick which he gripped two-handedly.

The Komuso stepped into the darkness. What looked like a kendo stick was only his bamboo shakuhachi; a traditional musical instrument. With well-rehearsed rapidity he slid the thing into a sheath concealed behind the folds of his cloak. Then, with imperial slowness, he removed the wicker helmet. The Komuso's face was difficult to make out. His hair was brilliantined, slickly tied back in a scythe-shaped tail. His eyes were lost behind sleek assassin's goggles, infrared sensitive facets dully catching the room's tinted light.

The music had come to an abrupt stop, the girl with the teeconax vanishing magically from the stage.

'They think it's a police bust,' Hegazi breathed, the room quiet enough now that he didn't need to raise his voice. 'The local cops send in the basket-cases when they don't want to bloody their own hands.'

The Komuso swept the room, flylike eyes targeting the table where Hegazi and Volyova sat. His head seemed to move independently of the rest of his body, like some species of owl. With a bustle of his cloak he cruised towards them, appearing to glide more than locomote. Nonchalantly Hegazi kicked a spare seat out from under the table, simultaneously taking an unimpressed drag on his cigarette.

'Good to see you, Sajaki.'

He dropped the wicker helmet next to their drinks, ripping the goggles away from his eyes as he did so. He lowered himself into the vacant chair, then turned casually around to the rest of the bar. He made a drinking gesture, imploring the people to get on with their own business while he attended to his. Gradually the conversation rumbled back into life, although everyone was keeping half an eye on the three of them.

'I wish the circumstances merited a celebratory drink,' Sajaki said.

'They don't?' Hegazi said, looking as crestfallen as his extensively modified face permitted.

'No, most certainly not.' Sajaki examined the nearly spent glasses on the table and lifted Volyova's, downing the few drops which remained. 'I've been doing some spying, as you might gather from my disguise. Sylveste isn't here. He isn't in this system any more. As a matter of fact, he hasn't been here for somewhere in the region of fifty years.'

'Fifty years?' Hegazi whistled.

'That's quite a cold trail,' Volyova said. She tried not to sound gloating, but she had always known this risk existed. When Sajaki had given the order to steer the lighthugger towards the Yellowstone system, he had done so on the basis of the best information available to him at the time. But that was decades ago, and the information had been decades old even when he received it.

'Yes,' Sajaki said. 'But not as cold as you might think. I know exactly where he went to, and there's no reason to assume he's ever left the place.'

'And where would this be?' Volyova asked, with a sinking feeling in her stomach.

'A planet called Resurgam.' Sajaki placed Volyova's glass down on the table. 'It's quite some distance from here. But I'm afraid, dear colleagues, that it must be our next port of call.'

He fell into his past again.

Deeper this time; back to when he was twelve. Pascale's flashbacks were non-sequential; the biography was constructed with no regard for the niceties of linear time. At first he was disorientated, even though he was the one person in the universe who ought not to have been adrift in his own history. But the confusion slowly gave way to the realisation that her way was the right one; that it was right to treat his past as shattered mosaic of interchangeable events; an acrostic embedded with numerous equally legitimate interpretations.

It was 2373; only a few decades after Bernsdottir's discovery of the first Shroud. Whole academic disciplines had sprung up around the central mystery, as well as numerous government and private research agencies. The Sylveste Institute for Shrouder Studies was only one of dozens of such organisations, but it also happened to be backed by one of the wealthiest – and most powerful – families in the whole human bubble. But when the break came, it was not via the calculated moves of large scientific organisations. It was through one man's random and dedicated madness.

His name was Philip Lascaille.

He was a SISS scientist working at one of the permanent stations near what was now called Lascaille's Shroud, in the trans Tau Ceti sector. Lascaille was also one of a team kept on permanent stand-by should there ever be a need for human delegates to travel to the Shroud, although no one considered that this was very likely. But the delegates existed, with a ship kept in readiness to carry them the remaining five hundred million kilometres to the boundary, should the invitation ever arrive.

Lascaille decided not to wait.

Alone, he boarded and stole the SISS contact craft. By the time anyone realised what was happening, it was far too late to stop him. A remote destruct existed, but its use might have been construed by the Shroud as an act of aggression, something no one wanted to risk. The decision was to let fate take its course. No one seriously expected to see Lascaille come back alive. And though he did eventually return, his doubters had in a sense been right, because a large portion of his sanity had not come back with him.

Lascaille had come very close indeed to the Shroud before some force had propelled him back out again – perhaps only a few tens of thousands of kilometres from the surface, although at that range there was no easy way of telling where space ended and the Shroud began. No one doubted that he had come closer than any other human being, or for that matter any living creature.

But the cost had been horrific.

Not all of Philip Lascaille – not even most of him – had come back. Unlike those who had gone before him, his body had not been pulped and shredded by incomprehensible forces near the boundary. But something no less final appeared to have happened to his mind. Nothing remained of his personality, except for a few residual traces which served only to heighten the almost absolute obliteration of everything else. Enough brain function remained for him to keep himself alive without machine assistance, and his motor control seemed completely unimpaired. But there was no intelligence left; no sense that Lascaille perceived his surroundings except in the most simplistic manner; no indication that he had any grasp of what had happened to him, or was even aware of the passage of time; no indication that he retained the ability to memorise new experiences or retrieve those that had happened to him before his trip to the Shroud. He retained the ability to vocalise, but while Lascaille occasionally spoke well-formed words, or even fragments of sentences, nothing he uttered made the slightest sense.

Lascaille – or what remained of Lascaille – was returned to the Yellowstone system, and then to the SISS habitat, where medical experts desperately tried to construct a theory for what might have happened. Eventually – and it was more out of desperation than logic – they decided that the fractal, restructured spacetime around the Shroud had not been able to support the information density of his brain. In passing through it, his mind had been randomised on the quantum level, although the molecular processes of his body had not been noticeably affected. He was like a text which had been transcribed imprecisely – so that much of the meaning was lost – and then retranscribed.

Yet Lascaille was not the last person to attempt such a suicide mission. A cult had grown up around him, its chief rumour being that, despite his exterior signs of dementia, the passage close to the Shroud had bestowed on him something like Nirvana. Once or twice every decade, around the known Shrouds, someone would attempt to follow Lascaille into the boundary, and the results were miserably uniform, and no improvement on what Lascaille himself had achieved. The lucky ones came back with half their minds gone, while the unlucky ones never made it back at all, or did so in ships so mangled that their human remains resembled a salmon-coloured paste.

While Lascaille's cult bloomed, people soon forgot about the man himself. Perhaps the salivating, mumbling reality of his existence was a touch too uncomfortable.

Sylveste, however, did not forget. More than that, he had become obsessed with teasing a last, vital truth out of the man. His familial connections guaranteed him an audience with Lascaille whenever he wanted – provided he ignored Calvin's forebodings. And so he had taken to visiting, and waiting in absolute patience while Lascaille attended to his pavement drawings, ever watchful for the one, transient clue which he knew the man would eventually bequeath him.

In the end, it was a lot more than a clue.

It was difficult to remember how long he had waited, on that day when the waiting finally paid off. For all that he intended to focus his mind with absolute attentiveness on what Lascaille was doing, he had been finding it increasingly difficult. It was like staring intently at a long series of abstract paintings – one's concentration inevitably began to wane, no matter how much one tried to keep it fresh. Lascaille had been halfway through the sixth or seventh hopeless chalk mandala of the day, executing the task with the same fervent dedication he brought to every mark he made.

Then, with no forewarning, he had turned to Sylveste and said, with complete clarity: 'The Jugglers offer the key, Doctor.'

Sylveste was too shocked to interrupt.

'It was explained to me,' Lascaille continued blithely. 'While I was in Revelation Space.'

Sylveste forced himself to nod, as naturally as possible. Some still-calm part of his mind recognised the phrase which Lascaille had spoken. As far as anyone had ever been able to tell, it was what Lascaille now called the Shroud boundary – 'space' in which he had been granted certain 'revelations' too abstruse to relate.

Yet now his tongue seemed to have been loosened.

'There was a time when the Shrouders travelled between the stars,' Lascaille said. 'Much as we do now – although they were an ancient species and had been starfaring for many millions of years. They were quite alien, you know.' He paused to switch a blue chalk for a crimson one, placing it between his toes. With that, he continued his work on the mandala. But with his hand – now free from that task – he began to sketch something on an adjacent patch of ground. The creature he drew was multi-limbed, tentacled, armour-plated, spined, barely symmetrical. It looked less like a member of a starfaring alien culture than something which might have flopped and oozed its way across the bed of a Precambrian ocean. It was utterly monstrous.

'That's a Shrouder?' Sylveste said, with a shiver of anticipation. 'You actually met one?'

'No; I never truly entered the Shroud,' Lascaille said. 'But they communicated with me. They revealed themselves to my mind; imparted much of their history and nature.'

Sylveste tore his gaze away from the nightmarish creature. 'Where do the Jugglers come into it?'

'The Pattern Jugglers have been around for a long time and

they're to be found on many worlds. All starfaring cultures in this part of the galaxy encounter them sooner or later.' Lascaille tapped his sketch. 'Just like we did, so did the Shrouders, only very much earlier. Do you understand what I'm saying, Doctor?'

'Yes . . .' He thought he did, anyway. 'But not the point of it.'

Lascaille smiled. 'Whoever – or whatever – visits the Jugglers is remembered by them. Remembered absolutely, that is – down to the last cell; the last synaptic connection. That's what the Jugglers are. A vast biological archiving system.'

This was true enough, Sylveste knew. Humans had gleaned very little of significance concerning the Jugglers, their function or origin. But what had become clear almost from the outset was that the Jugglers were capable of storing human personalities within their oceanic matrix, so that anyone who swam in the Juggler sea – and was dissolved and reconstituted in the process – would have achieved a kind of immortality. Later, those patterns could be realised again; temporarily imprinted in the mind of another human. The process was muddy and biological, so the stored patterns were contaminated by millions of other impressions, each subtly influencing the other. Even in the early days of Juggler exploration it had been obvious that the ocean had stored patterns of alien thought; hints of otherness bleeding into the thoughts of the swimmers – but these impressions had always remained indistinct.

'So the Shrouders were remembered by the Jugglers,' Sylveste said. 'But how does that help us?'

'More than you realise. The Shrouders may look alien, but the basic architectures of their minds were not completely dissimilar to our own. Ignore the bodyplan; realise instead that they were social creatures with a verbal language and the same perceptual environment. To some degree, a human could be made to think like a Shrouder, without becoming completely inhuman in the process.' He looked at Sylveste again. 'It would be within the capabilities of the Jugglers to instil a Shrouder neural transform within a human neocortex.'

It was a chilling thought: achieve contact not by meeting an alien, but by becoming it. If that was what Lascaille meant. 'How would that help us?'

'It would stop the Shroud from killing you.'

'I don't follow you.'

'Understand that the Shroud is a protective structure. What lies within are . . . not just the Shrouders themselves, but technologies which are simply too powerful to be allowed to fall into the wrong hands. Over millions of years, the Shrouders combed the galaxy seeking harmful things left over by extinct cultures – things which I can almost not even begin to describe to you. Things which may once have served good, but which are also capable of being used as weapons of unimaginable horror. Technologies and techniques which may only be deployed by ascended races: means of manipulating spacetime, or of moving faster-than-light . . . other things which your mind literally can't encompass.'

Sylveste wondered if that really were the case. 'Then the Shrouds are – what? Treasure chests, where only the most advanced races get the keys?'

'More than that. They defend themselves against intruders. A Shroud's boundary is almost a living thing. It responds to the thought patterns of those who enter it. If the patterns do not resemble those of the Shrouders . . . it fights back. It alters spacetime locally, creating vicious eddies of curvature. Curvature equals gravitational sheer stress, Doctor. It rips you apart. But the right kinds of mind . . . the Shroud admits them; guides them closer, protects them in a pocket of quiet space.'

The implications, Sylveste saw, were shattering. Think like a Shrouder and one could slip past those defences . . . into the glittering heart of the treasure box. So what if humans were not advanced enough by Shrouder reckoning to behold that treasure? If they were clever enough to break open the box, were they not entitled to take what they found? According to Lascaille, the Shrouders had assumed the role of galactic matron when they secreted those harmful technologies . . . but had anyone asked them to do it? Then another question ghosted into his mind.

'Why did they let you know this, if what was inside the Shrouds had to be protected at all costs?'

'I don't know if it was intentional. The barrier around the Shroud that bears my name must have failed to identify me as alien, if only fleetingly. Perhaps it was damaged, or perhaps my . . . state of mind . . . confused it. Once I had begun to penetrate the Shroud, information began to flow between us. That was how I learned these things. What the Shroud contained, and how its defences might be circumvented. It's not a trick machines can learn, you know.' The last remark seemed to have come from nowhere; for a moment it hung there before Lascaille continued. 'But the Shroud must have begun to suspect that I was foreign. It rejected me; flung me back out into space.'

'Why didn't it just kill you?'

'It must not have been completely confident in its judgement.' He paused. 'In Revelation Space, I did sense doubt. Vast arguments taking place around me, quicker than thought. In the end, caution must have won the day.'

Now another question; the one he had wanted to ask since the moment Lascaille had opened his mouth.

'Why have you waited until now to tell us these things?'

'I apologise for my earlier reticence. But first I had to digest the knowledge that the Shrouders had placed in my mind. It was in their terms, you see – not ours.' He hesitated, his attention seemingly drawn to a smudge of chalk which was marring the mathematical purity of his mandala. He licked his finger and rubbed it away. 'That was the easy part. Then I had to remember how humans communicate.' Lascaille looked at Sylveste, his animal eyes veiled by a Neanderthal tangle of uncombed hair. 'You've been kind to me, not like the others. You had patience with me. I thought this might help you.'

Sylveste sensed that this window of lucidity might soon be closing. 'How exactly do we persuade the Jugglers to imprint the Shrouder consciousness pattern?'

'That's the easy part.' He nodded at the chalk drawing. 'Memorise this figure, and hold it in mind when you swim.'

'That's all?'

'It will suffice. The internal representation of this figure in your mind will instruct the Jugglers as to your needs. You'd better take them a gift, of course. They don't do something of this magnitude for free.'

'A gift?'

Sylveste was wondering what kind of gift one could possibly offer to an entity which resembled a floating island of seaweed and algae.

'You'll think of something. Whatever it is, make sure it's information-dense. Otherwise you'll bore them. You wouldn't want to bore them.' Sylveste wanted to ask further questions, but

Lascaille's attention had returned to his chalk drawings. 'That's all I have to say,' the man said.

It turned out to be the case.

Lascaille never spoke to Sylveste, or anyone else again. A month later they found him dead, drowned in the fishpond.

'Hello?' Khouri said. 'Is there anyone here?'

She had awoken, that was all she knew. Not from a catnap, either, but from something much deeper, longer and colder. A reefersleep fugue, almost certainly – they were not something you forgot, and she had woken from one before, around Yellowstone. The physiological and neural signs were exactly right. There was no sign of a reefersleep casket – she was lying, fully-clothed, on a couch – but someone could easily have moved her before she was properly conscious. Who, though? And where was she? It seemed as if someone had tossed a grenade into her memory, blowing it into frags. The place where she found herself now was only teasingly familiar.

Someone's hallway? Wherever it was, it was filled with ugly sculptures. She had either walked past these things a matter of hours ago, or else they were recessive figments from the depths of her childhood; nursery horrors. Their curved, jagged and burnt shapes loomed over her, casting demonlike shadows. Groggily she intuited that these things fitted together in some way, or had once done so, though they were perhaps too warped and torn for that now.

Footsteps padded unsteadily across the hallway.

She twisted her head to view the approaching person. Her neck felt stiffer than cured wood. Years of experience had told her that the rest of her body would be no more supple after the sleep fugue.

The man stopped a few paces from her bed. In the moonlight glow of the chamber it was hard to read his features, but there was a familiarity within the shadowed jowliness that tugged at her memory. Someone she had known, many years ago.

'It's me,' he said, the voice wet and phlegmatic. 'Manoukhian. The Mademoiselle thought you might appreciate a familiar face when you woke up.'

The names meant something to her, but exactly what, it was hard to say. 'What happened?'

'Simple. She made you an offer you couldn't refuse.'

'How long have I been asleep?'

'Twenty-two years,' Manoukhian said, offering her a hand. 'Now, shall we go and see the Mademoiselle?'

Sylveste woke facing a wall of black which swallowed half the sky – a black so total that it seemed like a nullification of existence itself. He had never noticed it before, but now he saw – or imagined he saw – that the ordinary darkness between the stars was in fact aglow with its own milky luminosity. But there were no stars in the circular pool of emptiness which was Lascaille's Shroud; no source of any light whatsoever, no photons arriving from any part of the detectable electromagnetic spectrum; no neutrinos of any flavour, no particles, exotic or otherwise. No gravity waves, electrostatic or magnetic fields – not even the slight whisper of Hawking radiation which, according to the few extant theories of Shroud mechanics, ought to be bleeding out of the boundary, reflecting the entropic temperature of the surface.

None of these things happened. The only thing a Shroud did – so far as anyone had ever been able to tell – was to comprehensively obstruct all forms of radiation attempting to pass through it. That, of course, and the other thing: which was to shred any object daring to pass too close to its boundary.

They had woken him from reefersleep, and now he was in the state of sickening disorientation which accompanied the crash revival, yet young enough to weather the effects: his physiological age was only thirty-three, despite the fact that more than sixty years had passed since his birth.

'Am I . . . all right?' he struggled to ask the revival medicos, while all the time his attention was being snared by the nothingness beyond the station window, like someone staring into the black counterpart of a snowstorm.

'You're almost clear,' said the medico next to him, watching neural readouts scroll through midair, digesting their import with quiet taps of a stylus against his lower lip. 'But Valdez faded. That means Lefevre's bumped up to primary. Think you can work with her?'

'Bit late for doubts now, isn't it?'

'It's a joke, Dan. Now, how much do you remember? Revival amnesia's the one thing I haven't scanned for.'

It seemed like a stupid question, but as soon as he interrogated his memory, he found it responding sluggishly, like a document retrieval system in an inefficient bureaucracy.

'Do you remember Spindrift?' the medico asked, with a note of concern in his voice. 'It's vital that you remember Spindrift . . .'

He remembered it, yes – but for a moment he could not connect it with any other memories. What he remembered – the last thing he remembered which was not adrift – was Yellowstone. They left it twelve years after the Eighty; twelve years after Calvin's corporeal death; twelve years after Philip Lascaille had spoken to Sylveste; twelve years after the man had drowned himself, his purpose seemingly fulfilled.

The expedition was small but well equipped – a lighthugger crew, partially chimeric, Ultranauts who seldom mingled with the other humans; twenty scientists largely culled from SISS, and four potential contact delegates. Only two of the four would actually travel to the surface of the Shroud.

Lascaille's Shroud was their objective, but not their first port of call. Sylveste had heeded what Lascaille had told him; the Pattern Jugglers were vital to the success of his mission. It was first necessary to visit them on their own world, tens of light-years from the Shroud. Even then Sylveste had little idea of what to expect. But, rash as it seemed, he trusted Lascaille's advice. The man would not have broken his silence for nothing.

The Jugglers had been a curiosity for more than a century. They existed on a number of worlds, all of them dominated by single planet-sized oceans. The Jugglers were a biochemical consciousness distributed through each ocean, composed of trillions of co-acting micro-organisms, arranged into island-sized clumps. All the Jugglers' worlds were tectonically active, and it was theorised that the Jugglers drew their energy from hydrothermal outlet vents on the seabed; that the heat was converted to bioelectrical energy and transferred to the surface via tendrils of organic superconductor draping down through kilometres of black cold. The Jugglers' purpose – assuming they had a purpose – remained completely unknown. It was clear that they had the ability to mediate the biospheres of the worlds in which they had been seeded, acting like a single, intelligently acting mass of phytoplankton – but no one knew if this was merely secondary to some hidden, higher function. What was known – and again not properly understood – was that the Jugglers had the capacity to store and retrieve information, acting like a single, planet-wide neural net. This information was stored on many levels, from the gross connectivity patterns of surface-floating tendrils, down to free-floating strands of RNA. It was impossible to say where the oceans began and the Jugglers ended – just as it was impossible to say whether each world contained many Jugglers or merely one arbitrarily extended individual, for the islands themselves were linked by organic bridges. They were world-sized living repositories of information; vast informational sponges. Almost anything entering a Juggler ocean would be penetrated by microscopic tendrils, partially dissolved, until its structural and chemical properties had been revealed, and that information would then be passed into the biochemical storage of the ocean itself. As Lascaille had intimated, the Jugglers could imprint these patterns as well as encode them. Supposedly those patterns could include the mentalities of other species which had come into contact with the Jugglers – such as the Shrouders.

Human study teams had been investigating the Pattern Jugglers for many decades. Humans swimming in the Juggler-infested ocean were able to enter rapport states with the organism, as Juggler micro-tendrils filtered temporarily into the human neocortex, establishing quasi-synaptic links between the swimmers' minds and the rest of the ocean. It was, they said, like communing with sentient algae. Trained swimmers reported feeling their consciousness expand to include the entire ocean, their memories becoming vast, verdant and ancient. Their perceptual boundaries became malleable, although at no point was there any sense that the ocean itself was truly self-aware; more that it was a mirror, massively reflecting human consciousness: the ultimate solipsism. Swimmers made startling breakthroughs in mathematics, as if the ocean had enhanced their creative faculties. Some even reported that these boosts persisted for some time after they had left the oceanic matrix and returned to dry land or orbit. Was it possible that some physical change had taken place in their minds?

So it was that the concept of the Juggler transform arose. With additional training, the swimmers learned how to select specific forms of transform. Neurologists stationed on the Juggler world attempted to map the brain alterations wrought by the aliens, but with only partial success. The transformations were extraordinarily subtle, more akin to retuning a violin than ripping it apart and building it from scratch. They were rarely permanent – days, weeks or, very occasionally, years later, the transform would fade.

Such was the state of knowledge when Sylveste's expedition reached the Juggler world Spindrift. Now he remembered it, of course – the oceans; the tides; the volcanic chains and the constant, overpowering seaweedy stench of the organism itself. Smell unlocked the rest. All four potential Shrouder contact delegates had learnt the chalk diagram on a deep level of recall. After months of training with expert swimmers, the four entered the ocean and filled their minds with the form Lascaille had given them.

The Juggler had reached into them, partially dissolved their minds, and then restructured them according to its own embedded templates.

When the four emerged, it seemed at first that Lascaille had been crazy after all.

They did not exhibit freakishly alien modes of behaviour, nor had they suddenly gained answers to the great cosmic mysteries. Questioned, none of them reported feeling particularly different, nor were they any the wiser about the identity or nature of the Shrouders. But sensitive neurological tests probed deeper than human intuition. The spatial and cognitive skills of the four had changed, though in ways that were perplexingly difficult to quantify. As days passed, they reported experiencing states of mind that were – paradoxically – both familiar and yet utterly alien. Evidently something had changed, though no one could be sure that the states of mind they were experiencing had any connection with the Shrouders.

Nonetheless, they had to move quickly.

As soon as the initial tests were complete, the four delegates entered reefersleep. The cold prevented the Juggler transforms from decaying, though they would inevitably begin to fade once the four were awakened, despite a complicated regimen of experimental neuro-stabilising drugs. They were kept asleep throughout the voyage to Lascaille's Shroud, then for weeks in the vicinity of the object itself, as their study station was manoeuvred closer, within the nominal 3 AU safe distance which it had maintained until that point. Even then, the delegates were not awoken until the eve of their trip to the surface.

'I . . . remember,' Sylveste said. 'I remember Spindrift.' And then there was a moment while the medico kept tapping his stylus against his lips, assimilating the reams of information pouring from the medical analysis systems, before nodding and passing him fit for the mission.

'The old place has changed a bit,' Manoukhian said.

He was right, Khouri saw. She was looking out over something she hardly recognised as Chasm City. The Mosquito Net was gone. Now the city was open to the elements once more, its buildings rising nakedly into Yellowstone's atmosphere where once they had sheltered beneath the merged drapery of the domes. The Mademoiselle's black château was no longer amongst the tallest structures. Tiered, aeroformed monsters knifed into the broiling brown sky, like sharks' fins, or blades of spinifex, slashed by countless scores of tiny windows, emblazoned with the giant Boolean-logic symbols of the Conjoiners. Like yacht sails, the buildings rose from what remained of the Mulch on slim masts so that their leading edges cut into the wind. Only a scattering of the old gnarled architecture remained, and only a vestigial remnant of the Canopy. The old city forest had been slashed into history by the shining bladelike towers.

'They grew something in the chasm,' Manoukhian said. 'Right down in the depths. They call it the Lilly.' His voice took on a tone of fascinated repulsion. 'People who've seen it say it's like a huge piece of breathing viscera, like a piece of God's stomach. It's fastened to the walls of the chasm. The stuff belching out of the depths is poisonous, but by the time it's been through the Lilly it's just about breathable.'

'All this in twenty-two years?'

'Yes,' someone answered. Movement played in the gloss-black armour of the shutters. Khouri turned around in time to catch a palanquin resting silently. Seeing it, she remembered the Mademoiselle, and much else too. It was as if no more than a minute had elapsed since their last meeting.

'Thank you for bringing her here, Carlos.'

'Will that be all?'

'I think so.' Her voice echoed slightly. 'Time is of the essence, you see. Even after all these years. I've located a crew who need someone like Khouri, but they won't wait for more than a few days before leaving the system. She will need to be educated, primed in her role, and introduced to them before we lose this opportunity.'

'What if I say no?' Khouri said.

'But you won't, will you? Not now that you know what I can do for you. You do remember, don't you?'

'It's not something you forget very easily.' She remembered clearly now what the Mademoiselle had shown her: that the other reefersleep casket held someone. The person inside had been Fazil, her husband. Despite what she had been told, she had never been separated from him. The two of them had both come from Sky's Edge, the clerical error more benign than she had imagined. Yet she had still been deceived. Evidence of the Mademoiselle's handiwork was clear from the outset. Khouri's job working as a Shadowplay assassin had come about a little too easily: in hindsight, the role had served only to demonstrate her fitness for the task ahead. As for ensuring her compliance, that was simplicity itself. The Mademoiselle had Fazil. If Khouri refused to do what was required of her, she would never see her husband again.

'I knew you would see sense,' the Mademoiselle said. 'What I ask of you is really not so difficult, Khouri.'

'What about the crew you've found?'

'They're just traders,' Manoukhian said soothingly. 'I used to be one myself, you know. That's how I came to rescue . . .'

'Enough, Carlos.'

'Sorry.' He looked back at the palanquin. 'All I'm saying is, how bad can they be?'

By accident or subconscious design – it was never entirely clear – the SISS contact craft resembled an infinity symbol: two lobelike modules packed with life support equipment, sensors and comms gear, spaced by a collar rimmed with thrusters and additional sensor arrays. Two people could fit into either of the lobes, and in the event of a mid-mission neural fadeout, one or both of the lobes could be ejected.

Ramping up thrust, the contact craft fell towards the Shroud, while the station made a retreat back beyond the safe range, towards the waiting lighthugger. Pascale's narrative showed the craft dwindling to ever-smaller size, until only the livid glare of its thrust and the pulsing red and green of its running lights remained, and then grew steadily fainter; the surrounding blackness seeming to occlude it like spreading ink.

No one could be certain of what happened thereafter. In the events which followed, most of the information gleaned by Sylveste and Lefevre on their approach was lost, including the data transmitted back to the station and the lighthugger. Not only were the timescales uncertain, but even the precise order of events was questionable. All that was known was what Sylveste himself remembered – and as Sylveste, by his own admission, underwent periods of altered or diminished consciousness in the vicinity of the Shroud, his memories could not be taken as the literal truth of events.

What was known was this.

Sylveste and Lefevre approached closer to the Shroud than any human being had ever done, even Lascaille. If what Lascaille had told them was true, then their transforms were fooling the Shroud's defences; forcing it to envelop them in a pocket of flattened spacetime while the rest of the boundary seethed with vicious gravitational riptides. No one, even now, pretended to understand how this might be happening: how the Shroud's buried mechanisms were able to curve spacetime through such insanely sharp geometries, when a folding a billion times less severe should have required more energy than was stored in the entire rest-mass of the galaxy. Nor did anyone understand how consciousness could bleed into the spacetime around the Shroud, so that the Shroud itself could recognise the sorts of minds which were attempting to gain passage into its heart, and at the same time reshape the thoughts and memories of those same minds. Evidently there was some hidden link between thought itself and the underlying processes of spacetime; the one influencing the other. Sylveste had found references to an antiquated theory, centuries dead, which had proposed a link between the quantum processes of consciousness and the quantum-gravitational mechanisms which underpinned spacetime, through the unification of something called the Weyl curvature tensor . . . but consciousness was no better understood now; the theory was as speculative as it had ever been. Perhaps, though, in the vicinity of the Shroud, any faint linkage between consciousness and spacetime was massively amplified. Sylveste and Lefevre were thinking their way through the storm, their reshaped minds calming the gravitational forces which seethed around them, only metres from the skin of their ship. They were like snake-charmers, moving through a pit of cobras, their music defining a tiny region of safety. Safe, that was, until the music stopped playing – or began to grow discordant – and the snakes began to break out of their hypnotic placidity. It would never be entirely clear how close Sylveste and Lefevre got to the Shroud before the music soured and the cobras of gravity began to stir.

Sylveste claimed they were never within the Shroud boundary itself – by his own visual evidence, more than half of the sky remained full of stars. Yet what little data was salvaged from the study ship suggested that the contact module was by then well inside the fractal foam surrounding the Shroud – well within the object's own infinitely blurred boundary, well within what Lascaille had called Revelation Space.

She knew when it began to happen. Terrified, but icily calm, she told Sylveste the news. Her Shrouder transform was breaking up, her veil of alien perception beginning to thin, leaving only human thoughts. It was what they had feared all along, but prayed would not happen.

Quickly they informed the study station and ran psych tests to verify what she was saying. The truth was appallingly clear. Her transform was collapsing. In a few minutes, her mind would lack the Shrouder component and would be unable to calm the snakes through which they walked. She was forgetting the music.

Even though they had prayed this would not happen, they had taken precautions. Lefevre retreated into the opposite half of the module and fired the separation charges, amputating her part of the ship from Sylveste's. By then her transform was almost gone. Via the audio-visual link between the two separated parts of the craft, she informed Sylveste that she could feel gravitational forces building, twisting and pulling at her body in viciously unpredictable ways.

Thrusters sought to move her module away from the curdled space around the Shroud, but the object was just too large, and she too small. Within minutes the stresses were tearing at the craft's thin hull, though Lefevre remained alive, huddled foetally in the last dwindling pocket of quiet space focused on her brain. Sylveste lost contact with her just as the craft burst asunder. Her air was sucked quickly out, but the decompression did not happen quickly enough to entirely snatch away her screams.

Lefevre was dead. Sylveste knew it. But his transform was still holding the snakes at bay. Bravely, more alone than any human being in history, Sylveste continued his descent into the Shroud boundary.

Some time later Sylveste awoke in the silence of his craft. Disorientated, he tried to contact the study station which was supposedly awaiting his return. But there was no answer. The study station and the lighthugger were lifeless, almost destroyed. Some kind of gravitational spasm had passed him by and peeled them open, eviscerating them just as thoroughly as Lefevre's craft had been. The crew and back-up members of his team had been killed instantly, along with the Ultras. He alone had survived.

But for what? To die, only far more slowly?

Sylveste steered his module back to what remained of the station and the lighthugger. For a moment his thoughts were empty of the Shrouders, focused only on survival.

Working alone, living within the cramped confines of the pod, Sylveste spent weeks learning how to jump-start the lighthugger's crippled repair systems. The Shroud spasm had vaporised or shredded thousands of tonnes of the lighthugger's mass, but it only had to carry one man home now. When the recuperative processes were in swing he was able to sleep, finally – not daring to believe that he would actually succeed. And in those dreams, Sylveste gradually became aware of a momentous, paralysing truth. After Carine Lefevre was killed, and before he regained consciousness, something had happened. Something had reached into his mind and spoken to him. But the message that was imparted to him was so brutally alien that Sylveste could not begin to put it into human terms.

He had stepped into Revelation Space.

FIVE

Carousel New Brazilia, Yellowstone, Epsilon Eridani, 2546

'I'm at the bar,' Volyova said into her bracelet, pausing at the entrance to the Juggler and the Shrouder. She regretted suggesting that this be the meeting point – she despised the establishment almost as much as she despised its clientele – but when she had arranged a rendezvous with the new candidate she had not been able to suggest an alternative.

'Is the recruit there yet?' Sajaki's voice said.

'Not unless she's very early. If she arrives on time, and our meeting proceeds favourably, we should be leaving in an hour.'

'I'll be ready.'

Squaring her shoulders she pushed on in, instantly assembling a mental map of the occupants. The air was still full of cloying pink perfume. Even the girl playing the teeconax was making the same nervous moves. Disturbingly liquid sounds emanated from the girl's cortex, amplified by the instrument and then modulated by the pressure of her fingers on its complex, spectrally coloured touch-sensitive fretboard. Her music toiled up staircase-like ragas, then splintered into nerve-shredding atonal passages which sounded like a pride of lions dragging their foreclaws down sheets of rusty iron. Volyova had heard that you had to have specialised neuro-auditory implants before teeconax music made any sense.

She found a barside stool and ordered a single vodka; a hypo was stashed in her pocket ready to blast her back to sobriety when she needed it. She was resigned to the fact that it might be a very long evening waiting for the recruit to show up. Usually this would have made her impatient but – to her surprise – she felt relaxed and attentive, despite the surroundings. Perhaps the air was spiked with psychotropic chemicals, but she felt better than she had in months, even allowing for the news that the crew were now to journey to Resurgam. Yet it was good to be around humans again, even the specimens who frequented the bar. Whole minutes passed while she watched their animated faces, serenely entranced by conversations she could not hear, imagining for herself the travellers' tales they were imparting. A girl inhaled from a hookah and blew out a long jetstream of smoke before cracking up as her partner reached the punchline in some outlandish joke. A bald man with a dragon tattoo on his scalp was boasting about how he had flown through a gas giant's atmosphere with his autopilot dead, his Juggler-configured mind solving atmospheric flow equations like he had been born to it. Another group of Ultras, turned ghostly by the wan blue lighting above their alcove, played a heated card game. One man was having to pay off his debt by losing a lock from his hair. His friends were holding him down while the winner claimed his pleated prize, slicing through the man's braid with a pocket knife.

What did Khouri look like again?

Volyova fished the card from her jacket, palming it unobtrusively and taking a last look at it. Ana Khouri, the name said, along with a few terse lines of biographical data. There was nothing about this woman that would make her stand out in any normal bar, but here her very ordinariness would have the same effect. Judging by the photograph, she would look slightly more out of place than Volyova herself, if that was possible.

Not that Volyova was complaining. Khouri looked like a remarkably suitable candidate for the vacant position. Volyova had already hacked into the system's remaining data-networks – those which still functioned after the plague – and drawn up a shortlist of individuals who might suit her needs. Khouri had been among that number; an ex-soldier from Sky's Edge. But Khouri had been impossible to trace, and eventually Volyova had given up, concentrating on other candidates. None of the others had really been what she was looking for, but she had kept searching anyway, growing steadily more despondent as each candidate failed to fit the bill. More than once Sajaki had suggested they just kidnap someone – as if recruiting someone under false pretences was somehow less of a crime. But kidnapping was too random: it still did not guarantee she would end up with someone she could work with.

Then Khouri had approached them out of the blue. She had heard that Volyova's crew were looking for someone to join their ship, and she was ready to leave Yellowstone. She had not mentioned her military background, but Volyova already knew about that; doubtless Khouri was just being cautious. The odd thing was, Khouri had not actually approached them until Sajaki – in accordance with the standard protocols of trade – had announced the change of destination.

'Captain Volyova? It's you, isn't it?'

Khouri was small, wiry and dourly dressed, and did not subscribe to any recognisable Ultra fashions. Her black hair was cut only an inch longer than Volyova's; short enough to make it obvious that her skull was not pierced by any clumsy input jacks or nerve-link interfaces. No guarantee that her head was not jam-packed with humming little machines, but it was certainly nothing she flaunted. The woman's face was a neutral composite of the gene-types which predominated on her homeworld, Sky's Edge; harmo-nious without being striking. Her mouth was small, straight and inexpressive, but that blandness was counterbalanced by the woman's eyes. They were dark, almost colourlessly so, but they glistened with a disarming inner prescience. For a tiny fraction of a moment, Volyova believed that Khouri had already seen through her tawdry skein of lies.

'Yes,' Volyova said. 'You must be Ana Khouri.' She kept her voice low, for having reached Khouri, the last thing she wanted was any other hopefuls within earshot trying to barge aboard. 'I understand you contacted our trade persona regarding possibilities for crewing with us.'

'I only just reached the carousel. I thought I'd try you first, before I went on to the crews who are advertising now.'

Volyova sniffed at her vodka. 'Odd strategy, if you don't mind my saying so.'

'Why? The other crews are getting so many applicants they're only interviewing via sim.' She took a perfunctory sip of her water. 'I prefer dealing with humans. It was just a question of going after a different crew.'

'Oh,' Volyova said. 'Ours is very different, believe me.'

'But you're traders, right?'

Volyova nodded enthusiastically. 'We've almost finished our dealings around Yellowstone. Not too productive, I must say. Economy's in the doldrums. We'll probably pop back in a century or two and see if things have picked up, but personally, I wouldn't mind if I never saw the place again.'

'So if I wanted to sign up for your ship I'd have to make my mind up pretty soon?'

'Of course, we'd have to make our minds up about you first.'

Khouri looked at her closely. 'There are other candidates?'

'I'm not really at liberty to discuss that.'

'I imagine there would be. I mean, Sky's Edge . . . there must be plenty of people who'd want to hop a lift there, even if they had to crew to pay their way.'

Sky's Edge? Volyova tried to keep a straight face, marvelling at their luck. The only reason Khouri had come forward was because she still thought they were going to the Edge, rather than Resurgam. Somehow she remained unaware of Sajaki's announced change of destination.

'There are worse places one could imagine,' Volyova said.

'Well, I'm keen to jump to the head of the line.' A perspex cloud sailed between them, dangling from its ceiling track, wobbling with its cargo of drinks and narcotics. 'What exactly is this position you have open?'

'It would be a lot easier if I explained things aboard the ship. You didn't forget that overnight bag, did you?'

'Of course not. I want this position, you know.'

Volyova smiled. 'I'm very glad to hear it.'

Cuvier, Resurgam, 2563

Calvin Sylveste was manifesting in his luxurious seigneurial chair at one end of the prison room. 'I've got something interesting to tell you,' he said, stroking his beard. 'Though I don't think you're going to like it.'

'Make it quick; Pascale will be here shortly.'

Calvin's permanent look of amusement deepened. 'Actually, it's Pascale I'm talking about. You're rather fond of her, aren't you?'

'It's no concern of yours whether I am or not.' Sylveste sighed; he had known this would lead to difficulties. The biography was nearing completion now and he had been privy to most of it. For all its technical accuracies, for all the myriad ways in which it could be experienced, it remained what Girardieau had always planned: a cunningly engineered weapon of precision propaganda.

Through the biography's subtle filter, there was no way to view any aspect of his past in a light which was not damaging to him; no way to avoid his depiction as an egomaniacal, single-minded tyrant: capacious of intellect, but utterly heartless in the way he used people around him. In this, Pascale had been undoubtedly clever. If Sylveste had not known the facts himself, he would have accepted the biography's slant uncritically. It had the stamp of truth.

That was hard enough to accept, but what made it immeasurably harder was how much of this harming portrait had been shaped by the testimonials of people who had known him. And chief among these – the most hurting of all – had been Calvin. Reluctantly, Sylveste had allowed Pascale access to the beta-level simulation. He had done so under duress, but there had been – at the time – what appeared to be compensations.

'I want the obelisk relocated and excavated,' Sylveste said. 'Girardieau promised me access to field data if I assisted in destroying my own character. I've kept my side of the deal handsomely. How about the government reciprocating?'

'It won't be easy . . .' Pascale had begun.

'No; but neither will it be a massive drain on Inundationist resources.'

'I'll speak to him,' she said, without much in the way of assurance. 'Provided you let me talk to Calvin whenever I want.'

It was the devil of all deals; he had known so at the time. But it had seemed worth it, if only to see the obelisk again, and not just the tiny part which had been uncovered before the coup.

Remarkably, Nils Girardieau had kept his word. It had taken four months, but a team had found the abandoned dig and removed the obelisk. It had not been painstakingly done, but Sylveste had not expected otherwise. It was enough that the thing had been unearthed in one piece. Now a holographic representation of it could be called into existence in his room at his whim; any part of the surface enlarged for inspection. The text had been beguiling; difficult to parse. The complicated map of the solar system was still unnervingly accurate to his eyes. Below it – too deep to have been seen before – was what looked like the same map, on a much larger scale, so that it encompassed the entire system out to the cometary halo. Pavonis was actually a wide binary; two stars spaced by ten light-hours. The Amarantin seemed to have known that, for they had marked the second star's orbit conspicuously. For a moment, Sylveste wondered why he had never seen the other star at night: it would be dim, but still much brighter than any of the other stars in the sky. Then he remembered that the other star no longer shone. It was a neutron star; the burnt-out corpse of a star which would once have shone hot and blue. It was so dark that it had not been detected before the first interstellar probes. A cluster of unfamiliar graphicforms attended the neutron star's orbit.

He had no idea what it meant.

Worse, there were similar maps lower down the obelisk which were at least consistent with other solar systems, although it was nothing he could prove. How could the Amarantin have obtained such data – the other planets, the neutron star, other systems – without a spacefaring capability comparable to humankind's?

Perhaps the crucial question was the age of the obelisk. The context layer suggested nine hundred and ninety thousand years, placing the burial within a thousand years of the Event – but in terms of validating his theory, he needed a much more precise estimate than that. On her last visit he had asked Pascale to run a TE measurement on the obelisk; he hoped she was going to give him the answer when she arrived.

'She's been useful to me,' he said to Calvin, who responded with a look of derision. 'I don't expect you to understand that.'

'Perhaps not. I could still tell you what I've learned.'

There was no point delaying it. 'Well?'

'Her surname isn't Dubois.' Calvin smiled, drawing out the moment. 'It's Girardieau. She's his daughter. And you, dear boy, have been had.'

They exited the Juggler and the Shrouder into the carousel's sweaty impression of planetary night. Outlaw capuchin monkeys were descending from the trees which lined the mall, ready for a session of prehensile pickpocketing. Burundi drums pounded from somewhere around the curve. Neon lightning strobed in serpentlike shapes in the billowing clouds which hung from the rafters. Khouri had heard that it sometimes rained, but so far she had been spared this particular piece of meteorological verisimilitude.

'We've a shuttle docked at the hub,' Volyova said. 'We'll just need to take a spoke elevator and clear outbound customs.'

The elevator car they rode in was rattling, unheated, piss-smelling and empty, apart from a helmeted Komuso who sat pensively on a bench, his shakuhachi resting between his knees. Khouri assumed that his presence had made other people decide to wait for the next car in the endless paternoster which rode between the hub and the rim.

The Mademoiselle stood next to the Komuso, hands clasped matronly behind her back, dressed in a floorlength electric-blue gown, black hair pulled into a severe bun.

'You're much too tense,' she said. 'Volyova will suspect you have something to hide.'

'Go away.'

Volyova glanced in her direction. 'Did you say something?'

'I said it's cold in here.'

Volyova seemed to take far too long to digest the statement. 'Yes. I suppose it is.'

'You don't have to speak out loud,' the Mademoiselle replied. 'You don't even have to subvocalise. Just imagine yourself speaking what you wish me to hear. The implant detects the ghost impulses generated in your speech area. Go on; try it.'

'Go away,' Khouri said, or rather imagined herself thinking it. 'Get the hell out of my head. This was never in the contract.'

'My dear,' the Mademoiselle said, 'there never was any contract, merely a – what shall I say? A gentlewomen's agreement?' She looked directly at Khouri as if expecting some kind of response. Khouri merely stared, venomously. 'Oh, very well,' the woman said. 'But I promise you I shall be back before very long.'

She popped out of existence.

'Can't wait,' Khouri said quietly.

'Pardon?' Volyova asked.

'I said I can't wait,' Khouri answered. 'I mean until we get out of this damn elevator.'

Before very long they reached the hub, cleared customs and boarded the shuttle, a non-atmospheric craft consisting of a sphere with four thruster pods splayed out at right angles. The ship was called the *Melancholia of Departure*, the kind of ironic name Ultras favoured for their craft. The interior had the ribbed look of a whale's gut. Volyova told her to go forward through a series of bulkheads and gullet-like crawlspaces until they reached the thing's bridge. There were a few bucket seats, together with a console displaying reams of avionics gibberish, latticed by delicate entoptics. Volyova thumbed one of the visual readouts, causing a small, traylike device to chug out of a black recess in the side of the console. The tray was gridded with an oldstyle keyboard. Volyova's fingers danced on the keys, causing a subtle change to sweep through the avionics data.

Khouri realised with a tingling feeling that the woman had no implants; that her fingers were actually one of the ways by which she communicated.

'Buckle in,' Volyova said. 'There's so much garbage floating round Yellowstone we might have to pull some gee-loads.'

Khouri did as she was told. For all the discomfort which ensued, it was her first chance to relax in days. Much had happened since her revival, all of it hectic. In all the time she had been asleep in Chasm City, the Mademoiselle had been waiting for a ship to arrive which was carrying on to Resurgam, and – given Resurgam's lack of importance in the ever-shifting web of interstellar commerce – the wait had been a long one. That was the trouble with lighthuggers. No individual, no matter how powerful, could ever own one now unless it had already been in their possession for centuries. The Conjoiners were no longer manufacturing drives and people who already owned ships were in no mind to sell them.

Khouri knew that the Mademoiselle had not been searching passively. Nor had Volyova. Volyova – so the Mademoiselle said – had unleashed a search program into Yellowstone's data network, what she called a bloodhound. A mere human – even a mere computerised monitor – could not have detected the dog's elaborate sniffing. But the Mademoiselle was seemingly neither of these things, and she sensed the dog the way a pond-skater feels ripples in the membrane on which it walks.

What she did next was clever.

She whistled to the bloodhound until it came bounding towards her. Then she casually broke the thing's neck, but not before she had flensed it open and examined its informational innards, working out just what it was that the dog had been sent to find. The gist was that the dog had been sent to retrieve supposedly secret information relating to individuals who had had slaver experience; exactly what one would have expected from a group of Ultras who were searching for a crewperson to fill a vacancy on their ship. But there was something else. Something a tiny bit strange, which pricked the Mademoiselle's curiosity.

Why were they looking for someone with military activity in their backgrounds?

Perhaps they were disciplinarians: professional traders who were operating one level above the normal state of play of commerce, ruthless experts who used slippery constructs to glean the knowledge they wanted, and who were not averse to travelling to backwater colonies like Resurgam when they saw a chance of some massive reward, perhaps centuries hence. It was probable that their entire organisation was structured along military lines, rather than the quasi-anarchy which existed on most trade craft. So by searching for military experience in the backgrounds of their candidates, what they were doing was ensuring themselves that the candidate would fit into their crew.

That was it, naturally.

Things had gone well so far, even allowing for the strange way in which Volyova had not corrected Khouri when she made obvious her ignorance of the ship's true destination. Khouri had known all along that the destination was Resurgam, of course – but if the Ultras knew this was where she really wanted to go to, she would have been forced to use one of several cover stories to explain her motivations for visiting the backwater colony. She had been ready to employ one of the stories as soon as Volyova corrected her – except she had failed to do so, seemingly willing to let her recruit keep on thinking they were really travelling to Sky's Edge.

That was indeed odd, though understandable if one assumed they were now desperate to recruit anyone who came forward. It said little for their honesty, of course, but then again, it saved Khouri using a cover story. It was, she decided, nothing to worry about. It would, in fact, all have been roses, were it not for what the Mademoiselle had placed in her head while she was sleeping. The implant was tiny and would not elicit suspicion from the Ultras, designed to resemble – and function as – a standard entoptic splice. If they got too inquisitive and removed the damn thing, all its incriminating parts would self-erase or reorganise. But that was not the point. Khouri's objection to the implant was not on the grounds that it was risky or unnecessary, but rather that the last person she wanted in her head on a daily basis was the Mademoiselle. Of course, it was just a beta-level simulation constructed to mimic her personality, projecting an image of the Mademoiselle into Khouri's visual field and tickling her aural centre to allow her to hear what the ghost said. No one else would be privy to the woman's apparitions, and Khouri would be able to communicate silently with her.

'Call it need to know,' the ghost had said. 'As an ex-soldier, I'm certain you understand this principle.'

'Yes, I understand it,' Khouri said with sullen acceptance. 'And it stinks, but I don't suppose you're about to take the damned thing out of my head just because I don't like it.'

The Mademoiselle smiled. 'To burden you with too much knowledge at this point would be to risk a momentary indiscretion in the presence of the Ultras.'

'Wait a minute,' Khouri said. 'I already know you want me to kill Sylveste. What more could there possibly be to find out?'

The Mademoiselle repeated her smile, maddeningly. Like many beta-level sims, her compendium of facial expressions was small enough to make repetition inevitable, like a bad actor constantly falling into the same characterisations.

'I'm afraid,' she said, 'that what you now know is not even a fragment of the whole story. Not even a splinter.'

When Pascale arrived, Sylveste made a point of studying her face, matching it against his memories of Nils Girardieu. As usual he rammed against the limitations of his vision. His eyes were poor at curves, tending to approximate the nuances of the human face as a series of stepped edges.

But what Calvin had said was not obviously untrue. Pascale's hair was Bible-black and straight; Girardieu's curly and red. But the bone structure had too many points of similarity for coincidence. If Calvin had not made the remark, perhaps Sylveste would never have guessed ... but now that the idea was there, it explained far too much.

'Why did you lie to me?' he said.

She seemed genuinely taken aback. 'About what?'

'Everything. Starting with your father.'

'My father?' She was quiet now. 'Ah. Then you know.'

He nodded, tight-lipped. Then, 'That was one of the risks you ran by collaborating with Calvin. Calvin is very clever.'

'He must have established some kind of data link with my compad; accessed private files. The bastard.'

'Now you know how I feel. Why did you do it, Pascale?'

'At first, because I had no choice. I wanted to study you. And the only way I could earn your trust was under another name. It was possible; few people even knew I existed, much less what I looked like.' She paused. 'And it worked, didn't it? You did trust me. And I did nothing to betray that trust.'

'Is that the truth? You never told Nils anything that might have helped him?'

She looked wounded. 'You had forewarning of the coup, remember? If anyone was betrayed in all this, it was my father.'

He tried to find an angle that would prove her wrong, without really being sure he wanted to. Perhaps what she said was true. 'And the biography?'

'That was my father's idea.'

'A tool to discredit me?'

'There's nothing in the biography which isn't truthful – unless you know otherwise.' She paused. 'It's nearly ready for release, actually. Calvin's been very helpful. It'll be the first major work of indigenous art produced on Resurgam, do you realise? Since the Amarantin, of course.'

'It's a piece of art all right. Are you going to release it under your real name?'

'That was always the idea. I was hoping you wouldn't find out until then, of course.'

'Oh, don't worry about that. None of this will change our working relationship, believe me. After all, I always knew Nils was the real author behind it.'

'That makes it easier for you, doesn't it? To write me off as an irrelevance?'

'Do you have the TE dates you promised me?'

'Yes.' She passed a card to him. 'I don't break my promises, Doctor. But I'm afraid the little respect I have for you is in serious danger of vanishing altogether.'

Sylveste glanced at the trapped-electron summary scrolling down the card as he flexed it between thumb and forefinger. Some part of his mind was entirely unable to detach itself from what the numbers represented, even as he spoke to Pascale. 'When your father told me about the biography, he said the woman who would be authoring it was someone whose illusions were on the point of being shattered.'

She stood up. 'I think we should leave this until another time.'

'No; wait.' Sylveste reached out and held her hand. 'I'm sorry. I need to talk to you about this, do you understand?'

She flinched at the contact, then slowly relaxed. Her expression was still watchful. 'About what?'

'This.' He tapped his thumb against the TE summary. 'It's very interesting.'

Volyova's shuttle was approaching a shipyard; up near the Lagrange point between Yellowstone and its moon, Marco's Eye. About a dozen lighthuggers were parked in the yard; more ships than Khouri had ever seen in her life. At the yard's hub was a major carousel, smaller in-system vessels attached to the wheel's rim like suckling pigs. A few of the lighthuggers were encased in skeletal support structures for major ice-shield or Conjoiner-drive over-hauls (Conjoiner ships were here, too: sleek and black, as if chiselled from space itself); but the rest of the starships were basically drifting, following lazy and slow orbits around the Lagrange point's centre of gravity. Khouri guessed that there must be complex rules of etiquette governing the way those ships were parked; who had to move out the way of whom to avoid a collision which a computer might predict days in advance. The expenditure of fuel which might have to be burned to nudge a ship off a collision course would be tiny against the profit margin of a typical trade stopover . . . but the loss of face would be much harder to amortise. There had never been as many ships as this parked around Sky's Edge, but even then she had heard of skirmishes between crews over issues of parking priority and trade rights. It was a common groundsider's misapprehension that Ultras were a homogeneous splinter of humanity. In truth, they were as factional, and as paranoid about one another, as any other human strain.

Now they were approaching Volyova's ship.

The thing, like all the other lighthuggers, was improbably streamlined. Space only approximated a vacuum at slow speeds. Up near lightspeed – which was where these ships spent most of their time – it was like cutting through a howling gale of atmosphere. That was why they looked like daggers: conic hull tapering to a needle-sharp prow to punch the interstellar medium, with two Conjoiner engines braced at the back on spars like an ornate hilt. The ship was sheathed in ice, so glisteningly pure that it looked like diamond. The shuttle swooped in low over Volyova's ship, and for a moment Khouri apprehended the ship's vastness. It was like flying over a city, not another vessel. Then a door irised open in the hull, revealing a glowing docking bay. Volyova guided the shuttle home with expert taps on her thruster controls, latching onto a berthing cradle. Khouri heard thumps as umbilicals and docking connectors thudded home.

Volyova was first out of her seat restraints. 'Shall we step aboard?' she asked, with something that was not quite the politeness Khouri had been expecting.

They propelled themselves through the shuttle and out into the spacious environment of the ship. They were still in free-fall, but at the end of the corridor they were facing Khouri could see a complex arrangement where the stationary and rotating sections were joined together.

She was beginning to feel nauseous, but she was damned if she was going to let Volyova see this.

'Before we go ahead,' the Ultra woman said, 'there's someone you have to meet.'

She was looking over Khouri's shoulder, back towards the corridor that led to the shuttle which had brought them aboard. Khouri heard the shuffling sound of someone working hand-over-hand along the rails which ribbed the passage. But that could only mean that there had been another person aboard the shuttle.

Something was wrong here.

Volyova's attitude was not that of someone who was trying to impress a potential recruit. It was more as if she cared little what Khouri thought; as if it was of no consequence at all. Khouri looked around, in time to see the Komuso who had come with them in the elevator. His face was lost under the expressionless wicker helmet they all wore. He carried his shakuhachi in the crook of his arm.

Khouri started to speak, but Volyova silenced her. 'Welcome aboard the *Nostalgia for Infinity*, Ana Khouri. You've just become our new Gunnery Officer.' Then she nodded towards the Komuso. 'Do me a favour, will you, Triumvir?'

'Anything particular?'

'Knock her out before she tries to kill either one of us.'

The last thing Khouri saw was a golden blur of bamboo.

*

Sylveste thought he smelt Pascale's perfume before his eyes separated her from the crowd outside the prison building. He made a reflex move towards her, but the two burly militiamen who had escorted him from his room quickly restrained him. Catcalls and muffled insults came from the cordoned-off crowd, but Sylveste barely noticed them.

Pascale kissed him diplomatically, half hiding the conjunction of their mouths behind her lace-gloved hand.

'Before you ask,' she said, her voice barely audible above the noise of the crowd, 'I have no more idea what this is about than you.'

'Is Nils behind it?'

'Who else? Only he's got the clout to get you out of that place for more than a day.'

'Pity he's not so keen to prevent me returning.'

'Oh, he might – if he didn't have to placate his own people, and the opposition. It's about time you stopped thinking of him as your worst enemy, you know.' They stepped into the sterile hush of the waiting car. The vehicle was adapted from one of the smaller surface exploration buggies, four balloon wheels at the extremities of its air-smoothed body, comms gear stowed in a matt-black hump on the roof. It was painted Inundationist purple, with Hokusai wave pendants mounted on the front.

'If it wasn't for my father,' Pascale continued, 'you'd have died during the coup. He protected you from your worst enemies.'

'That doesn't make him a very competent revolutionary.'

'And what does that say about the regime he managed to overthrow?'

Sylveste shrugged. 'Fair point, I suppose.'

A guard climbed into the front seat, behind a partition of armoured glass, and then they were moving, rushing through the crowd, speeding towards the edge of the city. They passed through one of the arboreta, then descended down one of the ramps which passed beneath the perimeter. Two other government cars accompanied them, also modified from surface buggies, but painted black and with masked militia riding postilion, holding rifles to their shoulders. After travelling for a kilometre along an unlit tunnel, the convoy arrived in an airlock and halted while the breathable city air was exchanged for Resurgam's atmosphere. The guards remained at their posts, pausing only to adjust their breather masks and goggles. Then the vehicles moved on, ascending back towards the surface. They arrived in greyish daylight, surrounded by concrete blast walls, driving across a surface patterned in red and green lights.

An aircraft was waiting for them, parked on the apron on a tripod of skids, the undersides of its wings already uncomfortably bright to look at, already beginning to ionise the boundary layer of air below them. The driver reached into a dashboard compartment and removed breather masks, passing them back through the security grill, motioning for them to place them over their faces.

'Not that you have to,' he said. 'Oxygen's up two hundred per cent since you were last outside Resurgam City, Doctor Sylveste. Some people have breathed naked atmosphere for tens of minutes with no longterm effects.'

'Those must be the dissidents I keep hearing about,' Sylveste said. 'The renegades Girardieau betrayed during the coup. The ones that are supposed to be communicating with True Path's leaders in Cuvier. I don't envy them. The dust must clog their lungs almost as much as it clogs their minds.'

The escort looked unimpressed. 'Scavenger enzymes process the dust particles. It's old Martian biotech. Anyway; dust levels are down. All the moisture we pumped into the atmosphere allowed the dust particles to bind into bigger grains which aren't so easily transported by the wind.'

'Very good,' Sylveste applauded. 'Pity it's still such a miserable hellhole.'

He palmed the mask to his face and waited for the door to open. A moderate wind was blowing, no more than a stinging abrasion.

They dashed across the ground.

The aircraft was a welcome oasis of space and quiet, its sumptuous interior outfitted in governmental purple. The occupants of the other two cars boarded by a different door, Sylveste catching a glimpse of Nils Girardieau crossing the apron. Girardieau walked with a swaying motion that began somewhere near his shoulders, like a pair of architect's dividers being walked across a drawing board point to point. There was a momentum to him, like a glacier compressed into a man's volume. The leader vanished out of sight and then a few minutes later the visible edge of the closest wing turned violet, enveloped in a nimbus of excited ions, and the aircraft climbed from the apron.

Sylveste sketched a window for himself and watched Cuvier – or Resurgam City, as they now called it – grow small beneath him. It was the first time he had seen the place in its entirety since the coup, back before the statue of the French naturalist had been toppled. The old simplicity of the colony was gone. A froth of human habitation extended messily beyond the dome perimeters; air-sealed structures linked by covered roads and walkways. There were many smaller outlying domes, emerald-green with plantations. Even a few undomed strips of trial organisms laid out in eye-hurting geometric patterns, waiting to be unleashed far beyond the city.

They circled the city and then took off on a northerly course. Lacework canyons furled below. Occasionally they overflew a small settlement, usually just an opaque dome or streamlined shack, the glare from the wings momentarily illuminating whatever they overflew. Mostly it was wilderness, uncrossed by road, pipe or power line.

Sylveste catnapped intermittently, waking to see tropical deserts of ice and imported tundra washing below. Presently a settlement came over the horizon and the aircraft made loitering spirals towards the ground. Sylveste moved his window to get a better look.

'I recognise this area. It's where we found the obelisk.'

'Yes,' Pascale said.

The landscape was craggy and mostly unvegetated, the horizon ruined by uprearing broken arches and improbable rock pillars, all of which looked on the point of imminent collapse. There was little flat ground, just deep fissures, like a calcified unmade bed. They came in over a solidified lava stream then landed on a flat hexagonal pad surrounded by armoured surface buildings. It was only midday, yet the dust in the air attenuated the sunlight so severely that it was necessary to bathe the pad in floodlights. Militia dashed across the ground to meet the flight, hiding their eyes against the light from the aircraft's underside.

Sylveste grabbed his mask, regarded it disdainfully, then left it on the seat. He needed no help making it the short distance to the building, and if he did, no one was going to know about it.

The militia escorted them into the shack. It was years since Sylveste had been this close to Girardieau. He was shocked at how small his adversary now seemed. Girardieau was built like some piece of squat mining machinery. He looked capable of scrabbling his way through solid basalt. His red hair was short and wirelike, sprinkled with white. His eyes were wide and quizzical, like a startled Pekinese pup.

'Strange allegiances,' he said, as one of the guards sealed the door behind them. 'Who'd have thought you and I would ever find ourselves with so much in common, Dan?'

'Less than you imagine,' Sylveste said.

Girardieau led the team forward through a ribbed corridor lined with discarded machines, grimed beyond recognition. 'I suppose you're wondering what all this is about.'

'I have my suspicions.'

Girardieau's laughter boomed off the derelict equipment around them. 'Remember that obelisk they dug up hereabouts? Of course – it was you who pointed out the phenomenological difficulty with the TE dating method used on the rock.'

'Yes,' Sylveste said tartly.

The implications of the TE dating had been enormous. No natural crystalline structure was ever completely perfect in its lattice geometry. There would always be gaps in the lattice where atoms were missing, and in those holes, electrons would gradually build up over time, knocked out of the rest of the lattice by cosmic-ray bombardments and natural radioactivity. Since the holes tended to fill up with electrons at a steady rate, the number of trapped electrons provided a dating method which could be used on inorganic artefacts. There was a catch, of course: the TE method was only useful if the traps had been emptied at some point in the past. Luckily, firing or exposure to light was enough to bleach – empty – the outermost traps in the crystal. TE analysis of the obelisk had shown that all the surface-layer traps had been bleached at the same time, which happened to be nine hundred and ninety thousand years earlier, within the errors of the measurement. Only something like the Event could have bleached an object as large as the obelisk.

There was nothing new in this; thousands of Amarantin artefacts had been dated back to the Event using the same technique. But none of them had been buried deliberately. The obelisk, on the other hand, had been emplaced deliberately in a stone sarcophagus after it had been bleached.

After the Event.

Even in the new regime, this realisation had been enough to draw attention to the obelisk. It had stimulated renewed interest in the inscriptions over the last year. On his own, Sylveste's interpretation had been sketchy at best, but now what remained of the archaeological community came to his aid. There was a new freedom in Cuvier; Girardieau's regime had relaxed some of its proscriptions on Amarantin research, even as the True Path opposition grew more fanatical.

Strange allegiances, as Girardieau had said.

'Once we had an idea of what the obelisk was telling us,' Girardieau said, 'we sectioned the whole area and excavated down sixty or seventy metres. We found dozens more of them – all bleached prior to burial, all carrying basically the same inscriptions. It isn't a record of something that happened in this area at all. It's a record of something buried here.'

'Something big,' Sylveste said. 'Something they must have planned before the Event – perhaps even buried before it, and then placed the markers afterwards. The last cultural act of a society poised on annihilation. Just how big, Girardieau?'

'Very.' And then Girardieau told him how they had surveyed the area first using an array of thumpers: devices for generating ground-penetrating Rayleigh waves, sensitive to the density of buried objects. They'd had to use the largest thumpers, Girardieau said, which meant that the depth of the object had to be at the extreme range of the technique; hundreds of metres down. Later they had brought in the colony's most sensitive imaging gravitometers, and only then had they gained any idea of what it was they were seeking.

It was nothing small.

'Is this dig connected with the Inundationist program?'

'Completely independent. Pure science, in other words. Does that surprise you? I always promised we'd never abandon the Amarantin studies. Maybe if you'd believed me all those years ago we'd be working together now, opposing the True Pathers – the real enemy.'

Sylveste said, 'You showed no interest in the Amarantin until the obelisk was discovered. But that scared you, didn't it? Because for once it was incontrovertible evidence; nothing I could have faked or manipulated. For once you had to allow the possibility that I might have been right all along.'

They stepped into a capacious elevator, outfitted with plush seats, Inundationist aquatints on the walls. A thick metal door hummed shut. One of Girardieau's aides flipped open a panel and palmed a button. The floor fell away sickeningly, their bodies only sluggishly catching up.

'How far down are we going?'

'Not far,' Girardieau said. 'Only a couple of kilometres.'

When Khouri awakened they had already left orbit around Yellowstone. She could see the planet through a porthole in her quarters, much smaller than it had looked before. The region around Chasm City was a freckle on the surface. The Rust Belt was only a tawny smoke ring, too far away for any of its component structures to be visible. There would be no stopping the ship now: it would accelerate steadily at one gee until it had left the Epsilon Eridani system completely, and it would not stop accelerating until it was moving barely a whisker below the speed of light. It was no accident that they called these vessels lighthuggers.

She had been tricked.

'It's a complication,' the Mademoiselle said, after long minutes of silence. 'But no more than that.'

Khouri rubbed at the painful lump on her skull where the Komuso – Sajaki was his name, she now knew – had knocked her out with his shakuhachi.

'What do you mean, a complication?' she shouted. 'They've kidnapped me, you stupid bitch!'

'Keep your voice down, dear girl. They don't know about me now and there's no reason they have to in the future.' The entoptic image smiled jaggedly. 'In fact, I'm probably your best friend right now. You should do your best to safeguard our mutual secret.' She examined her fingernails. 'Now, let's approach this rationally. What was our objective?'

'You know damn well.'

'Yes. You were to infiltrate this crew and travel with them to Resurgam. What is now your status?'

'The Volyova bitch keeps calling me her recruit.'

'In other words, your infiltration has been spectacularly successful.' She was strolling nonchalantly around the room now, one hand on her hip, the other tapping an index finger against her lower lip. 'And where exactly are we now headed?'

'I've no reason to suspect it isn't still Resurgam.'

'So in all the essential details, nothing has happened to compromise the mission.'

Khouri wanted to strangle the woman, except it would have been like strangling a mirage. 'Has it occurred to you that they might have their own agenda? You know what Volyova said just before I was knocked out? She said I was the new Gunnery Officer. What do you suppose she meant by that?'

'It explains why they were looking for military experience in your background.'

'And what if I don't go along with her plans?'

'I doubt it matters to her.' The Mademoiselle stopped her strolling, adopting an expression of seriousness from her internal compendium of facial modes. 'They're Ultras, you see. Ultras have access to technologies considered taboo on colony worlds.'

'Such as?'

'Instruments for manipulating loyalty might be among them.'

'Well, thanks for giving me this important information well in advance.'

'Don't worry – I always knew there was a chance of this.' The Mademoiselle paused and touched the side of her own head. 'I took precautions accordingly.'

'That's a relief.'

'The implant I put inside you will fabricate antigens for their neural medichines. More than that, it will also broadcast subliminal reinforcement messages into your subconscious mind. Volyova's loyalty therapies will be completely neutralised.'

'So why bother even telling me this is going to happen?'

'Because, dear girl, once Volyova begins the treatment, you'll have to let her think it's working.'

The descent took only a few minutes, the air-pressure and temperature stabilised at surface normal. The shaft which the car descended was walled in diamond, ten metres wide. Occasionally there were recesses, stash-holes for equipment or small operations shacks, or switching points where two elevators could squeeze past one another before continuing their journeys. Servitors were working the diamond, extruding it in atomic-thickness filaments from spinnerettes. The filaments zipped neatly into place under the action of protein-sized molecular machines. Looking through the glass ceiling, the faintly translucent shaft seemed to reach towards infinity.

'Why didn't you tell me you'd found this?' Sylveste asked. 'You must have been here for months at the very least.'

'Let's just say your input wasn't critical,' Girardieau said, and then added, 'until now, that is.'

At the shaft's bottom, they exited into another corridor, silver-clad, cleaner and cooler than the one they had walked through at ground level. Windows along its length offered glimpses into a disarmingly large cavern filled with geodesic scaffolding and industrial structures. Sylveste was able to freezeframe the view with his eyes, then do some image-processing and expand the captured view when he was ten paces further along the corridor. For that he offered grudging thanks to Calvin.

What he saw was enough to quicken his heartbeat.

Now they pushed through a pair of armoured doors ghosted by security entoptics, writhing snakes which seemed to hiss and spit at the group. They trooped on through into an ante-room with another set of doors at the far end, flanked by militia. Girardieau waved them aside, then turned to Sylveste. The roundness of his eyes, the Pekinese aspect of his features, suddenly made him think of a painted Japanese devil on the point of belching fire.

'Now this,' Girardieau said, 'is where you either ask for your money back or stand in awed silence.'

'Impress me,' Sylveste said, with as much droll nonchalance as he could muster, despite his racing pulse and feverish internal excitement.

Girardieau opened the rear doors. They walked into a room half the size of the freight elevator, empty apart from a row of simple escritoires inlaid into the wall. A headset and wraparound mike lay on one of them, next to a compad displaying pencil-sketch engineering diagrams. The walls sloped outwards, the area of the ceiling greater than the floor. Combined with the huge glass windows set in three of the walls, it made Sylveste feel as if he was in the gondola of an airship, cruising under a starless night sky across an unnavigated ocean.

Girardieau killed the lights, enabling them to see what lay beyond the glass.

Floods swung from the roof of the chamber beyond, curving down towards the Amarantin object which lay below. It was emerging from one nearly sheer wall of the cave; a hemisphere of pure black, hemmed by gantries and geodesic scaffolding. Scabrous lumps of hardened magma still clung to it, yet across the large areas where the magma had been chipped away, the thing was as smooth and dark as obsidian. The underlying shape was spherical; at least four hundred metres wide, although more than half still lay entombed.

'You know who made this?' Girardieau said, finally whispering. He did not wait for an answer: 'It's older than human language, but my goddamn wedding ring has more scratches on it.'

Girardieau led the party back to the elevator shaft for the final short descent down to the operations floor of the hollowed-out chamber. The ride lasted no more than thirty seconds, but for Sylveste it seemed like a grindingly slow Homeric odyssey. The object felt like his own personal prize; as hard-won as if he had unearthed it with his own bloodied fingernails. It loomed over them now, its curved, rock-encrusted side jutting unsupported into the air. There was a faint groove scored around the object, running obliquely from one side to the other. It looked like little more than a shallow hairline fracture from where he was, but it was a metre or so wide, and probably just as deep.

Girardieau led them into the nearest chock: a concrete structure with its own inner rooms and operations levels abutting the object. Inside they took another elevator, rising up through the building into the haze of scaffolding which erupted from it. Sylveste's stomach crawled with conflicting impulses of claustro- and agoraphobia. He felt hemmed in by the unthinkable mega-tonnes of rock looming hundreds of metres over his head, while simultaneously racked with vertigo as they ascended the scaffold-ing high up the side of the object.

Small shacks and equipment huts floated in the geodesic framework. The lift connected with one of these structures and they trooped out into a complex of rooms still abuzz with the afterhum of recently curtailed activity. All the warning signs and notices were decals or painted, the area too makeshift for entoptic generators.

They walked over a tremoring girderwork bridge which extended through a loom of scaffolding towards the black skin of the Amarantin object. They were halfway up the object's height, level with the groove. The object no longer seemed spherical; they were too close for that. It was a single black wall blocking their progress, as vast and depthless as the view of Lascaille's Shroud he remembered after he had travelled from Spindrift. They walked onwards, until the bridge took them into the groove.

The path immediately swung to the right. On three sides – to the left, and above and below – they were hemmed in by the eerily unmarked black substance of the artefact. They walked on a trelliswork path fixed to the underlying floor via suction pads, since the alien material was nearly frictionless. To the right was a waist-high safety railing and then several hundred metres of nothing. Every five or six metres on the inside wall was a lamp, attached via epoxy pads, and every twenty or so metres was a panel marked with cryptic symbols.

They continued along the steep incline of the groove for three or four minutes until Girardieau brought them to a halt. The place where they had arrived was a tangled nexus of power lines, lamps and communications consoles. The left-hand wall of the groove folded inwards here.

'Took us weeks to find the way in,' Girardieau said. 'Originally the trench was plugged by basalt. It was only after we'd chipped it all out that we found this one place where the basalt seemed to continue inwards, as if it were plugging some kind of radial tunnel which emerged in the trench.'

'You've been busy little beavers, I can see.'

'Digging it out was hard work,' Girardieau said. 'Excavating the trench was easy by comparison, but here we had to drill and remove material through the same tiny hole. Some of us wanted to use boser torches to cut a few secondary tunnels in to make the job easier, but we never went that far. And our mineral-tipped drills couldn't touch the stuff.'

Sylveste's scientific curiosity momentarily beat his urge to belittle Girardieau's attempts at impressing him. 'You know what this material is?'

'Basically carbon, with some iron and niobium and a few rare metals as trace elements. But we don't know the structure. It's not simply some allotropic form of diamond we haven't invented yet, or even hyperdiamond. Maybe the top few tenths of a millimetre are close to diamond, but the stuff seems to undergo some kind of complex lattice transformation deeper down. The ultimate form – far deeper then we've yet sampled – may not even be a true crystal at all. It could be that the lattice breaks up into trillions of carbon-heavy macromolecules, locked together in a co-acting mass. Sometimes these molecules seem to work their way to the surface along lattice flaws, which is the only time we see them.'

'You're talking as if it's purposeful.'

'Maybe it is. Maybe the molecules are like little enzymes tooled-up to repair the diamond crust when it becomes damaged.' He shrugged. 'But we've never isolated one of the macromolecules, or at least not in a stable form. They seem to lose coherence as soon as they're removed from the lattice. They fall apart before we can get a look inside them.'

'What you're describing,' Sylveste said, 'sounds very much like a form of molecular technology.'

Girardieau smiled at Sylveste, seeming to acknowledge the private game in which they were enmeshed.

'Except we know that the Amarantin were far too primitive for such a thing.'

'Of course.'

'Of course.' Girardieau smiled again, only this time to the group as a whole. 'Shall we forge inwards?'

Navigating the tunnel system which led from the groove was trickier than Sylveste had at first imagined. He had assumed that the radial tunnel would continue inwards for the necessary distance to traverse the shell of the object, and they would then enter the thing's hollow interior. But it was not like that at all. The thing was a deliberate labyrinth. The path did progress radially, for perhaps ten metres, but then it jerked to the left and soon branched into multiple tunnel systems. The routes were colour-coded with adhesive markers, but the coding system was too cryptic to make much sense to Sylveste. Within five minutes he was thoroughly disorientated, though he had the suspicion that they had not strayed very deep into the object. It was as if the tunnel system was the work of a demented maggot which preferred the part of the apple immediately under the skin. Eventually, however, they crossed what seemed to be a regular fissure in the fabric of the object. Girardieau explained that the thing was structured in a series of concentric shells. They continued to worm their way through another confusing tunnel system while Girardieau regaled them with dubious stories about the initial exploration of the object.

They had known about it for two years – ever since Sylveste had drawn Pascale's attention to the oddity of the obelisk's burial sequence. Excavating the chamber had taken most of that time, detailed study of the object's warrenlike interior only happening in the last few months. There had been a few deaths in those early days. Nothing mysterious, it eventually transpired – just teams getting lost in unmapped sections of the labyrinth and stumbling into vertical shafts in the tunnel system where the safety flooring had not yet been fixed. One worker had starved to death when she ventured too far without laying a breadcrumb trail behind her – servitors found her two weeks after she went missing. She had been wandering in a series of doodle-like circles, at times only a few minutes from the safe zones.

Progress through the final concentric shell was slower and more deliberate than the four they traversed before it. They worked downwards, eventually reaching a gratifyingly horizontal stretch of tunnel, the far end of which was milky with light.

Girardieau spoke to his sleeve and the light dimmed.

They moved on in semi-darkness. Gradually their breathing ceased to echo from the walls as the confining space opened out. The only sound came from the laboured purring of nearby air pumps.

'Hold on,' Girardieau said. 'Here it comes.'

Sylveste steeled himself for the inevitable disorientation when the lights returned. For once he did not mind Girardieau's theatrics. It permitted him a sense of discovery, albeit at second hand. Of course, he alone understood this surrogacy for what it was. But he did not begrudge the others the moment. That would have been churlish, for after all, they would never know what true discovery felt like. He almost pitied them, though in that moment the sight revealed in the lights purged all normal thought.

It was an alien city.

SIX

'I expect,' Volyova said, 'that you're one of those otherwise rational people who pride themselves on not believing in ghosts.'

Khouri looked at her, frowning slightly. Volyova had known from the outset that the woman was no fool, but it was still interesting to see how she reacted to the question.

'Ghosts, Triumvir? You can't be serious.'

'One thing you'll quickly learn about me,' Volyova said, 'is that I'm very seldom anything other than completely serious.' And then she indicated the door at which they had arrived, set unobtrusively into one rusty-red interior wall of the ship. The door was of heavy construction, a stylised drawing of a spider discernible through layers of corrosion and staining. 'Go ahead. I'll be right behind you.'

Khouri did as she was told without hesitation. Volyova was satisfied. In the three weeks since the woman had been snared – or recruited, if one wanted to be polite about it – Volyova had administered a complex regimen of loyalty-altering therapies. The treatment was almost complete, apart from the top-up doses which would continue indefinitely. Soon the woman's loyalty would be so strongly instilled that it would transcend mere obedience and become an animating compulsion, a principle to which she could no more fail to adhere than a fish could choose to stop breathing water. Taken to an extreme which Volyova hoped would prove unnecessary, Khouri could be made not only to desire to do the crew's will, but to love them for giving her the chance. But Volyova would relent before she programmed the woman that deeply. After her less than fruitful experiences with Nagorny, she was wary of creating another unquestioning guinea pig. It would not displease her if Khouri retained a trace of resentment.

Volyova did as she had promised, following Khouri into the

door. The recruit had halted a few metres beyond the threshold, realising that there was no way to go further.

Volyova sealed the great iron iris of a door behind them.

'Where are we, Triumvir?'

'In a little private retreat of my own,' Volyova said. She spoke into her bracelet and made a light come on, but the interior remained shadowy. The room was shaped like a fat torpedo, twice as long as it was wide. The interior was sumptuously outfitted, with four scarlet-cushioned seats installed on the floor, next to each other, and space for another two behind, though nothing remained but their anchor-points. Where they were not upholstered in cushioned velvet, the room's brass-ribbed walls were curved and glossily dark, as if made of obsidian or black marble. There was a console of black ebony, attached to the armrest of the front seat in which Volyova now sat. She folded down the console, familiarising herself with the inset dials and controls, all of which were tooled in brass or copper, with elaborately inscribed labels, offset by flowered curlicues of differently inlaid woods and ivories. Not that it took much familiarising, since she visited the spider-room with reasonable regularity, but she enjoyed the tactile pleasure of stroking her fingertips across the board.

'I suggest you sit down,' she said. 'We're about to move.'

Khouri obeyed, sitting next to Volyova, who threw a number of ivory-handled switches, watching some of the dials on the panel light up with roseate glows, their needles quivering as power entered the spider-room's circuits. She extracted a certain sadistic pleasure in observing Khouri's disorientation, for the woman clearly had no idea where she was in the ship, nor what was about to happen. There were clunking sounds, and a sudden shifting, as if the room were a lifeboat which had just come adrift from a mother vessel.

'We're moving,' Khouri diagnosed. 'What is this – some kind of luxury elevator for the Triumvirate?'

'Nothing so decadent. We're in an old shaft which leads to the outer hull.'

'You need a room just to take you to the hull?' Some of Khouri's scornful disregard for the niceties of Ultra life was coming to the fore again. Volyova liked that, perversely. It convinced her that the loyalty therapies had not destroyed the woman's personality, only redirected it.

'We're not just going to the hull,' Volyova said. 'Otherwise we'd walk.'

The motion was smooth now, but there were still occasional clunks as airlocks and traction systems assisted their passage. The shaft walls remained utterly black, but – Volyova knew – all that was about to change. Meanwhile, she watched Khouri, trying to guess whether the woman was scared or merely curious. If she had sense she would have realised by now that Volyova had invested too much time in her simply to kill her – but on the other hand, the woman's military training on Sky's Edge must have taught her to take absolutely nothing for granted.

Her appearance had changed considerably since her recruitment, but little of that was due to the therapies. Her hair had always been short, but now it was absent entirely. Only up close was the peachy fuzz of regrowth visible. Her skull was quilted with fine, salmon-coloured scars. Those were the incision marks where Volyova had opened her head in order to emplace the implants which had formerly resided in Boris Nagorny.

There had been other surgical procedures, too. Khouri's body was peppered with shrapnel from her soldiering days, in addition to the almost invisibly healed scars of beam-weapon or projectile impact points. Some of the shrapnel shards lay deep – too deep, it seemed, for the Sky's Edge medics to retrieve. And for the most part they would have caused her no harm, for they were biologically-inert composites not situated close to any vital organs. But the medics had been sloppy, too. Near the surface, dotted under Khouri's skin, Volyova found a few shards they really should have removed. She did it for them, examining each in turn before placing it in her lab. All but one of the shards would have caused no problems to her systems; non-metallic composites which could not interfere with the sensitive induction fields of the gunnery's interface machinery. But she catalogued and stored them anyway. The metal shard she frowned at, cursing the medics' procedures, and then laid it next to the rest.

That had been messy work, but not nearly as bad as the neural work. For centuries, the commonest forms of implant had either been grown *in situ* or were designed to self-insert painlessly via existing orifices, but such procedures could not be applied to the unique and delicate gunnery interface implants. The only way to get them in or out was with a bone-saw, scalpel and a lot of mopping up afterwards. It had been doubly awkward because of the routine implants already resting in Khouri's skull, but after giving them a cursory examination Volyova had seen no reason to remove them. Had she done so, she would sooner or later have had to re-implant very similar devices just so Khouri could function normally beyond the gunnery. The implants had grafted well, and within a day – with Khouri unconscious – Volyova had placed her in the gunnery seat and verified that the ship was able to talk to her implants and vice versa. Further testing had to wait until the loyalty therapies were complete. That would mainly be done while the rest of the crew were asleep.

Caution: that was Volyova's current watchword. It was incaution that had resulted in the whole unpleasantness with Nagorny.

She would not make that mistake again.

'Why do I get the idea this is some kind of test?' Khouri said.

'It isn't. It's just—' Volyova waved a hand dismissively. 'Indulge me, will you? It's not much to ask.'

'How do I oblige – by claiming to see ghosts?'

'Not by seeing them, Khouri, no. By hearing them.'

A light was visible now, beyond the black walls of the moving room. Of course, the walls were nothing but glass, and until that moment they had been surrounded only by the unlit metal of the shaft in which the room rested. But now illumination was shining from the shaft's approaching end. The rest of the short journey took place in silence. The room pushed itself towards the light, until the chill blue luminance was flooding in from all angles. Then the room pushed itself beyond the hull.

Khouri upped from her seat and went to the glass, edging towards it with trepidation. The glass was, of course, hyperdiamond, and there was no danger that it would shatter or that Khouri would stumble and plunge through it. But it looked ridiculously thin and brittle, and the human mind was able to take only so many things on trust. Looking laterally, she would have seen the articulated spider-legs, eight of them, anchoring the room to the exterior hull of the ship. She would have understood why Volyova called this place the spider-room.

'I don't know who or what built it,' Volyova said. 'My guess is that they installed it when the ship itself was constructed, or when it was due to change hands, assuming anyone could ever afford to buy it. I think this room was a very elaborate ploy for impressing potential clients – hence the general level of luxury.'

'Someone used it to make a sales pitch?'

'It makes a kind of sense – assuming one has any need in the first place to actually be outside a vessel like this. If the ship's under thrust, then any observation pod sent outside also has to match that level of thrust, or else it gets left behind. No problem if that pod's just a camera system, but as soon as you put people aboard it it gets a lot more complicated; someone actually has to fly the damned thing, or at the very least know how to program the autopilot to do what you want. The spider-room avoids that difficulty by physically attaching itself to the ship. It's child's play to operate; just like crawling around on all-eights.'

'What happens if . . .'

'It loses its grip? Well, it's never happened – even if it did, the room has various magnetic and hull-piercing grapples it can deploy; and even if those failed – which they wouldn't, I assure you – the room can propel itself independently; certainly for long enough to catch up with the ship. And even if that failed . . .' Volyova paused. 'Well, if that failed, I'd consider having a word with my deity-of-choice.'

Although Volyova had never taken the room more than a few hundred metres from its exit point on the hull, it would have been possible to crawl all around the ship. Not necessarily wise, however, for at relativistic speed the ship pushed through a blizzard of radiation which was normally screened by the hull insulation. The spider-room's thin walls only shielded a fraction of the flux, lending the whole exercise of being outside an odd and hazardous glamour.

The spider-room was her little secret; it was absent from the major blueprints, and to the best of her knowledge none of the others knew anything about it at all. In an ideal world, she would have kept it that way, but the problems with the gunnery had forced her into some necessary indiscretions. Even given the state of the ship's decay, Sajaki's network of surveillance devices was extensive, leaving the spider-room as one of the few places where Volyova could guarantee absolute privacy when she needed to discuss something sensitive with one of her recruits; something that she did not want the other Triumvirs to know about. She had been forced to reveal the spider-room to Nagorny so that she could talk with him frankly about the Sun Stealer problem, and for months – as his condition deteriorated – she had regretted that decision, always fearful that he would reveal the room's existence to Sajaki. But she need not have worried. By the end, Nagorny had been far too occupied with his nightmares to indulge in any subtleties of shipboard politick. Now he had taken the secret to his grave and for the time being Volyova had been able to sleep easy, safe in the knowledge that her sanctuary was not about to be betrayed. Perhaps what she was doing now was an error she would later regret – she had certainly sworn to herself not to violate the room's secrecy again – but as always, current circumstances had forced her to amend an earlier decision. There was something she needed to discuss with Khouri; the ghosts were merely a pretext so that Khouri would not become overly suspicious of Volyova's deeper motives.

'I'm not seeing any ghosts yet,' the recruit said.

'You'll see, or rather hear them, shortly,' Volyova said.

The Triumvir was acting oddly, Khouri thought. More than once she had hinted that this room was her private retreat aboard the ship, and that the others – Sajaki, Hegazi, and the other two women – were not even aware that it existed. It seemed strange indeed that Volyova was prepared to reveal the room to Khouri so soon in their working relationship. Volyova was a solitary, obsessive figure, even aboard a ship crewed by militaristic chimerics – not someone with a natural instinct for trustfulness, Khouri would have thought. Volyova was going through the motions of friendliness towards her, but there was something artificial about all her efforts . . . they were too planned, too lacking in anything resembling spontaneity. When Volyova made some kind of friendly overture to Khouri – a piece of smalltalk, shipboard gossip or a joke – there was always the feeling that Volyova had spent hours rehearsing, hoping she would sound off-the-cuff. Khouri had known people like that in the military; they seemed genuine at first, but they were usually the ones who turned out to be foreign spies or intelligence-gathering stooges from high command. Volyova was doing her best to act casually about the whole spider-room business, but it was obvious to Khouri that the ghost thing was not all that it appeared. A number of disquieting thoughts struck Khouri, prime among them the idea that perhaps

Volyova had brought her to this room with no intention of her ever leaving . . . alive, anyway.

But that turned out not to be the case.

'Oh, something I've been meaning to ask you,' Volyova said, breezily. 'Does the phrase Sun Stealer mean anything to you yet?'

'No,' Khouri said. 'Should it?'

'Oh; there's no reason it should – just a question, that's all. Too tedious to explain why, of course – don't worry about it, will you?'

She was about as convincing as a Mulch fortune-teller.

'No,' Khouri said. 'I won't worry, no . . .' And then added: 'Why did you say "yet"?'

Volyova cursed inwardly: had she blown it? Perhaps not; she had delivered the question as blithely as she dared, and there was nothing in Khouri's demeanour to suggest that she had taken it as anything other than a casual enquiry . . . and yet . . . now was emphatically *not* the time to start making errors.

'Did I say that?' she said, hoping to inject the right degree of surprise-mingled-with-indifference into her voice. 'Slip of the tongue, that's all.' Volyova groped for a change of subject, quickly. 'See that star, the faint red one?'

Now that their eyes had adjusted to the ambient light-levels of interstellar space, with even the blue radiance of the engine exhausts no longer seeming to blot out everything, a few stars were visible.

'That's Yellowstone's sun?'

'Epsilon Eridani, yes. We're three weeks beyond the system. Pretty soon you wouldn't have such an easy time finding it. We're not moving relativistically now – only a few per cent of light – but we're accelerating all the time. Soon the visible stars will move, the constellations warping, until all the stars in the sky are bunched ahead and behind us. It'll be as if we're poised midway down a tunnel, with light streaming in from either end. The stars will change colour as well. It isn't simple, since the final colour depends on the spectral type of each star; how much energy it emits in different wavelengths, including the infrared and ultraviolet. But the tendency will be for those stars ahead of us to shift to the blue; those behind us to the red.'

'I'm sure it'll be very pretty,' Khouri said, somewhat spoiling the moment. 'But I'm not quite sure where the ghosts come into it.'

Volyova smiled. 'I'd almost forgotten about them. That would have been a shame.'

And then she spoke into her bracelet, vocalising softly so that Khouri would not hear what it was she had to ask the ship.

Voices of the damned filled the chamber.

'Ghosts,' Volyova said.

Sylveste hovered in midair above the buried city, bodyless.

The encaging walls rose around him, densely engraved with the equivalent of ten thousand printed volumes of Amarantin writing. Although the graphicforms of the writing were mere millimetres high and he floated hundreds of metres from the wall, he only had to focus on any one part of it for the words to slam into clarity. As he did so, parallel translating algorithms processed the text into something approaching Canasian, while Sylveste's own quick semi-intuitive thought processes did likewise. More often than not he came to broad agreement with the programs, but occasionally they missed what might have been a crucial, context-dependent subtlety.

Meanwhile in his quarters in Cuvier, he made rapid, cursive notes, filling page after page of writing pad. These days, he favoured pen and paper over modern recording devices where possible. Digital media were too susceptible to later manipulation by his enemies. At least if his notes were pulped they would be lost for ever, rather than returning to haunt him in a guise warped to suit somebody else's ideology.

He finished translating a particular section, coming to one of the folded-wing glyphs which signified the end of a sequence. He pulled back from the dizzying textual precipice of the wall.

He slipped a blotter into the pad and closed it. By touch he slipped the pad back into a rack and removed the next pad along. He opened it at the page marked by its own blotter, then ran his fingers down the page until he felt the roughness of the ink vanish. Positioning the book exactly parallel with the desk, he stationed the pen at the start of the first new blank line.

'You're working too hard,' Pascale said.

She had entered the room unheard; now he had to visualise her standing at his side – or sitting, whichever was the case.

'I think I'm getting somewhere,' Sylveste said.

'Still banging your head against those old inscriptions?'

'One of us is beginning to crack.' He turned his bodyless point of view away from the wall, towards the centre of the enclosed city. 'Still, I didn't think it would take this long.'

'Me neither.'

He knew what she meant. Eighteen months since Nils Girardieau had shown him the buried city; a year since their wedding had been mooted and then put on hold until he had made significant progress on the translating work. Now he was doing exactly that – and it scared him. No more excuses, and she knew it as well as he did.

Why was that such a big problem? Was it only a problem because he chose to classify it as such?

'You're frowning again,' Pascale said. 'Are you having problems with the inscriptions?'

'No,' Sylveste said. 'They aren't the problem any more.' And it was the truth; it was now second nature for him to merge the bimodal streams of Amarantin writing into their implied whole, like a cartographer studying a stereographic image.

'Let me look.'

He heard her move across the room and address the escritoire, instructing it to open a parallel channel for her sensorium. The console – and, indeed, Sylveste's whole access to the data-model of the city – had come not long after that first visit. For once the idea had not been Girardieau's, but something Pascale had initiated. The success of *Descent into Darkness*, the recently published biography, and the upcoming wedding had increased her leverage over her father, and Sylveste had known better than to argue when she had offered him – literally – the keys to the city.

The wedding was the talk of the colony now. Most of the gossip which reached its way back to Sylveste assumed that the motives were purely political; that Sylveste had courted Pascale as a way of marrying his way back into something close to power; that – seen cynically – the wedding was only a means to an end, and that the end was a colonial expedition to Cerberus/Hades. Perhaps, for the briefest of instants, Sylveste had wondered that himself; wondered if his subconscious had not engineered his love for Pascale with this deeper ambition in mind. Perhaps there was the tiniest grain of truth in that, as well. But from his current standpoint, it was mercifully impossible to tell. He certainly felt as if he loved her – which, as far as he could tell, was the same thing as loving her –

but he was not blind to the advantages that the marriage would bring. Now he was publishing again; modest articles based on tiny portions of translated Amarantin text; co-authorship with Pascale; Girardieau himself acknowledged as having assisted in the work. The Sylveste of fifteen years ago would have been appalled, but now he found it hard to stir up much self-disgust. What mattered was that the city was a step towards understanding the Event.

'I'm here,' Pascale said – louder now, but just as bodyless as Sylveste. 'Are we sharing the same point of view?'

'What are you seeing?'

'The spire; the temple – whatever you call it.'

'That's right.'

The temple was at the geometric centre of the quarter-scale city, shaped like the upper third of an egg. Its topmost point extended upwards, becoming a spiriform tower which ascended – narrowing as it did – towards the roof of the city chamber. The buildings around the temple had the fused look of weaver-bird nests; perhaps the expression of some submerged evolutionary imperative. They huddled like misshapen orisons before the vast central spire which curled from the temple.

'Something bothering you about this?'

He envied her. Pascale had visited the real city dozens of times. She had even climbed the spire on foot, following the gulletlike spiral passage which wound up its height.

'The figure on the spire? It doesn't fit.'

It looked like a small, daintily carved figurine by comparison with the rest of the city, but was still ten or fifteen metres tall, comparable to the Egyptian figures in the Temple of Kings. The buried city was built to an approximate quarter-scale, based on comparisons with other digs. The full-size counterpart of the spire figure would have been at least forty metres tall. But if this city had ever existed on the surface, it would have been lucky to survive the firestorms of the Event, let alone the subsequent nine hundred and ninety thousand years of planetary weathering, glaciation, meteorite impacts and tectonics.

'Doesn't fit?'

'It isn't Amarantin – at least not any kind I've ever seen.'

'Some kind of deity, then?'

'Maybe. But I don't understand why they've given it wings.'

'Ah. And this is problematic?'

'Take a look around the city wall if you don't believe me.'

'Better lead me there, Dan.'

Their twin points of view curved away from the spire, dropping down dizzyingly.

Volyova watched the effect the voices had on Khouri, certain that somewhere in Khouri's armour of self-assurance was a chink of fearful doubt – the thought that maybe these really were ghosts after all, and that Volyova had found a way to tune into their phantom emanations.

The sound that the ghosts made was moaning and cavernous; long drawn-out howls so low that they were almost felt rather than heard. It was like the eeriest winter night's wind imaginable; the sound that a wind might make after blowing through a thousand miles of cavern. But this was clearly no natural phenomenon, not the particle wind streaming past the ship, translated into sound; not even the fluctuations in the delicately balanced reactions in the engines. There were souls in that ghost-howl; voices calling across the night. In the moaning, though not one word was understandable, there remained nonetheless the unmistakable structure of human language.

'What do you think?' Volyova asked.

'They're voices, aren't they? Human voices. But they sound so . . . exhausted; so sad.' Khouri listened attentively. 'Every now and then I think I understand a word.'

'You know what they are, of course.' Volyova diminished the sound, until the ghosts formed only a muted, infinitely pained chorus. 'They're crew. Like you and me. Occupants of other vessels, talking to each other across the void.'

'Then why—' Khouri hesitated. 'Oh, wait a minute. Now I understand. They're moving faster than us, aren't they? Much faster. Their voices sound slow because they are, literally. Clocks run slower on ships moving near the speed of light.'

Volyova nodded, the tiniest bit saddened that Khouri had understood so swiftly. 'Time dilation. Of course, some of those ships are moving towards us, so doppler-blueshifting acts to reduce the effect, but the dilation factor usually wins . . .' She shrugged, seeing that Khouri was not yet ready for a treatise on the finer principles of relativistic communications. 'Normally, of course, *Infinity* corrects for all this; removes the doppler and dilatory distortions, and translates the result into something which sounds perfectly intelligible.'

'Show me.'

'No,' Volyova said. 'It isn't worth it. The end product is always the same. Trivia, technical talk, boastful old trade rhetoric. That's the interesting end of the spectrum. At the boring end you get paranoid gossip or brain-damaged cases baring their souls to the night. Most of the time it's just two ships handshaking as they pass in the night; exchanging bland pleasantries. There's hardly ever any interaction since the light-travel times between ships are seldom less than months. And anyway, half the time the voices are just prerecorded messages, since the crew are usually in reefer-sleep.'

'Just the usual human babble, in other words.'

'Yes. We take it with us wherever we go.'

Volyova relaxed back in her seat, instructing the sound-system to pump out the sorrowful, time-stretched voices even louder than before. This signal of human presence ought to have made the stars seem less remote and cold, but it managed to have exactly the opposite effect; just like the act of telling ghost stories around a campfire served to magnify the darkness beyond the flames. For a moment – one that she revelled in, no matter what Khouri made of it – it was possible to believe that the interstellar spaces beyond the glass were really haunted.

'Notice anything?' Sylveste asked.

The wall consisted of chevron-shaped granite blocks, interrupted at five points by gatehouses. The gatehouses were surmounted by sculptural Amarantin heads, in a not-quite-realistic style reminiscent of Yucatán art. A fresco ran around the outer wall, made from ceramic tiles, depicting Amarantin functionaries performing complex social duties.

Pascale paused before answering, her gaze tracking over the different figures in the fresco.

They were shown carrying farming implements which looked almost like actual items from human agricultural history, or weapons – pikes, bows and a kind of musket, although the poses were not those of warriors engaged in combat, but were far more formalised and stiff, like Egyptian figurework. There were Amarantin surgeons and stoneworkers, astronomers – they had invented reflecting and refracting telescopes, recent digs had confirmed – and cartographers, glassworkers, kitemakers and artists, and above each symbolic figure was a bimodal chain of graphicforms picked out in gold and cobalt-blue, naming the flock which assumed the duty of the representational figure.

'None of them have wings,' Pascale said.

'No,' Sylveste said. 'What used to be their wings turned into their arms.'

'But why object to a statue of a god with a pair of wings? Humans have never had wings, but that's never stopped us investing angels with them. It strikes me that a species which really did once have wings would have even fewer qualms.'

'Yes, except you're forgetting the creation myth.'

It was only in the last years that the basic myth had been understood by the archaeologists; unravelled from dozens of later, embroidered versions. According to the myth, the Amarantin had once shared the sky with the other birdlike creatures which still existed on Resurgam during their reign. But the flocks of that time were the last to know the freedom of flight. They made an agreement with the god they called Birdmaker, trading the ability to fly for the gift of sentience. On that day, they raised their wings to heaven and watched as consuming fire turned them to ash, for ever excluding them from the air.

So that they might remember their arrangement, the Birdmaker gave them useless, clawed wing-stubs – enough to remind them of what they had forsaken, and enough to enable them to begin writing down their history. Fire burned in their minds too, but this was the unquenchable fire of being. That light would always burn, the Birdmaker told them – so long as they did not try to defy the Birdmaker's will by once more returning to the skies. If they did that, it was promised, the Birdmaker would take back the souls they had been given on the Day of Burning Wings.

It was, Sylveste knew, simply the understandable attempt of a culture to raise a mirror to itself. What made it significant was the complete extent to which it had permeated their culture – in effect, a single religion which had superseded all others and which had persisted, through different tellings, for an unthinkable span of centuries. Undoubtedly it had shaped their thinking and behaviour, perhaps in ways too complex to begin guessing.

'I understand,' Pascale said. 'As a species, they couldn't deal with being flightless, so they created the Birdmaker story so they could feel some superiority over the birds which could still fly.'

'Yes. And while that belief worked, it had one unexpected side-effect: to deter them from ever taking flight again: much like the Icarus myth, only exhibiting a stronger hold over their collective psyche.'

'But if that's the case, the figure on the spire . . .'

'Is a big two-fingered salute to whatever god they used to believe in.'

'Why would they do that?' Pascale said. 'Religions just fade away; get replaced by new ones. I can't believe they'd build that city, everything in it, just as an insult to their old god.'

'Me neither. Which suggests something else entirely.'

'Like what?'

'That a new god moved in. One with wings.'

Volyova had decided it was time to show Khouri the instruments of her profession. 'Hold on,' she said, as the elevator approached the cache chamber. 'People don't generally like this the first time it happens.'

'God,' Khouri said, instinctively pressing herself against the rear wall as the vista suddenly expanded shockingly; the elevator a tiny beetle crawling down the side of the vast space. 'It looks too big to fit inside!'

'Oh, this is nothing. There are another four chambers this large. Chamber two is where we train for surface ops. Two are empty or semi-pressurised; the fourth holds shuttles and in-system vehicles. This is the only one dedicated to holding the cache.'

'You mean those things?'

'Yes.'

There were forty cache-weapons in the chamber, though none exactly resembled any other. Yet in their general style of construction, a certain affinity was betrayed. Each machine was cased in alloy of a greenish-bronze hue. Though each of the devices was large enough to be a medium-sized spacecraft in its own right, none exhibited any indication that this was their function. There were no windows or access doors visible in what would have been their hulls, no markings or communications systems. While some of the objects were studded with what might have been vernier jets, they were only there to assist in the moving around and positioning of the devices, much as a battleship was only there to assist in moving around and positioning its big guns.

Of course, that was exactly what the cache devices were.

'Hell-class,' Volyova said. 'That was what their builders called them. Of course, we're going back a few centuries here.'

Volyova watched as her recruit appraised the titanic size of the nearest cache-weapon. Suspended vertically, its long axis aligned with the ship's axis of thrust, it looked like a ceremonial sword dangling from a warrior-baron's ceiling. Like all the weapons, it was surrounded by a framework which had been added by one of Volyova's predecessors, to which were attached various control, monitoring and manoeuvring systems. All the weapons were connected to tracks – a three-dimensional maze of sidings and switches – which merged lower down in the chamber, feeding into a much smaller volume directly below, large enough to contain a single weapon. From there, the weapons could be deployed beyond the hull, into space.

'So who built them?' Khouri said.

'We don't know for sure. The Conjoiners, perhaps, in one of their darker incarnations. All we know is how we found them – hidden away in an asteroid, circling a brown dwarf so obscure it has only a catalogue number.'

'You were there?'

'No; this was long before my time. I only inherited them from the last caretaker – and he from his. I've been studying them ever since. I've managed to access the control systems of thirty-one of them, and I've figured out – very roughly – about eighty per cent of the necessary activation codes. But I've only tested seventeen of the weapons, and of that number, only two in what you might term actual combat situations.'

'You mean you've actually used them?'

'It wasn't something I rushed into.'

No need, she thought, to burden Khouri with details of past atrocities – at least, not immediately. Over time, Khouri would come to know the cache-weapons as well as Volyova knew them – perhaps even more intimately, since Khouri would know them via the gunnery, through direct neural-interface.

'What can they do?'

'Some of them are more than capable of taking planets apart. Others . . . I don't even want to guess. I wouldn't be at all surprised if some of them did unpleasant things to stars. Exactly who'd want to use such weapons . . .' She trailed off.

'Who did you use them against?'

'Enemies, of course.'

Khouri regarded her for long, silent seconds.

'I don't know whether to be horrified that such things exist . . . or relieved to know that at least it's us who have our fingers on the triggers.'

'Be relieved,' Volyova said. 'It's better that way.'

Sylveste and Pascale returned to the spire, hovering. The winged Amarantin was just as they had left it, but now it seemed to brood over the city with imperious disregard. It was tempting to think that a new god really had moved in – what else could have inspired the building of such a monument, if not fear of the divine? But the accompanying text on the spire was maddeningly hard to unscramble.

'Here's a reference to the Birdmaker,' Sylveste said. 'So chances are good the spire had some bearing on the Burning Wings myth, even though the winged god clearly isn't a representation of the Birdmaker.'

'Yes,' Pascale said. 'That's the graphicform for fire, next to the one for wings.'

'What else do you see?'

Pascale concentrated for a few long moments. 'There's some reference here to a renegade flock.'

'Renegade in what sense?' He was testing her, and she knew it, but the exercise was valuable in itself, for Pascale's interpretation would give him some indication of how subjective his own analysis had been.

'A renegade flock which didn't agree to the deal with the Birdmaker, or reneged on the deal afterwards.'

'That's what I thought. I was worried I might have made an error or two.'

'Whoever they were, they were called the Banished Ones.' She read back and forth, testing hypotheses and revising her interpretation as she went. 'It looks like they were originally part of the flock who agreed to the Birdmaker's terms, but that they changed their minds sometime later.'

'Can you make out the name of their leader?'

She began: 'They were led by an individual called . . .' But then Pascale trailed off. 'No, can't translate that string; at least not right now. What does all this mean, anyway? Do you think they really existed?'

'Perhaps. If I had to take a guess, I'd say they were unbelievers who came to realise that the Birdmaker myth was just that – myth. Of course, that wouldn't have gone down very well with the other fundamentalist flocks.'

'Which is why they were banished?'

'Assuming they ever existed in the first place. But I can't help thinking, what if they were some kind of technological sect, like an enclave of scientists? Amarantin who were prepared to experiment, to question the nature of their world?'

'Like mediaeval alchemists?'

'Yes.' He liked the analogy immediately. 'Perhaps they even tried experimenting with flight, the way Leonardo did. Against the backdrop of general Amarantin culture, that would have been like spitting in God's eye.'

'Agreed. But assuming they were real – and were banished – what happened to them? Did they just die out?'

'I don't know. But one thing's clear. The Banished Ones were important – more than just a minor detail in the overall story of the Birdmaker myth. They're mentioned all over the spire; all over this damned city, in fact – far more frequently than in any other Amarantin relics.'

'But the city is late,' Pascale said. 'Apart from the marker obelisk, it's the most recent relic we've found. Dating from near the Event. Why would the Banished Ones suddenly crop up again, after so long an absence?'

'Well,' Sylveste said. 'Maybe they came back.'

'After – what? Tens of thousands of years?'

'Perhaps.' Sylveste smiled privately. 'If they did return – after that long away – it might be the kind of thing to inspire statue-building.'

'Then the statue – do you think it might portray their leader? The one called—' Pascale took another stab at the graphicform. 'Well, this is the symbol for the sun, isn't it?'

'And the rest?'

'I'm not sure. Looks like the glyph for the act of . . . theft – but how can that be?'

'Put the two together, what have you got?'

He imagined her shrugging, noncommittally. 'One who steals suns? Sun Stealer? What would that mean?'

Sylveste shrugged himself. 'That's what I've been asking myself all morning. That and one other thing.'

'Which would be?'

'Why I think I've heard that name before.'

After the weapons chamber, the three of them rode another elevator further into the ship's heart.

'You're doing well,' the Mademoiselle said. 'Volyova honestly believes that she's turned you to her side.'

She had, more or less, been with them the whole time – silently observing Volyova's guided tour, only occasionally interjecting with remarks or prompts for Khouri's ears only. This was extremely disquieting: Khouri was never able to free herself of the feeling that Volyova was also privy to these whispered asides.

'Maybe she's right,' Khouri answered, automatically thinking her response. 'Maybe she's stronger than you.'

The Mademoiselle scoffed. 'Did you listen to anything I told you?'

'As if I had any choice.'

Shutting out the Mademoiselle when she wanted to say something was like trying to silence an insistent refrain playing in her head. There was no respite from her apparitions.

'Listen,' the woman said. 'If my countermeasures were failing, your loyalty to Volyova would force you to tell her of my existence.'

'I've been tempted.'

The Mademoiselle looked at her askance, and Khouri felt a brief frisson of satisfaction. In some respects the Mademoiselle – or rather, her implant-distilled persona – seemed omniscient. But apart from the knowledge which had been instilled in it upon its creation, the implant's learning was restricted entirely to what it could perceive through Khouri's own senses. Maybe the implant could hook into data networks even if Khouri herself were not interfaced, but while that might have been possible, it seemed unlikely; there was too much risk of the implant itself being detected by the same systems. And although it could hear her thoughts when Khouri chose to communicate with it, it could not read her state of mind, other than by the most superficial biochemical cues in the neural environment in which it floated. So for the implant, there was a necessary element of doubt concerning the efficacy of its countermeasures.

'Volyova would kill you. She killed her last recruit, if you haven't worked that out for yourself.'

'Maybe she had good reason.'

'You don't know anything about her – or any of them. Neither do I. We haven't even met her Captain yet.'

There was no arguing with that. Captain Brannigan's name had come up once or twice when Sajaki or one of the others had been indiscreet in Khouri's presence, but in general they did not speak often of their leader. Clearly they were not Ultras in the usual sense, although they maintained a meticulous front even the Mademoiselle had not seen through. The fiction was so absolute that they went through the motions of trade just like all the other Ultra crews.

But what was the reality behind the façade?

Gunnery Officer, Volyova had said. And now Khouri had seen something of the cache of weapons stored within the ship. It was rumoured that many trade vessels carried discreet armaments, for resolving the worst sorts of breakdown in client-customer relations, or for staging acts of blatant piracy against other ships. But these weapons looked far too potent to be used in mere squabbles, and in any case, the ship clearly had an extra layer of conventional weaponry for just those circumstances. So what exactly was the point behind this arsenal? Sajaki must have had some long-term plan in mind, Khouri thought, and that was disturbing enough – but even more worrying was the thought that perhaps there was no plan at all; that Sajaki was carrying the cache around until he found an excuse for using it, like a tooled-up thug stumbling around in search of a fight.

Over the weeks, Khouri had considered and discarded numerous theories, without coming close to anything that sounded plausible. It was not the military side of the ship's nature that troubled her, of course. She had been born to war; war was her natural environment, and while she was ready to consider the possibility that there were other, more benign states of being, there was nothing about war that felt alien to her. But, she had to admit, the kinds of wars which she had known on Sky's Edge were hardly

151

comparable to any of the scenarios in which the cache-weapons might be used. Though Sky's Edge had remained linked to the interstellar trade network, the average technological level of the combatants in the surface battles had been centuries behind the Ultras who sometimes parked their ships in orbit. A campaign could be won just by one side gaining one item of Ultra weaponry . . . but those items had always been scarce; sometimes too valuable even to use. Even nukes had been deployed only a few times in the colony's history, and never in Khouri's lifetime. She had seen some vile things – things that still haunted her – but she had never seen anything capable of instant, genocidal death. Volyova's cache-weapons were much worse than that.

And perhaps they had been used, once or twice. Volyova had said as much – pirate operations, perhaps. There were plenty of thinly populated systems, only loosely connected to the trade nets, where it would be entirely possible to exterminate an enemy without anyone ever finding out. And some of those enemies might be as amoral as any of Sajaki's crew; their pasts littered with acts of random atrocity. So, yes, it was quite likely that parts of the cache had been tested. But Khouri suspected that this would only have ever been a means to an end; self-preservation, or tactical strikes against enemies with resources they needed. The heavier cache-weapons would not have been tested. What they eventually planned to do with the cache – how they planned to discharge the world-wrecking power they possessed – was not yet clear, perhaps not even to Sajaki. And perhaps Sajaki was not the man in whom the ultimate power lay vested. Perhaps, in some way, Sajaki was still serving Captain Brannigan.

Whoever the mysterious Brannigan was.

'Welcome to the gunnery,' Volyova said.

They had arrived somewhere near the middle of the ship. Volyova had opened a hole in the ceiling, folded down a telescopic ladder and beckoned Khouri to climb its sharp-edged rungs.

Her head was poking into a large spherical room full of curved, jointed machinery. At the centre of this halo of bluish-silver was a rectilinear hooded black seat, festooned with machinery and a seemingly random tangle of cables. The seat was fixed within a series of elegant gyroscopic axes, arranged so that its motion would be independent of that of the ship. The cables passed into sliding armatures which transmitted power between each concentric shell, before the final thigh-thick clump dove into the machinery-clotted spherical wall of the room. The room reeked of ozone.

There was nothing in the gunnery which looked much newer than a few hundred years old, and plenty that looked as if it had been around for considerably longer. All of it, though, had been scrupulously cared for.

'This is what it's all been building up to, isn't it?' Khouri pushed herself through the trapdoor into the heart of the chamber, slithering between the curved skeletal shells until she reached the seat. Massive as it was, it seemed to beckon to her with promises of comfort and security. She could not stop herself from sliding into it, letting its cumbersome black bulk softly encase her with a whir of buried servomechanisms.

'How does it feel?'

'Like I've been here before,' she said wonderingly, voice distorted by the bulk of the studded black helmet which had slid over her head.

'You have,' Volyova answered. 'Before you were properly conscious. Besides, the gunnery implant in your head already knows its way around here – that's where half the sense of familiarity comes from.'

What Volyova said was true. Khouri felt as if the chair were some familiar piece of furniture she had grown up around, its every wrinkle and scratch known to her. She already felt powerfully relaxed and calm, and the urge to actually do something – to use the power that the chair bestowed on her – was building by the second.

'I can control the cache-weapons from here?'

'That's the intention,' Volyova said. 'But not just the cache, of course. You'll also be directing every other major weapon system aboard the *Infinity* – with as much fluency as if these instruments were simply extensions of your own anatomy. When you're fully subsumed by the gunnery, that's how it'll feel – your own body image swelling out to take in the ship itself.'

Khouri had already begun to feel something similar; the sense at least that her body was blurring into the chair. Tantalising as it was, she had no wish for the sense of subsumption to continue any further. With a conscious effort she eased herself from the chair, its enfolding panels whirring aside to release her.

'I'm not sure I like this,' the Mademoiselle said.

SEVEN

Never quite forgetting that she was aboard a ship (it was the ever-so-slightly irregular pattern of the induced gravity, caused by tiny imbalances in the thrust stream, which in turn reflected mysterious quantum capriciousness in the bowels of the Conjoiner drives) Volyova entered the green seclusion of the glade alone and hesitated at the top of the rustic staircase which led down to the grass. If Sajaki was aware of her presence, he chose not to show it, kneeling silently and motionlessly next to the gnarled tree stump which was their informal meeting place. But he undoubtedly sensed her. Volyova knew that Sajaki had visited the Pattern Jugglers on the aquatic world Wintersea, accompanying Captain Brannigan, back when Captain Brannigan was capable of leaving the ship. She did not know what the purpose of that trip had been – for either of them – but there had been rumours that the Pattern Jugglers had tampered with his neocortex, embossing neural patterns which configured an unusual degree of spatial awareness: the ability to think in four or five dimensions. The patterns had been the rarest kind of Juggler transform: one that lingered.

Volyova ambled down the staircase and allowed her foot to creak on the lowest tread. Sajaki turned to regard her with no visible hint of surprise.

'Something up?' he asked, reading her expression.

'It concerns the *stavlennik*,' she said, momentarily lapsing back into Russish. 'The protégée, I mean.'

'Tell me about it,' Sajaki said absently. He wore an ash-grey kimono, damp grass darkening his knees to olive-black. His Komuso's shakuhachi rested on the stump's mirror-smooth, elbow-polished surface. He and Volyova were now the only two crewmembers yet to enter reefersleep, two months out from Yellowstone.

'She's one of us now,' Volyova said, kneeling opposite him. 'The core of her indoctrination is complete.'

'I welcome this news.'

Across the glade a macaw screeched, then left its perch in a flurry of clashing primary colours. 'We can introduce her to Captain Brannigan.'

'No time like the present,' Sajaki said, smoothing a wrinkle from his kimono. 'Or do you have second thoughts?'

'About meeting the Captain?' She clucked nervously. 'None at all.'

'Then it's deeper than that.'

'What?'

'Whatever's on your mind, Ilia. Come on. Spit it out.'

'It's Khouri. I'm no longer willing to risk her suffering the same kind of psychotic episodes as Nagorny.' She stopped, expecting – hoping, even – for some response from Sajaki. But instead all she got was the white-noise of the waterfall, and a total absence of expression on her crewmate's face. 'What I mean,' she continued – almost stammering with her own uncertainty – 'is that I'm no longer sure she's a suitable subject at this stage.'

'At this stage?' Sajaki spoke so softly she largely read his lips.

'I mean, to go into the gunnery immediately after Nagorny. It's too dangerous, and I think Khouri is too valuable to risk.' She stopped, swallowed, and drew breath into her lungs for what she knew would be the hardest thing to say. 'I think we need another recruit – someone less gifted. With an intermediate recruit I can iron out the remaining wrinkles before going ahead with Khouri as primary candidate.'

Sajaki picked up his shakuhachi and sighted along it thoughtfully. There was a little raised burr at the end of the bamboo, perhaps from the time when he had used the stick on Khouri. He rubbed it with his thumb, smoothing it back down.

When he spoke, it was with a calm so total that it was worse than any possible display of anger.

'You're suggesting we look for another recruit?'

He made it sound as if what she was proposing was easily the most absurd, deranged thing he had ever heard uttered.

'Only in the interim,' she said, aware that she was speaking too quickly, hating herself for it, despising her sudden deference to the man. 'Just until everything's stable. Then we can use Khouri.'

Sajaki nodded. 'Well, that sounds sensible. Goodness knows why we didn't think of it earlier, but I suppose we had other things on our minds.' He put down the shakuhachi, although his hand did not stray far from its hollow shaft. 'But that can't be helped. What we have to do now is find ourselves another recruit. Shouldn't be too hard, should it? I mean, we hardly taxed ourselves recruiting Khouri. Admittedly we're two months into interstellar space and our next port of call is a virtually unheard-of outpost – but I don't envisage any great problem in finding another subject. I expect we'll have to turn them away in droves, don't you?'

'Be reasonable,' she said.

'In what sense am I being anything other than reasonable, Triumvir?'

A moment ago she had been scared; now she was angry. 'You haven't been the same, Yuuji-san. Not since . . .'

'Not since what?'

'Not since you and the Captain visited the Jugglers. What happened there, Yuuji? What did the aliens do to your head?'

He looked at her oddly, as if the question were a perfectly valid one which it had never struck him to ask himself. It was, fatefully, a ruse. Sajaki moved quickly with the shakuhachi, so that all Volyova really saw was a teak-coloured blur in the air. The blow was relatively soft – Sajaki must have pulled at the last moment – but, gashing into her side, it was still sufficient to send her sprawling into the grass. For the first instant, it was not the pain or the shock of being attacked by Sajaki that overwhelmed her, but the prickly cold wetness of the grass brushing against her nostrils.

He stepped casually round the stump.

'You're always asking too many questions,' Sajaki said, and then drew something from his kimono that might have been a syringe.

Nekhebet Isthmus, Resurgam, 2566

Sylveste reached anxiously into his pocket, feeling for the vial which he felt sure would be missing.

He touched it; a minor miracle.

Down below, dignitaries were filing into the Amarantin city, moving slowly towards the temple at the city's heart. Snatches of their conversation reached him with perfect clarity, though never long enough for him to hear more than a few words. He was hundreds of metres above them, on the human-installed balustrade which had been grafted to the black wall of the city-englobing egg.

It was his wedding day.

He had seen the temple in simulations many times, but it had been so long since he had actually visited the place that he had forgotten how overpowering its size could be. That was one of the odd, persistent defects of simulations: no matter how precise they became, the participant remained aware that they were not reality. Sylveste had stood beneath the roof of the Amarantin spire-temple, gazing up to where the angled stone arches intersected hundreds of metres above, and had felt not the slightest hint of vertigo, or fear that the age-old structure would choose that moment to collapse upon him. But now – visiting the buried city for only the second time in person – he felt a withering sense of his own smallness. The egg in which it was encased was itself uncomfortably large, but that at least was the product of a recognisably mature technology – even if the Inundationists elected to ignore the fact. The city which rested within, on the other hand, looked more like the product of some fifteenth-century fever-dream fantasist, not least because of the fabulous winged figure which rested atop the temple spire. And all of it – the more he looked – seemed to exist only to celebrate the return of the Banished Ones.

None of it made sense. But at least it forced his mind off the ceremony ahead.

The more he looked, the more he realised – against his first impression – that the winged thing really *was* an Amarantin, or, more accurately, a kind of hybrid Amarantin/angel, sculpted by an artist with a deep and scholarly understanding of what the possessing of wings would actually entail. Seen without his eyes' zoom facility, the statue was cruciform, shockingly so. Enlarged, the cruciform shape became a perched Amarantin with glorious, outspread wings. The wings were metalled in different colours, each small trailing feather sparkling with a slightly different hue. Like the human representation of an angel, the wings did not simply replace the creature's arms, but were a third pair of limbs in their own right.

But the statue seemed more real than any representation of an angel Sylveste had ever seen in human art. It appeared – the thought seemed absurd – anatomically correct. The sculptor had not just grafted the wings onto the basic Amarantin form, but had subtly re-engineered the creature's underlying physique. The manipulatory forelimbs had been moved slightly lower down the torso, elongated to compensate. The chest of the torso swelled much wider than the norm, dominated by a yokelike skeletal/muscular form around the creature's shoulder area. From this yoke sprouted the wing, forming a roughly triangular shape, kitelike. The creature's neck was longer than normal, and the head seemed even more streamlined and avian in profile. The eyes still faced forwards – though like all Amarantin, its binocular vision was limited – but were set into deep, grooved bone channels. The creature's upper mandible nostril parts were flared and rilled, as if to draw the extra air into the lungs required for the beating of the wings. And yet not everything was right. Assuming that the creature's body was approximately similar in mass to the Amarantin norm, even those wings would have been pitifully inadequate for the task of flying. So what were they – some kind of gross ornamentation? Had the Banished Ones gone in for radical bio-engineering, only to burden themselves with wings of ridiculous impracticality?

Or had there been another purpose?

'Second thoughts?'

Sylveste was jolted suddenly from his contemplation.

'You still don't think this is a good idea, do you?'

He turned around from the balustrade which looked across the city.

'It's a little late to voice my objections, I think.'

'On your wedding day?' Girardieau smiled. 'Well, you're not home and dry yet, Dan. You could always back out.'

'How would you take that?'

'Very badly indeed, I suspect.'

Girardieau was dressed in starched city finery, cheeks lightly rouged for the attendant swarms of float-cams. He took Sylveste by the forearm and led him away from the edge.

'How long have we been friends, Dan?'

'I wouldn't exactly call it friendship; more a kind of mutual parasitism.'

'Oh come on,' Girardieau said, looking disappointed. 'Have I made your life any more of a misery these last twenty years than was strictly necessary? Do you think I took any great pleasure in locking you away?'

'Let's say you approached the task with no little enthusiasm.'

'Only because I had your best interests at heart.' They stepped off the balcony into one of the low tunnels which threaded the black shell around the city. Cushioned flooring absorbed their footsteps. 'Besides,' Girardieau continued, 'if it wasn't transparently obvious, Dan, there was something of a feeding frenzy at the time. If I hadn't put you in custody, some mob would eventually have taken out their anger on you.'

Sylveste listened without speaking. He knew much of what Girardieau said was true on a theoretical level, but that there was no guarantee that it reflected the man's actual motives at the time.

'The political situation at the time was much simpler. Back then we didn't have True Path making trouble.' They reached an elevator shaft and entered the carriage, its interior antiseptically clean and new. Prints hung on the wall, showing various Resurgam vistas before and after the Inundationist transformations. There was even one of Mantell. The mesa in which the research outpost was embedded was draped in foliage, a waterfall running off the top, blue, cloud-streaked skies beyond it. In Cuvier, there was a whole sub-industry devoted to creating images and simulations of the future Resurgam, ranging from water-colour artists to skilled sensorium designers.

'And on the other hand,' Girardieau said, 'there are radical scientific elements coming out of the woodwork. Only last week, one of True Path's representatives was shot dead in Mantell, and believe me, it wasn't one of our agents who did it.'

Sylveste felt the carriage begin to convey them down, towards the city level.

'What are you saying?'

'I'm saying that with fanatics on both sides, you and I are beginning to look like distinct moderates. Depressing thought, isn't it?'

'Out-radicalised on both fronts, you mean.'

'Something like that.'

They emerged through the black, graven wall of the city-shell into a small crowd of media types who were running through last-minute preparations for the event. Reporters wore buff-coloured float-cam glasses, choreographing the cams which hovered around them like drab party balloons. One of Janequin's genetically engineered peacocks was pecking around the group, its tail hissing behind it. Two security officers stepped forwards garbed in black with gold Inundationist sigils on their shoulders, surrounded by flocks of deliberately threatening entoptics. Servitors loitered behind them. They ran full-spectrum ident scans on Sylveste and Girardieau, then motioned them to a small temporary structure which had been placed near a nestlike froth of Amarantin dwellings.

The inside was almost bare, apart from a table and two skeletal chairs. There was a bottle of Amerikano red wine on the table, next to a pair of wine goblets, engraved with frosted-glass landscapes.

'Sit down,' Girardieau said. He swaggered around the table and decanted measures of wine into both glasses. 'I don't know why you're so damned nervous. It isn't as if this is your first time.'

'My fourth, actually.'

'All Stoner ceremonies?'

Sylveste nodded. He thought of the first two: small-scale affairs, to minor-league Stoner women, the faces of whom he could almost not separate in his memory. Both had withered under the glare of publicity that the family name attracted. By contrast, his marriage to Alicia – his last wife – had been sculpted as a publicity move from the onset. It had focused attention on the upcoming Resurgam expedition, giving it the final monetary push it needed. The fact that they had been in love had been almost inconsequential, merely a happy addendum to the existing arrangement.

'That's a lot of baggage to be carrying around in your head now,' Girardieau said. 'Don't you ever wish you could be rid of the past each time?'

'You find the ceremony unusual.'

'Perhaps I do.' Girardieau wiped a red smear of wine from his lips. 'I was never part of Stoner culture, you see.'

'You came with us from Yellowstone.'

'Yes, but I wasn't born there. My family were from Grand Teton. I only arrived on Yellowstone seven years before the Resurgam expedition departed. Not really enough time to become culturally adapted to Stoner tradition. My daughter, on the other hand . . . well, Pascale's never known anything but Stoner society. Or at least the version of it we imported when we came here.' He lowered his voice. 'You must have the vial with you now, I suppose. May I see it?'

'I could hardly refuse you.'

Sylveste reached in his pocket and removed the little glass cylinder he had been carrying with him all day. He passed it to Girardieau, who nervously tinkered with it, tipping it this way and that. He watched the bubbles within, slipping to and fro as if in a spirit level. Something darker hung within the fluid, fibrous and tendrilled.

He placed the vial down; it made a delicate glassy chime as it settled on the tabletop. Girardieau studied it with barely masked horror.

'Was it painful?'

'Of course not. We're not sadists, you know.' Sylveste smiled, secretly enjoying Girardieau's discomfort. 'Would you rather we exchanged camels, perhaps?'

'Put it away.'

Sylveste slipped the vial back into his pocket. 'Now tell me who's the nervous one, Nils.'

Girardieau poured himself another measure of wine. 'Sorry. Security are edgy as hell. Don't know what's got them so bothered, but it's rubbing off on me, I suppose.'

'I didn't notice anything.'

'You wouldn't.' Girardieau shrugged; a bellows-like movement that began somewhere below his abdomen. 'They claim everything's normal, but after twenty years I read them better than they imagine.'

'I wouldn't worry. Your police are very efficient people.'

Girardieau shook his head briefly, as if he had taken a bite from a particularly sour lemon. 'I don't expect the air between us to ever be completely cleared, Dan. But you could at least give me the benefit of the doubt.' He nodded towards the open door. 'Didn't I give you complete access to this place?'

Yes, and all that had done was to replace a dozen questions with a thousand more. 'Nils . . .' he began, 'how are the colony's resources these days?'

'In what sense?'

'I know things have been different since Remilliod came through. Things which would have been unthinkable in my day . . . could be done now, if the political will was there.'

'What kinds of things?' Girardieau asked dubiously.

Sylveste reached into his jacket again, but this time, instead of the vial, he removed a piece of paper which he spread before Girardieau. The paper was marked with complex circular figures. 'You recognise these marks? We found them on the obelisk and all over the city. They're maps of the solar system, made by the Amarantin.'

'Somehow, having seen this city, I find that easier to believe now than I once did.'

'Good, then hear me out.' Sylveste drew his finger along the widest circle. 'This represents the orbit of the neutron star, Hades.'

'Hades?'

'That was the name it was given when they first surveyed the system. There's a lump of rock orbiting it, too – about the size of a planetary moon. They called it Cerberus.' Then he brushed his finger across the cluster of graphicforms attending the neutron star/planet double system. 'Somehow, this was important to the Amarantin. And I think it might have some bearing on the Event.'

Girardieau buried his head in his hands theatrically, then looked back at Sylveste. 'You're serious, aren't you?'

'Yes.' Carefully – never allowing his gaze to move from Girardieau's eyes – he folded away the paper and replaced it in his pocket. 'We have to explore it, and find out what killed the Amarantin. Before it kills us as well.'

When Sajaki and Volyova came to Khouri's quarters, they told her to put on something warm. Khouri noticed that they were both wearing heavier than usual shipwear – Volyova in a zipped-up flying jacket, Sajaki in muffled, high-collared thermals, quilted in a mosaic of nova-diamond patches.

'I've screwed up, haven't I?' Khouri said. 'This is where I get the airlock treatment. My scores in the combat simulations haven't been good enough. You're going to ditch me.'

'Don't be stupid,' Sajaki said, only his nose and forehead protruding above the furline of his collar. 'If we were going to kill you, do you think we'd worry about you catching a chill?'

'And,' Volyova said, 'your indoctrination finished weeks ago. You're now one of our assets. To kill you now would be a form of treason against ourselves.' Beneath the bill of her cap only her mouth and chin were visible; she exactly complemented Sajaki, the two of them forming one bland composite face.

'Nice to know you care.'

Still unsure of her position – the possibility that they might be planning something nasty was still looming large – she dug through what passed for her belongings until she found a thermal jacket. Manufactured by the ship, it was similar to Sajaki's harlequin job, except that it fell almost to her knees.

An elevator journey took them into an unexplored region of the ship – at least, well away from what Khouri considered known territory. They had to change elevators several times, walking through interconnecting tunnels which Volyova said were necessary because of virus damage taking out large sections of the transit system. The décor and technological level of the walk-through areas was always subtly different, suggesting to Khouri that whole districts of the ship had been left fallow at different stages over the last few centuries. She remained nervous, but something in Sajaki and Volyova's demeanour told her that what they had in mind was more akin to an initiation ceremony than a cold execution. They reminded her of children embarked on some piece of malicious tomfoolery – Volyova at least, though Sajaki looked and acted a good deal more authoritarian, like a functionary carrying out a grim civic duty.

'Since you're part of us now,' he said, 'it's time you learnt a little more about the set-up. You might also appreciate knowing our reason for going to Resurgam.'

'I assumed it was trade.'

'That was the cover story, but let's face it, it was never very convincing. Resurgam doesn't have much in the way of an economy – the purpose of the colony is pure research – and it certainly lacks the resources to buy much from us. Of course, our data on the colony is necessarily old, and once we're there we'll trade what we can, but that could never be the sole reason for our voyage there.'

'So what is?'

The lift they were in was decelerating. 'The name Sylveste mean anything to you?' Sajaki asked.

Khouri did her best to act normally, as if the question were reasonable, and not one which had gone off in her cranium like a magnesium flare.

'Well, of course. Everyone on Yellowstone knew about Sylveste. Guy was practically a god to them. Or maybe the devil.' She paused, hoping her reactions sounded normal. 'Wait though; which Sylveste are we talking about here? The older one, the guy who botched up those immortality experiments? Or his son?'

'Technically speaking,' Sajaki said, 'both.'

The lift thundered to a halt. When the doors opened it was like being slapped in the face with a cold wet cloth. Khouri was glad for the advice about the warm clothes, although she still felt mortally chilled. 'Thing was,' she continued, 'they weren't all bastards. Lorean was the old guy's father, and he was still some kind of a folk hero, even after he died, and the old guy – what was his name again?'

'Calvin.'

'Right. Even after Calvin killed all those people. Then Calvin's son came along – Dan, that would have been – and he tried to make amends, in his own way, with the Shrouder thing.' Khouri shrugged. 'I wasn't around then, of course. I only know what people told me.'

Sajaki led them through gloomy grey-green lit corridors, huge and perhaps mutant janitor-rats scrabbling away as their footfalls neared. What he took them into resembled the inside of a choleraic's trachea – corridors thick and glutinous with dirty carapacial ice; venous with buried tentacular ducts and power lines, slick with something nastily like human phlegm. Ship-slime, Volyova called it – an organic secretion caused by malfunctioning biological recycler systems on an adjacent level.

Mostly, though, it was the cold of which Khouri took heed.

'Sylveste's part in things is rather complex,' Sajaki said. 'It'll take a while to explain. First, though, I'd like you to meet the Captain.'

Sylveste walked around himself, checking that nothing was seriously out of place. Satisfied, he cancelled the image and joined Girardieau in the pre-fab's ante-room. The music reached a crescendo, then settled into a burbling refrain. The pattern of lights altered, voices dropping to a hush.

Together, they stepped into the glare, into the basso sound-field of the organ's drone. A meandering path led to the central temple, carpeted for the occasion. Chime-trees lined it, cased in protective domes of clear plastic. The chime-trees were spindly, articulated sculptures, their many arms tipped with curved, coloured mirrors. At odd times, the trees would click and reconfigure themselves, moved by what seemed to be million-year-old clockwork buried in pedestals. Current thinking had it that the trees were elements of some city-wide semaphore system.

The organ's noise magnified as they stepped into the temple. Its egg-shaped dome was permeated by petal-shaped expanses of elaborate stained-glass, miraculously intact despite the slow preda- tions of time and gravity. Filtered through the toplights, the air in the temple seemed suffused with a calming pink radiance. The central portion of the enormous room was taken up by the rising foundation of the spire which rose above the temple; wide and flared like the base of a sequoia. Temporary seating for a hundred top-level Cuvier dignitaries bowed out in a fan-shape from one side of the pillar; easily accommodated by the building, despite its one- quarter scale. Sylveste scanned the racks of watchers, recognising about a third of them. Perhaps a tenth had been his allies before the coup. Most of them wore heavy outer garments, plump with furs. He recognised Janequin amongst them, sagelike with his smoke-white goatee and long silvery hair waterfalling from his bald pate. He looked more simian than ever. Some of his birds were in the hall, released from a dozen bamboo boxes. Sylveste had to admit that they were now strikingly good facsimiles, even down to the bobbed crest and the speckle-shimmer of their turquoise plumage. They had been adapted from chickens by careful manipulation of homeobox genes. The audience, many of whom had not seen the birds before today, applauded. Janequin turned the colour of bloodied snow, and seemed anxious to sink into his brocade overcoat.

Girardieau and Sylveste reached a sturdy table at the focus of the audience. The table was ancient: its woodwork eagle and Latinate inscriptions dated back to the Amerikano settlers on Yellowstone. Its corners were chipped. A varnished mahogany box sat on the table, sealed by delicate gold clasps.

A woman of serious demeanour stood behind the table, dressed in an electric-white gown. The gown's clasp was a complex dual sigil, combining the Resurgam City/Inundationist governmental seal with the emblem of the Mixmasters: two hands holding a cat's cradle of DNA. She was, Sylveste knew, not a true Mixmaster. The Mixmasters were a cliquish guild of Stoner bioengineers and geneticists, and none of their sanctum had journeyed to Resurgam. Yet their symbol – which *had* travelled – denoted general expertise in life-sciences: genesculpting, surgery or medicine.

Her unsmiling face was sallow in the stained light, hair collected in a bun, pierced by two syringes.

The music quietened.

'I am Ordinator Massinger,' she said, voice ringing out across the chamber. 'I am empowered by the Resurgam expeditionary council to marry individuals of this settlement, unless such union conflicts with the genetic fitness of the colony.'

The Ordinator opened the mahogany box. Just below the lid lay a leather-bound object the size of a Bible. She removed it and placed it on the table, then folded it open with a creak of leather. The exposed surfaces were matt grey, like wet slate, glistening with microscopic machinery.

'Place one hand each on the page nearest you, gentlemen.'

They placed their palms on the surface. There was a fluorescent sweep as the book took their palm-prints, followed by a brief tingle as biopsies were taken. When they were done, Massinger took the book and pressed her own hand against the surface.

Massinger then asked Nils Girardieau to state his identity to the gathered. Sylveste watched faint smiles ghost the audience. There was something absurd about it, after all, though Girardieau made no show of this himself.

Then she asked the same of Sylveste.

'I am Daniel Calvin Lorean Soutaine-Sylveste,' he said, using the form of his name so rarely employed that it almost took an effort of memory to bring it to mind. He went on, 'The only biological son of Rosalyn Soutaine and Calvin Sylveste, both of Chasm City, Yellowstone. I was born on the seventeenth of January, in the hundred and twenty-first standard year after the resettlement of Yellowstone. My calendrical age is two hundred and twenty-three. Allowing for medichine programs, I have a physiological age of sixty, on the Sharavi scale.'

'How do you knowingly manifest?'

'I knowingly manifest in one incarnation only, the biological form now speaking.'

'And you affirm that you are not wittingly manifested via alpha-level or other Turing-capable simulacra, in this or any other solar system?'

'None of which I am aware.'

Massinger made small annotations in the book using a pressure stylus. She had asked Girardieau precisely the same questions: standard parts of the Stoner ceremony. Ever since the Eighty, Stoners had been intensely suspicious of simulations in general, particularly those that purported to contain the essence or soul of an individual. One thing they especially disliked was the idea of one manifestation of an individual – biological or otherwise – making contracts to which the other manifestations were not bound, such as marriage.

'These details are in order,' Massinger said. 'The bride may step forward.'

Pascale moved into the roseate light. She was accompanied by two women wearing ash-coloured wimples, a squad of float-cams and personal security wasps and a semi-transparent entourage of entoptics: nymphs, seraphim, flying-fish and hummingbirds, star-glitter dew-drops and butterflies, in slow cascade around her wedding dress. The most exclusive entoptic designers in Cuvier had created them.

Girardieau raised his thick, hauserlike arms and bid his daughter forward.

'You look beautiful,' he murmured.

What Sylveste saw was beauty reduced to digital perfection. He knew that Girardieau saw something incomparably softer and more human, like the difference between a swan and a hard glass sculpture of a swan.

'Place your hand on the book,' the Ordinator said.

An imprint of moisture from Sylveste's hand was still visible, like a wider shoreline around Pascale's island of pale flesh. The Ordinator asked her to verify her identity, in the same manner as she had asked Girardieau and Sylveste. Pascale's task was simple enough: not only had she been born on Resurgam, but she had never left the planet. Ordinator Massinger delved deeper into the mahogany box. While she did so, Sylveste's eyes worked the audience. He saw Janequin, looking paler than ever, fidgety. Deep within the box, polished to a bluish antiseptic lustre, lay a device like a cross between an old-style pistol and a veterinarian's hypodermic.

'Behold the wedding gun,' the Ordinator said, holding the box aloft.

*

Bone-splinteringly cold as it was, Khouri soon stopped noticing the temperature except as an abstract quality of the air. The story that her two crewmates was relating was far too strange for that.

They were standing near the Captain. His name, she now knew, was John Armstrong Brannigan. He was old, inconceivably so. Depending on the system one adopted in measuring his age, he was anywhere between two hundred and half a thousand years old. The details of his birth were unclear now, hopelessly tangled in the countertruths of political history. Mars, some said, was the place where he had been born, yet it was equally possible that he had been born on Earth, Earth's city-jammed moon or in any one of the several hundred habitats which drifted through cislunar space in those days.

'He was already over a century old before he ever left Sol system,' Sajaki said. 'He waited until it was possible to do so, then was among the first thousand to leave, when the Conjoiners launched the first ship from Phobos.'

'At least, someone called John Brannigan was on that ship,' Volyova said.

'No,' Sajaki said. 'There's no doubt. I know it was him. Afterwards . . . it becomes less easy to place him, of course. He may have deliberately blurred his own past, to avoid being tracked down by all the enemies he must have made in that time. There are many sightings, in many different systems, decades apart . . . but nothing definite.'

'How did he come to be your Captain?'

'He turned up centuries later – after several landfalls elsewhere, and dozens of unconfirmed apparitions – on the fringe of the Yellowstone system. He was ageing slowly, due to the relativistic effects of starflight, but he was still getting older, and longevity techniques were not as well developed as in our time.' Sajaki paused. 'Much of his body was now prosthetic. They said that John Brannigan no longer needed a spacesuit when he left his ship; that he breathed vacuum, basked in intolerable heat and quenching cold, and that his sensory range encompassed every spectrum imaginable. They said that little remained of the brain with which he had been born; that his head was merely a dense loom of intermeshed cybernetics, a stew of tiny thinking machines and precious little organic material.'

'And how much of that was true?'

'Perhaps more of it than people wished to believe. There were certainly lies: that he had visited the Jugglers on Spindrift years before they were generally discovered; that the aliens had wrought wondrous transformations on what remained of his mind, or that he had met and communicated with at least two sentient species so far unknown to the rest of humanity.'

'He did meet the Jugglers eventually,' Volyova said, in Khouri's direction. 'Triumvir Sajaki was with him at the time.'

'That was much later,' Sajaki snapped. 'All that's germane here is his relationship with Calvin.'

'How did they cross paths?'

'No one really knows,' Volyova said. 'All that we know for sure is that he became injured, either through an accident or some military operation that went wrong. His life wasn't in danger, but he needed urgent help, and to go to one of the official groups in the Yellowstone system would have been suicide. He'd made too many enemies to be able to place his life in the hands of any organisation. What he needed were loosely scattered individuals in whom he could place personal trust. Evidently Calvin was one of them.'

'Calvin was in touch with Ultra elements?'

'Yes, though he would never have admitted so in public.' Volyova smiled, a wide toothy crescent opening beneath the bill of her cap. 'Calvin was young and idealistic then. When this injured man was delivered to him, he saw it as a godsend. Until then he had had no means of exploring his more outlandish ideas. Now he had the perfect subject, the only requirement being total secrecy. Of course, they both gained from it: Calvin was able to try out his radical cybernetic theories on Brannigan, while Brannigan was made well and became something more than he had been before Calvin's work. You might describe it as the perfect symbiotic relationship.'

'You're saying the Captain was a guinea pig for that bastard's monstrosities?'

Sajaki shrugged, the movement puppetlike within his swaddling clothes.

'That was not how Brannigan saw it. As far as the rest of humanity was concerned, he was already a monster before the accident. What Calvin did was merely take the trend further. Consummate it, if you like.'

Volyova nodded, although there was something in her expression which suggested she was not quite at ease with her crewmate. 'And in any case, this was prior to the Eighty. Calvin's name was unsullied. And among the more overt extremes of Ultra life, Brannigan's transformation was only slightly in excess of the norm.' She said it with tart distaste.

'Carry on.'

'Nearly a century passed before his next encounter with the Sylveste clan,' Sajaki said. 'By which time he was commanding this ship.'

'What happened?'

'He was injured again. Seriously, this time.' Gingerly, like someone testing himself against a candle flame, he whisked his fingers across the limiting extent of the Captain's silvery growth. The Captain's outskirts looked frothy, like the brine left on a rockpool by the retreating tide. Sajaki delicately swabbed his fingers against the front of his jacket, but Khouri could tell that they did not feel clean; that they itched and crawled with subepidermal malignance.

'Unfortunately,' Volyova said, 'Calvin was dead.'

Of course. He had died during the Eighty; had in fact been one of the last to lose his corporeality.

'All right,' Khouri said. 'But he died in the process of having his brain scanned into a computer. Couldn't you just steal the recording and persuade it to help you?'

'We would, had that been possible.' Sajaki's low voice reverberated from the throated curve of the corridor. 'His recording, his alpha-level simulation, had vanished. And there were no duplicates – the alphas were copy-protected.'

'So basically,' Khouri said, hoping to shatter the morguelike atmosphere of the proceedings, 'you were up shit creek without a Captain.'

'Not quite,' Volyova said. 'You see, all this took place during a rather interesting period in Yellowstone's history. Daniel Sylveste had just returned from the Shrouders, and was neither insane nor dead. His companion hadn't been so lucky, but her death only gave additional poignancy to his heroic return.' She halted, then asked, with birdlike eagerness: 'Did you ever hear of his "thirty days in the wilderness", Khouri?'

'Maybe once. Remind me.'

'He vanished for a month a century ago,' Sajaki said. 'One minute the toast of Stoner society, the next nowhere to be found. There were rumours that he'd gone out of the city dome; jammed on an exosuit and gone to atone for the sins of his father. Shame it isn't true; would have been quite touching. Actually,' Sajaki nodded at the floor, 'he came here for a month. We took him.'

'You kidnapped Dan Sylveste?' Khouri almost laughed at the audaciousness of it all. Then she remembered they were talking about the man she was meant to kill. Her impulse to laugh evaporated quickly.

'Invited aboard is probably a preferable term,' Sajaki said. 'Though I admit he didn't have a great deal of choice in the matter.'

'Let me get this straight,' Khouri said. 'You kidnapped Cal's son? What good was that going to do you?'

'Calvin took a few precautions before he subjected himself to the scanner,' Sajaki said. 'The first was simple enough, although it had to be initiated decades before the culmination of the project. Simply put, he arranged to have every subsequent second of his life monitored by recording systems. Every second: waking, sleeping, whatever. Over the years, machines learnt to emulate his behaviour patterns. Given any situation, they could predict his responses with astonishing accuracy.'

'Beta-level simulation.'

'Yes, but a beta-level sim orders of magnitude more complex than any previously created.'

'By some definitions,' Volyova said, 'it was already conscious; Calvin had already transmigrated. Calvin may or may not have believed that, but he still kept on refining the sim. It could project an image of Calvin which was so real, so like the actual man, that you had the forceful sense that you were really in his presence. But Calvin took it a step further. There was another mode of insurance available to him.'

'Which was?'

'Cloning.' Sajaki smiled, nodded almost imperceptibly in Volyova's direction.

'He cloned himself,' she said. 'Using illegal black genetics techniques, calling in favours from some of his shadier clients. Some of them were Ultra, you see – otherwise we wouldn't know any of this. Cloning was embargoed technology on Yellowstone;

young colonies almost always outlaw it in the interests of ensuring maximum genetic diversity. But Calvin was cleverer than the authorities, and wealthier than those he was forced to bribe. That way he was able to pass off the clone as his son.'

'Dan,' Khouri said, the monosyllabic word carving its own angular shape in the refrigerated air. 'You're telling me Dan is Calvin's clone?'

'Not that Dan knows any of this,' Volyova said. 'He'd be the last person Calvin wanted to know. No; Sylveste is as much party to the lie as any of the populace ever were. He thinks he's his own man.'

'He doesn't realise he's a clone?'

'No, and as time goes by his chances of ever finding out get smaller and smaller. Beyond Calvin's Ultra allies, almost no one knew, and Calvin set up incentives to keep those that did quiet. There were a few unavoidable weak links – Calvin had no choice but to recruit one of Yellowstone's top geneticists – and Sylveste picked the same man for the Resurgam expedition, not realising the intimate connection they shared. But I doubt that he's learnt the truth since, or even come close to guessing it.'

'But every time he looks in a mirror . . .'

'He sees himself, not Calvin.' Volyova smiled, evidently enjoying the way their revelation was upsetting some of Khouri's basic certainties. 'He was a clone, but that didn't mean he had to resemble Cal down to the last skin pore. The geneticist – Janequin – knew how to induce cosmetic differences between Cal and Dan's makeup, enough so that people would see only the expected familial traits. Obviously, he also incorporated traits from the woman who was supposed to be Dan's mother, Rosalyn Soutaine.'

'The rest was simple,' Sajaki said. 'Cal raised his clone in an environment carefully structured to emulate the surroundings he had known as a boy – even down to the same stimuli at certain periods in the boy's development, because Cal couldn't be sure which of his own personality traits were due to nature or nurture.'

'All right,' Khouri said. 'Accepting for the moment that all of this is true – what was the point? Cal must have known Dan wouldn't follow the same developmental path, no matter how closely he manipulated the boy's life. What about all those decisions that take place in the womb?' Khouri shook her head. 'It's insane. At the very best, all he'd end up with would be a crude approximation to himself.'

'I think,' Sajaki said, 'that that was all that Cal hoped for. Cal cloned himself as a precaution. He knew the scanning process that he and the other members of the Eighty would have to endure would destroy his material body, so he wanted a body to which he could return if life in the machine turned out not to be to his liking.'

'And did it?'

'Maybe, but that was beside the point. At the time of the Eighty, the retransfer operation was still beyond the technology of the day. There was no real hurry: Cal could always have the clone put in reefersleep until he needed it, or simply reclone another one from the boy's cells. He was thinking well ahead.'

'Assuming the retransfer ever became possible.'

'Well, Calvin knew it was a long shot. The important thing was that there was a second fall-back option apart from retransfer.'

'Which was?'

'The beta-level simulation.' Sajaki's voice had become as slow, cold and icy as the breezes in the Captain's chamber. 'Although not formally capable of consciousness, it was still an incredibly detailed facsimile of Calvin. Its relative simplicity meant it would be easier to encode its rules into the wetware of Dan's mind. Much easier than imprinting something as volatile as the alpha.'

'I know the primary recording – the alpha – disappeared,' she said. 'There was no Calvin left to run the show. And I guess Dan began to act a little more independently than Calvin might have wished.'

'To put it mildly,' Sajaki said, nodding. 'The Eighty marked the beginning of the decline of the Sylveste Institute. Dan soon escaped its shackles, more interested in the Shrouder enigma than cybernetic immortality. He kept possession of the beta-level sim, though he never realised its exact significance. He thought of it more as an heirloom than anything else.' The Triumvir smiled. 'I think he would have destroyed it had he realised what it represented, which was his own annihilation.'

Understandable, Khouri thought. The beta-level simulation was like a trapped demon waiting to inhabit a new host body. Not properly conscious, but still dangerously potent, by virtue of the subtle ingenuity with which it mimicked true intelligence.

'Cal's precautionary measure was still useful to us,' Sajaki said. 'There was enough of Cal's expertise encoded in the beta to mend the Captain. All we had to do was persuade Dan to let Calvin temporarily inhabit his mind and body.'

'Dan must have suspected something when it worked so easily.'

'It was never easy,' Sajaki admonished. 'Far from it. The periods when Cal took over were more akin to some kind of violent possession. Motor control was a problem: in order to suppress Dan's own personality, we had to give him a cocktail of neuro-inhibitors. Which meant that when Cal finally got through, the body he found himself in was already half-paralysed by our drugs. It was like a brilliant surgeon performing an operation by giving orders to a drunk. And – by all accounts – it wasn't the most pleasant of experiences for Dan. Quite painful, he said.'

'But it worked.'

'Just. But that was a century ago, and now it's time for another visit to the doctor.'

'Your vials,' said the Ordinator.

One of the wimpled aides from Pascale's party stepped forward, brandishing a vial identical in size and shape to the one which Sylveste removed from his pocket. They were not the same colour: the fluid in Pascale's vial had been tinted red, against the yellow hue of Sylveste's. Similar darkish fronds of material orbited within. The Ordinator took both vials and held them aloft for a few moments before placing them side by side on the table, in clear view of the audience.

'We are ready to begin the marriage,' she said. She then performed the customary duty of asking if there were anyone present who had any bioethical reasons as to why the marriage should not take place.

There was, of course, no objection.

But in that odd, loaded moment of branching possibilities, Sylveste noted a veiled woman in the audience reach into a purse and uncap a dainty, jewel-topped amber perfume jar.

'Daniel Sylveste,' said the Ordinator. 'Do you take this woman to be your wife, under Resurgam law, until such time as this marriage is annulled under this or any prevailing legal system?'

'I do,' Sylveste said.

She repeated the question to Pascale.

'I do,' Pascale said.

'Then let the bonding be done.'

Ordinator Massinger took the wedding gun from the mahogany box and snapped it open. She loaded the reddish vial – the one Pascale's party had delivered – into the breech, then reclosed the instrument. Status entoptics briefly haloed it. Girardieau placed his hand on Sylveste's upper arm, steadying him as the Ordinator pressed the conic end of the instrument against his temple, just above his eye-level. Sylveste had been right when he told Girardieau that the ceremony was not painful, but neither was it entirely pleasant. What it was was a sudden flowering of intense cold, as if liquid helium were being blasted into his cortex. The discomfort was brief, however, and the thumb-sized bruise on his skin would not last more than a few days. The brain's immune system was weak by comparison with the body as a whole, and Pascale's cells – floating as they did in a stew of helper medichines – would soon bond with Sylveste's own. The volume was tiny – no more than a tenth of one per cent of the brain's mass – but the transplanted cells carried the indelible impression of their last host: ghost threads of holographically distributed memory and personality.

The Ordinator removed the spent red vial and slotted the yellow one in its place. It was Pascale's first wedding under the Stoner custom, and her trepidation was not well disguised. Girardieau held her hands as the Ordinator delivered the neural material, Pascale visibly flinching as it happened.

Sylveste had let Girardieau think the implant was permanent, but this was never the case. The neural tissue was tagged with harmless radioisotope trace elements, enabling it to be routed out and destroyed, if necessary, by divorce viruses. So far, Sylveste had never taken that option, and imagined he never would, no matter how many marriages down the line he was. He carried the smoky essences of all his wives – as they carried him – as he would carry Pascale. Indeed, on the faintest level, Pascale herself now carried traces of his previous wives.

That was the Stoner way.

The Ordinator carefully replaced the wedding gun in its box. 'According to Resurgam law,' she began, 'the marriage is now formalised. You may—'

Which was when the perfume hit Janequin's birds.

The woman who had uncapped the amber jar was gone, her seat glaringly vacant. Fragrant, autumnal, the odour from the jar made Sylveste think of crushed leaves. He wanted to sneeze.

Something was wrong.

The room flashed turquoise blue, as if a hundred pastel fans had just opened. Peacocks' tails, springing open. A million tinted eyes.

The air turned grey.

'Get down!' Girardieau screamed. He was scrabbling madly at his neck. There was something hooked in it, something tiny and barbed. Numbly, Sylveste looked at his tunic and saw half a dozen comma-shaped barbs clinging to it. They had not broken the fabric, but he dared not touch them.

'Assassination tools!' Girardieau shouted. He slumped under the table, dragging Sylveste and his daughter with him. The auditorium was chaos now, a frenzied mass of agitated people trying to escape.

'Janequin's birds were primed!' Girardieau said, virtually screaming in Sylveste's ear. 'Poison darts – in their tails.'

'You're hit,' Pascale said, too stunned for her voice to carry much emotion. Light and smoke burst over their heads. They heard screams. Out of the corner of his eye, Sylveste saw the perfume woman holding a sleekly evil pistol in a two-handed grip. She was dousing the audience with it, its fanged barrel spitting cold pulses of boser energy. The float-cams swept round her, dispassionately recording the carnage. Sylveste had never seen a weapon like the one the woman used. He knew it could not have been manufactured on Resurgam, which left only two possibilities. Either it had arrived from Yellowstone with the original settlement, or it had been sold by Remilliod, the trader who had passed through the system since the coup. Glass – Amarantin glass that had survived ten thousand centuries – broke shrilly above. Like pieces of shattered toffee, it crashed down in jagged shards into the audience. Sylveste watched, powerless, as the ruby planes buried themselves in flesh, like frozen lightning. The terrified were already screaming loud enough to drown out the cries of those in pain.

What remained of Girardieau's security team was mobilising, but terribly slowly. Four of the militia were down, their faces punctured by the barbs. One had reached the seating, struggling with the woman who had the gun. Another was opening fire with his own sidearm, scything through Janequin's birds.

Girardieau meanwhile was groaning. His eyes were rolling, bloodshot, hands grasping at thin air.

'We have to get out of here,' Sylveste said, shouting in Pascale's ear. She seemed still dazed from the neural transfer, blearily oblivious to what was happening.

'But my father . . .'

'He's gone.'

Sylveste eased Girardieau's dead weight onto the cold floor of the temple, careful to keep behind the safety of the table.

'The barbs were meant to kill, Pascale. There's nothing we can do for him. If we stay, we'll just end up following him.'

Girardieau croaked something. It might have been 'Go', or it might only have been a final senseless exhalation.

'We can't leave him!' Pascale said.

'If we don't, his killers end up winning.'

Tears slashed her face. 'Where can we go?'

He looked around frantically. Smoke from concussion shells was filling the chamber, probably from Girardieau's own people. It was settling in lazy pastel spirals, like scarves tossed from a dancer. Just when it was almost too dark to see, the room plunged into total blackness. The lights beyond the temple had obviously been turned off, or destroyed.

Pascale gasped.

His eyes slipped into infrared mode, almost without him having to think about it.

'I can still see,' he whispered to her. 'As long as we stay together, you don't have to worry about the darkness.'

Praying that the danger from the birds was gone, Sylveste rose slowly to his feet. The temple glowed in grey-green heat. The perfume woman was dead, a fist-sized hot hole in her side. Her amber jar was smashed at her feet. He guessed it had been some kind of hormonal trigger, keyed to receptors Janequin had put in the birds. He had to have been part of it. He looked – but Janequin was dead. A tiny dagger sat in his chest, trailing hot rivulets down his brocade jacket.

Sylveste grabbed Pascale and shoved her along the ground towards the exit, a vaulted archway gilded with Amarantin figurines and bas-relief graphicforms. It seemed that the perfume woman had been the only assassin actually present, if one discounted Janequin. But now her friends were entering, garbed in chameleoflage. They wore close-fitting breather masks and infrared goggles.

He pushed Pascale behind a jumble of upturned tables.

'They're looking for us,' he hissed. 'But they probably think we're already dead.'

Girardieau's surviving security people had fallen back and taken up defensive positions, kneeling within the fan-shaped auditorium. It was no match: the newcomers carried much heavier weapons, heavy boser-rifles. Girardieau's militia countered with low-yield lasers and projectile weapons, but the enemy were cutting them apart with blithe, impersonal ease. At least half the audience were unconscious or dead; they had caught the brunt of the peacock venom salvo. Hardly the most surgically precise of assassination tools, those birds – but they had been allowed into the auditorium completely unchecked. Sylveste observed that two were still alive, despite what he had at first imagined. Still triggered by trace molecules of the perfume which remained aloft, their tails were flicking open and shut like the fans of nervous courtesans.

'Did your father carry a weapon?' Sylveste said, instantly regretting his use of the past tense. 'I mean, since the coup.'

'I don't think so,' Pascale said.

Of course not; Girardieau would never have confided such a thing to her. Quickly Sylveste felt around the man's still body, hoping to find the padded hardness of a weapon beneath his ceremonial clothes.

Nothing.

'We'll have to do without,' Sylveste said, as if the stating of this fact would somehow alleviate the problem it encapsulated. 'They're going to kill us if we don't run,' he said, finally.

'Into the labyrinth?'

'They'll see us,' Sylveste said.

'But maybe they won't think it's us,' Pascale said. 'They might not know you can see in the dark.' Though she was effectively blind, she managed to look him square in the face. Her mouth was open, an almost circular vacancy of expression or hope. 'Let me say goodbye to my father first.'

She found his body in the darkness, kissed him for the last time. Sylveste looked to the exit. At that moment the soldier guarding it was hit by a shot from what remained of Girardieau's militia. The masked figure crumpled, his body heat pooling liquidly into the floor around his body, spreading smoky white maggots of thermal energy into the stonework.

The way was clear, for the moment. Pascale found his hand and together they began to run.

EIGHT

'I take it you've heard the news concerning the Captain,' Khouri said, when the Mademoiselle coughed discreetly from behind her. Other than the Mademoiselle's illusory presence, she was alone in her quarters, digesting what Volyova and Sajaki had told her of the mission.

The Mademoiselle's smile was patient. 'Rather complicates matters, doesn't it? I'll admit I considered the possibility that the crew might have some connection with him. It seemed logical, given their intention of travelling to Resurgam. But I never extrapolated anything this convoluted.'

'I suppose that's one word for it.'

'Their relationship is . . .' The ghost seemed to take a moment to choose her words, though Khouri knew it was all annoying fakery. 'Interesting. It may limit our options in the future.'

'Are you still sure you want him killed?'

'Absolutely. This news merely heightens the urgency. Now there is the danger that Sajaki will try to bring Sylveste aboard.'

'Won't it be easier for me to kill him then?'

'Certainly, but at that point killing him would not suffice. You would then have to find a way of destroying the ship itself. Whether or not you found a way to save yourself in the process would be your problem.'

Khouri frowned. Perhaps it was her, but very little of this made very much sense.

'But if I guarantee that Sylveste's dead . . .'

'That would not suffice,' said the Mademoiselle, with what Khouri sensed was a new candour. 'Killing him is part of what you must do, but not the entirety. You must be specific in the manner of killing.'

Khouri waited to hear what the woman had to say.

'You must allow him absolutely no warning; not even seconds. Furthermore, you must kill him in isolation.'

'That was always part of the plan.'

'Good – but I mean precisely what I say. If it isn't possible to ensure solitude at any given moment, you must delay his death until it is. No compromises, Khouri.'

This was the first time they had discussed the manner of his death in any detail. Evidently the Mademoiselle had decided that Khouri was now fit to know slightly more than before, if not the whole picture.

'What about the weapon?'

'You may use any which suits you, provided the weapon incorporates no cybernetic components above a certain level of complexity, which I will stipulate at a later date.' Before Khouri could object she added, 'A beam weapon would be acceptable, provided the weapon itself was not brought into proximity with the subject at any stage. Projectile and explosive devices would also serve our purpose.'

Given the nature of the lighthugger, Khouri thought, there ought to be enough suitable weapons lying around for her use. When the time came, she should be able to appropriate something moderately lethal and allow herself time to learn its nuances before deploying it against Sylveste.

'I can probably find something.'

'I'm not finished. You must not approach him, nor must you kill him when he is in the proximity of cybernetic systems – again, I will stipulate my requirements nearer the time. The more isolated he is, the better. If you can manage to do it when he is alone and far from help, on Resurgam's surface, you will have accomplished your task to my complete satisfaction.' She paused. Evidently all this was hugely important to the Mademoiselle, and Khouri was doing her best to remember it, but so far it sounded no more logical than the incantations of a Dark Age prescription against fever. 'But on no account must he be allowed to leave Resurgam. Understand that, because when a lighthugger arrives around Resurgam – even this lighthugger – Sylveste will try and find a way to get himself aboard. That must not be allowed to happen, under any circumstances.'

'I get the message,' Khouri said. 'Kill him down below. Is that everything?'

'Not quite.' The ghost made a smile; a ghoulish one Khouri had never seen before. Maybe, she thought, the Mademoiselle had yet to exhaust her reservoir of expressions, keeping a few in store for moments such as this. 'Of course I want proof of his death. This implant will record the event, but on your return to Yellowstone I also want physical evidence to corroborate what the implant records. I want remains, and more than just ashes. Preserve what you can in vacuum. Keep the remains sealed and isolated from the ship. Bury them in rock if that suits you, but just bring them back to me. I must have proof.'

'And then?'

'Then, Ana Khouri, I will give you your husband.'

Sylveste did not stop to catch his breath until he and Pascale had reached and passed the ebony shell encasing the Amarantin city, taking several hundred footsteps into the tangled maze which wormholed through it. He chose his directions as randomly as was humanly possible, ignoring the signs added by the archaeologists, desperately trying to avoid following a predictable path.

'Not so quickly,' Pascale said. 'I'm worried about getting lost.'

Sylveste put a hand to her mouth, even though he knew that her need to talk was only a way to obliterate the fact of her father's assassination.

'We have to be quiet. There must be True Path units in the shell, waiting to mop up escapees. We don't want to draw them down on us.'

'But we're lost,' she said, her voice now hushed. 'Dan, people died in this place because they couldn't find their way out before they starved.'

Sylveste pushed Pascale down a constricting bolthole into steadily thickening darkness. The walls were slippery here; no friction flooring had been installed. 'The one thing that isn't going to happen,' he said, more calmly than he felt, 'is that we get lost.' He tapped his eyes, though it was already much too gloomy for Pascale to notice the gesture. Like a seeing person among the blind, he had trouble remembering that much of his nonverbal communication was wasted. 'I can replay every step we take. And the walls reflect infrared from our bodies reasonably well. We're safer here than back in the city.'

She panted along behind him, saying nothing for long minutes.

Finally she mumbled, 'I hope this isn't one of the rare occasions when you're wrong. That would be a particularly inauspicious start to our marriage, don't you think?'

He did not much feel like laughing; the hall's carnage was still garishly fresh in his mind. He laughed all the same, and the gesture seemed to lessen the reality of it all. Which was all for the better, because when he thought about it rationally, Pascale's doubts were perfectly justified. Even if he knew the precise way out of the maze, that knowledge might be unusable, if the tunnels were too slippery to climb, or if, as rumour had it, the labyrinth occasionally changed its own configuration. Then, magic eyes or no, they would starve along with all the other poor fools who had wandered away from the marked path.

They worked deeper into the Amarantin structure, feeling the lazy curve of the tunnel as it wound its way maggottishly through the inner shell. Panic was as much an enemy as disorientation, of course. But forcing oneself to stay calm was never easy.

'How long do you think we should stay here?'

'A day,' Sylveste said. 'Then we leave after them. By then, reinforcements will have arrived from Cuvier.'

'Working for whom?'

Sylveste shouldered into a wasp-waist in the tunnel. Beyond, it bottled out into a triple-junction; he made a mental coin-flip and took the left way. 'Good question,' he said, too softly for his wife to hear him.

But what if the incident had merely been part of a colony-wide coup, rather than an isolated act of publicly visible terrorism? What if Cuvier was now out of Girardieau government control, fallen to True Path? Girardieau's death left behind a lumbering party machine, but many of its cogs had been removed in the wedding hall. In this moment of weakness, blitzkrieg revolutionaries might accomplish much. Perhaps it was already over, Sylveste's former enemies dethroned, strange new faces assuming power. In which case, waiting in the labyrinth might be completely futile. Would True Path regard him as an enemy, or as something infinitely more ambiguous; an enemy's enemy?

Not that Girardieau and he had even been enemies, at the end.

Finally, they came to a wide, flat-bottomed throat where a number of tunnels converged. There was room to sit down, and the air was fresh and breezy; pumped air currents reached this far.

In infrared, Sylveste watched Pascale slump cautiously down, hands scrabbling the frictionless floor for rats, sharp stones or grinning skulls.

'It's all right,' he said. 'We're safe here.' As if by the very act of saying as much, he made it more likely. 'If anyone comes, we can pick our escape routes. We'll lie low and see what happens.'

Of course, now that the immediate flight was over, she would begin thinking about her father again. He did not want that; not now.

'Stupid dumb Janequin,' he said, hoping to steer her thoughts at least tangentially away from what had happened. 'They must have blackmailed him. Isn't that the way it always happens?'

'What?' Pascale asked labouredly. 'Isn't that the way what always happens?'

'The pure becomes corrupted.' His voice was so low it threatened to crack into a whisper. The gas used in the auditorium attack had not properly reached his lungs, but he could still feel its effect on his larynx. 'Janequin was working on those birds for years; all the time I knew him in Mantell. They started as innocent living sculptures. He said any colony orbiting a star named Pavonis ought to have a few peacocks around the place. Then someone thought of a better use for them.'

'Perhaps they were all poisonous,' Pascale said, stretching the final word into a long slither of sibilant esses. 'Primed like little walking bombs.'

'Somehow I doubt he tampered with more than a few of them.' Maybe it was the air, but Sylveste felt suddenly weary, needful of immediate sleep. He knew they were safe for now. If the killers had been following them – and the killers might not even realise they were not among the dead – they would have reached this part of the shell already.

'I never believed he had real enemies,' Pascale said, her sentence seeming to writhe unattached in the confined space. He imagined her fear: without vision, with only his assurances, this dark place must be exquisitely frightening. 'I never thought anyone would kill him for what they wanted. I didn't think anything was worth that much.'

Along with the rest of the crew, Khouri would eventually enter reefersleep for the bulk of the time that the ship took to reach

Resurgam. But before then she spent much of her waking time in the gunnery, being subjected to endless simulations.

After a while it began to invade her dreams, to the point where boredom was no longer an adequate term to encompass the repetitiousness of the exercises Volyova had conceived for her. Yet losing herself in the gunnery environment was something she began to welcome, since it offered temporary respite from her worries. In the gunnery, the whole Sylveste problem became a small anxious itch, nothing more. She remained aware that she was in an impossible situation, but that fact no longer seemed critical. The gunnery was all, and that was why she no longer feared it. She was still herself after the sessions, and she began to think that the gunnery hardly mattered at all; that it would not ultimately make any difference to the outcome of her mission.

All that changed when the dogs came home.

They were the Mademoiselle's bloodhounds: cybernetic agents she had unleashed into the gunnery during one of Khouri's sessions. The dogs had clawed their way into the system itself via the neural interface, exploiting the system's one forgivable weakness. Volyova had hardened it against software attack, but had obviously never imagined that the attack might come from the brain of the person hooked into the gunnery. The dogs barked back safe assurances that they had entered the gunnery's core. They had not returned to Khouri during the session in which they were unleashed, since it would take more than a few hours for them to sniff every nook and cranny of the gunnery's Byzantine architecture. So they had stayed in the system for more than a day, until Volyova once again hooked Khouri in.

Then the dogs returned to the Mademoiselle, and she decrypted them and unravelled the prey they had located.

'She has a stowaway,' the Mademoiselle said when she and Khouri were alone after a session. 'Something has hidden itself in the gunnery system, and I'm prepared to bet she knows nothing about it at all.'

Which was when Khouri stopped regarding the gunnery chamber with such total equanimity. 'Go on,' she said, feeling her body temperature plummet.

'A data entity; that's as well as I can describe it.'

'Something the dogs encountered?'

'Yes, but . . .' Once again the Mademoiselle sounded lost for words. Occasionally Khouri suspected it was genuine: the implant was having to deal with a situation light-years away from anything in the real Mademoiselle's expectations. 'It's not that they saw it, or even saw a part of it. It's too subtle for that, or else Volyova's own counter-intrusion systems would have caught it. It's more that they sensed the absences where it had just been; sensed the breeze it stirred when it moved around.'

'Do me a favour,' Khouri said. 'Try not to make it sound so damned scary, will you?'

'I'm sorry,' the Mademoiselle answered. 'But I can't deny that the thing's presence is disturbing.'

'Disturbing to you? How do you think I feel?' Khouri shook her head, stunned at the casual viciousness of reality. 'All right; what do you think it is? Some kind of virus, like all the others which are eating away this ship?'

'The thing seems much too advanced for that. Volyova's own defences have kept the ship operational despite the other viral entities, and she's even kept the Melding Plague at bay. But this . . .' The Mademoiselle looked at Khouri with a convincing facsimile of fear. 'The dogs were frightened by it, Khouri. In the way it evaded them, it revealed itself to be much cleverer than almost anything in my experience. But it didn't attack them, and that troubles me even more.'

'Yes?'

'Because it suggests that the thing is biding its time.'

Sylveste never found out how long they had slept. It might only have been minutes, packed with fevered, adrenalin-charged dreams of chaos and flight, or it might have been hours, or even a whole portion of the day. No way of knowing. Whatever the case, it had not been natural fatigue that sent them under. Roused by something, Sylveste realised with a stunned jolt that they had been breathing sleeping gas, pumped into the tunnel system. No wonder the air had seemed so fragrant and breezy.

There was a sound like rats in the attic.

He pawed Pascale awake; she came to consciousness with a plaintive moan, assimilating her surroundings and predicament in a few troubled seconds of reality-denial. He studied the heat-signature of her face, watching waxy neutrality cave in to an expressive mélange of remorse and fear.

'We have to move,' Sylveste said. 'They're after us – they gassed the tunnels.'

The scrabbling sound grew closer by the second. Pascale was still somewhere between wakefulness and dream, but she managed to open her mouth – it sounded as if she were speaking through cotton wool – and ask him, 'Which way?'

'This way,' Sylveste said, grabbing her and propelling her forwards, down the nearest valvelike opening. She stumbled on the slipperiness. Sylveste helped her up, squeezed beyond her and took her hand. Gloom lay ahead, his eyes revealing only a few metres of the tunnel beyond their position. He was, he realised, only slightly less blind than his wife.

Better than nothing.

'Wait,' Pascale said. 'There's light behind us, Dan!'

And voices. He could hear their wordless, urgent babble now. The rattle of sterile metal. Chemosensor arrays were probably already tracking them; pheromonal sniffers were reading the airborne human effluent of panic, graphing data directly into the sensoria of the chasers.

'Faster,' Pascale said. He snatched a glance back, his eyes momentarily overloaded by the new light. It was a bluish radiance limning the shaft's far reach, quivering, as if someone were holding a torch. He tried to increase speed, but the tunnel was steepening, making it harder to find traction on the glassily smooth sides: too much like trying to scramble up an ice chimney.

Panting sounds, metal scraping against the walls, barked commands.

Too steep now. It was now a constant battle just to hold balance, just to keep from slipping backwards. 'Get behind me,' he said, turning to face the blue light.

Pascale rushed past him.

'What now?'

The light wavered, crept in intensity. 'We have no choice,' Sylveste said. 'We can't outrun them, Pascale. Have to turn and face them.'

'That's suicide.'

'Maybe they won't kill us if they see our faces.'

He thought to himself that four thousand years of human civilisation put the lie to that hope, but, given that it was the only one he had, it hardly mattered that it was forlorn. His wife locked her arms round his chest and pressed her head against his, looking the same way. Her breathing was pulsed and terrified. Sylveste had no doubt that his own sounded much the same.

The enemy could probably smell their fear, quite literally.

'Pascale,' Sylveste said. 'I need to tell you something.'

'Now?'

'Yes, now.' He could no longer separate his own rapid breathing from hers, each exhalation a quick hard beat against the skin. 'In case I don't get a chance to tell anyone else. Something I've kept a secret for too long.'

'You mean in case we die?'

He avoided answering her question directly, one half of his mind trying to guess how many seconds or tens of seconds they had left. Perhaps not enough for what had to be said. 'I lied,' he said. 'About what happened around Lascaille's Shroud.'

She started to say something.

'No, wait,' Sylveste said. 'Hear me out. I have to say this. Have to get it out.'

Her voice was barely audible. 'Say it.'

'Everything that I said happened out there was true.' Her eyes were wide now; oval voids in the heat-map of her face. 'It just happened in reverse. It wasn't Carine Lefevre's transform that began to break down when we were close to the Shroud.'

'What are you saying?'

'That it was mine. I was the one who nearly got both of us killed.' He paused, waiting either for her to say something, or for the chasers to erupt from the blue light which was slowly creeping closer. When neither happened he continued, lost in the momentum of confession. 'My Juggler transform started to decay. The gravity fields around the Shroud began to lash at us. Carine was going to die unless I separated my half of the contact module from hers.'

He could imagine the way she was trying to fit this over the existing template she carried in her mind, part of the consensus history with which she had been born. What he was saying was not, could not, should not be the truth. The way it was was very simple. Lefevre's transform had begun to decay; Lefevre had made the supreme sacrifice, jettisoning her half of the contact module so that Sylveste stood a chance at surviving this bruising encounter with the totally alien. It could not be any other way. It was what she knew.

Except it was all untrue.

'Which is what I should have done. Easy to say now, after the fact. But I couldn't, not there and then.' She could not read his expression, and he was unsure whether this pleased or displeased him at this moment. 'I couldn't blow the separation charges.'

'Why not?'

And he thought: what she wants me to say is that it was not physically possible; that the quiet space had become too restricted for physical movement; that the gravity vortices were pinning him immobile, even as they worked to rip him flesh from bone. But that would have been a lie, and he was beyond that now.

'I was scared,' Sylveste said. 'More scared than I've ever been in my life. Scared of what dying in an alien place would mean. Scared of what would happen to my soul, around that place. In what Lascaille called Revelation Space.' He coughed, knowing there wasn't much time left. 'Irrational, but that was how I felt. The simulations hadn't prepared us for the terror.'

'Yet you made it.'

'Gravity torsions ripped the craft apart; did the job the explosive charges were meant to do. I didn't die ... and that I don't understand, because I should have.'

'And Carine?'

Before he could answer – as if he even had an answer – a sickly-sweet smell hit them. Sleeping gas again, only this time in a much thicker dose. It flooded his lungs. He wanted to sneeze. He forgot about Lascaille's Shroud, forgot Carine, forgot his own part in whatever had become of her. Sneezing was suddenly the most important thing in his universe.

That and clawing his skin off with his fingers.

A man stood against the blue. His expression was unreadable beneath his mask, but his stance conveyed nothing more than bored indifference. Languidly, he raised his left arm. At first it appeared that he was holding a trigger-grip megaphone, but the way he held the device was infinitely more purposeful. Calmly he sighted until the flared weapon was pointed straight at Sylveste's eyes.

He did something – it was completely silent – and molten agony spiked into Sylveste's brain.

NINE

'Sorry about the eyes,' the voice said, after an eternity of pain and motion.

For a moment Sylveste drifted in confused thought, trying to arrange the order of recent events. Somewhere in his recent past lay the wedding, the murders, their flight into the labyrinth, the tranquilliser gas, but nothing connected with anything else. He felt as if he were trying to reassemble a biography from a handful of unnumbered fragments, a biography whose events seemed tantalisingly familiar.

The unbelievable pain in his head when the man had pointed the weapon at him—

He was blind.

The world was gone, replaced by an unmoving grey mosaic; the emergency shutdown mode of his eyes. Severe damage had been wrought on Calvin's handiwork. The eyes had not merely crashed; they had been assaulted.

'It was better that you not see us,' said the voice, very close now. 'We could have blindfolded you, but we weren't sure what those little beauties could do. Maybe they could see through any fabric we used. It was simpler this way. Focused mag pulse . . . probably hurt a bit. Blitzed a few circuits. Sorry for that.'

He managed not to sound sorry at all.

'What about my wife?'

'Girardieau's kid? She's okay. Nothing so drastic was required in her case.'

Perhaps because he was blind, Sylveste was more sensitive to the motion of his environment. They were in an aircraft, he guessed, steering through canyons and valleys to avoid dust storms. He wondered who owned the aircraft, who was now in charge. Were Girardieau government forces still holding Cuvier, or had the whole colony fallen to the True Path uprising? Neither was particularly appealing. He might have struck an alliance with Girardieau, but he was dead now and Sylveste had always had enemies in the Inundationist power structure; people who resented the way Girardieau had allowed Sylveste to live after the first coup.

Still, he was alive. And he had been blind before. The state was not unfamiliar to him; he knew it was something he could survive.

'Where are we going?' he asked. They had bound him with tight, circulation-inhibiting restraints. 'Back to Cuvier?'

'What if we were?' asked the voice. 'I'm surprised you'd be in much of a hurry to get there.'

The aircraft tilted and banked sickeningly, plummeting and jerking aloft like a toy yacht in a squall. Sylveste tried to relate the turns to his mental map of the canyon systems around Cuvier, but it was hopeless. He was probably much closer to the buried Amarantin city than home, but he could also be anywhere on the planet by now.

'Are you . . .' Sylveste hesitated. He wondered if he ought to fake some ignorance about his situation, then crushed the idea. There was little he needed to fake. 'Are you Inundationists?'

'What do you think?'

'I think you're True Path.'

'Give the man a round of applause.'

'Are you running things now?'

'The whole show.' The guard tried to put some swagger into his answer, but Sylveste caught the momentary hesitation. Uncertainty, Sylveste thought. Probably they had no real idea how well their takeover was going. What he said could have been true, but, given that communications across the planet might have been damaged, there was no way of knowing; no way of confirming the thoroughness of their control. It could easily be that Girardieau-loyal forces retained the capital, or another faction entirely. These people must be acting out of faith, hoping that their allies had also succeeded.

They could, of course, be completely right.

Fingers placed the mask over his face, its hard edges knifing into his skin. The discomfort was tolerable, though: against the permanent pain from his damaged eyes it hardly registered at all.

Breathing with the mask in place took some effort. He had to work hard to draw air through the dust-collector built into the mask's snout. Two-thirds of the oxygen which entered his lungs would now come from Resurgam's atmosphere, while the remaining third came from a pressurised canister slung beneath the proboscis. It was doped with enough carbon dioxide to trigger the body's breathing response.

He had barely felt the aircraft touch down – had not even been certain that they had arrived somewhere until the door was opened. Now the guard undid his restraints and shoved him peremptorily towards the coldness and the wind of the exit.

Was it dark or daytime out there?

He had no idea; no way of telling.

'Where are we?' he called. The mask muffled his voice and made him sound moronic.

'You imagine it makes any difference?' The guard's voice was not distorted. He was breathing the air directly, Sylveste realised. 'Even if the city was within walking distance – which it isn't – you wouldn't get beyond spitting distance of where you are now without killing yourself.'

'I want to speak to my wife.'

The guard grabbed his arm and pivoted it back to the point where Sylveste felt it was going to be dislocated. He stumbled, but the guard refused to let him fall. 'You'll speak to her when we're good and ready. Told you she was fine, didn't I? You don't trust me or something?'

'I just watched you kill my new father-in-law. What do you think?'

'I think you should keep your head down.'

A hand ducked him, forcing him into shelter. The wind ceased stinging his ears; voices suddenly had an echoey quality. Behind, a pressure door hove shut and amputated the sound of the storm. Though blind, he sensed that Pascale was nowhere near him, and hoped that that meant she had been escorted separately, and that his captors were not lying when they said she was safe.

Someone snatched the mask away.

What followed was a forced march down narrow, shoulder-bruising corridors which stank of brutal hygiene. His escort helped him descend rattling stairwells and ride two lurching elevators down an unguessable distance. They exited into an echoey subterranean space, the air metallic and breezy. They walked past a gusting air duct; from the surface came the shrill proclamation of the wind. Intermittently he heard voices, and though he thought he recognised intonations, he could not begin to put names to the sounds.

Finally there was a room.

He was sure it was painted white. He could almost sense the blank cubic pressure of its walls.

Someone stepped next to him; cabbage breath. He felt fingers touch his face, delicately. They were sheathed in something textureless, reeking faintly of disinfectant. The fingers touched his eyes, tapping their facets with something hard.

Each tap was a small nova of pain behind his temples.

'Fix them when I say,' said a voice which, beyond any doubt, he knew. It was female, but with a throaty quality which rendered it almost masculine. 'For now keep him blind.'

Footsteps left; the speaker must have dismissed the escort with a silent gesture. Alone now, with no reference points, Sylveste felt his balance go. No matter how he moved, the grey matrix remained in front of him. His legs felt weak, but there was nothing with which to support himself. For all he knew he was standing on a plank of wood ten storeys above the floor.

He began to topple, arms flailing pathetically.

Something snatched at his forearm and stabilised him. He heard a pulsing rasp, like someone sawing through timber.

His breathing.

He heard a moist click, and knew that she had opened her mouth to speak again. Now she must be smiling, contemplating.

'Who are you?' he asked.

'You hopeless bastard. You don't even remember my voice.'

Her fingers gouged his forearm, expertly locating nerves and pinching them in the appropriate place. He let out a doglike yelp; it was the first stimulus which had made him forget the pain in his eyes. 'I swear,' Sylveste said, 'I don't know you.'

She released the pressure. As his nerves and tendons sprang back into place there was more pain, subsiding into a numb discomfort which gloved his entire arm and shoulder.

'You should,' said the wrecked voice. 'I'm someone you think died a long time ago, Dan, buried under a landslide.'

'Sluka,' he said.

*

194

Volyova was on her way to the Captain when the disturbing thing happened. Now that the rest of the crew were sleeping out the journey to Resurgam – including Khouri – Volyova had again fallen into her old habit of conversing with the slightly warmed Captain; elevating his brain temperature by the fraction of a kelvin necessary to allow him some kind of consciousness, however fragmentary. This had been her routine now for the better part of two years, and would continue for another two and half, until the ship arrived around Resurgam and the others came out of reefersleep. Of course, the conversations were infrequent – she could not risk warming the Captain too often, for with each warming the plague claimed a little more of both him and the surrounding matter – but they were little oases of human interaction in weeks otherwise filled only with the contemplating of viruses, weapons and the general matter of the ship's ailing fabric.

So, in her own way, Volyova looked forward to their talks, even though the Captain seldom showed much sign of remembering what they had talked about previously. Worse, a certain frostiness had entered their relationship of late. Partly this was due to Sajaki's lack of fortune in locating Sylveste in the Yellowstone system, condemning the Captain to another half-decade of torment at the very least – or longer, if Sylveste could not be found on Resurgam either, which struck Volyova as an at least theoretical possibility. What made matters difficult was that the Captain kept asking her how the search for Sylveste was going, and she kept having to break the news to him that it was not going as auspiciously as one might wish. The Captain would become sullen at that point – she could hardly blame him for that – and the tone of the conversation would darken, often to the point where the Captain became completely incommunicative. When, days or weeks later, she tried to speak to him again, he would have forgotten what she had told him before and they would go through the same process again, except this time Volyova would do her best to break the bad news more gently, or put some kind of optimistic spin on it.

The other thing that was casting a shadow over their talks stemmed from Volyova's side, which was her nagging insistence on probing the Captain about the visit he and Sajaki had made to the Pattern Jugglers. It was only in the last few years that Volyova had become interested in the details of the visit, for it now seemed to her that Sajaki's change of personality had occurred around the same time. Of course, having one's mind altered was the whole point of visiting the Jugglers – but why would Sajaki have allowed the aliens to change him for the worse? He was crueller than he had been before; despotic and single-minded where once he had been a firm but fair leader; a valued member of the Triumvirate. Now she hardly trusted him at all. And yet – instead of casting some light on the change – the Captain deflected her questions aggressively, and left her even more obsessed with what had happened.

She was on her way to speak to him, then, with these things foremost in her mind; wondering how she would deal with the inevitable question about Sylveste, and what new approach she would take when probing the Captain about the Jugglers. And, because she was taking her usual route, she was obliged to pass through the cache-chamber.

And she saw that one of the weapons – one of the most feared, as it happened – appeared to have moved.

'There have been developments,' said the Mademoiselle. 'Both fortuitous and otherwise.'

It was a surprise to be conscious at all; let alone to hear the Mademoiselle. The very last thing Khouri remembered was climbing into a reefersleep casket with Volyova looking down on her, tapping commands into her bracelet. Now she could neither see nor feel anything, not even a sense of cold, yet she knew she was still – somehow – in the reefer, and still by some measure asleep.

'Where – when – am I?'

'Still aboard the ship; about halfway to Resurgam. We are moving very quickly now; less than one per cent slower than light. I have raised your neural temperature slightly – enough for conversation.'

'Won't Volyova notice?'

'Her noticing may be the least of our problems, I am afraid. Do you remember the cache, how I found something hiding in the gunnery architecture?' The Mademoiselle did not wait for an answer. 'The message that the bloodhounds brought back was not easy to decipher. Over the subsequent three years . . . their auguries have become clearer, now.'

Khouri had a vision of the Mademoiselle disembowelling her dogs, studying the topology of the outspilled entrails.

'So is the stowaway real?'

'Oh yes. And hostile too, though we'll come to that in a moment.'

'Any idea what it is?'

'No,' she said, though the answer was guarded. 'But what I have learnt is almost as interesting.'

What the Mademoiselle had to say related to the gunnery's topology. The gunnery was an enormously complex assemblage of computers: layers accreted over decades of shiptime. It was doubtful that any one mind – even Volyova's – could have grasped more than the very basics of that topology; how the various layers interpenetrated each other and folded back on themselves. But in one sense the gunnery was easy to visualise, since it was almost totally disconnected from the rest of the ship, which was why most of the higher cache-weapon functions could only be accessed by someone physically present in the gunnery seat. The gunnery was surrounded by a firewall, and data could only pass from the rest of the ship to the gunnery. The reasons for this were tactical; since the gunnery's weapons (and not just those in the cache) would project outside the ship when they were used, they potentially offered routes for enemy weapons to penetrate the ship by viral means. So the gunnery was isolated: protected from the rest of the ship's dataspace by a one-way trapdoor. The door only allowed data to enter the gunnery from the rest of the ship; nothing within the gunnery could traverse it.

'Now,' said the Mademoiselle, 'given that we have discovered something in the gunnery, I invite you to draw the logical conclusion.'

'Whatever it was got there by mistake.'

'Yes.' The Mademoiselle sounded pleased, almost as if the thought had not struck her. 'I suppose we must consider the possibility that the entity found its way into the gunnery via the weapons, but I think it is far more likely it entered via the trapdoor. I also happen to know when the door was last traversed.'

'How long ago?'

'Eighteen years ago.' Before Khouri could interject, the Mademoiselle added, 'Shiptime, that is. In worldtime, I estimate between eighty and ninety years prior to your recruitment.'

'Sylveste,' Khouri said, wonderingly. 'Sajaki said that the reason Sylveste went missing was because they brought him aboard this ship, to fix Captain Brannigan. Do the dates tie together?'

'Conclusively, I would say. This would have been 2460 – twenty or so years after Sylveste returned from the Shrouders.'

'And you think he brought – whatever it is – with him?'

'All we know is what Sajaki told us, which is that Sylveste accepted the Calvin simulation in order to heal Captain Brannigan. At some point during the operation Sylveste must have been connected to the ship's dataspace. Perhaps that was how the stowaway gained access. Thereafter – very soon after, I suspect – it entered the gunnery through the one-way door.'

'And it's been there ever since?'

'So it appears.'

This seemed to be a pattern: whenever Khouri felt she had things ordered in her head, or at least approximately so, some new fact would dash her scheme to shreds. She felt like a mediaeval astronomer, creating ever more intricate clockwork cosmologies to incorporate every new observational oddity. Now, in some way she could not begin to guess, Sylveste was related to the gunnery. At least she could take comfort in her ignorance. Even the Mademoiselle was foxed.

'You mentioned the thing was hostile,' she said carefully, not really sure she wanted to ask any more questions, in case the answers were too difficult to assimilate.

'Yes.' Hesitating now. 'The dogs were a mistake,' she said. 'I was too impetuous. I should have realised that Sun Stealer—'

'Sun Stealer?'

'What it calls itself. The stowaway, I mean.'

This was bad. How did she know the thing's name? Fleetingly, Khouri remembered that Volyova had once asked her if that name meant anything to her. But there was more to it than that. It was as if she had been hearing that name in her dreams for some time now. Khouri opened her mouth to speak, but the Mademoiselle was already talking. 'It used the dogs to escape, Khouri. Or at least for a part of itself to escape. It used them to get into your head.'

Sylveste had no reliable way of marking the time in his new prison. All he remained certain of was that many days had passed since his capture. He suspected he was being drugged, forced into comalike sleep, barren of dreams. When he did dream, which was rarely, he had sight, but his dreams always revolved around his imminent blindness and the preciousness of the sight he retained. When he awoke he saw only grey, but after some time – days, he guessed – the grey had lost its geometric structure. The pattern had been imposed on his brain for too long; now his brain was simply filtering it out. What remained was a colourless infinity, no longer even recognisably grey, but simply a bright absence of hue.

He wondered what he was missing. Perhaps his actual surroundings were so dull and Spartan that his mind would sooner or later have performed the same filtering trick, even if he still had his sight. He sensed only the echoless enclosure of rock; many megatonnes of it. He thought constantly of Pascale, but it became harder by the day to hold her in his mind. The grey seemed to be seeping into his memories, smearing over them like wet concrete.

Then there came a day, just after Sylveste had finished his rations, when the cell door was unlocked and two voices joined him.

The first was that of Gillian Sluka.

'Do what you can with him,' her croak of a voice said. 'Within limits.'

'He should be put under while I operate,' said the other voice, male and treacle-thick. Sylveste recognised the cabbagy smell of the man's breath.

'He should, but he won't be.' The voice hesitated, then added: 'I'm not expecting any miracles, Falkender. I just want the bastard to see me.'

'Give me a few hours,' Falkender said. There was a thump as the man placed something down on the cell's blunt-edged table. 'I'll do my best,' he said, almost mumbling. 'But from what I know, these eyes were nothing special before you had him blinded.'

'One hour.'

She slammed the door as she exited. Sylveste, cocooned in silence since his capture, felt its reverberations jar his skull. For too long he had been striving to pick up the softest of noises, clues to his fate. There had been none, but in the process he had become sensitised to silence.

He smelled Falkender loom nearer. 'A pleasure to work with you, Dr Sylveste,' he said, almost diffidently. 'I'm confident I can undo most of the damage she had inflicted on you, given time.'

'She gave you one hour,' Sylveste said. His own voice sounded foreign; it had been too long since he had done much except mumble incoherently to himself in his sleep. 'What can you possibly do in one hour?'

He heard the man rummage through his tools. 'At the very least improve things for you.' He punctuated his remarks with clucking noises. 'Of course, I can do more if you don't struggle. But I can't promise that this will be pleasant for you.'

'I'm sure you'll do your best.'

The man's fingers skated over his eyes, lightly probing.

'I always admired your father, you know.' Another cluck, reminding Sylveste of one of Janequin's chickens. 'It's well known that he fashioned these eyes for you.'

'His beta-level simulation,' Sylveste corrected.

'Of course, of course.' He could visualise Falkender waving aside this vaporous distinction. 'And not the alpha, either – we all know that vanished years ago.'

'I sold it to the Jugglers,' Sylveste said blankly. After years of holding it in, the truth had popped out of his mouth like a small sour pip.

Falkender made an odd tracheal sound which Sylveste eventually decided might be the man's mode of chuckling. 'Of course, of course. You know, I'm surprised no one ever accused you of that. But that's human cynicism for you.' A shrill whirring sound filled the air, followed by a nerve-searing vibration. 'I think you can say goodbye to colour perception,' Falkender said. 'Monochrome's going to be about the best I can manage.'

Khouri had been hoping for some mental breathing-space, some time in which to collect her thoughts, in which to listen quietly for the breathing of the invasive presence in her head. But the Mademoiselle was still speaking.

'I believe Sun Stealer has already attempted this once before,' she said. 'I'm speaking of your predecessor, of course.'

'You mean the stowaway tried to get into Nagorny's head?'

'Exactly that. Except in Nagorny's case, there would have been no bloodhounds on which to hitch a ride. Sun Stealer must have had to resort to something cruder.'

Khouri considered what she had learnt from Volyova about this whole incident.

'Crude enough to drive Nagorny mad?'

'Evidently so,' her companion nodded. 'And perhaps Sun Stealer only attempted to impose his will on the man. Escape from the gunnery was impossible, so Sun Stealer merely tried to make Nagorny his puppet. Perhaps it was all done via subconscious suggestion, while he was in the gunnery.'

'Exactly how much trouble am I in?'

'Little, for now. There were only a few dogs – not enough for him to do much damage.'

'What happened to the dogs?'

'I decrypted them, of course – learnt their messages. But in doing so, I opened myself up to him. To Sun Stealer. The dogs must have limited him somewhat, because his attack on me was far from subtle. Fortunately, because otherwise I might not have deployed my defences in time. He was not particularly hard to defeat, but of course I was only dealing with a tiny part of him.'

'Then I'm safe?'

'Well, not quite. I ousted him – but only from the implant in which I reside. Unfortunately my defences do not extend to your other implants, including those Volyova installed in you.'

'He's still in my head?'

'He may not have even needed the dogs,' the Mademoiselle said. 'He might have entered Volyova's implants as soon as she placed you in the gunnery for the first time. But he certainly found the dogs advantageous. If he hadn't tried to invade me with them, I might not have sensed his presence in your other implants.'

'I feel the same.'

'Good. It means my countermeasures are effective. You recall how I used countermeasures against Volyova's loyalty therapies?'

'Yes,' Khouri said, gloomily uncertain that those had worked quite as well as the Mademoiselle liked to imagine.

'Well, these are much the same. The only difference is, I'm using them against those sites in your mind which Sun Stealer has occupied. For the last two years, we've been waging a kind of . . .' She paused, and then seemed to experience a moment of epiphany. 'I suppose you could call it a cold war.'

'It would have to be cold.'

'And slow,' the Mademoiselle said. 'The cold robbed us of the energies for anything more. And, of course, we had to be careful that we did not harm you. Your being injured was no use to either myself or Sun Stealer.'

Khouri remembered why this conversation was possible in the first place.

'But now that I'm warmed . . .'

'You understand well. Our campaign has intensified since the warming. I think Volyova may even suspect something. A trawl is reading your brain even now, you see. It may have detected the neural war Sun Stealer and I are waging. I would have relented – but Sun Stealer would have used the moment to overwhelm my counter-measures.'

'But you can hold him at bay . . .'

'I believe so. But should I not succeed in holding Sun Stealer at bay, I felt you needed to know what happened.'

That much was reasonable: better to know that Sun Stealer was in her than to suffer the delusion that she was clean.

'I also wished to warn you. The bulk of him remains in the gunnery. I've no doubt that he will try to enter you fully, or as fully as is possible, when he finds the chance.'

'You mean, next time I'm in the gunnery?'

'I admit the options are limited,' the Mademoiselle said. 'But I thought it best that you knew the entirety of the situation.'

Khouri was, she thought, still a long way from anything that approximated that. But what the ghost said was correct. Better to appreciate the danger than ignore it.

'You know,' she said, 'if Sylveste really was responsible for this thing, killing him won't pose too many problems for me.'

'Good. And the news is not unremittingly bad, I assure you. When I sent those dogs into the gunnery I also sent in an avatar of myself. And I know from the reports that the dogs returned that my avatar remained undetected by Volyova, at least during those early days. That was, of course, more than two years ago . . . but I've no reason to suspect that the avatar has been found since.'

'Assuming it hasn't been destroyed by Sun Stealer.'

'A reasonable point,' she conceded. 'But if Sun Stealer is as intelligent as I suspect, he won't do anything that might draw attention to himself. He can't know for certain that this avatar isn't something Volyova has sent into the system. She has enough doubts of her own, after all.'

'Why did you do it?'

'So that, if necessary, I might gain control of the gunnery.'

*

If Calvin had had any grave, Sylveste thought, then his father would be spinning in it faster than Cerberus spun around the neutron star Hades, aggrieved at the abuse of his own handiwork. Except Calvin had already been dead, or at least non-corporeal, long before his simulation had engineered Sylveste's vision. Such thought-games held the pain at bay, at least part of the time. And, in truth, there had never really been a time since his capture when he had not been in pain. Falkender was flattering himself if he imagined his surgery was exacerbating Sylveste's agony to any significant degree.

Eventually – miraculously – it began to abate.

It was like a vacuum opening in his mind, a cold, void-filled ventricle which had not been there before. Taking the pain away was like taking away some inner buttress. He felt himself collapsing, whole eavestones of his psyche grinding loose under their suddenly unsupported weight. It took an effort to restore some of his own internal equilibrium.

And now there were colourless, evanescent ghosts in his vision.

By the second they hardened into distinct shapes. The walls of a room – as bland and unfurnished as he had imagined – and a masked figure crouched low over him. Falkender's hand was immersed in a kind of chrome glove which ended not in fingers but in a crayfish-like explosion of tiny glistening manipulators. One of the man's eyes was monocled by a lens system, connected to the glove by a segmented steel cable. His skin had the pallor of a lizard's underbelly: his one visible eye was unfocused and cyanotic. Dried specks of blood sprinkled his brow. The blood was grey-green, but Sylveste knew well enough what it was.

In fact, now that he noticed, everything was grey-green.

The glove retracted, and Falkender pulled it from his wrist with the other hand. A caul of lubricant sheened the hand which had been under the glove.

He began to pack his kit away. 'Well, I never promised miracles,' he said. 'And you shouldn't have been expecting any.'

When he moved, it was jerkily, and it took moments for Sylveste to grasp that his eyes were only perceiving three of four images a second. The world moved with the stuttering motion of the pencil cartoons children made in the corners of books, flicked into life between thumb and forefinger. Every few seconds there were upsetting inversions of depth, when Falkender would appear to be a man-shaped recess carved into the cell's wall, and sometimes part of his visual field would jam, not changing for ten or more seconds, even if he looked to another part of the room.

Still, it was vision, or at least vision's idiot cousin.

'Thank you,' Sylveste said. 'It's . . . an improvement.'

'I think we'd better move,' said Falkender. 'We're five minutes behind schedule as it is.'

Sylveste nodded, and just the action of tipping his head was enough to spark pulsing migraines. Still, they were nothing compared with what he had endured until Falkender's work.

He helped himself from the couch and stepped towards the door. Maybe it was because he now moved to the door with a purpose – because, for the first time, he actually expected to step through it – but the action suddenly seemed perverse and alien. He felt as if he were casually stepping off a precipice. He now had no balance. It was as if his inner equilibrium had become accustomed to no vision, and was now thrown by its return. The dizziness faded, though, just as two True Path heavies emerged from the outer corridor and took him by the elbows.

Falkender trailed behind. 'Be careful. There may be perceptual glitches . . .'

But though Sylveste heard his words, they meant nothing to him. He knew where he was now, and that knowledge was momentarily too overpowering. He was back home, after more than twenty years of exile.

His prison was Mantell, a place he had not seen – and barely even visited in his memory – since the coup.

TEN

Approaching Delta Pavonis, 2564

Volyova sat alone in the huge sphere of the bridge, under the holographic display of the Resurgam system. Her seat, like the other vacant ones around her, was mounted on a long, telescopic, highly articulated arm, so that it could be steered to almost any point in the sphere. Hand under chin, she had been staring into the orrery for hours, like a child transfixed by some glittery toy.

Delta Pavonis was a chip of warm-red ambergris fixed at the middle, the system's eleven major planets spaced around it on their respective orbits, positioned at their true positions; smears of asteroidal debris and comet-shards following their own ellipses; the whole orrery haloed by a tenuous Kuiper belt of icy flotsam; tugged into slight asymmetry by the presence of the neutron star which was Pavonis's dark twin. The picture was a simulation, rather than an enlargement of what lay ahead. The ship's sensors were acute enough to glean data at this range, but the view would have been distorted by relativistic effects, and – worse – would have been a snapshot of the system as it was years earlier, with the relative positions of the planets bearing no resemblance to the present situation. Since the ship's approach strategy would depend critically on using the system's larger gas giants for camouflage and gravitational braking, Volyova needed to know where things would be when they got there, not how they had been five years ago. And not only that. Before the ship arrived in the Resurgam system, its advance envoys would already have skimmed by invisibly, and it was just as crucial to arrange their passage at the optimum planetary alignment.

'Release pebbles,' she said, satisfied now that she had run enough simulations. Heeding her, *Infinity* deployed one thousand of the tiny probes, firing them ahead of the decelerating ship in a slowly spreading pattern. Volyova spoke a command into her bracelet and a window opened ahead of her, captured by a camera on the hull. The entire ensemble of pebbles contracted into the distance, apparently tugged away by an invisible force. The cloud diminished as it fell further and further ahead of the ship, until all Volyova could see was a blurred nimbus, diminishing quickly. The pebbles were moving at almost the speed of light, and would reach the Resurgam system months ahead of the ship. The swarm, by then, would be wider than the orbit of Resurgam around the sun. Each tiny probe would align itself towards the planet and catch photons across the electromagnetic spectrum. The data from each pebble would be sent in a tightly focused laser pulse back towards the ship. The resolution of any one unit in the swarm would be tiny, but by combining their results, a very sharp and detailed picture of Resurgam could be assembled. It would not tell Sajaki where Sylveste was, but it would give him an idea of the likely centres of power on the planet, and – more importantly – what kind of defences they were capable of mustering.

That was one thing on which Sajaki and Volyova had been in complete agreement. Even if they found Sylveste, it seemed unlikely that he would agree to come aboard without coercion.

'Do you know what they did to Pascale?' Sylveste said.

'She's safe,' said the eye surgeon, as he led Sylveste along tracheal, rock-clad tunnels deep in Mantell. 'That's what I've heard, at least,' he added, lessening Sylveste's ease. 'But I could be wrong. I don't think Sluka would have killed her without good reason, but she may have had her frozen.'

'Frozen?'

'Until she's useful. You'll understand by now that Sluka thinks long-term.'

Continual waves of nausea kept threatening to overwhelm him. His eyes hurt, but, as he kept reminding himself, it was vision. That at least was something. Without it he was powerless, not even capable of effective disobedience. With it, escape might still be impossible, but at least he was spared the stumbling indignity of the blind. What vision he had, though, would have shamed the lowliest invertebrate. Spatial perception was haphazard, and colour existed in his world now only via nuances of grey-greens.

What he knew – what he remembered – was this.

He had not seen Mantell since the night of the coup twenty years earlier. The *first* coup, he corrected himself. Now that Girardieau had been overthrown, Sylveste had to get used to thinking of his own dethronement in purely historical terms. Girardieau's regime had not immediately closed the place down, even though its Amarantin-directed research conflicted with their Inundationist agenda. For five or six years after the coup they had kept the place running, but one by one they had moved Sylveste's best researchers back to Cuvier, replacing them with eco-engineers, botanists and geopower specialists. Finally, Mantell had been reduced to a skeleton-crewed test station, whole portions moth-balled or derelict. It should have stayed that way, but trouble was already looming from outside elements. For years it had been rumoured that True Path's leaders in Cuvier, Resurgam City, or whatever they were calling it now, were under direction from individuals beyond, a clique of one-time Girardieau sympathisers who had fallen out of favour during the machinations of the first coup. Supposedly, these brigands had altered their physiologies to cope with the dusty, oxygen-depleted atmosphere beyond the domes, using biotech purchased from Captain Remilliod.

Stories like that could be expected. But after sporadic attacks against a number of outposts, they began to look far less speculative. Mantell had been abandoned at some point, Sylveste knew, which meant that the current occupants might have been here for much longer than the time since Girardieau's assassination. Months, or possibly even years.

Certainly they acted as if they owned the place. He knew when they entered a room that it was the one where Gillian Sluka had addressed him upon his arrival, however long ago that was. He failed to recognise it, though: it was entirely possible that during his tenancy in Mantell he had known this room intimately, but there were no longer any points of reference to aid him. The room's décor and furnishings – such as there were – had been completely replaced. She stood with her back to him, next to a table, gloved hands knitted primly above her hip. She wore a knee-length fluted jacket with leather shoulder patches, the colour rendered as murky olive by his eyes. Her hair was collected in a braided tail which hung between her shoulder blades. She was not projecting entoptics. On either side of the room, planetary globes orbited on slender, swan-necked plinths. Something approximating daylight slatted down from the ceiling, though his eyes leeched it of any warmth.

'When we first spoke after your imprisonment,' she said, in her croak of a voice, 'I almost had the impression you couldn't place me.'

'I'd always assumed you were dead.'

'That was what Girardieau's people wished you to think. The story about our crawler being hit by a landslide – all lies. We were attacked – they thought you were aboard, of course.'

'Why didn't they kill me later, when they found me at the dig?'

'They realised you were more useful to them alive than dead, of course. Girardieau was no fool – he always used you profitably.'

'If you'd stayed with the dig, none of it would have happened. How did you survive, anyway?'

'Some of us got out of the crawler before Girardieau's henchmen reached it. We took what equipment we could; made it into the Bird's Claw canyons and set up bubbletents. That's all I saw for a year, you know: the inside of a bubbletent. I was hurt quite badly in the attack.'

Sylveste brushed his fingers over the mottled surface of one of Sluka's pedestal-mounted globes. What they represented, he saw now, was the topography of Resurgam at different epochs during the planned Inundationist terraforming program. 'Why didn't you join Girardieau in Cuvier?' he asked.

'He considered me too embarrassing to admit back into his fold. He was prepared to let us live, but only because killing us would have attracted too much attention. There were lines of communication, but they broke down.' She paused. 'Fortunately we took some of Remilliod's trinkets with us. The scavenger enzymes were the most useful. The dust doesn't hurt us.'

He studied the globes again. With his impaired vision, he could only guess at the colours of the planetscapes, but he assumed that the spheres represented a steady march towards blue-green verdure. What were now merely upraised plateaux would become landmasses limned by ocean. Forests would fester across steppes. He looked to the furthest globes, which represented some remote version of Resurgam several centuries hence. Nightside, cities glistened in chains, and a spray of tinkertoy habitats girdled the planet. Gossamer starbridges reached from the equator towards orbit. How would that delicate future vision fare, he wondered, if Resurgam's sun again erupted, as it had done nine hundred and ninety thousand years ago, just when Amarantin civilisation was approaching a human level of sophistication?

Not, he ventured, terribly well.

'Apart from the biotech,' he said, 'what else did Remilliod give you? You appreciate I'm curious.'

She seemed ready to humour him.

'You haven't asked me about Cuvier. That surprises me.' She added: 'Or your wife.'

'Falkender told me Pascale was safe.'

'She is. Perhaps I'll allow you to join her at some point. For now, I wish your attention. We haven't secured the capital. The rest of Resurgam is ours, but Girardieau's people still hold Cuvier.'

'The city's still intact?'

'No,' she said. 'We . . .' She looked over his shoulder, directly at Falkender. 'Fetch Delaunay, will you? And have him bring one of Remilliod's gifts.'

Falkender left, leaving them alone.

'I understand there was some agreement between you and Nils,' Sluka said. 'Although the rumours I've heard are too contradictory to make much sense. Do you mind enlightening me?'

'There was never anything formal,' Sylveste said. 'No matter what you may have heard.'

'I understand his daughter was brought in to paint you in an unflattering light.'

'It made sense,' Sylveste said wearily. 'There'd be a certain cachet in having the biography scripted by a member of the family who was holding me prisoner. And Pascale was young, but not so young that it wasn't time for her to make her mark. There were no losers: Pascale could hardly fail, though in fairness she applied herself to the task excellently.' He winced inwardly, remembering how close she had come to exposing the truth about Calvin's alpha-level simulation. More than ever he was convinced that she had correctly guessed the facts, but had held back from committing them to the biography. Now, of course, she knew much more: what had happened around Lascaille's Shroud, and how Carine Lefevre's death was not the clear-cut thing he had made it seem upon his return to Yellowstone. But he had not spoken to her since that announcement. 'As for Girardieau,' he said, 'he had the satisfaction of seeing his daughter associated with a genuinely important project. Not to mention the fact that I was opened to the world for closer scrutiny. I was the prize butterfly in his collection, you see – but until the biography, he'd had no easy means of showing me off.'

'I've experienced the biography,' Sluka said. 'I'm not entirely sure Girardieau got what he wanted.'

'All the same, he promised to keep his word.' His eyes faltered, and for a moment the woman he was addressing seemed to be a woman-shaped hole cut in the fabric of the room's volume, a hole through which infinities lay.

The odd moment passed. He continued, 'I wanted access to Cerberus/Hades. I think – towards the end – Nils was almost ready to give it to me, provided the colony had the means.'

'You think there's something out there?'

'If you're acquainted with my ideas,' Sylveste said, 'then you must bow to their logic.'

'I find them intriguing – like any delusional construct.'

As she spoke, the door opened and a man Sylveste had not seen before entered, shadowed by Falkender. The new man – whom he assumed to be Delaunay – was bulldog-stocky. His wore several days' growth of beard, a purple beret resting on his scalp. There were red weals around his eyes and a pair of dust goggles around his neck. His chest was crossed by webbing and his feet vanished into ochre mukluks.

'Show the nasty little thing to our guest,' Sluka said.

Delaunay was carrying an obviously heavy black cylinder in one hand, gripped in a thick handle.

'Take it,' Sluka told Sylveste.

He did; it was as heavy as he had expected. The handle was attached to the top of the cylinder; beneath it was a single green key. Sylveste put the cylinder down on the table; it was too heavy to hold comfortably for any length of time.

'Open it,' Sluka said.

He pressed the key – it was the obvious thing to do – and the cylinder split open like a Russian doll, the top half rising on four metal supports which surrounded a slightly smaller cylinder hidden until now. Then the inner cylinder split open similarly, revealing another nested layer, and the process continued until six or seven shells had been revealed.

Inside was a thin silver column. There was a tiny window set into the column's side, showing an illuminated cavity. Cradled in the cavity was what looked like a bulbous-headed pin.

'I assume by now you understand what this is,' Sluka said.

'I can guess it wasn't manufactured here,' Sylveste said. 'And I know nothing like this was brought with us from Yellowstone. Which leaves our excellent benefactor Remilliod. He sold this to you?'

'This and nine others,' she said. 'Eight now, since we used the tenth against Cuvier.'

'It's a weapon?'

'Remilliod's people called it hot-dust,' she said. 'Antimatter. The pinhead contains only a twentieth of a gramme of antilithium, but that's more than sufficient for our purposes.'

'I didn't realise such a weapon was possible,' he said. 'Something so small, I mean.'

'That's understandable. The technology's been outlawed for so long almost nobody remembers how to actually make one.'

'What yield does this have?'

'About two kilotonnes. Enough to put a hole in Cuvier.'

Sylveste nodded, absorbing the implication of what she had said. In his mind's eye he tried to imagine what it must have been like, for those who had either died in or had been blinded by the pinhead True Path had used against the capital. The slight pressure differential between the domes and the outside air would have led to ferocious winds combing through the ordered municipal spaces. He imagined the trees and plants of the arboreta uprooted and shredded by the force of it, the birds and other animals carried aloft on the hurricane. Those people who survived the initial breach – no guessing how many – would have had to seek shelter underground, quickly, before the choking outside air replaced the leaking dome air. Admittedly the air was closer to being breathable now than it had been twenty years ago, but it took skill to learn how to do it, even for a few minutes only. Most of the inhabitants of the capital had never left it. He did not greatly value their chances.

'Why?' he asked.

'It was a . . .' She paused. 'I was going to call it a mistake, but you could argue that there are no mistakes in war, only fortunate and less fortunate events. The intention, at least, was not to use the pinhead. Girardieau's loyals were to surrender the city once they knew we possessed the weapon. But it didn't work like that. Girardieau himself had known of the existence of the pinheads, but he hadn't communicated that knowledge to his subordinates. No one would believe we had it.'

It was not necessary for her to tell him the rest; what had taken place was clear enough. Frustrated by the fact that their weapon was not taken seriously, the brigands had used it anyway. Yet the capital was still inhabited; Sluka had made that clear early on. Girardieau's loyals still held it. He imagined them running things from subsurface bunkers, while overhead dust storms fingered through the open latticework of the ruined domes.

'So you see,' the woman said, 'no one should underestimate us, much less anyone who retains any lingering attachment to Girardieau's rule.'

'What do you plan to use the others for?'

'Infiltration. Remove the shrouding, and the pinhead itself is tiny enough to be implanted in a tooth. You'd never find it, except with the most detailed medical scan.'

'Is that your plan?' he asked. 'To find eight volunteers, and have those things surgically implanted? Then have your eight infiltrate the capital again? This time they'd believe you, I think.'

'Except we don't even need volunteers,' Sluka said. 'They might be preferable, but they're not necessary.'

Ignoring his own better judgement, Sylveste said, 'Gillian, I think I liked you better fifteen years ago.'

'You can take him back to his cell,' she said to Falkender. 'I'm bored with him for now.'

He felt the surgeon tug at his sleeve.

'May I spend more time with his eyes, Gillian? There was more I could do, but at the expense of greater discomfort.'

'Do what you like,' Sluka said. 'But don't feel any obligation. Now that I have him, I have to confess I'm a little disappointed. I think I liked him better in the past as well, before Girardieau turned him into a martyr.' She shrugged. 'He's too valuable to throw away, but in the absence of anything better, I might just have him frozen, until I find a use for him. That might be a year from now, or it might be five years. All I'm saying is, it would be a shame to invest very much time in something we might soon tire of, Dr Falkender.'

'Surgery has its own rewards,' the man said.

'I can see well enough now,' Sylveste said.

'Oh no,' Falkender answered. 'There's much more I can do for you, Dr Sylveste. Very much more. I've barely begun.'

Volyova was down with Captain Brannigan when a janitor-rat informed her that the pebbles had sent back their reports. She was gathering fresh samples from the Captain's periphery, encouraged by recent successes of one of her retrovirus strains against the plague. Her virus was adapted from one of the military cyberviruses which had struck the ship, suitably modifed for Plague-compatibility. Amazingly, it actually seemed to be working – at least against the tiny samples she had so far tried it against. How irritating to be snatched from this by something she had set in motion nine months earlier, and had in the meantime all but forgotten. For a moment she refused to believe that so much time could possibly have passed. Yet she was excited by what she might learn.

She took the lift upship. Nine months, yes. It hardly seemed possible – but that was what happened when you were working. And she should have been expecting it. Rationally she had known that so much time had passed – but the information had managed not to tunnel into the part of her mind where she actually acknowledged such things and began to deal with them. But the clues had been there all along. The ship was now cruising at only one quarter of lightspeed. In about a hundred days they would be making final insertion into Resurgam orbit, and they would need a strategy when they got there. That was where the pebbles came in.

Snapshots of Resurgam and near-Resurgam space were assembling in the bridge, in various EM and exotic-particle bands. It was the first recent glimpse of a possible enemy. Volyova let the salient facts mole deep into her consciousness, so that she could recall them with instinctive ease during a crisis. The pebbles had whipped past either side of Resurgam so that there was data from both its day and night sides. Additionally, the pebble cloud had elongated itself in the line of flight until fifteen hours spaced the passage of its first and last unit through the system, enabling the entire surface of Resurgam to be glimpsed under both illumination and darkness. The dayside pebbles were looking away from Delta Pavonis, so they snooped for neutrino leakage from fusion and antimatter power units on the surface. The nightside pebbles snooped for the heat signatures of population centres and orbital facilities. Other sensors sniffed the atmosphere, measuring oxygen, ozone and nitrogen levels; sensing the extent to which the colonists had tampered with the native biome.

Given that the colonists had been here for more than half a century, it was striking how much they had managed to live without. There were no large structures in orbit; no evidence of local spaceflight within the system. Only a few comsats girdled the planet, and given the lack of large-scale industrialisation on the surface, it was doubtful whether they could be repaired or replaced if any were damaged. It would be a simple matter to disable or confuse those that remained, if that fitted in with the as yet unformulated plan.

Yet they had not been entirely idle; the atmosphere showed signs of extensive modification, with free oxygen now well above what Volyova would have expected. The infrared sensors revealed geothermal taps aligned along what were certainly continental subduction zones. Neutrino leakage from the polar zones hinted at oxygen factories; fusion-powered units which would crack open water-ice molecules to extract oxygen and hydrogen. The oxygen would be bled into the atmosphere – or pumped to domed-over communities – while the hydrogen was cycled back into the fusors. Volyova identified upwards of fifty communities, but most were small affairs, and none approximated the size of the main settlement. She assumed there were other, tinier outposts – family-tended stations and homesteads – but the pebbles would miss these.

So what did she have to report? No orbital defences, almost certainly no capability for spaceflight, and most of the planet's inhabitants still crammed into one community. At least from a standpoint of relative strengths, persuading the Resurgamites to give up Sylveste ought to be the simplest of matters.

But there was something else.

The Resurgam system was a wide binary. Delta Pavonis was the life-giving star, but – as she had known – it possessed a dead twin. The dark companion was a neutron star, separated by ten light-hours from Pavonis, far enough for stable planetary orbits to be possible around both stars. And indeed, the neutron star had claimed a planet of its own. The fact of the planet's existence was known to her in advance of the information from the pebbles. All

214

it warranted in the ship's database was a line of comment and a scrawl of terse numerics. These worlds were invariably chemically dull, atmosphereless and biologically inert, flensed sterile by the wind that the neutron star had blown when it was a pulsar. Little more, Volyova thought, than lumps of stellar slag-iron, and about as interesting.

But near this world was a neutrino source. It was weak – almost at the limit of detectability – but nothing she could ignore. Volyova digested this knowledge for a few moments before regurgitating it as a tiny, troublesome cud of certainty. Only a machine could create such a signature.

And that worried her.

'You've really been awake all this time?' Khouri asked, shortly after waking herself, as she and Volyova journeyed down to see the Captain.

'Not literally,' Volyova said. 'Even my body needs sleep occasionally. I tried dispensing with it once; there are drugs you can take. And implants which can be put into the RAS . . . that's the reticular activating system, the region of the brain which mediates sleep – but you still need to clean out those fatigue poisons.' She winced. It was evident to Khouri that Volyova found the topic of implants about as pleasant as toothache.

'Much happen?' Khouri asked.

'Nothing you need concern yourself with,' Volyova said, taking a drag on a cigarette. Khouri assumed that would be the end of it, but then her tutor fixed her with an uneasy expression. 'Well, now you mention it, there was something. Two things, in fact, though I'm not sure to which I should attach the greater significance. The first need not concern you immediately. As for the second . . .'

Khouri searched Volyova's face for concrete evidence of the seven additional years the woman had aged since their last meeting. There was nothing; not a hint of it, which meant that she had balanced the seven years with infusions of anti-senescence drugs. She looked different, but only because she had permitted her hair to grow out from her usual crop. It was still short, but the extra volume served to ameliorate the sharp lines of her jaw and cheekbones. If anything, Khouri thought, Volyova looked seven years younger, rather than older. Not for the first time, she attempted to assess the woman's actual physiological age, and failed miserably.

'What was it?'

'There was something unusual about your neural activity while you were in reefersleep. There shouldn't have been any. But what I saw didn't even look normal for someone awake. It looked like a small war going on in your head.'

The elevator had arrived at the Captain's level. 'That's an interesting analogy,' Khouri said, stepping into the chill of the corridor.

'Assuming it is one. I doubted that you'd have been aware of much, of course.'

'I don't remember anything,' Khouri said.

Volyova was silent until they reached the human nebula which was the Captain. Glittering and uncomfortably mucoid, he less resembled a human being than an angel which had dropped from the sky onto a hard, splattering surface. The antiquated reefer which had until recently cased him was now shattered and fissured. It still functioned, but only barely, and the cold it offered was no longer adequate to stifle the plague's relentless encroachment. Captain Brannigan had sunk dozens of tendril-like roots into the ship now, roots which Volyova tracked but was powerless to prevent spreading. She could sever them, but what effect would that have on the Captain? For all she knew, the roots were all that was keeping him alive, if she dared dignify his state with the word. Eventually, Volyova said, the roots would permeate the whole vessel, and by then it would probably be unwise to make much of a distinction between the ship and the Captain. Of course, she could arrest that spread if she wished, by the simple expedient of ejecting this portion of the ship; cutting it entirely free from the rest of the vessel, the way an oldtime surgeon might have dealt with a particularly voracious tumour. The volume Brannigan had subsumed was tiny now, and the ship would certainly not miss it. Undoubtedly his transformations would continue, but lacking sustaining material they would be turned incestuously inwards, until entropy drove the life from what he had become.

'You'd consider doing that?' Khouri asked.

'Consider it, yes,' Volyova replied. 'But I'm hoping it won't come to that. All these samples I've been taking – I think I'm actually getting somewhere. I've found a counteragent – a retrovirus which seems stronger than the plague. It subverts the plague machinery faster than the plague subverts it. Only tested it on tiny pieces so far – and there's really no way I can do any better than that, because testing it on the Captain would be a medical matter, and I'm not qualified to do that.'

'Of course,' Khouri said hastily. 'But if you won't do that, you're really trusting all on Sylveste, aren't you?'

'Maybe, but one shouldn't underestimate his skills. Or Calvin's, I should say.'

'And he'll help you, just like that?'

'No, but he didn't willingly help us the first time either, and we still found a way.'

'Persuasion, you mean?'

Volyova took a moment to take a scraping from one of the pipelike tendrils, just before it dove into an intestinal mass of ship plumbing. 'Sylveste is a man with obsessions,' she said. 'And people like that are more easily manipulated than they imagine. They're so intent on whatever goal it is they have in mind that they don't always notice that they're being bent to someone else's will.'

'Like yours, for instance.'

She took the sliver-thin sample and popped it away for analysis. 'Sajaki told you that we brought him aboard during his missing month?'

'Thirty days in the wilderness.'

'Stupid name, that,' Volyova said, gritting her teeth. 'Did they have to make it sound so damned Biblical? Wasn't as if he didn't already have a messiah complex, if you ask me. Anyway, yes, that was when we brought him aboard. And the interesting thing was, this was fully thirty years before the Resurgam expedition ever left Yellowstone. Now, I'll let you in on a secret. Until we returned to Yellowstone and recruited you, we didn't even know of the existence of this expedition. We still expected to find Sylveste on Yellowstone.'

Khouri knew well enough from her own experience with Fazil the kind of difficulty Volyova's crew must have faced, but she decided a little fake ignorance would seem more plausible.

'Careless of you not to check firsthand.'

'Not at all. In fact we did – it was just that our best information was already decades old before we obtained it. And then by the time we'd acted on it – made the hop to Yellowstone – it was twice as old again.'

'I suppose it wasn't a bad gamble. The family had always been associated with Yellowstone, so you'd have expected to find the rich young brat still hanging around the old place.'

'Except we were wrong. But the interesting thing is, it looks as if we could have spared ourselves the bother all along. Sylveste may have had the Resurgam expedition in mind when we first brought him aboard. If only we'd listened, we could have gone there directly.'

As they traversed the complicated series of elevators and access tunnels which led from the Captain's corridor to the glade, Volyova spoke beneath audibility into the bracelet which she never let slip from her wrist. Khouri knew that she must be addressing one of the ship's many artificial personae, but Volyova gave no hint of what it was she was arranging.

The green light of the glade was a sensual feast after the unremitting cold and gloom of the Captain's corridor. The air was warm and bouquet-fresh, and the painted birds which owned the aerial spaces of the chamber were almost too gaudy for Khouri's dark-adapted eyes. For a moment she was too overwhelmed to notice that Volyova and she were not alone. Then she saw the three other people who were present. The trio sat facing each other around a stump of wood, kneeling in the dew-moistened grass. Sajaki was one of them, though he wore his hair in a different style from those Khouri had seen before: he was entirely bald apart from a topknot. The second person she recognised was Volyova herself – hair short now, which accentuated the angular form of her skull and made her look older than the version of Volyova which was standing next to Khouri. The third person, Khouri realised, was Sylveste himself.

'Shall we join them?' Volyova said, leading the way down the rickety staircase which descended to the lawn.

Khouri followed. 'This dates from . . .' She paused and recalled the date when Sylveste had gone missing from Chasm City. 'Around 2460, right?'

'Spot on,' Volyova said, turning to fix Khouri with a look of mild amazement. 'What are you, an expert on Sylveste's life and times? Oh, never mind. The point is, we recorded his entire visit, and I knew there was one particular remark he made which . . . well, in the light of what we now know, I find curious.'

'Intriguing.'

Khouri jumped, because it was not she who had spoken, and the voice had appeared to come from behind her. It was then that she became conscious of the Mademoiselle, loitering some distance up the staircase.

'I should have known you'd show your ugly face,' Khouri said, not even bothering to subvocalise, since the constant chatter of the songbirds served to mask her words from Volyova, who had gone on ahead to the others. 'You're like a bad penny, you know.'

'At least you know I'm still around,' she said. 'If I weren't, you'd have real grounds to worry. It would mean Sun Stealer had overwhelmed my countermeasures. Your sanity would be next, and I hate to speculate about what that would do for your employment prospects where Volyova's concerned.'

'Shut up and let me concentrate on what Sylveste has to say.'

'Be my guest,' the Mademoiselle said curtly, not straying from her vantage point.

Khouri joined Volyova next to the trio.

'Of course,' the standing Volyova said, addressing Khouri, 'I could have replayed this conversation from any point in the ship. But it took place here, so this is where I chose to re-enact it.' As she spoke, she reached into her jacket pocket and slipped out a pair of smoke-coloured goggles which she proceeded to place over her eyes. Khouri understood: lacking implants, Volyova could only witness this playback with the aid of direct retinal projection. Until she slipped on the goggles, she would not have seen the figures at all.

'So you see,' Sajaki was saying, 'it's in your best interests to do what we want. You've made use of Ultra elements in the past – your trip out to Lascaille's Shroud, for instance – and it's highly probable you'll want to do so in the future.'

Sylveste placed his elbows on the tree stump. Khouri studied the man. She had seen plenty of lifelike evocations of Sylveste before, but this image seemed more real than any she had yet experienced. She guessed it was because Sylveste was in conversation with two people she knew, rather than anonymous figures from Yellowstone's history. That made a lot of difference. He was handsome; improbably so, in her opinion, but she doubted that the image had been cosmetically doctored. His long hair hung in tangles either side of his magisterial brow; his eyes were acutely green. Even if she had to look him in the eyes before killing him – and the Mademoiselle's specifications about the killing did not make that unlikely – it would be something to see those eyes for real.

'That sounds awfully like blackmail,' Sylveste said, his voice the lowest of those present. 'You talk as if you Ultras have some kind of binding agreement. It might fool some people, Sajaki, but I'm afraid I'm not one of them.'

'Then you may be in for a surprise the next time you attempt to enlist Ultra assistance,' Sajaki answered, toying with a splinter of wood. 'Let's be quite clear on this. If you refuse us – in addition to whatever else that might bring upon yourself – you'd ensure that you never leave your home planet.'

'I doubt that that would greatly inconvenience me.'

Volyova – the seated version – shook her head. 'Not what our spies tell us. Rumour has it you're trying to find funding for an expedition to the Delta Pavonis system, Dr Sylveste.'

'Resurgam?' Sylveste snorted. 'I don't think so. There's nothing there.'

The real, standing Volyova said, 'He's clearly lying. It's obvious now, though at the time I just assumed the rumour I had heard was false.'

Sajaki had replied to Sylveste, and now Sylveste was speaking again, defensively. 'Listen,' he said. 'I don't care what rumours you've heard – you'd better ignore them. There's not a scrap of a reason to go there. Check the records if you don't believe me.'

'But that's the odd thing,' the standing Volyova said. 'I did just that, and damned if he wasn't right. Based on what was known at the time, there was absolutely no reason to consider an expedition to Resurgam.'

'But you just said he was lying . . .'

'And he was, of course – hindsight proves that much.' She shook her head. 'You know, I've never really thought about this, but it's actually very strange – paradoxical, even. Thirty years after this meeting took place the expedition left for Resurgam, which means the rumour was correct after all.' She nodded at Sylveste, embroiled in heated discussion with her seated image. 'But back then nobody knew about the Amarantin! So what in hell's name gave him the idea to go to Resurgam in the first place?'

'He must have known he'd find something there.'

'Yes, but where did that information come from? There were automated surveys of the system prior to his expedition, but none of them were thorough. As far as I know, none of them scanned the planetary surfaces close enough to find evidence that there'd once been intelligent life on Resurgam. Yet Sylveste knew.'

'Which makes no sense.'

'I know,' Volyova said. 'Believe me, I know.'

At which point she joined her twin next to the stump and leant so close to the image of Sylveste that Khouri could see the reflection of his unwavering green eyes in the smoky facets of her goggles. 'What did you know?' she asked. 'More to the point, how did you know?'

'He isn't going to tell you,' Khouri said.

'Maybe not now,' Volyova said. And then smiled. 'But before very long it'll be the real one sitting there. And then we may get some answers.'

As she was speaking, her bracelet began to emit a sonorous chiming. The sound was unfamiliar, but it obviously connoted alarm. Above, without any fuss, the synthetic daylight turned blood-red and began to pulse in rhythm with the chiming.

'What's that?' Khouri asked.

'An emergency,' Volyova said, holding the bracelet close to her jaw. She snatched the retinal-projection goggles from her face and studied a little display inset into the bracelet. It was also pulsing red, in perfect time with the sky and the chiming. Khouri could see words trickling onto the display, but not clearly enough to read them.

'What sort of emergency?' Khouri breathed, wary of disturbing the woman's attention. Though she had not noticed their departure, the trio had vanished quietly back into whatever portion of the ship's memory had tricked them to life.

Volyova looked up from the bracelet, face quite pale. 'One of the cache-weapons.'

'Yes?'

'It's arming itself.'

ELEVEN

Approaching Delta Pavonis, 2565

They were running down a curving corridor, one that led from the glade towards the nearest radial elevator shaft.

'What do you mean?' Khouri shouted, straining to be heard above the klaxon. 'What do you mean it's arming itself?'

Volyova wasted no breath replying, not until they had reached the waiting elevator car, and she had ordered the thing to shuttle them straight to the nearest spinal-trunk elevator shaft, ignoring all the usual acceleration limits. When the car began to move she and Khouri were rammed back into its glass walling, almost knocking what wind they had left from their chests. The car's interior lights were pulsing red; Volyova could feel her heart starting to pulse in sympathy. But somehow she managed to talk.

'Exactly what I said. There are systems monitoring each cache-weapon – and one has just detected a power-surge in its weapon.'

Volyova did not add that the reason she had installed those monitors in the first place was because of the weapon which had appeared to move. Ever since, she had clung to the hope that the move had been imagined – a hallucination brought on by the loneliness of her vigil – but she now knew that it had been nothing of the sort.

'How can it arm itself?'

The question was perfectly reasonable. It was one for which Volyova had a decided absence of glib answers.

'I'm just hoping the glitch is in the monitoring systems,' she said, if only to be saying something. 'Not the weapon itself.'

'Why would it be arming itself?'

'I don't know! Haven't you noticed I'm not exactly taking this calmly?'

The axial lift decelerated abruptly, transitioning to the trunk shaft with a series of nauseous lurches. Then they were dropping quickly, so fast that their apparent weight dwindled almost to nothing.

'Where are we going?'

'The cache chamber, of course.' Volyova glared at the recruit. 'I don't know what's going on, Khouri, but whatever it is, I want visual confirmation. I want to see what the damned things are actually doing.'

'It arms itself, what else can it do?'

'I don't know,' Volyova said, as calmly as possible. 'I've tried all the shutdown protocols – nothing worked. This isn't exactly a situation I anticipated.'

'But surely it can't deploy? It can't actually find a target and go off?'

Volyova glanced down at her bracelet. Maybe the readings were going haywire; maybe there really had been a glitch in the watchdog systems. She hoped that was the case, because what the bracelet was telling her now was very bad news indeed.

The cache-weapon was moving.

Falkender was true to his word: the operations he performed on Sylveste's eyes were seldom pleasant and frequently much worse, with occasional forays into absolute agony. For days now Sluka's surgeon had been exploring the envelope of his skill, promising to restore such basic human functions as colour perception and the ability to sense depth and smooth movement, but not quite convincing Sylveste that he had the means or the expertise to do so. Sylveste had told Falkender that the eyes had never been perfect in the first place; Calvin's tools had been too limited for that. But even the crude vision which Calvin had given him would have been preferable to the insipidly coloured, flicker-motion parody of the world through which he now moved. Not for the first time, Sylveste found himself doubting that the discomfort of the repair was likely to be justified by the results.

'I think you should give up,' he said.

'I fixed Sluka,' Falkender said, a lividly coloured laminate of flat, man-shaped apertures dancing into Sylveste's visual field. 'You're no great challenge.'

'So what if you restore my vision? I can't see my wife because Sluka won't let us be together. And a cell wall's a cell wall, no matter how clearly you see it.' He stopped as waves of pain lashed his temples. 'Matter of fact, I'm not sure it isn't better being blind. At least that way you don't have reality rammed down your optic nerve every time you open your eyes.'

'You don't have eyes, Doctor Sylveste.' Falkender twisted something, sending pink pain-rosettes into his vision. 'So stop feeling sorry for yourself, please; it's most unbecoming. Besides, it's possible you won't have to stare at these particular walls for very much longer.'

Sylveste perked up.

'Meaning what?'

'Meaning things may soon start moving, if what I've heard is halfway to the truth.'

'Very informative.'

'I've heard that we may soon have visitors,' Falkender said, punctuating his remark with another stab of pain.

'Stop being cryptic. When you say "we", which faction do you mean? And what kind of visitors?'

'All I've heard is rumour, Doctor Sylveste. I'm sure Sluka will tell you in good time.'

'Don't count on it,' Sylveste said, who happened to be under no illusions as to his usefulness from Sluka's point of view. Since the time of his arrival in Mantell he had come to the forcible conclusion that Sluka was retaining him only because he offered her some transient entertainment; that he was some fabulous captured beast of dubious use but undoubted novelty. It was not at all clear that she would ever confide in him regarding any matter of true seriousness – and even if she did, it would be for only one of two reasons: either because she wanted something other than a wall to talk to, or because she had devised some new means of tormenting him verbally. More than once she had spoken of putting him to sleep until she thought of a use for him. 'I was right to capture you,' she would say. 'And I'm not saying you don't have your uses – they're just not immediately apparent to me. But I don't see why anyone else should be allowed to exploit you.' From that point of view, as Sylveste had soon realised, it mattered little to Sluka whether or not she kept him alive. Alive, he provided her with some amusement – and there was always the possibility he might become more useful to her in the future, as the colony's balance of power shifted. But, equally, it would not greatly inconvenience her to have him killed now. At least that way he would never become a liability; could never turn against her.

Eventually there came an end to the tenderly administered agonies, a passage into calmer light and almost plausible colours. Sylveste held his own hand before his gaze and turned it slowly, absorbing its solidity. There were furrows and traceries embossed into his skin which he had almost forgotten, yet it could not be more than tens of days – a few weeks – since he had been blinded in the Amarantin tunnel system.

'Good as new,' Falkender said, placing his tools back into their wooden autoclave. The strange, ciliated glove went last of all; as Falkender peeled it from his womanly fingers, it twitched and spasmed like a beached jellyfish.

'Get some illumination here,' Volyova said into her bracelet as the elevator entered the cache chamber.

Weight rushed back as the box slowed to a halt. Immediately they had to squint as the chamber lights glared on, shining on the enormous, cradled shapes of the weapons.

'Where is it?' Khouri asked.

'Wait,' Volyova said. 'I have to get my orientation.'

'I don't see anything moving.'

'Me neither . . . yet.'

Volyova was squashed flat against the glass side of the elevator, straining to peer around the corner of the weapon which bulked largest. Swearing, she made the elevator descend another twenty, thirty metres, then found the order which killed the pulsing red lighting and the interior klaxon.

'Look,' Khouri said, in the relative calm which followed. 'Is that something moving?'

'Where?'

She pointed, almost vertically downwards. Volyova squinted after her, then spoke into the bracelet again. 'Auxiliary lighting – cache chamber quadrant five.' Then to Khouri: 'Let's see what the *svinoi*'s up to.'

'You weren't really serious, were you?'

'About what?'

'A glitch in the monitoring systems.'

'Not really,' Volyova said, squinting even more as the auxiliaries came online, spotlighting a portion of the chamber far beneath their feet. 'It's called optimism – but I'm losing the hang of it fast.'

The weapon, Volyova said, was one of the planet-killers. She was not really sure how it functioned; still less exactly what it was capable of doing. But she had her suspicions. She had tested it years ago at the very lowest range of its destructive settings . . . against a small moon. Extrapolating – and she was very good at extrapolating – the weapon would have no trouble dismantling a planet even at a range of hundreds of AU. There were things inside it which had the gravitational signatures of quantum black holes, yet which, strangely, refused to evaporate. Somehow the weapon created a soliton – a standing-wave – in the geodesic structure of spacetime.

And now the weapon had come alive, without her bidding. It was gliding through the chamber, riding the network of tracks which would eventually deliver it to open space. It was like watching a skyscraper crawl through a city.

'Can we do anything?'

'I'm open to suggestions. What did you have in mind?'

'Well, you have to appreciate I haven't given this a hell of a lot of thought . . .'

'Say it, Khouri.'

'We could try blocking it.' Khouri's forehead was furrowed, as if, on top of all this, she was battling with a sudden migraine attack. 'You've got shuttles on this thing, haven't you?'

'Yes, but—'

'Then use one to block the exit. Or is that too crude for you?'

'Right now, the expression "too crude" isn't in my vocabulary.'

Volyova glanced at her bracelet. All the while the weapon was moving down the chamber wall, for all the world like an armoured slug retracing its own slime-trail. At the bottom of the chamber a vast iris was opening; the track led through the aperture into the dark chamber nested below this one. The weapon was almost level with the aperture.

'I can move one of the shuttles . . . but it'll take too long to get it outside the ship. I don't think we'd get there in time . . .'

'Do it!' Khouri said, every muscle in her face screaming tension. 'Piss around any more and we won't even have this option!'

Volyova nodded, regarding the recruit suspiciously. What did Khouri know about all this? She seemed less bewildered than

Volyova, although she also looked far more agitated than Volyova would have expected. But she had a point; the shuttle idea was worth a try, even though it was unlikely to succeed.

'We need something else,' she said, calling up the shuttle-control subpersona.

The weapon was halfway through the transfer iris, sliding into the second chamber.

'Something else?'

'In case this doesn't work. The problem's in the gunnery, Khouri – and maybe that's where we should attack it.'

She blanched. 'What?'

'I want you in the seat.'

While they dropped towards the gunnery, accelerating so hard that the floor inverted to become the ceiling – and Khouri's stomach felt like it had done something similar – Volyova whispered frantic, breathless instructions into her bracelet. It took a maddening few seconds to access the right subpersona, another few to bypass the safeguards which prevented unauthorised remote control of the shuttles. Still more to warm up the engines of one of the shuttles, and then longer still while the machine declamped from the docking restraints and vectored out of its holding bay, beyond the hull, handling – Volyova said – like the damn thing was still half asleep. The lighthugger was still under thrust, so the manoeuvre was doubly tricky.

'What worries me,' Khouri said, 'is what the weapon plans to do once it gets outside. Are we in range of anything?'

'Resurgam, conceivably.' Volyova raised her eyes from the bracelet. 'But maybe now it won't get a chance.'

The Mademoiselle chose that moment to blink into existence, somehow managing to accommodate herself within the elevator without intruding on the volume already claimed by Khouri and the Triumvir. 'She's wrong. This isn't going to work. I control more than just the cache-weapon.'

'Admitting it now, are you?'

'What's to deny?' The Mademoiselle smiled pridefully. 'You recall that I downloaded an avatar of myself into the gunnery? Well my avatar now controls the cache. Nothing I can do can influence her actions. She's as far beyond my reach as I am beyond the reach of my original self on Yellowstone.'

The elevator was slowing now, Volyova engrossed by the complex little readouts patterning her bracelet. A schematic holo showed the shuttle moving along the lighthugger's hull; a tiny remora nosing along the smooth flank of a basking shark.

'But you gave her orders,' Khouri said. 'You know what the hell she's up to, don't you.'

'Oh, her orders were very simple. If control of the gunnery placed at her disposal any systems which could quicken the completion of the mission, she was to make whatever arrangements were necessary to hasten that end.'

Khouri shook her head in abject disbelief.

'I thought you wanted me to kill Sylveste.'

'The weapon may now make that end achievable rather sooner than I anticipated.'

'No,' Khouri said, after the Mademoiselle's remark had had time to settle in. 'You wouldn't wipe out a planet just to kill one man.'

'Discovered a conscience all of a sudden, have we?' The Mademoiselle shook her head, lips pursed. 'You exhibited no qualms over Sylveste. Why should the deaths of others trouble you so much? Or is it simply a question of scale?'

'It's just . . .' Khouri hesitated, knowing what she was about to say would not trouble the Mademoiselle. 'Inhuman. But I don't expect you to understand that.'

The elevator halted, door opening to reveal the semi-flooded access way which led to the gunnery. Khouri took a moment to get her bearings. Ever since the descent had begun, she had been suffering the worst headache imaginable. It seemed to be lessening now, but she had no wish to dwell on what might have caused it.

'Quickly,' Volyova said, traipsing out.

'What you don't understand,' the Mademoiselle said, 'is why I would go to the trouble of destroying an entire colony just to ensure one man's death.'

Khouri followed Volyova, boots disappearing to the knees in the flood.

'Damn right I don't. And I'd try and stop you whether I did or not.'

'Not if you grasped the facts, Khouri. You'd actually be urging me on.'

'Then it's your fault for not telling me.'

They pushed through bulkhead seals, dead janitor-rats bobbing by as the water levels equalised, loosened from the little crannies where they had curled up to expire.

'Where's the shuttle?' Khouri called.

'Parked over the space-door,' Volyova said, turning back to look Khouri in the eye. 'And the weapon hasn't emerged yet.'

'Does that mean we won?'

'Means we haven't lost yet. But I still want you in the gunnery.'

The Mademoiselle had gone now, but her disembodied voice lingered, wrongly echoless in the cramped corridor.

'It won't do you any good. There's no system in the gunnery that I can't override, so your presence would be futile.'

'So why are you obviously so keen to talk me out of going in there?'

The Mademoiselle did not answer.

Two bulkheads further, they reached the ceiling access point which led to the chamber. They were running by that point, and it took a few moments for the water to stop sloshing up and down the angled sides of the corridor. When it did, Volyova frowned.

'Something's up,' she said.

'What?'

'Can't you hear it? There's a noise.' She angled her head. 'Seems to be coming from the gunnery itself.'

Khouri could hear it for herself now. It was a high-pitched mechanical sound, like ancient industrial machinery going haywire.

'What is it?'

'I don't know.' Volyova paused. 'At least, I hope I don't. Let's get inside.'

Volyova reached up and tugged at the overhead access door, budging it open, a small shower of ship-sludge loosening from its seals, spattering their shoulders. The alloy ladder descended, the industrial noise intensifying. It was clearly coming from the gunnery itself. The gunnery's bright internal lights were on, but they appeared to be unsteady, as if something were moving around up there interrupting the light-beams. Whatever it was was moving quickly as well.

'Ilia,' she said. 'I'm not sure I like this.'

'Join the club.'

Her bracelet chimed. Volyova was bending to examine it when

an almighty shudder rammed through the entire fabric of the ship. The two of them slipped into the floodwater, falling against the slippery corridor-sides. Khouri was struggling to her feet when a tiny tidal wave of viscous sludge upended her. She hit the deck. For a moment she was swallowing the stuff, the closest to eating shit since her army days. Volyova hooked her by the elbows, hauling her to her feet. Khouri gagged and spat out the sludge, though the awful taste lingered.

Volyova's bracelet was in scream-mode again.

'What the hell . . .'

'The shuttle,' Volyova said. 'We just lost it.'

'What?'

'I mean it just got blown up.' Volyova coughed. Her face was wet; she must have taken a good mouthful of the stuff herself. 'Far as I can tell, the cache-weapon didn't even have to push its way out. Secondary weapons did the job – turned on the shuttle.'

Above, the gunnery was still making frightening noises.

'You want me to go up there, don't you?'

Volyova nodded. 'Right now, getting you in the chair is the only option we have left. But don't worry. I'm right behind you.'

'Listen to her,' the Mademoiselle said, quite suddenly. 'All ready to have you do what she hasn't the guts to do herself.'

'Or the implants,' Khouri shouted, aloud.

'What?' Volyova said.

'Nothing.' Khouri planted one foot on the lowest rung. 'Just telling an old friend to go stuff herself.' Her foot slid off the slime-encrusted rung. Next attempt, she found something approximating a grip and planted her second foot on the same rung. Her head was poking into the little access tunnel which fed into the gunnery, no more than two metres above.

'You won't get in,' the Mademoiselle said. 'I'm controlling the chair. As soon as you put your head into the chamber, you lose it.'

'I'd love to see the look on your face, in that case.'

'Khouri, haven't you grasped things yet? The loss of your head would be no more than a minor inconvenience.'

Her head was just below the chamber entrance now. She could see the gimballed chair, moving in whiplash arcs through the chamber's volume. It had never been designed for such acrobatics; Khouri could smell the ozone of fried power-systems greasing the air. 'Volyova,' she called, shouting above the din. 'You built this set-up. Can you cut the power to the chair from below?'

'Cut power to the chair? Certainly – but what good would it do us? I need you linking in to the gunnery.'

'Not everything – just enough to stop the bastard moving around.'

There was a brief pause, during which Khouri imagined Volyova summoning ancient wiring diagrams to mind. The woman had constructed the gunnery herself – but it might have been decades and decades of subjective time ago, and something as vulgarly functional as the main power trunk had probably never needed to be upgraded since.

'Well,' Volyova said, eventually. 'There's a main feed line here – I suppose I could sever it . . .'

Volyova left, trudging quickly out of sight below. It sounded simple; severing the power feed. Maybe, Khouri thought, Volyova would have to fetch a specialised cutter from elsewhere. Surely there was not that much time. But no; Volyova had something. There was that little laser, the one she used to flense away samples from Captain Brannigan. She always carried it. Agonising seconds passed, Khouri thinking of the cache-weapon, easing slowly beyond the hull, entering naked space. By now it would be locking on target – Resurgam – going to final power-up, preparing to unleash a pulse of gravitational death.

Above, the noise stopped.

All was still, the light steady. The chair hung motionless within its gimbals, a throne imprisoned within an elegantly curved cage.

Volyova shouted, 'Khouri, there's a secondary power-source. The gunnery can tap it, if it senses a drain from the main feed. Means you might not have much time to reach the chair . . .'

Khouri sprang into the gunnery, heaving her body weight out of the hole in the floor. The slender alloy gimbals now looked sharper than before. She moved fast, monkeying through the feed lines, hopping under or above the gimbals. The chair was still static, but the closer she got, the less room she would have if the apparatus swung into motion again. If it happened now, she thought, the walls would be rapidly redecorated in sticky, coagulating red.

And then she was in. Khouri buckled, and the instant she closed the clasp, the chair whined and shot forwards. The gimbals rolled about her, swerving the chair backwards and forwards, upside down and sideways, until all sense of orientation was lost. The motion was neck-breaking, and Khouri felt her eyeballs bulging out of their sockets with each hairpin reversal – but the motion was surely less vicious than before.

She wants to deter me, Khouri thought, but not kill me . . . yet.

'Don't attempt to hook in,' the Mademoiselle said.

'Because it might screw up your little plan?'

'Not at all. Might I remind you of Sun Stealer? He's waiting in there.'

The chair was still bucking, but not so violently as to hinder conscious thought.

'Maybe he doesn't exist,' Khouri said, subvocalising. 'Maybe you invented him to have more leverage over me.'

'Go ahead then.'

Khouri made the helmet lower itself down over her head, masking the whirling motion of the chamber. Her palm rested on the interface control. All it would take was slight pressure to initiate the link; to close the circuit which would result in her psyche being sucked into the military data-abstraction known as gunspace.

'You can't do it, can you? Because you believe me. Once you open that connection, there's no going back.'

She increased the pressure, feeling the slight give as the control threatened to close. Then – either via some unconscious neuro-muscular twitch, or because part of her knew it had to be done, she closed the connection. The gunnery environment enfolded around her, as it had done in a thousand tactical simulations. Spatial data came first: her own body-image become nebulous, replaced by the lighthugger and its immediate surroundings, and then a series of hierarchical overlays conveying the tactical/strategic situation, constantly updating, self-checking its own assumptions, running frantic realtime-extrapolated simulations.

She assimilated.

The cache-weapon was holding station, several hundred metres away from the hull. Its prong was pointed in the direction of flight, straight towards Resurgam – allowing, Khouri knew, for the tiny relativistic light-bending effects caused by their moderate velocity. Near the space-door from which the weapon had emerged, the shuttle had left a black smear along the side of the hull. There were damage-points there; Khouri felt them as little pricks of discomfort, numbing as auto-repair systems phased in. Gravity sensors felt ripples emanating from the weapon; Khouri felt periodic – and quickening – breezes wash over her. The black holes in the weapon must be spinning up, orbiting quicker and quicker around the torus.

A presence sniffed her, not from outside, but from within the gunnery itself.

'Sun Stealer's detected your entry,' the Mademoiselle said.

'No problem.' Khouri reached out into gunspace, slipping abstract hands into cybernetically realised gauntlets. 'I'm accessing ship's defences. A few seconds is all I need.'

But something was wrong. The weapons felt differently from the way they had in simulation; unwilling to budge to her whims. Quickly she intuited: they were being fought over, and she was merely joining in the struggle.

The Mademoiselle – or rather, her avatar – was trying to block the hull defences, prevent them from being turned on the cache-weapon. The weapon itself was firmly out of Khouri's reach, veiled by numerous firewalls. But who – or what – was resisting the Mademoiselle, trying to bring those weapons to bear? Sun Stealer, of course. She could sense him now. Vast, powerful, but also intent on invisibility and slyness, careful to camouflage his actions behind routine data movements. For years that had worked, and Volyova had known nothing of his presence. But now Sun Stealer was driven to recklessness, like a crab forced to scuttle from one hideaway to another by the retreating tide. Nothing remotely human; no sense that this third presence in the gunnery was anything so mundane as another downloaded personality simulation; what Sun Stealer felt like was pure mentality, as if this data-representation was all that he had ever been; all that he ever would be.

It felt like absolutely nothing – but a locus of nothingness which had somehow achieved a terrifying degree of organisation.

Was she seriously contemplating joining forces with this thing?

Maybe. If that was what it took to stop the Mademoiselle.

'You can still back out,' the woman said. 'He's busy at the moment – can't spare his energies to invade you. But in a moment that won't be the case.'

Now the aiming systems were at least under her control,

although they operated sluggishly. She bracketed the cache-weapon, encasing the whole bulk in a potential sphere of annihilation. Now all that had to happen was for the Mademoiselle to surrender control of the weapons, if only for the microsecond necessary for them to slew, target and fire.

She felt them loosen. She – or rather, she and Sun Stealer – seemed to be winning.

'Don't do this, Khouri. You don't know what's at stake . . .'

'Then clue me in, bitch. Tell me what's so important.'

The cache-weapon was moving away from the hull, surely a sign that the Mademoiselle was worried about its safety. But the pulses of gravitational radiation were quickening, now coming almost too rapidly to separate. No guessing how long it would be before the cache-weapon fired, but Khouri suspected it could only be seconds away.

'Listen,' the Mademoiselle said. 'You want the truth, Khouri?'

'Damn right I do.'

'Then you'd better brace yourself. You're about to get the whole thing.'

And then – as soon as she had adjusted to being sucked into gunspace – she felt herself being sucked somewhere else entirely. The odd thing was that it seemed to be a part of herself she had until that moment completely overlooked.

They were on a battlefield, surrounded by the chameleoflaged bubbletents, the temporary enclosures of some hospital or forward command post. The sky above the compound was azure, cloud-streaked, but littered with dirty, intermingling vapour trails. It was as if some world-spanning squid were spilling its viscera into the stratosphere. Sowing the trails, and darting between them, were numerous arrow-winged jet aircraft. Lower, there were drone-dirigibles and, lower still, bulbous-bodied transport helicopters, tilt-wings and veetols, skimming the periphery of the compound, occasionally dropping to disgorge armoured personnel carriers or walking troops, ambulances or armed servitors. There was a scorched, grass-covered apron to one side of the compound, where six delta-winged, windowless aircraft were parked on skids, their upper surfaces precisely mimicking the sun-bleached hue of the ground, their VTOL irises open for inspection.

Khouri felt herself stumbling, falling towards the grass at her feet. She wore chameleoflage fatigues, currently emitting in dappled khaki. There was a lightweight projectile weapon in her hands, its alloy grip contour-moulded to match her palm. She was helmeted, a two-d readout monocle dangling down from the helmet's rim, showing a false-colour heat-map of the battlezone, telemetered from one of the dirigibles.

'This way, please.'

A whitehat was directing her into one of the bubbletents. Inside, an aide took her gun, ident-chipped it and racked it with eight other weapons, varying in firepower from projectile units like her own to medium-yield party-poopers and a ferocious shoulder-held ack-am weapon, something one would really not want to use on the same continent as one's adversary. The feed from the dirigibles fuzzed and vanished, occluded by the anti-surveillance shroud around the bubbletent. She reached up with her now free hand and flicked the monocle back over the helmet rim, raking a strand of sweaty hair away from her eye with the same movement.

'Through here, Khouri.'

They led her into a partitioned back area of the tent, through a room filled with bunkbeds, injured, and quietly humming med-servitors, craning over their patients like mechanised green swans. From outside she heard a shriek of jets, then a series of concussive explosions, but no one inside the tent seemed to even notice the sound.

Finally they let her into a tiny, square-walled room outfitted with a single desk. The walls were draped with the transnational flags of the Northern Coalition and there was a large bronze-mounted globe of Sky's Edge on one corner of the desk. The globe was currently in geological mode, showing only the varying landmasses and terrain-types on the surface, rather than the hotly contested political boundaries. But Khouri paid it no more than cursory attention, because what snared her attention was the person sitting behind the desk, in full military dress: cross-buttoned olive-drab tunic, gold epaulettes, a conspicuous panoply of NC medals ranked across his chest, his black hair slicked back in brilliant grooves.

'I'm sorry,' Fazil said. 'That it had to happen this way. But now that you're here . . .' He motioned across the room. 'Have a seat; we need to talk. Rather urgently, as it happens.'

Khouri recalled, distantly, another place. She remembered a

chamber, metallic, containing a seat, but while there was some-thing about the memory that made her nervous – as if time were precious – it felt unreal compared to the present, which was this room. Fazil absorbed her attention totally. He looked exactly as she remembered him (remembered him from where, she wondered?), although his cheek bore evidence of a scar she did not recall, and he had grown a moustache, or at least (she could not be sure) changed something about the one he had worn last time; thickened it or allowed it to grow out from simply thick black stubble, to the point where it now had the onset of a rakish droop on either side of his upper lip.

She did as he had suggested, easing herself into a folding chair.

'She – the Mademoiselle – worried that it might come to this,' Fazil said, his lips barely moving, or seeming to move, beneath the moustache. 'So she took certain measures. While you were still on Yellowstone, she implanted a series of closed-access memories. They were tagged to activate – to become accessible to your conscious mind – only when she deemed them useful.' He reached across the desk and spun the globe, allowing it to whir before stopping it abruptly. 'As a matter of fact, the process of unlocking those memories began some while ago. Do you remember a slight migraine attack in the elevator?'

Khouri grasped for some anchor-point; some objective reality she could place her trust in.

'What is this?'

'A convenience,' Fazil said. 'Woven partially out of existing memory patterns the Mademoiselle appropriated and found use-ful. This meeting, for instance – isn't it a little like how we first met, darling? That time in the ops unit on Hill Seventy-Eight, in the central provinces campaign, before the second red-peninsula offensive? You'd been sent to me because I needed someone for an infiltration mission; someone with knowledge of the unshielded SC-controlled sectors. We made a great team, didn't we? In more ways than one.' He fondled his moustache and tapped the globe again. 'Of course, I didn't – or rather she didn't – bring you here just to reminisce. No; the mere fact that this memory has been accessed means that certain truths have to be revealed to you. The question is, are you ready for them?'

'Of course I'm . . .' Khouri trailed off. What Fazil was saying made no sense, but she was being troubled by that memory of the other place; of the brutal chair in the metallic room. She had the feeling something was unresolved there – even, possibly, in the process of being resolved. She felt that, wherever that room was, she was meant to be there, adding her weight to the struggle. Whatever that struggle concerned, she had the sense that there was not much time left, and certainly not enough for this diversion.

'Oh, don't worry about that,' Fazil said, appearing to read her mind. 'None of this is really taking place in realtime; not even the accelerated realtime of the gunnery. Haven't you ever had it happen to you that someone wakes you abruptly from a dream, and yet somehow their actions were incorporated into the dream's narrative, long before they actually woke you? You know what I mean: your dog licks your face to wake you, and in your dream you fall overboard from a ship into the sea. Yet you'd been on that ship for the entirety of the dream.' He paused. 'Memory, Khouri. Memory being laid down instantaneously. The dream felt real, but it was created in an instant when the dog began licking your face. Back-constructed. You never actually lived through it. It's the same with these memories.'

Fazil's mention of the gunnery had crystallised the concept of the room. More than ever she felt as if she had to be back there, engaging in a struggle. The details of it still escaped her, it seemed very important that she rejoin it.

'The Mademoiselle,' Fazil continued, 'could have selected any venue from your past, or manufactured one from scratch. But she felt that – in some way – it would assist matters if you were put in a frame of mind where the discussion of military matters seemed natural.'

'Military matters?'

'Specifically, a war.' He smiled then, causing the tips of his moustache to angle momentarily upwards, like a demonstration of the engineering principles of a cantilever bridge. 'But not one you're likely to have ever read about. No; I'm afraid it happened rather too long ago for that.' He stood without warning, pausing to straighten his tunic, tugging down the belt. 'It might help if we adjourned to the briefing room, actually.'

TWELVE

The briefing room into which Fazil escorted Khouri was unlike any she had ever visited. It was clearly far too large for the bubbletent to have ever held it. And while Khouri had experienced many projection devices, none of them would have been capable of displaying the thing that was now being presented to her. It covered the entire floor, across a space about twenty metres wide, and was circumnavigated by a metal-railinged walkway.

It was a map of the entire galaxy.

And what made it impossible that the map could ever have been projected by the devices with which she was familiar was one simple fact. Looking at it, she apprehended – saw, and, somehow noted – every single star in the galaxy, from the coolest, barely fusing brown dwarf up to the brightest, transient white-hot supergiant. And it was not just that every star in the galaxy was there to be noticed, if her gaze chanced upon it. It went beyond that. It was, simply, that the galaxy was knowable in one glance. She was assimilating it in its entirety.

She counted the stars.

There were four hundred and sixty-six billion, three hundred and eleven million, nine hundred and twenty-two thousand, eight hundred and eleven of them. As she watched, one of the white supergiants expired in a supernova, so she revised her count down by one.

'It's a trick,' Fazil said. 'A codification. There are more stars in the galaxy than there are cells in the human brain, so for you to know them all would tie up an undesirable fraction of your total connective memory. Which doesn't mean that the sensation of omniscience can't be simulated, of course.'

The galaxy was in fact too perfectly detailed to really be described as a map. Not only had every star been accorded due prominence – colours, sizes, luminosities, binary associations, positions and space velocities all represented with absolute fidelity – but there were also star-forming regions, wispish, gently glowing veils of condensing gas, in which were embedded the hottening embers of embryo suns. There were newly formed stars surrounded by disks of protoplanetary material, and – where she cared to apprehend them – planetary systems themselves, ticking round their central suns like microscopic orreries, at a vastly accelerated rate. There were also aged stars which had ejected shells of their own photospheres into space, enriching the tenuous interstellar medium: the basic protoplasmic reservoir from which future generations of stars, worlds and cultures would eventually be created. There were regular or irregular supernova remnants, cooling as they expanded and shed their energy to the interstellar medium. Sometimes, at the heart of one of these stellar death-events, she observed a newly forged pulsar, emitting radio bursts with ever-slowing but stately precision, like the clocks in some forgotten imperial palace which had been wound one final time and would now tick until they died, the time between each tick lengthening towards some chill eternity. There were also black holes in the hearts of some of these remnants, and one massive (though now dormant) one at the heart of the galaxy, surrounded by an attendant shoal of doomed stars which would one day spiral into its event-horizon and fuel an apocalyptic burst of X-rays as they were ripped asunder.

But there was more to this galaxy than astrophysics. As if a new layer of memories had been quietly overlaid over her previous ones, Khouri found herself knowing something more. That the galaxy was teeming with life; a million cultures dispersed pseudo-randomly across its great slowly rotating disk.

But this was the past – the deep, deep past.

'Actually,' Fazil said, 'somewhere in the region of a billion years ago. Given that the Universe is only about fifteen times older than that, that's quite a hefty chunk of time, especially on the galactic timescale.' He was leaning over the railinged walkway next to her, as if they were a couple pausing to stare at their reflections in a dark, bread-strewn duckpond. 'To give you some perspective, humanity didn't exist a billion years ago. In fact, neither did the dinosaurs. They didn't get around to evolving until less than two hundred million years ago; a fifth of the time we're dealing with here. No; we're deep into the Precambrian here. There was life on Earth, but nothing multicellular – a few sponges if you were lucky.' Fazil looked at the galaxy representation again. 'But that wasn't the case everywhere.'

The million or so cultures (although she could be infinitely precise about the number, it suddenly struck her as childishly pedantic to do so, like specifying one's age to the nearest month) had not all arisen at the same time, nor they did all hang around for the same length of time. According to Fazil (though she understood it on some basic level) it had taken until four billion years ago for the galaxy to reach the required state at which intelligent cultures could begin to arise. But once that point of minimal galactic maturity had been reached, the cultures had not all suddenly appeared in unison. It had been a progressive emergence of intelligence, some cultures having arisen on worlds where, for one reason or another, the pace of evolutionary change was slower than the norm, or life's ascendancy was subject to more than the usual quota of catastrophic setbacks.

But eventually – two or three billion years after life had first arisen on their homeworlds – some of these cultures had become spacefaring. When that point was reached, most cultures expanded rapidly into the galaxy, although there were always a few stay-at-homes who preferred to colonise only their own solar systems, or sometimes even just their own circum-planetary environments. But generally the pace of expansion was rapid, with a mean drift rate between one tenth and one hundredth of the speed of light. That sounded slow, but was in fact blindingly fast, given that the galaxy was billions of years old and only a hundred thousand light-years wide. Unrestricted, any of these spacefarers could have dominated the entire galaxy in the totally inconsequential time of a few tens of millions of years. And maybe if it had happened like that – a neatly imperialist domination by one power – things would have been very different.

But instead, the first culture had been at the slower end of the expansionist speed-range, and had impacted on the expansion wave of a second, younger upstart. And while younger, the second civilisation was not technologically inferior to the first, nor less capable of mustering aggression when it was required. There was what – for want of a better word – one might describe as a galactic war; a sudden sparking friction where these two swelling empires brushed against one another, grinding like vast flywheels. Soon, other ascendant cultures were embroiled in the conflict. Eventually – to one degree or another – several thousand spacefaring civilisations fell into the fray. They had many names for it, in the thousand primary languages of the combatants. Some of these names could not easily be translated into any meaningful human referent. But more than one culture called it something which might – with due allowance for the crudities of interspecies communication – be termed the Dawn War.

It was a war encompassing the entire galaxy (and the two smaller satellite galaxies which orbited the Milky Way) – one which consumed not just planets, but whole solar systems, whole star systems, whole clusters of stars, and whole spiral arms. She understood that evidence of this war was visible even now, if one knew where to look. There were anomalous concentrations of dead stars in some regions of the galaxy, and still-burning stars in odd alignments; husked components of weapons-systems light-years wide. There were voids where there ought to have been stars, and stars which – according to the accepted dynamics of solar-system formation – ought to have had worlds, but which lacked them: only rubble, cold now. The Dawn War had lasted a long, long time – longer even than the evolutionary timescale of the hottest stars. But on the timescale of the galaxy, it had indeed been mercifully brief; a transforming spasm.

It was possible that no culture emerged intact; that none of the players who entered the Dawn War actually emerged, victorious or otherwise. The lengthscale of the war, while short by galactic time, was nonetheless hideously long by species-time. It was long enough for species to self-evolve, to fragment, to coalesce with other species or assimilate them, to remake themselves beyond recognition, or even to jump from organic to machine-life substrates. Some had even made the return trip, becoming machine, then returning to the organic when it suited their purposes. Some had sublimed, vanishing from the theatre of the war entirely. Some had converted their essences to data and found immortal storage in carefully concealed computer matrices. Others had self-immolated.

Yet in the aftermath, one culture emerged stronger than the others. Possibly they had been a fortunate small-time player in the main fray, now rising to supremacy amongst the ruins. Or possibly they were the result of a coalition, a merging of several battle-weary species. It hardly mattered, and they themselves probably had no hard data on their absolute origin. They were – at least then – a hybrid machine-chimeric species, with some residual vertebrate traits. They did not bother giving themselves a name.

'Still,' Fazil said, 'they acquired one, whether they liked it or not.'

Khouri looked at her husband. As he had been relating to her the story of the Dawn War, she had come to a kind of understanding about where she was, and the unreality of it all. What Fazil had said about the Mademoiselle had finally connected with some lingering memory of the true-present. She remembered the gunnery room clearly now, and knew that this place, this tampered-with shard of her past – was no more than an interlude. And this was not properly Fazil, though – because he had been resurrected from her memories – he was at least as real as the Fazil she recalled.

'What were they called?' she asked.

He waited before answering, and when he did, it was with almost theatrical gravity. 'The Inhibitors. For a very good reason, which will shortly become apparent.'

And then he told her, and she knew. The knowledge crashed home, vast and impassive as a glacier, something she could never begin to forget. And she knew something else, which was, she supposed, the whole point of this exercise. She understood why Sylveste had to die.

And why – if it took the death of a planet to ensure his death – that was an entirely reasonable price to pay.

Guards came just as Sylveste was falling into shallow dreams, exhausted by the latest operation.

'Wake up, sleepy-head,' said the taller of the two, a stocky man with a drooping grey moustache.

'What have you come for?'

'Now that would spoil the surprise,' said the other guard, a weasely individual hefting a rifle.

The route along which they took him was clearly intended to disorientate, its convolutions too frequent to be accidental. Quickly they succeeded in their aim. The sector where they arrived was unfamiliar; either an old part of Mantell extensively refurbished by Sluka's people, or else a completely new set of tunnel workings dug since the occupation. For a moment he wondered if he were being moved permanently to a differerent cell, but that seemed unlikely – they had left his other clothes in the first room, and had only just changed the bedsheets. But Falkender had spoken of the possibility of his status altering, in connection with the visitors he had mentioned, so maybe there had been a sudden change of plan.

But there been no change of plan, as he soon discovered.

The room where they left him was no less Spartan than his own; a virtual duplicate down to the same blank walling and food hatch; the same crushing sense that the walls were infinitely thick, reaching endlessly back into the mesa. So similar, in fact, that for a moment he wondered if his senses had deceived him, and all that had happened was the guards had frogmarched him in a loop which eventually returned to his own place of imprisonment. He would not have put it past them . . . and at least it was exercise.

But as soon as he had absorbed the room's contents fully, he knew it was not his own. Pascale was sitting on her bed – and when she glanced up, he could tell she was just as astonished as Sylveste.

'You've got an hour,' the moustachioed guard said, patting his partner on the back.

And then he closed the door, Sylveste having already entered the room without their bidding.

The last time he had seen her, she had been wearing the wedding dress; her hair sculpted in brilliant purple waves, entoptics adorning her like an army of attendant fairies. He might as well have dreamt that. Now she wore overalls, as drab and shapeless as those Sylveste himself was dressed in. Her hair was a lank black bowl, eyes rouged by sleeplessness or bruising, possibly both. She looked thinner and smaller than he remembered – probably because she was hunched over, bare feet hooked under her calves, and the room's whiteness seemed so large.

He was unable to remember a time when she had looked more fragile or beautiful; when it had been harder to believe that she was his wife. He thought back to the night of the coup, when she had waited in the dig with her patient, probing questions; questions which would later open a wound into the very core of who he was; what he had done and was capable of doing. It seemed very strange indeed that a confluence of events had brought them together, in this loneliest of rooms.

'They kept telling me you were alive,' he said. 'But I don't think I ever really believed them.'

'They told me you'd been hurt,' Pascale said, her voice quiet, as if she dared not shatter a dream by speaking aloud. 'They wouldn't say what – and I didn't want to ask too much – in case they told me the truth.'

'They blinded me,' Sylveste said, touching the hard surface of his eyes; the first time he had done so since the surgery. Instead of the little nova of pain to which he had become accustomed there was only a vague fog of discomfort which faded as soon as he removed his fingers.

'But you can see now?'

'Yes. As a matter of fact you're the first thing it's been worth having sight for.'

And then she rose from the bed, slipping into his arms, hooking a leg round his own. He felt her lightness and delicacy; was almost afraid to return her embrace in case he crushed her. Yet he drew her nearer, and she reciprocated, seemingly just as nervous of damaging him, as if the two of them were spectres uncertain of each other's reality. They held each other for what seemed like many more hours than the one they had been allocated; not because time dragged, but because for now time was unimportant; it was in abeyance, and it seemed as if it could be held that way by the act of will alone. Sylveste drank in the vision of her face; her eyes found something human even in the blankness of his own. There had been a time when Pascale had lacked the courage to look at him face-on, let alone stare into his eyes – but that time had long passed. And for Sylveste, gazing into Pascale's eyes had never been difficult, since she need never be aware of his scrutiny. Now, though, he wished she could tell when he was staring; wished her the vicarious pleasure of knowing that he found her intoxicating.

Soon they were kissing, and then they slumped awkwardly to the bed. In a moment they were free of their Mantell clothes, shucking them in drab heaps beside the bed. Sylveste wondered if they were being observed. It seemed possible – likely even. It also seemed possible not to care. For now – for as long as this hour lasted – he and Pascale were absolutely alone; the room's walls really infinite; the room the only open enclosure in the whole universe. It was not the first time they had made love, though the previous occasions had been rare indeed; in those few instances when the opportunity for privacy had arisen. Now – the thought almost made Sylveste laugh – they were married, and there was even less need for any subterfuge. And yet here they were again, once more snatching what intimacy they could. He felt an edge of guilt, and for a long time he wondered where it came from. Eventually, as they lay together, his head buried softly in her chest, he realised why he felt that way. Because there was so much to speak about, and instead they had squandered their time in the fevered archaeology of their bodies. But it had to be that way, Sylveste knew.

'I wish there was longer,' he said, when his sense of time had returned to something like normality, and he began to wonder how much of the hour remained.

'The last time we spoke,' Pascale said, 'you told me something.'

'About Carine Lefevre, yes. It was something I had to tell you, do you understand? It sounds ridiculous, but I thought I was going to die. I had to tell you; tell anyone. It was something I'd kept inside me for years.'

Pascale's thigh was a cool pressure against his own. She drew her hand across his chest, mapping it. 'Whatever happened out there, there's no way I or anyone else can begin to judge you.'

'It was cowardice.'

'No, it wasn't. Just instinct. You were in the most terrifying place in the universe, Dan, don't forget that. Philip Lascaille went there without a Juggler transform – look what happened to him. That you stayed sane at all was a kind of bravery. Insanity would have been a lot easier on you.'

'She could have lived. Hell, even leaving her to die the way I did – even that would have been acceptable if I'd had the courage to tell the truth about it afterwards. That would have been some atonement; God knows she deserved better than to be lied about, even after I'd killed her.'

'You didn't kill her; the Shroud did.'

'I don't even know that.'

'What?'

He leant on his side, momentarily pausing to study Pascale. Before, his eyes could have frozen her image for posterity. But that feature no longer functioned.

'What I mean is,' Sylveste said, 'I don't even know she died out there – I mean, not at first. I survived, after all – and I was the one

245

who lost the Juggler transform. Her chances would have been better, though not by much. But what if she came through it, the way I did? What if she found a way to stay alive, but just couldn't communicate her presence to me? She might have drifted halfway to the edge of the Shroud before I came round. After I'd repaired the lighthugger, I never thought to look for her. It never crossed my mind she might still be alive.'

'For a very good reason,' Pascale said. 'She wasn't. You can question what you did now, but back then intuition told you she was dead. And if she didn't die – she'd have found a way to get in touch with you.'

'I don't know that. I never can.'

'Then stop dwelling on it. Or else you'll never escape the past.'

'Listen,' he said, thinking of something else Falkender had said. 'Do you ever speak to anyone apart from the guards? Like Sluka, or anyone like that?'

'Sluka?'

'The woman who's holding us here.' Sylveste realised with a yawning sensation that they had told her next to nothing. 'There isn't time for me to explain in anything but the simplest terms. The people who killed your father were True Path Inundationists, as near as I can tell, or at least one offshoot of the movement. We're in Mantell.'

'I knew it had to be somewhere outside Cuvier.'

'Yes, and from what they told me Cuvier has been attacked.' He held back from telling her the rest, which was that the city had most probably been rendered uninhabitable above ground. She did not have to know that – not just yet, when it was the only place she had ever known properly. 'I'm not really sure who's running it now – whether people loyal to your father, or a rival group of True Pathers. The way Sluka tells it, your father didn't exactly welcome her with open arms once he'd gained control of Cuvier. Seems there was enough enmity there for her to arrange his assassination.'

'That's a long time to hold a grudge.'

'Which is why Sluka is possibly not the most stable person on this planet. Actually, I don't think capturing us figured in her plans – but now she's got us, she isn't quite sure what to do. Clearly we're too potentially valuable to discard ... but in the meantime—'

Sylveste paused. 'Anyway, something may be about to change. The man who fixed my eyes told me there was a rumour about visitors.'

'Who?'

'My question as well. But that's as much as he said.'

'It's tempting to speculate, isn't it?'

'If anything was likely to change things on Resurgam, it would be the arrival of Ultras.'

'It's a bit soon for Remilliod to return.'

Sylveste nodded. 'If there really is a ship coming in, you can bet it isn't Remilliod. But who else would want to trade with us?'

'Maybe trade isn't what they've come for.'

Possibly it was a sign of arrogance, but Volyova was not physically capable of letting someone else do her work, no matter how absurd the alternative. She was perfectly happy – if happy was the word – to let Khouri sit in the gunnery and do her best at shooting the cache-weapon out of the sky. She was also willing to admit that using Khouri was the only sensible option available. But that did not mean that she was prepared to sit calmly by and await the outcome. Volyova knew herself too well for that. What she needed – what she craved – was some way to attack the problem from another angle.

'*Svinoi*,' she said, because, no matter how hard she tried, an answer obdurately failed to pop into her mind. Every time she thought she had hit on an approach, a way to circumvent the weapon's progress, another part of her mind had already jumped ahead and found some impasse further down the logical chain. It was, in a way, a testament to the fluidity of her thought that she was able to critique her own solutions as soon as they came to mind; in fact, almost before she became consciously aware of them. But it also felt – maddeningly – as if she was doing her level best to sabotage her own chances of success.

And now there was this aberration to deal with.

She called it that now, because the word served to contain the mélange of incomprehension and disgust she felt whenever she forced her mind onto the topic. The topic was whatever was going on inside Khouri's head. And, now that Khouri was immersed in the abstracted mental landscape of gunspace, the aberration necessarily included the gunnery itself, and by extension Volyova, since it was her handiwork. She was monitoring the situation closely, via neural readouts on her bracelet. There was quite a storm going on in that woman's skull; no doubt about it. And the storm was extending troubled, flickering tendrils into gunspace.

Volyova knew that, somehow, all of this had to be related. The whole problem with the gunnery, from the beginning: Nagorny's madness, the Sun Stealer business, and latterly the self-activation of the cache-weapon. Somehow, also, the storm in Khouri's head – the aberration – also fitted in with things. But knowing that a solution existed, or at the very least an answer – a unifying picture which would explain everything – did not help at all.

Perhaps the most annoying aspect was that, even in a moment like this, part of her mind was dwelling on that problem, not giving itself over fully to the more pressing issue at hand. Volyova felt as if her brain consisted of a room full of precocious schoolchildren: individually bright, and – if only they would pool themselves – capable of shattering insights. But some of those schoolchildren were not paying attention; they were staring dreamily out of the window, ignoring her protestations to focus on the present, because they found their own obsessions more intellectually attractive than the dull curriculum she was intent on dispensing.

A thought budged to the front of her mind; a recollection. It concerned a series of firewall systems she had installed in the ship, upwards of four decades earlier by shiptime. She had intended that they be called into use as a final countermeasure against incursion by subversive viruses. It had not occurred to her that they would ever really be needed, and most certainly not under circumstances like this.

But all the same, she remembered them.

'Volyova,' she said, almost gasping, into her bracelet, straining to tug the requisite commands from her memory. 'Access counter-insurgent protocols; lambda-plus severity, maximum battle-readiness concurrence and counter-check to be assumed, full autonomous denial-suppression, criticality-nine Armageddon defaults, red-one-alpha security-bypass, all Triumvirate privileges invoked at all levels; all non-Triumvirate privileges rescinded.' She collected her breath; hoping that the string of incantations had opened enough doors for her into the heart of the ship's operational matrix. 'Now,' she said. 'Retrieve and run the executable coded Palsy.' To herself she muttered, 'And do it damned quickly!'

Palsy was the program which initiated the sealing of the firewalls she had installed. She had written Palsy herself – but it was so long ago that she barely remembered what Palsy did, or how much of the ship Palsy was liable to affect. It was a gamble – she wanted to immobilise enough to inconvenience the cache-weapon, but most certainly not enough to hamper her own attempts at stopping it.

'*Svinoi, svinoi, svinoi . . .*'

Error-messages were scrolling across her bracelet. They were telling her, very helpfully, that the various systems which Palsy had attempted to access and disable were no longer within Palsy's remit; they were out-of-bounds to the program's interference. Most of them, anyway – especially the deeper ship systems. If Palsy had functioned correctly, it would have had the same general effect on the ship as a blow on the head had to a human being – massive shut-down of all nonessential systems, and a general collapse into a state of recuperative immobility. Real damage would have been done, but mostly on a superficial level, and of a sort that Volyova would have been able to fix, disguise or invent lies about before the other crewmembers were awakened. But Palsy had worked differently. If likened to a human affliction, what the ship had suffered was more akin to an episode of mild paralysis immobilising only the epidermal layers, and then only partially. That was not at all in accordance with Volyova's plans.

But, she realised, it would have immobilised the autonomous hull weapons, those which were not directly slaved to the gunnery and which had already blown up the shuttle. Now at least she could try the same gambit again. Of course, the weapon would have advanced further now; there was no longer an option of simply obstructing it. But if she could at least get another shuttle out into space, certain possibilities presented themselves.

A second or so later, her optimism had been shattered into a few dismal crumbs of dejection. Maybe Palsy had been meant to work this way, or maybe in the intervening forty years various ship-systems had become tangled up and interconnected, so that Palsy killed certain parts Volyova had never meant it to touch . . . but, for whatever reason, the shuttles were inoperative, locked out by firewalls. She tried, perfunctorily, the usual Triumvirate-level bypass commands, but none of them worked. Hardly surprising: Palsy had set up physical breaks in the command network, chasms that no amount of software intervention could possibly bridge. To get the shuttles online, Volyova would have to physically reset all those breaks – and to do that, she would have to find the map she had made, four decades earlier, of the installations. That would entail, conservatively, several days' work.

Instead, she had minutes in which to act.

She was sucked into – not so much a pit of despondency, as a bottomless, endlessly plummeting gravitational well. But, when she had dropped deep into its maw – and several of those precious minutes had elapsed – she remembered something; something so obvious she should have thought of it long before.

Volyova began running.

Khouri crashed back into the gunnery.

A quick check on the status-clocks confirmed what Fazil had promised her, which was that no real time had passed. That was some trick; she really felt as if she had spent the best part of an hour in the bubbletent, when in fact the whole experience had just been laid down a fraction of a second earlier. She had lived through none of it, but that was almost impossible to accept. Yet she could not now relax – events had been frantic enough even before the memories had been triggered. The situation had not lost any of its urgency.

The cache-weapon must be nearly ready to blow now: its gravitational emissions were no longer detectable by the ship, like a whistle which had passed into the ultrasonic. Maybe the weapon was already able to fire. Was the Mademoiselle actually holding back? Was it important to her that Khouri come over to her side? If the weapon failed, Khouri would again be her only means of acting.

'Relinquish,' the Mademoiselle said. 'Relinquish, Khouri. You must realise by now that Sun Stealer is something alien! You're assisting it!'

The mental effort involved in subvocalising was almost too much for her now.

'Yeah, I'm quite prepared to believe that it's alien. The trouble is, what does that make you?'

'Khouri, we don't have time for this.'

'Sorry, but now seems as good a time as ever to get this into the open.' While she communicated her thoughts, Khouri kept up her side in the struggle, though part of her – the part that had been swayed by what she had been shown in the memories – implored her to give up; to let the Mademoiselle assume total control of the cache-weapon. 'You led me into thinking Sun Stealer was something Sylveste brought back from the Shrouders.'

'No; you saw the facts and jumped to the only logical conclusion.'

'Did I hell.' Khouri found new strength now, though it remained insufficient to tip the balance. 'All along, you were desperate to turn me against Sun Stealer. Now, that may or may not have been justified – maybe he is an evil bastard – but it does beg a question. How would you know? You wouldn't. Not unless you were alien yourself.'

'Assuming – for the moment – that that were the case—'

Something new snared Khouri's attention. Even given the severity of the battle she was waging, this new thing was sufficiently important for her to relax momentarily; allocating some additional part of her conscious mind to assess the situation.

Something else was joining the fray.

This newcomer was not in gunspace; it was not another cybernetic entity, but a physical object, one which until now had not been present – or at least not noticed – in the arena of battle. At the moment Khouri had detected it, it was very close to the lighthugger; dangerously close by her reckoning – in fact, so close that it seemed to be physically attached, parasitic.

It was the size of a very small spacecraft, its central mass no more than ten metres from end to end. It resembled a fat, ribbed torpedo, sprouting eight articulated legs. It was walking along the hull of the ship. Most miraculously, it was not being shot at by the same defences which had destroyed the shuttle.

'Ilia . . .' Khouri breathed. 'Ilia, you aren't seriously thinking—' And then, a moment later, 'Oh shit. You were, weren't you?'

'What foolishness,' the Madmemoiselle said.

The spider-room had detached itself from the hull, each of its eight legs releasing its grip simultaneously. Since the ship was still decelerating, the spider-room seemed to fall forwards with increasing speed. Ordinarily, so Volyova had said, the room would have fired its grapples at that point, to reestablish contact with the ship. Volyova must have disabled them, because the room kept falling, until its thrusters kicked in. Although Khouri was perceiving the scene via many different routes, and in some modes which would not have been assimilable to someone lacking the gunspace implants, a small aspect of that sensory stream was devoted to the optical, relayed from the external cameras on the ship. Via that channel she saw the thrusters burn violet-hot, jetting from pinprick-apertures around the midsection of the spider-room, where the torpedo-shaped body was attached to the turret from which sprouted the now purchaseless legs. The glare underlit the legs, picking them out in rapid strobing flashes as the room adjusted its fall, negated it and began to heave-to alongside the ship once more. But Volyova did not use the thrusters to bring the room within grasping range. After loitering for a few seconds, the room fell laterally away, accelerating towards the weapon.

'Ilia . . . I really don't think—'

'Trust me,' the Triumvir's voice replied, cutting into gunspace as if she were speaking from halfway across the universe, not merely a few kilometres from Khouri's position. 'I've got what you might charitably refer to as a plan. Or at the very least an option on going out fighting.'

'I'm not sure I liked the last bit.'

'Me neither, in case you were wondering.' Volyova paused. 'Incidentally, Khouri, when all this is over – assuming we both survive all of this, which I admit isn't exactly guaranteed at this juncture . . . I rather think we ought to set aside time for a little chat.'

Maybe she was talking to blank out the fear she must be feeling. 'A little chat?'

'About all of this. The whole problem with the gunnery. It might also be a chance for you to ease yourself of any . . . niggling little burdens you might have been well advised to share with me much earlier.'

'Like what?'

'Like who you are, for a start.'

The spider-room covered the distance to the weapon rapidly, using its thrusters to slow down, but still holding station relative to the ship, maintaining a standard one-gee aft burn. Even with its legs splayed, the spider-room was less than a third the size of the cache-weapon. It looked less like a spider now, and more like a hapless squid, about to vanish into the maw of a slowly cruising whale.

'That's going to take more than a little chat,' Khouri said, feeling

– with, she suspected, no little justification – that there was really no point holding much back from Volyova any more.

'Good. Now excuse me for a moment; what I'm about to try is somewhat on the tricky side of downright impossible.'

'She means suicidal,' the Mademoiselle said.

'You're enjoying all this, aren't you?'

'Immensely – more so given that I have no control over anything that transpires.'

Volyova had positioned the spider-room near the projecting spike of the cache-weapon, although she was too far from it for the wriggling mechanical legs to gain a scramblehold on the pitted surface. In any case, the weapon was moving around now, oscillating slowly and randomly from side to side with fierce bursts of its own thrusters, seemingly trying to evade Volyova's approach, but restricted in its movements by its own inertia – just as if the mighty hell-class weapon was scared of a tiny little spider. Khouri heard four rapid pops, almost too closely spaced to discriminate, as if a projectile weapon had emptied its chamber.

She watched as four grapple lines whipped out from the body of the spider-room, impacting silently with the cache-weapon's spike. The grapples were penetrators; designed to burrow a few tens of centimetres into their target before widening, so once they had bitten home there was no possibility of their breaking loose. The guy lines were illuminated by the arcing thrusters, taut now, and the spider-room was already hauling itself in, even though the weapon had kept up its ponderous evasions.

'Great,' Khouri said. 'I was all ready to shoot the bastard – now what do I do?'

'You get a chance, you shoot,' Volyova said. 'If you can focus the blast away from me, I'll take my chances – this room's better armoured than you'd think.' A moment's silence, then: 'Ah, good. Got you, you vicious piece of junk.'

She had the legs of the spider-room wrapped around the spike now. The weapon appeared to have given up all hope of dislodging her, and perhaps with good reason: it struck Khouri that Volyova had not achieved much, despite her valiant attempt. In all probability, the cache-weapon was not going to be greatly hindered by the arrival of the spider-room.

The struggle for control of the hull weapons had, meanwhile, resumed in earnest. Occasionally Khouri felt them budge slightly, the Mademoiselle's systems momentarily losing the battle, but these tiny slippages were never enough to allow Khouri to target and deploy. And if Sun Stealer was assisting her, she did not feel it, although possibly that absence of presence was simply an artefact of his extreme cunning. Perhaps if Sun Stealer had not been there, she would have lost the battle completely, and – freed of this diversion – the Mademoiselle would already have unleashed whatever it was that the weapon held. Right now the distinction felt rather irrelevant. She had just noticed what it was that Volyova was doing. The spider-room's thrusters were firing in concert now, resisting the thrust that the larger but clumsier weapon was applying.

Volyova was dragging the weapon downship, towards the spewing blue-white radiance that was the lighthugger's nearest thrust-beam. She was going to kill the damned thing by taking it into the searing exhaust of the Conjoiner drive.

'Ilia,' Khouri said. 'Are you sure this is . . . considered?'

'Considered?' This time there was no mistaking the woman's clucking laughter, even though it sounded institutional. 'It's the most ill-considered thing I've ever done, Khouri. But right now I don't see many alternatives. Not unless you get those guns online damn quickly.'

'I'm . . . working on it.'

'Well work on it some more and stop bothering me. In case it hadn't occurred to you, I've got rather a lot on my mind right now.'

'Her whole life flashing before her eyes, I should imagine.'

'Oh, you again.' Khouri ignored the Mademoiselle, realising by now that her interjections served the sly purpose of distracting her; that by doing so she was indeed interfering in the course of the battle; not nearly so ineffective a bystander as she maintained.

Volyova had now less than five hundred metres to go before she dragged the cache-weapon into the flames. It was putting up a fight, thrusters going haywire, but its overall thrust capacity was less than that of the spider-room. Understandable, Khouri thought. When its designers had conceived the ancillary systems which would be required to move and position the device, the idea that it would also have to fend for itself in a wrestling match had probably not been uppermost in their minds.

'Khouri,' Volyova said, 'in about thirty seconds I'm going to release the *svinoi*. Assuming my sums are right, no amount of corrective thrust will be able to stop it drifting into the beam.'

'That's good, isn't it?'

'Well, sort of. But I feel I ought to warn you . . .' Volyova's voice faded in and out of clarity, reception compromised by the broiling energies of the propulsion beam, which she was now approaching at distances not usually considered wise for the organic. 'It's occurred to me that even if I succeed in destroying the cache-weapon . . . some part of the blast – something exotic, perhaps – might get sent back up the drive beam, into the propulsion core.' A pause that was definitely intentional. 'If that happens, the results might not be . . . optimal.'

'Well, thanks,' Khouri said. 'I appreciate the morale-building.'

'Damn,' Volyova said, quietly and calmly. 'There's a slight flaw in my plan. The weapon must have hit the spider-room with some kind of defensive EM-pulse; either that or the radiation from the drive is interfering with the hardware.' There was the sound – possibly – of someone making repeated attempts to throw antique metal switches on a console. 'What I mean,' Volyova said, 'is that I don't seem to be able to break free. I'm stuck to the bastard.'

'Then shut off the damned drive – you can do that, can't you?'

'Of course; how do you think I killed Nagorny?' But she didn't sound optimistic. '*Nyet* – I'm locked out of the drive; must have blocked my intercession pathways when I ran Palsy . . .' She was practically gabbling now. 'Khouri, this is getting a tiny bit desperate . . . if you have those weapons . . .'

The Mademoiselle spoke now, sounding appropriately smug. 'She's dead, Khouri. And at the angle you'd now have to fire, half those weapons would be disabled to prevent them inflicting damage on the ship. You'll be lucky to scorch the cache-weapon's hull with what remains.'

She was right – almost without Khouri noticing, whole blocks of potentially available armament had safed themselves, since she was now requesting them to point dangerously close to critical ship components. What remained were the lightest armaments, almost by definition incapable of doing any serious damage.

Perhaps sensing this, something relented.

The weapons were suddenly more under Khouri's control than not, and – she realised – the fact that the remaining systems were limited in their firepower was actually to her advantage. Her plan had changed. What she needed now was surgical precision, not brute force.

In the hiatus, before the weapons were regained by the Mademoiselle, Khouri ditched the prior target pattern and issued re-aiming orders. Her instructions were specific in the extreme. Now, oozing into position as if immersed in toffee, the weapons aligned themselves on the impact points she had selected. Not the cache-weapon now, but something else entirely . . .

'Khouri,' the Mademoiselle began, 'I really think you should consider this . . .'

But by then Khouri had already fired.

Gouts of plasma streamed out towards the cache-weapon connecting – not with the weapon itself, but with the spider-room, neatly severing all eight of its legs, and then all four of its grapple-lines. The room flung itself away from the lancing spear of the drive, its legs truncated abruptly at the knees.

The cache-weapon drifted into the beam, like a moth brushing into an incandescent lamp.

What happened thereafter took place in an inhumanly brief series of instants; almost too rapid for Khouri to comprehend until afterwards. The physical exterior of the cache-weapon evaporated in a millisecond, boiling away in a gasp of predominantly metallic vapour. It was impossible to tell whether it was the touching of the beam which led to what followed, or whether, at the instant of its destruction, the cache-weapon was already committed to the act of turning itself inside out.

Either way, things did not proceed quite as its builders had intended.

Simultaneously – or as near as mattered – what was left of the cache-weapon beneath its eviscerated hide emitted a prolonged gravitational eruction, a burp of shearing spacetime. Something very horrible was happening to the fabric of reality in the immediate vicinity of the weapon, but not in the way which had been planned. A rainbow of bent starlight flickered around the curdling mass of plasma-energy. For a millisecond the rainbow was approximately spherical and stable, but then it began to wobble, oscillating unevenly like a soap-bubble on the point of bursting. A fraction of a millisecond later, it collapsed inwards, and accelerating exponentially, vanished.

For another moment there was nothing left, not even debris, just the normal star-speckled backdrop of space.

Then a glint of light appeared, shading to ultraviolet. The glint magnified and swelled, bloating into an intense, malignant sphere. The wave of expanding plasma hit the ship, juddering it so violently that Khouri felt the impact even with the cushioning gimbals of the gunnery. Data rushed in, telling her – not that she was particularly keen on knowing – that the blast had not seriously compromised any hull-based systems, and that the brief spike of background radiation from the flash was within tolerable norms. Gravimetric scans had abruptly returned to normal.

Spacetime had been punctured, penetrated at the quantum level, releasing a minuscule glint of Planck energy. Minuscule, that is, compared with the normally seething energies present in the spacetime foam. But beyond normal confinement that negligible release had been like a nuke going off next door. Spacetime had instantly healed itself, knitting back together before any real damage was done, leaving only a few surplus monopoles, low-mass quantum black holes and other anomalous/exotic particles as evidence that anything untoward had happened.

The cache-weapon had malfunctioned, badly.

'Oh, very good,' the Mademoiselle said, sounding more disappointed than anything. 'I hope you're proud of what you've done.'

But what had Khouri's attention now was the absence streaking towards her, rushing through gunspace. She tried to back out in time; tried to disengage the link—

But she was not quite fast enough.

THIRTEEN

Resurgam Orbit, 2566

'Seat,' Volyova said, entering the bridge.

A chair craned eagerly towards her. She buckled herself in and then gunned the seat away from the bridge's tiered walls, until she was orbiting the enormous holographic projection sphere which occupied the room's middle.

The sphere was showing a view of Resurgam, although one might have easily concluded that it was really the desiccated eyeball of an ancient and mummified corpse, magnified several hundred times. But Volyova knew that the image was more than just an accurate portrayal of Resurgam dredged from the ship's database. It was being imaged in realtime; captured by the cameras which were even now pointing down from the lighthugger's hull.

Resurgam was not a beautiful planet, by anyone's standards. Apart from the sullied white of the polar caps, the overall colour was a skullish grey, offset by scabs of rust and a few desultory chips of powder-blue near the equatorial zones. The larger oceanic water masses were still mostly cauled under ice, and those motes of exposed water were almost certainly being artificially warmed against freeze-over; either by thermal energy grids or carefully tailored metabolic processes. There were clouds, but they were wispy plumes rather than the great complex features Volyova knew one could usually expect from planetary weather systems. Here and there they thickened towards white opacity, but only in small gangliar knots near the settlements. Those were the places where the vapour factories were working, sublimating polar ice into water, oxygen and hydrogen. There were few patches of vegetation large enough to be seen without magnification down to kilometre-resolution, and by the same token no obvious visible evidence of human presence, save for a sprinkling of settlement lights when the planet's nightside rolled around every ninety minutes. Even with the zoom, the settlements were elusive, since – with the exception of the capital – they tended to be sunk into the ground. Often, very little projected beyond the surface apart from antennae, landing pads and air-smoothed greenhouses. Of the capital . . .

Well, that was the disturbing part.

'When does our window with Triumvir Sajaki open?' she asked, snapping her gaze across the faces of the other crewmembers, whose seats were arranged in a loosely defined cluster, facing each other beneath the ashen light of the imaged planet.

'Five minutes,' Hegazi said. 'Five tortuous minutes and then we'll know what delights dear Sajaki has to share with us regarding our new colonist friends. Are you sure you can bear the agony of waiting?'

'Why don't you have a guess, *svinoi*?'

'That wouldn't be much of a challenge, would it?' Hegazi was grinning, or at least trying very hard to approximate the gesture; no mean feat given the amount of chimeric accessories which encrusted his face. 'Funny, if I didn't know you better, I'd say you weren't exactly enthralled by any of this.'

'If he hasn't found Sylveste . . .'

Hegazi raised a gauntleted hand. 'Sajaki hasn't even made his report yet. No sense jumping the gun . . .'

'You're confident he'll have found him, then?'

'Well, no. I didn't say that.'

'If there's one thing I hate,' Volyova said, looking coldly at the other Triumvir, 'it's mindless optimism.'

'Oh, cheer up. Worse things happen.'

Yes, she had to admit, they did. And with an annoying regularity, they seemed to have decided to keep happening to her. What was astonishing about her recent run of misfortune was that it had managed to keep escalating with each new bout of bad luck. It had reached the point where she was beginning to look back nostalgically on the merely irksome problems she had encountered with Nagorny; when all she had to deal with was someone trying to kill her. It made her wonder – without a great deal of enthusiasm – if there would soon come a day when she would look back even on this period with longing.

The trouble with Nagorny had been the precursor, of course. It was obvious now; at the time she had regarded the whole thing as an isolated incident, but what it had really been was just the initial indications of something far worse in the future, like a heart murmur presaging an attack. She had killed Nagorny – but in doing so, she had not come to any understanding of the problem that had driven him psychotic. Then she had recruited Khouri, and the problems had not so much repeated themselves as reiterated a grander theme, like the second movement of a grim symphony. Khouri was not obviously mad – yet. But she had become a catalyst for a worse, less localised madness. There had been the storms in her head, beyond anything Volyova had ever seen. And then there had been the incident with the cache-weapon, which had almost killed Volyova, and might have gone on to kill all of them, and perhaps a significant number of the people on Resurgam as well.

'It's time for some answers, Khouri,' she had said, before the others were revived.

'Answers about what, Triumvir?'

'Forget the charade of innocence,' Volyova said. 'I'm far too tired for it, and I assure you I will get to the truth one way or the other. During the crisis with the cache-weapon, you gave too much away. If you were hoping I would forget some of the things you said, you were mistaken.'

'Like what?' They were down in one of the rat-infested zones; it was, Volyova reckoned, as safe from Sajaki's listening devices as any area of the ship save the spider-room itself.

She shoved Khouri against the wall, hard enough to knock some wind out of the woman; letting her know Volyova's wiry strength should not be underestimated, nor her patience stretched too far. 'Let me make something clear to you, Khouri. I killed Nagorny, your predecessor, because he failed me. I successfully concealed the truth of his death from the rest of the crew. Be under no illusions that I will do the same to you, if you give me sufficient justification.'

Khouri pushed herself back from the wall, regaining some colour. 'What is it you want to know, exactly?'

'You can start by telling me who you are. Begin with the assumption that I know you are an infiltrator.'

'How can I be an infiltrator? You recruited me.'

'Yes,' Volyova said, for she had already thought this through. 'That was the way it was made to seem, of course . . . but it was deception, wasn't it? Whatever agency is behind you managed to manipulate my search procedure, making it seem as if I had selected you . . . whereas the choice was ultimately not mine at all.' Volyova had to admit to herself that she had no direct evidence to support this, but it was the simplest hypothesis which fitted all the facts. 'So, are you going to deny this?'

'Why would you think I was an infiltrator?'

Volyova paused to light up a cigarette; one of those she had bought from the Stoners in the carousel where Khouri had been recruited, or found. 'Because you seem to know too much about the gunnery. You seem to know something about Sun Stealer . . . and that troubles me deeply.'

'You mentioned Sun Stealer shortly after you brought me aboard, don't you remember?'

'Yes, but your knowledge goes deeper than can be explained by the information you could have gleaned from me. In fact there are times when you seem to know somewhat more about the whole situation than I do.' She paused. 'There's more to it than that, of course. The neural activity in your brain, during reefersleep . . . I should have examined the implants you came aboard with more carefully. They obviously aren't all that they seem. Do you want to have a stab at explaining any of this?'

'All right . . .' Khouri's tone of voice was different now. It was clear that she had given up any hope of bluffing her way out of this one. 'But listen carefully, Ilia. I know you've got your little secrets, too – things you really don't want Sajaki and the others to find out about. I'd already guessed about Nagorny, but there's also the business with the cache-weapon. I know you don't want that to become common knowledge, or you wouldn't be going to such lengths to cover up the whole thing.'

Volyova nodded, knowing it would be fruitless to deny these things. Maybe Khouri even had an inkling of her relationship with the Captain. 'What are you saying?'

'I'm saying, whatever I say to you now, it had better stay between us. Isn't that reasonable of me?'

'I just said I could kill you, Khouri. You're not exactly in a strong bargaining position.'

'Yes, you could kill me – or at least have a go – but despite what you said, I doubt you'd manage to cover up my death as easily as you did Nagorny's. Losing one Gunnery Officer is bad luck. Two begins to look like carelessness, doesn't it?'

A rat scampered by, splashing them. Irritatedly, Volyova flicked her cigarette butt towards the animal, but it had already vanished through a duct in the wall. 'So you're saying I don't even tell the others I know you're an infiltrator?'

Khouri shrugged. 'You do what you like. But how do you think Sajaki would take that? Whose fault would it have been that the infiltrator ever came aboard in the first place?'

Volyova took her time before answering. 'You've got it all worked out, haven't you?'

'I knew you'd want to ask me some questions sooner or later, Triumvir.'

'So let's start with the obvious one. Who are you, and who are you working for?'

Khouri sighed and spoke with resignation. 'A lot of what you already know is the truth. I'm Ana Khouri and I was a soldier on Sky's Edge ... although about twenty years earlier than you thought. As for the rest ...' She paused. 'You know, I could really use some coffee.'

'There isn't any, so get used to it.'

'All right. I was in the pay of another crew. I don't know their names – there was never any direct contact – but they've been trying to get their hands on your cache-weapons for some time.'

Volyova shook her head. 'Not possible. No one else knows about them.'

'That's what you'd like to think. But you have used parts of the cache, right? There must have been survivors, witnesses, you never knew about. Gradually word got about that your ship was carrying some serious shit. Maybe no one knew the whole picture, but they knew enough of it to want to have their own slice of the cache.'

Volyova was silent. What Khouri was saying was shocking – like finding out that her most private of habits was public knowledge – but, she had to admit, not beyond the bounds of possibility. Conceivably there had been a leak. Crew had left the ship, after all – not always willingly – and while those who had done so were not supposed to have had access to anything sensitive – certainly nothing pertaining to the cache – there was always the chance that an error had been made. Or perhaps, as Khouri had said, someone had witnessed the cache being used and had lived to pass on that information.

'This other crew – you may not have known their names, but did you know what their ship was called?'

'. . . no. That would have been just as sloppy as letting me know who they were, wouldn't it?'

'What *did* you know, in that case? How were they expecting to steal the cache from us?'

'That's where Sun Stealer comes into it. Sun Stealer was a military virus they snuck aboard your ship when you were last in the Yellowstone system. A very smart, adaptive piece of infiltration software. It was designed to worm its way into enemy installations and wage psychological warfare on the occupants, driving them mad through subliminal suggestion.' Khouri paused, giving Volyova time to digest that. 'But your own defences were too good. Sun Stealer was weakened, and the strategy never really worked. So they bided their time. They didn't get another chance until you were back in the Yellowstone system, nearly a century later. I was the next line of attack: get a human infiltrator aboard.'

'How was the original viral attack made?'

'They got it in via Sylveste. They knew all about you bringing him aboard to fix up your Captain. They planted the software on him without him knowing, then let it infect your systems while he was hooked in to your medical suite, fixing the Captain.'

There was, Volyova thought, something deeply and worryingly plausible about that. It was just an example of another crew being as predatory as they were. It would be arrogance in the extreme to assume that only Sajaki's Triumvirate were capable of such subterfuge.

'And what was your function?'

'To assess the state of Sun Stealer's corruption of your gunnery systems. If possible, to gain control of the ship. Resurgam was a good destination for that – sufficiently out of the way not to be under any kind of system-wide police jurisdiction. If a takeover could be staged, there would be no one to observe it except maybe a few colonists.' Khouri sighed. 'But believe me, that plan's well and truly shit-canned. The Sun Stealer program was flawed; too dangerous and too adaptive. It drew too much attention to itself when it drove Nagorny mad – but on the other hand, he was the only one it could reach. Then it started screwing around with the cache itself . . .'

'The rogue weapon.'

'Yeah. That scared me, as well.' Khouri shivered. 'I knew Sun Stealer was too powerful by then. There was nothing I could do to control it.'

Over the next few days, Volyova would ask Khouri more questions, testing different aspects of her story against what passed for the known facts. Certainly, Sun Stealer could have been some kind of infiltration software . . . even if it was more subtle, more insidious, than anything she had heard of in all her years of experience. But did that mean she could dismiss it? No; of course not. After all, she knew the thing existed. Khouri's story, in fact, was the first explanation she had encountered that made any kind of objective sense at all. It explained why her attempts to cure Nagorny had failed. He had not been sent mad by any subtle combination of effects stemming from her gunnery implants. He had been driven mad, purely and simply, by an entity that had been designed for just that purpose. No wonder it had been so hard to find any explanation for Nagorny's problems. Of course, there remained the irksome question of why exactly Nagorny's madness had expressed itself so forcefully in the manner it had – all those fevered sketches of nightmarish birds' parts, and the designs on his coffin – but who was to say that Sun Stealer had not simply amplified some pre-existing psychosis, letting Nagorny's subconscious work with whatever imagery suited it?

The mysterious other crew could also not be dismissed too easily. Shipboard records revealed that another lighthugger – the *Galatea* – had been present in Yellowstone on both occasions when they had last visited the system. Could they have been the crew responsible for sending Khouri aboard?

For now, it was as good an explanation as any. And one thing was absolutely clear. Khouri was quite right in saying that none of this information could be presented to the rest of the Triumvirate. Sajaki would indeed blame Volyova totally for what was a grievous lapse in security. He would punish Khouri, of course . . . but Volyova could also expect some kind of retribution. The way their relationship had been strained of late, it was entirely possible that Sajaki would try and kill her. He might succeed, too – he was at least as strong as Volyova. It would not greatly trouble him that he would be losing his chief weapons expert and the only person who had any real insight into the cache. His argument would no doubt be that she had already demonstrated her incompetence in that regard. But there was something else, too: something Volyova could not entirely dismiss. No matter what had really transpired with the cache-weapon, the unavoidable truth was that Khouri had saved Volyova's life.

Hateful though the thought was, she owed the infiltrator.

Her only option, when she considered the situation dispassionately, was to proceed as if nothing had happened. Khouri's mission was in any case no longer viable; there would be no attempted takeover now. The woman's hidden reason for being aboard the ship had no impact on the upcoming attempt to bring Sylveste aboard again, and in many respects Khouri would be needed simply as a crewmember. Now that Volyova knew the truth, and now that the original purpose of Khouri's mission had been abandoned, Khouri would surely do everything in her power to fit into her pre-assigned position. It hardly mattered whether the loyalty treatments were working or not: Khouri would have to behave as if they were, and gradually the act would become indistinguishable from the truth. She might not even want to leave the ship when the opportunity arose to do so. After all, there were worse places to be. Over months or years of subjective time, she would become one of the crew, and her past duplicity could remain a secret shared only by her and Volyova. In time, it might even be something Volyova almost forgot.

Eventually, Volyova managed to convince herself that the infiltration question had been settled. Sun Stealer would remain a problem, of course – but now Khouri would be working with her to conceal it from Sajaki. And in the meantime, there were other things that needed to be concealed from the Triumvir. Volyova had set herself the task of eradicating every shred of evidence that the cache-weapon incident had ever happened. She had intended to do this before Sajaki and the others were revived, but it had not proved easy. Her first task had been to repair the damage to the lighthugger itself, patching the areas of the hull which had been hurt by the weapon's detonation. Largely this consisted of coaxing the auto-repair routines to work faster, but she also had to ensure that all pre-existing scars, impact-craters, or areas of imperfect repair were precisely duplicated. She then had to hack into the auto-repair memory and erase the knowledge that the repairs had been orchestrated at all. She had to repair the spider-room, even though Sajaki and the others were not meant to know it even existed. Better to be safe than sorry, though, and that had been by far the simplest of the repairs. Next, she had to erase all evidence that the Palsy routine had been run; at least a week's work.

The loss of the shuttle was much harder to hide. For a while, she considered making a new one: harvesting tiny amounts of raw materials from all over the ship, until she had what she needed. She would only have to use one ninety-thousandth of the entire mass of the ship. But it was too risky, and she doubted her ability to weather the shuttle authentically; to make it look as old as it should have been. Instead, she took the simpler option of editing the ship's database so that it would always look as if there had been one shuttle fewer aboard. Sajaki might notice – all the crew might notice – but there would be absolutely nothing that anyone could prove. Finally, of course, she remade the cache-weapon. It was only a façade; a replica designed to lurk in the cache chamber and look threatening on the rare occasions when Sajaki paid a visit to her domain. Covering her tracks took six days of manic work. On the seventh day she rested, and endeavoured to compose herself, so that none of the others would guess what labours she had been through. On the eighth day Sajaki had awakened and asked her what she had been up to in the years he had been in reefersleep.

'Oh,' she had said. 'Nothing to write home about.'

His reaction – like much else about Sajaki these days – had been difficult to judge. Even if she had succeeded this time, she thought, she could not risk another mistake. Yet, already – though they had not even made contact with the colonists – things were drifting beyond the arena of her understanding. Her thoughts returned to the neutrino signature she had detected around the system's neutron star, and of the feeling of unease which had been with her ever since. The source was still there, and while it remained weak, she had now studied it well enough to know that it was in orbit not just around the neutron star, but also around the moon-sized rocky world which attended the star. It had certainly not been present when the system had been surveyed decades earlier, immediately suggesting that it was something to do with the colony on Resurgam. But how could they have sent it? The colonists did not even seem capable of reaching orbit, let alone sending some kind of probe to the edge of their system. Even the ship which should have brought them here was missing; she had expected to find the *Lorean* in orbit around Resurgam, but there was no sign of it. Now, no matter what the evidence said, she kept in the back of her mind the possibility that the colonists might be capable of something completely unexpected. It was another burden to add to her mounting stockpile of worries.

'Ilia?' said Hegazi. 'We're almost ready now. The capital's about to emerge from nightside.'

She nodded. The ship's high-magnification cameras, dotted around the hull, would be zooming in on a very specific site several kilometres beyond the city boundary, focusing on a spot which had been identified and agreed upon before Sajaki's departure. If no misfortune had befallen him, he should now be waiting at that spot, standing on the upper surface of an unshielded mesa, looking directly towards the rising sun. Timing was critical here, but Volyova did not doubt that Sajaki would be on the mark.

'Got him,' Hegazi said. 'Image stabilisers phasing in . . .'

'Show us.'

A window opened in the globe near the capital, rapidly swelling. At first what lay within the window was unclear; a blurred smear that might have been a man standing on a rock. But the image quickly sharpened, until the figure was recognisably Sajaki. In place of the bulky adaptive armour which Volyova had last seen him wearing, Sajaki wore an ash-coloured overcoat, its long tails flapping around his booted legs, evidencing the mild wind playing over the mesa's topside. The suit's collar was drawn up around his ears, but his face was unobstructed.

It was not quite his own. Prior to leaving the ship, Sajaki's features had been subtly remoulded, according to an averaged ideal derived from the genetic profiles of the original expedition members who had travelled to Resurgam from Yellowstone, in turn reflecting the Franco-Sino genes of the Yellowstone settlers. Sajaki would arouse nothing more than a curious glance if he chose to walk through the capital's streets at midday. There was nothing to betray him as a newcomer, not even his accent. Linguistic software had analysed the dozen or so Stoner dialects carried by the expedition members, applying complex lexicostatistic models to merge these modes of speech into a new, planetwide dialect for Resurgam as a whole. If Sajaki chose to communicate with any of the settlers, his look, cover-story and manner of speaking would convince them that he was merely from one of the remoter planetary settlements, not an offworlder.

That at least was the idea.

Sajaki carried no technological implements which would give him away, save the implants beneath his skin. A conventional surface-to-orbit communication system would have been too susceptible to detection, and far too difficult to explain had he been captured for some reason or other. Yet now he was speaking; reciting a phrase repeatedly, while the ship's infrared sensors examined the bloodflow around Sajaki's mouth region, assembling a model of his underlying muscular and jaw movements. By correlating these movements against the extensive archives of actual conversation already recorded, the ship could begin to guess the sounds he was making. The final step was to include grammatical, syntactical and semantic models for the words Sajaki was likely to be saying. It sounded complex – it was – but to Volyova's ears there was no perceptible timelag between his lip movements and the simulated voice she was hearing, eerily clear and precise.

'I must presume you can now hear me,' he said. 'For the record, let this be my first report from the surface of Resurgam after landing. You will forgive me if I occasionally digress from the point, or express myself with a certain inelegance. I did not write this report down beforehand; it would have constituted too great a security risk if I were found with it while leaving the capital. Things are very different than we expected.'

True enough, Volyova thought. The colonists – or at least a faction of them – certainly knew that a ship had arrived around Resurgam. They had bounced a radar beam off it, surreptitiously. But they had made no attempt to contact *Infinity* – no more so than the ship had attempted to contact anyone on the ground. As much as the neutrino source, that worried her. It spoke of paranoia, and hidden intentions – and not just her own. But she forced herself not to think about that now, for Sajaki was still speaking, and she did not want to miss any of what he had to report.

'I have much to tell concerning the colony,' he said, 'and this window is short. So I will begin with the news you are undoubtedly waiting for. We have located Sylveste; now it is simply a matter of bringing him into our custody.'

*

268

Sluka was pushing coffee down her throat, sitting across from Sylveste with a black oblong table positioned between them. Early morning Resurgam sun was filtering into the room via half-closed jalousies, casting fiery contours across her skin.

'I need your opinion on something.'

'Visitors?'

'How astute.' She poured him a cup, offered the palm of her hand towards the chair. Sylveste sank down into the seat, until he was the lower of the two. 'Indulge my curiosity, Doctor Sylveste, and tell me exactly what you've heard.'

'I've heard nothing.'

'Then it won't take much of your time.'

He smiled through the fog of tiredness. For the second time in a day he had been awakened by her guards, dragged in a state of semi-consciousness and disorientation from his room. He still smelt Pascale, her scent cloaking him, and wondered if she was still sleeping in her own cell somewhere across Mantell. As lonely as he now felt, the feeling was tempered by the gladdening news that she was alive and unharmed. They had told him as much in the days before their meeting, but he had had no reason to believe Sluka's people were telling the truth. What use, after all, was Pascale to the True Pathers? Even less than he – and it was already clear enough that Sluka had been debating the value of retaining him alive.

Yet now, perceptibly, things were changing. He had been allowed time with Pascale, and he believed that this would not be the only occasion. Did this development stem from some basic humanity on Sluka's behalf, or did it imply something entirely different – perhaps that she might have need of one of them in the near future, and that now was the time when she had to begin winning favour?

Sylveste swigged the coffee, blasting away his residual tiredness. 'All I've heard is that there may be visitors. From then on I drew my own conclusions.'

'Which I presume you'd care to share with me.'

'Perhaps we could discuss Pascale for a moment?'

She peered at him over the rim of her cup, before nodding with the delicacy of a clockwork marionette. 'You're venturing an exchange of knowledge in return for – what? Certain relaxations in the regime under which you're held?'

'That wouldn't be unreasonable, I feel.'

'It would all depend on the quality of your speculations.'

'Speculations?'

'As to who these visitors might be.' Sluka glanced towards the slatted rising sun, eyes narrowed against the ruby-red glare. 'I value your point of view, though heaven knows why.'

'First you'd have to tell me what it is you know.'

'We'll come to that.' Sluka bit on a smile. 'First I should admit that I have you at something of a disadvantage.'

'In what way?'

'Who are these people, if they aren't Remilliod's crew?'

Her remark meant that his conversations with Pascale – and by implication everything that had gone on between them – had been monitored. The knowledge shocked him less than he would have expected. He had obviously suspected it must be so the whole time, but perhaps he had preferred to ignore his own qualms.

'Very good, Sluka. You ordered Falkender to mention the visitors, didn't you? That was quite clever of you.'

'Falkender was just doing his job. Who are they, then? Remilliod already has experience trading with Resurgam. Wouldn't it make sense for him to return here for a second bite?'

'Much too soon. He'll have barely had time to reach another system, let alone anything with trading prospects.' Sylveste freed himself of the chair's embrace, strolling to the slatted window. Through the iron jalousies he watched the northerly faces of the nearest mesas radiate cool orange, like stacked books on the point of bursting into flame. The thing he noticed now was the bluer tone of the sky; no longer crimson. That was because megatonnes of dust had been removed from the winds; replaced with water vapour. Or maybe it was a trick of his impaired colour perception.

Fingering the glass, he said, 'Remilliod would never return so quickly. He's among the shrewdest of traders, with very few exceptions.'

'Then who is it?'

'It's the exceptions I'm bothered about.'

Sluka called an aide to remove the coffee. With the table bare, she invited Sylveste back to his seat. Then she printed a document from the table and offered it to him.

'The information you're about to see reached us three weeks ago, from a contact in the East Nekhebet flare-watch station.'

Sylveste nodded. He knew about the flare-watches. He had pushed to set them up himself; small observatories dotted around Resurgam, monitoring the star for evidence of abnormal emission.

Reading was too much like trying to decipher Amarantin script: creeping letter by letter along a word until the meaning snapped into his mind. Cal had known that much of reading boiled down to mechanics – the physiology of eye movement along the line. He had built routines into Sylveste's eyes to accommodate this need, but it had not been within Falkender's gift to restore everything.

Still, this much was clear:

The flare-watch in East Nekhebet had picked up an energy pulse, much brighter than anything seen previously. Briefly, there was the worrying possibility that Delta Pavonis was about to repeat the flare which had wiped out the Amarantin: the vast coronal mass ejection known as the Event. But closer examination revealed that the flare did not originate from the star, but rather from something several light-hours beyond it, on the edge of the system.

Analysis of the spectral pattern of the gamma-ray flash indicated that it was subject to a small but measurable Doppler shift; a few per cent of the speed of light. The conclusion was inescapable: the flash originated from a ship, on the final phase of deceleration from interstellar cruising speed.

'Something happened,' Sylveste said, absorbing the news of the ship's demise with calm neutrality. 'Some kind of malfunction in the drive.'

'That was our guess as well.' Sluka tapped the paper with her fingernail. 'A few days later we knew it couldn't possibly be the case. The thing was still there – faint, but unmistakable.'

'The ship survived the blast?'

'Whatever it was. By then we were getting a detectable blueshift off the drive flame. Deceleration was continuing normally, as if the explosion had never happened.'

'You've got a theory for this, I presume.'

'Half of one. We think the blast originated from a weapon. What kind, we haven't a clue. But nothing else could have liberated so much energy.'

'A weapon?' Sylveste tried to keep his voice completely calm, allowing only natural curiosity to show, purging it of the emotions he really felt, which were largely variations on pure dread.

'Odd, don't you think?'

Sylveste leant forwards, a damp chill along his spine.

'These visitors – whoever they are, I presume they understand the situation here.'

'The political picture, you mean? Unlikely.'

'But they'd have attempted contact with Cuvier.'

'That's the funny thing. Nothing from them. Not a squeak.'

'Who knows this?'

His voice by now was almost inaudible, even to himself, as if someone were standing on his windpipe.

'About twenty people on the colony. People with access to the observatories, a dozen or so of us here; somewhat fewer in Resurgam City . . . Cuvier.'

'It isn't Remilliod.'

Sluka let the paper be reabsorbed by the table, its sensitive content digested away.

'Then do you have any suggestions as to who it might be?'

Sylveste wondered how close to hysteria his laugh sounded. 'If I'm right about this – and I'm not often wrong – this isn't just bad news for me, Sluka. This is bad news for all of us.'

'Go on.'

'It's a long story.'

She shrugged. 'I'm not going anywhere in a hurry. Nor are you.'

'Not for now, certainly.'

'What?'

'Just a suspicion of my own.'

'Stop playing games, Sylveste.'

He nodded, knowing there was no real point in holding back. He had shared the deepest of his fears with Pascale already, and for Sluka it would now be just a case of filling in the gaps; things which were unobvious from her eavesdropping. If he resisted, he knew, she would find a way to learn what she wished, either from him or – worse – Pascale.

'It goes back a long way,' he said. 'Way back, to the time when I'd just returned to Yellowstone from the Shrouders. You recall that I disappeared back then, don't you?'

'You always denied anything had happened.'

'I was kidnapped by Ultras,' Sylveste said, not waiting to observe her reaction. 'Taken aboard a lighthugger in orbit around Yellowstone. One of their number was injured, and they wanted me to . . . "repair" him, I suppose.'

'Repair him?'

'The Captain was an extreme chimeric.'

Sluka shivered. It was clear that – like most colonialists – her experience with the radically altered fringes of Ultra society had been confined largely to lurid holo-dramas.

'They were not ordinary Ultras,' Sylveste said, seeing no reason not to play on Sluka's phobias. 'They'd been out there too long; too long away from what we'd think of as normal human existence. They were isolated even by normal Ultra standards; paranoid; militaristic . . .'

'But even so . . .'

'I know what you're thinking – that, even if these were some outlandish offshoot culture, how bad could they be?' Sylveste deployed a supercilious smile and shook his head. 'That's exactly what I thought, at first. Then I found out more about them.'

'Such as?'

'You mentioned a weapon? Well, they have them. They have weapons which could comfortably dismantle this planet, should they wish.'

'But they wouldn't use them without reason.'

Sylveste smiled. 'We'll find out when they reach Resurgam, I think.'

'Yes . . .' Sluka said this last word on a falling note. 'Actually, they're already here. The explosion happened three weeks ago, but the – um – significance of it was not immediately clear. In the meantime they've decelerated and assumed orbit around Resurgam.'

Sylveste took a moment to regulate his breathing, wondering just how deliberate Sluka's piecewise revelation was. Had she really neglected to mention this detail – or had she spared it, disclosing the facts in a manner calculated to keep him permanently disorientated?

If so, she was succeeding admirably.

'Wait a minute,' Sylveste said. 'Just now you said only a few people knew about this. But how easy would it be to miss a lighthugger orbiting a planet?'

'Easier than you imagine. Their ship's the darkest object in the system. It radiates in the infrared, of course – it must do – but it seems able to tune its emissions to the frequencies of our atmospheric vapour bands; the frequencies which don't penetrate down to the surface. If we hadn't spent the last twenty years putting so much water into the atmosphere . . .' Sluka shook her head ruefully. 'In any case, it doesn't matter. Right now, no one's paying much attention to the sky. They could have arrived lit up in neon and no one would have noticed.'

'But instead they haven't even announced their presence.'

'Worse than that. They've done everything possible not to let us know they're here. Except for that damn weapon blast . . .' For a moment she trailed off, looking towards the window, before snapping her attention back to Sylveste. 'If these people are who you think, you must have an idea what it is they want.'

'That's easy enough, I think. What they want is me.'

Volyova listened intently to the rest of Sajaki's report from the surface. 'Very little information had reached Yellowstone from Resurgam; even less after the first mutiny. We now know that Sylveste survived the mutiny, but was ousted in a coup ten years later; ten years ago from the present date. He was imprisoned – in some luxury, I might add – at the expense of the new regime, who saw him as a useful political tool. Such a situation would have suited us extremely well, since Sylveste's whereabouts would have been easy to deduce. We would also have been in the fortunate position of being able to negotiate with people who might have had few qualms about turning him over to us. Now, however, the situation is immeasurably more complex.'

Sajaki paused at this point, and Volyova noticed that he had turned slightly, bringing a new background into view behind him. Their angle of sight was altering as they passed overhead and to the south, but Sajaki was aware of this and was making the necessary adjustments in his position to keep his face in view of the ship at all times. To an observer on one of the other mesas he would have looked strange indeed: a silent figure facing the horizon, whispering unguessable incantations, slowly pivoting on his heels with almost watchlike precision. No one could have guessed that he was engaged in one-way communication with an orbiting spacecraft, rather than lost in the observances of some private madness.

'As we ascertained as soon as we were in scan range, the capital Cuvier has been gutted by a number of large explosions. As we were also able to deduce by examining the degree of reconstruction, these events happened very recently on the colonial timescale. My investigations here have established that the second coup – when these weapons were used – took place barely eight months ago. However, the coup was not entirely successful. The old regime still control what remains of Cuvier, though their leader – Girardieau – was killed during the disturbance. The True Path Inundationists – those responsible for the attacks – control many of the outlying settlements, but they seem to lack cohesion, and may even have fallen into factional squabbles. In the week in which I have been here there have been nine attacks against the city, and some suspect internal saboteurs: True Path infiltrators working from within the ruins.' Sajaki collected his thoughts at this point, and Volyova wondered if he felt some distant kinship with the infiltrators he had mentioned. If so, there was not a hint of it in his expression.

'Concerning my own actions, my first task, of course, was to order the suit to dismantle itself. It would have been tempting to use it to make the journey overland to Cuvier, but the risk would have been excessive. Yet the journey was easier than I had feared, and on the outskirts I hitched a ride with a gang of pipeline technicians returning from the north, using them as cover to enter Cuvier. They were suspicious at first, but the vodka soon persuaded them to take me aboard their vehicle. I told them we distilled it in Phoenix, the settlement where I said I'd come from. They'd never heard of Phoenix, but they were more than happy to drink to it.'

Volyova nodded. The vodka – along with a satchel-full of trinkets – had been manufactured aboard ship shortly before Sajaki's departure.

'People mostly live underground now, in catacombs which were dug fifty or sixty years ago. Of course, the air is tolerably adapted for breathing, but you have my assurance that the procedure is not exactly comfortable, and one is never far away from the onset of hypoxia. The exertion which was required to reach this mesa was considerable.'

Volyova smiled to herself. If Sajaki even admitted such a thing, his ascent of the mesa must have been close to torture.

'They say that the True Pathers have access to Martian genetic technology,' he continued, 'which facilitates easier breathing, though I've seen nothing to prove this. My pipeline friends helped me find a room in a hostel used by miners from beyond the city, which of course fitted in perfectly with my cover story. I wouldn't describe the accommodation as salubrious, but it suited my purpose well enough, which was of course to gather data. In the course of my enquiries,' Sajaki added, 'I learnt much that was contradictory, or at best vague.'

Sajaki had now turned almost from horizon to horizon. The sun was now beyond his right shoulder, making his image increasingly difficult to interpret. The ship, of course, would simply switch to infrared, reading Sajaki's speech in the shifting blood-patterns of his face.

'Eyewitnesses say Sylveste and his wife managed to escape the assassination attempt which killed Girardieau, but they have not resurfaced since. That was eight months ago. The people I have spoken to, and the covert data sources I have intercepted, lead me to one conclusion. Sylveste is someone's prisoner again, except this time he is being held outside the city, probably by one of the True Path cells.'

Volyova was tense now. She could see where all this was leading: there had always been a kind of inevitability to it. The only difference was that in this case it stemmed from what she knew about Sajaki, rather than the man he sought.

'It would be futile to negotiate with the official powers here – whoever they are,' Sajaki said. 'I doubt that they could give us Sylveste even if they wanted to hand him over, which of course they wouldn't. Which unfortunately leaves us only one option.'

Volyova bridled. Here it was.

'We must arrange things so that it is in the best interests of the colony as a whole to give us Sylveste.' Sajaki smiled again, teeth flashing against the shadow of his face. 'Needless to say, I have already begun laying the necessary groundwork.' And now he really was addressing her directly, no doubt about it. 'Volyova; you may make the necessary formal overtures at your discretion.'

Ordinarily she might have felt some consolatory pleasure at having judged Sajaki's intentions so accurately. Not now. All she felt was a slow-burning horror, the realisation that, after all this time, he was going to ask her to do it again. And the worst component of her horror stemmed from the realisation that she would probably do what he wanted.

*

'Go on,' Volyova said. 'It won't bite.'

'I do know suits, Triumvir.' Khouri paused, and took a step into the room's whiteness. 'It's just I didn't think I'd see one again. Let alone get to actually wear the bastard.'

The four waiting suits rested against the wall in the oppressively white storage room, six hundred levels below the bridge, adjacent to Chamber Two, where the training session would take place.

'Listen to her,' one of the two other women present said. 'Talking as if she's going to do more than just wear the damn thing for a few minutes. It's not like you're going down with us, Khouri, so don't wet yourself.'

'Thanks for the advice, Sudjic – I'll bear it it in mind.'

Sudjic shrugged – a sneer would have been too much of an emotional expenditure, Khouri figured – and stepped towards her designated suit, followed by her companion, Sula Kjarval. Preparing to welcome their occupants, the suits resembled frogs which had been exsanguinated, eviscerated, dissected, stretched and pinned out on a vertical table. In their current configurations the suits were at their most androform, with well-defined legs and outstretched arms. There were no fingers on the 'hands' – for that matter, no obvious hands at all, simply streamlined flippers – although at the user's wish the suits could extrude the necessary manipulators and digits.

Khouri did indeed know suits, just as she had claimed. The suits on Sky's Edge had been rare imports, purchased from Ultra traders who made stopover around the war-torn planet. No one on the Edge had the expertise to actually duplicate them, which meant that those units which her side had bought were fabulously valuable: powerful totems dispensed from gods.

The suit scanned her, assessing her bodily dimensions before adjusting its own interior to precisely match her contours. Khouri then allowed it to step forward and surround her, suppressing the tinge of claustrophobia that accompanied the process. Within a few seconds the suit had locked tight and filled itself with gel-air, enabling manoeuvres which would otherwise have crushed its occupant. The suit's persona interrogated Khouri regarding small details she might wish changed, allowing her to customise her weapons suite and adjust its autonomous routines. Of course, none but the lightest weapons would actually be deployed in Chamber Two; the combat scenarios which were to be enacted would be a seamless mixture of real, physical action and simulated weapons-usage, but it was the point that counted. One had to treat every aspect of the enterprise with the utmost seriousness, including the limitless choices which the suit offered for the convenience of despatching any enemies who might have the misfortune to stray into its sphere of superiority.

There were three of them, apart from Khouri herself, but she was the only one who was not in serious contention for the surface operation. Volyova took the lead. Although her conversations with Khouri suggested that she had been born in space, she had visited planets on more than one occasion, and had acquired the appropriate, near-instinctive reflexes which bettered the chances of surviving a planetary excursion; not least amongst these being a profound respect for the law of gravitation. The same went for Sudjic; she had been born in a habitat, or possibly a lighthugger, but had visited enough worlds to gain the right moves. Her bladelike thinness, which made it look as if she could not possibly have taken a footstep on a large planet without breaking every bone in her body, did not fool Khouri for a moment; Sudjic was like a building designed by a master architect, who knew the precise stresses which had to be obeyed by every articulation and strut, and took an aesthetic pride in allowing for no additional tolerances. Kjarval, the woman who was always with Sudjic, was different again. Unlike her friend, she exhibited no extreme chimeric traits; all her limbs her own. But she resembled no human Khouri had ever known. Her face was sleek, as if optimised for some unspecified aquatic environment. Her catlike eyes were gridded red orbs with no pupils. Her nostrils and ears were rilled apertures, and her mouth was a largely expressionless slot; one that barely moved when the woman spoke, but was permanently curved in an expression of mild exaltation. She wore no clothes; not even in the relative cool of the suit storage room, yet to Khouri's eyes she did not seem truly naked. Rather, she looked like a naked woman who had been dipped in some infinitely flexible, quick-drying polymer. A true Ultra, in other words, of uncertain and almost certainly non-Darwinian provenance. Khouri had heard tales of bioengineered human splinter-species cultured under the ice of worlds like Europa, or of merpeople, bio-adapted for life in totally flooded spacecraft. Kjarval seemed to be the living, freakishly hybrid embodiment of these myths. Alternatively, she might be something else entirely. Maybe she had wrought these transformations on herself for a whim. Maybe they were purposeless, or served only the deeper purpose of masking another identity entirely. Whatever; she knew worlds, and that – seemingly – was all that mattered.

Sajaki knew worlds as well, of course, but he was already on Resurgam, and it was not clear what role he would play in the recovery of Sylveste, if and when it happened. Of Triumvir Hegazi Khouri knew little, but through chance remarks, she had gleaned enough to know that the man had never set foot on anything which had not been manufactured. It was no wonder that Sajaki and Volyova had relegated Triumvir Hegazi to the more clerical aspects of their profession. He would not be allowed – nor did he even wish – to make the journey to Resurgam's surface, when the time came.

Which left Khouri. There was no arguing with her experience; unlike any of the crew, she had demonstrably been born and raised on a planet, and – vitally – had seen action on one. It was probable – nothing she had heard led her to doubt the fact – that the Sky's Edge war had placed her in situations far graver than any the crew had experienced beyond their ship. Their excursions had been shopping trips, trade missions or simple tourism; coming down to gloat at the compressed lives of ephemerals. Khouri had been in situations where, at times, it had seemed very unlikely that she would survive. Yet – because she had never been anything less than a competent soldier, and she was also lucky – she had come through relatively unscathed.

No one aboard the ship actually argued with this.

'It's not that we wouldn't want you along,' Volyova had said, not long after the incident with the cache-weapon. 'Far from it. I've no doubt that you'd handle a suit as well as any of us, and you wouldn't be likely to freeze under fire.'

'Well, then . . .'

'But I can't risk losing my Gunnery Officer again.' They had been having the discussion in the spider-room, but Volyova had lowered her voice all the same. 'Only three people need to go down to Resurgam, and that means we don't have to use you. Apart from me, Sudjic and Kjarval can handle the suits. In fact we've already begun training up.'

'Then at least let me join in the sessions.'

Volyova had raised an arm, apparently to dimiss this suggestion. But as soon as she had done so she relented. 'All right, Khouri. You get to train with us. But it doesn't mean anything, understand?'

Oh yes, she understood. Things were different between Khouri and Volyova now – they had been ever since Khouri had told Volyova the lie about being an infiltrator for another crew. The Mademoiselle had long ago primed her for that particular little chat and it seemed to have worked perfectly, even down to the sly way the *Galatea* – completely innocent, of course – had deliberately not been mentioned, leaving Volyova to make that deduction herself, and thereby allowing her to feel some quiet satisfaction in the process. It was a red herring, but it mattered only that Volyova found it a plausible one. Volyova had also accepted the story about Sun Stealer being a piece of human-designed infiltration software, and for now her curiosity seemed satisfied. Now they were almost equals, both having something to hide from the rest of the crew, even if what Volyova thought she had on Khouri was not even close to the truth.

'I understand,' Khouri said.

'Still, it's a shame, though.' Volyova smiled. 'I get the impression you always wanted to meet Sylveste. You'll get your chance, of course, once we bring him aboard . . .'

Khouri smiled. 'That'll have to do then, won't it?'

Chamber Two was an empty twin of the chamber where the cache-weapons were kept.

Unlike the weapon-filled chamber, it had been pressurised up to one standard atmosphere. This was no mere extravagance; it constituted the largest single pocket of breathable air aboard the lighthugger, and was therefore used as a reservoir for supplying normally vacuum-filled regions of the ship with air when they needed to be entered by unsuited humans.

Usually the drive would have supplied an illusory one-gee of gravity, acting along the long axis of the ship, which was also the long axis of the roughly cylindrical chamber. But now that the drive had been quenched – now that the ship was in orbit around Resurgam – the illusion of gravity came from rotating the whole chamber, which meant that gravity acted at ninety degrees to the long axis, pushing radially outwards from the chamber's middle.

Near the middle, there was almost no gravity at all; objects could free-float there for minutes before their inevitable small initial drift slowly pushed them away from the middle. Thereafter, the increasing wind-pressure of the co-rotating air would tug them faster and lower. But nothing 'fell' in straight lines in the chamber, at least not from the point of view of someone standing on the rotating wall.

They entered at one end of the cylinder, via an armoured clamshell door whose inner face was pitted with blast-marks and projectile impact-craters. Every visible surface of the chamber was similarly weathered; as far as Khouri could see (and the suit's vision-augmentation routines meant she could see as far as she wished) there was no square metre of the chamber's skin which had not been harried, scarred, gouged, buckled, assaulted, melted or corroded by some kind of weapon. It might once have been silver; now it was purple, like an all-enveloping metallic bruise. Illumination was supplied not from a stationary light source, but from dozens of free-floating drones, each of which picked out a spot on the chamber's wall with a floodlight of actinic brilliance. The drones were constantly moving around, like a swarm of agitated glow-worms. The result was that no shadow in the chamber stayed still for more than a second or so, and it was impossible to look in any direction for more than a second before a blinding light-source entered it, washing everything else out.

'You sure you can handle this?' Sudjic said, as the door locked shut behind them. 'You wouldn't want to damage that suit. You break it, you bought it, you know?'

'Concentrate on not damaging your own,' Khouri said. Then she switched to the private channel, addressing Sudjic alone. 'Maybe it's just my imagination, but do I get the impression you don't like me very much?'

'Now why would you think that?'

'I think it might have something to do with Nagorny.' Khouri paused. It had occured to her that the private channels might not be private at all, but then again, nothing she was about to say would not already be completely obvious to anyone listening in; most especially not to Volyova. 'I don't know exactly what happened with him, except that you were close.'

'Close isn't the word for it, Khouri.'

'Lovers, then. I wasn't going to say that in case I offended you.'

'Don't worry about offending me, kid. It's way too late for that.'

Volyova's voice interrupted them. 'Kick off and descend to the chamber wall, you three.'

They obeyed her, using their suits on mild amplification to jump away from the plate which capped the end of the cylinder. They had been in freefall from the moment they entered the place, but now, as they descended towards the wall/floor, and picked up circumferential speed, their sense of weight mounted. The change was small, cushioned within the gel-air, but it gave enough small cues to engender a sense of up and down.

'I understand why you resent me,' Khouri said.

'Bet you do.'

'I took his position. Filled his role. After . . . whatever happened to him, you suddenly had me to deal with.' Khouri did her best to sound reasonable, as if she was taking none of this personally. 'If I was in your shoes, I think I'd feel the same. In fact I'm sure of it. But that doesn't make it right, either. I'm not your enemy, Sudjic.'

'Don't delude yourself.'

'About what?'

'That you understand one tenth of what this is about.' Sudjic had positioned her suit close to Khouri's now: seamless white armour stark against the damaged wall of the chamber. Khouri had seen images of ghostly white whales which lived – or used to live; she wasn't sure – in Earth's seas. Belugas, they were called, and they came to mind now. 'Listen,' Sudjic said. 'Do you think I'm simplistic enough that I'd hate you just because you fill the space Boris left? Don't insult me, Khouri.'

'Not my intention, believe me.'

'If I hate you, Khouri, it's for a perfectly good reason. It's because you belong to her.' She emitted the last word as a gasp of pure animosity. 'Volyova. You're her trinket. I hate her, so naturally I hate her possessions. Especially those whom she values. And of course – if I found a way to harm one of her possessions – do you imagine I wouldn't do it?'

'I'm nobody's possession,' Khouri said. 'Not Volyova's; not anyone's.' She immediately hated herself for protesting so vigorously, and then began to hate Sudjic for pushing her to the cusp of this defensiveness. 'Not that it's any of your business. You know what, Sudjic?'

'I'm dying to hear.'

'From what I heard, Boris wasn't the sanest individual who ever lived. From what I hear, Volyova didn't so much drive him mad as try and use his madness for something constructive.' She felt her suit decelerate, softly depositing her feet-first on the crumpled wall. 'So it didn't work. Big deal. Maybe you two deserved each other.'

'Yeah, maybe we did.'

'What?'

'I don't necessarily like anything that you just said, Khouri. Fact is, if we didn't have company, and if we weren't suited up, I might take a few moments to teach you how easily I could break your neck. Might still do it, one of these days. But I've got to admit. You've got spite. Most of her puppets usually lose that straight away; if she doesn't fry them first.'

'You're saying you misjudged me? Excuse me if I don't sound grateful.'

'I'm saying maybe you aren't as much her possession as she imagines.' Sudjic laughed. 'It's not a compliment, kid – just an observation. It might be worse for you once she realises. It doesn't mean you're off my shit-list, either.'

Khouri might have replied, but anything she intended to say was drowned out by Volyova, who was again speaking over the general suit channel, addressing the three of them from her vantage point high above, near the chamber's middle. 'There is no structure to this exercise,' she said. 'At least none that you need know about. Your sole obligation is to stay alive until the scenario is over. That's all there is to it. The exercise begins in ten seconds. I won't be available for questions during the course of it.'

Khouri absorbed this without any undue worry. There had been many unstructured exercises on the Edge, and many more in the gunnery. All it meant was that the deeper purpose of the scenario was masked, or that it was – literally – an exercise in disorientation intended to represent the chaos which might follow an operation which had gone badly wrong.

They began with warm-up exercises. Volyova watched them from on high while a variety of drone-targets emerged from previously concealed trapdoors in the wall of the chamber. The targets were not much of a challenge; at least, not at first. At the beginning the suits retained enough autonomy to detect and react to the targets before the wearer had even noticed them, so that all

283

the wearer needed to do was issue consent for the kill. But it became harder. The targets stopped being passive and began to shoot back – usually indiscriminately, but with steadily mounting firepower, so that even wide-shots posed a threat. The targets also got smaller and faster, popping out of the trapdoors with increasing frequency. And – keeping pace with the increasing danger posed by the enemy – the suits suffered progressive losses of functionality. By the sixth or seventh round most of the suit autonomy had been eroded, and the sensor webs which each suit draped around itself were breaking up, so that the wearers had to rely increasingly on their own visual cues. Yet though the exercise had increased in difficulty, Khouri had worked through similar scenarios so often that she did not begin to lose her cool. One had to remember how much of the suit functionality remained: one still had the weapons, the suit power and flight-capability.

The three of them did not communicate during the initial exercises; they were too intent on finding their own mental edges. Eventually it was like getting a second wind; a state of stability which lay beyond what at first seemed like the limits of normal performance. Getting there was a little like entering a trance state. There were certain tricks of concentration one could call into play: rote mantras which mediated the transition. It was never just a matter of wishing it and being there; it was more like climbing onto some awkward ledge. But as one did it – and did it over again – one found that the move became more fluid, and the ledge no longer seemed quite so high or inaccessible. But it was never reached simply, or without some expenditure of mental effort.

It was during the ascension to that state that Khouri half thought she had seen the Mademoiselle.

It was not even a glimpse, just a peripheral awareness that – momentarily – there had been another body out there in the chamber, and that its shape might have been that of the Mademoiselle. But the sensation vanished as quickly as it had come.

Could it have been her?

Khouri had not seen or heard from the Mademoiselle since the incident in the gunnery room. The Mademoiselle's last communiqué to her had been more pique than anything else; delivered after Khouri had helped Volyova finish off the cache-weapon. She had warned her that by remaining in the gunnery so long she had brought Sun Stealer on herself. And – indeed – the moment that Khouri tried to leave gunspace, she had felt something rushing towards her. It had come at her like a largening shadow, but she had not felt anything when the shadow seemed to engulf her. It was if a hole had opened in the shadow and she had passed unscathed through it, but she doubted that that had really been the case. The truth was almost certainly less palatable. Khouri did not want to consider the possibility that the shadow might have been Sun Stealer, but it was a conclusion she could not ignore. And in accepting that, she also had to accept the likelihood that Sun Stealer had now managed to ensconce a much larger part of himself in her skull.

It had been bad enough knowing that a small part of that thing had come back with the Mademoiselle's bloodhounds. But that at least had been contained; it had been within the Mademoiselle's powers to hold him at bay. Now Khouri had to accept that a more substantial fragment of Sun Stealer had reached her. And the Mademoiselle had been curiously absent ever since – until this voiceless half-glimpse, which might have been nothing at all; less than a figment of her imagination; something which any sane person would have dismissed as a trick of the light at the edge of vision.

If it had been her . . . what did it mean, after all this time?

Eventually the initial phase of exercises finished, and some of the suit functionality was reinstated. Not everything, but enough to let the three of them know that a certain slate had been wiped clean, and that from now the rules would be different.

'All right,' Volyova said. 'I've seen worse.'

'I'd take that as a compliment,' Khouri said, hoping to elicit some vague camaraderie from her compatriots. 'But the trouble with Ilia is she means it literally.'

'At least one of you gets it,' Volyova said. 'But don't let it go to your head, Khouri. Especially as it's about to get serious.'

At the far end of the chamber another clamshell door was easing open. Because of the constantly shifting light, Khouri saw what happened more as a series of frozen, glare-saturated images than actual motion. Things were spilling out: an expanding mass of ellipsoidal objects, each perhaps half a metre long, metallic-white in colour, with various protrusions, gun-nozzles, manipulators and apertures interrupting its surface.

Sentry drones. She knew them – or something similar – from the Edge. They had called them wolfhounds, because of the ferocity of their attack, and the fact they always moved in packs. Although their main military use was as an instrument of demoralisation, Khouri knew what they could do, and she knew that wearing a suit was no guarantee of safety. Wolfhounds were built for viciousness, not intelligence. They carried relatively light weapons – but they did so in large numbers, and, more to the point, they acted in unison. A pack of wolfhounds could collectively target their fire against a single individual, if their pooled-processors deemed that the action was strategically useful. It was that singlemindedness which made them terrifying.

But there was more. Embedded in the mass of erupting drones were several larger objects, also metallic-white in colour, but lacking the spherical symmetry of the wolfhounds. It was difficult to make them out clearly in the intermittent bursts of illumination, but Khouri thought she knew what they were. They were other suits, and they were very unlikely to be friendly.

The wolfhounds and the enemy suits were dropping away from the central axis now, vectoring towards the three waiting trainees. Perhaps two seconds had elapsed since the other door had opened, but it had seemed much longer as Khouri's mind easily switched to the mode of rapid consciousness which combat demanded. Many of the suit's higher autonomous functions were disabled, but its target-acquisition routines were still operable, so she ordered the suit to lock onto the wolfhounds, not actually firing, but keeping a bead on each one. She knew that her suit would confer with its two partners; between them devising a moment-by-moment strategy and allocating targets to each other, but that process was largely invisible to the wearer.

Where the hell was Volyova?

Was it possible she could have moved from one end of the chamber to the other, in time to appear in the pack? Yes, probably – motion in a suit, at least on a scale this compressed, could be so rapid that a person might seem to disappear from one point and appear hundreds of metres further away an eyeblink later. But the enemy suits Khouri had seen had definitely come through the other door, which would have necessitated Volyova leaving the chamber and making her way to the other end through normal ship corridors and accessways. Even in a suit, even with the route keyed in beforehand, Khouri doubted that anyone could do that so quickly; not without becoming liquid en route. But maybe Volyova had a short-cut; a clear shaft through which she could move much more rapidly . . .

Shit.

Khouri was being shot at.

The wolfhounds were firing, lancing her with small-grade laser fire, emerging in twin beams from malignant, closely spaced eyes in the upper hemisphere of their ellipsoid shells. By now their chameleoflage had adapted to the floor metal, turning them into purple lozenges which seemed to dance in and out of clarity. Her suit skin had silvered to an optically perfect mirror, deflecting most of the energy, but some of the initial blasts had done real damage to the suit integrity. She would lose points for that – she had been too busy cogitating on Volyova's vanishing act to pay attention to the attack. That diversion, of course, had almost certainly been Volyova's intention. She looked around, confirming what the suit readouts were telling her, which was that her compatriots had all survived. Flanking her, Sudjic and Kjarval resembled androform blobs of mercury, but they were not hurt and were returning fire.

Khouri set her escalation protocols to stay one offensive step ahead of the enemy, but not to obliterate them. Her suit sprouted low-yield lasers, popping up on both shoulders, pivoting on turrets. She watched the beams converge ahead of her, knifing forwards, each burst leaving a lilac contrail of ionised air. When hit, the shining, flying purple wolfhounds tended to crash out of the sky, bouncing to the ground or just exploding in hot blossoms. It would have been unwise in the extreme to be out in the chamber without a suit.

'You were slow,' Sudjic said, on the general-suit, even as the attack continued. 'This was real, we'd be hosing you off the walls.'

'How many times you seen close-quarters action, Sudjic?'

Kjarval – who until then had said next to nothing – cut in on them. 'We've all seen action, Khouri.'

'Yeah? And did you ever get close enough to the enemy to hear them scream for mercy?'

'What I mean is . . . fuck.' Kjarval had just taken a hit. Her suit spasmed momentarily, flicking through a series of incorrect chameleoflage modes: space-black; snow-white and then florid, tropical foliage, making it look as if Kjarval were a door leading out of the chamber into the heart of some remote planetary jungle.

Her suit stammered, and then regained its reflective sheen.

'I'm worried about those other suits.'

'That's what they're for. To make you worry, and louse up.'

'We need help to louse up? That's a new one.'

'Shut it, Khouri. Just concentrate on the damned war.'

She did. That part was easy.

Roughly a third of the attacking wolfhounds had been shot down, and no new forces were emerging through the chamber's still-open end door. But the other suits – there were three of them, Khouri saw – had done nothing so far except loiter near the hole, and were now slowly moving towards the floor, correcting their descent with bursts of needle-thin thrust from their heels. As they did so they too assumed a colour and texture which matched the shot-up floor. It was impossible to tell which – if any – were occupied.

'This is part of the scenario; those suits – they've got to mean something.'

'I said shut it, Khouri.'

But she continued, 'We're on a mission, right? We have to assume that much. We have to impose some structure on the damned thing or we don't know who the hell's the enemy!'

'Good idea,' Sudjic said. 'Let's schedule a meeting.'

By now the wolfhounds, and their fire-returning suits, were using particle-beams. Maybe the lasers had been real – it was just within the bounds of possibility – but it seemed certain that any significantly more powerful weapon would be only simulated. After all, it would not be an auspicious end to the exercise if one of them blasted a hole in the chamber wall and vented all the air into space.

'Let's assume,' Khouri said, 'that we know who the hell we are and why we're here – wherever here happens to be. The next question is, do we know those bastards in the other three suits?'

'This is getting way too philosophical for me,' Kjarval said, loping away to draw fire.

'If we're having this conversation,' Khouri said, doggedly talking over Sudjic's interjections, 'then we have to assume we don't know who they are. That they're hostile. And that means we should shoot the scum first, before they do whatever they're going to do to us.'

'I think you could be fucking up big-time, Khouri.'

'Yeah, well, as you kindly pointed out, I'm the one who isn't going down anyway.'

'Amen to that.'

'Er . . . people . . .' This was Kjarval, who had noticed what it took Khouri and Sudjic another moment to absorb. 'I don't like the look of that.'

What she had seen was that the wrists of the three other suits were morphing, each extruding an as yet unformed weapon. The process was unnervingly rapid, like watching a party balloon inflate into the shape of an animal.

'Shoot the fuckers,' Khouri said, with a voice so calm it almost scared her. 'Full fire-convergence on the leftmost suit. Go to minimum-yield ack-am pulse mode, conic dispersal with lateral cross-sweep.'

'Since when are you giving . . .'

'Just fucking do it, Sudjic!'

But she was already firing, Kjarval too; the three of them were now standing apart by ten metres, directing their suits' fire towards the enemy. The accelerated antimatter pulses were simulated . . . of course. If they had been real, there would have been little of the chamber left to stand on.

There was a flash, one so bright that Khouri felt it reach out and push taloned fingers into her eyes. It felt too intense to have been properly simulated . . . too concussive. The noise of the blast hit with a force that seemed almost gentle by comparison, but the shock was still enough to throw her backwards, keeling into the mottled chamber wall. The bump was like bouncing onto a mattress in an expensive hotel room. For a moment her suit was out cold; even when her eyes began to clear she could see that the readouts had either died or turned to unreadably cryptic mush. They lingered in that state for a few agonising seconds before the suit's back-up brain staggered on line, reinstating what it could. A simpler – but at least comprehensible – display returned to life, detailing what remained and what had been destroyed. Most of the major weapons were out. Suit autonomy was down by fifty per cent, the persona slipping towards machine autism. There was extensive loss of servo-assistance in three articulation points. Flight capability was impaired, at least until the repair protocols could get to work, and they needed a minimum two hours to finesse a bypass solution.

Oh, and – according to the bio-medical readout – she was now minus one upper limb, from the elbow down.

She struggled to a sitting position and – though every instinct told her to spend the time getting safe and assessing the surroundings – she had to look at the shot-away limb. Her right arm ended just where the med-readout said it would; truncating in a crumpled mass of scorched bone, flesh and intermingled metal. Further up the stump, the gel-air would have shock-congealed to prevent pressure and blood loss, but that was a detail she had to take for granted. There was no pain, of course – another aspect in which the simulation was utterly realistic, since the suit would be telling her pain centre to shut down for the time being.

Assess, assess . . .

She had lost her orientation completely in the blast. She looked around, but the suit's head articulation was jammed. There was suddenly an awful lot of smoke out there; hanging in coils in the air venting from the chamber itself. The intermittent illumination provided by the aerial drones was now only a stuttering strobe-effect. There were the wrecks of two suits over there, suffering the kind of comprehensive damage which might indicate that they had been hit by combined ack-am pulses. But the suits were too mangled up for her to tell if they had – or had ever had – occupants. A third suit – less critically damaged, and perhaps only stunned, as her own had been – rested ten or fifteen metres away around the great curve of the chamber's scarred wall. The wolfhounds were gone, or destroyed; it was impossible to tell which.

'Sudjic? Kjarval?'

Silence; not even her own voice properly audible, and certainly nothing resembling a reply. Intersuit comms were compromised, she saw now – a detail on the damage readout she had ignored until then. Bad, Khouri. Very bad.

Now she had no idea who the enemy was.

The ruined suit arm was fixing itself by the second, scorched parts sloughing to the ground, while the exterior skin crawled forwards to envelop the stump. It was faintly disgusting to watch, even though Khouri had seen it happen many times before, in other simulation scenarios on the Edge. What was really nauseating was knowing that no such immediate repair was possible for her own wounds; that they would have to wait until she was med-evacked out of the zone.

The other suit, the one less damaged, was moving now, raising itself to a standing position, just as she was doing. The other suit had a full complement of limbs, and many of its weapons were still deployed, jutting from various apertures. They were locking onto Khouri, like a dozen vipers poising for the strike.

'Who's that?' she asked, before remembering that the comms were offline, probably for good. Out of the corner of her eye she saw another two suits off to one side, emerging from banners of languid, charcoal-dark smoke. Who were they? Remnants of the original three which had come down with the wolfhounds, or her comrades?

The single suit with the weapons was approaching her, very slowly, as if she were a bomb which might go off at any moment. The suit stopped, motionless. Its skin was trying to mimic the combination of the background colour of the chamber wall and the smoke screens, with only moderate success. Khouri wondered how her own suit was doing. Was her faceplate opaque or transparent? It was impossible to tell from inside, and the minimalist readout told her nothing. If the one with the weapons saw a human face within, would that incite it to kill or hold fire? Khouri had locked her own usable weapons on the figure, but nothing she had seen told her whether she was pointed at the enemy or a mute comrade.

She moved to raise her good arm, to indicate her face, asking the other to make its faceplate transparent.

The other fired.

Khouri was blown back into the wall, an invisible piledriver ramming into her stomach. Her suit started screaming, all manner of gibberish scrolling across her vision. There was a roar of sound before she hit the wall, the compressed burst of a frantic return-fire from her own available weapons.

Fuck, Khouri thought. That actually hurt, at the visceral level which somehow betrayed it as not having been simulated.

She struggled to her feet again, just as another charge from the attacker slammed past and the third caught her on the thigh. She started wheeling back, both arms flailing at the periphery of vision.

There was something wrong with her arms; or more accurately, something not wrong where something should have been. They were completely intact; no sign that one of them had just been blasted off.

'Shit,' she said. 'What the fuck is happening?'

The attack was continuing, each blast impacting her and driving her back.

'This is Volyova,' said a voice, not in any way calm and detached. 'Listen to me carefully, all of you! Something's going wrong with the scenario! I want you all to stop firing—'

Khouri had hit the deck again, this time with enough force that she felt it through the gel-air cushion, like a slap against her spine. Her thigh felt injured, and the suit was doing nothing to ameliorate the discomfort.

It's gone live, she thought.

The weapons were for real now; or at least those which belonged to the suit attacking her.

'Kjarval,' Volyova said. 'Kjarval! You have to stop firing! You're killing Khouri!'

But Kjarval – Khouri guessed that she was the attacker – was not listening, or not capable of listening, or, more terrifyingly, not capable of stopping.

'Kjarval,' the Triumvir said again, 'if you don't stop, I'm going to have to disarm you!'

But Kjarval did not stop. She kept on firing, Khouri feeling each impact like a lash, writhing under the assault, desperate to claw her way through the tortured alloy of the chamber into the sanctuary beyond.

And then Volyova descended from the chamber's middle, where she had apparently been all along, unseen. As she descended, she opened fire on Kjarval, at first with the lightest weapons she had, but with steadily mounting force. Kjarval countered by directing some portion of her fire upwards, towards the lowering Triumvir. The blasts hit Volyova, gouging black scars into her armour, chipping fragments from the flexible integument, slicing off weapons as her suit tried to extrude and deploy them. But Volyova maintained an edge on the trainee. Kjarval's suit began to wilt, losing integrity. Its weapons went haywire, missing their targets and then shooting haphazardly around the chamber.

Eventually – it could not have been more than a minute after she had first started firing on Khouri – Kjarval dropped to the ground. Her suit, where it was not blackened by the hits it had sustained, was a quilt of mismatched psychedelic colours and rapidly morphing hyper-geometric textures, sprouting half-realised weapons and devices. Her limbs were thrashing crazily. The ends of the limbs had gone berserk, extruding – and then budding off – various manipulators and rough, baby-sized approximations of human hands.

Khouri got to her feet, stifling a scream of pain as her thigh protested against the movement. Her suit was a stiffening deadweight around her, but somehow she managed to walk, or at least totter, to the place where Kjarval lay.

Volyova and another suited figure – she had to be Sudjic – were already there, leaning over what remained of the suit, trying to make some sense of its medical diagnostic readouts.

'She's dead,' Volyova said.

FOURTEEN

On the day that the newcomers announced their presence, Sylveste was woken by a stab of unforgiving white light. He held his arm up in supplication while he waited for his eyes to cycle through their initialisation routines. It was almost useless speaking to him in those moments; Sluka evidently realised this. With so many of their original functions gone, the eyes took longer than ever now to reach functionality. Sylveste experienced a slow rote of errors and warnings, little spectral prickles of pain as the eyes investigated critically impaired modes.

He was half aware of Pascale sitting up in bed next to him, lifting the sheets around her chest.

'You'd better wake up,' Sluka said. 'Both of you. I'll wait outside while you dress.'

The two of them struggled into clothes. Beyond the room, Sluka stood patiently with two guards, neither conspicuously armed. Sylveste and his wife were escorted towards Mantell's commons, where the morning shift of True Path Inundationists were gathered around an oblong wallscreen. Flasks of coffee and breakfast rations lay undisturbed on the commons table. Whatever was going on, Sylveste surmised, was enough to kill any normal appetite. And the screen evidently held the key. He could hear a voice speaking, amplified and harsh, as if from a loudspeaker. There was so much background conversation taking place that he could do no more than snatch the odd word from the narrative. Unfortunately, that odd word tended to be his own name, spoken at too-frequent intervals by whoever was booming from the screen.

He pushed to the front, aware that the watchers deferred to him with more respect than he'd felt for several decades. But was it possibly only pity being afforded to a condemned man?

Pascale joined him at his side. 'Do you recognise that woman?' she asked.

'What woman?'

'On the screen. The one you're standing in front of.'

What Sylveste saw was only an oblong of pointillist silver-grey pixels.

'My eyes don't read video too well,' he said, addressing Sluka as much as Pascale. 'And I can't hear a damned thing. Maybe you'd better tell me what I'm missing.'

Falkender had appeared out of the crowd. 'I'll patch you in neurally, if you wish. It'll only take a moment.' He shunted Sylveste away from the watchers, towards a private alcove in one corner of the commons, Pascale and Sluka following. There, he opened his toolkit and removed a few glistening instruments.

'Now you're going to tell me this won't hurt at all,' Sylveste said.

'I wouldn't dream of it,' Falkender said. 'After all, it wouldn't be the complete truth, would it?' Then he clicked his fingers, either at an aide or Pascale; Sylveste was unsure, and his visual field was now too restricted to discriminate. 'Get the man a mug of coffee; that'll take his mind off it. In any case, when he's able to read that screen, I think he'll need something stronger.'

'That bad?'

'I'm afraid Falkender isn't joking,' Sluka said.

'My, aren't you all enjoying yourselves.' Sylveste bit his lip at the first cascade of pain from Falkender's probings, although, as the minor operation proceeded, the pain never worsened. 'Are you going to put me out of my misery? After all, it seemed important enough to wake me.'

'The Ultras have announced themselves,' Sluka said.

'That much I extrapolated for myself. What have they done? Landed a shuttle in the middle of Cuvier?'

'Nothing so obtrusive. Yet. There may be worse to come.'

Someone pushed a mug of coffee into his hands; Falkender relented in his ministrations long enough for Sylveste to sip a mouthful. It was acrid and not entirely warm, but sufficed to propel him fractionally closer towards alertness. He heard Sluka say, 'What we're showing on the screen is a repeating audiovisual message, one that's been transmitting continuously now for about thirty minutes.'

'Transmitted from the ship?'

'No, seems they've managed to tap straight into our comsat girdle, piggybacking their message on our routine transmissions.'

Sylveste nodded, then regretted the movement. 'Then they're still edgy about being detected.' Or else, he thought, they merely want to reaffirm their absolute technological superiority over us; their ability to tap into and manipulate our existing data systems. That seemed more likely: it smacked not only of the arrogant Ultra way of doing things, but of one Ultra crew in particular. Why announce your presence in a mundane way, when you can do a full burning bush and impress the natives? But he hardly needed confirmation that he knew these people. He had known ever since the ship had entered the system.

'Next question,' he said. 'Who was the message directed to? Do they still think there's some kind of planetary authority with whom they can deal?'

'No,' Sluka said. 'The message was addressed to the citizens of Resurgam, irrespective of political or cultural affiliation.'

'Very democratic,' Pascale said.

'Actually,' Sylveste said, 'I rather doubt that democracy comes into it. Not if I know who we're dealing with.'

'Regarding that,' Sluka said, 'you never did quite explain to my total satisfaction why these people might . . .'

Sylveste cut her off. 'Before we go into any detailed analysis, do you think I could see the message for myself? Particularly as I seem to hold something of a personal stake in the matter.'

'There.' Falkender retreated and closed his toolkit with a decisive snap. 'I told you it wouldn't take a moment. Now you can jack straight into the screen.' The surgeon smiled. 'Now, do me a favour and be sure not to kill the messenger, won't you?'

'Let me see the message,' Sylveste said. 'Then I'll decide.'

It was far worse than he had feared.

He pushed to the front again, though by now the watchers had thinned out, dispersed reluctantly to duties elsewhere in Mantell. It was much easier to hear the speaker now, and he recognised cadences in the woman's speech as she repeated phrases which had cycled around a few minutes earlier. The message was not a long one, then. Which was ominous in itself. Who crossed light-years of interstellar space, only to announce their arrival around a colony in terms which were, frankly, curt? Only those who had no interest whatsoever in ingratiating themselves, and whose demands were supremely clear. And again that suspicion accorded well with what he already knew of the crew he believed had come for him. They had never been talkative.

He could not yet see the face, although the voice was already whispering across the years to him. When vision came – when Falkender completed the neural interface – he remembered.

'Who is she?' Sluka asked.

'Her name – when last we met – was Ilia Volyova.' Sylveste shrugged. 'It may or may not have been real. All I do know is that whatever threats she goes on to make, she's fully capable of backing them up.'

'And she's – what? The Captain?'

'No,' Sylveste said, distracted. 'No, she's not.'

The woman's face was unremarkable. Almost monochromatically pale of complexion, short dark hair, and a facial structure somewhere between elfin and skeletal, framing deepset, narrow, slanted eyes which dispensed little compassion. She had hardly changed at all. But then, that was the point of Ultras. If subjective decades had passed for Sylveste since their last meeting, then for Volyova it might only have been a handful of years; a tenth or a twentieth of the time. For her, their last meeting would be a thing of the relatively recent past, whereas for Sylveste it felt like an event consigned to the dusty annals of history. It placed him at a disadvantage, of course. For Volyova, his mannerisms – the more predictable aspects of his behaviour – would still be fresh in her mind; he would be an adversary not long met. But Sylveste had barely recognised Volyova's voice until now, and when he tried to recall whether she had been more or less sympathetic to him on their previous meeting, his memory failed him. Of course, it would all come back, but it was that very slowness of recall which gave Volyova her undoubted edge.

Odd, really. He had assumed – stupidly, perhaps – that it would be Sajaki who was making this announcement. Not the true Captain, of course, or else why would they have come for him? The Captain had to be ill again.

But then where was Sajaki?

He forced his mind to disregard these questions and concentrate on what Volyova had to say.

After two or three repetitions, he had the whole of her

monologue assembled in his head, and was almost certain he could have regurgitated it word for word. It was indeed curt. They knew what they wanted, these Ultras. And they knew what it would take to get it. 'I am Triumvir Ilia Volyova of the lighthugger *Nostalgia for Infinity*' was how she introduced herself. No helloes; not even a perfunctory admission of gratitude for the fates having allowed them to cross space to Resurgam.

Such niceties, Sylveste knew, were not exactly Ilia Volyova's style. He had always thought of her as the quiet one; more concerned with housekeeping her hideous weapons than condescending to engage in anything resembling normal social intercourse. More than once he had heard the other crewmembers joke – and they hardly ever joked – about how Volyova preferred the company of the vessel's indigenous rats over her human crewmates.

Perhaps they had not really been joking.

'I am addressing you from orbit,' was how she continued. 'We have studied your state of technological advancement and concluded that you pose us no military threat.' And then she paused, before continuing in what to Sylveste sounded like the tones of a schoolteacher warning pupils against committing an act of minor disobedience, like gazing out the window, or not keeping their compads well organised. 'However, should any act be construed as a deliberate attempt at inflicting damage on us, we will retaliate in a massively disproportionate sense.' She almost smiled at that point. 'Not so much an eye for an eye, so to speak, as a city for an eye. We are fully capable of destroying any or all of your settlements from orbit.'

Volyova leant forwards, her leonine grey eyes seeming to fill the screen. 'More importantly, we also have the resolve to do it, should the need arise.' Volyova again allowed herself an over-dramatic pause, doubtless aware that she had a captive audience at this point. 'If I chose, it could happen in a matter of minutes. Don't imagine I'd lose much sleep over it.'

Sylveste could see where all this was heading.

'But let us put aside such vulgarities, at least for the moment.' She really smiled at that point, though as smiles went, it was near-cryogenic in its frostiness. 'You're doubtless wondering why we're here.'

'Not me,' Sylveste said, loud enough that Pascale heard him.

'There is a man amongst you we seek. Our desire to find him is so absolute, so pressing, that we have decided to bypass the usual . . .' Volyova's smile reappeared; an even colder phantom of itself. '. . . diplomatic channels. The man's name is Sylveste; no further explanation should be necessary, if his reputation hasn't waned since our last meeting.'

'Tarnished, perhaps,' Sluka commented. Then, to Sylveste, 'You're really going to have to tell me more about this prior meeting, you know. It can hardly do you any harm.'

'And knowing the facts won't do you a blind bit of good,' Sylveste said, immediately returning his attention to the broadcast.

'Ordinarily,' Volyova said, 'we'd establish lines of dialogue with the proper authorities and negotiate for Sylveste's handover. Possibly that was our original intention. But a cursory scan of your planet's main settlement from orbit – Cuvier – convinced us that such an approach would be doomed to failure. We surmised that there was no longer any power worth dealing with. And I'm afraid we don't have the patience to bargain with squabbling planetary factions.'

Sylveste shook his head. 'She's lying. They never intended to negotiate, no matter what state we were in. I know these people; they're vicious scum.'

'So you keep telling us,' Sluka said.

'Our options are therefore rather limited,' Volyova continued. 'We want Sylveste, and our intelligence has confirmed that he is not . . . how shall I put it – at large?'

'All that from orbit?' Pascale asked. 'That's what I call good intelligence.'

'Too good,' Sylveste said.

'This then,' Volyova added, 'is how things will proceed. Within twenty-four hours Sylveste will make his presence and location known to us via a radio-frequency broadcast. Either he emerges from hiding or those who are holding him set him free. We leave the details to you. If Sylveste is dead, then irrefutable evidence of his death must be offered in place of the man himself. Whether we accept it will be entirely at our discretion, of course.'

'Good job I'm not dead, in that case. I doubt there's anything you could do to convince Volyova.'

'She's that intransigent?'

'Not just her; the whole crew.'

But Volyova was still speaking: 'Twenty-four hours, then. We will be listening. And if we hear nothing, or suspect deception in any form, we will enact a punishment. Our ship has certain capabilities – ask Sylveste, if you doubt us. If we have not heard from him within the next day, we will use that capability against one of your planet's smaller surface communities. We have already selected the target in question, and the nature of the attack will be such that no one in the community will survive. Is that clear? No one. Twenty-four hours after that, if we have still heard nothing of the elusive Dr Sylveste, we will escalate to a larger target. Twenty-four hours after that, we will destroy Cuvier.' And Volyova proffered another brief smile at that point. 'Though you seem to be doing an admirable job there yourselves.'

The message ended, then recommenced from the beginning, with Volyova's blunt introduction. Sylveste listened to it in its entirety twice more before anyone dared interrupt his concentration.

'They wouldn't do it,' Sluka said. 'Surely not.'

'It's barbaric,' Pascale added, eliciting a nod from their captor. 'No matter how much they need you – they couldn't possibly intend to do what she said. I mean, destroy a whole settlement?'

'That's where you're wrong,' Sylveste said. 'They've done it before. And I don't doubt that they'll do it again.'

There had been never been any real certainty in Volyova's mind that Sylveste was alive – but on the other hand, the fact that he might not be present was something she had carefully avoided dwelling on, because the consequences of failure were too unpleasant to bring to mind. It mattered not that this was Sajaki's quest, rather than her own. If it failed, he would punish her just as severely as if she had contrived the whole thing herself; as if it were Volyova who had brought them to this dispiriting place.

She had not really expected anything to happen in the first few hours. That was too optimistic; it presumed that Sylveste's captors were awake and immediately aware of her warning. Realistically, it might be a fraction of a day before the news was passed along the chain of command to the right people; yet more time while it was verified. But as the hours became tens of hours, and then most of a day, she was forced to the conclusion that her threat would have to be enacted.

Of course, the colonists had not been entirely silent. Ten hours earlier, one unnamed group had come forward with what they claimed were Sylveste's remains. They had left them on the top of a mesa, then retreated into caves through which the ship's sensors could not peer. Volyova sent down a drone to examine the remains, but while they were a close genetic match, they did not agree precisely with the tissue samples retained since Sylveste's last visit to the ship. It would have been tempting to punish the colonists for this, but on reflection she decided against such a course of action: they had acted solely out of fear, with no prospect of personal gain except their own – and everyone else's – survival, and she did not want to deter any other parties coming forward. Likewise she had stilled her hand when two independently acting individuals announced themselves as Sylveste, since it was obvious that the people in question were not really lying, but genuinely believed themselves to be the man himself.

Now, however, there was not even time left for deception.

'I'm actually rather surprised,' she said. 'I thought by now they would have given him over. But evidently one party in this arrangement is seriously underestimating the other.'

'You can't back down now,' Hegazi said.

'Of course not.' Volyova said it with surprise, as if the thought of clemency had never once occurred to her.

'No; you have to,' Khouri said. 'You can't go through with this.'

This was almost the first thing she had said all day. Perhaps she was having trouble coming to terms with the monster for whom she now worked: this suddenly tyrannical incarnation of the previously fair Volyova. It was difficult not to sympathise. When she examined herself, what she saw was indeed something monstrous, even if it was not entirely the truth.

'Once a threat's made,' Volyova said, 'it's in everyone's interests to carry it through if the terms aren't met.'

'What if they can't keep the terms?' Khouri said.

Volyova shrugged. 'That's their problem, not mine.'

She opened the link to Resurgam and said her piece – reiterating the demands she had made, and stating her deep disappointment that Sylveste had not been brought to light. She was wondering how convincing she sounded – whether the colonists truly believed her threats – when she was struck by an inspirational idea. She unclipped her bracelet, whispering the command which would instruct it to accept limited input from a third party, rather than injuring them.

She passed the bracelet to Khouri.

'You want to salve your conscience, be my guest.'

Khouri examined the device as if it might suddenly extrude fangs, or spit venom into her face. Finally she raised it to her mouth, not actually slipping it around her wrist.

'Go ahead,' Volyova said. 'I'm serious. Say whatever you want – I assure you it won't do a blind bit of good.'

'Speak to the colonists?'

'Certainly – if you think you can convince them better than I can.'

For a moment Khouri said nothing. Then – diffidently – she started speaking into the bracelet. 'My name is Khouri,' she said. 'For whatever it's worth, I want you to know I'm not with these people. I don't agree with what they're doing.' Khouri's large and frightened eyes scanned the bridge, as if she expected any moment to be punished for this. But the others showed only mild interest in what she had to say.

'I was recruited,' she said. 'I didn't understand what they were. They want Sylveste. They're not lying. I've seen the weapons they've got in this ship, and I think they will use them.'

Volyova affected a look of bored indifference, as if all of this were exactly what she would have expected; tiresomely so.

'I'm sorry none of you have brought Sylveste forward. I think Volyova's serious when she says she's going to punish you for that. All I want to say is, you'd better believe her. And maybe if some of you can bring him forward now it won't be too—'

'Enough.'

Volyova took back the bracelet. 'I'm extending my deadline by one hour only.'

But the hour passed. Volyova barked cryptic commands into her bracelet, causing a target-designator to spring into place over the northerly latitudes of Resurgam. The red cross-hairs hunted with sullen, sharklike calm, until they latched onto a particular spot near the planet's northern icecap. Then they pulsed a bloodier red, and status graphics informed Volyova that the ship's orbital-suppression elements – almost the puniest weapons system it could deploy – were now activated, armed, targeted and ready.

Then she resumed her address to the colonists.

'People of Resurgam,' Volyova said. 'Our weapons have just aligned themselves on the small settlement of Phoenix; fifty-four degrees north by twenty west of Cuvier. In fractionally less than thirty seconds Phoenix and its immediate environs will cease to exist.'

The woman dampened her lips with the tip of her tongue before continuing. 'This will be our last announcement for twenty-four hours. You have until then to produce Sylveste, or we escalate to a larger target. Count yourselves lucky that we began with one as small as Phoenix.'

The general tenor of her pronouncements, Khouri realised, had been that of a schoolteacher patiently explaining why the punishment she was about to visit upon her pupils was both in their best interests and entirely brought about by their own actions. She avoided saying, 'This will hurt me more than it hurts you,' but if she had, Khouri would not have been at all surprised. In fact, she wondered if there was anything Volyova could now do which would surprise her in any way. It seemed that she had not so much misjudged the woman as assigned her to completely the wrong species. And not just Volyova, but the entire crew. Khouri felt a pang of revulsion, shuddering to think how much a part of them she had recently dared imagine herself to be. It was as if they had all pulled masks from their faces, revealing snakes.

Volyova fired.

For a moment – a long, pregnant moment – there was nothing. Khouri began to entertain the idea that maybe the entire thing had been a bluff after all. But that hope lasted until the walls of the bridge shuddered, as if the entire ship were an ancient sea vessel scraping past an iceberg. Khouri felt none of the motion, since the articulated seat boom moved to smother the vibrations. But she had no doubts that she had seen it, and seconds later she heard what sounded like distant thunder.

The hull weapons had discharged.

On the projected image of Resurgam, the weapons readouts recast themselves, changing to illuminate the conditions of the armaments in the moments after they had been deployed. Hegazi consulted his seat readouts, his eyepiece clicking and whirring as it assimilated the news.

'Suppression elements discharged,' he said, voice clipped and devoid of emphasis. 'Targeting systems confirm correct acquisition.' Then, with magisterial slowness, he elevated his gaze to the globe.

Khouri looked with him.

There was – where previously there had been nothing – a tiny red-hot smear near the edge of Resurgam's northern polar cap, like a foul rat's eye in the crust of the world. It was darkening now, like a hot needle just pulled from a brazier. But it was still hurtingly bright, darkening less through its own cooling than because it was being progressively shrouded by titanic veils of uplifted planetary debris. In windows which opened fleetingly in the curdling dark storm, Khouri observed dancing tendrils of lightning, their bright ignitions strobing the landscape for hundreds of kilometres around. A near-circular shockwave was racing from the site of the attack. Khouri observed its movement via a subtle change in the refractive index of the air, the way a ripple in shallow water caused the rocks below to acquire a momentary fluidity of their own.

'Preliminary sit-rep coming in now,' Hegazi said, still managing to sound like a bored acolyte reciting the dullest of scriptures. 'Weps functionality: nominal. Ninety-nine point four per cent probability that target was completely neutralised. Seventy-nine per cent probability that no one within two hundred kilometres could have survived, unless they were behind a kilometre of armour.'

'Good enough odds for me,' Volyova said. She studied the wound in the surface of Resurgam for a moment longer, evidently satiating herself with the thought of planetary-scale destruction.

FIFTEEN

Mantell, North Nekhebet, 2566

'They bluffed,' Sluka said, just as a sudden, false dawn shone over the north-easterly horizon, turning the intervening ridges and bluffs into serrated black cutouts. The glare was magnesium-bright, edged in purple. Briefly it overloaded whole strips of Sylveste's vision, leaving numb voids where it had burned.

'Care to take another guess?' he asked.

For a moment Sluka seemed unable to answer. She only stared at the flare, mesmerised by its radiance and the message of atrocity it brought.

'He told you they'd do it,' Pascale said. 'You should have listened to him. He knew these people. He knew they'd do exactly what they promised.'

'I never thought they would,' Sluka said, her voice so quiet that it seemed she was talking to herself. Despite the glare, it was still a totally silent evening, free even of the usual music of Resurgam's winds. 'I thought their threat was too monstrous to take seriously.'

'Nothing's too monstrous for them.' Sylveste's eyes were returning to normality now; enough that he could read the expressions of the women who were standing next to him on Mantell's mesa. 'From now on, you'd better take Volyova at her word. She means what she said. In twenty-four hours she'll do it all again, unless you turn me over.'

It was as if Sluka had not heard him. 'Perhaps we ought to get down,' was all she said.

Sylveste agreed, though before they headed back into the mesa they took time to crudely measure the direction from which the flash had come. 'We know when it happened,' Sylveste said. 'And we know the direction. When the pressure wave comes through, we'll know how far away it was. Settlements on Resurgam are still widely spread, so we should be able to pinpoint it.'

'She said the name of the place,' Pascale said.

Sylveste nodded.

'But while I'd believe any threat she made, I also know Volyova's not to be trusted.'

'I don't know anything about Phoenix,' Sluka said, as they descended via a cargo elevator. 'I thought I knew most of the recent settlements. But then again I've not exactly been at the heart of government these last few years.'

'She would have started with something small,' Sylveste said. 'Otherwise she wouldn't have room to escalate. We can assume Phoenix was a soft target; a scientific or geological outpost; something on which the rest of the colony wasn't materially dependent. Just people, in other words.'

Sluka shook her head. 'We're talking about them in the past tense, and we never even discussed them in the present. It's like their only reason for existing was so they could die.'

Sylveste felt physically sick; on the nauseous cusp of actually vomiting. It was, he thought, the only occasion in his life when this feeling had been engendered by an external event; something in which he was not directly participating. He had not even felt this way when Carine Lefevre had died. The mistake – the error – had not been his to commit. And while he had argued with Sluka that the crew would inflict what they threatened, some part of him had clung to the idea that, ultimately, they would not; that he was wrong and Sluka and the other humanitarians were correct. Perhaps, had he been in Sluka's position, he too would have ignored the warning, irrespective of how sure he had felt before the attack. The cards always look different when it's your turn to play them; loaded with subtly different possibilities.

The pressure wave came three hours later. By then it was little more than a gust, but it was a gust completely out of place on such a still night. After it had passed, the air was turbulent, prone to sudden squalls, as if a full-blooded razorstorm was on the verge. Timing of the shock indicated that the site of the attack was somewhat less than three and a half thousand miles away (seismic data also confirmed this); almost due north-east, according to the visual evidence. Retiring under guard to Sluka's stateroom, they pushed themselves beyond sleep with strong coffee, calling up global maps of the colony from Mantell's archives.

Feeling edgy, Sylveste sipped his drink.

'Like you say, it could be a new settlement they've hit. Are these maps up to date?'

'As good as,' Sluka said. 'They were refreshed from Cuvier's central cartographics section about a year ago, before things became too serious around here.'

Sylveste looked at the map, projected over Sluka's table like a ghostly, topographic tablecloth. The area displayed by the map was two thousand kilometres square, large enough to contain the destroyed colony, even if their directional estimate was crude.

But there was no sign of Phoenix.

'We need more recent maps,' he said. 'It's possible this place was founded in the last year.'

'That's not going to be easy to arrange.'

'Then you'd better find a way. You have to make a decision in the next twenty-four hours. Probably the biggest of your life.'

'Don't flatter yourself. I've as good as decided to let them have you.'

Sylveste shrugged, as if it were of no consequence to him. 'Even so, you should still be in possession of the facts. You're going to be dealing with Volyova. If you can't be sure that her threats are genuine, you might be tempted to call her bluff.'

She looked at him, long and hard.

'We do still have – in principle – data links to Cuvier, via what remains of the comsat girdle. But they've barely been used since the domes were blown. It would be risky to open them – the data-trail could lead back to us.'

'I'd say that's the least of anyone's worries right now.'

'He's right,' Pascale said. 'With all this going on, who's going to care about a minor breach of security in Cuvier? I'd say it would be worthwhile just to get the maps updated.'

'How long will it take?'

'An hour; two hours. Why, were you planning on going somewhere?'

'No,' Sylveste said, conspicuously failing to smile. 'But someone else might be deciding for me.'

They went surfaceside again while they were waiting for the maps to be revised. There were no stars visible in the low north-east; just a hump of sooty nothingness, as if a gargantuan crouched figure were looming over the horizon. It must have been an uplifted wall of dust, edging towards them. 'It'll blanket the world for months,' Sluka said. 'Just as if a massive volcano had gone off.'

'The winds are getting stronger,' Sylveste said.

Pascale nodded. 'Could they have done that – changed the weather, this far from the attack? What if the weapon they used caused radioactive contamination?'

'It needn't have been,' Sylveste said. 'Some kind of kinetic-energy weapon would have sufficed. Knowing Volyova, she wouldn't have done anything more than was absolutely necessary. But you're right to worry about radiation. That weapon probably opened a hole right through the lithosphere. It's anyone's guess what was released from the crust.'

'We shouldn't spend too much time surfaceside.'

'Agreed – but that probably goes for the colony as a whole.'

One of Sluka's aides appeared in the exit door.

'You've got the maps?' she asked.

'Give us another half-hour,' he said. 'We've got the data, but the encryption's pretty heavy. There's news from Cuvier, though. We just picked it up, publicly broadcast.'

'Go on.'

'It seems the ship took pictures of the – uh – aftermath. They transmitted them to the capital, and now they've been sent around the planet.' The aide took a battered compad from his pocket, its flatscreen throwing his features into lilac relief. 'I have the images.'

'You'd better show us.'

The aide placed the compad on the mesa's gritty, wind-smoothed surface. 'They must have used infrared,' he said.

The pictures were awesome and terrifying. Molten rock was still snaking from the crater and beyond, or spraying in fountainlike cascades from dozens of suddenly birthed baby volcanoes. All evidence of the settlement had been obliterated, completely swallowed by the wide cauldron of the crater, which must have been a kilometre or two across. There were vast patches of glassy smoothness near its centre, like solidified tar; black as night.

'For a moment I hoped we were wrong,' Sluka said. 'I hoped that the flash, even the pressure-wave – I hoped that somehow they'd been faked, like a theatrical effect. But I can't see how they could have faked this without actually blowing a hole in the planet.'

'We'll know in a while,' the aide said. 'I presume I can speak freely?'

'This concerns Sylveste,' Sluka said. 'So he may as well hear it.'

'Cuvier has a plane heading towards the site of the attack. They'll be able to confirm that this imagery wasn't fabricated.'

By the time they returned underground the maps had been cracked, replacing the outdated copies in Mantell's archive. Once again they retired to Sluka's stateroom to view the data. This time the map's accompanying information showed that it had been updated only a few weeks earlier.

'They've done pretty well,' Sylveste said. 'To have kept up with the business of cartography while the city was crumbling around them. I admire their dedication.'

'Never mind their motives,' Sluka said, brushing her fingers against one of the pedestal-mounted globes which flanked the room, seemingly to anchor herself to the planet which now seemed to be spinning irrevocably beyond her control. 'As long as Phoenix – or whatever they called it – is there, that's all I care.'

'It's there all right,' Pascale said.

Her finger penetrated the projected terrain, arrowing a tiny, labelled dot in the otherwise unpopulated north-eastern ranges. 'It's the only thing so far north,' she said. 'And the only settlement in remotely the right direction. It's called Phoenix, too.'

'What else do you have on it?'

Sluka's aide – he was a small man with a delicately oiled moustache and goatee – spoke softly into his sleeve-mounted compad, instructing the map to zoom in on the settlement. A series of demographic icons popped into existence above the table. 'Not much,' he said. 'Just a few multi-family surface shacks linked by tubes. A few underground workings. No ground connections, although they did have a landing pad for aircraft.'

'Population?'

'I don't think population's quite the word for it,' the man said. 'Just a hundred or so; about eighteen family units. Most of them from Cuvier, by the look of this.' He shrugged. 'Actually, if this was her idea of a strike against the colony, I think we did remarkably well. A hundred or so people – well, it's a tragedy. But I'm surprised she didn't play her hand against a more populous target. The fact that none of us really knew this place existed – it almost nullifies the act, don't you think?'

'A splendidly inept thing,' Sylveste said, nodding despite himself.

'What?'

'The human capacity for grief. It just isn't capable of providing an adequate emotional response once the dead exceed a few dozen in number. And it doesn't just level off – it just gives up, resets itself to zero. Admit it. None of us feels a damn about these people.' Sylveste looked at the map, wondering what it must have been like for the inhabitants, given those few seconds of warning which Volyova had prescribed them. He wondered if any of them had taken the trouble to leave their dwellings and face the sky, in order to quicken – fractionally – the coming annihilation. 'But I do know one thing. We have all the evidence we need that she's a woman of her word. And that means you have to let me go to them.'

'I'm reluctant to lose you,' Sluka said. 'But it isn't like I have much choice in the matter. You'll be wanting to contact them, of course.'

'Naturally,' Sylveste said. 'And of course Pascale will be coming with me. But there's one thing I'd like you to do for me first.'

'A favour?' Sluka sounded amused, as if this were the last thing in the world she would have expected from him. 'Well, what can I do for you, now that we've become such firm friends?'

Sylveste smiled. 'Actually it's not so much what you can do for me as what Doctor Falkender can. It concerns my eyes, you see.'

From the vantage point of her floating, boom-suspended seat, the Triumvir observed the handiwork she had wrought on the planet below. It was all perfectly clear, imaged precisely on the bridge's projection sphere. In the last ten hours she had observed the wound extend dark cyclonic tendrils away from its focus, evidence that the weather in that region – and, by implication, elsewhere on the planet – had been tipped towards a violent new equilibrium. According to the locally culled data, the colonists on Resurgam called such phenomena razorstorms, on account of the merciless flensing quality of the airborne dust. It was fascinating to watch, much like the dissection of some unfamiliar animal species. Although she had had more experience with planets than many of her crewmates, there were still things about them which she found surprising and not a little disturbing. It was disturbing that simply puncturing a hole in the planet's integument could have this much effect – not just on the immediate locality of the place she had attacked, but thousands of kilometres beyond. Eventually, she knew, there would not be a spot on the planet which had not been in some measurable way affected by her action. The dust she had caused to be elevated would eventually settle; a fine blackened, faintly radioactive caul deposited fairly uniformly around the planet. In the temperate regions it would soon be washed away by the weather processes which the colonists had instigated, assuming of course that those processes still functioned. But in the arctic regions there was never any rain, so the fine fall of dust would remain unperturbed for centuries to come. Eventually other deposits would cover it, and it would become part of the irrevocable geological memory of the planet. Perhaps, the Triumvir mused, in a few million years other beings would arrive on Resurgam, sharing something of humanity's curiosity. They would want to learn of the planet's history, and in doing so they would take core samples, reaching far back into Resurgam's past. Doubtless that deposited layer of dust would not be the only mystery they had to solve, but nonetheless they would mull on it, if only fleetingly. And she had no doubt that those hypothetical future investigators would come to a totally wrong conclusion regarding the layer's origin. It would never occur to them that it had been put there by an act of conscious volition . . .

Volyova had slept only a few hours in the last thirty, but her nervous energy currently seemed limitless. She would, of course, pay a price for it at some point in the near future, but for now she felt like she was careering, imbued with unstoppable momentum. Even so, she did not immediately snap to alertness when Hegazi steered his chair next to hers.

'What is it?'

'I'm getting something which might very much be our boy.'

'Sylveste?'

'Or someone pretending to be him.' Hegazi entered one of his intermittent phases of fugue, which to Volyova signified that he was in deep rapport with the ship. 'Can't trace the communication route he's using. It's coming from Cuvier, but you can bet Sylveste isn't physically there.'

She did not raise her voice, even though the two of them were quite alone in the bridge.

'What's he saying?'

'He's just asking to speak to us. Over and over again.'

*

Khouri heard footsteps sloshing through the inch-thick sludge which flooded the entire Captain's level.

She did not have a rational answer for why she had come down here. Perhaps that was the point, really: now that she no longer trusted Volyova – the one person she had thought she could place her faith in – and now that the Mademoiselle was absent, as she had been ever since the attack against the cache-weapon, Khouri had to turn to the irrational. The only person left on the ship who had not in some way betrayed her, or had not earned her hatred, was the one she could never expect an answer from.

She knew almost immediately that the footsteps did not belong to Volyova, but there was a purposefulness to them which suggested that the person knew exactly where they were going, and had not simply strolled into this area of the ship by accident.

Khouri got up out of the muck. The seat of her trousers was wet and cold with the stuff, but the darkness of the fabric concealed most of the damage.

'Relax,' said the person, strolling casually round the bend, her boots sloshing through the sludge. There was a glint of metal from the woman's free-swinging arms and a multicoloured glow from the holographic designs worked into the arms' metalwork.

'Sudjic,' Khouri identified. 'How the hell did you—'

Sudjic shook her head with a tight-lipped smile. 'How did I find my way down here? Simple, Khouri. I followed you. Once I saw which general direction you'd gone, it was obvious you must be headed here. So I came after you, because I reckon you and I could use a little chat.'

'A chat?'

'About the situation here.' Sudjic gestured expansively. 'On this ship. More specifically, the fucking Triumvirate. It can't have escaped you that I have a grievance against one of them.'

'Volyova.'

'Yes, our mutual friend Ilia.' Sudjic managed to make the woman's name sound like a particularly unsavoury expletive. 'She killed my lover, you know that.'

'I understand there'd been . . . problems.'

'Problems, ha. That's a good one. Do you call turning someone psychotic a problem, Khouri?' She paused, stepped a little closer, but still kept a respectful distance from the fused, angelic core of the Captain. 'Or maybe I should call you Ana, now that we're on – uh – closer terms.'

'Call me what you want. It doesn't alter anything. I may hate her guts right now, but that doesn't mean I'm about to betray her. We shouldn't even be having this conversation.'

Sudjic nodded sagely. 'She really hit you with that loyalty therapy, didn't she? Look, Sajaki and the others are not nearly as omniscient as you'd think. You can tell me everything.'

'There's a lot more to it than that.'

'Such as?' Sudjic was standing akimbo now, her gauntleted hands placed daintily against her narrow hips. The woman was beautiful, in the emaciated way which was common among the spaceborn. Her physiology was wraith-like; had her underlying skeletal-muscular structure not been chimerically enhanced, it was doubtful she would have been fully ambulatory in normal gravity. But now, with those subcutaneous augmentations, Sudjic was undoubtably stronger and faster than any non-augmented human. Her strength was double-edged, because she looked so fragile. She was like an origami sculpture of a woman folded from razor-sharp paper.

'I can't tell you,' Khouri said. 'But Ilia and I – we have mutual secrets.' Instantly she regretted saying that, but she wanted to deflate the smug superiority of the Ultra. 'What I mean is—'

'Listen, I'm sure that's the way she wants you to feel. But ask yourself this, Khouri. How much of what you remember is real? Isn't it possible that Volyova's been screwing with your memories? She tried it with Boris. She tried to cure him by erasing his past, but it didn't work. He still had the voices to deal with. That go for you too? Any new voices floating around in your head?'

'If there are,' Khouri said, 'they haven't got anything to do with Volyova.'

'So you admit it.' Sudjic smiled primly, like a valiant schoolgirl acknowledging victory in a game, but hoping not to look too proud of the fact. 'Well, whether you do or don't, it doesn't matter. The fact is you're disillusioned with her. With the Triumvirate as a whole. You can't kid yourself you liked what they just did.'

'I'm not sure I understand what it was they just did, Sudjic. There are a few things I haven't got right in my head.' Khouri felt the cold, wet fabric of her trousers clinging to her buttocks. 'That's why I came down here, as a matter of fact. For some peace and quiet. To get my head together.'

'And see if he had wisdom to spare?'

Sudjic had nodded towards the Captain.

'He's dead, Sudjic. I may be the only person here who recognises that, but it's true all the same.'

'Maybe Sylveste can cure him.'

'Even if he could, would Sajaki want it to happen?'

Sudjic nodded knowingly. 'Of course, of course. I understand totally. But listen.' Her voice lowered to a conspiratorial whisper, though the only possible eavesdroppers were the skulking rats. 'They've found Sylveste – I just heard, before I came down.'

'Found him? You mean he's here?'

'No, of course not. They've just made contact. They don't even know where he is yet, just that he's alive. Still got to get the bastard aboard somehow. And that's where you come in. Me too, in fact.'

'What do you mean?'

'I don't pretend to understand what happened with Kjarval in the training chamber, Khouri. Maybe she just cracked, although I knew her better than anyone else on this ship, and I'd say she wasn't really the cracking type. Whatever it was, it gave Volyova an excuse to finish her off – not that I ever thought the bitch really hated her that much . . .'

'It wasn't Volyova's fault . . .'

'Whatever.' Sudjic shook her head. 'That's not important – just now. But what it means is she needs you for the mission. You and me, Khouri – and maybe the bitch-queen herself – are going down there to retrieve him.'

'You can't know that yet.'

Sudjic shook her head. 'Not officially I can't. But when you've been aboard this ship as long as I have, you'll know a thing or two about bypassing the usual channels.'

For a moment there was only silence, broken by the distant dripping of a leaking conduit, some distance down the flooded corridor.

'Sudjic, why are you telling me this? I thought you hated my guts.'

'Maybe I did,' the woman said. 'Once. But now we need all the allies we can get. And I thought you might appreciate forewarning. Especially if you've got any sense, and you know who to trust.'

*

Volyova addressed her bracelet. '*Infinity*, I want you to correlate the voice you're about to hear against shipboard records of Sylveste. If you can't confirm a match, let me know immediately via secure readout.'

Sylveste's voice burst in on them, mid-sentence: '. . . if you are reading me. Repeat, I need to know if you are reading me. I demand that you acknowledge me, bitch. I demand that you fucking acknowledge me!'

'That's him all right,' Volyova said, speaking over the man's voice. 'I'd know that petulant tone anywhere. Better put him out of it. I presume we still don't have a fix on him?'

'Sorry. You're going to have to address the colony as a whole and assume he has a means of reading you.'

'I'm sure he won't have neglected that detail.' Volyova consulted her bracelet, observing that the ship could so far not disprove the hypothesis that the voice she was hearing belonged to Sylveste. There was room for error, since the Sylveste who had come aboard the ship once before was a much younger counterpart of the one they were now looking for, and so the voice match was not expected to be perfect. But even allowing for that, it looked increasingly likely that they had found him, and that this was not simply another hapless impersonator coming forward to 'save' the colony. 'All right, patch me through. Sylveste? This is Volyova. Tell me if you're hearing this.'

His voice was clearer now. 'About fucking time.'

'I think we'll take that as a "yes",' Hegazi said.

'We need to discuss the logistics of picking you up, and I believe it would be very much easier if we could do so on a secure channel. If you give me your current location, we can make a detailed sensor-sweep of that region and pick up your transmission at source, avoiding the relay at Cuvier.'

'Now why would you need to do that? Is there something you want me to know that the colony as a whole can't share?' Sylveste paused, but Volyova mentally inserted a sneer at that point. 'After all, you haven't been slow in bringing them into it so far.' Another pause. 'Incidentally, it troubles me that I'm dealing with you and not Sajaki.'

'He's indisposed,' Volyova said. 'Give me your position.'

'Sorry, but that isn't possible.'

'You'll have to do better than that.'

'Why should I bother? You're the ones with all the firepower. You figure out a solution.'

Hegazi waved his hand, signalling Volyova to cut the audio link. 'Maybe he can't reveal his position.'

'Can't?'

Hegazi tapped a steel forefinger against his steel-bridged nose.

'His captors might not let him. They're ready to let him go, but they don't want to give up their position.'

Volyova nodded, admitting that Hegazi's suggestion was probably close to the truth. She reinstated the link. 'All right Sylveste. I think I understand your predicament. I propose the following compromise, assuming that you have the means to move around. Your – uh – hosts can doubtless arrange something at short notice, I presume?'

'We have transportation, if that's what you're asking.'

'You have six more hours, in that case. Enough time to get to a location sufficiently far from where you are now that you won't compromise it when you reveal your position. But if in six hours we don't hear from you, we will bring forward the attack against the next target. Is that perfectly clear to all concerned?'

'Oh yes,' Sylveste said, tartly. 'Perfectly clear.'

'There's one more thing.'

'Yes?'

'Bring Calvin with you.'

SIXTEEN

North Nekhebet, 2566

Sylveste felt the aircraft haul itself aloft, at first moving horizontally to clear Mantell's dugout hangar, then making rapid height and swerving to avoid dashing itself against the stacked strata of the adjacent mesa wall. He made himself a window, but the thickening dust allowed him only a glimpse of the base, the mesa in which it had been tunnelled falling away below the brilliant undercurve of the plasma-wing. He knew, with absolute certainty, that he would not be returning. It was not just Mantell that he sensed he was seeing for the last time, but – and he could not have articulated exactly why – the colony itself.

The machine was the smallest and least valuable aircraft that the settlement could muster; barely larger than one of the volantors which he had flown in Chasm City a lifetime earlier. It was also fast enough to make that six hours of grace count; capable of putting a useful distance between itself and the mesa. The aircraft could have carried four, but only Sylveste and Pascale were riding it. Yet – insofar as their freedom of movement went – they were still Sluka's captives. Her people had programmed the aircraft's route before it left Mantell, and it would only deviate from that flight-plan if the autopilot judged that the weather conditions merited a different course. Unless ground conditions at the site became intolerable, it would deposit Sylveste and his wife at a pre-agreed location which had still not been revealed to Volyova and her crew. If conditions were bad, another site could be picked in the same area.

The plane would not linger at the delivery point. After Sylveste and Pascale had been let off – with enough provisions to survive in the storm for a few hours at most – the plane would return swiftly to Mantell, evading the few extant radar systems which could have alerted Resurgam City to its trajectory. Sylveste would then contact

Volyova and inform her of his location, although, because he would then be broadcasting directly, she would have no difficulty triangulating his position. Thereafter things would be in Volyova's hands. Sylveste had no real idea how events would proceed, how she would bring him aboard the ship. That was her problem, not his. All he knew was that it was very unlikely that this whole affair was a trap. Although the Ultras wanted access to Calvin, Calvin was essentially useless without Sylveste. They would want to take very good care of him indeed. And if the same logic did not automatically apply to Pascale, Sylveste had taken steps to amend that deficiency.

The aircraft levelled now. It was flying below the average height of the mesas, using their bulk for cover. Every few seconds it would veer, steering through the narrow, canyonlike corridors which spaced the mesas. Visibility was near zero. Sylveste hoped that the terrain map on which the plane was basing its manoeuvres had not been compromised by any recent landfalls, or else the ride would be very much shorter than the six hours Volyova had allocated.

'Where the hell . . .' Calvin, who had just appeared in the cabin, looked around frantically. He was, as usual, reclining in an enormous, fussily upholstered chair. There was not enough room for its bulk in the fuselage, so its extremities had to vanish awkwardly into the walls. 'Where the hell am I? I'm not getting anything! What the hell's happened? Tell me!'

Sylveste turned to his wife. 'The first thing he does, on being woken, is sniff the local cybernetic environment – allows him to get his bearings, establish the time frame, and so on. Trouble is, right now there isn't a local cybernetic environment, so he's a bit disorientated.'

'Stop talking about me like I'm not here. Wherever the hell here is!'

'You're in a plane,' Sylveste said.

'A plane? That's novel,' Cal nodded, regaining some of his composure. 'Very novel indeed. Don't think I've ever been in one of those before. I don't suppose you'd mind filling your old dad in on a few key facts?'

'That's exactly why I've woken you.' Sylveste paused to cancel the windows; there was no view now and the unchanging pall of dust served only to remind him of what lay ahead once the plane had deposited them. 'Don't for one moment imagine it was because I felt in need of a fireside chat, Cal.'

'You look older, son.'

'Yes, well, some of us have to get on with the business of being alive in the entropic universe.'

'Ouch. That hurts, you know.'

Pascale said, 'Stop it, will you? There isn't time for this bickering.'

'I don't know,' Sylveste said. 'Five hours – seems like more than enough to me. What do you think, Cal?'

'Too right. What does she know anyway?' Cal glared at her. 'It's traditional, dearie. It's how we – how shall I put it? Touch base. If he showed even the remotest hint of cordiality towards me, then I'd really start worrying. It would mean he wanted some excruciatingly difficult favour.'

'No,' Sylveste said. 'For merely excruciatingly difficult favours, I'd just threaten you with erasure. I haven't needed anything big enough from you to justify being pleasant, and I doubt I ever will.'

Calvin winked at Pascale. 'He's right, of course. Silly me.'

He was manifesting in a high-collared ash-coloured frockcoat, its sleeves patterned with interlocked gold chevrons. One booted foot was resting on the knee of his other leg, and the frock's tail draped over the raised leg in a long curtain of gently rippling fabric. His beard and moustache had attained some realm beyond the merely fussy, sculpted into a whole of such complexity that it could only have been maintained by the fastidious attention of an army of dedicated grooming-servitors. An amber data-monocle rested in one socket (an affectation, since Calvin had been implanted for direct interfacing since birth), and his hair (long now) extended beyond the back of his skull in an oiled handle, reconnecting with his scalp somewhere above his nape. Sylveste attempted to date the ensemble, but failed. It was possible that the look referred to a particular era from Calvin's days on Yellowstone. It was equally possible that the simulation had invented it entirely from scratch, to kill the time while all his routines booted.

'So, anyway . . .'

'The plane's taking me to meet Volyova,' Sylveste said. 'You remember her, of course?'

'How could we forget?' Calvin removed the monocle, polishing it absently against his sleeve. 'And just how did all this come about?'

'It's a long story. She's put the squeeze on the colony. They had little choice but to hand me over. You too, in fact.'

'She wanted me?'

'Don't look all surprised about it.'

'I'm not; just disappointed. And of course this is rather a lot to take in all of a sudden.' Calvin popped the monocle back in, one eye glaring magnified behind the amber. 'Do you think she wanted us together as a safeguard, or because she has something specific in mind?'

'Probably the latter. Not that she's been exactly open about her intentions.'

Calvin nodded thoughtfully. 'So you've been dealing only with Volyova, is that it?'

'Does that strike you as odd?'

'I would have expected our friend Sajaki to show his face at some point.'

'Me too, but she hasn't made any reference to his absence.' Sylveste shrugged. 'Does it really matter? They're all as bad as each other.'

'Granted, but at least with Sajaki we knew where we were.'

'Shafted, you mean?'

Calvin rocked his head equivocally. 'Say what you like about the man, at least he kept his word. And he – or whoever is running things – has at least had the decency not to bother you again until now. How long has it been since we were last aboard that Gothic monstrosity they call *Nostalgia for Infinity*?'

'About a hundred and thirty years. A lot less for them, of course – only a few decades as far as they were concerned.'

'I suppose we'd better assume the worst.'

'The worst what?' Pascale said.

'That,' Calvin began, with laboured patience, 'we have a certain task to perform, in connection with a certain gentleman.' He squinted at Sylveste. 'How much does she know, anyway?'

'Rather less than I imagined, I suspect.' Pascale did not look amused.

'I told her the minimum,' Sylveste said, glancing between his wife and the beta-level simulation. 'For her own good.'

'Oh, thanks.'

'Of course, I had some doubts of my own . . .'

'Dan, just what is it these people want with you and your father?'

'Ah, well, that's another very long story, I'm afraid.'

'You've got five hours – you just said so yourself. Assuming, of course, you two can bear to break off from your mutual admiration session.'

Calvin raised one eyebrow. 'Never heard it called that before. But maybe she's got something, eh, son?'

'Yes,' Sylveste said. 'What she's got is a severe misapprehension of the situation.'

'Nonetheless, maybe you should tell her a bit more – keep her in the picture and all that.'

The aircraft executed a particularly abrupt turn, Calvin the only one amongst them impervious to the motion. 'All right,' Sylveste said. 'Though I still say she'd be better off knowing less rather than more.'

'Why don't you let me be the judge of that?' Pascale said.

Calvin smiled. 'Start by telling her about dear Captain Brannigan, that's my advice.'

So Sylveste told her the rest of it. Until then, he had deliberately skirted the issue of what exactly it was that Sajaki's crew wanted of him. Pascale had always had every right to know, of course . . . but the subject itself was so unpalatable to Sylveste that he had done his best to avoid it at all times. It was not that he had anything personal against Captain Brannigan, or even any lack of sympathy for what had become of the man. The Captain was a unique individual with a uniquely horrifying affliction. Even if he was not in any sense aware now (to the best of Sylveste's knowledge), he had been in the past, and could be again in the future, in the admittedly unlikely event that he could be cured. So what if the Captain's murky past quite possibly contained crimes? Surely the man had atoned for prior sins a thousand times over in his present state. No; anyone would have wished the Captain well, and most people would have been willing to expend some energy in helping him, provided they ran no risk to themselves. Even some small risk might have been accepted.

But what the crew were asking of Sylveste was much more than just the acceptance of personal risk. They would require him to submit to Calvin; to allow Cal to invade his mind and take command of his motor functions. The thought alone was repulsive. It was bad enough dealing with Cal as a beta-level simulation; as bad as being haunted by his father's ghost. He would have destroyed the beta-level years ago if it had not proven so intermittently useful, but just knowing it existed made him uncomfortable. Cal was too perceptive; too shrewd in his . . . in *its* judgements. It knew what he had done with the alpha-level simulation, even if it had never come out and said it. But every time he allowed it into his head, it seemed to sink deeper tendrils into him. It seemed to know him better each time; seemed able to predict his own responses more closely. What did that make him, if what seemed like his own free will was so easily mimicked by a piece of software which had no theoretical consciousness of its own? It was worse than simply the dehumanising aspect of the channelling process, of course. The physical procedure was itself far from pleasant, for his own voluntary motor signals had to be blocked at source, obstructed by a stew of neuro-inhibitory chemicals. He would be paralysed, yet moving – as close to demonic possession as anyone ever came. It had always been a nightmarish experience; never one he was in a hurry to repeat.

No, he thought. The Captain could go to hell, for all he cared. Why should he lose his own humanity to save someone who had lived longer than most people in history? Sympathy be damned. The Captain should have been allowed to die years ago, and the greater crime now was not the Captain's suffering, but what his crew were prepared to put Sylveste through to alleviate it.

Of course, Calvin saw it differently . . . less an ordeal, more an opportunity . . .

'Of course, I was the first,' Calvin said. 'Back when I was still corporeal.'

'The first what?'

'First to serve him. He was heavily chimeric even then. Some of the technologies holding him together dated from before the Transenlightenment. God knows how old the flesh parts of him were.' He fingered his beard and moustache, as if needing to remind himself how artful the combination was. 'This was before the Eighty, of course. But I was known even then as an experimenter on the fringe of the radical chimeric sciences. I wasn't just content with renovating the techniques developed before the Transenlightenment. I wanted to go beyond what they'd attained.

I wanted to leave them in my dust. I wanted to push the envelope so far it ripped into shreds, and then remake it from the pieces.'

'Yes, enough about you Cal,' Sylveste said. 'We were discussing Brannigan, remember?'

'It's called setting the scene, dear boy.' Calvin blinked. 'Anyway, Brannigan was an extreme chimeric, and I was someone prepared to consider extreme measures. When he became sick, his friends had no choice but to hire my services. Of course, this was all strictly below-board – and it was a total diversion, even for me. I was increasingly uninterested in physiological modifications, at the expense of a growing fascination – obsession, if you will – with neural transformations. Specifically, I wanted to find a way of mapping neural activity straight into—' Calvin broke off, biting his lower lip.

'Brannigan used him,' Sylveste continued. 'And in return, helped him to establish ties with some of the Chasm City rich; potential clients for the Eighty program. And if he'd done a good job of healing Brannigan, that would have been the end of the story. But he botched the job – did the minimum he could get away with, to get Brannigan's allies off his back. If he'd taken the trouble to do it properly, we wouldn't be in this mess now.'

'What he means,' Calvin cut in, 'is that my repair of the Captain could not be considered permanent. It was inevitable, given the nature of his chimerism, that some other aspect of his physiology would eventually need our attention. And by then – because of the complexity of the work I'd done on him – there was literally no other person they could turn to.'

'So they came back,' Pascale said.

'This time he was commanding the ship we're about to board.' Sylveste looked at the simulation. 'Cal was dead; the Eighty a publicly staged atrocity. All that remained of him was this beta-level simulation. Needless to say Sajaki – he was with the Captain by then – was not best pleased. But they found a way, all the same.'

'A way?'

'For Calvin to work on the Captain. They found he could work through me. The beta-level sim provided the expertise in chimeric surgery. I provided the meat it needed to move around to get the job done. "Channelling" was what the Ultras called it.'

'Then it needn't have been you at all,' Pascale said. 'Provided they had the beta-level simulation – or a copy of it – couldn't one of them have acted as the – as you so charmingly put it – meat?'

'No, though they probably would have preferred it that way: it would have freed them of any dependency on me. But channelling only worked when there was a close match between the beta-level sim and the person it was working through. Like a hand fitting into a glove. It worked with me and Calvin because he was my father; there were many points of genetic similarity. Slice open our brains and you'd probably have trouble telling them apart.'

'And now?'

'They're back.'

'Now if only he'd done a good job last time,' Calvin said, dignifying his remark with a thin smile of self-satisfaction.

'Blame yourself; you were in the driving seat. I just did what you told me.' Sylveste scowled. 'In fact for most of it I wasn't even what you'd term conscious. Not that I didn't hate every minute of it, all the same.'

'And they're going to make you do it again,' Pascale said. 'Is that all it's about? Everything that's happened here? The attack on that settlement? Just to get you to help their Captain?'

Sylveste nodded. 'In case it hasn't escaped your attention, the people we're about to do business with are not what you'd properly term human. Their priorities and timescales are a little ... abstract.'

'I wouldn't call it business, in that case. I'd call it blackmail.'

'Well,' Sylveste said. 'That's where you're wrong. You see, this time Volyova made a small miscalculation. She gave me some warning of her arrival.'

Volyova glanced up at the imaged view of Resurgam. At the moment Sylveste's location on the planet's surface was completely unknown, like a quantum wave function which had not yet collapsed. Yet in a moment they would have an accurate triangulation fix on his broadcast, and that wave function would shed a myriad unselected possibilities.

'You have him?'

'Signal's weak,' Hegazi said. 'That storm you made is causing a lot of ionospheric interference. I bet you're really proud, aren't you?'

'Just a get a fix, *svinoi*.'

'Patience, patience.'

Volyova had not really doubted that Sylveste would call in on time. Nonetheless, when she heard from him, she could not help but feel relief. It meant that another element in the tricky business of getting him aboard had been achieved. She did not, however, deceive herself that the job was in any way complete. And there had been something arrogant about Sylveste's demands – the way he seemed to be ordering how things should happen – which left her wondering if her colleagues really did have the upper hand. If Sylveste had set out to sow a seed of doubt in her mind, the man had certainly succeeded. Damn him. She had prepared herself, knowing that Sylveste was adept at mind games, but she had not prepared herself enough. Then she took a mental back step and asked herself how things had so far proceeded. After all, Sylveste was shortly to be in their custody. He could not possibly desire such an outcome, especially as he would know just what it was they wanted from him. If he were in control of his destiny, he would not now be on the verge of being brought aboard.

'Ah,' Hegazi said. 'We have a fix. You want to hear what the bastard has to say?'

'Put him on.'

The man's voice burst in on them again, as it had done six hours previously, but there was a difference now, very obviously. Every word Sylveste spoke was backgrounded – almost drowned out – by the continuous howl of the razorstorm.

'I'm here, where are you? Volyova, are you listening to me? I said are you listening to me? I want an answer! Here are my coordinates relative to Cuvier – you'd better be listening.' And then he recited – several times, for safety – a string of numbers which would pinpoint him to within one hundred metres; redundant information, given the triangulation which had now been performed. 'Now get down here! We can't wait for ever – we're in the middle of a razorstorm, we're going to die out here if you don't hurry.'

'Mmm,' Hegazi said. 'I think at some point it might not be a bad idea to answer the poor fellow.'

Volyova took out and lit a cigarette. She savoured a long intake before replying. 'Not yet,' she said. 'In fact, maybe not for an hour or two. I think I'll let him get really worried first.'

Khouri heard only the faintest of scuffling sounds as the open suit shuffled towards her. She felt its gently insistent pressure against her spine and the backs of her legs, arms and head. In her peripheral vision she observed the wet-looking side-parts of the head fold around her, and then felt the legs and arms of the suit meld around her limbs. The chest cavity sealed, with a sound like someone taking the last slurp from a pudding bowl.

Her vision was restricted now, but she could see enough to watch the suit's limbs closing up along their dissection-lines. The seals lingered for a second or so before becoming invisible, lost in the bland whiteness of the rest of the suit's hide. Then the head formed over her own, and for a moment there was darkness before a transparent oval appeared ahead of her. Smoothly, the darkness around the oval lit up with numerous readouts and status displays. Later the suit would flood itself with gel-air, to protect its occupant against the gee-loads of flight, but for now Khouri was breathing mintily fresh oxygen/nitrogen air at shipboard pressure.

'I have now run through my safety and functionality tests,' the suit informed her. 'Please confirm that you wish to accept full control of this unit.'

'Yes, I'm ready,' Khouri said.

'I have now disabled the majority of my autonomous control routines. This persona will remain online in an advisory capacity, unless you request otherwise. Full suit-autonomous control can be reinstated by—'

'I get the deal, thanks. How are the others doing?'

'All other units report readiness.'

Volyova's voice cut in: 'We're set, Khouri. I'll lead the team; triangular descent formation. I shout, you jump. And don't make a move unless I authorise it.'

'Don't worry; I had no plans to.'

'I see you have her well under your thumb,' Sudjic said, on the open channel. 'Does she shit to order as well?'

'Shut it, Sudjic. You're only along because you know worlds. One step out of line . . .' Volyova paused. 'Well, put it this way; Sajaki won't be around to intercede if I lose my temper, and I've got a lot of firepower with which to lose it.'

'Talking of firepower,' Khouri said, 'I'm not seeing any weapons data on my readout.'

'That's because you're not authorised,' Sudjic said. 'Ilia doesn't trust you not to shoot at the first thing that moves. Do you, Ilia?'

'If we run into trouble,' Ilia said, 'I'll let you have weps usage, trust me.'

'Why not now?'

'Because you don't need it now, that's why. You're along for the ride; to assist if things deviate from the plan. Which of course they won't . . .' She drew breath audibly. 'But if they do, you get your precious weapons. Just try and be discreet if you have to use them, that's all.'

Once outside, the shipboard air was purged and replaced by gel-air: breathable fluid. For a moment it felt like drowning, but Khouri had made the transition enough times on Sky's Edge not to feel much discomfort. Normal speech was impossible now, but the suit helmets contained trawls which were able to interpret subvocal commands. Speakers in the helmets shifted incoming sounds by the appropriate frequency to compensate for the gel-air-induced distortions, which ensured that the voices she heard sounded perfectly normal. Although it was a harder and heavier descent than any shuttle insertion, it felt easier, apart from an occasional pressure above Khouri's eyeballs. It was only by reference to the suit's readouts that she knew they were routinely exceeding six gees of acceleration, impelled by the tiny antilithium-fed thrusters buried in the suit's spine and heels. With Volyova leading the descent, the suits formed a deltoid pattern, the two inhabited suits following her and the three slaved empty suits trailing behind. For the first part of the descent, the suits remained in the configuration they had assumed aboard the lighthugger, making a rough concession to human anatomy. But by the time the first traces of Resurgam's upper atmosphere began to glow around them, the suits had silently transformed their exteriors. Now – although none of this was obvious from within – the membrane linking the arms to the body had thickened, until the arms and body were no longer easily divisible. The angle of the arms had altered as well; now they were held rigid but slightly bent, at an angle of forty-five degrees to the body. Since the head had retracted and flattened, there was now a smooth arc running from the tip of each arm, over the head and down again. The columnar legs had fused into a single flared tail, and any transparent patches defined by the user had been forcibly re-opaqued, to protect against the glare of re-entry. The suits met the atmosphere chest-on, with the tail hanging slightly lower than the head: complex shockwave patterns being tamed and exploited by the morphing geometry of the suit hide. While direct vision was no longer possible, the suits were continuing to perceive their surroundings in other EM bands, and were perfectly capable of adapting this data for human senses. Looking around and below, Khouri saw the other suits, each seemingly immersed in a radiant teardrop of pinkish plasma.

At twenty kilometres' altitude the suits used their thrusters to drop to merely supersonic speeds. Now they remoulded themselves to adapt to the thickening atmosphere, transforming into human-sized aircraft. The suits grew stabilising fins along their backs, and the face parts again returned to transparency. Snug in the suit's embrace, Khouri barely felt these changes, only a slight pressure from the surrounding suit material which nudged her limbs from one position to another.

At fifteen kilometres, the sixth suit broke formation and went hypersonic, configuring itself into an aerodynamically optimum shape into which no human could have fitted without drastic surgery. It disappeared over the horizon in a few seconds, probably moving faster than any artificial object which had ever entered Resurgam's atmosphere, exerting upward thrust to keep itself from escaping from the planet entirely. Khouri knew that the suit was heading to pick up Sajaki – it would meet with him near the designated site where he had last communicated with the ship, now that his work on Resurgam was complete.

At ten kilometres – maintaining silence, even though the com-laser links between the suits were totally secure – they hit the first traces of the razorstorm Volyova had stirred to life. From space it had looked black and impenetrable, like a plateau of ash. Inside, there was more illumination than Khouri had expected. The light was gritty and sepia, like a bad afternoon in Chasm City. A muddyish rainbow haloed the sun, and then that too vanished as they sank deeper into the storm. Now light did not so much stream down to them as stumble haphazardly, navigating layer upon layer of elevated dust like a drunkard descending stairs. Since there was no feeling of weight in the gel-air, Khouri rapidly lost all sensation of up and down, but she instinctively trusted the suit's own inertial systems to figure things out. Now and again – even though the thrusters were trying to smooth out the ride – she felt lurches as the suit hit a pressure cell. As the speed of the ensemble dropped below that of sound, the suits reconfigured again, becoming more statuesque. The ground was only a few kilometres below, and the highest peaks of the mesa system were only hundreds of metres under them, though they remained unseen. It was increasingly hard now to make out the other four suits in the formation; they kept fading in and out of the dust.

Khouri began to get a little concerned. She had never used a suit in conditions anything like this. 'Suit,' she asked. 'Are you quite sure you can handle this stuff? I wouldn't want you dropping out of the sky on me.'

'Wearer,' it said, managing to sound sniffy. 'When the dust becomes a problem I shall immediately inform you of that fact.'

'All right; just asking.'

Now there was hardly anything to see. It was like swimming through mud. There were occasional rents in the storm which afforded glimpses of towering canyon and mesa walls, but most of the time the dust was completely featureless. 'Can't see anything,' she said.

'Is this an improvement?'

It was. The storm had casually blinked out of existence. She could see around her for tens of kilometres; all the way to the relatively near horizon, where it was unobstructed by closer rock walls. It was just like flying on a dazzlingly clear day, except that the entire scene was rendered in sickly variations of pale green. 'A montage,' the suit said. 'Constructed from ambient infrared, interpolated random-pulse/snapshot sonar and gravimetric data.'

'Very nice, but don't get cocky about it. When I get annoyed with machines, even very sophisticated ones, I have a nasty habit of abusing them.'

'Duly noted,' the suit said, shutting up.

She called up an overlay which gave her some idea where she was on a larger scale. The suit knew exactly where to go – homing in on the coordinates where Sylveste had called from – but it made her feel more professional to actually take an active interest in things. Three and a half hours had passed now since Volyova and Sylveste had spoken, which, assuming he was on foot, would not allow Sylveste to get seriously far from the agreed rendezvous point. Even if, for some reason, he now tried to evade the pick-up, the suit's sensors would have no trouble locating him, unless he had found a conveniently deep cave in which to ensconce himself:

but then the suit's detector systems would do their level best to track him down, using the thermal and biochemical evidence he would have unavoidably left behind on his route.

'Listen up,' Volyova said, using the intersuit com for the first time since they had entered the atmosphere. 'We'll be at the reception point in two minutes. I've just had a signal from orbit. Triumvir Sajaki's suit has located him and made successful pick-up. He's currently en route to meet us, but because his suit can't move so quickly now he won't make it for another ten minutes.'

'He's meeting us?' Khouri asked. 'Why doesn't he just return to the ship? Doesn't he believe we can do the job without him breathing down our necks?'

'Are you kidding?' Sudjic asked. 'Sajaki's waited years – decades – for this. He wouldn't miss it for the world.'

'Sylveste won't put up a struggle, will he?'

'Not unless he's feeling incredibly lucky,' Volyova said. 'But don't take anything for granted. I've dealt with this bastard before; you two haven't.'

Khouri felt her suit slither to a configuration very similar to the one it had first had aboard the ship. The wing membrane had vanished entirely now, and her limbs were properly defined and articulated, rather than just being flattened winglike appendages. The tips of the arms had bifurcated into mittenlike claws, but a more developed hand could be formed, if she needed to do delicate manipulations. Now she was tipping back into a near-vertical posture, while still moving forwards. The suit was now maintaining altitude solely by thrust, utterly impervious to the dust.

'One minute,' Volyova said. 'Altitude two hundred metres. Expect visual acquisition of Sylveste any moment now. And remember we'll also be looking for his wife; I doubt they'll be far apart.'

Tiring of the pale-green false image, Khouri reverted to normal vision. She could hardly make out the other suits. They were now a long way from the canyon walls of any major rock features or crevasses. The terrain was flat for thousands of metres in any direction, apart from the odd boulder or gully. But even when pockets opened in the storm, calm ventricles in the chaos, it was impossible to see more than a few tens of metres, and the ground was ceaselessly aswirl in dust eddies. Yet in the suit it was totally cool and silent, lending the whole situation a dangerous air of unreality. If she had wished it, the suit could have relayed the ambient sound to her, but it would have told her nothing except that it was hellishly windy out there.

She returned to the pale-green.

'Ilia,' she said. 'I'm still weaponless here. Starting to feel a bit itchy.'

'Give her something to play with,' Sudjic said. 'It can't hurt, can it? She can go away and shoot some rocks while we take care of Sylveste.'

'Fuck you.'

'In spades, Khouri. Didn't it occur to you I might be trying to do you a favour? Or do you think you can persuade Ilia all on your lonesome?'

'All right Khouri,' Volyova said. 'I'm enabling your minimal-volition defence protocols. That suit you?'

Not exactly, no. While Khouri's suit had now been given the autonomous privileges to defend itself against external threats – even, to some extent, to act proactively towards that goal – Khouri still did not have her finger on the trigger. And that might prove to be a problem if she wanted to kill Sylveste, which was an objective she had not entirely jettisoned.

'Yeah, thanks,' she said. 'Excuse me if I don't whoop for joy.'

'My pleasure . . .'

A second or so later they landed, soft as five feathers. Khouri felt a shiver as her suit depowered its thrusters, then made a further series of minute readjustments to its anatomy. The status readouts had now flicked over from flight to ambulatory mode, signifying that she could, if she wished, walk around normally. At this point she could even ditch the suit entirely, but without protective gear she would not have lasted long in the razorstorm. She was more than happy to remain encased in the suit's silence, even if it meant that she did not feel entirely participatory.

'We split,' Volyova said. 'Khouri; I'm assigning control of the two empty suits to your own; they'll shadow you when you move. The three of us move apart for one hundred paces; initiate active sensor sweep in all EM and supplemental bands. If Sylveste is anywhere nearby we'll find the *svinoi*.'

The two empty suits had shuffled next to Khouri already, latching onto her like stray dogs. This was, she knew, definitely the short straw choice; Volyova was letting her look after the empty units as a consolation prize for not being better armed. But there was no point whining. Her only reasonable argument for being properly armed was so that she could use those defences to kill Sylveste. It was probably not an argument which would prove entirely effective against Volyova. Still, it was worth bearing in mind that the suits could be deadly even without their armaments. In training on Sky's Edge, she had been shown how someone wearing a suit could inflict damage on an enemy by the exertion of sheer brute force, literally tearing an opponent apart.

Khouri watched Sudjic and Volyova move off in their respective directions, walking with the deceptively plodding slowness of the suits in their default ambulatory modes. Deceptive, because the suits were capable of moving with gazelle-like speed if required, but there was no need to deploy such swiftness at the moment. She switched off the pale-green overlay, returning to normal vision. Sudjic and Volyova were not visible at all now, unsurprisingly. And while occasional pockets continued to open in the storm, Khouri was generally unable to see beyond the end of her own out-stretched arm.

With a jolt, though, she realised she had seen something – someone – moving in the dust. It had only been there for a moment; not even something she could properly dignify by calling it a glimpse. Khouri was just beginning – without too much concern – to rationalise the apparition as a chance swirling of dust, momentarily assuming a vaguely human shape. But then she saw it again.

Now the figure was better defined. It lingered, teasingly. And stepped out of the maelstrom, into clear vision.

'It's been a long time,' the Mademoiselle said. 'I thought you'd be happier to see me.'

'Where the hell have you been?'

'Wearer,' the suit said. 'I am not able to interpret your last subvocalised statement. Would you mind rephrasing what you had to say?'

'Tell it to ignore you,' the Mademoiselle's dust-ghost said. 'I don't have very long.'

Khouri told the suit to ignore what she was subvocalising, until she gave a codeword. The suit acceded with a note of stuffy displeasure, as if it had never ever been asked to do something so irregular, and that it would have to seriously rethink the terms of their working relationship in future.

'All right,' she said. 'It's just you and me, Mad. Care to tell where you've been?'

'In a moment,' the woman's projected image said. She had stabilised now, but was certainly not rendered with the fidelity Khouri had come to expect. She looked more like a crude sketch of herself, or a blurred photograph, subject to rippling waves of distortion. 'Firstly I'd better do what I can for you, or else you'll be forced into foolishness like trying to ram Sylveste. Now let's see; accessing primary suit systems . . . bypassing Volyova's restriction codes . . . remarkably simple, in fact – I'm rather disappointed she didn't give me more of a challenge, especially as this is the last time I'm likely—'

'What are you talking about?'

'I'm talking about giving you firepower, dear girl.' As she was speaking, the status-readouts reconfigured, indicating that a number of previously locked-out suit weapons systems had just come online. Khouri appraised the sudden arsenal at her fingertips, only half believing what she had just witnessed. 'There you are,' Mademoiselle said. 'Anything else you'd like me to kiss better before I go?'

'I suppose I should say thanks . . .'

'Don't bother, Khouri. The last thing I'd expect from you would be gratitude.'

'Of course, now I actually have no choice but to kill the bastard. Am I supposed to thank you for that as well?'

'You've seen the – uh – evidence. The case for the prosecution, if you will.'

Khouri nodded, feeling her scalp squidging against the suit's internal matrix. You were not meant to make gestures in a suit. 'Yes, that stuff about the Inhibitors. 'Course, I still don't know if any of it's true . . .'

'Consider the alternative, in that case. You refrain from killing Sylveste, and yet what I've told you turns out to be the truth. Imagine how bad you'd feel after that, especially if Sylveste,' the dust apparition attempted a grisly smile, 'fulfils his ambition.'

'I'd still have a clear conscience, wouldn't I?'

'Undoubtedly. And I hope that would be sufficient consolation while your entire species is being eradicated by Inhibitor systems.

Of course, in all likelihood you wouldn't even be around to regret your mistake. They're rather efficient, the Inhibitors. But you'll find that out in due course . . .'

'Well, thanks for the advice.'

'That isn't all, Khouri. Did it not occur to you that there might have been a very good reason for my absence until now?'

'Which is?'

'I'm dying.' The Mademoiselle let the word hover in the dust storm before continuing. 'After the incident with the cache-weapon, Sun Stealer managed to inject another portion of himself into your skull – but of course, you're aware of that. You felt him enter, didn't you? I remember your screams. They were graphic. How odd it must have felt; how invasive.'

'Sun Stealer hasn't exactly made an impression on me since.'

'But did it ever occur to you to ask why?'

'What do you mean?'

'I mean, dear girl, that I've spent the last few weeks doing my damnedest to stop him spreading further into your head. That's why you haven't heard anything from me. I've been too preoccupied with containing him. It was bad enough dealing with the part of him that I inadvertently let return with the bloodhounds. But at least then we reached a kind of stalemate. This time, though, it's been rather different. Sun Stealer has become stronger, while I have become successively weaker with each of his onslaughts.'

'You mean he's still here?'

'Very much so. And the only reason you haven't heard from him is that he's been equally preoccupied in the war the two of us have been waging within your skull. The difference is, he's been making progress all the time – corrupting me, co-opting my systems, exploiting my own defences against me. Oh, he's a crafty one, take my word for it.'

'What's going to happen?'

'What's going to happen is that I'm going to lose. I can be quite certain about this; it's a mathematical certainty based on his current rate of gains.' The Mademoiselle smiled again, as if she were perversely proud of this analytical detachment. 'I can delay his onslaught for a few days more, and then it's all over. It might even be shorter. I've significantly weakened myself just by the act of presenting myself to you now. But I had no choice. I had to sacrifice time in order to reinstate your weapons privilege.'

'But when he wins . . .'

'I don't know, Khouri. But be prepared for anything. He's likely to be a rather less charming tenant than I've endeavoured to be. After all, you know what he did to your predecessor. Drove the poor man psychotic.' The Mademoiselle stepped back, seeming to partially cloak herself in the dust, as if she were stepping offstage via the curtains. 'It's doubtful that we'll have the pleasure again, Khouri. I feel I should wish you well. But right now I ask only one thing of you. Do what you came here to do. And do it well.' She retreated further, her form breaking up, as if she were no more than a charcoal sketch of a woman, dispersed by wind. 'You have the means now.'

The Mademoiselle was gone. Khouri waited a moment – not so much collecting her thoughts as kicking them into some vaguely cohesive mass which she hoped might stay bundled together for more than a few seconds. Then she issued the codeword which put the suit back online. The weapons, she observed with nothing remotely resembling relief, were all still functioning, just as the Mademoiselle had promised.

'I'm sorry to interrupt,' the suit said. 'But if you'd care to reinstate full-spectrum vision you'll observe that we have company.'

'Company?'

'I've just alerted the other suits. But you're the closest.'

'Sure this isn't Sajaki?'

'It isn't Triumvir Sajaki, no.' It might have been Khouri's imagination, but the suit sounded peeved that she had even doubted its judgement in this matter. 'Even if it exceeds all safety limits, the Triumvir's suit will not arrive here for another three minutes.'

'Then it must be Sylveste.'

Khouri had by then switched to the recommended sensory overlay. She could see the approaching figure – or more accurately, figures, since there were two of them, easily resolved. The other two occupied suits were converging on the location, at the same unhurried pace with which they had first departed. 'Sylveste, I'm assuming you can hear us,' Volyova said. 'Stop where you are. We're zeroing in on you from three sides.'

His voice cut across the suit channel. 'I assumed you'd left us here to die. Nice of you to say you were coming.'

'I'm not in the habit of breaking my word,' Volyova said. 'As you undoubtedly know by now.'

Khouri began to make preparations for the kill she was still not sure she could commit herself to. She called up a target overlay, boxing Sylveste, then allocated one of her less ferocious suit-weapons: a medium-yield laser built into the head. It was puny by comparison with the other suit armaments; really just intended to warn prospective attackers to go away and pick another target. But against an unarmoured man, at virtually zero-range, it would more than suffice.

It would take only an eyeblink now, and Sylveste would die, in strict compliance with the Mademoiselle's terms.

Sudjic was moving more rapidly now, moving more swiftly towards Volyova than Sylveste. It was then that Khouri noticed something odd about the suit Sudjic was wearing. There was something projecting from one end of her clawed arm, something small and metallic. It looked like a weapon, a light hand-held boser-pistol. She was raising her arm with unhurried calm, the way a professional would have done. For an instant Khouri experienced a shocking sense of dislocation. It was as if she were seeing herself from beyond her own body; watching herself raise a weapon in readiness to kill Sylveste.

But something was wrong.

Sudjic was pointing the weapon at Volyova.

'I take it you have a plan here—' Sylveste said.

'Ilia!' Khouri shouted. 'Get down, she's going to—'

Sudjic's weapon was more powerful than it looked. There was a flash of horizontal light – the containment laser for the coherent matter-beam – streaking laterally across Khouri's field of view, knifing into Volyova's suit. Various warning alarms went haywire, signifying an excessive energy-discharge in the vicinity. Khouri's suit automatically jumped to a higher, more hair-trigger level of battle readiness, indices on the display changing to indicate that their respective subordinated weapons systems were set to go off without her conscious say-so if her suit were similarly threatened.

Volyova's suit was badly hit; a significant acreage of the chest was gone, revealing densely laminated hypodermal armour layers and outspilling cabling and power lines.

Sudjic took aim again, fired.

This time the blast went deeper, cutting into the wound it had already opened. Volyova's voice cut across the channel, but it sounded weak and distant. All Khouri could make out was a kind of questioning groan; more of shock than pain.

'That was for Boris,' Sudjic said, her own voice obscenely clear. 'That was for what you did to him in your experiments.' She levelled the gun again, no less calmly than if she were an artist about to put the finishing dab of paint on a masterpiece. 'And this is for killing him.'

'Sudjic,' Khouri said, 'stop it.'

The woman's suit did not turn to look at her. 'Why stop, Khouri? Didn't I make it clear I had a grudge against her?'

'Sajaki'll be here in minute or so.'

'By which time I'll have made it look like Sylveste fired at her.' Sudjic snorted derisively. 'Shit; didn't it occur to you I'd have thought of that? I wasn't going to let myself get stuffed just to get revenge on the old hag. She isn't worth the expense.'

'I can't let you kill her.'

'Can't let me? Oh, that's funny, Khouri. What are you going to stop me with? I don't recall her reinstating your weapons privilege, and right now I don't think she's in much of a state to do it.'

Sudjic was right.

Volyova was slumped over now, her suit having lost integrity. Maybe the wound reached into her by now. If she were making any sound, her suit was too damaged to amplify it.

Sudjic relevelled the boser, aiming low now. 'One shot to finish you off, Volyova – then I plant the gun on Sylveste. He'll deny everything, of course – but there'll only be Khouri as a witness, and I don't think she's going to go out of her way to back up his story. I'm right, aren't I? Admit it, Khouri, I'm about to do you a favour. You'd kill the bitch if you had the means.'

'That's where you're wrong,' Khouri said. 'On two counts.'

'What?'

'I wouldn't kill her, despite everything she's done. And I do have the means.' She took a moment – not even a fraction of second – to target the laser. 'Goodbye, Sudjic. Can't say it's been a pleasure.'

And fired.

By the time Sajaki arrived, not much more than a minute later, what was left of Sudjic was not worth burying.

Her suit had retaliated, of course, escalating to a higher level of response, directed plasma bolts emitting from projectors which had popped up on either side of her head. But Khouri's suit had been expecting something like that. In addition to changing the exterior state of its armour to maximally avert the plasma (retexturing itself and applying massive plasma-deflective electric currents to its own hide), it was already returning fire at a yet higher level of aggression, dispensing with childish weapons like plasma and particle-beams and opting for the more decisive deployment of ack-am pulses, releasing tiny nano-pellets from its own antilithium reservoir; each pellet caulked in a shield of ablative normal-matter, and the whole thing accelerated up to a significant fraction of the speed of light.

Khouri had not even had time to gasp. After issuing the initial fire-order, her suit had done all the rest on its own.

'There's been . . . trouble,' she said, as the Triumvir descended and made touch-down.

'You don't say,' he said, surveying the carnage: the wounded husk of a suit containing Volyova; the liberally strewn and now radioactive residual pieces of what had once been Sudjic, and – in the middle of it – unharmed by the blast, but seemingly too stunned to speak or try to evade capture, Sylveste and his wife.

SEVENTEEN

Rendezvous Point, Resurgam, 2566

Sylveste had rehearsed the meeting in his head many times.

He had done his best to consider every possible eventuality; even those that – based on his understanding of the situation – seemed fantastically unlikely to actually occur. But he had considered nothing like this, and with good reason. Even as it happened around him, he could not begin to make sense of what was going on; let alone why it deviated so far from the path of sanity.

'If it's any consolation,' Sajaki said, his voice booming above the wind, amplified from the head of his monstrous suit, 'I don't understand much of this either.'

'That consoles me no end,' Sylveste said, speaking on the same radio frequency channel he had used for all his negotiations with the crew, even though their representatives – or what remained of them – were now standing within shouting distance. In the unrelenting howl of the razorstorm, shouting was not much of an option. 'Call me naïve but at this point I was hoping you'd have taken things over with your usual ruthless efficiency, Sajaki. All I can say is that you appear to be slacking.'

'I don't like it any more than you do,' the Ultra said. 'But you'd better believe me – for your sakes – that things are now very much under control. Now, I'm about to divert my attention to my wounded colleague. At this point I strongly recommend that you resist the temptation to do anything foolhardy. Not that the thought ever crossed your mind, eh, Dan?'

'You know me better than that.'

'The problem, Dan, is that I know you only too well. But let's not dwell on the past.'

'Let's not.'

Sajaki moved over to the wounded one. Sylveste had known he was dealing with Triumvir Yuuji Sajaki even before the man had spoken. As soon as his suit hove into view, emerging from the storm, his faceplate had been rendered transparent, the man's over-familiar features peering intently at the damage he surveyed. Although it was hard to tell, Sajaki looked largely unchanged from their last meeting. For him, only a few years of subjective time would have elapsed. Sylveste by contrast had squeezed the equivalent of two or three old-style human lives into that space. It was a dizzying moment.

But Sylveste could not establish the identities of the other two crew. There had been a third, of course . . . but he or she was now past the point at which he could ever hope to make acquaintance. And of the two who were not obviously dead, one was perhaps perilously close – this was the one now receiving Sajaki's ministrations – and one was standing in what looked like shocked silence off to one side. Oddly, the uninjured one was keeping some suit weapons trained on Sylveste, even though he was unarmed and had no intention – no intention whatsoever – of resisting capture.

'She'll live,' Sajaki said, after a moment in which his suit must have communed with the suit of the fallen one. 'But we need to get her back to the ship fast. Then we can find out what actually happened down here.'

'It was Sudjic,' said a voice Sylveste didn't know; female. 'Sudjic tried to kill Ilia.'

Then the wounded one was the bitch herself: Triumvir Ilia Volyova.

'Sudjic?' Sajaki said. For a moment the word hung between them, and it seemed as if Sajaki could not – or would not – accept what the other, nameless woman was saying. But then, after the wind had torn at them for several more seconds, he said the name again, only this time on a falling note of acceptance. 'Sudjic. Yes, it would make sense.'

'I think she planned—'

'You can tell me later, Khouri,' Sajaki said. 'There'll be plenty of time – and your role in the incident of course will have to be explained to my total satisfaction. But for now we should deal with priorities.' He nodded down at the injured Volyova. 'Her suit will keep her alive for a few more hours, but it isn't capable of reaching the ship.'

'I take it,' Sylveste said, 'that you envisaged a way of getting us off the planet?'

'A word of advice,' Sajaki said. 'Don't irritate me too much, Dan. I've expended a considerable amount of trouble in getting you. But don't imagine I wouldn't stretch to killing you just to see how it feels.'

Sylveste had expected something like that from Sajaki – he would have been more worried if the man had said something dissimilar, downplaying the act of finding him. But if Sajaki believed a word of what he said – which was doubtful – then he was a fool. He had come from at least as far away as the Yellowstone system, perhaps even further, in his quest for Sylveste. No guessing what the human costs of it had actually been; quite aside from the sheer number of years which had been consumed.

'Good for you,' Sylveste said, injecting as much insincerity into his voice as he could muster. 'But as a scientific man you must respect my impulse to experiment; to determine the limits of your tolerance.' He whipped his arm out from under his windcloak, holding something tightly between two fingers of his gloved hand. He had almost expected the one with the guns to fire at him at that point, thinking that he was drawing a weapon. It was, he considered, a reasonable risk to take. But he had not produced a gun. What he held was a smallish sliver of quantum-state memory.

'You see this?' he said. 'This is what you asked me to bring. Calvin's beta-level simulation. You need it, don't you? You need it very badly.'

Sajaki watched him without a word.

'Well fuck you,' Sylveste said, crushing the simulation, until its dust was blown away into the storm.

EIGHTEEN

Resurgam Orbit, 2566

They lifted from Resurgam, quickly lancing into the clear skies above the storm. Eventually there was something above Sylveste, small at first and really only visible because it occasionally occluded the stars behind it. It looked no larger than a sliver of coal, but it kept on growing, until its roughly conical shape became obvious, and what had at first seemed like a silhouette of total blackness began to show faint details within its own shape, gloomily underlit by the world around which it was orbiting. The lighthugger grew until it seemed impossibly large, blocking half the sky, and then kept on growing. The ship had not changed greatly since his last trip aboard. Sylveste knew – without being much impressed by the fact – that ships like this were always redesigning themselves, although the changes would usually be subtle modifications of the interior, rather than radical overhauls of the exterior layout (although that did happen as well, perhaps once every century or two). For a moment he worried that it might now lack the capability he wished – but then he remembered what the ship had done to Phoenix. It was hard to forget, in truth, since the evidence of that attack was still glaringly visible below him; a lotus-bloom of grey destruction set into the face of Resurgam.

A door had opened in the dark hull of the ship. The door looked far too small to accept even one of the suited, let alone all of them, but as they neared it became obvious that the door was tens of metres wide and would admit them all with ease. Sylveste, his wife and the other two Ultras from the ship, one of whom held the wounded Volyova, vanished inside, and the door closed on them.

Sajaki brought them to a holding area where they sloughed the suits and breathed normally. There was a taste to the air which slammed him back to his last visit aboard. He had forgotten how the ship smelled.

'You wait here,' Sajaki said, while their suits tidied themselves up and moved to one wall. 'I have to attend to my colleague.'

He knelt down and busied himself with Volyova's armour. Sylveste toyed with the idea of telling Sajaki not to expend too much effort in helping the other Triumvir, then decided that was possibly not the best course of action. He might have already pushed Sajaki to the edge of his patience when he crushed the Cal sim. 'What exactly happened down there?'

'I don't know.' That was typical Sajaki; like all the genuinely clever people Sylveste had met he knew better than to feign understanding where none existed. 'I don't know and for the moment – for the moment – it doesn't matter.' He studied a readout in Volyova's suit. 'Her injuries, while serious, don't seem to be fatal. Given time, she can be healed. Also, I now have you. Everything else is detail.' Then he cocked his head towards the other woman, who had slipped out of her suit. 'Still, something troubles me, Khouri . . .'

'What?' she said.

'It doesn't matter . . . for the moment.' He looked back at Sylveste. 'Incidentally, that little trick you did with the sim – don't imagine for one instant that I was impressed by that.'

'You should be. How are you going to get me to fix the Captain now?'

'With Calvin's help, of course. Don't you remember that I kept a back-up the last time you brought Cal aboard? Granted, it's slightly out-of-date, but the surgical expertise is all there.'

It was a good bluff, Sylveste thought, but that was all it was. Still, there *was* a back-up, of sorts . . . or else he would never have destroyed the sim.

'Talking of which . . . is the Captain so grievously unwell that he can't meet me in person?'

'You'll meet him,' Sajaki said. 'All in good time.'

The other woman and Sajaki were removing scabs of damaged hide from Volyova's suit, a process which resembled the shelling of a crab. Eventually Sajaki murmured something to the woman and they halted their work, evidently deciding that it was too delicate to be continued here. Presently a trio of servitors glided into the room. Two of the machines lifted Volyova between them and then left with her, accompanied by Sajaki and the woman. Sylveste had not seen her during his last visit aboard, but she seemed to have assumed a fairly elevated role in the ship's hierarchy. The third servitor squatted down and observed Sylveste and Pascale with one sullen camera eye.

'He didn't even ask me to take off my mask and goggles,' Sylveste said. 'It's like he hardly cares that he has me.'

Pascale nodded. She was fingering her clothes, seemingly convinced that the suit's gel-air should have left some sticky residue behind on them. 'Whatever happened down there must have thrown his plans completely. Maybe he'd be more triumphant if things had gone according to plan.'

'Not Sajaki; triumphant just isn't his style. But I'd at least have expected him to spend a few minutes gloating.'

'Maybe the fact that you destroyed the sim . . .'

'Yes; that'll have thrown him.' As he spoke, he did so in the knowledge that his words were almost certainly being recorded. 'There may still be some residual functionality in the copy he made of Cal, even allowing for the self-destruct routines, though probably not enough for any kind of channelling, even with one-to-one neural congruency between sim and recipient.' Sylveste found a pair of storage crates and moved them over to use for chairs. 'I'm sure he already tried to run the sim in some poor fool's body, though.'

'And it must have failed.'

'Messily, probably. He's probably hoping now that I can work with the damaged copy without channelling; just relying on my knowledge of Cal's instincts and methodologies.'

Pascale nodded. She was shrewd enough not to ask the obvious question: what kind of plan would Sajaki have if his own copy was too damaged even for that? Instead, she said, 'Do you have any idea what happened down there?'

'No – and I think Sajaki was telling the truth when he said the same thing. Whatever it was, it wasn't to plan. Maybe some kind of power-struggle within the crew, acted out on the surface because whoever was involved never got a chance aboard.' But while the idea sounded halfway plausible to him, that was as far as his thinking took him. Too much time had gone by, even within Sajaki's reference frame, for Sylveste to trust his usually infallible processes of insight.

He would have to play things very carefully indeed until he

understood the dynamics of the current crew. Assuming they gave him the luxury of time . . .

Pascale knelt down next to her husband. They had both removed their masks now, but only Pascale had removed her dust-goggles. 'We're in a lot of danger, aren't we? If Sajaki decides he can't use you . . .'

'He'll return us to the surface unharmed.' Sylveste took Pascale's hands. Ranks of empty suits towered around them, as if the two of them were unwanted despoilers in an Egyptian tomb and the suits were mummies. 'Sajaki can't ever rule out my being useful to him again, in the future.'

'I hope you're right . . . because that was quite a risk you took.' She looked at him now with an expression he had rarely seen before. It was one of quiet, calm warning. 'With my life as well.'

'Sajaki isn't my master. I just had to remind him of that; to let him know no matter how clever he gets, I'll always be ahead of him.'

'But he is your master now, don't you understand? He may not have the sim, but he's got you. That still puts him ahead in my book.'

Sylveste smiled and reached for an answer that was both true and exactly what Sajaki would expect of him. 'But not as far as he thinks.'

Sajaki and the other woman came back less than an hour later, accompanied by a huge chimeric. Sylveste recognised the man from his previous trip aboard as Triumvir Hegazi, but only just. Hegazi had always been an extreme example of his kind – almost as comprehensively cyborgised as his Captain – but in the intervening time, Hegazi had further submerged his core humanity in machine supplements, exchanging various prosthetic parts for newer or more elegant substitutes, and had gained a whole new entourage of entoptics, most of which were designed to interact with the motion of his body parts, creating an off-spilling cascade of rainbow-coloured ghost limbs which lingered in the air for a second or so before fading. Sajaki wore unassuming shipboard clothes devoid of rank or ornamentation, emphasising the light-ness of his build. But Sylveste was wise enough not to judge the man by his lack of bulk and absence of obvious weapons prosthetics. Machines undoubtedly seethed beneath his skin, giving him inhuman speed and strength. He was at least as dangerous as Hegazi and a good deal quicker, Sylveste knew.

'I can't exactly say it's entirely a pleasure,' Sylveste said, addressing Hegazi. 'But I admit to experiencing a mild *frisson* of surprise at the fact that you haven't imploded under the weight of your prosthetics, Triumvir.'

'I suggest you take that as a compliment,' Sajaki said to the other Triumvir. 'It's the closest you'll get from Sylveste.'

Hegazi fingered the moustache which he still cultivated, despite the encroaching prosthetics which cased his skull.

'Let's see how witty he sounds when you've shown him the Captain, Sajaki-san. That'll wipe the smile off his face.'

'Undoubtedly,' Sajaki said. 'And talking of faces, why don't you show us a little more of yours, Dan?' Sajaki fingered the haft of a gun resting in a hip-holster.

'Gladly,' Sylveste said. He reached up and pulled away the dust-goggles. He let them clatter to the floor, watching the expressions – or what passed for expressions – on the faces of the people who had taken him prisoner. For the first time they were seeing what had become of his eyes. Perhaps they knew already, but the shock of seeing Calvin's handiwork could never be underestimated. His eyes were not sleek improvements on the originals, but brutalist substitutes which only approximated the functionality of the human eye. There were more sophisticated things in ancient medical textbooks ... not far removed from wooden legs. 'You knew that I lost my sight, of course?' he said, examining each of them in turn with his blank, eyeless gaze. 'It's common knowledge on Resurgam ... hardly even worth mentioning.'

'What kind of resolution do you get out of those?' Hegazi said, with what sounded like genuine interest. 'I know they're not completely state-of-the-art, but I bet you've got full EM sensitivity from the IR into the UV, right? Maybe even acoustic imaging? Got a zoom capability?'

Sylveste looked at Hegazi long and hard before answering. 'You need to understand one thing, Triumvir. In the right light, when she's not standing too far away, I can just about recognise my wife.'

'That good ...' Hegazi kept looking at him, fascinated.

They were escorted deeper into the ship. The last time he had been aboard, they had taken him straight to the medical centre.

The Captain had been more or less capable of walking then, at least for short distances. But they were not taking him anywhere he recognised now. Which was not necessarily to say that he was far from the medical centre, for the ship was as intricate as a small city and as difficult to memorise, even though he had once spent nearly a month aboard it. But he sensed that this was entirely new territory; that he was passing through regions of the ship – what Sajaki and the crew called districts – which he had never been shown before. If his reckoning was good, the elevator was carrying them away from the ship's sleek prow, down to where the conic hull broadened to its maximum width.

'Minor technical defects in your eyes don't concern me,' Sajaki said. 'We can repair them easily enough.'

'Without a working version of Calvin? I don't think so.'

'Then we rip out your eyes and replace them with something better.'

'I wouldn't do that. Besides . . . you still wouldn't have Calvin, so what good would it do you?'

Sajaki said something beneath his breath and the elevator crawled to a halt. 'So you never believed me when I said we had a back-up? Well, you're right, of course. Our copy had some strange flaws in it. Became quite useless long before we asked anything of it.'

'That's software for you.'

'Yes . . . perhaps I may kill you after all.' With one smooth movement he drew the gun from his holster, giving Sylveste time enough to notice the bronze snake which spiralled around the barrel. The weapon's mode of killing was not at all obvious; it might have been a beam or projectile gun, but he had no doubts that he was comfortably within its lethal range.

'You wouldn't kill me now; not after all the time you spent looking for me.'

Sajaki's finger tightened on the trigger. 'You underestimate my propensity for acting on a whim, Dan. I might kill you just for the sheer cosmic perversity of the act.'

'Then you'd have to find someone else to heal the Captain.'

'What would I have lost?' Under the snake's jaw, a status light flicked from green to red. Sajaki's finger whitened.

'Wait,' Sylveste said. 'You don't have to kill me. Do you honestly think I'd have destroyed the only copy of Cal left in existence?'

Sajaki's relief was evident. 'There's another?'

'Yes.' Sylveste nodded towards his wife. 'And she knows where to find it. Don't you, Pascale?'

Some hours later Cal said, 'I always knew you were a cold, calculating bastard, son.'

They were near the Captain. Sajaki had taken Pascale away, but now she was back again – along with all the other crew-members Sylveste knew about, and the apparition he had hoped never to see again. 'An insufferable, treacherous . . . nonentity.' The apparition was speaking quite calmly, like an actor running through lines purely to judge the timing, without imparting any actual emotion. 'You unthinking rat.'

'From nonentity to rat, eh?' Sylveste said. 'From some perspectives, that's almost an improvement.'

'Don't believe it, son.' Calvin leered at him, stretching forward from the seat which held him. 'Think you're so intolerably clever, don't you? Well now I've got you by the balls; assuming you have any. They told me what you did. How you killed me purely on the pretext of ruining their plans.' He raised his eyes to the ceiling. 'I mean, what a pathetic justification for patricide! I'd have at least thought you'd do me the courtesy of killing me for a halfway decent reason. But no. That would have been asking too much. I'd almost say I was disappointed, except that would imply I once had higher expectations.'

'If I'd actually killed you,' Sylveste said, 'this conversation would pose certain ontological problems. Besides, I always knew there was another copy of you.'

'But you murdered one of me!'

'Sorry, but that's a category mistake if ever I heard one. You're just software, Cal. Being copied and erased is your natural state of being.' Sylveste steeled himself for another protest from Cal, but for the moment he was silent. 'I didn't do it to ruin Sajaki's plans. I need his . . . co-operation as much as he needs mine.'

'My co-operation?' The Triumvir's eyes narrowed.

'We'll get to that. All I'm saying is that when I destroyed the copy, I knew another existed and that you'd soon force me into revealing its whereabouts.'

'So the act was pointless?'

'No; not at all. For a while I had the pleasure of seeing you imagine your plans in ruins, Yuuji-san. The risk was worth it for that glimpse into your soul. It wasn't a pretty sight, either.'

'How did you . . . know?' Cal said. 'How did you know I'd been copied?'

'I thought you couldn't copy him,' said the woman he had been introduced to as Khouri. She was small and foxlike, but perhaps, like Sajaki, not entirely to be trusted. 'I thought they had spoilers . . . copy-protection . . . that kind of shit.'

'That's alpha-level simulations, dear,' Calvin said. 'Which – for better or for worse – I happen not to be. No; I'm just a lowly beta-level. Capable of passing all the standard Turings, but not – from a philosophical standpoint – actually capable of consciousness. Hence, no soul. And therefore no ethical problems about there being more than one of me. However . . .' He drew in breath, filling the silence which someone else might have been tempted to fill with their own thoughts '. . . I no longer believe any of that neuro-cognitive rubbish. I can't speak for my alpha-level self, since my alpha-level self disappeared some two centuries ago, but for whatever reason, I am now fully conscious. Perhaps all beta-levels are capable of this, or perhaps my sheer connectional complexity ensured that I exceeded some state of critical mass. I have no idea. All I know is that I think, and therefore I'm exceedingly angry.'

Sylveste had heard all this before. 'He's a Turing-compliant beta-level. They're meant to say this sort of thing. If they didn't claim to be conscious, they'd automatically fail the standard Turings. But that doesn't mean that what he says – the noises he makes . . . the noises *it* makes – have any validity.'

'I could apply the same reasoning to you,' Calvin said. 'And where it's leading to, dear son, is this: since I can't speculate about the alpha, I have to assume that I'm all that remains. Now, this may be hard for you to understand, but the mere fact that I'm something precious and unique makes me object even more strenuously to the idea of anyone making a copy of me. Every act of copying me cheapens what I am. I am reduced to a mere commodity; something to be created, duplicated and disposed of whenever I happen to fit someone else's inadequate notion of usefulness.' He paused. 'So – while I'm not saying I wouldn't take steps to increase my likelihood of survival – I would not willingly have consented to be copied by anyone.'

'But you did. You allowed Pascale to copy you into *Descent into*

Darkness.' She had been clever about it, too; for years he had never suspected a thing. He had given her access to Calvin to assist with the construction of the biography. She had allowed him to return to the object of his obsession, the Amarantin, with access to research tools and his dwindling network of sympathisers.

'It was his idea,' Pascale said.

'Yes . . . I admit that much.' Cal drew in a lungful of breath, appearing to take stock before his next utterance, despite the fact that the Calvin simulation 'thought' far more rapidly than unaugmented humans. 'Those were dangerous times – no worse than now, of course, from what I've gathered since my re-awakening – but hazardous all the same. It seemed prudent to ensure some part of me would survive my original's destruction. I wasn't thinking of a copy, though – more a sketch, a likeness; perhaps not even fully Turing-compliant.'

'What made you change your mind?' Sylveste said.

'Pascale began to embed parts of me in the biography over a period of time – months, in fact. The encryption was very subtle. But once she had copied enough of the original for the copied parts to start interacting, they – or rather me – became rather less enthralled by the notion of committing cybernetic suicide just to prove a point. In fact I felt rather more alive – more myself – than I ever had before.' He vouchsafed his audience a smile. 'Of course, I soon realised why this was the case. Pascale had copied me into a more powerful computer system; the governmental core in Cuvier, where *Descent* was being assembled. The system was connected to more archives and networks than you ever allowed me, even back in Mantell. For the first time I actually had something to justify the attentions of my massive intellect.' He held their gaze for a moment before adding, very softly: 'That's a joke, by the way.'

'Copies of the biography were freely available,' Pascale said. 'Sajaki had already obtained one without even realising it contained a version of Calvin. How did you know he was in it, though?' She was looking at Sylveste now. 'Did the copied version of Cal tell you?'

'No, and I'm not even sure he would have wanted to if a way had existed. I figured it out for myself. The biography was too large for the amount of simulational data it contained. Oh, I know you'd been clever – encoding Cal into least significant digits of data files – but there was just too much of Cal to hide away that easily. *Descent*

350

was fifteen per cent longer than it should have been. For months I thought there had to be a whole hidden layer of scenarios; aspects of my life not supposedly documented but which you'd put in anyway, for anyone persistent enough to find them. But finally I realised that the missing capacity was enough to store a copy of Cal, and then it made sense. Of course I could never be completely sure . . .' He looked at the projected image. 'Though I suppose you'd say you're the real Cal now and what I erased was just a copy?'

Cal raised a hand from the armrest, disputatiously. 'No; that would be much too simplistic a version of things. After all, I was that copy, once. But what I was then – and what the copy remained, until you killed it – was just a shadow of what I am now. Let's just say I had a moment of epiphany, shall we, and leave it at that?'

'So . . .' Sylveste stepped forward, finger tapping against his lip. 'In that case, I never really killed you, did I?'

'No,' Calvin said, with deceptive placidity. 'You didn't. But it's what you might have been doing that counts. And on that score, dear boy, I'm afraid you're still a callous, patricidal bastard.'

'Touching, isn't it?' Hegazi said. 'Nothing I like better than a good old family reunion.'

They proceeded to the Captain. Khouri had been here before, but despite her minor familiarity with the place, she still felt unnerved; obtrusively aware of the contaminating matter which was only barely contained by the envelope of cold which been caulked around the man.

'I think I should know what you want from me,' Sylveste said.

'Isn't it obvious?' Sajaki said. 'Do you think we went to all this trouble just to ask you how you were doing these days?'

'I wouldn't put it past you,' Sylveste said. 'Your behaviour never made much sense to me in the past, so why should it start doing so now? And besides, let's not deceive ourselves that what went on back there was everything it seemed.'

'What do you mean?' Khouri asked.

'Oh, don't tell me you haven't figured it out yet?'

'Figured what out?'

'That it never actually happened.' Sylveste fixed her with the blank depths of his eyes; a scrutiny which felt more like the scanning of a mindless automatic surveillance system than any human apperception. 'Or perhaps not,' he added. 'Perhaps you haven't actually figured it out yet. Who are you anyway?'

'You'll get your chance to ask all the questions you want,' Hegazi said, edgy now that they were within a stone's throw of the Captain.

'No,' Khouri said. 'I want to know. What do you mean, none of that actually happened?'

Sylveste's voice was slow and calm. 'I'm talking about that business with the settlement Volyova wiped out.'

Khouri stepped ahead of the entourage, blocking their progress. 'You'd better explain that.'

'That can wait,' Sajaki said, stepping forward to push her aside. 'Certainly until you've explained your role in things to my complete satisfaction, Khouri.' The Triumvir was eyeing her suspiciously all the time now, convinced that the two deaths in her presence had to be more than coincidence. With Volyova out of the way – and the Mademoiselle silent – she had no one to shelter her. It would be only a matter of time before Sajaki acted on his suspicions and did something drastic.

But Sylveste said, 'No. Why need it wait? I think we should all be absolutely clear about what's going on here. Sajaki; you didn't go down to Resurgam just to obtain a copy of the biography, did you? What would have been the point? You had no knowledge that *Descent* contained a copy of Cal until I told you. You only picked up the biography because it might have come in useful in your negotiations with me. But it wasn't the reason you went down there. That was something else entirely.'

'Intelligence gathering,' Sajaki said, carefully.

'More than that. You went there to glean information, yes. But you also had to plant some.'

'About Phoenix?' Khouri said.

'Not just about Phoenix, the place itself. It never existed.' Sylveste allowed a pause before continuing. 'It was a ghost planted there by Sajaki. It wasn't even on the old maps we kept at Mantell, but as soon as we updated them from the master copies in Cuvier it appeared. We just assumed it was a new settlement; too recent to show up on the previous maps. That was stupid, of course – I should have seen through it then. But we assumed the master copies hadn't been corrupted.'

'Doubly stupid,' Sajaki said. 'Given that you must have wondered where I was.'

'If I'd given it more than a moment's thought . . .'

'Pity you didn't,' Sajaki said. 'Or we might not be having this conversation. But then again, we'd have only resorted to another means of securing you.'

Sylveste nodded. 'I suppose your next logical step would have been to blow up a bigger fictitious target. But I'm not entirely sure you could have pulled off the same trick twice. I've a nasty suspicion you might have had to hit somewhere real.'

The cold had a steely texture to it, like a thousand pieces of barbed metal constantly scraping softly against the skin; threatening to pierce to the bone with each movement. But as soon as they were truly in the Captain's realm, it became impossible to notice the cold, since the cold in which he was imprisoned was so obviously deeper.

'He's sick,' Sajaki said. 'With a variant of the Melding Plague. You know all about that, of course.'

'We heard reports from Yellowstone,' Sylveste said. 'I can't say they were exceptionally detailed.' All the while he had not actually looked directly at the Captain.

'We haven't been able to contain it,' Hegazi said. 'Not properly, anyway. Extreme cold goes some way to slowing it, but no more than that. It – or rather, he – is spreading slowly, incorporating the mass of the ship into his own template.'

'Then he's still alive, at least by some biological definition?'

Sajaki nodded, 'Of course, no organism can really be said to be alive at these temperatures. But if we were to warm the Captain now . . . parts of him would function.'

'That's hardly reassuring.'

'I brought you aboard to heal him, not to hear reassurances.'

What the Captain resembled was a statue smeared in ropelike silver tendrils, extending tens of metres in either direction; beautifully aglisten with sinister biochimeric malignancy. The reefersleep unit at the heart of the frozen explosion was still, by some miracle of design or accident, nominally functional. But its once symmetrical form had been tugged and warped by the glacially slow but unyielding forces of the Captain's spread. Most of its status readouts were now dead; there were no active entoptics surrounding it. Of the display devices which still worked, some showed unreadable mush; the senseless hieroglyphics of machine senility. Khouri was grateful that there were no entoptics. She had the feeling that if there had been any, they too would have been corrupted; a host of malignant seraphim or disfigured cherubim signifying the excessive state of the Captain's illness.

'You don't need a surgeon here,' Sylveste said. 'You need a priest.'

'That isn't what Calvin thought,' Sajaki said. 'He was rather eager to begin the work.'

'Then the copy they had in Cuvier must have been delusional. Your Captain isn't sick. He isn't even dead, since there isn't enough left which was ever alive in the first place.'

'Nonetheless,' Sajaki said. 'You will help us. You'll have Ilia's assistance, as well – as soon as she's well herself. She thinks that she has created a counteragent for the plague – a retrovirus. I'm told it works on small samples. But she's a weaponeer. Applying it to the Captain would be strictly a medical matter. But at least she can provide you with a tool.'

Sylveste directed a smile at Sajaki. 'I'm sure you've discussed the matter with Calvin already.'

'Let's just say he's been briefed. He's willing to try it – he thinks it might even work. Does this encourage you?'

'I would have to bow to Calvin's wisdom,' Sylveste replied. 'He's the medical man, not me. But before I enter into any commitment we'd have to negotiate terms.'

'There won't be any,' Sajaki said. 'And if you resist us, don't imagine we won't consider ways of persuading you via Pascale.'

'You'd probably regret it.'

Khouri prickled. For the dozenth time this day, something felt seriously wrong. She sensed that the others were also attuned to it, though there was nothing to read in their expressions. Sylveste sounded too cocksure; that was it. Too cocksure for someone who had been abducted and was about to be forced to undergo a painful ordeal. Instead he sounded like someone who was about to reveal a winning hand.

'I'll fix your damn Captain,' Sylveste said. 'Or at least prove it can't be done; one of the two. But in return, there's a small favour you have to do for me.'

'Excuse me,' Hegazi said, 'but when negotiating from a position of weakness, you don't ask for favours.'

'Who said anything about weakness?' Sylveste smiled again, this time with unconcealed ferocity, and something which looked dangerously like joy. 'Before I left Mantell, my captors did me a small, final favour. I don't think they particularly felt they owed me anything. But the act was a small thing, and it allowed them to spite you, which did, I think, rather appeal to them. They were losing me, after all – but they saw no reason why you should get quite what you thought you were getting.'

'I don't like this at all,' Hegazi said.

'Believe me,' Sylveste said, 'you're about to like it a lot less. Now; I have to ask a question, just to clarify our positions.'

'Go ahead,' Sajaki said.

'Are you all completely familiar with the concept of hot-dust?'

'You're talking to Ultras,' Hegazi said.

'Well, of course. Just wanted to make sure you weren't under any illusions. And you'll know that hot-dust fragments can be sealed within containment devices smaller than pinheads? Of course you do.' He tapped his finger against his chin, extemporising like an expert lawyer. 'You heard about Remilliod's visit, of course? The last lighthugger to trade with the Resurgam system before you came?'

'We heard about it.'

'Well, Remilliod sold hot-dust to the colony. Not many frag-ments; just enough for a colony which might want to do some hefty landscape-rearranging in the near future. Of his sample, a dozen or less fell into the hands of the people who were holding me prisoner. Do you want me to continue, or are you ahead of me already?'

'I fear I may be,' Sajaki said. 'But continue anyway.'

'One of those pinheads is now installed in the vision system which Cal made for me. It draws no current, and even if you dismantled my eyes, you would not be able to tell which component was the bomb. But you wouldn't want to try that, because even tampering with my eyes will detonate the pinhead, with a yield sufficient to turn the front kilometre of this ship into a very expensive and useless piece of glass sculpture. Kill me, or even harm me to the extent that certain bodily functions are compromised beyond a preset limit, and the device triggers. Clear on that?'

'As crystal.'

'Good. Harm Pascale and the same thing happens: I can trigger it deliberately, by executing a series of neural commands. Or I could of course simply kill myself – the result would be indistinguishable.' He clasped his hands together, beaming like a statue of Buddha. 'So. How does a little negotiation sound to you?'

Sajaki said nothing for what seemed like an eternity; doubtless considering every ramification of what Sylveste had said. Finally he said, without having consulted Hegazi: 'We can be . . . flexible.'

'Good. Then I expect you're keen to hear my terms.'

'Burning with enthusiasm.'

'Thanks to the recent unpleasantness,' Sylveste said, 'I have a reasonably good idea what this ship can do. And I suspect that little demonstration was very much at the timid end of things. Am I right?'

'We have . . . capabilities, but you'd have to talk to Ilia. What did you have in mind?'

Sylveste smiled.

'First you have to take me somewhere.'

NINETEEN

Delta Pavonis system, 2566

They retired to the bridge.

Sylveste had visited this room during his previous period aboard the ship and had spent hundreds of hours in it then, but it still impressed him. With the encircling ranks of empty seats rising towards the ceiling, it felt more like a court of law where some momentous case was about to be tried; the jurors about to take their places in the concentric seats. Judgement seemed to be waiting in the air, about to be voiced into being. Sylveste examined his state of mind and found nothing resembling guilt, so he did not place himself in the role of the accused. But he felt a weight. It was the weight that some legal functionary might feel; the burden of a task which had to be performed not only in public but to the highest possible standards of excellence. If he failed, more than his own dignity might be at stake. A long and elaborately connected chain of events leading to this point would be severed, a chain that stretched unimaginably far into the past.

He looked around and made out the holographic projection globe which jutted into the chamber's geometric centre, but his eyes were barely able to make out the object which it was imaging, though there were enough ancillary clues to suggest it was a realtime representation of Resurgam.

'Are we still in orbit?' he asked.

'Now that we've got you?' Sajaki shook his head. 'That would be pointless. We have no more business with Resurgam.'

'You're worried about the colonists trying something?'

'They could inconvenience us, I admit.'

For a moment they were silent, before Sylveste said, 'Resurgam never interested you, did it? You came all this way just for me. I find that singleminded to the point of monomania.'

'It was only the work of a few months, if that.' Sajaki smiled.

'From our perspective, of course. Don't flatter yourself that I'd have chased you for years.'

'From my perspective, of course, that's just what you did.'

'Your perspective isn't valid.'

'And yours is? Is that what you're saying?'

'It's . . . longer. That has to count for something. Now; to answer your earlier question, we've left orbit. We've been accelerating away from the ecliptic ever since you came aboard.'

'I haven't told you where I want us to go.'

'No, our plan was simply to put an AU or so between us and the colony, then lock into a constant-thrust holding pattern while we think things over.' Sajaki clicked his fingers, causing a robotic seat to angle down beside him. He boarded it, then waited while another quartet of seats appeared for Sylveste and Pascale, Hegazi and Khouri. 'During which time, of course, we anticipated that you'd assist with the Captain.'

'Did I say I wouldn't do it?'

'No,' Hegazi said. 'But you sure as hell came with some unanticipated fine print.'

'Don't blame me for making the best of a bad situation.'

'We're not, we're not,' Sajaki said. 'But it would help if you were a little clearer on your requirements. Isn't that reasonable?'

Sylveste's seat was hovering next to the one holding Pascale. She was looking at him now, as much in expectation as any of the crew who had captured him. Except that she knows so much more, he thought, almost everything there was to know, in fact – or at least as much as he knew, however insignificant a part of the truth that knowledge actually constituted.

'Can I call up a map of the system from this position?' Sylveste asked. 'I mean, of course I can, in principle – but will you give me the freedom to do so and some instructions?'

'The most recent maps were compiled during our approach,' Hegazi said. 'You can retrieve them from ship memory and project them into the display.'

'Then show me how. I'm going to be more than just a passenger for some time to come – you might as well get used to it.'

It took a minute or so to find the right maps; another half a minute to project the right composite into the projection sphere in the form Sylveste desired, eclipsing the realtime image of Resurgam. The image had the form of an orrery, the orbits of the system's eleven planets and largest minor planets and comets denoted by elegant coloured tracks, with the positions of the bodies themselves shown in their current relative positions. Because the scale adopted was large, the terrestrial planets – Resurgam included – were crammed into the middle; a tight scribble of concentric orbits banded around the star Delta Pavonis. The minor planets came next, followed by the gas giants and comets, occupying the system's middle ground. Then came two smaller sub-Jovian gas worlds, hardly giants at all, then a Plutonian world – not much more than a captured cometary husk, with two attendant moons. The system's Kuiper belt of primordial cometary matter was visible in infrared as a curiously distorted shoal, one nubby end pointing out from the star. And then there was nothing at all for twenty further AU, more than ten light-hours out from the star itself. Matter here – such as there was – was only weakly bound to the star; it felt its gravitational field, but orbits here were centuries long and easily disrupted by encounters with other bodies. The protective caul of the star's magnetic field did not extend this far out, and objects here were buffeted by the ceaseless squall of the galactic magnetosphere; the great wind in which the magnetic fields of all stars were embedded, like tiny eddies within a vaster cyclone.

But that enormous volume of space was not completely empty. It appeared at first only as one body – but that was because the default magnification scale was too large to show its duplicity. It lay in the direction in which the Kuiper halo was pointing; its own gravitational drag had pulled the halo out of sphericity towards that bulged configuration, betraying its existence. The object itself would have been utterly invisible to the naked eye, unless one were within a million kilometres of it; at which point seeing the object would have been the least of one's problems.

'You'll know of this,' Sylveste said. 'Even though you might not have paid it very much attention until now.'

'It's a neutron star,' Hegazi said.

'Good. Remember anything else?'

'Only that it has a companion,' Sajaki said. 'Which doesn't in itself make it unusual, of course.'

'Not really, no. Neutron stars often have planets – they're supposed to be the condensed remnants of evaporated binary stars. Either that or the planet somehow managed to avoid being destroyed when the pulsar was formed during the supernova explosion of a heavier star.' Sylveste shook his head. 'But not unusual, no. So – you may be asking – why am I interested in it?'

'That's a reasonable question,' Hegazi said.

'Because there's something strange about it.' Sylveste enlarged the image, until the planet was clearly visible, streaking around the neutron star in its ludicrously rapid orbit.

'The planet was of extraordinary significance to the Amarantin. It appears in their late-phase artefacts with increasing frequency as one approaches the Event – the stellar flare which wiped them out.'

He knew he had their attention now. If the threat to destroy their ship had appealed to them on the level of self-preservation, now he had fully snared their intellects. He had never doubted that this part would be simpler than with the colonists, for Sajaki's crew already had the advantage of a cosmic perspective.

'So what is it?' Sajaki said.

'I don't know. That's what you're going to help me find out.'

Hegazi said, 'You think there might be something on the planet?'

'Or inside it. We won't know for sure until we get a lot closer, will we?'

'It could be a trap,' Pascale said. 'I don't think we should dismiss that possibility – especially if Dan's right about the timing.'

'What timing?' Sajaki said.

Sylveste steepled his fingers. 'It's my suspicion – no; not a suspicion, my conclusion – that the Amarantin eventually progressed to the point where they could achieve space travel.'

'From what I gathered on the surface,' Sajaki said, 'there's very little in the fossil record to substantiate that.'

'But there wouldn't be, would there? Technological artefacts are inherently less durable than more primitive items. Pottery endures. Microcircuits crumble to dust. Besides, it took a technology comparable to our own to bury the city under the obelisk. If they were capable of that, we've no grounds for presuming they weren't also capable of reaching the edge of their solar system – perhaps even interstellar space.'

'You don't think the Amarantin reached other systems?'

'I don't rule it out, no.'

Sajaki smiled. 'Then where are they now? I can accept one

technological civilisation being wiped out without a trace, but not one spread across many worlds. They would have left something behind.'

'Perhaps they did.'

'The world around the neutron star? You think that's where you'll find the answers to your questions?'

'If I knew that, I wouldn't need to go there. All I'm asking is that you let me find out, which means taking me there.' Sylveste rested his chin on his steepled fingers. 'You'll get me as close to the planet as possible, and ensure my safety at the same time. If that means putting the nastier capabilities of this vessel at my disposal, so be it.'

Hegazi looked fascinated and fearful. 'Do you think we'll encounter something when we get there – something we need the weapons for?'

'There's no harm in taking precautions, is there?'

Sajaki turned to his fellow Triumvir. For a moment it was as if none of the others were present at all as something flickered between them, perhaps on the level of machine thought. When they spoke, it might only have been to repeat the discussion for Sylveste's benefit. 'What he said about the device in his eyes – is that possible? I mean, assuming what we know of the technical expertise on Resurgam, could they have installed such an implant in the time we gave them?'

Hegazi took his time before answering. 'I think, Yuuji-san, that we should seriously consider the possibility.'

Most of Volyova woke up in the recovery suite of the medical bay. She did not need to be told that she had been unconscious for more than a few hours. She had only to examine her state of mind, the feeling that she had been dreaming, deeply so – for centuries – to know that her injuries, and her recuperation, had not been trivial. Sometimes one could feel like one had been dreaming for a lifetime in the shortest of catnaps. But not now, for these dreams were as long, and as saturated with event, as the most turgid of pretechnological fables. She felt that she had lived through dusty, deathless volumes of her own wanderings.

Yet she remembered very little. She had been aboard this ship, yes, and then not aboard it – somewhere else, though where, she was not yet clear – and then something dreadful had happened. All she really remembered was the sound and the fury – but what did they signify? Where had she been?

Dimly – at first wary that it was merely a dislodged fragment of the dream – she remembered Resurgam. And then, slowly, events returned, not as a tidal wave, or even as a landslide, but as a slow, squelching slippage: a disembowelment of the past. They did not even have the decency to return in anything like chronological order. But when she ordered things to her own satisfaction, she remembered the delivering of ultimata, in her voice, oddly enough, announced from orbit to the waiting world below. And then waiting in the storm, and feeling at first a terrible hotness and then an equally terrible coolness in her stomach, and seeing Sudjic standing over her, dispensing pain.

The room's door opened; Ana Khouri entered, alone.

'You're awake,' she said. 'Thought so. I had the system advise me when your neural activity passed a certain level consistent with conscious thought. It's good to have you back, Ilia. We could use some sanity around here.'

'How long . . .' Volyova swallowed her words – they sounded broken and slurred – before beginning again. 'How long have I been here? And where are we now?'

'Ten days since the attack, Ilia. We're – well, I'll come to that. It's a long story. How do you feel?'

'I've felt worse.' Then she wondered why she had said it, because she could not think of an occasion when she had felt this bad, ever. But it seemed to be what one said under the circumstances. 'What attack?'

'I don't think you remember much, do you?'

'I did just ask that question, Khouri.'

She had joined Volyova, the room extruding a blocky chair by the bedside for her comfort. 'Sudjic,' she said. 'She tried to kill you when we were on Resurgam – you remember, don't you?'

'Not really.'

'We'd gone down to escort Sylveste up to the ship.'

Volyova was silent for a moment, the man's name ringing in her head with a peculiarly metallic quality, as if a scalpel had just crashed to the floor. 'Sylveste, yes. I remember that we were about to bring him in. Did it work, then? Did Sajaki get what he wanted?'

'Yes and no,' Khouri said, after deliberation.

'And Sudjic?'

'She wanted to kill you because of Nagorny.'

'No pleasing some people, is there?'

'I think she'd have found some excuse, whatever happened. She thought I'd join with her, as well.'

'And?'

'I killed her.'

'Then I'd hazard a guess that you saved my life.' For the first time Volyova lifted her head from the pillow; it felt as if it were attached to the bed by elastic cables. 'You really ought to cut down on it, Khouri, before it becomes a habit. But if there was another death . . . you can probably expect Sajaki to start asking questions.' That was as much as she would risk saying now; the warning she had just given was exactly what any senior crewperson might give to an understudy; it did not necessarily mean – to anyone listening in – that Volyova knew anything more about Khouri than the other Triumvirs.

But the warning was sincere enough. First the killing in the training chamber . . . then another on Resurgam. In neither situation had Khouri exactly instigated the trouble, but if her proximity to both happenings was enough to trouble Volyova, it would certainly give Sajaki pause for thought. Asking questions was probably at the milder end of the Triumvir's likely interrogative process, if it came to that. Sajaki might opt for torture . . . perhaps even a dangerous deep-memory trawl. Then – if he did not fry Khouri's mind in the process – he might learn her identity as infiltrator, put aboard to steal the cache. His next question would almost certainly be: how much of this did Volyova know? And if he deemed it worthwhile to trawl Volyova as well . . .

It must not come to that, she thought.

As soon as she was well enough, she would have to get Khouri to the spider-room where they could talk more freely. For now, it was senseless to dwell on things beyond her control.

'What happened afterwards?' she asked.

'After Sudjic bought it? Everything continued according to plan, believe it or not. Sylveste still had to be escorted aboard the ship, and Sajaki and I hadn't been injured.'

She thought of Sylveste, somewhere in the ship now. 'Then Sajaki really did get what he wanted.'

'No,' Khouri said, guardedly. 'That's only what he thought he'd got. But the truth was a bit different.'

Over the next hour she told Volyova everything that had happened since Sylveste had been brought back aboard the lighthugger. It was all general ship-knowledge; nothing that Sajaki would not expect her to tell Volyova. But all the while, Volyova reminded herself that she was being told events as filtered by Khouri's perception of things, which might not necessarily be complete, or even reliable. There were nuances of shipboard politics which would elude Khouri; would, indeed, elude anyone who had not been aboard for years. But at the end it seemed unlikely that any large portion of the truth had not been related, whether Khouri knew it or not. And what Volyova had been told was not good; not good at all.

'You think he lied?' Khouri asked.

'About the hot-dust?' Volyova approximated a shrug. 'It's certainly possible. Granted, Remilliod did sell hot-dust to the colony – we've seen the evidence of that already – but manipulating it isn't child's play. And they wouldn't have had long to install it in his eyes, assuming they waited until the strike against Phoenix had already taken place, which seems likely. On the other hand . . . the risk's just too great to assume he was lying. No remote-scan could detect hot-dust without risking a trigger . . . it puts Sajaki in a double-bind. He can't not assume Sylveste was telling the truth. He has to take Sylveste at his word, or risk everything. At least this way the risk's marginally quantifiable.'

'You call Sylveste's request a quantifiable risk?'

Volyova clucked, thinking of his demands. In all her life, she had never been near anything potentially alien; anything so potentially outside of her experience. There would surely be much there that could teach her . . . many lessons she could absorb. Sylveste need hardly have bothered with his threat . . .

'He should have known better than to offer us such a tantalising lure,' she said. 'I've been intrigued by that neutron star ever since we entered the system, do you know? I found something near it on our approach – a weak neutrino source. It seems to be orbiting the planet, which itself orbits the neutron star.'

'What could produce neutrinos?'

'Many things – but of this energy? I can only think of machinery. Advanced machinery.'

'Left there by the Amarantin?'

'It's a possibility, isn't it?' Volyova smiled, with effort. That was exactly what she was thinking, but there was no sense in stating her desires so blatantly. 'I suppose we will find out when we get there.'

Neutrinos are fundamental particles; spin-half leptons. They come in three forms, or flavours: electron, mu- or tau-neutrinos, depending on the nuclear reactions which have birthed them. But because they have mass – because they move fractionally slower than the speed of light – neutrinos oscillate between flavours as they fly. By the time the ship's sensors intercepted these neutrinos, they were a blend of the three possible flavour states, difficult to untangle. But as the distance to the neutron star decreased – and with it the time available for the neutrinos to oscillate away from their creation state – the blend of flavours became increasingly dominated by one type of neutrino. The energy spectrum became easier to read, too, and the time-dependent variations in the source strength were now much simpler to follow and interpret. By the time the distance between the ship and the neutron star had narrowed to one-fifth of one AU – about twenty million kilometres – Volyova had a much clearer idea about what was causing the steady flux of particles, dominated by the heaviest of the neutrino flavours, tau-neutrinos.

And what she learned disturbed her enormously.

But she decided to wait until they were closer before announcing her fears to the rest of the crew. Sylveste was, after all, still controlling them; it seemed unlikely that her worries would greatly dissuade him from his current course of action.

Khouri was getting used to dying.

One of the niggling aspects of Volyova's simulations was the way they routinely carried on beyond the point where any real observer would have been killed, or at the very least so gravely injured as to be incapable of perceiving any subsequent events, let alone capable of having any influence over them. Like this time. Something had lanced out from Cerberus – an unspecified weapon of arbitrary destructiveness – and casually shredded the entire lighthugger. Nothing could have survived that attack, but Khouri's disembodied consciousness was still stubbornly present, watching the riven shards drift lazily apart in a pinkish halo of their own ionised guts. It was, she supposed, Volyova's way of rubbing it in.

'Haven't you ever heard of morale-building?' Khouri had asked.

'Heard of it,' Volyova said. 'Don't happen to agree with it. Would you rather be happy and dead, or scared and alive?'

'But I keep dying anyway. Why are you so convinced we're going to run into trouble when we get there?'

'I'm only assuming the worst,' Volyova said, depressingly.

The next day Volyova felt strong enough to talk to Sylveste and his wife. She was sitting up in bed when they came into the medical bay, a compad propped on her lap, scrolling through a plethora of attack scenarios which she would later test against Khouri. She hastily closed the display and replaced it with something less ominous, though she doubted that the cryptic code of her simulations would have made much sense to Sylveste anyway; even to herself, her scribbles sometimes resembled a private language in which she had only passing fluency.

'You're healed now,' Sylveste said, sitting next to her, flanked by Pascale. 'That's good.'

'Because you care about my well-being, or because you need my expertise?'

'The latter, obviously. There's no love lost between us, Ilia, so why pretend otherwise?'

'I wouldn't dream of it.' She put the compad aside. 'Khouri and I had a discussion about you. I – or we – concluded that it was better to give you the benefit of the doubt. So for the time being, assume that I assume that everything you've told us,' she touched a finger against her brow, 'is completely true. Of course, I reserve the right to alter this judgement at any point in the future.'

'I think it's best for all of us if we adopt that line of thinking,' Sylveste said. 'And I assure you, scientist to scientist, it's utterly true. Not just about my eyes, either.'

'The planet.'

'Cerberus. yes. I presume they briefed you?'

'You expect to find something there which may relate to the Amarantin extinction. Yes; that much I gleaned.'

'You know about the Amarantin?'

'Orthodox thinking, yes.' She lifted the compad again, quickly scrolling to a cache of documents uplinked from Cuvier. 'Of course, very little of this is your work. But I have the biography, as well. It conveys a great deal of your speculation.'

'Framed from the point of view of a sceptic,' Sylveste said, glancing towards Pascale – a visible shift in the angle of his head, for it was impossible to judge the direction of his gaze from his eyes.

'Naturally. But the essence of your thinking comes through. Within that paradigm . . . I concur that Cerberus/Hades is of some interest.'

Sylveste nodded, clearly impressed that she had remembered the proper nomenclature for the planet/neutron-star binary system they were now approaching. 'Something drew the Amarantin there, in their end days. I want to know what it was.'

'And does it concern you that this something might have been related to the Event?'

'It concerns me, yes.' His answer was not quite what she was expecting. 'But it would concern me more if we were to ignore it entirely. After all, the threat to our own safety might be just as present. At least if we learn something we have a chance of avoiding the same fate.'

Volyova tapped a finger against her lower lip, thoughtfully. 'The Amarantin may have thought similarly.'

'Better, then, to approach the situation from a standpoint of power.' Sylveste looked to his wife again. 'It was providential that you arrived, in all honesty. There was no way for Cuvier to finance an expedition out here, even if I had been able to persuade the colony of its importance. And even if they had, nothing they could have prepared would have equalled the offensive capabilities of this ship.'

'That little demonstration of our fire-power was really rather ill-judged, wasn't it?'

'Perhaps – but without it, I might never have been released.'

She sighed. 'That, unfortunately, is precisely my point.'

The better part of a week later – when the ship had arrived within twelve million kilometres of Cerberus/Hades, and had assumed orbit around the neutron star – Volyova convened a meeting of the entire crew, and their guests, in the ship's bridge. Now, she thought, was the time to reveal that her deepest fears had indeed been justified. It was hard enough for her, but how would Sylveste take matters? What she was about to tell him not only confirmed that they were approaching something dangerous, but it also touched on something of deep personal significance for him. She was not an adept judge of character at the best of times – and Sylveste was entirely too complex a beast to submit to easy analysis – but she saw no way that her news could be anything other than painful.

'I found something,' she said, when she had everyone's attention. 'Quite some time ago, in fact: a source of neutrinos, near Cerberus.'

'How long ago?' Sajaki said.

'Before we arrived around Resurgam.' Watching his expression darken, she added: 'There was nothing worth telling you, Triumvir. We did not even know we would be sent out here at that point. And the nature of the source was very unclear.'

'And now?' Sylveste said.

'Now I have ... a clearer idea. As we approached Hades, it became obvious that the emissions at source were pure tau-neutrinos of a particular energy spectrum; unique, in fact, amongst the signatures of any human technology.'

'Then it's something human that you've found out here?' Pascale said.

'That was my assumption.'

'A Conjoiner drive,' Hegazi said, and Volyova nodded slightly.

'Yes,' she said. 'Only Conjoiner drives produce tau-neutrino signatures which match the source around Cerberus.'

'Then there's another ship out here?' Pascale said.

'That was my first thought,' Volyova said, sounding uneasy. 'And, in fact, it isn't entirely wrong, either.' Then she whispered commands into her bracelet, causing the central display sphere to warm to life and begin running through a pre-programmed routine she had set up just before the meeting. 'But it was important to wait until we were close enough for visual identification of the source.'

The sphere showed Cerberus. The moon-sized world was like a less inviting version of Resurgam: monotonously grey, densely cratered. It was dark, too: Delta Pavonis was ten light-hours away, and the other nearby star – Hades – offered almost no light at all. Although it had been born furiously hot in a supernova explosion, the tiny neutron star had long since cooled into the infrared, and to the naked eye it was only visible when its gravitational field tricked background stars into arcs of lensed light. But even if Cerberus had been bathed in light, there was no suggestion of anything which might have lured the Amarantin. Even the best of Volyova's scans, however, had only mapped the surface at a resolution of kilometres, so very little could be ruled out at this stage. But she had studied the object orbiting Cerberus in considerably greater detail.

She zoomed in on it now. At first it was just a slightly elongated whitish-grey smudge, backdropped by stars, with one edge of Cerberus visible to one side. That was how it had looked to her days ago, before the ship had deployed all its long-baseline eyes. But even then she had found it hard to ignore her suspicions. As more details appeared, it became harder still.

The smudge took on definite attributes of solidity and form now. It was a vaguely conic shape, like a splinter of glass. Volyova made a dimensional grid envelop the object, showing its approximate size. It was clearly several kilometres from end to end: three or four, easily.

'At this resolution,' Volyova said, 'the neutrino emission resolved into two distinct sources.' She showed them: grey-green blurs spaced either side of the thickened end of the conic shape. As more details phased in, the blurs could be seen to be attached to the body of the splinter by elegant, back-swept spars.

'A lighthugger,' Hegazi said. He was right; even at this relatively crude resolution, there was no doubt about it. What they were looking at was another ship, much like their own. The two individual sources of neutrino emission originated from the two Conjoiner engines mounted either side of the hull.

'The engines are dormant,' Volyova said. 'But they still give off a stable flux of neutrinos even when the ship's not under thrust.'

'Can you identify the ship?' Sajaki said.

'It isn't necessary,' Sylveste said, the deep calm in his voice surprising them all. 'I know which ship it is.'

On the display, the final wave of detail shimmered across the ship, and the view enlarged until the craft filled almost the entire sphere. It was obvious now, even if it had not been completely so before. The ship was damaged; gutted: pocked by great spherical indentations, acres of the hull flensed open to reveal an intricate and queasy complexity of sub-layers which ought never to have been exposed to vacuum.

'Well?' Sajaki said.

'It's the wreck of the *Lorean*,' Sylveste said.

TWENTY

Calvin assumed existence in the lighthugger's medical suite, still incongruously posed in his enormous hooded chair.

'Where are we?' he asked, rummaging in the corner of one eye with his finger, as if he had just awoken from a satisfactorily deep sleep. 'Still around that shithole of a planet?'

'We've left Resurgam,' said Pascale, who sat in the seat next to Sylveste, who in turn was reclining on the operation couch, fully clothed and conscious. 'We're on the edge of Delta Pavonis's heliosphere, near the Cerberus/Hades system. They've found the *Lorean*.'

'Sorry; I think I misheard you.'

'No; you heard me perfectly well. Volyova showed it to us – it's definitely the same ship.'

Calvin frowned. Like Pascale – like Sylveste – he had assumed that the *Lorean* was no longer anywhere near the Resurgam system. Not since Alicia and the other mutineers had stolen it to return to Yellowstone back in the early days of the Resurgam colony. 'How can it be the *Lorean*?'

'We don't know,' Sylveste said. 'All we know is what we've told you. You're as much in the dark as the rest of us.' At such a point in their conversation, he normally inserted a barb against Calvin, but for once something made him hold his tongue.

'Is it intact?'

'Something must have attacked it.'

'Survivors?'

'I doubt it. The ship was heavily damaged . . . whatever it was came suddenly, or they would have tried moving out of range.'

Calvin was silent for a few moments before answering. 'Alicia must have died, then. I'm sorry.'

'We don't know what it was, or how the attack came about,' Sylveste said. 'But we may learn something shortly.'

'Volyova's launched a probe,' Pascale said. 'A robot – capable of crossing over to the *Lorean* very quickly. It should have arrived by now. She said it will enter the ship and find whatever electronic records have survived.'

'And then?'

'We'll know what killed them.'

'But that won't be enough, will it? No matter what you learn from the *Lorean*, it won't be enough to make you turn back, Dan. I know you better than that.'

'You only think you do,' Sylveste said.

Pascale stood up, coughing. 'Can we save this for later? If you can't work together, Sajaki's not going to have much use for either of you two.'

'Irrelevant what he thinks about me,' Sylveste said. 'Sajaki still has to do whatever I say.'

'He has a point,' Calvin said.

Pascale asked the room to extrude an escritoire, with controls and readouts in the Resurgam style. She made a seat and sat herself beneath the escritoire's curved ivory fascia. Then she called up a map of the data connections in the suite, and set about establishing the necessary links between Calvin's module and the suite's medical systems. She looked like she was spinning an elaborate cat's cradle in thin air. As the connections were created, Calvin acknowledged them, and told her whether to increase or decrease bandwidth along certain pathways, or whether additional topologies were needed. The procedure lasted only a few minutes, and when it was complete Calvin was able to operate the medical suite's servo-mechanical equipment, causing a mass of tipped alloy arms to descend from the ceiling, like the sculpture of a medusa.

'You have no idea how this feels,' Calvin said. 'It's the first time in years I've been able to act on a part of the physical universe – not since I first repaired your eyes.' And as he spoke, the multi-jointed arms executed a shimmering dance, blades, lasers, claws, molecular-manipulators and sensors scything the air in a whirl of vicious silver.

'Very impressive,' Sylveste said, feeling the breeze on his face. 'Just be careful.'

'I could rebuild your eyes in a day,' Calvin said. 'I could make

them better than they ever were. I could make them look human –
hell; with the technology here I could implant biological eyes just
as easily.'

'I don't want you to rebuild them,' Sylveste said. 'Right now
they're all I have on Sajaki. Just repair Falkender's work.'

'Ah, yes – I'd forgotten about that.' Calvin, who remained
essentially immobile, raised an eyebrow. 'Are you sure this
procedure is wise?'

'Just be careful what you poke.'

Alicia Keller Sylveste had been his last wife before Pascale. They
had married on Yellowstone, during the long years when the
Resurgam expedition had been planned in excruciating detail.
They had been together at the founding of Cuvier and had worked
in harmony during the earliest years of the digs. She had been
brilliant; too much so, perhaps, to stay comfortably within his
orbit. Independently minded, she had begun to draw away from
him – both personally and professionally – as their time on
Resurgam entered its third decade. Alicia was not alone in her
conviction that enough had been learned of the Amarantin; that it
was time for the expedition – never meant to be permanent – to
return to Epsilon Eridani. After all, if they had not learned
anything shattering in thirty years, there was no promise that the
next thirty years, or the next century, would bring anything more
overwhelming. Alicia and her sympathisers believed that the
Amarantin did not merit further detailed study; that the Event had
only been an unfortunate accident of no actual cosmic significance. It was not hard to see the sense in this. The Amarantin, after
all, were not the only dead species known to humankind. Out in
the ever-expanding bubble of explored space, it was entirely
possible that other cultures were about to be discovered, potent
with archaeological treasures waiting to be unearthed. Alicia's
faction felt that Resurgam should be abandoned; that the colony's
finest minds should return to Yellowstone and select new targets of
study.

Sylveste's faction, of course, disagreed in the strongest terms. By
then Alicia and Sylveste were estranged, but even in the depths of
their enmity they preserved a cool respect of each other's abilities.
If love had withered, detached admiration remained.

Then came the mutiny. Alicia's faction had done just what they always threatened to do: abandoned Resurgam. Unable to convince the rest of the colony to travel with them, they had stolen the *Lorean* from its parking orbit. The mutiny had been quite bloodless, but in their theft of the ship, Alicia's faction had inflicted a much more insidious harm upon the colony. The *Lorean* had contained all the intra-system vessels and shuttles, meaning that the colonists were confined to Resurgam's surface. They had no means to repair or upgrade the comsat girdle until Remilliod's arrival, decades later. Servitors, replicating technology and implants had all been in excruciatingly short supply after Alicia's departure.

But, in fact, Sylveste's faction had been the fortunate ones.

'Log entry,' said Alicia's ghost, floating disembodied in the bridge. 'Twenty-five days out from Resurgam. We've decided – against my better judgement – to approach the neutron star on our way out. The alignment's propitious; it doesn't take us very far from our planned heading for Eridani, and the net delay to our journey will be tiny compared with the years of flight that are ahead of us in any case.'

She was not quite what Sylveste remembered. It had been a long time, in any case. She no longer seemed hateful to him; merely errant. She wore dark green clothes of a kind no one had worn in Cuvier since the mutiny itself, and her hairstyle seemed almost theatrical in its antiquity.

'Dan was convinced there was something important out here, but the evidence was always lacking.'

That surprised him. She was speaking from a time long before the unearthing of the obelisk with its curious orrery-like inscriptions. Had his obsession been that strong, even then? It was entirely possible, but the realisation was not a comfortable one. Alicia was right in what she said. The evidence had been lacking.

'We saw something strange,' Alicia said. 'A cometary impact on Cerberus, the planet orbiting the neutron star. Such impacts must be quite rare, this far out from the main Kuiper swarm. It naturally drew our attention. But when we were close enough to examine the surface of Cerberus, there was no sign of a new impact crater.'

Sylveste felt the hairs on the back of his neck tingle. 'And?' he found himself mouthing, almost silently, as if Alicia were standing before them in the bridge, and not a projection dredged from the memory banks of the wrecked ship.

'It was not something we could ignore,' she said. 'Even if it seemed to lend tacit support to Dan's theory that there was something strange about the Hades/Cerberus system. So we altered our course to come in closer.' She paused. 'If we find something significant . . . something we can't explain . . . I don't think we'll have any ethical choice but to inform Cuvier. Otherwise we could never again hold our heads high as scientists. We will know better tomorrow, anyway. We'll be within probe range by then.'

'How much more of this is there?' Sylveste asked Volyova. 'How much longer did she continue with log entries?'

'About a day,' Volyova said.

Now they were in the spider-room, safe – or so Volyova wished to believe – from the prying eyes of Sajaki and the others. They had still not listened to everything Alicia had to say, for the very act of sifting through the spoken records was time-consuming and emotionally draining. Yet the basic shape of the truth was emerging, and it was far from encouraging. Alicia's crew had been attacked by something near Cerberus, suddenly and decisively. Shortly Volyova and her crewmates would know a great deal more about the danger they were being impelled towards.

'You realise,' Volyova said, 'that if we encounter trouble, you may have to enter the gunnery.'

'I don't think that would necessarily be for the best,' Khouri said. Justifying herself, she added, 'We both know there have been some worrying events related to the gunnery recently.'

'Yes. As a matter of fact . . . during my convalescence, I convinced myself that you know more than you admit.' Volyova relaxed back into the maroon plush of her seat, toying with the brass controls in front of her. 'I think you told me the truth when you said you were an infiltrator. But I think that was as far as it went. The rest was a lie, designed to satisfy my curiosity and yet stop me taking the matter to the rest of the Triumvirate . . . which worked, of course. But there were too many things you didn't explain to my satisfaction. Take the cache-weapon, for instance. When it malfunctioned, why did it point itself at Resurgam?'

'It was the closest target.'

'Sorry; too glib. It was something *about* Resurgam, wasn't it? And the fact that you infiltrated this ship only when you knew our destination . . . yes; an out-of-the-way place would have made a good venue for staging an attempted take-over of the cache – but that was never on the cards anyway. You may have been resourceful, Khouri, but there was no way you were ever going to wrest control of those weapons from either myself or the rest of the Triumvirate.' She put her hand beneath her chin now. 'So – the obvious question. If your initial story was untrue, what exactly are you doing aboard this ship?' She looked at Khouri, awaiting an answer. 'You may as well tell me now, because I swear the next person to ask you will be Sajaki. It can't have escaped your notice that Sajaki has his suspicions, Khouri – especially since Kjarval and Sudjic died.'

'I didn't have anything to do with . . .' Then her voice lost conviction. 'Sudjic had her own vendetta against you; that was none of my doing.'

'But I had already disabled your suit's weapons. Only I could have undone that order, and I was too busy being killed to do so. How did you manage to override the lock in order to kill Sudjic?'

'Someone else did it.' Khouri paused before continuing. 'Some-*thing* else, I should say. It was the same something that got into Kjarval's suit and made her turn against me in the training session.'

'That wasn't Kjarval's doing?'

'No . . . not really. I don't think I was her favourite person in the universe . . . but I'm fairly sure that she wasn't planning to kill me in the training chamber.'

This was a lot to take in, even if it did finally feel like the truth. 'So what happened, exactly?'

'The thing inside my suit had to arrange matters so I'd be on the team to recover Sylveste. Getting Kjarval out of the picture was the only option.'

Yes; she could almost see the logic in that. She had never once questioned the manner in which Kjarval had died. It had seemed so predictable that one of the crew would turn against Khouri – especially Kjarval or Sudjic. Equally, one or other would surely have turned against Volyova before too long. Both things had happened, but now she saw them as part of something else . . . ripples of something she did not pretend to understand, but which moved with sharklike stealth beneath the surface of events.

'What was so important about being in on the Sylveste recovery?'

'I . . .' Khouri had been on the verge of saying something, but now she faltered. 'I'm not sure this is the best time, Ilia – not when we're so close to whatever destroyed the *Lorean*.'

'I didn't bring you here just to admire the view, in case you thought otherwise. Remember what I said about Sajaki? It's either me, now – the closest thing on this ship you have to either an ally or a friend – or it's Sajaki, later, with some hardware you probably don't want to even think about.' That was no great exaggeration, either. Sajaki's trawl techniques were not exactly state-of-the-art in their subtlety.

'I'll start at the beginning, then.' What Volyova had just said seemed to have done the trick. That was good – or else she would have to think about dusting off her own coercion methods. 'The part about being a soldier . . . all that was true. How I got to Yellowstone is . . . complicated. Even now I'm not sure how much of it was an accident; how much of it was her doing. All I know is, she singled me out early on for this mission.'

'Who was she?'

'I don't really know. Someone with a lot of power in Chasm City; maybe the whole planet. She called herself the Mademoiselle. She was careful never to use a real name.'

'Describe her. She may be someone we know; someone we've had dealings with in the past.'

'I doubt it. She wasn't . . .' Khouri paused. 'She wasn't one of you. Maybe once, but not now. I got the impression she'd been in Chasm City for a long time. But it wasn't until after the Melding Plague that she came to power.'

'She came to power and I haven't heard of her?'

'That was the whole point of her power. It wasn't blatant, and she didn't have to make her presence known to get something done. She just made shit happen. She wasn't even rich – but she controlled more resources than anyone else on the planet, by sleight of hand. Not enough to conjure up a ship, though – which is why she needed you.'

Volyova nodded. 'You said she might have been one of us, once. What did you mean by that?'

Khouri hesitated. 'It wasn't anything obvious. But the man working for her – Manoukhian, he called himself – definitely used to be an Ultra. He dropped enough clues to suggest that he'd found her in space.'

'Found – as in rescued?'

'That was how it sounded to me. She had these jagged metal sculptures, too – at least I thought they were sculptures to start with. Later, they began to look like parts of a wrecked spaceship. Like she was keeping them around her as a reminder of something.'

Something tugged at Volyova's memory, but for the moment she allowed the thought process to remain below the level of consciousness. 'Did you get a good look at her?'

'No. I saw a projection, but it needn't have been accurate. She lived inside a palanquin, like the other hermetics.'

Volyova knew a little about the hermetics. 'She needn't have been one at all. A palanquin could simply have been a way of masking her identity. If we knew more about her origin . . . Did this Manoukhian tell you anything else?'

'No; he wanted to – I could tell that much – but he managed not to give anything useful anyway.'

Volyova leaned closer. 'Why do you say he wanted to tell you?'

'Because that was his style. The guy never stopped mouthing off. The whole time I was being driven around by him, he never stopped telling me stories about all the things he'd done; all the famous people he'd known. Except for anything to do with the Mademoiselle. That was a closed subject; maybe because he was still working for her. But you could tell he was just itching to tell me stuff.'

Volyova drummed her fingers on the fascia. 'Maybe he found a way.'

'I don't understand.'

'No; I wouldn't expect you to. It was nothing he told you, either . . . but I think he *did* find a way to tell you the truth.' The memory process she had suppressed a moment earlier had indeed dredged something. She thought back to the time of Khouri's recruitment; to the examination she had given the woman after she had been brought aboard. 'I can't be sure yet, of course . . .'

Khouri looked at her. 'You found something on me, didn't you? Something Manoukhian planted?'

'Yes. It seemed quite innocent, at first. Fortunately, I have an odd character defect, common amongst those of us who indulge in the sciences . . . I never, *ever* throw anything away.' It was true; disposing of the thing she had found would have demanded a greater expenditure of effort than simply leaving it in her lab. It had seemed pointless at the time – the thing was just a shard, after all – but now she could run a compositional analysis on the metal splinter she had pulled from Khouri. 'If I'm right, and this was Manoukhian's doing, it may tell us something about the Mademoiselle. Perhaps even her identity. But you still need to tell me what exactly she wanted you to do for her. We already know it involves Sylveste in some way or another.'

Khouri nodded. 'It does. And I'm afraid this is the part you're *really* not going to like.'

'We've completed a more detailed inspection of the surface of Cerberus from our present orbit,' Alicia's projection said. 'And there's still no evidence of the cometary impact point. Plenty of cratering, yes – but none of it recent. Which just doesn't make any sense.' She elaborated the one plausible theory they had, which was that the comet had been destroyed just before impact. Even that explanation implied the use of some form of defensive technology, but at least it avoided the paradox of the unchanged surface features. 'But we saw no sign of anything like that, and there's certainly no evidence of any technological structures on the surface. We've decided to launch a squadron of probes down to the surface. They'll be able to hunt for anything we might have missed – machines buried in caves, or sunk in canyons below our viewing angle – and they might provoke some kind of response, if there are automated systems down there.'

Yes, Sylveste thought acidly. They had indeed provoked some kind of response. But it was almost certainly not the kind Alicia had anticipated.

Volyova located the next segment in Alicia's narrative. The probes had been deployed; tiny automated spacecraft as fragile and nimble as dragonflies. They had fallen towards the surface of Cerberus – there was no atmosphere to retard them – only arresting their descent at the last moment, with quick spurts of fusion flame. For a while, seen from the vantage point of the *Lorean*, they had been sparks of brightness against the unremitting grey of Cerberus. But as the sparks had become tiny, they were a reminder that even this tiny, dead world was orders of magnitude larger than most human creations.

'Log entry,' said Alicia, after a gap in the narrative. 'The probes are reporting something unusual – it's just coming in now.' She looked to one side, consulting a display beyond the projection volume. 'Seismic activity on the surface. We were expecting to see it already, but until now the crust hasn't moved at all, even though the planet's orbit isn't quite circularised and there should be tidal stresses. It's almost as if the probes have triggered it, but that's quite ridiculous.'

'No more so than a planet that erases all evidence of a cometary impact on its surface,' Pascale said. Then she looked at Sylveste. 'I didn't mean that as a criticism of Alicia, by the way.'

'Perhaps you didn't,' he said. 'But it would have been valid.' Then he turned to Volyova. 'Did you recover anything other than Alicia's log entries? There must have been telemetered data from her probes . . .'

'We have it,' Volyova said cautiously. 'I haven't cleaned it up. It's a little on the raw side.'

'Patch me in.'

Volyova breathed a string of commands into the bracelet she always wore and the bridge burned away, a barrage of synaesthesia jumbling Sylveste's senses. He was being immersed in the data from one of Alicia's probes – the surveyor's sensorium fully as raw as Volyova had warned. But Sylveste had known more or less what to expect; the transition was merely jarring rather than – as could easily have been the case – agonising.

He floated above a landscape. Altitude was difficult to judge, since the fractal surface features – craters, clefts and rivers of frozen grey lava – would have looked very similar at any distance. But the surveyor told him he was only half a kilometre above Cerberus. He looked down at the plain, hunting for some sign of the seismic activity Alicia had mentioned. Cerberus looked eternally old and unchanging, as if nothing had happened to it for billions of years. The only hint of motion came from the fusion jets, casting radial shadows away from his position as the machine loitered.

What had the drones seen? Certainly nothing in the visual band. Feeling his way into the sensorium – it was like slipping on an unfamiliar glove – Sylveste found the neural commands which accessed different data channels. He turned to thermal sensors, but the plain's temperature showed no signs of variation. Across the complete EM spectrum there was nothing anomalous. Neutrino and exotic particle fluxes remained steadfastly within expectation.

Yet when he switched to the gravitational imagers, he knew that something was very wrong with Cerberus. His visual field was overlaid with coloured, translucent contours of gravitational force. The contours were moving.

Things – huge enough to register via the mass sensors – were travelling underground, converging in a pincer movement directly below the point where he was hovering. For a moment, he allowed himself to believe that these moving forms were only vast, buried flows of lava – but that comforting delusion lasted no more than a second.

This was nothing natural.

Lines appeared on the plain, forming a starlike mandala centred on the same focus. Dimly, on the limits of his perception, he was aware that similar starlike patterns were opening below the other probes. The cracks widened, opening into monstrous black fissures. Through the fissures, Sylveste had a glimpse into what seemed to be kilometres of luminous depth. Coiled mechanical shapes writhed, sliding blue-grey tendrils wider than canyons. The motion was busy; orchestrated, purposeful, machinelike. He felt a special kind of revulsion. It was the feeling of biting an apple and exposing a colony of wrigglingly industrious maggots. He knew now. Cerberus was not a planet.

It was a mechanism.

Then the coiled things erupted through the star-shaped hole in the plain, rushing dreamily towards him, as if reaching to snatch him out of the sky. There was a horrible moment of whiteness – a whiteness in every sense he had – before Volyova's sensorium-feed ended with screaming suddenness, Sylveste almost shrieking with existential shock as his sense of self crashed back into his body in the bridge.

He had time enough, after he had gathered his faculties, to observe Alicia mouthing something soundlessly, her face carved in what might have been fear, and what might equally have been the dismay at learning – in the instant prior to her death – that she had been wrong all along.

Then her image dissolved into static.

'Now at least we know he's mad,' Khouri said, hours later. 'If that didn't persuade him against going any closer to Cerberus, I don't think anything will.'

'It may well have had the opposite effect,' Volyova said, voice low despite the relative security furnished by the spider-room. 'Now Sylveste knows there is something worth investigating, rather than merely suspecting so.'

'Alien machinery?'

'Evidently. And perhaps we can even guess at the purpose, too. Cerberus clearly isn't a real world. At the very least, it's a real world surrounded by a shell of machines, with an artificial crust. That explains why the cometary impact-point was never found – the crust, presumably, repaired itself before Alicia's crew could get close enough.'

'Some kind of camouflage?'

'So it would seem.'

'So why draw attention by attacking those probes?'

Volyova had evidently given the matter some prior thought. 'The illusion of verisimilitude obviously can't be foolproof at distances less than a kilometre or so. My guess is the probes were about to learn the truth just before they were destroyed, so the world lost nothing and gained some additional raw material in the bargain.'

'Why, though? Why surround a planet with a false crust?'

'I have no idea, and neither, I suspect, does Sylveste. That's why he's now even more likely to insist on going closer.' She lowered her voice. 'He's already asked me to devise a strategy, in fact.'

'A strategy for what?'

'For getting him inside Cerberus.' She paused. 'He knows about the cache-weapons, of course. He presumes they'll be sufficient to achieve his aims, by weakening the crustal machinery in one area of the planet. More than that will be needed, of course . . .' Her tone of voice shifted. 'Do you think this Mademoiselle of yours always knew this would be his objective?'

'She was pretty damn clear he shouldn't be allowed aboard the ship.'

'The Mademoiselle told you that before you joined us?'

'No; afterwards.' She told Volyova about the implant in her head; how the Mademoiselle had downloaded an aspect of herself into Khouri's skull for the purposes of the mission. 'She was a pain,' she said. 'But she made me immune to your loyalty therapies, which I suppose was something to be grateful for.'

'The therapies worked as intended,' Volyova said.

'No, I just pretended. The Mademoiselle told me what to say and when, and I guess she didn't do too bad a job, or else we wouldn't be having this discussion.'

'She can't rule out the possibility that the therapies worked partially, can she?'

Khouri shrugged again. 'Does it matter? What kind of loyalty would make any sense now? You've as good as told me you're waiting for Sajaki to make the wrong move. The only thing holding this crew together is Sylveste's threat to kill us all if we don't do what he wants. Sajaki's a megalomaniac – maybe he should have double-checked the therapies he was running on you.'

'You resisted Sudjic when she tried to kill me.'

'Yeah, I did. But if she'd told me she was going after Sajaki – or even that prick Hegazi – I don't know what I would have said.'

Volyova spent a moment in consultation with herself.

'All right,' she said finally. 'I suppose the loyalty issue is moot. What else did the implant do for you?'

'When you hooked me into the weapons,' Khouri said, 'she used the interface to inject herself – or a copy of herself – into the gunnery. To begin with I think she just wanted to assume control of as much of the ship as possible, and the gunnery was her only point of entry.'

'The architecture wouldn't have allowed her to reach beyond it.'

'It didn't. To the best of my knowledge, she never gained control of any part of the ship other than the weapons.'

'You mean the cache?'

'She was controlling the rogue weapon, Ilia. I couldn't tell you at the time, but I knew what was happening. She wanted to use the weapon to kill Sylveste at long-range, before we'd ever arrived at Resurgam.'

'I suppose,' Volyova said, heavy with resignation, 'that it makes a kind of twisted sense. But to use that weapon just to kill a man . . . I told you, you're going to have to tell me why she wanted him dead so badly.'

'You won't like it. Especially not now, with what Sylveste wants to do.'

'Just tell me.'

'I will, I will,' Khouri said. 'But there's one other thing – one other complicating factor. It's called Sun Stealer, and I think you may already be acquainted with it.'

Volyova looked as if some recently healed internal injury had just relapsed; as if some painful seam had opened in her like ripping cloth. 'Ah,' she said eventually. 'That name again.'

TWENTY-ONE

Approaching Cerberus/Hades, 2566

Sylveste had always known this point would come. But until now he had managed to keep it quarantined from his thoughts, acknowledging its existence without focusing his attention on what it actually entailed, the way a mathematician might ignore an invalidated part of a proof until the rest was rigorously tested and found to be free not just of glaring contradictions but of the least hint of error.

Sajaki had insisted that they journey alone to the Captain's level, forbidding Pascale or any of the crew to accompany them. Sylveste did not argue the point, although he would have preferred his wife to be with him. It was the first time that Sylveste had been alone with Sajaki since arriving on the *Infinity*, and as they took the elevator downship, Sylveste ransacked his mind for something to talk about; anything except the atrocity that lay ahead of them.

'Ilia says her machines aboard the *Lorean* will need another three or four days,' Sajaki said. 'You're quite certain you wish her work to continue?'

'I have no second thoughts,' Sylveste said.

'Then I have no choice but to comply with your wishes. I've weighed the evidence and decided to believe your threat.'

'You imagine I hadn't worked that out for myself already? I know you too well, Sajaki. If you didn't believe me, you'd have forced me into helping the Captain while we were still around Resurgam, and then quietly disposed of me.'

'Not true, not true.' Sajaki's voice had an amused quality to it. 'You underestimate my sheer curiosity. I think I'd have indulged you this far just to see how much of your story was true.'

Sylveste was incapable of believing that for a moment, but equally, he saw no point in debating it. 'Just how much of it don't you believe, now that you've seen Alicia's message?'

'But that could so easily have been faked. The damage to her ship could have been inflicted by her own crew. I shan't believe things entirely until something jumps out of Cerberus and starts attacking us.'

'I rather suspect you'll get your wish,' Sylveste said. 'In four or five days. Unless Cerberus really is dead.'

They spoke no more until they had reached their destination.

It was not, of course, the first time he had seen the Captain – not even during this visit. But the totality of what had become of the man was still shocking; each time it was as if Sylveste had never properly set eyes on the scene before. True enough: this was his first visit to the Captain's level since Calvin had renewed his eyes using the ship's superior medical capabilities, but there was more to it than that. It was also the case that the Captain had changed since last time; perceptibly now – as if his rate of spread was accelerating, racing towards some unguessable future state even as the ship raced towards Cerberus. Perhaps, Sylveste thought, he had arrived in the nick of time – assuming that any intervention at all could help the Captain now.

It was tempting to think that this quickening was significant; perhaps even symbolic. The man, after all, had been sick – if one could properly call this state sickness – for many decades, and yet he had chosen this period in which to enter a new phase of his malady. But that was an erroneous view. One had to consider the Captain's time-frame: relativistic flight had compressed those decades to a mere handful of years. His latest blooming was less unlikely than it seemed; there was nothing ominous about it.

'How does this work?' Sajaki asked. 'Do we follow the same procedures as last time?'

'Ask Calvin – he'll be running things.'

Sajaki nodded slowly, as if the point had only just occurred to him. 'You should have a say in things, Dan. It's you he'll be working through.'

'Which is exactly why you don't need to consider my feelings – I won't even be present.'

'I don't believe that for one moment. You'll be there, Dan – fully aware, too, from what I remember last time. Maybe not in control, but you'll be participating. And you won't like it – we know that much from last time.'

'You're an expert all of a sudden.'

'If you didn't hate this, why would you have kept away from us?'

'I didn't. I wasn't in any position to run.'

'I'm not just talking about the time when you were in prison. I'm talking about you coming here in the first place; to this system. What were you doing if you weren't running from us?'

'Maybe I had reasons for coming here.'

For a moment Sylveste wondered if Sajaki was going to push the matter further, but the moment passed and the Triumvir seemed to mentally discard that line of enquiry. Perhaps the topic bored him. It struck Sylveste that Sajaki was a man who existed in the present and thought largely about the future, and for whom the past held few enticements. He was not interested in sifting through possible motivations or might-have-beens, perhaps because, on some level, Sajaki was not really capable of grasping these issues.

Sylveste had heard that Sajaki had visited the Pattern Jugglers, as he himself had done prior to the Shrouder mission. There was only one reason for visiting the Jugglers, which was to submit oneself to their neural transformations, opening the mind to new modes of consciousness unavailable through human science. It was said – rumoured, perhaps – that no Juggler transform was without its deficits; that there was no resculpting of the human mind which did not result in some pre-existing faculty being lost. There were, after all, only a finite number of neurones in the human brain, and a corresponding finite limit to the number of possible interneuronal connections. The Jugglers could rewire that network, but not without destroying prior connectional pathways. Perhaps Sylveste himself had lost something, but if that were the case, he could not locate the absence. In Sajaki's case, it might be more obvious. The man was missing some instinctive grasp of human nature, almost an autism. There was an aridity in his conversations, but it was only clear if one paid proper attention. In Calvin's laboratories back on Yellowstone, Sylveste had once spoken to an early, historically preserved computer system which had been created several centuries before the Transenlightenment, during the first flourishing of artificial intelligence research. The system purported to mimic natural human language, and initially it did, answering inputted questions with apparent cognisance. But the illusion lasted for no more than a few exchanges; eventually one realised that the machine was steering the conversation away from itself, deflecting questions with a sphinxlike impassiveness. It was far less extreme with Sajaki, but the same sense of evasion was present. It was not even particularly artful. Sajaki made no effort to disguise his indifference to these matters; there was no sociopathic gloss of superficial humanity. And why should Sajaki even bother to deny his nature? He had nothing to lose, and in his own way, he was no more or less alien than any of the other crew.

Eventually, when it became obvious that he was not going to pursue Sylveste any further about his reasons for coming to Resurgam, Sajaki addressed the ship, asking it to invoke Calvin and project his simulated image onto the Captain's level. The seated figure appeared almost immediately. As usual Calvin subjected his witnesses to a brief pantomime of burgeoning awareness, stretching in his seat and looking around him, though without a glimmer of real interest.

'Are we about to begin?' he asked. 'Am I about to enter you? Those machines I used on your eyes were like a tantalus, Dan – for the first time in years I remember what I've been missing.'

''Fraid not,' Sylveste said. 'This is just a – how should we call it? Exploratory dig?'

'Then why bother invoking me?'

'Because I'm in the unfortunate position of requiring your advice.' As he spoke, a pair of servitors emerged from the darkness along the corridor. They were hulking machines which rode on tracks and whose upper torsos sprouted a glistening mass of specialised manipulators and sensors. They were antiseptically clean and highly polished, but they looked about a thousand years old, as if they had just trundled out of a museum. 'There's nothing in them that the plague can touch,' Sylveste said. 'No components small enough to be invisible to the naked eye; nothing replicating, self-repairing or shape-shifting. All the cybernetics are elsewhere – kilometres away upship, with only optical connections to the drones. We won't hit him with anything replicating until we use Volyova's retrovirus.'

'Very thoughtful.'

'Of course,' Sajaki said, 'for the delicate work, you'll have to hold the scalpel yourself.'

Sylveste touched his brow. 'My eyes aren't so immune. You'll have to be very careful, Cal. If the plague touches them . . .'

'I'll be more than careful, believe me.' From the monolithic enclosure of his seat, Calvin threw back his head and laughed like a drunkard amused by his own drollery. 'If your eyes go up, even I won't get a chance to put my affairs in order.'

'Just so long as you appreciate the risk.'

The servitors lurched forwards, approaching the shattered angel of the Captain. More than ever he looked like something which had not so much crept with glacial slowness from his reefer, but had burst with volcanic ferocity, only to be frozen in a strobe flash. He radiated in every direction parallel to the wall, extending far into the corridor on either side, for dozens of metres. Nearest to him, his growth consisted of trunk-thick cylinders, the colour of quicksilver, but with the texture of jewel-encrusted slurry, constantly shimmering and twinkling, hinting at phenomenally industrious buried activity. Further away, on his periphery, the branches subdivided into a bronchial-like mesh. At its very boundary, the mesh grew microscopically fine and blended seamlessly with the fabric of its substrate: the ship itself. It was glorious with diffraction patterns, like a membrane of oil on water.

The silver machines seemed to dissolve into the silver background of the Captain. They positioned themselves on either side of the wrecked shell of the reefer unit at his heart, no more than a metre from the violated carapace. It was still cold there – if Sylveste had touched any part of the Captain's reefer, his flesh would have stayed there, soon to be incorporated into the chimeric mass of the plague. When the operation proper began, they would have to warm him just to work. He would quicken then – or rather, the plague would seize the opportunity to increase its rate of transformation – but there was no other way to work on him, for at the temperature he had reached now, all but the crudest of tools would themselves become inoperable.

The machines now extended booms tipped with sensors; magnetic resonance imagers to peer deep into the plague, differentiating between the machine, chimeric and organic strata which had once been a man. Sylveste had the drones pass what they saw to his eyes, appearing as a lilac-tinged overlay superimposed on the Captain. It was only with effort that he could make out the residual outline of the human instar which had become this; it was like a ghostly outline beneath the paint on a recycled canvas. But as the MRI sweep continued, the details grew progressively sharper, the man's plague-distorted anatomy bleeding into clarity. That was when the horror of it could no longer be ignored. But Sylveste just stared.

'Where are we – I mean you – going to begin?' he asked, towards Calvin. 'Are we healing a man or sterilising a machine?'

'Neither,' Calvin said drily. 'We're fixing the Captain, and I'm afraid he's rather transcended both those categories.'

'You understand magnificently,' Sajaki said, standing back from the cold tableau to allow the Sylvestes an unimpeded view. 'It's no longer a matter of healing, or even repairing. I prefer to think of it as restoration.'

'Warm him,' Calvin said.

'What?'

'You heard. I want him warmed – just temporarily, I assure you. But long enough to take a few biopsies. I understand Volyova restricted her examinations to the plague periphery. That was diligent of her; she did well, and the samples she obtained are invaluable indices of the growth pattern, and of course she couldn't have engineered her retrovirus without them. But now we need to reach into the core; to where there's still living meat.' He smiled, undoubtedly enjoying the revulsion which flickered across Sajaki's face. So maybe there was some empathy there after all, Sylveste thought – or at least the atrophied stump of what it had once been. For an instant he felt kinship with the Triumvir.

'What are you so interested in?'

'His cells, of course.' Calvin fingered the curlicued arm of his seat. 'They say the Melding Plague corrupts our implants, blends them into the flesh, by subverting their replicating machinery. I think it goes beyond that. I think it tries to hybridise – tries to achieve some harmony between the living and the cybernetic. That's what it's doing here, after all – nothing more malign than trying to hybridise the Captain with his own cybernetics and the ship. It's almost benign; almost artistic, almost purposeful.'

'You wouldn't be saying that if you were where he is now,' Sajaki said.

'Of course not. That's why I want to help him. And why I need to see into his cells. I want to know if the plague has touched his DNA – whether it's tried to hijack his own cellular machinery.'

Sajaki extended a hand towards the chill. 'Go ahead, in that case. You've permission to warm him. But only for as long as it takes.

Then I want him back under, until it's time to operate. And I don't want those samples leaving here.'

Sylveste noticed that the Triumvir's outstretched hand was shaking.

'All this has something to do with a war,' Khouri said in the spider-room. 'That much I'm clear about. The Dawn War, they called it. It was a long time ago. Millions of years back.'

'How would you know?'

'The Mademoiselle gave me a lesson in galactic history, just so I'd appreciate what was at stake. And it worked, too. Can't you accept that going along with Sylveste is not a good idea?'

'I was never remotely of the opinion it was.'

Pull the other one, Khouri thought. Volyova was still childishly curious about Cerberus/Hades, even now that she knew it contained something dangerous. More so, in fact. Before, the mystery had consisted of a single anomalous neutrino signature. Now she had seen the alien machinery for herself, via Alicia's recording. No; in some respects Volyova was as fascinated by the place as Sylveste. The difference was, she could still be reasoned with. Volyova still had a residual core of sanity.

'Do you think we'd stand a chance of persuading Sajaki of the risks?'

'Not much. We've kept too much from him. He'd kill us just for that. I'm still worried about him trawling you. He mentioned it again just now, you know. I managed to deflect him, but . . .' She sighed. 'In any case, Sylveste is the one pulling the strings now. What Sajaki does or doesn't want is almost irrelevant.'

'Then we have to get to Sylveste.'

'It won't work, Khouri. No amount of rational argument is going to sway him now – and I'm afraid what you've told me doesn't even qualify as that.'

'But you believe it.'

Volyova raised a hand. 'I believe some of it, Khouri – but that isn't the same thing. I've witnessed some of the things you claim to understand, like the incident with the cache-weapon. And we know alien forces are involved on some level, which makes it difficult for me to dismiss your Dawn War story completely. But we still don't have anything resembling the big picture.' She paused. 'Maybe when I've finished analysing that splinter . . .'

'What splinter?'

'The one Manoukhian planted on you.' Volyova told her the rest; how she had found the splinter during the medical examination she had conducted after Khouri's recruitment. 'At the time I just assumed it was a piece of shrapnel from your soldiering days. Then I wondered why your own medics hadn't removed it earlier. I suppose I should have realised there was something strange about it even then ... but it clearly wasn't any kind of functional implant, just a piece of jagged metal.'

'And you haven't worked out what it is yet?'

'No, I ...' But that was the truth of it, as Khouri learned. There was a lot more to that little shard than met the eye. The blend of metals was fairly unusual, even for someone who had worked with some very strange alloys indeed. Also, Volyova said, it had what looked like odd manufacturing flaws, but which could just as easily have been stresses worked into the metal long afterwards; bizarre nanoscale fatigue patterns. 'Still, I'm nearly there,' she said.

'Maybe it'll tell us what we need. But one thing won't change. I can't do the one thing which would get us out of this mess, can I? I can't kill Sylveste.'

'No. But if the stakes become higher – if it becomes absolutely clear that he must be killed – then I think we have to begin thinking about what would be required.'

It took a moment for the true meaning of what Volyova was saying to sink in.

'Suicide?'

Volyova nodded dourly. 'Meanwhile I have to do the best possible job I can of granting Sylveste's wish, or else I put us all in danger.'

'That's what you don't understand,' Khouri said. 'I'm not saying that we'll all die if the attack against Cerberus isn't successful, which is what you seem to assume. I'm saying that something terrible is going to happen, even if the attack works. That's exactly why the Mademoiselle wanted him dead.'

Volyova had sealed her lips and shaken her head slowly, for all the world like a parent admonishing a child.

'I can't start a mutiny on the basis of some vague premonition.'

'Then maybe I'll have to start it myself.'

'Be careful, Khouri. Be very careful indeed. Sajaki's a more dangerous man than you can even begin to imagine. He's waiting for any excuse to crack your head open and see what's inside. He might not even wait for one. Sylveste is . . . I don't know. I'd think twice about crossing him as well. Especially now that he has the smell of it.'

'Then we have to get to him indirectly. Through Pascale. Do you understand? I'll tell her everything, if I think she can get him to see sense.'

'She won't believe you.'

'She might if you back me up. You'll do it, won't you?' Khouri looked at Volyova. The Triumvir stared back for a long moment, and might have been on the verge of answering when her bracelet began chirping. She pulled back the cuff of her sleeve and looked at the readout. She was wanted upship.

The bridge, as always, seemed too large for the few people in it, dispersed sparsely throughout the chamber's enormous and redundant volume. Pathetic, Volyova thought – and for a moment considered calling up some of her beloved dead, to at least fill out the place a bit and add a sense of ceremony to the occasion. But that would be demeaning, and in any case – despite the amount of thought she had expended on this project – she was not feeling remotely elated. Her recent discussions with Khouri had killed any lingering positive feelings she might have had for this whole enterprise. Khouri was right, of course – they really were taking an unthinkable risk just by being near to Cerberus/Hades – but there was nothing she could do about that. It was not simply that they ran the risk of the ship being destroyed. According to Khouri, that might actually be preferable to having Sylveste succeed in getting inside Cerberus. The ship and its crew might just survive that . . . but their short-term good fortune would be only a prelude to something much, much worse. If what Khouri had told her about the Dawn War was halfway to being the truth, it would be very bad indeed, not just for Resurgam – not just for this system – but for humanity as a whole.

She was about to make what might be the worst mistake of her career, and it was not even properly a mistake, since she had no choice in the matter.

'Well,' Triumvir Hegazi said, lording over her from his seat, 'I hope this is worth it, Ilia.'

So did she – but the last thing she was going to do was concede any of her feelings of unease to Hegazi. 'Bear in mind,' she said, addressing them all, 'that as soon as this is done, there won't be any going back. This is going to look like bad news in anyone's book. We might elicit an immediate response from the planet.'

'Or we might not,' Sylveste said. 'I've told you repeatedly, Cerberus won't do anything to draw unwarranted attention to itself.'

'Then we'd better hope your theories are right.'

'I think we can trust the good doctor,' Sajaki said from Sylveste's flank. 'He's just as vulnerable as the rest of us.'

Volyova felt an urge to get things over with. She illuminated the previously dark holo, filling it with a realtime image of the *Lorean*. The wreck showed no sign of having changed in any way since they had first found it – the hull was still peppered with awful wounds, inflicted, as they now knew, immediately after Cerberus had attacked and destroyed the probes. But within the ship, Volyova's machines had been busy. There had been only a tiny swarm of them at first, spawned by the robot she had sent to find Alicia's log entries. But the swarm had grown swiftly, consuming metal in the ship to fuel expansion, interfacing with the ship's own self-replicating repair and redesign systems, most of which had failed to reboot after the Cerberus attack. Other populations would have followed – and then, a day or so after the first impregnation, the work proper would commence: transformation of the ship's interior and skin. To a casual observer, none of this activity would have been apparent, but any kind of industry produced heat, and the outer layer of the wrecked ship had grown slightly warmer over the last few days, betraying the furious activity inside.

Volyova stroked her bracelet, doublechecking that all the indications were nominal. In a moment it would begin; there was now nothing that she could do to arrest the process.

'My God,' Hegazi said.

The *Lorean* was changing: shedding its skin. Sections of the damaged outer hull were flaking away in great acres, the ship enveloping itself in a slowly expanding cocoon of shards. What was revealed underneath still had the same form as the wreck, but it was smoothly carapaced, like a snake's new skin. The transformations had been really rather easy to impose – the *Lorean*, unlike the *Infinity*, did not fight back with replicating viruses of its own; did not resist her sculpting hand. If reshaping the *Infinity* was like trying to carve fire, the other ship had been clay in her hands.

The angle of the view shifted, as the sloughing debris caused the *Lorean* to turn about its long axis. The Conjoiner engines were still attached and working – and now she had control of them, delegated to her bracelet. They would probably never have reached sufficient functionality to push the ship to the edge of light, but that was not Volyova's intention. The journey it had to make – the last journey it would ever make – was almost insultingly small for such a ship. And now the ship was mostly hollow, the interior volume compressed into the thickened walls of the conic hull. The cone was open at the base; the ship was like a huge pointed thimble.

'Dan,' she said. 'My machines found Alicia's body, and the other crew, of course. Most of the mutineers had been in reefersleep . . . but even they didn't survive the attack.'

'What are you saying?'

'I can have them returned here, if you wish. There'll be a delay, of course – we'd have to send a shuttle over to retrieve them.'

Sylveste's answer, when it came, was swifter than she had expected. She had assumed he would want to dwell on it for anything up to an hour or so. Instead, he said: 'No. There can't be any delay now. You're right – Cerberus will have witnessed this activity.'

'Then the bodies?'

When he spoke, it was as if his answer were the only reasonable course of action. 'They'll have to go down with it.'

TWENTY-TWO

Cerberus/Hades Orbit, Delta Pavonis Heliopause, 2566

It was beginning.

Sylveste sat with steepled fingers before a luminous entoptic projection which occupied a good fraction of the volume of his quarters. Pascale, half consumed by shadow, was a series of abstract sculptural curves on their bed; he was cross-legged on a tatami mat, reeling in the delicious reprisals from a few millimetres of ship-distilled vodka he had downed minutes earlier. After years of forced abstinence, his tolerance for alcohol was abysmally low, which in this instance was a distinct advantage, hastening the process by which he negated the outside world. The vodka did not quell his inner voices, and, if anything, the withdrawal served only to create an echo-chamber, in which the voices took on an additional insistence. One in particular rose above the clamour. It was the voice which dared ask exactly what it was he expected to find in Cerberus; what it was that would make any kind of objective sense. And he had no idea. Not having an answer to that question was like descending a staircase in darkness and miscounting the number of steps; expecting floor and feeling sudden, heart-stopping vertigo.

Like a shaman shaping air-spirits with his fingers, Sylveste made the orrery which was projected ahead of him tick to life. The entoptic was a schematic of the little pocket of space englobing Hades, encompassing the orbit of Cerberus and – at its very limit – the approaching human machines, no longer cloaked by an asteroid. At the geometric centre was Hades itself, burning foul, abscessive red. The tiny neutron star was only a few kilometres wide, yet it dominated all around it; its gravitational field was whirlpool-fierce.

Objects which were two hundred and twenty thousand kilometres from the neutron star orbited twice an hour. Now that they had more thoroughly investigated Alicia's testimony, they knew that another of the surveyor probes had been destroyed near that point, so Sylveste marked the radius with a red death-line. Cerberus had killed it, just as if the little world were as intent on protecting the secrets of Hades as its own felicities. Another mystery – what possible advantage lay in that? Sylveste had grasped for an answer and failed. But it had told him one thing: nothing here was predictable, or even logical. If he kept those two truths foremost, he might stand a chance where the dumb machines – and his wife – had failed.

Cerberus orbited further out; nine hundred thousand kilometres from Hades, in an orbit which whipped it around once every four hours and six minutes. He had marked its orbit in cool emerald – it seemed safe, at least until one strayed too close to the planet itself.

Now Volyova's weapon – what had once been the *Lorean* – had moved under its own power to a lower orbit; it had not so far triggered a response from Cerberus. But Sylveste did not doubt for one moment that something down there knew they were here; that something had its eye on the waiting weapon. It was just waiting to see what would happen next.

He made the orrery contract, until the lighthugger hove into proper view. It was two million kilometres from the neutron star; a mere six light-seconds, which was within the conceivable strike range of energy weapons, although they would have to be very large indeed to do their job: the targeting arrays alone would have to be kilometres wide just to resolve the ship. No material weapons could touch them at this range, save for a brute-force swarm attack by relativistic weapons, but that again was unlikely – the lesson of the *Lorean* was that the planet acted swiftly and discreetly, rather than in some gauche display of firepower which would betray the careful camouflaging of the crust.

Oh yes, he thought – all so neatly predictable. And there was the trap.

'Dan,' said Pascale, who had stirred awake. 'It's late. You need to rest before tomorrow.'

'Was I talking aloud?'

'Like a true madman.' Her eyes moved nervously around the room, alighting on the entoptic map. 'Is it really going to happen? It all feels so unreal.'

'Are you talking about this or the Captain?'

'Both, I suppose. It's not like we can separate them any more. The one depends on the other.' She stopped speaking and he moved from the mat to her bedside, stroking her face, old buried memories stirring, those he had held sacrosanct during all the years of imprisonment on Resurgam. She reciprocated his caress and in minutes they were making love, with all the efficiency of those on the eve of something epochal – knowing that there might never be another moment like this, and that every second was therefore heightened in its preciousness. 'The Amarantin have waited long enough,' Pascale said. 'And that poor man they want you to help. Can't we leave both of them alone?'

'Why would I want to do that?'

'Because I don't like what it's doing to you. Don't you feel you've been driven here, Dan? Don't you feel that none of this was really of your own doing?'

'It's too late to stop now.'

'No! It isn't, and you know it. Tell Sajaki to turn back now. Offer to do what you can for his Captain if you wish, but I'm sure he's sufficiently scared of you now that he'll accede to any terms you propose. Abandon Cerberus/Hades before it does to us what it did to Alicia.'

'They weren't prepared for the attack. We will be, and that will make all the difference in the world. In fact, we'll be attacking first.'

'Whatever you're hoping to find in there, it just isn't worth this kind of risk.' She held his face in her hands now. 'Don't you understand, Dan? You've won. You've been vindicated. You've got what you always wanted.'

'It isn't enough.'

She was cold, but she stayed beside him as he passed in and out of shallow dreams. It was never anything that felt like true sleep. She was almost correct. The Amarantin did not have to flock through his mind; not for one night. She wanted him to forget them for eternity. No; that had never been remotely an option – more so now. But even willing them away for a few hours took more strength than he had. His dreams were Amarantin dreams. And whenever he woke, which was often, beyond the curved silhouette of his wife, the walls were alive with interlocking wings, balefully regarding wings, waiting.

For what was on the eve of beginning.

*

'You won't feel much,' Sajaki said.

The Triumvir was telling the truth, at least initially. Khouri felt no sensation when the trawl began, except for the slight pressure of the helmet, locking itself rigid against her scalp so that its scanning systems could be targeted with maximum accuracy. She heard faint clicks and whines, but that was all: not even the tingling sensation she had half expected.

'This isn't necessary, Triumvir.'

Sajaki was finessing the trawl parameters, tapping commands into a grotesquely outdated console. Cross-sections of Khouri's head – quick, low-resolution snapshots – were springing up around him. 'Then you have nothing to fear, do you? Nothing to fear at all. It's a procedure I should have run on you when you were recruited, Khouri. Of course, my colleague was against the idea . . .'

'Why now? What have I done to make you do this?'

'We're nearing a critical time, Khouri. I can't afford not to be able to trust any of my crewmembers totally.'

'But if you fry my implants, I won't be any use to you at all!'

'Oh; you shouldn't pay too much attention to Volyova's little scare stories. She only wanted to keep her little trade secrets from me, in case I decided I could do her job as well as she does.' Her implants were showing up on the scans now; little geometric islands of order amid the amorphous soup of neural structure. Sajaki tapped in commands and the scan image zoomed in on one of the implants. Khouri felt her scalp tingle. Layers of structure peeled away from the implant, exposing its increasingly intricate innards in a series of dizzying enlargements, like a spysat gazing at a city, resolving first districts, then streets and then the details of buildings. Somewhere in that intricacy, stored in some ultimately physical form, was the data from which the Mademoiselle's simulation sprang.

It had been a long time since her last visitation. Then – in the midst of the storm on Resurgam – the Mademoiselle had told Khouri that she was dying; losing the war against Sun Stealer. Had Sun Stealer won since then, or was the continued silence of the Mademoiselle simply evidence that she was putting all her energies into prolonging the war? Nagorny had gone mad as soon as Sun Stealer established tenancy in his head. Did that still lie ahead for Khouri, or was Sun Stealer's residency in her going to be more stealthy? Perhaps – it was a disquieting thought – he had learnt from his mistakes with Nagorny. How much of this would be evident to Sajaki, after he had run the trawl?

He had taken her from her quarters; Hegazi there to add back-up. The other Triumvir was gone now, but even if Sajaki had come alone, Khouri would not have considered resisting him. Volyova had already warned her that Sajaki was stronger than he looked, and, adept at close-quarters combat as Khouri was, she had very little doubt that Sajaki would have been better than her.

The trawling room had the atmosphere of a torture chamber. There had been terror here, once – maybe not for decades, but it was not something that could ever be erased. The trawl equipment was ancient, as bulky and monstrous as anything Khouri had seen on the ship so far. Even if the gear had been subtly modified to work better than its original spec, it was never going to be as sophisticated as the kind of trawls her side's intelligence wing had possessed on Sky's Edge. Sajaki's trawl was the kind that left a trail of neural damage behind as it scanned, like a frantic burglar ransacking a house. It was scarcely more advanced than the destructive scanning machines which Cal Sylveste had used during the Eighty . . . perhaps less so.

But he had her now. He was already learning things about her implants . . . unravelling their structures, reading out their data. Once he had those, he would adjust the trawl to resolve cortical patterns, pulling webs of neuronal connectivity from her skull. Khouri knew a lot about trawling just by knowing people in intelligence. Embedded in those topologies lay longterm memories and personality traits, tangled together in ways that were not easy to separate. But if Sajaki's equipment was not the best, chances were good that he had excellent algorithms to distil memory traces. Over centuries, statistical models had studied patterns of memory storage in ten billion human minds, correlating structure against experience. Certain impressions tended to be reflected in similar neural structures – internal qualia – which were the functional blocks out of which more complex memories were assembled. Those qualia were never the same from mind to mind, except in very rare cases, but neither were they encoded in radically different ways, since nature would never deviate far from the minimum-energy route to a particular solution. The statistical models could identify those qualia patterns very efficiently, and then map the connections between them out of which memories were forged. All Sajaki had to do was identify enough qualia structures, map enough hierarchical linkages between them, and then let his algorithms chew through them, and there would be nothing about her that he could not in principle know. He could sift through her memories at leisure.

An alarm sounded. Sajaki glanced up at one of the displays, seeing how Khouri's implants were now glowing red; red which was leaking into surrounding brain areas.

'What's happening?' she asked.

'Inductive heat,' Sajaki said, unconcernedly. 'Your implants are getting a little hot.'

'Shouldn't you stop?'

'Oh; not yet. Volyova would have hardened them against EM pulse attack, I think. A little thermal overload won't do any irreversible damage.'

'But my head hurts . . . it doesn't feel right.'

'I'm sure you can take it, Khouri.'

The migrainous pressure had come from nowhere, but it was really quite unbearable now, as if Sajaki had her head in a vice and was screwing it tighter. The heat build-up in her skull must be a lot worse than the scans suggested. Doubtless Sajaki – who must seldom have had the best interests of his clients at heart – had calibrated the displays not to show lethal brain temperature until it was already much too late . . .

'No, Yuuji-san. She can't take it. Get her out of that thing.'

The voice, miraculously, was Volyova's. Sajaki looked to the door. He must have been aware of her entrance long before Khouri, but even now he only affected a look of bored indifference.

'What is it, Ilia?'

'You know exactly what it is. Stop the trawl before you kill her.' Volyova stepped into view now. Her tone of voice had been authoritative, but Khouri could see that she was unarmed.

'I haven't learned anything useful yet,' Sajaki said. 'I need a few more minutes . . .'

'A few more minutes and she'll be dead.' With typical pragmatism, she added: 'And her implants will be damaged beyond repair.'

Perhaps the second thing worried Sajaki more than the first. He made a tiny adjustment to the trawl. The red hue faded to a less alarming pink. 'I thought these implants would be adequately hardened.'

'They're just prototypes, Yuuji-san.' Volyova stepped closer to the displays and surveyed them for herself. 'Oh, no . . . you fool, Sajaki. You damned fool. I swear you may have already damaged them.' It was as if she were talking to herself.

Sajaki waited silently for a moment. Khouri wondered if he was going to lash out and kill Volyova in an eyeblink of furious motion. But then, scowling, the Triumvir snapped the trawl controls to their off settings, watched the displays pop out of existence, then hoisted the helmet off Khouri's head.

'Your tone of voice – and choice of wording – was inappropriate there, Triumvir,' Sajaki said. Khouri saw his hand slip into his trouser pocket and finger something – something that, for an instant, looked like a hypodermic syringe.

'You nearly destroyed our Gunnery Officer,' Volyova said.

'I'm not finished with her. Or you, for that matter. You rigged something to this trawl, didn't you, Ilia? Something to alert you when it was running? Very clever.'

'I did it to protect a shipboard resource.'

'Yes, of course . . .' Sajaki left his answer hanging in the air, its threat implicit, and then quietly walked out of the trawl room.

TWENTY-THREE

Cerberus/Hades Orbit, Delta Pavonis Heliopause, 2566

It was, Sylveste thought, a situation of disturbing symmetry. In a matter of hours Volyova's cache-weapons would begin to combat the buried immunological systems of Cerberus; virus against virus, tooth against tooth. And here, on the eve of that attack, Sylveste was preparing to go to war against the Melding Plague which was consuming – or, depending on one's point of view, grotesquely enlarging – Volyova's afflicted Captain. The symmetry seemed to hint at an underlying order to which he was only partly privy. It was not a feeling he enjoyed; like being a participant in a game and realising, halfway through, that the rules were far more complicated than he had so far imagined.

In order that Calvin's beta-level simulation be allowed to work through him, Sylveste had to slip into a state of ambulatory semiconsciousness akin to sleepwalking. Calvin would puppet him, receiving sensory input directly through Sylveste's own eyes and ears, tapping directly into his nervous system to achieve mobility. He would even speak through Sylveste. The neuro-inhibitor drugs had already kicked him into a queasy full-body paralysis; as unpleasant as he remembered from the last time.

Sylveste thought of himself as a machine in which Calvin was about to become the ghost . . .

His hands worked the medical analysis tools, skirting the periphery of the growth. It was dangerous to stray too close to the heart; too high a risk of plague transmission into his own implants. At some point – this session, or perhaps the next – they would have to skirt the heart; that was inevitable, but Sylveste did not really want to think about that. For now, when they needed to work closer, Calvin used the simple, mindless drones which were slaved from elsewhere in the ship, but even those tools were susceptible. One drone had malfunctioned close to the Captain, and was even now being enmeshed in fine, fibrous plague tendrils. Even though the machine contained no molecular components, it still seemed that it was of use to the plague; still able to be digested into the Captain's transformative matrix; fuel for his fever. Calvin was having to resort to cruder instruments now, but this was only a stopgap: at some point – soon now, undoubtedly – they would have to hit the plague with the only thing which could really work against it: something very like itself.

Sylveste could feel Calvin's thought processes churning somewhere behind his own. It was nothing that could be called consciousness – the simulation which was running his body was no more than mimesis, but somewhere in the interfacing with his own nervous system ... it was as if something had arisen, something which was riding that chaotic edge. The theories and his own prejudices denied that, of course – but what other explanation could there be for the sense of divided self Sylveste felt? He did not dare ask if Calvin experienced something similar, and would not necessarily have trusted any answer he received.

'Son,' Calvin said. 'There's something I've waited until now before discussing. I'm rather worried about it, but I didn't want to discuss it in front of, well ... our clients.'

Sylveste knew that only he could hear Calvin's voice. He had to subvocalise to respond, Calvin momentarily relinquishing vocal control to his host. 'This isn't the time, either. In case you weren't paying attention, we're in the middle of an operation.'

'It's the operation I want to talk about.'

'Make it quick, in that case.'

'I don't think we're meant to succeed.'

Sylveste observed that his hands – driven by Calvin – had not ceased working during this last exchange. He was conscious of Volyova, who was standing nearby, awaiting instructions. He subvocalised, 'What the hell are you talking about?'

'I think Sajaki is a very dangerous man.'

'Great – that makes two of us. But it hasn't stopped you cooperating with him.'

'I was grateful to begin with,' Calvin admitted. 'He saved me, after all. But then I started wondering how things must seem from his side. I began to wonder if he wasn't just a touch insane. It struck me that any sane man would have left the Captain for dead years ago. The Sajaki I knew last time was fiercely loyal, but at least then there was some sense to his crusade. At least then there was a hope we could save the Captain.'

'And now there isn't?'

'He's been infected with a virus which the entire resources of the Yellowstone system couldn't combat. Admittedly, the system itself was under attack from the same virus, but there were still isolated enclaves which survived for months – places where people with techniques as sophisticated as our own struggled to find a cure – and yet they never succeeded. Not only that, but we don't even know which blind alleys they pursued, or which approaches might almost have worked, if they'd had more time.'

'I told Sajaki he needed a miracle worker. It's his problem if he didn't believe me.'

'The problem is, I think he did believe you. That's what I mean when I said we weren't meant to succeed.'

Sylveste happened to be looking at the Captain, Calvin having judiciously arranged the view. Confronted with the thing before his eyes, he experienced a moment of epiphany in which he knew that Calvin was absolutely right. They could go through the preliminary motions of healing the Captain – the rituals of establishing just how corrupted the man's flesh was – but it could never progress beyond that. Whatever they tried, no matter how intelligent, no matter how conceptually brilliant, could not possibly succeed. Or, more significantly, could not be permitted to succeed. It was that latter realisation which was the most disturbing, because it had come from Calvin, rather than Sylveste. He had seen something which to Sylveste was still opaque, and now it seemed obvious; shatteringly so.

'You think he'll hinder us?'

'I think he already has. We both observed that the Captain's rate of growth had accelerated since we were brought aboard, but we dismissed it – either just a coincidence or our imaginations. But I don't think so. I think Sajaki allowed him to warm.'

'Yes . . . I was drawn to that conclusion myself. There's something else, isn't there?'

'The biopsies – the tissue samples I asked for.'

Sylveste knew where this was leading. The drone that they had sent in to extract the cell samples was now half-digested by the plague. 'You don't think that was a genuine malfunction, do you? You think Sajaki made it happen.'

'Sajaki, or one of his crewmates.'

'Her?'

Sylveste felt himself glance towards the woman. 'No,' Calvin said, effecting an entirely unnecessary murmur. 'Not her. That doesn't mean I trust her, but on the other hand, I don't see her as one of Sajaki's automatic minions.'

'What are you discussing?' asked Volyova, stepping towards them.

'Don't come too close,' Calvin said, speaking through Sylveste, who, for the moment, was unable to form his own sounds even subvocally. 'Our investigations may have unleashed plague spore – you wouldn't want to inhale them.'

'It wouldn't harm me,' Volyova said. 'I'm *brezgatnik*. I have nothing in me that the plague can touch.'

'Then why are you looking so stand-offish?'

'Because it's cold, *svinoi*.' She paused. 'Wait a minute. Which one of you am I actually talking to? It's Calvin, isn't it? I suppose I owe you fractionally more respect – it isn't you holding us to ransom, after all.'

'You're too kind,' Sylveste found himself saying.

'I trust you've arrived at a strategy here? Triumvir Sajaki won't be pleased if he suspects you aren't keeping up your side of the bargain.'

'Triumvir Sajaki,' Calvin said, 'may well be part of the problem.'

She had come closer now, even though she was visibly shivering, lacking the thermal protection which Sylveste wore. 'I'm not sure I understand that remark.'

'Do you honestly think he wants us to heal the Captain?'

She looked as if he had slapped her across the face. 'Why wouldn't he?'

'He's had a long time to get used to being in command. This Triumvirate of yours is a farce – Sajaki's your Captain in all but name, and you and Hegazi know it. He isn't going to relinquish that without a fight.'

She answered too hastily to be totally convincing. 'If I were you I'd concentrate on the job in hand and stop worrying about the Triumvir's wishes. He brought you here, after all. He came light-years for your services. That's hardly the work of a man who doesn't want to see his Captain reinstated.'

'He'll ensure that we fail,' Calvin said. 'But in the course of our

406

failure, he'll find another glimmer of hope; something or someone else who can heal the Captain, if only he can find it or them. And before you know it, you'll be on another century-long quest.'

'If that's the case,' she said slowly, as if fearful of being drawn into a trap, 'then why hasn't Sajaki already killed the Captain? That would safeguard his position.'

'Because then he'd have to find a use for you.'

'A use?'

'Yes, think about it.' Calvin let go of the medical tools and stepped away from the Captain, like an actor preparing to enter the limelight for his soliloquy. 'This quest to heal the Captain is the only god you're capable of serving. Maybe there was a time when it was a means to an end . . . but that end never came, and after a while it didn't even matter. You have the weapons aboard this ship; I know all about those, even the ones you don't really like talking about. For now, the only purpose they serve is bargaining power when you need someone like me – someone who can go through the motions of healing the Captain, without actually making any real difference.' Sylveste was glad when Calvin did not speak for a few seconds, for he needed to catch his breath and lubricate his mouth. 'Now, if Sajaki suddenly became Captain, what would he do next? You'd still have the weapons – but who could you use them against? You'd have to invent an enemy from scratch. Maybe they wouldn't even have something you wanted – after all, you're the ones with the ship; what else do you need? Ideological enemies? Tricky, because the one thing I haven't noticed among you is an ideological attachment to anything, except perhaps your own survival. No; I think Sajaki knows what would happen, deep down. He knows that if he became Captain, sooner or later you'd have to use those weapons just because they existed. And I don't mean the kind of minimalist intervention you demonstrated on Resurgam. You'd have to go all the way: use every one of those horrors.'

Volyova was quick; Sylveste had already been impressed by that. 'In which case, we owe Triumvir Sajaki our gratitude, don't we? By not killing the Captain, he's keeping us from the brink.' But the way she spoke, it was as if she were reciting the argument of a devil's advocate, saying it aloud only to better illuminate its heresies.

'Yes,' Calvin said, dubiously. 'I suppose you're right.'

'I don't believe any of this,' Volyova said, with sudden fire. 'And if you were one of us, it would be treason just to entertain those thoughts.'

'Suit yourself. But we've already seen evidence that Sajaki wants to sabotage the operation.'

For a moment curiosity flashed in her expression, but she crushed it just as efficiently. 'I'm not interested in your paranoia, Calvin – assuming it's Calvin I'm talking to. I have an obligation to Dan, which is to get him into Cerberus. And I have an obligation to you, which is to help with the healing. The discussion of any other topics is superfluous.'

'So you have the retrovirus, I take it?'

Volyova reached into her jacket and removed the vial she had been carrying. 'It works against the plague samples I was able to isolate and keep in culture. Whether or not it will work against *that* is another question entirely.'

Sylveste felt his hands jerk forward to catch the vial as she threw it. The tiny glass autoclave reminded him of the vial he had carried before his wedding, but only fleetingly.

'It's a pleasure doing business with you,' Calvin said.

Volyova left Calvin or Dan Sylveste – she had never been entirely sure who she had been dealing with – having given the man explicit instructions concerning the administration of the counter-agent. Her relationship to him had been that of an apothecary to a surgeon, she thought: she had formulated a serum which worked in the laboratory, and she could offer broad guidelines regarding the manner in which it should be administered, but the ultimate decisions, the true life-and-death questions; those were at the discretion of the surgeon only, and she had no desire to intervene. After all, if the manner of the administration had not been so critical, there would have been no need to bring Sylveste aboard in the first place. And her retrovirus would form only one element of the treatment, though it might prove decisive.

She rode the elevator back to the bridge, trying hard not to think about what Calvin (it had been him, surely?) had been saying to her about Sajaki. But it was difficult; there was too much internal logic – too much reason to what he said. And what was she to make of the alleged sabotage against the healing process? She had almost dared ask, but was perhaps too fearful of hearing something she could not refute. As she had said – and it was true, in a way – just thinking along those lines was treasonable.

But in many ways she had already committed treason.

Sajaki was beginning to have his doubts about her; that much was obvious. Disagreeing with him over whether or not Khouri should have been trawled was one thing. But rigging the trawl to inform her when Sajaki activated it was something else entirely – not the act of someone exhibiting mild professional concern over her charge, but one which spoke of quiet paranoia, fear and brooding hatred. Luckily she had reached him in time. The trawl had not done any lasting damage and it was doubtful that Sajaki had mapped enough neural volume in sufficient detail to pull out anything more than blurred impressions, rather than fully fledged incriminating memories. Now, she thought, Sajaki would be more cautious: it would be no good losing their Gunnery Officer now. But what if he turned the focus of his suspicion towards Volyova herself? She could be trawled, too. Sajaki would have few qualms about that, other than the fact that it would completely destroy any lingering sense of equality between them. Certainly she had no implants to damage. And to some extent, with the work aboard the *Lorean* progressing autonomously, her period of maximum usefulness to him had passed.

She consulted her bracelet. That little splinter she had pulled from Khouri was causing more headaches than she had ever thought possible. Now she had the composition and stress patterning more or less pinned down, she had asked the ship to match the sample against something in its memory. Her hunch about it being Manoukhian's doing was looking good, for the shard had clearly not originated on Sky's Edge. But the ship was still searching, burrowing deeper and deeper into its memory. Now it was working through technological data from nearly two centuries previously. Absurd to search such antiquity . . . but, on the other hand, why stop now? In a matter of hours the ship would have correlated right back to the founding of the colony; to the few records surviving from the Amerikano era. She would at least be able to tell Khouri that the search had been exhaustive – even if it had been futile.

She entered the bridge, alone.

The gigantic chamber was dark except for the glow cast by the display sphere, which was locked in a schematic of the whole

Pavonis-Hades binary. There were no other crewmembers (of the few who remained alive, she thought), and none of the dead were currently being recalled from archival posterity to share their views in languages hardly anyone now spoke. The solitude suited Volyova. She had no wish to deal with Sajaki (most especially not him), and Hegazi's was a species of company she did not especially prize. She did not even want to talk to Khouri; not just now. Being with Khouri raised too many questions; forced her mind onto topics with which it did not wish to be preoccupied. Now, for a few minutes at least, Volyova could be alone, and in her element, and – however foolishly – forget everything that threatened to transform order into chaos.

She could be with her beautiful weapons.

The transfigured *Lorean* had dropped to an even lower orbit without provoking a response from Cerberus – only ten thousand kilometres above the planet's surface. She had named the vast conic object the bridgehead, because that was its function. As far as the others were concerned, it was just Volyova's weapon, if they bothered calling it anything. The thing was four thousand metres long; almost the same length as the lighthugger which had given birth to it. Very little of it was solid; even the walls were honeycombed with pores, in which lay clades of primed military cyberviruses, similar in structure to the counteragent about to be used against the Captain. Larger energy and projectile weapons were set inside caverns in the walls. The whole thing was sheathed in several metres of hyperdiamond which would be ablated sacrificially upon impact. Shock waves would rush up the length of the bridgehead as it hit the surface, but piezoelectric crystal boundaries would gradually bleed energy from the shock waves, energy which could be redirected into weapons systems. The impact speed would be relatively slow, in any case – less than a kilometre a second, since the bridgehead would decelerate massively just before puncturing the crust. And the crust would be softened up beforehand; apart from the bridgehead's own frontal guns, Volyova would deploy as much of the cache armament as she dared.

She interrogated the weapon via her bracelet. It was not the most riveting of conversations. The device's controlling personality was rudimentary; nothing more could be expected from something mere days old. In a sense that was good. Better that the thing be pigeon-minded, or it might start getting ideas above its station. And, as she reminded herself, the bridgehead might not have very long to enjoy its sentience in the first place.

Numerics dancing in the sphere told her of the bridgehead's total readiness. She had to trust what the summarising systems told her, for the weapon was in many ways unknown to her. She had sketched out her basic requirements, but the dogwork had been done by autonomous design programs, and they had not deigned to inform her of every technical problem and solution encountered along the way. But as profound as her ignorance of the bridgehead might be, it was not so very different from the way a mother managed to create a child without knowing the precise location of every artery and nerve ... or even the precise biochemistry of its metabolism. It was no less her creation for that – no less her child.

A child she was consigning to an early, ignominious death – but by no means a meaningless one.

Her bracelet chirped. She glanced down at it, expecting that it would be a technical squirt from the bridgehead; a brief update concerning some last-minute inflight redesign which had been put in place by the replicating systems still at work in its core.

But it was not that at all.

It was from the ship, and it had found a match for the splinter. It had needed to look back into technical files more than two centuries old, but it had found a match all the same. And apart from the stress patterning – which must have come after the shard's manufacture – the agreement was absolute, within the errors of measurement.

She was still alone in the bridge.

'Put it on the display,' Volyova said.

A magnified, visible-light image of the splinter appeared in the sphere. A series of zoom-ins appeared, beginning with a grey-scale electron-microscopy view which showed the shard's tortured crystalline structure, and ending with a gaudily hued atomic-scale resolution ATM image, individual atoms blurred together. X-ray crystallographic and mass spectrograph plots popped into separate windows, jostling for her attention with reams of technical summary data. Volyova paid no attention to these results; they were completely familiar to her for she had made most of the measurements herself.

Instead, she waited while the entire display shuffled to one side and a very similar set of graphics sprang into existence next to it, arrayed around a sliver of similar-looking material, identical at atomic resolution, but showing none of the stress patterning. The compositions, isotopic ratios and lattice properties were identical: lots of fullerenes, knitted into structural allotropes, threading a bafflingly complex matrix of sandwiched metal layers and odd alloys. Spikes of yttrium and scandium, with a whole slew of stable-island transuranic elements in trace quantities, presumably adding some arcane resilience to the shard's bulk properties. Still, by Volyova's reckoning, there were stranger substances aboard the ship, and she had synthesised a few of them herself. The splinter was unusual, but it was clearly human technology – the buckytube filaments, in fact, were a typical Demarchist signature, and stable-island transuranics had been in massive vogue in the twenty-fourth and -fifth centuries.

The shard, in fact, looked a lot like the kind of thing a spacecraft hull from that era might have been made of.

The ship seemed to think so too. What was Khouri doing with a piece of hull buried in her? What kind of message had Manoukhian intended by that? Perhaps she was wrong, and this was none of Manoukhian's doing – just an accident. Unless this had been a very specific spacecraft . . .

It seemed that it was. The technology was typical for that era, but in every specific, the shard was unique – manufactured to tighter tolerances than would have been required even in a military application. In fact, as Volyova digested the results, it became clear that the shard could only have come from one kind of ship: a contact vessel owned by the Sylveste Institute for Shrouder Studies.

Subtleties of isotopic ratio established that it had come from one ship in particular: the contact vessel that had carried Sylveste to the boundary of Lascaille's Shroud. For a moment, that discovery was enough for Volyova. There was a circularity about it; confirmation that Khouri's Mademoiselle really did have some connection with Sylveste. But Khouri already knew that . . . which meant that the message must be telling them something more profound. Of course, Volyova had already seen what it must be. But for an instant she flinched at the enormity of it. There was no way it could be her, could it? No way she could have survived what had happened around Lascaille's Shroud. But Manoukhian had always told Khouri that he had found his paymistress in space. And it was entirely possible that her disguise of a hermetic masked an injury more savage than anything the plague could have inflicted . . .

'Show me Carine Lefevre,' Volyova said, retrieving the name of the woman who should have died around the Shroud.

Vast as a goddess, the face of the woman stared down at her. She was young, and from the little of her that was visible below her face, it could be seen that she was dressed in the fashions of the Yellowstone Belle Epoque, the glittering golden age before the Melding Plague. And her face was familiar – not shatteringly so, but enough for Volyova to know she had seen this woman before. She had seen this woman's face in a dozen historical documentaries, and in every one of them the assumption had been made that she was long dead; murdered by alien forces beyond human comprehension.

Of course. Now it was obvious what caused that stress patterning. The gravitational riptides around Lascaille's Shroud had squeezed matter until it bled.

Everyone thought Carine Lefevre had died the same way.

'*Svinoi*,' said Triumvir Ilia Volyova, because now there could be no doubt.

Ever since she was a child, Khouri had noticed that something happened when she touched something that was too hot, like the barrel of a projectile rifle which had just discharged its clip. There would be a flash of premonitory pain, but so brief that it was hardly pain at all; more a warning of true pain which was about to come. And then the premonitory pain would subside, and there would be an instant when there was no sensation at all, and in that instant she would snatch back her hand, away from whatever it was that was too hot. But it would be too late; the true pain was already coming, and there was nothing she could do about it except ready herself for its arrival, like a housekeeper forewarned about the imminent arrival of a guest. Of course, the pain was never so bad, and she had usually withdrawn her hand from whatever was its source, and there would usually not even be a scar afterwards. But it always made her wonder. If the premonitory pain was enough to persuade her to remove the hand – and it always was – what was the purpose of the *tsunami* of true pain which lagged behind it? Why did it have to come at all, if she had already received the message and removed her hand from harm? When, later, she found out that there was a sound physiological reason for the delay between the two warnings, it still seemed almost spiteful.

That was how she felt now, sitting in the spider-room with Volyova, who had just told her who she thought the face belonged to. Carine Lefevre; that was what she had said. And there had been a flash of premonitory shock, like an echo from the future of what the real shock of it was going to be like. A very faint echo indeed, and then – for an instant – nothing.

And then the true force of it.

'How can it be her?' Khouri said, afterwards, when the shock had not so much subsided as become a normal component of her emotional background noise. 'It isn't possible. It doesn't make any sense.'

'I think it makes too much sense,' Volyova said. 'I think it fits the facts too well. I think it's something we can't ignore.'

'But we all know she died! And not just on Yellowstone, but halfway across colonised space. Ilia, she died, violently. There's no way it can be her.'

'I think it can. Manoukhian said he found her in space. So perhaps he did. Perhaps he found Carine Lefevre drifting near Lascaille's Shroud – he might have been looking to salvage something from the wreckage of the SISS facility – and then rescued her and took her back to Yellowstone.' Volyova stopped, but before Khouri could speak, or even think about speaking, the Triumvir was on a roll again. 'That would make sense, wouldn't it? We'd at least have a connection to Sylveste – and maybe even a reason for her wanting him dead.'

'Ilia, I've read what happened to her. She was shredded by the gravitational stresses around the Shroud. There wouldn't have been anything left for Manoukhian to bring home.'

'No . . . of course not. Unless Sylveste was lying. Remember that we have only Sylveste's word that any of it happened the way he said it did – none of the recording systems survived the encounter.'

'She didn't die, is that what you're saying?'

Volyova raised a hand, the way she always did when Khouri failed to read her mind perfectly.

'No . . . not necessarily. Perhaps she did die – just not in the way Sylveste had it. And maybe she didn't die in the way we understand, and perhaps she isn't really alive, even now – despite what you saw.'

'I didn't see much of her, did I? Just the box she used to move around in.'

'You assumed she was a hermetic, because she rode something like a hermetic's palanquin. But that might have been a piece of mis-direction on her behalf.'

'She'd have been shredded. Nothing changes that.'

'Perhaps the Shroud didn't kill her, Khouri. Perhaps something dreadful happened to her, but something kept her alive afterwards. Perhaps something actually saved her.'

'Sylveste would know.'

'Even if he doesn't admit it to himself. We have to talk to him, I think – here, where we won't we bothered by Sajaki.' Volyova had hardly finished speaking when her bracelet chirped and filled with a human face, eyes lost behind blank globes. 'Speak of the devil,' Volyova murmured. 'What is it, Calvin? You are Calvin, aren't you?'

'For now,' the man said. 'Though I fear my usefulness to Sajaki may be coming to an ignominious end.'

'What are you talking about?' Quickly she added: 'There's something I have to discuss with Dan; it's rather on the urgent side, if you'd oblige.'

'I think what I have to say is more urgent,' Calvin said. 'It's your counteragent, Volyova. The retrovirus you fabricated.'

'What about it?'

'It doesn't seem to be working quite as intended.' He took a step backwards; Khouri glimpsed part of the Captain behind him, silvery and muculent, like a statue covered with a palimpsest of snail tracks. 'As a matter of fact, it seems to be killing him faster.'

TWENTY-FOUR

Cerberus/Hades, Delta Pavonis Heliopause, 2566

Sylveste did not have long to wait. When Volyova arrived, she was accompanied by Khouri; the woman who had saved Volyova's life on the surface. If Volyova was something of a rogue variable in his plans then Khouri was worse, because he had not so far ascertained where her loyalties lay; whether to Volyova or Sajaki, or somewhere else entirely. But for now he suppressed his concerns, sharing Calvin's urgency.

'What do you mean, it's killing him faster?'

'I mean just that,' Calvin made him say, before either of the two women had drawn breath. 'We administered it according to your instructions. But it's as if we've given the plague a massive shot in the arm. It's spreading faster than ever. If I didn't know better I'd say your retrovirus has actually helped it.'

'Damn,' Volyova said. 'I'm sorry, but you'll have to excuse me. It's been a wearying few hours.'

'Is that all you're going to say?'

'I tested the counteragent against small samples of isolated plague,' she said defensively. 'It worked against them. I couldn't promise it would work against the main body of the plague so effectively . . . but at the very least, in the worst possible scenario . . . I assumed it would have some effect, however limited. The plague has to expend *some* of its resources against the counteragent; there's no getting around that. It has to direct some of the energy it would ordinarily use for expansion into resisting the agent. I hoped it would kill it – subvert it, I mean, into a form we could manipulate – but even when I was being pessimistic, I assumed the plague would catch a cold; that it would slow down perceptibly.'

'That's not what we're seeing,' Calvin said.

'But she has a point,' Khouri said, and Sylveste felt himself glare at her, as if questioning the very reason for her existence.

'What are you seeing?' Volyova asked. 'You understand, I'm more than a little curious.'

'We've stopped administering,' Calvin said. 'So for now the growth has stabilised. But when we gave the Captain the counteragent, he spread faster. It was as if he were incorporating the mass of the counteragent into his matrix more rapidly than he could convert the substrate of the ship.'

'But that's ridiculous,' Volyova said. 'The ship doesn't even resist the plague. For him to spread faster . . . that would mean that the counteragent was giving itself over to him; converting itself faster than the plague could subvert it.'

'Like frontline soldiers defecting before they've even heard any propaganda,' Khouri said.

'Exactly like that,' Volyova said, and for the first time, Sylveste sensed something between the two women, something suspiciously like mutual respect. 'But that just isn't possible. For that to happen, the plague would have to have hijacked the replication routines almost without trying – almost as if they were willingly hijacked. I'm telling you, it isn't possible.'

'Well, try it for yourself.'

'No thanks. It isn't that I don't believe you, but you have to see it from my side. From my point of view – and I engineered the damn thing – it doesn't make much sense.'

'There is something,' Calvin said.

'What?'

'Could sabotage have done this? I told you already that we think someone doesn't want this operation to succeed. You know who I'm talking about.' He was being circumspect now, unwilling to say too much in Khouri's presence, or within range of Sajaki's listening systems. 'Could your counteragent have been tampered with?'

'I'll have to think about it,' she said.

Sylveste had not administered all of the vial Volyova had given him, so she was able to run a check on the molecular structure of that sample and the other batches which remained in her laboratory, using the same tools she had employed on Khouri's splinter. When she compared the sample against her lab batches, they were identical, within the normal boundaries of quantum accuracy. The sample Calvin had given to the Captain was exactly as she had intended it to be, down to the humblest chemical bond linking the least significant atoms in the smallest and least essential molecular component . . .

Volyova checked the counteragent's structure against her records, and observed that it had not deviated from the blueprint she had held in her head for subjective years. It was exactly as she had planned it. Her virus had not been tampered with; its teeth had not been pulled. So much for Calvin's sabotage theory. She felt a surge of relief – she had not really wanted to believe that Sajaki was actually hampering the whole process; the notion that he might be consciously prolonging the Captain's illness was too hideous, and she was glad when examination of the counteragent gave her a justification for flushing the idea of sabotage from her mind. She still had misgivings about Sajaki, of course; but there was at least no evidence that he had become something as monstrous as that.

But there was another possibility.

Volyova left the lab and returned to the Captain, cursing herself for not thinking of this earlier and sparing herself the runaround. Sylveste asked what she was doing now. She looked at him for long moments before speaking. Yes, there was a connection with Lascaille's Shroud; she was sure of that. Was it purely revenge on the Mademoiselle's part – in payment for his cowardice, or treachery, or whatever it was that had almost killed her in the Shroud boundary? Or did it go beyond that, connected in some way with the aliens themselves; the ancient, protective minds Lascaille had touched during his own flyby? Was it human spite they were dealing with here, or some imperative as alien and old as the Shrouders themselves? There was much she needed to discuss with Sylveste – but it would have to be in the sanctuary of the spider-room.

'I need another sample,' she said. 'From the infection boundary, where you administered the counteragent.' And she fished out her laser-curette, made the deft light-guided incisions and popped the sample – it felt like a metallic scab – into a waiting autoclave.

'What about the counteragent? Was it altered?'

'It hadn't been touched,' she said. Then she turned down the curette's yield and used it to scratch in tiny letters a quick message in the ship's fabric, just ahead of the Captain's encroachment.

Long before Sajaki stood a chance of reading it, the Captain would have flowed over it like an erasing tide.

'What are you doing?' Sylveste said.

But before the man could ask anything else, she was gone.

'You were right,' Volyova said, when they were safely beyond the hull of the *Nostalgia for Infinity*, perched on its outer carapace like some adventurous steel parasite. 'It was sabotage. But not in the way I first imagined.'

'What do you mean?' said Sylveste, who by now was grudgingly impressed by the existence of the spider-room. 'I thought you cross-referenced the retrovirus against your earlier batches, those which worked against small samples of the plague.'

'I did, and – as I said – there was no difference. Which only left one possibility.'

Silence hung in the air. Finally, it was Pascale Sylveste who broke it. 'He – it – must have been inoculated. That's what must have happened, isn't it? Someone must have stolen a batch of your retrovirus and denatured it – removed its lethality, its urge to replicate – and then shown it to the Melding Plague.'

'It's the only thing which would explain it,' Volyova said.

Khouri said, 'You think Sajaki did it, don't you?' She was talking to Sylveste.

He nodded. 'Calvin had as good as predicted that Sajaki would try and ruin the operation.'

'I don't follow,' Khouri said. 'You're talking about the Captain being inoculated – isn't that for the better?'

'Not in this case – and it wasn't the Captain who was inoculated, really, but the plague resident in him.' It was Volyova speaking now. 'We've always known that the Melding Plague is hyperadaptive. That's always been the problem – every molecular weapon we throw at it ends up being co-opted, smothered and reprocessed into the plague's own all-consuming offensive. But this time I hoped we'd steal an advantage. The retrovirus was extraordinarily potent – there was a chance it could outmanoeuvre the plague's normal corruption pathways. But what happened was that the plague got a sneak look at the enemy before it ever encountered it in its active form. It got a chance to dismantle and know the counteragent before it ever posed a threat to it. And by the time Calvin administered it, the plague already knew all its tricks. It had

419

worked out a way to disarm the virus and persuade it to join the plague without even expending any energy in the process. So the Captain grew faster.'

'Who could have done this?' Khouri asked. 'I thought you were the only person on this ship who could do something like that.'

Sylveste nodded. 'As much as I still think Sajaki's trying to sabotage the operation . . . this doesn't look like it could be his handiwork.'

'I agree,' Volyova said. 'Sajaki just doesn't have the expertise to have done this.'

'What about the other man?' Pascale asked. 'The chimeric.'

'Hegazi?' Volyova shook her head. 'You can ignore him. He might become a problem if any of us ever move against the Triumvirate, but this isn't within his capabilities any more than Sajaki's. No; the way I see it, there are only three people on this ship who could have done it, and I'm one of them.'

'Who are the other two?' Sylveste asked.

'Calvin is one of them,' she said. 'Which rather removes him from suspicion as well.'

'And the other?'

'That's the problematic part,' she said. 'The only other person who could do this to a cybervirus is the one we've been trying to heal all this time.'

'The Captain?' Sylveste said.

'He could have done it – from a theoretical standpoint, I mean.' Volyova clucked. 'Were he not already dead.'

Khouri wondered how Sylveste would react to that, but he seemed unimpressed. 'It doesn't matter who it was – if it wasn't Sajaki himself, it was someone acting for him.' Now he addressed Volyova. 'I take it this convinces you.'

She graced him with a nod. 'Regrettably, yes. What does it mean to you and Calvin?'

'Mean to us?' Sylveste seemed surprised by the question. 'It means absolutely nothing. I never promised we could heal the Captain in the first place. I told Sajaki I considered the task impossible, and I wasn't exaggerating. Calvin agreed with me as well. In all honesty, I'm not even sure Sajaki had to sabotage the operation. Even if your retrovirus hadn't been denatured, I doubt that it would have given the plague much trouble. So what has changed? Calvin and I will continue with the pretence of healing the Captain, and at some point it will be clear that we can't succeed. We won't let Sajaki know that we're aware of his sabotage. We don't want a confrontation with the man – especially not now, with the attack against Cerberus about to happen.' Sylveste smiled placidly. 'And I don't think Sajaki will be particularly disappointed to hear that our efforts have been in vain.'

'You're saying that nothing changes, is that it?' Khouri looked around at the others for support, but their expressions were inscrutable. 'I don't believe this.'

'The Captain doesn't matter to him,' said Pascale Sylveste. 'Isn't that obvious to you? He's only doing this to keep his side of the bargain with Sajaki. Cerberus is all that matters to him. It's been like a magnet to Dan.' She was talking as if her husband were somewhere else entirely.

'Yes,' Volyova said. 'Well, I'm glad you raised that subject, because there's something Khouri and I need to discuss with all of you. It concerns Cerberus.'

Sylveste looked scornful. 'What do you know about Cerberus?'

'Too much,' Khouri said. 'Too damned much.'

She began where it made sense to begin, at the beginning, with her revival on Yellowstone, her work as an assassin in Shadowplay, and how the Mademoiselle had recruited her and made it very difficult for her not to accept the woman's offer.

'Who was she?' Sylveste asked, when the preliminaries had been dispensed with. 'And what did she want you to do?'

'We'll come to that,' Volyova said. 'Just be patient.'

Khouri continued; repeating to Sylveste the story that she had not long ago told Volyova, though it felt that an eternity spaced the two recitations. How she had infiltrated the ship, and how – simultaneously – she had been tricked by Volyova, who needed a new Gunnery Officer, irrespective of whether anyone volunteered for that role. How the Mademoiselle had been in her head all this time, revealing only as much information as Khouri needed at any moment. How Volyova had interfaced Khouri into the gunnery, and how the Mademoiselle had detected something lurking in the gunnery, something – a software entity – that called itself Sun Stealer.

Pascale looked at Sylveste. 'That name,' she said. 'It . . .

means something. I've heard it before; I'd swear it. Don't you remember?'

Sylveste looked at her, but said nothing.

'This thing,' Khouri said. 'Whatever it was – it had already tried to get out of the gunnery into the head of the last poor sucker Volyova recruited. Drove him insane.'

'I don't see where this concerns me,' Sylveste said.

So Khouri told him. 'The Mademoiselle worked out that this thing had to have entered the gunnery at a certain time.'

'Very good; continue.'

'Which was when you were last aboard this ship.'

She had wondered what it would take to shut Sylveste up, or at the very least wipe the look of smug superiority off his face. Now she knew, and realised that in the midst of everything, this achievement had been one of life's small and unexpected pleasures. Breaking the spell, with admirable self-control, Sylveste said: 'What does that mean?'

'It means what you think it means, but don't want to consider.' The words had tumbled out of her mouth. 'Whatever it was, you brought it with you.'

'Some kind of neural parasite,' Volyova said, taking the burden of explication from Khouri. 'It came aboard with you and then hopped into the ship. It could have ridden your implants, or perhaps your mind itself, independent of any hardware.'

'This is ridiculous.' But something in his tone of voice failed to convince.

'If you weren't aware of it,' Volyova said, 'then you could have been carrying it around for years. Maybe even since you came back.'

'Came back from where?'

'Lascaille's Shroud,' Khouri said, and, for the second time, her words seemed to lash against Sylveste like squalls of wintery rain. 'We checked the chronology; it fits. Whatever it was, it got into you around the Shroud, and stayed with you until you came here. Maybe it didn't even leave you; just split off part of itself into the ship, hedging its bets.'

Sylveste stood up, motioning for his wife to do likewise. 'I'm not staying to hear any more of this madness.'

'I think you should,' Khouri said. 'We still haven't told you about the Mademoiselle, or what she wanted me to do.'

He just looked at her, poised on the verge of leaving, his face a study in disgust. Then – perhaps a minute later – he returned to his seat and waited for her to continue.

TWENTY-FIVE

Cerberus/Hades, Delta Pavonis Heliopause, 2566

'I'm sorry,' Sylveste said. 'But I don't think this man can be cured.'

His only companions, save the Captain himself, were the two members of the Triumvirate other than Volyova.

The closest, Sajaki, stood with his arms folded in front of the Captain, as if inspecting a challengingly modern fresco, his head tilted just so. Hegazi maintained a respectful distance from the plague, refusing to approach within three or four metres of the outer extent of the Captain's recently invigorated growth. He was doing his best to look nonchalant, but, despite the relatively sparse acreage of his face which was actually visible, fear was written across it like a tattoo.

'He's dead?' Sajaki asked.

'No, no,' said Sylveste hastily. 'Not at all. It's just that all our therapies have failed, and our one best shot turned out to hurt him more than to heal him.'

'Your one best shot?' Hegazi parroted, his voice echoing from the walls.

'Ilia Volyova's counteragent.' Sylveste knew he had to be very careful now; that it would not do for Sajaki to realise that his sabotage had come to light. 'For whatever reason, it didn't work in the way she thought it would. I don't blame Volyova for that – how could she predict how the main body of the plague would behave, when all she had to work on was tiny samples?'

'How indeed?' Sajaki said, and in that short declamation, Sylveste decided that he hated the man, with a hatred as irrevocable as death. But he also knew that Sajaki was a man he could work with, and that – as much as he despised him – nothing that had occurred here would make any difference to the attack against Cerberus. It was better than that, in fact: much better. Now that he was certain that Sajaki had no desire to see the Captain healed – quite the opposite – there was nothing to prevent Sylveste from turning his full attention to the matter of the imminent attack. Perhaps he would have to endure Calvin's presence in his head for a little while longer, until this charade had run its course, but that was a small price to pay, and he felt up to the task. Besides: now he rather welcomed Calvin's intrusion. There was too much going on; too much to be assimilated, and for the time being it was good to have a second mind parasitising his own, gleaning patterns and forging inferences.

'He's a lying bastard,' Calvin whispered. 'I had my doubts before, but now I know for sure. I hope the plague consumes every atom of the ship and takes him with it. It's all he deserves.'

Sylveste said to Sajaki, 'It doesn't mean we've given up hope. With your permission Cal and I will continue trying . . .'

'Do what you can,' Sajaki said.

'You want to let them continue?' Hegazi said. 'After what they've almost done to him?'

'You've got a problem with that?' said Sylveste, feeling that the conversation was as ritualised as a play; its conclusion just as preordained. 'If we don't take risks . . .'

'Sylveste is right,' Sajaki said. 'Who's to say how the Captain would respond to the most innocent of interventions? The plague is a living thing – it isn't necessarily obedient to any set of logical rules, so every act we make carries some risk, even something as seemingly harmless as sweeping it with a magnetic field. The plague might interpret it as a stimulus to shift to a new phase of growth, or it might cause the plague to turn to dust in seconds. I doubt that the Captain would survive either scenario.'

'In which case,' Hegazi said, 'we might as well give up now.'

'No,' Sajaki said, so calmly that Sylveste feared for the other man's well-being. 'It doesn't mean that we give up. It means that we need a new paradigm – something beyond surgical intervention. Here we have the finest cyberneticist born since the Transenlightenment, and no one has a finer grasp of molecular weapons than Ilia Volyova. The medical systems we have aboard this ship are as advanced as any in existence. And yet we've failed; for the simple reason that we're dealing with something stronger, faster and more adaptable than anything we can imagine. What we've always suspected is true: the Melding Plague is of alien origin. And that's why it will always beat us. Provided, that is, we continue to wage war against it on our terms, rather than on its own.'

Now, Sylveste thought, this play had arrived at an unwritten epilogue all of its own.

'What kind of new paradigm do you have in mind?'

'The only logical answer,' Sajaki said, as if what he was about to reveal had always been blindingly obvious. 'The only effective medicine against an alien illness would be an alien medicine. And that's what we have to seek now, no matter how long it takes us, or how far.'

'Alien medicine,' Hegazi said, as if trying on the phrase for size. Perhaps he imagined that he would be hearing it rather frequently in the future. 'And just what kind of alien medicine did you have in mind?'

'We'll try the Pattern Jugglers first,' Sajaki said, absently, as if no one else were present, merely toying with the notion. 'And if they can't heal him, we'll look further.' Suddenly his attention snapped back onto Sylveste. 'We visited them once, you know, the Captain and I. You aren't the only one to have tasted the brine of their ocean.'

'Let's not spend a second longer in the company of this madman than absolutely necessary,' Calvin said, and Sylveste nodded silent assent.

Volyova checked her bracelet again, for the sixth or seventh time in the last hour, even though what it had to tell her had barely changed. What it told her – and what she already knew – was that the calamitous marriage of bridgehead and Cerberus was due to happen in just under half a day, and that no one looked likely to voice any objections, let alone make any attempt to avert the union.

'You looking at that thing every other second isn't going to change anything,' said Khouri, who, together with Volyova and Pascale, remained in the spider-room. For most of the last few hours they had been beyond the outer hull, venturing inside only to return Sylveste into the ship so that he could meet the other Triumvirs. Sajaki had not queried Volyova's absence: doubtless he assumed she was busy in her quarters, putting the finishing touches to her attack strategy. But in an hour or two she would need to show her face if she wished to avoid suspicion. Not long after that, she would need to begin the softening-up procedure, deploying elements of the cache against the point on Cerberus where the bridgehead was scheduled to arrive. As she glanced at the bracelet again – involuntarily, this time – Khouri said, 'What are you hoping for?'

'Something unexpected from the weapon – a fatal malfunction would do very nicely.'

'Then you really don't want this to succeed, do you?' Pascale said. 'A few days ago you were gloating over that thing like it was your finest hour. This is quite some turnaround.'

'That was before I knew who the Mademoiselle was. If I'd had any idea earlier . . .' Volyova found herself running out of anything to say. It was obvious now that using the weapon was an act of almost staggering recklessness – but would knowing that have altered a thing? Would she have felt compelled to make the weapon just because she could; just because it was elegant and she wanted her peers to see what fabulous creatures could spring forth from her mind; what Byzantine engines of war? The thought that she might have done so was sickening, but – in its own way – entirely plausible. She would have given birth to the bridgehead and hoped that she could prevent it completing its mission at some later point. She would, in short, have been in exactly the position in which she now found herself.

The bridgehead – the converted *Lorean* – was nearing Cerberus now, slowing as it did so. By the time it touched Cerberus it would be moving no faster than a bullet, but it would be a bullet massing millions of tonnes. If the bridgehead hit an ordinary planetary surface at that speed, its kinetic energy would be converted into heat rather efficiently: there would be a colossal explosion and her toy would be destroyed in a flash. But Cerberus was not a normal planet. Her assumption – backed up by endless simulations – was that the sheer grinding bulk of the weapon would be sufficient to push it through the thin layer of artificial crust overlaying the world's interior. Once it had thrust below that, once it had impaled the world, she had no real idea what it would encounter.

And now that scared her beyond words. Intellectual vanity had brought Sylveste to this point – and something else, perhaps – but she was not unguilty of obeying the same unquestioning drive. She wished she had taken the project less seriously; made the bridge-head less likely to succeed. It terrified her to think what would happen if her child did not disappoint her.

'Had I known . . .' she said, finally. 'I don't know. But I didn't, so what does it matter?'

'If you'd listened to me,' Khouri said, 'I told you we had to stop this madness. But my word wasn't good enough; you had to let it come to this.'

'I was hardly going to confront Sajaki on the basis of a vision you had in the gunnery. He'd have killed both of us, I'm sure of it.' Although now, she thought, they might have to move against Sajaki anyway – they could only do so much from the spider-room, and soon that might not be nearly enough.

'You could have decided to trust me,' Khouri said.

If circumstances had been any different, Volyova thought, she might have hit Khouri at the point. Instead, mildly, she answered, 'You can talk to me about trust when you haven't lied and cheated your way aboard my ship, but not before.'

'What did you expect me to do? The Mademoiselle had my husband.'

'Did she?' Volyova leant forward now. 'Do you know that for sure, Khouri? I mean, did you ever meet him, or was that another of the Mademoiselle's little deceptions? Memories can be implanted easily enough, can't they?'

Khouri's voice was soft now; as if there had never been an angry word between the two of them. 'What do you mean?'

'I mean maybe he never made it, Khouri. Did you ever consider that? Maybe he never left Yellowstone; the way you always believed it had happened.'

Pascale pushed her face between the two of them. 'Look, stop arguing, will you? If something awful is going to happen here, the last thing we need is division amongst ourselves. In case it has escaped your attention, I'm the only person on this ship who didn't ask or want to come aboard.'

'Yeah, well that's just tough luck,' Khouri said.

Pascale glared at her. 'Well maybe what I just said wasn't all true. I *am* after something. I've got a husband as well, and I don't want him to hurt himself – or anyone around him – just because of something he wants so bad. And that's why I need you now – both of you, because you seem to be the only two around here who feel the same way I do.'

'How do you feel?' Volyova asked.

'That none of this is right,' she said. 'Not from the moment you mentioned that name.'

Volyova didn't have to ask what name Pascale meant. 'You acted as if you recognised it.'

'We did – both of us. Sun Stealer's an Amarantin name; one of their gods, or mythic figures – maybe even a real historical individual. But Dan was too pigheaded – or perhaps too scared – to admit it.'

Volyova checked her bracelet again, but there was still no news. Then she waited while Pascale told her story. She told it well; there was no preamble, no scene-setting, and with the few carefully chosen facts which Pascale deployed, Volyova found herself visualising all that was necessary; events sketched with artful economy. She could see now why Pascale had helmed Sylveste's biography. What she had to say concerned the Amarantin, the extinct avian-descended creatures who had lived on Resurgam. By now the crew had absorbed enough knowledge from Sylveste to place this story in its proper context, but it was still disturbing to find a connection to the Amarantin. After all, Volyova had found it troubling enough to think that her problems were in some way associated with the Shrouders. At least there the causality was clear enough. But how did the Amarantin fit into everything? How could there be a link between two radically different alien species, both now long since vanished from galactic affairs? Even the timescales were in radical disagreement: according to what Lascaille had told Sylveste, the Shrouders had vanished – perhaps by retreating into their spheres of restructured spacetime – millions of years before the Amarantin had ever evolved, taking with them artefacts and techniques too hazardous to be left within the reach of less experienced species. That, after all, was what had driven Sylveste and Lefevre to the Shroud boundary: the lure of that stored knowledge. The Shrouders were as alien in form as anything in human experience – carapacial, multi-limbed things brewed from nightmares. The Amarantin, by contrast, with their avian ancestry and four-limbed, bipedal body-plan, were less shatteringly alien.

Yet Sun Stealer showed a link. The ship had never before visited

Resurgam; had never had aboard it anyone openly familiar with any aspect of the Amarantin – and yet Sun Stealer had been part of Volyova's life for subjective years, and several decades of planetary time. Sylveste was clearly the key – but any kind of logical connection steadfastly refused to reveal itself to Volyova.

Pascale continued, while an unsupervised part of Volyova's mind raced ahead and tried to fit things into some kind of order. Pascale was talking about the buried city; a vast Amarantin structure discovered during Sylveste's imprisonment. About how the city's central feature, a huge spire, had been surmounted by an entity which was not quite Amarantin, but looked like the Amarantin analog of an angel – except that this was an angel designed by someone with a scrupulous attention to the limits of anatomy. An angel that almost looked like it could fly.

'And that was Sun Stealer?' Khouri asked, awed.

'I don't know,' Pascale said. 'All we know is that the original Sun Stealer was just an ordinary Amarantin, but one who formed a renegade flock – a renegade social clade, if you like. We think they were experimentalists, studying the nature of the world; questioners of myth. Dan had this theory that Sun Stealer was interested in optics; that he made mirrors and lenses; literally, that he stole the sun. He may also have experimented with flight; simple machines and gliders. Whatever it was, it was heresy.'

'So what was the statue?'

Pascale told them the rest; how the renegade flock became known as the Banished Ones; how they effectively disappeared from Amarantin history for thousands of years.

'If I can interject a theory at this point,' Volyova said, 'is it possible that the Banished Ones went away to a quiet corner of the planet and invented technology?'

'Dan thought so. He thought they went the whole way – until they had the power to leave Resurgam entirely. And then one day – not long before the Event – they came back, but by then they were like gods compared to those who had stayed behind. And that was what the statue was – something raised in honour of the new gods.'

'Gods who became angels?' Khouri asked.

'Genetic engineering,' Pascale said, with conviction. 'They could never have flown, even with those wings they gave themselves, but then again, they'd already left gravity behind; become spacefaring.'

'What happened?'

'Much later – centuries afterwards, or even thousands of years – Sun Stealer's people returned to Resurgam. It was almost the end. We can't resolve the archaeological timescale, it's so short. But it's as if they brought it with them.'

'Brought what?' Khouri said.

'The Event. Whatever it was that ended life on Resurgam.'

As they trudged through the effluent which lay ankle-deep along the corridor floor, Khouri said, 'Is there a way to stop your weapon reaching Cerberus? I mean, you still have control of it, don't you?'

'Be quiet!' Volyova hissed. 'Anything we say down here . . .' She trailed off, pointing to the walls, presumably indicating all manner of concealed spy devices; part of the surveillance web she believed Sajaki controlled.

'Might get back to the rest of the Triumvirate. So what?' Khouri kept her voice low – no point in taking needless risks, but she spoke anyway. 'The way things are going, we're going to be openly resisting them before too long. My guess is Sajaki's listening network isn't as comprehensive as you think, anyway – that's what Sudjic said. Even if it is, he's likely to be preoccupied right now.'

'Dangerous, very dangerous.' But perhaps recognising the sense in what Khouri had said – that at some very imminent time subterfuge would have to become rebellion – she elevated the cuff of her jacket to reveal her bracelet, glowing with schematics and slowly updating numerics. 'I can control almost everything with this. But what good does it do me? Sajaki'll kill me if he thinks I'm trying to sabotage the operation – and he'll know the instant the weapon deviates from its intended course. And let's not forget that Sylveste is holding all of us to ransom – I don't know how *he*'d react.'

'Badly, I suspect – but that doesn't change anything.'

Now Pascale spoke. 'He won't do what he's been threatening. There's nothing in his eyes; he told me. But because Sajaki could never be sure – because it was possible – Dan said he was sure it would work.'

'And you're absolutely certain he wasn't lying to you?'

'What kind of a question is that?'

'A perfectly legitimate one, under the circumstances. I fear

Sajaki, but I can confront him with force if the need arises. But not your husband.'

'It never happened,' Pascale said. 'Trust me on that.'

'Like we've got a choice,' Khouri said. They had arrived at an elevator; the door opened and they had to step up to reach the elevator's floor. Khouri kicked the slime from her boots, hammered the wall and said, 'Ilia, you have to stop that thing. If it reaches Cerberus, we're all dead. That's what the Mademoiselle knew all along; that's why she wanted to kill Sylveste. Because she knew that, one way or another, he was going to try and get there. Now, I haven't got all of this straight in my head, but I do know one thing. The Mademoiselle knew it was going to be really bad news for all of us if he ever succeeded. And I mean *really* bad news.'

The elevator was rising now, but Volyova had not stated their destination.

'It's like Sun Stealer was pushing him on,' Pascale said. 'Putting ideas in his head, shaping his destiny.'

'Ideas?' Khouri asked.

'Like coming here in the first place – to this system.' Volyova was animated now. 'Khouri; don't you remember how we retrieved that recording of Sylveste from ship's memory, from when he was last aboard?' Khouri nodded; she remembered it well enough: how she had looked into the eyes of the recorded Sylveste and imagined killing the real man. 'And how he dropped hints that he was already thinking of the Resurgam expedition? And that bothered us because there was no logical way he could know about the Amarantin? Well, now it makes perfect sense. Pascale's right. It was Sun Stealer, already in his head, pushing him here. I don't think he even knew it was happening himself, but Sun Stealer was in control, all that time.'

Khouri said, 'It's like Sun Stealer and the Mademoiselle are fighting each other, but they need to use us to wage their war. Sun Stealer's some kind of software entity, and she's confined to Yellowstone, in her palanquin . . . so they've been pulling our strings, puppeting us against each other.'

'I think you're right,' Volyova said. 'Sun Stealer has me worried. Deeply worried. We haven't heard from him since the cache-weapon went up.'

Khouri said nothing. What she knew was that Sun Stealer had entered her head during her last session in the gunnery. Later, during her final visitation, the Mademoiselle had appeared to tell her that Sun Stealer was consuming her; that he would inevitably overwhelm her in hours or – at most – days. Yet that had been weeks earlier. According to her estimated rate of losses, the Mademoiselle should by now be dead, and Sun Stealer victorious. Yet nothing had changed. If anything, her head had been quieter than at any time since she had been revived around Yellowstone. No damn Shadowplay proximity implant; no damn midnight apparitions from the Mademoiselle. It was as if Sun Stealer had died just as he triumphed. Not that Khouri believed that, and his utter absence was all the more stressing; heightening the waiting until – as she was sure would happen – he appeared. And somehow she sensed he would be even less pleasant company than her previous lodger.

'Why should he show his face?' Pascale said. 'He's almost won, in any case.'

'Almost won,' Volyova agreed. 'But what we're about to do might make him intervene. I think we should be ready for that – you especially, Khouri. You know he found his way into Boris Nagorny, and you can take it from me, it wasn't nice knowing either of them.'

'Maybe you should lock me up now, before it's too late.' Khouri hadn't given the statement much thought, but she said it with deadly seriousness. 'I mean it, Ilia – I'd rather you did that than be forced into shooting me later.'

'I'd love to do that,' said her mentor. 'But it isn't as if we're already vastly outnumbering the others. At the moment it's the three of us against Sajaki and Hegazi – and God only knows whose side Sylveste will choose, if it comes to that.'

Pascale said nothing.

They reached the warchive, the destination Volyova had always had in mind, though she had said nothing until they arrived. Khouri had never been to this sector of the ship, but she did not need to have it identified to her. She had been in plenty of armouries before and there was a smell to them.

'This is some heavy shit we're getting ourselves into,' she said. 'Right?'

The vast oblong room constituted the display and dispensary section of the warchive, with somewhere in the region of a thousand weapons racked for immediate use. Tens of thousands more could be manufactured in short order, assembled according to blueprints distributed holographically through the mass of the ship.

'Yes,' Volyova said, with something worryingly close to relish. 'In which case we'd better have some obnoxiously effective firepower at our disposal. So, use your skill and discretion, Khouri, and kit us up. And be quick about it – we don't want Sajaki locking us out before we've got what we came for.'

'You're actually enjoying this, aren't you?'

'Yes. And you know why? Suicidal or not, we're finally doing something. It might get us killed – and it might not do any good – but at least we'll go out with a fight, if it comes to that.'

Khouri nodded slowly. Now that Volyova put it like that, she was right. It was a soldier's prerogative not to let events take their course without some kind of intervention, no matter how futile. Quickly Volyova showed her how to use the warchive's lower-level functions – luckily, it was almost intuitive – then took Pascale by the arm and turned to leave.

'Where are you going?'

'The bridge. Sajaki will want me there for the softening-up operation.'

TWENTY-SIX

Cerberus/Hades, Delta Pavonis Heliopause, 2566

Sylveste had not seen his wife for hours, and now it seemed as if she would not even be present for the culmination of all that he had striven for. Only ten hours remained until Volyova's weapon was due to impact Cerberus, and in less than an hour from now, the first wave of her softening-up assault was scheduled to commence. This in itself was momentous – yet it appeared that he would have to witness it without Pascale's company.

The ship's cameras had never lost sight of the weapon, and even now it hovered in the bridge's display, as if only a few kilometres away, rather than more than a million. They were seeing it side-on, since it had begun its approach from the Trojan point, whereas the ship remained in a holding pattern ninety degrees clockwise, along the line which threaded Hades and its furtive planetary companion. Neither machine was in a true orbit, but the weak gravitational field of Cerberus meant that these artificial trajectories could be maintained with minimal expenditure of correcting thrust.

Sajaki and Hegazi were with him, bathed in the reddish light which spilled from the display. Everything was red now; Hades close enough that it was a perceptible prick of scarlet, and Delta Pavonis – faint as it was – also casting ruddy light on all that orbited it. And because the display was the only source of light in the room, some of that redness leaked into the bridge.

'Where the hell is that *brezgatnik* cow Volyova?' Hegazi said. 'I thought she was meant to be showing us her chamber of horrors in action by now.'

Had the woman actually done the unspeakable, Sylveste thought? Had she actually decided to ruin the attack, even though she had masterminded the whole thing? If that was the case, he had misread her badly. She had inflicted her misgivings on him, fuelled by the delusions of the woman Khouri, but surely she hadn't taken any of that seriously? Surely she had been playing devil's advocate; testing the limits of his own confidence?

'You'd better hope that's the case, son,' Calvin said.

'You're reading my thoughts now?' Sylveste said, aloud, nothing to conceal from the partial Triumvirate convened around him. 'That's quite a trick, Calvin.'

'Call it a progressive adaptation to neural congruency,' the voice said. 'All the theories said that if you allowed me to stay in your head for long enough, something like this would occur. Really all that's happening is that I'm constructing a steadily more realistic model of your neural processes. To begin with I could only correlate what I read against your responses. But now I don't even have to wait for the responses to guess what they'll be.'

So read this, Sylveste thought. *Piss off.*

'If you want rid of me,' Calvin said, 'you could have done so hours ago. But I think you're beginning to rather like having me where I am.'

'For the time being,' Sylveste said. 'But don't get used to it, Calvin. Because I'm not planning on having you around on a permanent basis.'

'This wife of yours worries me.'

Sylveste looked at the Triumvirs. Suddenly he did not want his half of the conversation to be public knowledge, so he switched to mentalising what he would say.

'I worry about her too, but that doesn't happen to be any of your business.'

'I saw the way she responded when Volyova and Khouri tried to turn her.'

Yes, Sylveste thought – and who could honestly blame her? It had been hard enough for him when Volyova had dropped Sun Stealer's name into the conversation, like a depth charge. Of course, Volyova had not known how significant that name was – and for a moment Sylveste had hoped that his wife would not remember where she had heard it, or even that she had ever heard it before. But Pascale was too clever for that; it was half the reason he loved her. 'It doesn't mean they managed, Cal.'

'I'm glad you're so sure.'

'She wouldn't try and stop me.'

'That rather depends,' Calvin said. 'You see, if she imagines that you're putting yourself in harm's way – and if she loves you as much as I think she does – then stopping you is going to be something she does as much out of love as logic. Maybe more so. It doesn't mean she's suddenly decided to hate you, or that she even gets pleasure out of denying you this ambition. Quite the opposite, in fact. I rather imagine it's hurting her.'

Sylveste looked at the display again; at the conic, sculpted mass of Volyova's bridgehead.

'What I think,' Calvin said, eventually, 'is that there may be rather more to any of this than meets your eye. And that we should proceed with caution.'

'I'm hardly being incautious.'

'I know, and I sympathise. The mere fact that there could be danger in this is fascinating in itself; almost an incentive to push further. That's how you feel, isn't it? Every argument they could use against you would only strengthen your resolve. Because knowledge makes you hungry, and it's a hunger you can't resist, even if you know that what you're feasting on could kill you.'

'I couldn't have put it better myself,' Sylveste said, and wondered, but only for an instant. Then he turned to Sajaki and spoke aloud. 'Where the hell is that damned woman? Doesn't she realise we have work to do?'

'I'm here,' Volyova said, stepping into the bridge, followed by Pascale. Wordlessly, she summoned a pair of seats, and the two women rose into the central volume of the room, positioning themselves near the others, where the spectacle playing on the display could best be appreciated.

'Then let battle commence,' Sajaki said.

Volyova addressed the cache; the first time she had accessed any of these horrors since the incident with the rogue weapon.

In the back of her mind was the thought that at any time one of these weapons could act in the same way; violently ousting her from the control loop and taking charge of its own actions. She could not rule that out, but it was a risk she was prepared to take. And if what Khouri had said was true, then the Mademoiselle – who had been controlling the rogue cache-weapon – was now dead, ruthlessly absorbed by Sun Stealer, then at the very least it would not be she who tried to turn the weapons renegade.

Volyova selected a handful of cache-weapons, those at (she assumed and hoped) the lower end of the destructive scale available, where their destructive potential overlapped with the ship's native armaments. Six weapons came to life and communicated their readiness via her bracelet, morbid skull-icons pulsing. The devices moved via the network of tracks, slowly threading their way out of the cache chamber into the smaller transfer chamber, and then deploying themselves beyond the hull, becoming, in effect, hugely overcannoned robotic spacecraft. None of the six devices resembled any of the others, except in the underlying signature of common design which was shared by all the hell-class weapons. Two were relativistic projectile launchers, and so bore a certain similarity, but no more than as if they were competing prototypes constructed by different design teams to satisfy a general brief. They looked like ancient howitzers; all elongated barrel, festooned with tubular complications and cancerous ancillary systems. The other four weapons, in no particular order of pleasantness, consisted of a gamma-ray laser (bigger by an order of magnitude than the ship's own units), a supersymmetry beam, an ack-am projector and a quark deconfinement device. There was nothing to compare with the planet-demolishing capability of the rogue weapon, but then again, nothing which one would wish to have pointed at oneself – or indeed, the planet one happened to be standing on. And, Volyova reminded herself, the plan was not to inflict arbitrary damage on Cerberus; not to destroy it – but merely to crack it open, and for that a certain amount of finesse was in order.

Oh, yes . . . this was finesse.

'Now give me something a novice can use,' Khouri said, dithering in front of the warchive's dispensary. 'I'm not talking about a toy, though – it's got to have real stopping power.'

'Beam or projectile, madame?'

'Make it a low-yield beam. We don't want Pascale putting holes in the hull.'

'Oh, marvellous choice, madame. Would madame care to rest her feet while I search for something which matches madame's discerning requirements?'

'Madame will stand, if you don't mind.'

She was being served by the dispensary's gamma-level persona, which consisted of a rather glum and simpering holographic head projected at chest height above the slot-topped counter. At first she had restricted her choices to those arms which were arrayed along the walls, stowed behind glass with little illuminated plaques detailing their operation, era-of-origin and history of usage. That was fine, in principle, and she had soon selected lightweight weapons for herself and Volyova, choosing a pair of electromagnetic needle-guns which were similar in design to Shadowplay equipment.

Volyova had, rather ominously, mentioned heavier ordnance, and Khouri had taken care of that as well, but only partially from the displayed wares. There had been a nice rapid-cycle plasma rifle, manufactured three centuries ago, but by no means outdated, and its neural-feed aiming system would make it very useful in close combat. It was light, as well, and when she hefted it, she felt that she knew the weapon immediately. There was also something obscenely alluring about the weapon's protective jacket of black leather: mottled and oiled to a high sheen, with patches cut away to expose controls, readouts and attachment points. It would suit her, but what could she bring back for Volyova? She perused the shelves for as long as she dared (which could not have been more than five minutes), and while there was no shortage of intriguing and even bewildering hardware, there was nothing which exactly matched what she had in mind.

Instead, she had turned to the warchive's memory. There were, Khouri was reliably informed, exemplars of in excess of four million hand weapons, spanning twelve centuries of gunsmithery, from the simplest spark-ignited projectile blunderbusses to the most gruesomely compact concentrations of death-directed technology imaginable.

But even that vast assortment was small compared to the warchive's total potential, because the warchive could also be creative. Given specifications, the warchive could sift its blueprints and merge the optimum characteristics of pre-existing weapons until it had forged something new and highly customised. Which, in minutes, it could synthesise.

When it was done – as it was with the little pistol Khouri had imagined for Pascale – the slot in the tabletop would whir open and the finished weapon would rise on a little felt-topped platter, gleaming with ultrasterility, still warm with the residual heat of its manufacture.

She lifted Pascale's pistol, sighting along the barrel, feeling the balance, running through the beam-yield settings, accessed by a stud recessed into the grip.

'Suits you, madame,' said the dispensary.

'It isn't for me,' Khouri said, hiding the gun in a pocket.

Volyova's six cache-weapons powered up their thrusters and vectored rapidly away from the ship, following a complex course which would position them to strike against the impact point, albeit obliquely. And the bridgehead, meanwhile, continued to reduce the distance between itself and the surface, always slowing. She was certain that the world had already decided that it was being approached by an artificial object, and a big one at that. The world might even recognise that the thing approaching it had once been the *Lorean*. Doubtless, somewhere down in that machine-permeated crust, a kind of debate was going on. Some components would be arguing that it was best to attack now; best to strike against the nearing thing before it became a real problem. Other components would be urging caution, pointing out that the object was still a long way from Cerberus, and that any attack against it now would have to be very large to ensure the object was annihilated before it could retaliate, and that such an open display of strength might attract more attention from elsewhere. And furthermore, the pacifist systems might say, so far this object had done nothing unambiguously hostile. It might not even suspect the artificiality of Cerberus. It might only want to sniff the world and leave it alone.

Volyova did not want the pacifists to win. She wanted the advocates of a massive pre-emptive strike to win, and she wanted it to happen now, before another minute passed. She wanted to observe Cerberus lash out and remove the bridgehead from existence. That would end their problems, and – because something similar had already happened to Sylveste's probes – they would not be any worse off than they were now. Perhaps the mere incitement of a counterstrike from Cerberus would not constitute the interference which the Mademoiselle had sought to prevent. After all, no one would have entered the place. And then they could admit defeat and go home.

Except none of that was going to happen.

'These cache-weapons,' Sajaki said, nodding at the display. 'Are you planning to arm and fire them from here, Ilia?'

'There's no reason not to.'

'I would have expected Khouri to direct them from the gunnery. After all, that's her role.' He turned to Hegazi and whispered, loud enough for everyone to hear, 'I'm beginning to wonder why we recruited that one – or why I allowed Volyova to stop the trawling.'

'I presume she has her uses,' said the chimeric.

'Khouri is in the gunnery,' Volyova lied. 'As a precaution, of course. But I won't call on her unless absolutely necessary. That's fair, isn't it? These are my weapons as well – you can't begrudge me the use of them when the situation is so controlled.'

The readouts on her bracelet – partially echoed on the display sphere in the middle of the bridge – informed her that in thirty minutes the cache-weapons would arrive at their designated firing positions nearly a quarter of a million kilometres away from the ship. At that point there would be no plausible reason not to fire them.

'Good,' Sajaki said. 'For a moment I worried that we didn't have your complete commitment to the cause. But that sounds suspiciously like a flash of the old Volyova.'

'How very gratifying,' Sylveste said.

TWENTY-SEVEN

Cerberus/Hades, Delta Pavonis Heliopause, 2566

The black icons of the cache-weapons swarmed towards their firing points, their terrible potency waiting to be unleashed against Cerberus. In all that time there had been no response from the world; no hint that it was anything other than what it appeared to be. It just hung there, grey and sutured, like the cranium of a skull tipped in prayer.

When, finally, the moment came, there was only a soft chime from the projection sphere, and the numerals briefly cycled through zero, before commencing the long count upwards.

Sylveste was the first to speak. He turned to Volyova, who had made no visible movement in minutes. 'Isn't something supposed to have happened? Aren't your damned weapons supposed to have gone off?'

Volyova looked up from the bracelet readout which was consuming her attention like someone snapping out of a trance.

'I never gave the order,' she said, so softly that it took conscious effort to hear her words. 'I never told the weapons to fire.'

'Pardon?' Sajaki said.

'You heard what I said,' she answered, with mounting volume. 'I didn't do it.'

Once again Sajaki's resolute calm managed to seem more threatening than any histrionics. 'There are a number of minutes remaining in which the attack may yet be made,' he said. 'Perhaps you had best consider utilising them, before the situation becomes irretrievable.'

'I think,' Sylveste said, 'that the situation did so some time ago.'

'That's a matter for the Triumvirate,' Hegazi said, his steel-clad knuckles glinting on the edge of his seat rests. 'Ilia, if you give the order now, maybe we can—'

'I'm not about to,' she said. 'Call it mutiny if you wish, or treason; I don't care. But my involvement in this madness ends here.' She looked at Sylveste with unexpected bile. 'You know my reasons, so don't pretend otherwise.'

'She's right, Dan.'

Now it was Pascale who had joined the conversation, and for a moment she had all their attention.

'You know what she's been saying is true; how we just can't take this risk, no matter how much you want it.'

'You've been listening to Khouri as well,' Sylveste said, although the news that his wife had gone over to Volyova's side was hardly surprising, drawing less bitterness than he might have expected. Aware of the perversity of his feelings, he nonetheless rather admired her for doing it.

'She knows things that we don't,' Pascale said.

'What the hell does Khouri have to do with any of this?' Hegazi asked, glancing peevishly towards Sajaki. 'She's just a grunt. Can we omit her from the discussion?'

'Unfortunately not,' Volyova said. 'Everything that you've heard is true. And carrying on with this really would be the worst mistake any of us have ever made.'

Sajaki veered his seat away from Hegazi, approaching Volyova.

'If you aren't going to give the attack order, at least surrender control of the cache to me.' And he reached out his hand, beckoning her to unclasp the bracelet and pass it to him.

'I think you should do what he says,' Hegazi said. 'It could be very unpleasant for you otherwise.'

'I don't doubt that for a moment,' Volyova said, and with one deft motion she snapped the bracelet from her hand. 'It's completely useless to you, Sajaki. The cache will only listen to me or Khouri.'

'Give me the bracelet.'

'You'll regret it, I'm warning you.'

She passed it to him all the same. Sajaki grasped it as if it were a valuable gold amulet, toying with it briefly before locking it around his wrist. He watched as the little display reignited, filling with the same schematic data which had flashed from Volyova's wrist a moment earlier.

'This is Triumvir Sajaki,' he said, licking his lips between each word, savouring the power. 'I'm not sure of the precise protocol required at this point, so I ask for your co-operation. But I want the six deployed cache-weapons to commence—'

Sajaki stopped mid-sentence. He looked down at his wrist, at first in puzzlement, and then, moments later, in something much closer to fear.

'You sly old dog,' Hegazi said, wonderingly. 'I imagined you might have a trick up your sleeve, but I never thought you'd have one literally.'

'I'm a very literal-minded person,' Volyova said.

Sajaki's face was a rigid mask of pain now, and the constricting bracelet had visibly cut into his wrist. His hand was locked open, now as white and bloodless as wax. With his free hand he was making a valiant effort to claw the bracelet free, but it was futile; she had seen to that. The clasp would have sealed shut now, and what remained was only a painful and slow process of constrictive amputation, as the memory-plastic polymer chains in the bracelet slithered ever tighter. The bracelet had known from the instant he placed it around his wrist that his DNA was not correct; that it failed to match her own. But it had not begun to constrict until he had tried to issue an order, which, she supposed, was a kind of leniency on her behalf.

'Make it stop,' he managed to say. 'Make it stop . . . you fucking bitch . . . please . . .'

Volyova estimated he had one to two minutes before the bracelet had his hand off; one to two minutes before the main sound in the room would be the cracking of bone, assuming it was audible above Sajaki's whimpers.

'Your manners let you down,' she said. 'What kind of a way to ask is that? You'd think now would be the one time when you had some courtesy to spare.'

'Stop it,' Pascale said. 'I'm begging you, please – whatever's happened, it isn't worth this . . .'

Volyova shrugged, and addressed herself to Hegazi. 'You may as well remove it, Triumvir, before it gets too messy. I'm sure you have the means.'

Hegazi held one of his own steel hands up for inspection, as if having to reassure himself that they were no longer flesh.

'Now!' Sajaki shrieked. 'Get it off me!'

Hegazi positioned his seat next to the other Triumvir and set to work. It was a process which seemed to cause Sajaki fractionally more pain than the constriction itself.

Sylveste said nothing.

Hegazi worked the bracelet free; his metal hands were lathered with human blood by the time he was done. What remained of the bracelet fell from his fingers, dropping to the floor twenty metres below.

Sajaki, who had not stopped moaning, looked with revulsion at the damage that had been wrought to his wrist. His hand was still attached, but the bones and tendons were hideously exposed, blood pulsing out in red gouts, cascading in a thin scarlet rope to the distant floor. Trying to stifle the loss, he pressed the agonised limb against his belly. Finally he ceased to make any sound, and after long moments, his blanched face turned to Volyova and spoke.

'You'll pay for this,' he said. 'I swear it.'

Which was when Khouri entered the bridge and began shooting.

Of course, she had always had a plan in mind, even if it was not a very detailed one. And when Khouri had taken her first step into the chamber, and seen the cataract of what was obviously blood, she had not taken the time to run her plan through a set of elaborate last-minute revisions. Instead, she had decided to start shooting the ceiling, until she had everyone's attention.

It had not taken very long.

Her weapon of choice was the plasma rifle, set to its lowest possible yield, with the rapid-fire mode disengaged so that she had to squeeze the trigger for each pulse. The first one bit a metre-wide crater into the ceiling, causing the cladding to rain down in jagged, heat-scorched shards. Wary of blasting right through, she directed her next pulse a little to the left, and then a little to the right. One of the shards crashed onto the glowing sphere of the holo-display, and for an eyeblink the sphere flickered and warped, before resuming stability. Then – because she had rather comprehensively announced her presence – she powered down the gun and slung it back over her shoulder. Volyova, who had obviously anticipated her next move, jetted her seat down towards Khouri, and when they were barely five metres apart, Khouri threw her one of the light-weight guns; the needle-projectors she had found on the warchive's wall. 'Take this for Pascale,' she said, throwing the low-yield beamer after it. Volyova caught both weapons expertly and quickly passed Pascale her own.

Khouri, who had by now assimilated the situation, observed that the rain of blood – which had now ceased – had originated from Sajaki. He looked in a bad way, cradling one arm as if it was broken or as if he had taken a hit.

'Ilia,' Khouri said, 'you started all the fun without me. I'm disappointed.'

'Events rather demanded it,' Volyova said.

Khouri looked at the display, trying to figure out what had happened beyond the ship. 'Did the weps fire?'

'No; I never gave the order.'

'And now she she can't,' Sylveste said. 'Because Hegazi just destroyed her bracelet.'

'Does that mean he's on our side?'

'No,' Volyova said. 'It just means he can't stand the sight of blood. Especially when it's Sajaki's.'

'He needs help,' Pascale said. 'For God's sake, you can't just let him bleed to death.'

'He won't,' Volyova said. 'He's chimeric, like Hegazi – just not so obviously. Already the medichines in his blood will be initiating cellular repair at a vastly accelerated rate. Even if the bracelet had taken his hand off, he'd have grown another one. Isn't that right, Sajaki?'

He looked at her with a face so drained of strength that it looked as if he'd have trouble growing a new fingernail, let alone a new hand. But eventually he nodded.

'Someone should still help me to the infirmary – there's nothing magical about my medichines; they have their limitations. And my pain receptors are alive and well, trust me.'

'He's right,' Hegazi said. 'You shouldn't overestimate the capabilities of his 'chines. Do you want him dead or not? You'd better decide now. I can help him to the infirmary.'

'And stop off for a browse at the warchive on the way?' Volyova shook her head. 'Thanks, but no thanks.'

'Then me,' Sylveste said. 'I'll take him. You trust me that far, don't you?'

'I trust you about as far as I could piss you, *svinoi*,' Volyova said. 'But on the other hand, you wouldn't know what to do at the warchive even if you got there. And Sajaki isn't in a fit state to give you any particularly cogent suggestions.'

'Is that a yes?'

'Be quick about it, Dan.' Volyova emphasised the point with a stab of the needler, her finger tense on the trigger. 'If you aren't back here in ten minutes I'm sending Khouri after you.'

In a minute the two men had left, Sajaki slumped on Sylveste, barely capable of walking without support from the other man. Khouri wondered if Sajaki would still be conscious by the time he was brought to the infirmary, and found that she did not particularly care.

'About the warchive,' she said. 'I don't think you have to worry too much about anyone else using it. I shot the fucking place to bits as soon as I had what I wanted.'

Volyova mulled on that and then nodded appreciatively.

'That was sound tactical thinking, Khouri.'

'Tactics didn't come into it. It was that persona running the place. I just decided to open up and torch the bastard.'

Pascale said, 'Does this mean we've won? I mean, have we actually achieved what we set out to do?'

'Guess so,' Khouri said. 'Sajaki's out of the picture, and I don't think our friend Hegazi is going to make too much trouble for himself. And it doesn't look like your husband is going to keep his word about killing us all if he doesn't get what he wants.'

'How very disappointing,' Hegazi said.

'I told you,' Pascale said. 'He was always bluffing. That's it, then? We can still call off those weapons, can't we?' She was looking at Volyova, who nodded instantly.

'Of course.' And then she reached in her jacket and snapped a new bracelet around her wrist, as if it were the most natural thing in the world. 'You think I'd be so foolish as not to carry a spare with me?'

'Not you, Ilia,' Khouri said.

She raised the bracelet to her mouth and spoke into it; a mantralike sequence of commands designed to bypass various levels of security. Finally, when everyone's attention was on the armillary, she said, 'All cache-weapons return to ship; repeat, all cache-weapons return to ship.'

But nothing happened; not even when enough seconds had elapsed for the expected light-travel timelag. Nothing, that is, except that the icons representing the cache-weapons changed from black to red, and began to flash with evil regularity.

'Ilia,' Khouri said. 'What does that actually mean?'

'It means they're arming up and preparing to fire,' she said, very evenly, as if barely surprised. 'It means that something very bad is about to happen.'

TWENTY-EIGHT

Cerberus/Hades, Delta Pavonis Heliopause, 2566

She had lost control again.

Volyova watched helplessly as the cache-weapons opened fire on Cerberus. The beam weapons found their mark first, of course, and the first indication that returned was a spark of blue-white light, winking open against the arid grey backdrop of the world, in the precise spot where, shortly, the bridgehead would reach the surface. The relativistic projectile weapons were only slightly tardier, and reports of their success followed a few seconds later; spectacular stuttering pulses as the projectiles rained home, slugs of neutronium and antimatter slamming into the world. All the while, she kept barking the disarming commands into the bracelet, but with steadily draining hope that she could have any influence over the weapons. For one foolish instant she had assumed that the replacement bracelet was faulty, but of course that could not be why the weapons were now behaving autonomously. They had fired for a purpose; just as they had disregarded her order to return to the bowels of the ship.

Because someone – or some*thing* – now had control.

'What's happening?' Pascale asked, in the tones of someone who did not honestly expect a comprehensible answer.

'It must be Sun Stealer,' Volyova said, finally giving up on the bracelet, relinquishing all hope of the weapons returning to her steerage. 'Because it can't possibly be Khouri's Mademoiselle. Even if she were still capable of influencing the cache, she'd be doing everything in her power to prevent this.'

'Part of him must have stayed behind in the gunnery,' Khouri said. She seemed to regret that, because she went quiet very abruptly, before adding, 'I mean, we always knew he could control the gunnery – that was why he resisted the Mademoiselle when she wanted to kill Sylveste with the other weapon.'

'But with this precision?' Volyova shook her head. 'Not all my commands to the cache-weapons are routed through the gunnery; I knew that was too big a risk to take.'

'And you're saying even those aren't working?'

'So it would appear.'

The display now showed that the weapons had ceased their attack, depleted of energy and munitions, drifting into useless orbits around Hades, where they would remain for millions of years, until swept by random gravitational perturbations into trajectories which would smash them into Cerberus or fling them out towards the Trojan points, where they would endure even the red-giant death of Delta Pavonis. Volyova extracted a residual grain of comfort in knowing that the weapons could not be used again; could not be turned against her. But it was far too late for such succour. The damage against Cerberus had already been done, and there would now be very little to hinder the bridgehead when it arrived. She could already see the evidence of their attack on the display, plumes of pulverised regolith fanning into space around the impact point.

Sylveste arrived at the ship's medical centre, Sajaki increasingly heavy against his shoulders. The man seemed to weigh far too much for his lean frame. Sylveste wondered if it was because of the sheer mass of machines streaming through his blood; waiting dormant in every cell, biding their time until a crisis such as this stirred them to life. Sajaki was hot too; feverishly so – perhaps evidence that the medichines had gone into an emergency breeding frenzy, building up their forces to deal with the situation, conscripting molecules from the man's 'normal' tissue until the hazard was averted. When Sylveste glanced reluctantly at the Triumvir's ruined wrist, he saw that the blood had stopped flowing, and the dreadful circumferential wound was now enveloped in a membranous caul. A faint amber luminosity shone through the tissue.

Servitors emerged from the centre as he approached, taking the burden from him, lifting Sajaki to a couch. The machines fussed over him for a few minutes, swanlike monitors angling over the bed; various neural monitors settled gently over his scalp. They did not seem overly concerned by the wound. Perhaps the medical systems were already communicating with his medichines, and there was no need for further intervention at this stage. He was still conscious, Sylveste observed, despite his weakness.

'You should never have trusted Volyova,' he said angrily. 'Now everything's ruined because she had too much power. That was a fatal mistake, Sajaki.'

His voice was barely there. 'Of course we trusted her. She was one of us, you fool! Part of the Triumvirate!' Then he added, in a croak, 'What is it you know about Khouri?'

'She was an infiltrator,' Sylveste said. 'Put aboard this ship to find me and kill me.'

Sajaki reacted to this as if it were only mildly diverting. 'That's all?'

'That's all I believed. I don't know who sent her, or why – but she had some absurd justification, which Volyova and my wife seem to have taken as the literal truth.'

'It isn't over yet,' Sajaki said, his eyes wide, rimmed in yellow.

'What do you mean, it isn't over?'

'I just know,' Sajaki said, and then closed his eyes, relaxing back into the couch. 'Nothing is finished.'

'He's going to survive,' Sylveste said, entering the bridge, obviously unaware of what had just taken place.

He looked around him, and Volyova could imagine his confusion. Superficially, nothing had changed in the time it had taken him to escort Sajaki to the infirmary – the same people holding the same guns, but the mood had undergone a dire transition. Hegazi, for instance, despite being on the wrong end of Khouri's needler, did not wear the expression of a man on the defeated side. Neither, however, did he look particularly jubilant.

It's out of all our hands now, Volyova thought, and Hegazi knows it.

'Something went wrong, didn't it?' Sylveste said, who had by then taken in the view of Cerberus on the display, with its ruptured crust bleeding into space. 'Your weapons actually opened fire, just as we wanted.'

'Sorry,' Volyova said, shaking her head. 'It was none of my doing.'

'You'd better listen to her,' Pascale said. 'Whatever's going on here, we don't want any part of it. It's bigger than us, Dan. Bigger than you, anyway – hard as that may be to believe.'

He looked scornful. 'Haven't you realised yet? This is exactly how Volyova wanted it to happen.'

'You're mad,' Volyova said.

'Now you get your chance,' Sylveste said. 'You get to see your planet-penetrator in action, while at the same time salving your conscience with this conveniently unsuccessful display of eleventh-hour caution.' He clapped his hands twice. 'No; honestly – I'm genuinely impressed.'

'You'll be genuinely dead,' Volyova said.

But while she hated him for saying what he had said, there was part of her which refused easy denial. She would have done anything in her power to stop the weapons from completing their mission – hell; she *had* done everything in her power, and none of it had worked. Even if she had not given the order to release them from the ship, Sun Stealer would surely have found a way; she was sure of that. But now that the attack had taken place, a kind of fatalistic curiosity had settled over her. The bridgehead's arrival would proceed as planned, unless she could find a way of stopping it, and thus far she had tried everything she knew. And therefore, because there was no way of preventing it from happening, a detached part of her was beginning to look forward to the event, tantalised not just by what would be learnt, but how well her child would endure its trials. Whatever happened, she knew – no matter how fearful the consequences might be – it could not help but be the most fascinating thing she had ever witnessed. And perhaps the most terrible.

There was nothing to do now except wait.

The hours passed neither swiftly nor slowly, because this was an event she was dreading as much as longing for. One thousand kilometres above Cerberus, the bridgehead commenced its final braking phase. The brilliance of the two Conjoiner drives was like a pair of miniature suns flaring into ignition above Cerberus, shocking the landscape into stark clarity, craters and ravines assuming enormously exaggerated prominence. For a moment, under that merciless glare, the world really did look artefactual; as if its makers had striven too hard to make Cerberus look weathered by aeons of bombardment.

On her bracelet now she was seeing images recorded from the downlooking cameras studded around the bridgehead's flanks. There were rings of cameras every hundred metres along the length of the four-kilometre cone, so that, no matter how deeply it penetrated, some cameras would always be above and below the crustal layer. She was looking through that crust now; through the still unhealed wound which had been opened by the cache.

Sylveste had not been lying.

There were things down there. Huge and organic and tubular, like a nest of snakes. The heat of the cache attack had dissipated now, and although greyish clouds were still smoking from the hole, Volyova suspected they were more to do with incinerated machinery than boiled crustal matter. None of the snakelike tubes were moving, and their segmented silvery sides were marred by black smears and hundred-metre-wide gashes, through which a whole intestinal mass of smaller snakes had exploded.

Volyova had hurt Cerberus.

She did not know if it was a mortal wound, or just a graze which would heal in days, but she had hurt it, and the realisation of that made her shiver. She had hurt something alien.

Soon, however, the alien thing retaliated.

She jumped when it happened, even though – intellectually, if not emotionally – she had been expecting it. It happened when the bridgehead was two kilometres from the surface – half its own length away.

The event itself was almost too swift to absorb. Between one moment and the next the crust changed with startling swiftness. A series of grey dimples had formed, ringed concentrically around the kilometre-wide wound, blistering like stone pustules. Almost as soon as Volyova noticed their existence, they ruptured, unleashing twinkling spore, silver glints which swarmed towards the bridgehead like fireflies. She had no idea what they were, whether they were chips of naked antimatter, tiny warheads, viral capsules or miniature gun batteries, except that they intended harm to her creation.

'Now,' she whispered. 'Now . . .'

She was not disappointed. Perhaps, on some level, it would have been better if her weapon had been destroyed in that moment – but then she would have been denied the thrill of seeing it react, and react with all the efficacy she had intended. The armaments in the bridgehead's circular rim erupted into life, tracking, lasering and bosering each of the glints before many of them had touched the conic weapon's hyperdiamond carapace.

The bridgehead accelerated now, covering the final two kilometres in a third of a minute, the crust around the wound constantly blistering and releasing glitter, the bridgehead parrying the strikes. There were craters in the weapon's hull now, where a few of the glitter-spore had impacted with brief pink radiance, but the bridgehead's operational integrity remained uncompromised. The needle-sharp tip pushed below the level of the crust, accurately positioned in the middle of the wound.

Seconds passed, and then the widening haft of the weapon began to brush against its ragged periphery. The ground began to rupture, fracture lines racing away. The blisters were still sprouting, but now at a greater radial distance from the wound, as if the underlying mechanisms were damaged or depleted within that circumference. The bridgehead was now hundreds of metres into Cerberus, shockwaves radiating out from the entry point and haring up the weapon's length. The piezoelectric crystal buffers which Volyova had integrated into the hyperdiamond would damp those shocks, converting their energy into heat which would then be channelled into the defensive armaments.

'Tell me we're winning,' Sylveste said. 'For God's sake, tell me we're winning!'

She speed-read the detailed status summaries spilling onto her bracelet. For a moment there was no antagonism between them; only a shared curiosity. 'We're coping,' she said. '. . . Weapon is now one kilometre in; maintaining steady descent rate at one kilometre every ninety seconds. Thrust level increasing to maximum; that must mean it's encountering mechanical resistance . . .'

'What is it passing through?'

'Can't tell,' she said. 'Alicia's data said the fake crust was no more than half a kilometre deep, but there are few sensors in the weapon's skin – they would have increased its vulnerability to cybernetic attack modes.'

What showed on the armillary, relayed from the ship's cameras, was a piece of abstract sculpture: a cone sliced off midway and positioned with its narrowest end resting on a scabrous grey surface. Anguished patterns were playing over the surrounding terrain, blisters spewing spore in random directions, as if their underlying targeting had gone awry. The weapon was slowing now, and though the scene was playing in absolute silence, Volyova could imagine the awful grinding friction; what it would have sounded like, had there been air to carry the sound and ears to be deafened by that titanic scraping roar. Now, her bracelet told her, the pressure on the tip had fallen drastically, as if the weapon had finally punctured all the way through the crust, and was now probing into the relative hollowness beneath: the domain of the snakes.

Slowing.

Skull-and-crossbones symbols danced on her bracelet, signifying the commencement of molecular weapon attack against the bridgehead. Volyova had expected as much. Already, antibodies would be oozing through the carapace, meeting and matching the alien attackers.

Slowing . . . and now stopping.

This was as deep as they were going to get. One and one-third of a kilometre of the cone still projected above the cracked surface of Cerberus; what it looked like was some kind of top-heavy cylindrical fortification. The rim armaments were still lancing away at the crustal countermeasures, but now the spore discharges were coming from tens of kilometres away, and it was clear that no immediate threat was posed, unless the crust was capable of improbably rapid regeneration.

The bridgehead would now commence anchoring itself, consolidating its gains, analysing the forms of the molecular weapons being used against it, devising subtly matched reverse strategies.

It had not let Volyova down.

She pivoted her couch round to face the others, noticing – for the first time in ages – that her fist was still locked around a needle-gun.

'We're in,' she said.

It looked like a biology lesson for gods, or a snapshot of the kind of pornography which might be enjoyed by sentient planets.

In the hours immediately after the weapon's anchoring, Khouri stayed in close consultation with Volyova, reviewing the constantly changing status of the sluggishly fought battle. The geometric forms of the two protagonists reminded her of a conic virus dwarfed by the much larger spherical cell which it was in the business of corrupting. Yet she had to keep reminding herself that even that insignificant cone was the size of a mountain; that the cell was a world.

Nothing very much seemed to be happening now, but that was only because the conflict was being waged primarily on the molecular level, across an invisible, near-fractal front which extended for tens of square kilometres. At first, and without success, Cerberus had tried to repel the invader with highly entropic weapons; trying to degrade the enemy into megatonnes of atomic ash. Now its strategy had evolved towards one of digestion. It was still trying to dismantle the enemy atom by atom, but systematically, like a child deconstructing a complex toy rather than smashing it to pieces, diligently placing each component into its assigned compartment so that it could be used again in the future, in some as yet undreamt-of project. There was logic to this, after all; a few cubic kilometres of the world had been annihilated by the cache-weapons, and Volyova's device presumably consisted of matter in much the same elemental and isotopic ratios as that which had been destroyed. The enemy was a huge potential reservoir of repair material, obviating the need for Cerberus to consume its own finite resources in the process. And perhaps it always sought motherlodes like this, to repair the inevitable damage wrought by millennia of meteorite strikes and the constant ablative toll of cosmic ray bombardment. Perhaps it had seized Sylveste's first probe more because it was hungry than out of a misguided sense that it was preserving its own secrecy; as much acting out of blind stimulus as a Venus flytrap, with no thought for the future.

But Volyova's weapon was not designed to be digested without putting up a struggle.

'See, Cerberus is learning from us,' she said from her bridge seat, graphing up schematics of the several dozen different components in the molecular arsenal which the world was now deploying against her weapon. What she was showing looked like a page from an entomology textbook: an array of metallic, differently specialised bugs. Some of them were disassemblers: the front line of the Amarantin defence system. These would physically attack the surface of the bridgehead, dislodging atoms and molecules with their manipulators, tugging apart chemical bonds. They would also engage in hand-to-hand combat with Volyova's own front-line forces. What matter they succeeded in wresting free they passed back to fatter bugs, behind the immediate battle-front. Like tireless clerks, these units endlessly categorised and sorted the chunks of matter they received. If it was structurally simple, like a single undifferentiated chunk of iron or carbon, they tagged it for recycling and passed it to other even fatter factory bugs which were manufacturing more bugs according to their internal templates. And if the chunks of matter had been organised so that within them was true structure, they were not passed for immediate recycling, but were instead passed to other bugs which dismantled the chunks and tried to figure out if they embodied any useful principles. If so, the principles would be learnt, tailored and passed to the factory bugs. That way, the next generation of bugs would be fractionally more advanced than the last. 'Learning from us,' Volyova said again, as if she found the prospect as glorious as it was disturbing. 'Unpicking our countermeasures and incorporating their design philosophies into its own forces.'

'You don't have to sound so cheerful about it.' Khouri was eating a ship-grown apple.

'But why not? It's an elegant system. I can learn from it, of course, but it isn't the same thing. What's happening down there is methodical, endless – and there isn't the tiniest grain of sentience behind any of it.'

She said it with genuine awe.

'Yes, very impressive,' Khouri said. 'Blind replication – nothing smart about it, but because it's happening simultaneously in a billion-odd places, they win over us by sheer weight of numbers. Isn't that what's going to happen? You're going to sit here and think like hell, and it won't make a bit of difference to the outcome. Sooner or later they'll learn every trick you have.'

'But not just yet.' Volyova cocked her head towards the schematic. 'You think I'd have been stupid enough to hit them with the most advanced countermeasures we have? You never do that in war, Khouri. You never expend any more energy – or intelligence – against an enemy than is absolutely appropriate to the situation at hand, just as you never play your best card first in a poker game. You wait, until the stakes justify it.' And then she explained how the current countermeasures being deployed by her weapon were really very old, and not especially sophisticated. She had adapted them from ancient entries in the holographically distributed database of the warchive. 'About three hundred years behind the current day,' she said.

'But Cerberus is catching up.'

'Correct, but that rate of technical gain is actually rather stable – probably because of the thoughtless way in which our secrets are being used. There are no intuitive jumps possible, so the Amarantin systems evolve linearly. It's like someone trying to crack a code by sheer brute-force computation. And because of that, I know rather precisely how long it will take for them to overtake our current level. At the moment they're catching up by about a decade for every three or four hours of shiptime. Which gives us slightly less than a week before things get interesting.'

'And this isn't?' Khouri shook her head, feeling – not for the first time – that there were many things she did not understand about Volyova. 'Just how do these escalations take place? Does your weapon carry a copy of the warchive?'

'No; too dangerous.'

'Right; it'd be like sending a soldier behind enemy lines with every secret you've got. How do you do it? Transmit the secrets down to the weapon only when they're needed? Isn't that just as risky?'

'That's how it happens, but it's much safer than you think. The transmissions are encrypted using a one-time pad; a randomly generated string of digits which specifies the change to be made to each bit in the raw signal; whether you add a zero or a one to it. After you've encrypted the signal with the pad, there's no way the enemy can recover the meaning without their own copy of the pad. The weapon needs one, of course – but the copy it carries is stored deep inside, beyond tens of metres of solid diamond, with hyper-secure optical links to the assembler control systems. Only if the weapon were under major attack would there be any risk of the pad being captured – and in that case, I'd simply refrain from transmitting anything.'

Khouri finished the apple down to the seedless core. 'So there is a way,' she said, after thinking for a moment.

'A way to what?'

'To end all this. We want to do that, don't we?'

'You don't think the damage has already been done?'

'We can't know for sure, but supposing it hasn't? After all, what we've seen so far is just a layer of camouflage, and below that a layer of defences designed to protect the camouflage. It's amazing, yes – and the mere fact that it's an alien technology means we could probably learn from it – but we still don't know what it's hiding.' She thumped her chair in emphasis, gratified to see Volyova react with a small shiver. 'It's something we haven't reached yet; haven't even glimpsed – and we won't, until Sylveste actually goes down there.'

'We'll stop him from leaving.' Volyova patted the needler which was tucked into her belt. 'We control things now.'

'And take the risk that he'll kill us all by triggering the thing in his eyes?'

'Pascale said it was a bluff.'

'Yeah, and I'm sure she believes it.' Khouri didn't need to say any more; it was obvious from the slow way she nodded that Volyova understood. 'There's a better way,' she continued. 'Let Sylveste leave if he wants, but we'll make damn sure he doesn't have an easy time getting inside.'

'By which you mean . . .'

'I'll say it, even if you won't. We have to let it die, Volyova. We have to let Cerberus win.'

TWENTY-NINE

Cerberus/Hades, Delta Pavonis Heliopause, 2566

'All we know,' Sylveste said, 'is that Volyova's weapon has reached below the outer skin of the planet; perhaps into the level occupied by the machines I saw in my first exploration.'

It was fifteen hours since the bridgehead had anchored itself, during which time Volyova had done nothing, refusing to send in the first of her mechanical spies until now.

'It seems that those machines are dedicated to maintaining the crust; keeping it repaired when it is punctured, maintaining the illusion of realism, and amassing raw material when it comes by. They're also the first line of defence.'

'But what lies below?' Pascale said. 'We didn't get a clear look the night you were attacked, and I don't think they're simply resting on bedrock; that there's a real rocky planet below this mechanised façade.'

'We'll know soon enough,' Volyova said, tight-lipped.

Her spies were laughable in their simplicity; cruder even than the robots which Sylveste and Calvin had used in their initial work on the Captain. It was all part of her philosophy of not letting Cerberus see any technology more sophisticated than was absolutely necessary for the task at hand. The drones were capable of being manufactured in vast numbers by the bridgehead, a profligacy which would outweigh their general lack of intelligence. Each was the size of a fist, equipped with just enough limbs for independent locomotion; just enough eyes to justify its existence in the first place. They had no brains; not even simple networks with a few thousand neurons; not even brains which would have made the average insect seem precociously cranial. Instead, they had little spinnerettes which extruded sheathed optical fibre. The drones were operated by her weapon; all commands and everything they saw routed back and forth through that cable, with quantum privacy guaranteed.

'I think we'll find another layer of automation,' Sylveste said. 'Perhaps another layer of defences. But there has to be something worth protecting.'

'Does there?' asked Khouri, who had kept her vicious-looking plasma-rifle pointing at him since this meeting had convened. 'Aren't you guilty of a few unwarranted assumptions? You keep talking as if there's something valuable in there we aren't meant to get our greasy fingers all over, and that's all that the camouflage is there for; to keep us monkeys out. But what if it's not like that at all? What if there's something bad in there?'

Pascale said, 'She could be right.'

Sylveste contemplated the gun.

'You shouldn't patronise yourself into imagining there's any possibility I haven't already considered,' he said, scarcely caring whether it was Khouri or his wife who thought they were being addressed.

'I wouldn't dream of it,' Khouri said.

Ninety minutes after the first spy had unwound its cable and dropped from the opening into the sub-crustal chamber, Sylveste had his first view of what awaited him. At first, he had no idea what it was he was seeing. The giant snakelike forms – damaged and, for all he knew, dead – towered over the drones like the limbs of fallen gods, tangled and haphazard. There was no guessing at the multitude of functions which these vast machines served, although the welfare of the overlying crust seemed likely to be paramount, and it was probably within them that the molecular weapons were first stirred to activity, before being released to attack newcomers. The crust itself was a machine of sorts, of course, but it was a machine constrained by the limitation of resembling a planet. The snakes had no such constraints.

It was less dark than he had been expecting, even though no light was straying through the wound now, which was plugged tight by the intruding weapon. Instead, the snakes themselves seemed to radiate a silvery glow, like the entrails of some phosphorescent deep-sea creature, radiant with bioluminous bacteria. It was impossible to guess at the function of this light; if there even was one. Perhaps it was an unavoidable byproduct of Amarantin nanotechnics. One could see for tens of kilometres, in any case – to the point where the ceiling of the overlying crust curved down to meet the horizon of the floor on which the snakes were coiled. Things with the gnarled, rooty shape of tree-trunks supported the roof at irregular intervals. It was like gazing into the moonlit depths of an arboreal forest; unable to glimpse the sky and barely able to glimpse the ground, so thick was the undergrowth. The roots of the trunks tangled and retangled with each other, until they formed a matrix of interlocked roots; graphite-coloured. That was the floor.

'I wonder what we'll find below,' Sylveste said.

Volyova considered infanticide. There was no escaping it: by denying the bridgehead the information it needed to keep evolving counteragents to the machinery being deployed by Cerberus, she was consigning it to a slow death. Without the necessary updates from the ship, the molecular weapon templates in the bridgehead's core could not be revised. They would remain frozen; capable only of generating spore which were more than two centuries out of date, incapable of parrying the relentless moronic march of progress exhibited by the alien defences. Her wonderful and brutal creation would be digested down to its last usable atom; spread thinly throughout the crustal matrix, where its remains would serve another function entirely, for uncountable millions of years.

Yet it had to be done.

Khouri was right: sabotaging the bridgehead was the only line of influence now remaining. They could not even destroy the weapon, since the cache was under Sun Stealer's jurisdiction. He would prevent any attempt at that. So what remained was to kill the weapon by slow starvation of knowledge.

Crueller by far.

Although none of the others could see it, her bracelet display was pulsing with the bridgehead's repeated requests for additional data. The weapon had noticed the omission an hour ago, when the scheduled update hadn't arrived. The first query had been merely technical; a check to see that the communication beam was still online. Later, the weapon had become more urgent; adopting tones of polite insistence. Now it was getting far less diplomatic, throwing the machine equivalent of a tantrum.

It was not yet harmed, since the Cerberus systems had not

exceeded its own retaliatory capabilities, but it was getting very agitated, even informing her of how many minutes it had left based on current escalation rates. There were not many. In rather less than two hours Cerberus would match it, and thereafter its fate would simply be a question of the sizes of the opposed forces. Cerberus would win, with absolute mathematical certainty.

Die quickly, Volyova thought.

But even as the plea ran through her mind, something impossible happened.

What little composure Volyova possessed dropped suddenly from her face.

'What's wrong?' said Khouri. 'You look like you've seen—'

'I have,' she said. 'A ghost, I mean. He's called Sun Stealer.'

'What's happened?' Sylveste asked.

She looked up from the bracelet, jaw slack. 'He's just reinstated the transmissions to the bridgehead.' Her gaze snapped back to her bracelet, as if hoping that whatever she had just seen there had been a mirage. But it was obvious from her expression that whatever inauspicious portent she had read was still there to be divined.

'What was it that had to be reinstated in the first place?' Sylveste asked. 'I'd rather you told me.'

Khouri tightened her grip on the warm leather-cladding of the plasma-rifle. She had been uncomfortable with the situation before, but now she was riding a knife-edge of constant terror.

'The weapon lacks the protocols for recognising its own obsolescence,' she said, and then seemed to shiver, as if shaking off possession. 'No . . . what I mean is . . . there are things the weapon can't be allowed to know, except when it needs to know them—' She paused, glancing anxiously around at her crewmates, unsure that she was making any sense. 'It can't be allowed to know how to evolve its own defences before the moment when that evolution has to be expedited; the timing of the upgrades is crucial—'

'You were trying to starve it,' Sylveste said. Hegazi, next to him, said nothing, but acknowledged his remark with a barely perceptible nod, like a despot casting judgement.

'No, I . . .'

'Don't apologise,' he said, with great insistence. 'If I wanted what you want – to sabotage this whole operation – I'm sure I'd have done something similar. Your timing was impeccable, as well – you waited until you'd had the satisfaction of seeing it work; the satisfaction of knowing that your toy functioned.'

'You prick,' Khouri said, spitting in the process. 'You narrow-minded, egotistical prick.'

'Congratulations,' Sylveste said. 'Now you can progress to words with six syllables. But in the meantime would you mind pointing that unpleasant piece of hardware somewhere other than my face?'

'With pleasure,' she said, not allowing the rifle to waver. 'I've got just the anatomical region in mind.'

Hegazi turned to the other member of the Triumvirate present. 'Would you mind explaining what's going on?'

'Sun Stealer must have control of the ship's communications systems,' Volyova said. 'That's the only possibility; the only way my command to stop the transmissions could have been rescinded.'

But even as she was speaking she was shaking her head.

'Which isn't possible. We know he's confined to the gunnery, and there's no physical link between the gunnery and comms.'

'There must be now,' Khouri said.

'But if there is . . .' The whites of her eyes were showing now; bright crescents against the gloom of the bridge. 'There are no logical barriers between comms and the rest of the ship. If Sun Stealer really has got that far, there isn't anything he can't touch.'

It was a long time before anyone spoke; as if everyone – even Sylveste – needed time to adjust to the gravity of the situation. Khouri tried to read him, but there was no way to tell how much of this he accepted, even now. She still suspected that he viewed everything as a paranoiac fantasy that she had woven from her own subconscious; one that had somehow infected both Volyova and, latterly, Pascale.

Perhaps a part of him was still refusing to believe, despite all the evidence.

What evidence, though? Apart from the reinstated signal – and all that it implied – there was nothing to suggest that Sun Stealer had reached beyond the gunnery. But if he had . . .

'You,' Volyova said, breaking the silence. She was pointing her gun at Hegazi. 'You, *svinoi*. You had to have a part in this, didn't you? Sajaki's out of the frame, and Sylveste doesn't have the expertise – so it had to be you.'

'I'm not sure what you're talking about.'

'Helping Sun Stealer. You did it, didn't you?'

'Get a grip, Triumvir.'

Khouri wondered in which direction she should be pointing the plasma-rifle. Sylveste looked as shaken as Hegazi; as surprised at Volyova's sudden line of enquiry.

'Listen,' Khouri said. 'Just because he's had his tongue up Sajaki's arse ever since I came aboard, it doesn't mean he'd do anything that stupid.'

'Thanks,' Hegazi said. 'I think.'

'You're not off the hook,' Volyova said. 'Not by a long mark. Khouri's right; doing what you did would have been an act of gross stupidity. But that hardly disqualifies you from having done it. You had enough expertise to do it. And you're chimeric as well – maybe Sun Stealer's in you too. In which case I'm afraid it's just too dangerous to have you around.'

She nodded at Khouri. 'Khouri; take him down to one of the airlocks.'

'You're going to kill me,' Hegazi said, as she prodded him along the flooded corridor with the barrel of the plasma-rifle, watching janitor-rats scatter ahead of them. 'That's what you're going to do, isn't it? You're going to space me.'

'She just wants you somewhere where you can't do any harm,' Khouri said, not especially in the mood for a protracted conversation with her prisoner.

'Whatever it was she thinks, I didn't do it. Sorry to admit it, but I haven't got the expertise. Does that satisfy you?'

Now he was annoying her, but she sensed that he would only shut up if she talked back to him.

'I'm not sure you did do it,' she said. 'After all, you'd have had to make the arrangements before you had any idea that Volyova was going to sabotage her weapon. You can't have done it since; you've been on the bridge the whole time.'

They had reached the nearest airlock. It was a small unit, just large enough to take a suited human. Like virtually everything else in this part of the ship, the controls on the door were caked in grime and corrosion and odd fungal growth. Yet it still functioned, miraculously.

'So why are you doing this?' Hegazi asked, as the door hummed open and she poked him into the cramped, sullenly lit interior. 'If you don't think I was capable of doing it?'

'It's because I don't like you,' she said, and closed the door on him.

THIRTY

When they were at last alone in their quarters, Pascale said, 'You can't go through with this, Dan. Do you understand what I'm saying?'

He was tired; they all were, but with his mind racing, the last thing he felt like now was sleep. Still, if the bridgehead survived long enough for his entry into Cerberus to proceed as planned, now might be the last opportunity he had for proper sleep for tens of hours; perhaps even days. He would need to be functioning as keenly as he ever had in his life when he descended beneath the alien world. Yet now, obviously, Pascale was going to do her best to talk him out of it.

'It's far too late now,' he said, wearily. 'We've already announced ourselves; done harm to Cerberus. The world knows of our presence; already knows something of our nature. My entering it won't make much difference now, except that I'll learn much more than Volyova's clunking spy robots will ever tell me.'

'You can't know what's waiting for you down there, Dan.'

'Yes, I can. An answer to what happened to the Amarantin. Can't you see that humanity needs to have that information?'

He could see that she did, if only on some theoretical level. But she said, 'What if it was the same kind of curiosity you're showing now that brought extinction upon them? You saw what happened to the *Lorean*.'

Once again he thought of Alicia, dying in that attack. What exactly was it that had made him so unwilling to spare the time that would have been needed to recover her body from the wreck? Even now, the way he had ordered that she go down with the bridgehead struck him as chillingly impersonal, as if – for a fleeting instant – it had not been him giving that order; not even Calvin, but something hiding behind both of them. The thought made him flinch, so he crushed it beneath conscious concern, the way one crushed an insect.

'Then we'll know, won't we?' he said. 'Finally, we'll know. And even if it kills us, someone else will know what happened – someone on Resurgam, or even in another system. You have to understand, Pascale, that I think it's worth that kind of risk.'

'There's more to it than just curiosity, isn't there?' She looked at him, obviously expecting some kind of answer. He just looked back at her, knowing how intimidating the lack of focus of his gaze could be, until she continued speaking. 'Khouri was put aboard to kill you. She even admitted as much. Volyova said she was sent here by someone who might have been Carine Lefevre.'

'That's not only impossible, it's insulting.'

'But it still might be the truth. And there might be more to it than just a personal vendetta, too. Maybe Lefevre did die, after all, but something assumed her shape, inherited her body, or whatever – something that knows the danger you're playing with. Can't you at least accept that as a remote possibility?'

'Nothing that happened around Lascaille's Shroud can have any bearing on what happened to the Amarantin.'

'How can you be so damned sure?'

Angry now, he said, 'Because I was there! Because I went where Lascaille went, into Revelation Space, and what they'd shown Lascaille, they showed to me.' He tried to calm his voice, taking both of Pascale's hands in his own. 'They were ancient; so alien they made me shiver. They touched my mind. I saw them . . . and they were nothing like the Amarantin.'

For the first time since leaving Resurgam, he thought back to that instant of screaming comprehension, as his damaged contact module had skirted the Shroud. Old as fossils, the Shrouders' minds had crawled into his; a moment of abyssal knowing. What Lascaille had said was true. They might have been alien in their biology, inspiring a kind of visceral revulsion simply because they were so far from what the human mind considered the right and proper form for sentience, but in the dynamics of their thought, they were a lot closer to people than their shapes would ever have implied. For a moment, the strangeness of that dichotomy troubled him . . . but it could not have been otherwise, for how else could the Pattern Jugglers have wired his mind to think like a Shrouder, if the basic modes of thought were not similar? Then he

468

remembered the festering queasiness of their communion – and a spillage of memory crashing over him, a glimpse of the vastness of Shrouder history. Across millions of years, they had scoured a younger galaxy than the present one, hunting down and collecting the discarded and dangerous playthings of other, even older, civilisations. Now those fabulous things were almost within reach; behind the membrane of the Shroud . . . and he had almost tricked his way inside. And then something else . . .

Something parting, momentarily, like a curtain, or a gap in clouds – something so fleeting, he had almost forgotten it until the present moment. Something revealed to him that should have remained hidden – hidden behind layers of identity. The identity and memories of a long-dead race . . . worn as camouflage . . .

And something else entirely within the Shroud; and another reason entirely for its existence . . .

But the recollection itself seemed elusive, seemed to slip out of mental reach, until he was left again with Pascale, and only the aftertaste of doubt.

'Promise me you won't go,' she said.

'We'll talk about it in the morning,' Sylveste said.

He woke in his quarters, the little sleep he had snatched insufficient to purge fatigue from his blood.

Something had stirred him awake, but for a moment he could not see or hear any disturbance. Then Sylveste noticed that the bedside holo screen was glowing palely, like a mirror turned to moonlight.

He moved to activate the link, taking care not to wake Pascale. Not that there seemed any danger of that; she was sleeping soundly. The discussion they had shared before sleeping seemed to have given her the mental calm she needed for that.

Sajaki's face appeared on the holo, backdropped by the apparatus of the clinic. 'Are you alone?' he asked, softly.

'My wife is here,' Sylveste said, whispering. 'She's sleeping.'

'Then I'll be brief.' He held up his damaged hand for inspection, revealing how the glistening caul had now filled out, returning his wrist to its normal profile, although the caul still glowed with subcutaneous industry. 'I am well enough to leave here. But I have no intention of duplicating Hegazi's current predicament.'

'Then you've got a problem. Volyova and Khouri have all the

weapons, and they've made sure we won't get our hands on any more.' He lowered his voice even further. 'I don't think it would take much to persuade her to lock me up as well. My threats against the ship don't seem to have impressed her.'

'She's assuming you'd never go that far.'

'What if she's right?'

Sajaki shook his head.

'None of this matters any more. In a matter of days – five at the most – her weapon will begin to fail. You have that window in which to get inside. And don't pretend that her little robots will teach you anything.'

'I know that much already.'

Next to him Pascale stirred.

'Then accept this proposition,' Sajaki said. 'I will lead you inside. The two of us; no one else. We can take two suits, of the same type that brought you here from Resurgam. We don't even need a ship. We'll reach Cerberus in less than a day. That gives you two days to get in, a day to look around and then a day to leave the way you came in. By which time of course you will know the route.'

'What about you?'

'I accompany you. I told you already how I believe we should proceed with the Captain.'

Sylveste nodded. 'You think you'll find something inside Cerberus; something that can heal him.'

'I have to start somewhere.'

Sylveste looked around. Sajaki's voice had been like the wind stirring trees, and the room seemed preternaturally still; more like a tableau glimpsed through a magic lantern than anything real. He thought of the fury taking place on Cerberus at that very moment; the fury of clashing machines, even if they were, for the most part, smaller than bacteria; and the din of their conflict inaudible to any human senses. But it was happening and Sajaki was right: they had only days before the numberless machines owing allegiance to Cerberus would begin to erode Volyova's mighty siege engine. Every second he delayed entering that place was a second less he would have to spend inside it, and a second which would make his eventual return take place that much closer to the end; that much more hazardous, since by then the bridge would be closing. Pascale stirred again, but he sensed that she was still deep in dream. She seemed no more present than the interlocked birds which mosaicked the room's walls; no more capable of being quickened to wakefulness.

'It's all very sudden,' he said.

'But you've waited for this moment all your life,' Sajaki said, his voice rising. 'Don't tell me you're not ready to seize it. Don't tell me you're scared of what you might find.'

Sylveste knew he had to make a decision before the true alienness of the moment had registered.

'Where do I meet you?'

'We'll meet outside the ship,' Sajaki said, and then explained why it had to be that way; why it was too risky for them to meet, because then Sajaki would run the risk of meeting Volyova or Khouri, or even Sylveste's wife. 'They still think I'm ill,' Sajaki added, rubbing the membrane casing his wounded wrist. 'But if they find me outside the clinic, they'll do to me what they did to Hegazi. But from here, I can reach a suit in a few minutes, without entering any areas of the ship still capable of registering my presence.'

'And me?'

'Go to the nearest elevator. I'll arrange for it to take you to a suit nearer to you. You don't have to do anything. The suit will take care of everything.'

'Sajaki, I . . .'

'Just be outside in ten minutes. Your suit will bring you to me.' Sajaki smiled before signing off. 'And I strongly advise that you don't wake your wife.'

Sajaki was true to his word: the elevator and the suit both seemed to know exactly where it was that Sylveste had to go. He met no one during his journey, and no one troubled him as the suit measured him, adjusted itself and then folded affectionately around him.

There was no indication that the ship even noticed as the airlock opened; still less as he reached space.

Volyova was startled awake, interrupted from monochromatic dreams of raging insect armies.

Khouri was banging on her door, shouting something, though Volyova was too bleary to make it out. When she opened the door she was looking down the barrel of the leatherclad plasma-rifle.

Khouri hesitated for a fraction of a second before lowering it, as if unsure just what she had been expecting beyond the door.

'What is it?' Volyova asked.

'It's Pascale,' Khouri said, sweat beading her forehead, shining in slick patches around the gun's grips. 'She woke up and Sylveste wasn't there.'

'Wasn't there?'

'He'd left this. She's pretty cut up about it, but she wanted me to show it to you.' Khouri let the gun drop in its sling and fished out a sheet of paper from her pocket.

Volyova rubbed her eyes and took the paper. Tactile contact activated its stored message; Sylveste's face appeared on it, sketched darkly against a background of interlocking birds.

'I'm afraid I've lied to you,' he said, his voice buzzing from the paper. 'Pascale, I'm sorry – you're entitled to hate me for this, but I hope you won't; not after what we went through.' His voice was very low now. 'You asked me to promise I wouldn't go into Cerberus. But I'm going, and by the time you read this I'll be well on my way, far too late to stop. There's no justification I can give for this, except it's something I have to do, and I think it's something you've always known I would do, if we ever got this close.' He paused, either to draw breath or think what he would say next. 'Pascale, you were the only one who guessed what really happened around Lascaille's Shroud. I admired you for that, you know. That was why I wasn't afraid to admit the truth to you. I swear, what I told you was the way I thought it happened; not just another lie. But now this woman – Khouri – says that she has been sent by someone who might have been Carine Lefevre, and that she's been sent to kill me because of what I might do.'

Again the paper was silent for a moment.

'I acted as if I didn't believe a word of it, Pascale, and maybe that was how I thought at the time. But I have to put those ghosts to rest; finally convince myself that none of this has any connection to what happened back around the Shroud.

'You understand that, don't you? I have to go this extra mile, just so I can silence these phantoms. Perhaps I owe Khouri thanks for that. She's given me a reason to take this step, when my fear of what I'll find is the greatest I've known. I don't believe she – or any of them – are bad people. And not you, either, Pascale. I know you were persuaded by what they said, but that wasn't your fault. You tried to talk me out of it because you love me. And what I was doing – what I was going to do – hurt me more, because I knew I was betraying that love.

'Does that make any sense to you? And will you be able to forgive me when I get back? It won't be long, Pascale – no more than five days; maybe a lot less.' He paused again, before adding a final postscript: 'I took Calvin with me. He's in me now, as I speak. I'd be lying if we said that the two of us haven't come to a new . . . equilibrium. I think he'll prove of value to me.'

And then the image on the paper faded.

'You know,' Khouri said, 'there have been moments when he almost had my sympathy. But I think he's just blown it.'

'You said Pascale had taken it badly.'

'Wouldn't you?'

'It depends. Maybe he was right: maybe she always knew it would come to this. Maybe she should have thought twice before marrying the *svinoi*.'

'You think he's got far?'

Volyova looked at the paper again, as if hoping to siphon fresh wisdom from its wrinkles.

'He must have had assistance. There aren't many of us left who could have helped him. No one, really, if you discount Sajaki.'

'Maybe we shouldn't have discounted him. Perhaps his medichines healed him faster than we expected.'

'No,' Volyova said. She tapped her magic bracelet. 'I know where the Triumvirate is at any moment. Hegazi's still in the airlock; Sajaki's in the clinic.'

'You mind if we check on them, just in case?'

Volyova grabbed another layer of clothing, warm enough that she could enter any of the pressurised parts of the ship without catching hypothermia. She slipped the needler into her belt, then slung over one shoulder the heavy ordnance Khouri had obtained from the warchive. It was a dual-gripped hypervelocity sports slug-gun from the twenty-third century; a product of the first Europan Demarchy, clad in curving black neoprene, ruby-eyed Chinese dragons in beaten gold and silver worked into the sides.

'Not in the slightest,' she said.

They reached the airlock where Hegazi had been waiting all this time, with nothing to amuse himself but the contemplation of his reflection in the chamber's burnished steel walls. That at least was how Volyova imagined it, in the rare moments when she bothered to give the imprisoned Triumvir any thought at all. She did not really hate Hegazi, or even particularly dislike him. He was too weak for that; too obviously a creature incapable of dwelling anywhere except in Sajaki's shadow.

'Did he give you any trouble?' Volyova asked.

'Not really, except that he kept protesting his innocence; saying it wasn't him who had released Sun Stealer from the gunnery. Sounded like he meant it as well.'

'It's an ancient technique known as lying, Khouri.'

Volyova shrugged back the Chinese-dragon gun and landed her fists on the handle which would open the airlock inner door. Her feet were already planted apart in the sludge.

She struggled.

'I can't open it.'

'Let me try.' Khouri pushed her gently aside and tried to work the handle. 'No,' she said, after grunting and then relenting. 'It's jammed tight. I can't move it.'

'You didn't weld it shut or anything like that?'

'Yes, stupid me, I forgot.'

Volyova knuckled the door. 'Hegazi, you hear me? What have you done to the door? It won't open.'

There was no answer.

'He's in there,' Volyova said, consulting her bracelet again. 'But maybe he can't hear us through the armour.'

'I don't like this,' Khouri said. 'There was nothing wrong with that door when I left it. I think we should shoot the lock.' Without waiting for Volyova's agreement, she said, 'Hegazi? If you can hear this, we're shooting our way in.'

In a flash she had the plasma-rifle in one hand, its weight drawing the muscles taut in her forearm. She was shielding her face with the other hand, looking away.

'Wait,' Volyova said. 'We're being too hasty. What if the outer door is open? The vacuum would trip the pressure-sensors and lock the inner door.'

'If that's the case, Hegazi isn't going to be causing us any more problems. Not unless he can hold his breath for a few hours.'

'Granted – but we still don't want to put a hole in that door.'

Khouri moved closer.

If there was a panel showing the pressure status beyond the door, it was well-concealed behind the grime.

'I can set the beam to its narrowest collimation. Put a needle-hole in the door.'

'Do it,' Volyova said, after a moment's hesitation.

'Change of plan, Hegazi. Gonna put a hole in the top of the door. If you're standing up, now would be a good time to sit down, maybe think about putting your affairs in order.'

There was still no answer.

It was almost an insult to the plasma-rifle to ask it to do this, Volyova thought – too precise and dainty an operation by far, like using an industrial laser to cut a wedding cake. But Khouri did it anyway. There was a flash and a crack, as the gun spat a tiny elongated seed of ball-lightning into the door. For a moment smoke coiled from the woodworm-sized hole which she had cut.

But only for a second.

Then something spurted from the door, in a dark hissing arc.

She wasted no time putting a bigger hole in the door. By then, neither Khouri nor Volyova considered it very likely that there was going to be anyone living behind the airlock. Either Hegazi was dead – and there was no guessing how – or Hegazi had already left the lock, and this jetting stream of high-pressure fluid was his perplexing idea of a message to his former captors.

Khouri shot through, and the stream became an arm-thick eruption of the brackish fluid, ramming out with such explosive force that she was thrown backwards into the ship-sludge under-foot, plasma-rifle clattering into the same pool of ankle-deep effluent. The stuff hissed fiercely as it touched the gun's hot maw. By the time she had struggled to her feet, however, the flow had dwindled to a dribble, slurping in noisy eructations through the punctured door. She picked up the gun and shook the muck off it, wondering if it would work again.

'It's ship-slime,' Volyova said. 'The same stuff we're standing in. I'd recognise that stench anywhere.'

'The lock was full of ship-slime?'

'Don't ask me how. Just open a bigger hole in the door.'

Khouri did so, until she could squeeze her arm through and work the lock's interior controls without brushing against the plasma-heated edges of the cut metal. Volyova was right, she thought, it had been the pressure switches which had tripped the locking mechanism. The chamber must have been pumped to bursting with ship-slime.

The door opened, allowing a final slick of slime to ooze into the corridor.

Along with what remained of Hegazi. It was unclear whether this stemmed from the pressure he had been subjected to, or its explosive release, but his metal and flesh components seemed to have arrived at a less than amicable separation.

THIRTY-ONE

Cerberus/Hades, Delta Pavonis Heliopause, 2566

'I think this calls for a cigarette,' Volyova said, and for a moment she had to remember where she had last stowed the smokes. When she found them, in a little-visited pocket of her flying jacket, she did not rush either to open the pack or fish out one of the crumpled, yellowing tubes which resided within. She took her time, and when at last she was ready, she took an unhurried inhalation and allowed her nerves to settle, like a blizzard of feathers slowly returning to the ground.

'The ship killed him,' she said, staring down at the remnants of Hegazi, but doing her best not to think too hard about what she was looking at. 'That's the only thing that makes sense.'

'Killed him?' Khouri asked, still directing the barrel of her plasma-rifle at the elements of the Triumvir which floated in suspension in the slick of ship-slime around their feet, as if nervous that his disassociated remains might be on the verge of spontaneously reassembling. 'You mean this wasn't an accident?'

'No, it wasn't an accident. I know he was in league with Sajaki, and therefore Sylveste. Yet Sun Stealer still killed him. Makes you think, doesn't it?'

'Yeah, I guess it does.'

Perhaps Khouri had already worked it out for herself, but Volyova decided to spell it out anyway. 'Sylveste is gone. He's on his way to Cerberus, and because I didn't manage to sabotage the weapon, there'll be very little to stop him getting inside. Do you understand? It means Sun Stealer has won. Nothing remains for him to achieve. The rest is only a question of time, and of maintaining the status quo. And what threatens that?'

'We do,' Khouri said, hesitantly, like a clever pupil who wanted to impress teacher but not draw the derision of her classmates.

'More than that. Not just you and I; not even when we include

Pascale. Hegazi was also a threat, as far as Sun Stealer was concerned. And for no other reason than that he was human.' She was guessing, of course, but it seemed to make complete sense to her. 'To something like Sun Stealer, human loyalty is fluid and chaotic – maybe not even properly comprehensible. He'd turned Hegazi – or at the very least those to whom Hegazi was already loyal. But did he understand the dynamics which governed that loyalty? I doubt it. Hegazi was a component which had served its usefulness, and which might malfunction at some point in the future.' She felt the icy calm which came from contemplating her own oblivion, knowing that there were few times when she had ever been so close to it. 'So he had to die. And now that his objective is almost achieved, I think Sun Stealer will want to do the same to all of us.'

'If he wanted to kill us . . .'

'He'd already have done so? He may well have already tried, Khouri. Whole parts of the ship are no longer under any central control, which means that Sun Stealer is limited in what he can do. He's taken possession of a body already half-paralysed; already half-leprous and half afflicted with the palsy.'

'Very poetic, but what does it mean to us, then?'

Volyova lit another cigarette; she had thoroughly seen off the first of them. 'It means he will try and kill us, but that his options are difficult to predict. He can't simply depressurise the whole ship, since there are no command channels which allow for that – even I couldn't do it, other than by physically opening all the locks, and to do that I'd have to disable thousands of electromechanical safeties. He would probably find it difficult to flood an area larger than the airlock. But he will think of something; I'm sure of it.'

Suddenly, and it was almost without thinking, she had the slug-gun in her hands and she was pointing it down the dark lengths of the flooded corridor which led to the lock.

'What is it?'

'Nothing,' Volyova said. 'I'm just scared. Remarkably so. I don't suppose you have any suggestions, Khouri?'

She did, as a matter of fact.

'We'd better find Pascale. She doesn't know her way around as well as we do. And if it gets nasty . . .'

Volyova stubbed out what was left of her cigarette, mashing it against the barrel of the slug-gun.

'You're right; we should stay together. And we will. Just as soon as . . .'

Something emerged noisily from the gloom and halted ten metres from them.

Volyova had the gun on it immediately, but she did not fire; some instinct was telling her that the thing had not come to kill them, or at least not yet. It was one of the tracked servitors which she had seen Sylveste using in the aborted operation to heal the Captain; one of the units lacking any great internal sophistication. One of those, in short, which was primarily controlled by the ship, rather than its own brain.

Its chunkily mounted sensor eyes locked onto them.

'It's not armed,' Volyova breathed, realising as she did so that whispering was useless. 'I think it's just been sent to scout us out. This is one of the parts of the ship which the ship can't see into; one of its blind spots.'

The servitor's sensors made little swivelling motions from side to side, as if triangulating their exact positions. Then it began to reverse back into the gloom.

Khouri shot it.

'Why did you do that?' Volyova asked, when the concussive echoes of the blast had died down and she no longer had to squint against the glare of the machine's demise. 'Whatever it saw was already transmitted back to the ship. Shooting it was pointless.'

'I didn't like the way it was looking at me,' Khouri said. Then she frowned. 'And besides – it's one less we have to worry about.'

'Yes,' Volyova said. 'And given the speed at which the ship can manufacture a drone that simple, it may be ten or twenty seconds before it's replaced.'

Khouri looked at her as if she'd just said a joke with an impenetrable punchline. But Volyova was serious. What she had just noticed had chilled her far more deeply than the appearance of the servitor. It was, after all, logical that the ship would soon resort to the drones for its sense-gathering operations; logical too that it would explore ways to outfit the machines for the murder of the remaining human crew and passengers. It was something she would have predicted herself, sooner or later. But not this. Not what had just poked itself above the ooze of the ship-slime; for the instant it took its black rodent eyes to spot her, before turning tail and swimming into the darkness.

Ship controlled the janitor-rats, she remembered.

When consciousness returned – and for a moment Sylveste did not remember precisely when it had left – he was surrounded by an audience of blurred stars. They were doing a very complex dance, and if he had not already felt nauseous, he felt sure that sight alone would have been sickening. What was he doing here? And why did he feel so strange; so much as if cotton-wool had been pressed into every cell in his body? Because he was in a suit, that was why. One of the special suits which the crew owned; of the sort which had carried him and Pascale up from the surface of Resurgam. The suit had forced his lungs to accept the fluid it filled itself with instead of air.

'What's happening?' he subvocalised, in the way he knew that the suit would be able to read, via the simple speech-centre trawl built into its helmet.

'I'm reversing,' the suit informed him. 'Midpoint thrust inversion.'

'Where the hell are we?' Picking through his memories was still arduous, like finding the end of a tangled rope. He had no idea where to begin.

'More than a million kilometres from the ship; somewhat less than that distance from Cerberus.'

'We've come all that way so—' He stopped. 'No, wait. I've no idea how long it's been.'

'We departed seventy-four minutes ago.' Hardly more than an hour, Sylveste thought. Yet if the suit had told him it had been a day he would have accepted it unquestioningly. 'Our average acceleration was ten gees. I was instructed to make all haste by Triumvir Sajaki.'

Yes, now he remembered more. Sajaki's midnight call, and the hurried rush to the suits. He remembered leaving a message for Pascale, though not the details. That had been his only concession; the one luxury he permitted himself. Yet even if there had been days to prepare for the entry, there would have been very little that he could have changed. He had no requirements for extra documentation or recording apparatus, since he had access to the suit's libraries and integral sensors. The suits were armed, he knew, and capable of defending themselves autonomously, against much the same modes of attack which Volyova's weapon was now experiencing. They were also able to extrude scientific analysis tools, or create compartments in themselves for the storing of samples. Quite apart from that, they were as independent as any spacecraft. He realised with a snap that he was thinking wrongly; the suits *were* actually spacecraft; just very flexible spacecraft with room inside for only one occupant; spacecraft which became their own atmospheric shuttles, and – if needed – their own surface rovers. Rationally, there was no other way he would rather be entering Cerberus.

'I'm glad I slept through that acceleration,' Sylveste said.

'You had no choice,' the suit said, evincing a complete lack of interest. 'Consciousness was suppressed. Now please ready yourself for the deceleration phase. When you resume wakefulness, we will have arrived in the vicinity of our destination.'

Sylveste began to frame a question in his head; intending to ask the suit why Sajaki had not yet shown himself, despite his assurance that he would accompany Sylveste. Yet, before he had even begun to concretise his thoughts into the unspoken state which the trawl could read, the suit made him sleep again, as dreamlessly as before.

While Khouri went to find Pascale Sylveste, Volyova made her way back up to the bridge. Now she dared not take the elevators, but thankfully there were fewer than twenty levels to climb; an exertion, but bearable. It was also relatively safe: the ship could not send drones into the stairwells, she knew; not even the floating machines which rode through the normal corridors on superconducting magnetic fields. All the same, she kept the slug-gun at readiness, sweeping it ahead of her as she endlessly rounded the ascending spiral, occasionally stopping and holding her breath, listening for the sounds of things following her, or lurking some distance ahead.

On the way up, she tried to think of the myriad ways in which the ship could kill her. It was an interesting intellectual challenge; testing her knowledge of the vessel in a way she had not previously considered. It made her look at things in a new light. Once – not so very long ago – she had been in much the same position as the ship was now. She had wanted to kill Nagorny, or at the very least prevent him from becoming a threat to her, which practically amounted to the same thing. In the end she had killed him because he first tried to kill her – but it was the manner of his execution that preyed on her mind now. She had killed Nagorny by accelerating and decelerating the ship so fiercely that he had been pulped alive. Sooner or later – and she could think of no pressing reason why it should not be the case – the ship would surely think of that for itself. When that happened, it would be a very good idea not to be in the ship any more.

She reached the bridge unhindered, although that did not stop her checking every shadow for a lurking machine, or – worse, now – rat. She did not know what the rats could do to her, but she was less than minded to find out.

The bridge was empty, much as when she had left it. The damage Khouri had wrought on it was still there; even the staining of Sajaki's blood on the floor of the vast spherical meeting place. The holo-display was still aglow, looming over her with its constantly updating progress report on the establishment of the Cerberus bridgehead. For a moment she could not help but take a proprietorial interest in her creation, which was still gamely holding its own against the antibiotic forces deployed by the alien world. Yet even as she experienced a flush of pride, she willed it to fail, so that Sylveste would be denied entry. Assuming that he had not already arrived.

'What have you come for?' asked a voice.

She whipped around, and there was a figure, looking down at her from one of the curved levels of the bridge. It was no one she recognised; just a darkly cloaked male with clasped hands and a sunken skull of a face. She blasted it, but the figure remained, even after the slug-gun's discharges had ripped through it, ion trails lingering in the air like banners.

Another figure, differently dressed, had appeared next to it. 'Your tenancy here has expired,' it said, in the oldest variant of Norte, Volyova's processing of it so tardy that she did not immediately understand his words.

'You must understand, Triumvir, that this domain is no longer yours,' said another, shivering to life on the chamber's opposite side, clad in the body section of a fantastically ancient spacesuit, ribbed with cooling lines and boxy attachments. The language he spoke was the oldest strain of Russish she could parse.

'What do you hope to achieve here?' asked the first figure, even as another appeared next to it, and began talking to her, and another; figures from the past hectoring her from all sides. 'This is outrageous . . .' But the voice blurred into that of another ghost, speaking to her from her right.

'. . . lack a mandate here, Triumvir. I have to tell you . . .'

'. . . gravely exceeded your authority and must now submit to . . .'

'. . . bitterly disappointed, Ilia, and must politely request that you . . .'

'. . . rescind . . . privileges . . .'

'. . . completely unacceptable . . .'

She screamed as the welter of voices became a constant wordless roar, the congregation of the dead filling the chamber totally, until all she could see in any direction was a mass of ancient faces, their mouths moving as if each one were the only one speaking; as if each imagined that he had her absolute attention. It was as if they were praying to her; as if they thought she was omniscient. Praying, but at the same time complaining; carpingly at first, as if disappointed, but – with every second – with more hate and scorn, as if she had not only let them down in the bitterest way possible, but that she had also committed some atrocity so dire it was unspeakable even now, but could only be acknowledged in the curved revulsion of their lips and the naked shame in their eyes.

She hefted the gun. The temptation to empty a slug-clip into the ghosts was overwhelming. She could not kill them, of course, but she could seriously disable their projection systems. But she needed to conserve her ammo now that the warchive was inaccessible.

'Go away!' she shouted. 'Get away from me!'

One by one, the dead grew silent and vanished. As each departed, each shook its head disappointedly, as if ashamed of staying in her presence a moment longer. Finally, she had the room to herself. She was breathing in hard rasps and needed to calm down. She lit another cigarette and smoked it slowly, trying to give her mind a few minutes' rest. She palmed the gun, glad she had not wasted the clip, for all the transient pleasure it would have given her to destroy the bridge. Khouri had chosen well. Emblazoned along the gun's flanks were silver and gold Chinese dragon motifs.

A voice spoke from the display.

Volyova looked up into the face of Sun Stealer.

It was as she had known it must be, after Pascale had first told her the significance of the creature's name. As she had known it must be, and yet also much worse. Because she was not simply seeing how the alien looked. She was seeing how the alien looked to itself – and there was evidently something very wrong with Sun Stealer's mind. She thought back to Nagorny, and understood how the man had been driven mad. She could hardly blame him, now – not if he had lived with this thing in his head all that time, and yet had lacked an inkling of where it came from or what it wanted from him. No; she sympathised with the dead Gunnery Officer, the poor, poor bastard. Perhaps she too would have sunk into psychosis when faced with this apparition, looming behind every dream, every waking thought.

Once Sun Stealer might have been Amarantin. But he had changed, perhaps deliberately, through the selective pressure of genetic engineering, sculpting himself and his banished brethren into a new species entirely. They had reshaped their anatomy for flight in zero-gravity; grown immense wings. She could see those wings now; looming behind the curved, sleek head which seemed to thrust down towards her.

The head was a skull. The eye sockets were not exactly vacant; not exactly hollow, but seemed abrim with reservoirs of something infinitely black and infinitely deep, as dark and depthless as she imagined the membrane of a Shroud. The bones of Sun Stealer shone with colourless lustre.

'Despite what I said earlier,' she said, when the initial shock of what she was seeing had passed, or at least subdued to a point where she could tolerate it, 'I think you could have found a way to kill me by now. If that was what you wanted.'

'You cannot guess what I want.'

When he spoke there was just a wordless absence which somehow made sense, as if carved from silence. The creature's complex jaw-bones did not move at all. Speech, she remembered of the Amarantin, had never been an important mode of communication. Their society had been based around visual display. Something so basic would surely have been preserved, even after Sun Stealer's flock had departed Resurgam and commenced their transformations; transformations so radical that when they later returned to the world they would be mistaken for winged gods.

'I know what you don't want,' Volyova said. 'You don't want

anything to stop Sylveste reaching Cerberus. That's why we have to die now; in case we find a way to stop him.'

'His mission is of great importance to me,' Sun Stealer said, then seemed to reconsider. 'To us. To us who survived.'

'Survived what?' Maybe this would be her one and only chance to come to any understanding. 'No; wait – what else could you have survived, but the death of the Amarantin? Is that what it was? Did you somehow find a way not to die?'

'You know by now the place where I entered Sylveste.' It was less a question, more a flat statement. Volyova wondered to how much of their discourse Sun Stealer had been privy.

'It had to be Lascaille's Shroud,' she said. 'That was the only thing that made sense – although not much, I admit.'

'That was where we sought sanctuary; for nine hundred and ninety thousand years.'

The coincidence was too great not to mean something. 'Ever since life ended on Resurgam.'

'Yes.' The word trailed off into a hiss of sibilance. 'The Shrouds were of our designing; the last desperate enterprise of our Flock, even after those who stayed behind on the surface were incinerated.'

'I don't understand. What Lascaille said, and Sylveste himself found out . . .'

'They were not shown the truth. Lascaille was shown a fiction – our identity replaced by that of a much older culture, utterly unlike ourselves. The true purpose of the Shrouds was not revealed to him. He was shown a lie which would encourage others to come.'

Volyova could see how that lie would have worked, now. Lascaille had been told that the Shrouds were repositories for harmful technologies – things humanity secretly craved, such as methods of faster-than-light travel. When Lascaille had revealed this to Sylveste, it had only increased Sylveste's desire to break into the Shroud. He had been able to muster the support of the entire Demarchist society around Yellowstone towards that goal, for the rewards would be dazzling beyond comprehension for the first faction to unlock such alien mysteries.

'But if it was a lie,' she said, 'what was the true function of the Shrouds?'

'We built them to hide inside, Triumvir Volyova.' It seemed to be playing with her, enjoying her confusion. 'They were places of sanctuary. Zones of restructured spacetime, within which we could shelter.'

'Shelter from whom?'

'The ones who survived the Dawn War. The ones who were given the name of the Inhibitors.'

She nodded. There was much she did not understand, but one thing was now clear to her. What Khouri had told her – the fragments that the woman remembered from the strange dream she had been vouchsafed in the gunnery – had been something like the truth. Khouri had not remembered everything, and the parts had not always been related to Volyova in the right order, but it was obvious now that this was only because Khouri had been expected to grasp something too huge, too alien – too apocalyptic – for her mind to comfortably hold. She had done her best, but her best had not been good enough. But now Volyova was being accorded disclosure of parts of the same picture, although from an oddly different perspective.

Khouri had been told about the Dawn War by the Mademoiselle, who had not wanted Sylveste to succeed. Yet Sun Stealer desired that outcome more than anything else.

'What is it about?' she asked. 'I know what you're doing here; you're delaying me; keeping me waiting because you know I'll do anything to hear the answers you have. And you're right, in a way. I have to know. I have to know everything.'

Sun Stealer waited, silently, and then continued to answer all the questions she had for it.

When she was done, Volyova decided that she could profitably use one of the slugs in her clip. She shot the display; the great glass globe shattered into a billion icy shards, Sun Stealer's face disrupting in the same explosion.

Khouri and Pascale took the circuitous route to the clinic, avoiding elevators and the kind of well-repaired corridors through which drones could easily travel. They kept their guns drawn at all times, and preferred to blast anything that looked even vaguely suspicious, even if it later turned out to be nothing more than a chance alignment of shadows or a disturbingly shaped accretion of corrosion on a wall or bulkhead.

'Did he give you any kind of warning he was going to leave so soon?' Khouri asked.

'No; not this soon. I mean, I thought he would try it at some point, but I tried talking him out of it.'

'How do you feel about him?'

'What do you expect me to say? He was my husband. We were in love.' Pascale seemed to collapse then; Khouri reached out to catch her. The woman wiped tears from her eyes, rubbing them red. 'I hate him for what he's done – you would as well. I don't understand him, either. But I still love him despite it. I keep thinking . . . maybe he's dead already. It's possible, isn't it? And even if he isn't, there's no guarantee I'll ever see him again.'

'It can't be a very safe place he's going to,' Khouri said, and then wondered if Cerberus was any more dangerous than the ship, now.

'No, I know. I don't think even he realises how much danger he's in – or the rest of us.'

'Still, your husband isn't just anyone. It's Sylveste we're talking about here.' Khouri reminded Pascale that Sylveste's life had been shot through with a core of rare luck, and that it would be strange if that fortune should desert him now, when the thing that he had always reached for was almost within his grasp. 'He's a slippery bastard, and I think there's still a good chance he'll find a way out of this.'

That seemed to calm Pascale, fractionally.

Then Khouri told her that Hegazi was dead and that the ship appeared to be trying to murder everyone else left aboard it.

'Sajaki can't be here,' Pascale said. 'I mean, he can't, can he? Dan wouldn't know how to find his own way to Cerberus. He'd need one of you to go with him.'

'That's what Volyova thought.'

'Then why are we here?'

'I guess Ilia didn't trust her convictions.'

Khouri pushed open the door which led into the clinic from the partially flooded access corridor, kicking a janitor-rat out of the way as she did so. The clinic smelt wrong. She knew it instantly.

'Pascale, something bad has happened here.'

'I'll . . . what is it I'm supposed to say at this point? Cover you?' Pascale had her low-yield beam gun out, without looking like she had much idea what to do with it.

'Yes,' Khouri said. 'You cover me. That's a very good idea.'

She entered the clinic, pushing the barrel of the plasma-rifle ahead of her.

As she moved in, the room sensed her presence and notched up its illumination. She had visited Volyova here after the Triumvir had been injured; she felt she knew the approximate geometry of the place.

She looked to the bed where she was sure Sajaki ought to have been. Above the bed floated an elaborate array of gimballed and hinged servo-mechanical medical tools, radiating down from a central point like a mutated steel hand with far too many fingers, all of which seemed tipped with talons.

There was not a single inch of metal which was not covered in blood; thickly congealed, like candle-wax.

'Pascale, I don't think—'

But she too had seen what lay on the bed below the machinery; the thing that might once have been Sajaki. There was also not a single inch of the bed which was not adorned in red. It was difficult to see where Sajaki ended and where his eviscerated remains began. He reminded her of the Captain; except here the Captain's silver borderlessness had been transfigured into scarlet; like an artist's reworking of the same basic theme in a different and more carnal medium. Two halves of the same morbid diptych.

His chest was bloated, raised above the bed, as if a stream of galvanising current were still slamming through him. His chest was also hollow; the gore pooled in a deep excavated crater which ran from his sternum to his abdomen, like a terrible steel fist had reached down and ripped half of him out. Perhaps that was the way it had happened. Perhaps he had not even been awake when it did. For confirmation of this theory she scrutinised his face, the little of his expression she could decipher beneath the veil of red.

No; Triumvir Sajaki had almost certainly been awake.

She felt Pascale's presence not far behind. 'You shouldn't forget I've seen death,' she said. 'I saw my father assassinated.'

'You've never seen this.'

'No,' she said. 'You're right. I've never seen anything like this.'

His chest exploded. Something burst out of it, at first so efficiently concealed by the fountain of blood that it had disturbed that it was not obvious what it was – until it landed on the blood-slicked floor of the room and scampered away, wormlike tail lashing behind it. Then three more rats elevated their snouts out of

Sajaki, sniffing the air, regarding Khouri and Pascale with matched pairs of black eyes. Then they too pulled themselves over the caldera which had been his rib-cage, landing on the floor, following the one who had just left. They vanished into the room's darker recesses.

'Let's get out of here,' Khouri said. But even as she was speaking it moved; the fist of steel fingers, activating with blinding speed, reaching out to her with a pair of its clawed, diamond-tipped digits, so quickly that she could only begin to scream. The claws snagged her jacket, ripping into it, and then she began to pull away, with all the strength she had.

She wrenched free, but not before it had located a purchase around her gun, dragging it with brutal force from her fingers. Khouri fell back into the mess on the floor; noticing how her jacket was soiled with Sajaki's blood; how at least some of the brighter red pooling from the rips must have been her own.

The surgical machine elevated the gun, cradling it for them to see, as if gloating at its acquisition of a hunting trophy. Now two of its more dextrous manipulators snaked into place and began to examine the gun's controls, stroking the leather casing in eerie fascination. Slowly, ever so slowly, the manipulators began to point the gun in Khouri's direction.

Pascale raised the beamer and blasted the whole assembly, blood-caked metallic chunks splattering over Sajaki's remains. The plasma-rifle crashed down, blackened and gushing smoke, bluish sparks dancing from its shattered casing.

Khouri picked herself up, oblivious to the filth in which she was liberally covered.

Her ruined plasma-rifle was now buzzing angrily, the sparks dancing with increased ferocity.

'It's going to blow,' Khouri said. 'We have to get away from here.'

They turned to the door, and then had a second to adjust to what was now blocking their exit. There had to be a thousand of them; piled three deep in the ship-slime, each individual careless of its own life, but acting for the greater good of the whole senseless mass. Behind, more rats; hundreds and then thousands more, piling back along the corridor; a vast rodent tidal wave, brimming at the aperture of the clinic, ready to surge forwards in one consuming *tsunami* of appetite.

She unsheathed the only weapon she now had left, the tiny, ineffectual needler she carried only because of the precision it allowed. She began to squirt it at the mass of rats while Pascale doused them with the beamer, which was hardly more suited to the task. Rats exploded and burned wherever they pointed their guns, but there were always more of them, and now the first rank of rats was beginning to creep into the clinic.

Brightness flared down the corridor, followed by a series of bangs spaced so closely together that they almost merged into a solid roar. The noise and the light came closer. Rats were flying through the air now, propelled by the approaching explosions. The stench of cooked rodent was overpowering; worse than the smell which already pervaded the clinic. Gradually, the wave of rats began to thin and disperse.

Volyova stood in the doorway, her slug-gun belching smoke, its barrel the colour of lava. Behind them, Khouri's ruined weapon grew suddenly and ominously silent.

'Now would be a good time to leave,' Volyova said.

They ran towards her, trampling over the dead rats and those still seeking shelter. Khouri felt something slam into her spine. There was a wind, hotter than any she had known. She felt herself lose contact with the floor, and then for a moment she was flying.

THIRTY-TWO

Approaching Cerberus Surface, 2566

This time the dislocation was briefer, even though the place in which he found himself was the most foreign he had known.

'On descent towards Cerberus bridgehead,' the suit informed him, voice pleasantly bland and drained of import, as if this were a perfectly natural destination. Graphics scrolled over the suit's faceplate window, but his eyes could not focus on them properly, so he told the suit to drop the imagery straight into his brain. Then it was much better. The fake contours of the surface – huge now, filling half the sky – were lined in lilac, their sinuous mock-geology rendering the world more folded and brainlike than ever before. There was very little natural illumination here, save for the twin beacons of dim ruddiness of Hades and, much further way, Delta Pavonis itself. But the suit compensated by shifting near-infrared photons into the visible.

Now something jutted over the horizon, blinkered in green by the overlay.

'The bridgehead,' Sylveste said, as much to hear a human voice as anything else. 'I see it.'

It was tiny, he saw now. It looked like the tip of an insignificant splinter blemishing the stone of God's own statue. Cerberus was two thousand kilometres across; the bridgehead a mere four in length, and most of that was now buried beneath the crust. In a way, it was the device's very tininess in relation to the world which best testified to Ilia Volyova's skill. It might be small, but it was still a thorn in the side of Cerberus. That much was obvious even from here; the crust around the bridgehead looked inflamed, stressed to some point beyond its inbuilt tolerances. For several kilometres around the weapon, the crust had given up any pretence of looking realistic. Now it had reverted to what he assumed was its native state: a hexagonal grid which blurred into rock on its fringes.

They would be over the maw – the cone's open end – in a few minutes. Sylveste could already feel gravity tugging at his viscera now, even though he was still immersed in the suit's liquid air. It was admittedly weak; a quarter of Earth normal – but a fall from his present height would still be adequately fatal, with or without the suit to protect him.

Now, finally, something else shared his immediate volume of space. He called in enhancements and saw a suit exactly like his own, twinkling brightly against the night. It was a little ahead of him, but following the same trajectory, heading for the circular entrance into the bridgehead. Two morsels of drifting marine food, he thought, about to be sucked into the enormous waiting funnel of the bridgehead, digested into the heart of Cerberus.

No going back now, he thought.

The three women ran down a corridor carpeted in dead rats and the blackened, stiff shells of things that might possibly once have been rats, though they did not invite close scrutiny. The trio had one big gun between the three of them now; one gun capable of despatching any servitor which the ship sent against them. The small pistols they also had might do the same job, but only if used with expertise and a certain degree of luck.

Occasionally, the floor shifted under their feet, unnervingly.

'What is it?' asked Khouri, limping now, after the bruising she had taken when the clinic had exploded. 'What does it mean?'

'It means Sun Stealer is experimenting,' Volyova said, pausing between every two or three words to catch her breath, her side aflame with pain now; every injury which had been healed since Resurgam seemed on the point of unstitching. 'So far he's moved against us with the less critical systems; the robots and the rats, for instance. But he knows that if he can understand the drive properly – if he can learn how to operate it within its safety margins – he can crush us just by ramping up the thrust for a few seconds.' She ran for a few more strides, wheezing. 'It's how I killed Nagorny. But Sun Stealer doesn't know the ship so well, even though he controls it. He's trying to adjust the drive very gradually; reaching an understanding of how it operates. When he has that—'

Pascale said, 'Is there anywhere we can go where we can be safe? Somewhere the rats and the machines can't reach?'

'Yes, but nowhere that the acceleration can't reach in and crush us.'

'So we should get off the ship, is that what you're saying?'

She stopped, audited the corridor they were in and decided it was not one of the ones in which the ship could hear their conversations. 'Listen,' she said. 'Don't be under any illusions. If we leave here, I doubt very much that we'll ever find a way to return. But on the other hand, we also have an obligation to stop Sylveste, if there's even a slim chance of doing so. Even if we kill ourselves in the process.'

'How could we reach Dan?' Pascale asked. Obviously, stopping Sylveste still amounted – in her mind – to catching him and talking him out of going further. Volyova decided not to disabuse her of that notion, not just yet; but it wasn't quite what she had in mind.

'I think your husband took one of our suits,' she said. 'According to my bracelet all the shuttles are still present. Besides, he could never have piloted one of them.'

'Not unless he had help from Sun Stealer,' Khouri said. 'Listen, can we keep moving? I know we don't have any particular direction in mind, but I'd feel a hell of a lot happier than standing around.'

'He'd have taken a suit,' Pascale said. 'That would have been his style. But he wouldn't have done so alone.'

'Is it possible he would have accepted Sun Stealer's help?'

She shook her head. 'Forget it. He didn't even believe in Sun Stealer. If he'd had an inkling that he was being led – pushed into something – no; he wouldn't have accepted it.'

'Maybe he didn't have any choice,' Khouri said. 'But anyway; assuming he took a suit, is there any way we can catch him?'

'Not before he reaches Cerberus.' There was no need to think about that. She knew just how quickly a million kilometres of space could be traversed if one could tolerate a constant ten gees of acceleration. 'It's too risky to take suits ourselves; not the kind your husband used. We'll have to get there in one of the shuttles. It'll be a lot slower, but there's less chance Sun Stealer will have infiltrated its control matrix.'

'Why's that?'

'Claustrophobia. The shuttles are about three centuries less advanced than the suits.'

'And that's supposed to help us?'

'Believe me, when you're dealing with infectious alien mind parasites, I always find primitive is best.' Then, calmly, almost as if it were a recognised form of verbal punctuation, she took aim with the needler and gutted a rat which had dared stray into the corridor.

'I remember this place,' Pascale said. 'This is where you brought us when—'

Khouri made the door open; the one marked with a barely legible spider.

'Get in,' she said. 'Make yourself at home. And start praying that I remember how Ilia worked this thing.'

'Where is she going to meet us?'

'Outside,' Khouri said. 'I sincerely hope.'

By which time she was already closing the spider-room's door; already looking at the brass and bronze controls and hoping for some spark of recognition.

THIRTY-THREE

Cerberus/Hades Orbit, 2566

Volyova slipped out the needler, approaching the Captain.

She knew that she had to get to the hangar chamber as quickly as possible; that any delay might give Sun Stealer the time he needed to find a way to kill her. But there was something she had to do first. There was no logic to it, no rationality – but she knew she had to do it anyway. So she took the stairwells to the Captain's level, into the deadening cold, her breath seeming to solidify in her throat. There were no rats down here: too cold. And servitors would not be able to reach him without running the risk of becoming part of him, subsumed by the plague.

'Can you hear me, you bastard?' She told her bracelet to warm him enough for conscious thought processes. 'If so, pay attention. The ship's been taken over.'

'Are we still around Bloater?'

'No . . . no, we're not still around Bloater. That was some time ago.'

After a few moments the Captain said, 'Taken over, did you say? Who by?'

'Something alien, with some unpleasant ambitions. Most of us are dead now – Sajaki, Hegazi; all the other crew you ever knew – and the few of us left are getting out while we can. I don't expect to ever come back aboard, which is why what I'm about to do might strike you as slightly drastic.'

She aimed the needler now; directing it towards the cracked, misshaped husk of the reefer encasing the Captain.

'I'm going to let you warm, do you understand? For the last few decades it's been all we can do to keep you as cool as possible – but it hasn't worked, so maybe it was never the right approach. Maybe what we need to do now is let you take over the damned ship, in whatever way you see fit.'

'I don't think—'

'I don't care what you think, Captain. I'm doing it anyway.'

Her finger grew tight against the needler's trigger; already she was mentally calculating how his rate of spread would increase as he warmed, and the numbers she was coming up with were not quite believable . . . but then, they had never considered doing this before.

'Please, Ilia.'

'Listen, *svinoi*,' she said, finally. 'Maybe it works; maybe it doesn't. But if I've ever shown any loyalty to you – if you even remember me – all I'm asking is that you do what you can for us.'

She was about to fire; about to unload the needler into the reefer, but then something made her hesitate.

'There's one other thing I have to say to you. Which is that I think I know who the hell you are, or rather who the hell you became.'

She was acutely conscious of the dryness of her mouth, and of the time she was wasting, but something made her continue.

'What do you have to say to me?'

'You travelled with Sajaki to the Pattern Jugglers, didn't you? I know. The crew spoke of it often enough – even Sajaki himself. What no one discussed was what happened down there: what the Jugglers did to the two of you. Oh, I know there were rumours – but that's all they were; engineered by Sajaki to throw me off the scent.'

'Nothing happened there.'

'No; what happened was this. You killed Sajaki, all those years ago.'

His answer came back, amused, as if he had misheard her. '*I* killed Sajaki?'

'You had the Jugglers do it; had them erase his neural patterns and overlay your own on his mind. You became him.'

Now she had to catch her breath, although she was almost done.

'One existence wasn't enough for you – and maybe by then you'd sensed that this body wasn't going to last too long; not with so many viruses flying around. So you colonised your adjutant, and the Jugglers did what you wished because they're so alien they couldn't even grasp the concept of murder. But that's the truth, isn't it?'

'No . . .'

'Shut up. That's why Sajaki never wanted you healed – because by then he *was* you, and he didn't need healing. And that's why Sajaki was able to denature my treatment for the plague – because he had all your expertise. I should let you die for this, *svinoi* – except of course you already are, because what's left of Sajaki is now redecorating the medical centre.'

'Sajaki – dead?' It was as if her news of the others' deaths had not reached him at all.

'Is that justice for you? You're alone now. All on your own. So the only thing you can do is protect your own existence against Sun Stealer by growing. By letting the plague have its way with you.'

'No . . . please.'

'Did you kill Sajaki, Captain?'

'It was . . . such a long time ago . . .' But there was something in his voice which was not quite denial. Volyova delivered the needler rounds into the reefer. Watched the few remaining indices on its shell flicker and die, and then felt the chill fading, by the second, ice on the shell already beginning to glisten with its own warming.

'I'm going now,' she said. 'I just wanted to get to the truth. I suppose I should wish you good luck, Captain.'

And then she was running, afraid of what might be happening behind her.

Sajaki's suit stayed tantalisingly ahead of Sylveste as they commenced the descent into the funnel of the bridgehead. The half-submerged, inverted cone of the device had seemed tiny only minutes ago, but now it was all he could see, its steep grey sides blocking the horizon in all directions. Occasionally the bridgehead shuddered, and Sylveste was reminded that it was fighting a constant battle with the crustal defences of Cerberus, and that he should not count blindly on its protection. If it failed, he knew, it would be consumed in hours; the wound in the crust would close, and with it his escape route.

'It is necessary to replenish reaction mass,' the suit said.

'What?'

Sajaki spoke for the first time since they had left the ship. 'We used a lot of mass getting here, Dan. We need to top up before we enter hostile territory.'

'Where from?'

'Look around you. There's an awful lot of reaction mass waiting to be used.'

Of course; there was nothing to stop them drawing resources from the bridgehead itself. He agreed, doing nothing while Sajaki took control of his suit. One of the steep, incurving walls loomed nearer, dense with ornate extrusions and random clusters of machinery. The scale of the thing was overwhelming now; like a dam wall which curved round until its ends met. Somewhere in that wall, he thought, were the bodies of Alicia and her fellow mutineers . . .

There was enough sense of gravity to engender a strong sense of vertigo, not aided by the way the bridgehead narrowed below, which made it seem like an infinitely deep shaft. The best part of a kilometre away, the star-shaped speck of Sajaki's suit had made contact with the precipitous wall on the far side. A few moments later Sylveste touched a narrow ledge, one that jutted no more than a metre beyond the wall. His feet made soft contact and suddenly he was poised there, ready to topple back into the nothingness behind him.

'What do I have to do?'

'Nothing,' Sajaki said. 'Your suit knows exactly what to do. I suggest you start trusting it: it's all that's keeping you alive.'

'Is that meant to reassure me?'

'Do you think reassurance would be especially appropriate at this point? You're about to enter one of the most alien environments that any human has ever known. I think the last thing you need is reassurance.'

While Sylveste watched, a trunk extruded from the suit's chest until it made contact with a section of the bridgehead's wall material. A few seconds later it began to pulse, bulges squirming along its length, back into the suit.

'Vile,' Sylveste said.

'It's digesting heavy elements from the bridgehead,' Sajaki said. 'The bridgehead gives of itself freely, since it recognises the suit as being friendly.'

'What if we run out of power inside Cerberus?'

'You'll be dead long before running out of power becomes a problem to your suit. But it needs to replenish reaction mass for its thrusters. It has all the energy it needs, but it still requires atoms to accelerate.'

'I'm not sure I like that last bit; about being dead.'

'It isn't too late to return.'

Testing me, Sylveste thought. For a moment he considered it rationally, but only for a moment. He was scared, yes – more so than he could comfortably remember; even if he went back to Lascaille's Shroud. But, as then, he knew that the only way to punch through his fear was to push on. To confront whatever it was that led to that fear. But, when the refuelling process was complete, it took all the nerve in the world to step off the ledge and continue the descent into the emptiness enclosed by the bridgehead.

They sank lower, dropping for long seconds before checking their fall with brief squirts of thrust. Sajaki was beginning to allow Sylveste some voluntary control of his suit now; slowly decreasing the suit's autonomic dominance until Sylveste was controlling most of it himself; the transition was barely noticeable. They were descending now at a rate of thirty metres per second, but it seemed to quicken as the walls of the funnel came closer together. Now Sajaki was only a few hundred metres away, but the facelessness of his suit offered little sense of human presence, no sense of companionship. Sylveste still felt dreadfully alone. And with good reason, he thought – it was possible that no thinking creature had been this close to Cerberus since it was last visited by the Amarantin. What ghosts had festered here in the intervening thousand centuries?

'Approaching the final injection tube,' Sajaki said.

The conic walls constricted now to a diameter of only thirty metres, then plunged vertically into darkness, as far as the eye could see. His suit veered towards the midline of the approaching hole without his bidding; Sajaki's suit lagged slightly behind.

'I wouldn't deny you the honour of being first in,' said the Triumvir. 'You've waited for it long enough, after all.'

They were in the shaft. Sensing their arrival, the walls lit up with recessed red lights. The impression of vertical speed was huge now, and more than a little sickening; too much like being injected down a syringe. Sylveste remembered the time when Calvin had shown him the passage of an endoscope through one of his patients; the ancient surgical tool with a camera eye at one end of its coiled length. He remembered the headlong rush along an artery. He remembered the night flight to Cuvier after he had been arrested at the obelisk excavation, streaking through canyons towards his political nemesis. He wondered if there had ever been a time in his life when he was certain of what lay at the end of those rushing walls.

Then the shaft vanished and they were dropping through emptiness.

Volyova reached the hangar chamber, pausing at one of the observation windows to check that the shuttles really were accounted for, and that the data she had seen on her bracelet had not been manipulated by Sun Stealer. The plasma-winged transatmospheric ships were still there, clamped in their holding pens like rows of arrowheads in a fletcher's workshop. She could begin powering one of them now, via the bracelet, but that was too dangerous, too likely to draw Sun Stealer's attention and alert him to what she was planning. At the moment she was safe enough, since she had not entered a part of the ship where Sun Stealer's senses could penetrate. At least, she hoped not.

She could not simply stroll aboard any of the shuttles. The usual access routes would take her through parts of the ship she did not dare enter; places where servitors had free range and janitor-rats were in direct biochemical consort with Sun Stealer. She had only one weapon now: the needler. She had left Khouri with the slug-gun, and while she did not doubt her proficiency, there were limits to what could be achieved by mere skill and determination. Especially as the ship would by now have had time to synthesise armed drones.

So now she found her way to an airlock chamber; not one which led to outside space, but one which accessed the depressurised vault of the hangar. The chamber was knee-deep in effluent, and all its lighting and heating systems had failed. Good. No chance then of Sun Stealer being able to watch her remotely, or even know she was there. She opened a locker and was relieved to find that the lightweight suit it was meant to contain was still present, and that it had not been visibly damaged by exposure to ship-slime. It was less bulky than the kind of suit Sylveste would have taken; less intelligent too, with no servosystems or integral propulsion. Before donning the suit she recited a series of words – well rehearsed –

into her bracelet, and then arranged the bracelet to respond to vocal commands spoken into her communicator, rather than via its own acoustic sensors. Then she had to latch on a thruster backpack, taking a moment to stare intently at its controls, as if knowledge of how to use it would bubble up from her memory by sheer force of will. She decided that the basics would come back to her as soon as she required them, and carefully stowed the needler on the suit's external equipment belt. She exited without fuss, jetting into the hangar, using a small constant thrust level to prevent herself drifting down the chamber. No part of the ship was in freefall, since the ship itself was not orbiting Cerberus, but holding itself artificially fixed in space, a tiny drain on the power of its engines.

She selected the shuttle she would use; the spherical *Melancholia of Departure*. Off to one side of the chamber, she watched a pair of bottle-green servitors detach from their mooring points and sidle towards her. They were free-fliers; spheres sprouting claws and cutting equipment for performing repair work on the shuttles. Evidently she had passed into Sun Stealer's perceptual domain when she entered the hangar. Well, she couldn't help that, and she had not brought the needler along to assist as an incentive in delicate negotiations with non-sentient machines. She shot them, each requiring more than one needle-strike before she interrupted a critical system.

Hit, both machines began to drift down the hangar, bleeding smoke.

She thumbed the backpack controls, imploring it to push her faster. The *Melancholia* loomed larger now; she could already see the tiny warning signs and technical phrases dotted around its fuselage, although most of them were in obsolete languages.

From around the curve of the shuttle hove another drone. This one was larger, its ochre body an ellipsoid studded with folded manipulators and sensors.

It was pointing something at her.

Everything turned a bright, hurting green which made her want to tear her eyeballs from their sockets. The thing was swiping a laser at her. She cursed – her suit had opaqued in time, but she was now effectively blind.

'Sun Stealer,' she said, presuming that he could hear her. 'You are making a very grave mistake.'

'I don't think so.'

'You're getting good now,' she said. 'You were a little stiff when we spoke earlier. What's happened? Did you access the natural language translators?'

'The more time I spend amongst you, the better I know you.'

The suit was de-opaquing as she spoke. 'Better than you did with Nagorny, at least.'

'I did not intend to give him nightmares.' Sun Stealer's voice was still the same absence as before; like a whisper heard against the white-noise of static.

'No, I doubt that you did.' She clucked. 'You don't want to kill me, do you? The others, perhaps – but not me; not just yet. Not while the bridgehead might still need my expertise.'

'That time has passed,' Sun Stealer said. 'Sylveste has now entered Cerberus.'

Not good news; not good news at all – although, rationally, she had known for some hours that it was probably the case.

'Then there must be another reason,' she said. 'Another reason why you need the bridgehead to stay open. It can't be that you care about Sylveste making it back. But if the bridgehead fails, you wouldn't necessarily know that he had progressed any deeper into the structure. You need to know, don't you? You need to know how deeply he gets; whether he achieves whatever it is you have in mind for him.'

She took Sun Stealer's lack of response as a tacit acknowledgement that she was not far from the truth. Perhaps the alien had not yet learnt all the ways of subterfuge, arts which might be uniquely human and therefore new to him.

'Let me take the shuttle,' she said.

'A vessel of this configuration is too large to enter Cerberus, even if you intend to reach Sylveste.'

Did it honestly imagine she had not thought of that herself? For a moment she felt pity that Sun Stealer was so singularly ill-equipped to grasp the way the human mind functioned. On one level he worked well enough; when he could lay lures of fear or reward; lures which depended on the emotions. It was not that his logic was faulty, either – more that he had an overestimation of how important it was in human affairs: as if pointing out to Volyova the essentially suicidal nature of her intended mission was going to suddenly deter her; turn her willingly to his side. Oh, you poor, pitiful monster, she thought.

'I've got one word for you,' she said, moving towards the airlock, daring the drone to intercept her. And then she said that word, having already recited the preliminary incantations which were required before the word itself could have any effect. It was a word she had not really expected that she would ever have to use in this context. But it had been enough of a surprise that she had been forced to use it once already; almost as surprising as the fact that she remembered it at all. Volyova had decided that the time to rely on expectation was long gone.

That word was *Palsy*.

It had an interesting effect on the servitor. The machine did not try and obstruct her as she reached the airlock and helped herself into the *Melancholia*. Instead, it hovered aimlessly for a few seconds and then darted towards one wall, suddenly out of contact with the ship and now relying on its limited reservoir of independent behaviour-modes. Nothing had happened to the servitor itself, since execution of the Palsy command only affected ship systems. But one of the first systems to crash would have been the radio/optical command net serving all the drones. Only the autonomous drones would continue functioning unaffected – and those machines had never come under Sun Stealer's influence. Now the thousands of supervised drones all over the ship would be scurrying to access terminals where they could tap into the controlling system directly. Even the rats would feel confused, since the aerosols dispersing their biochemical instructions would be among the affected systems. Unshackled from relentless machine control, the rodents would begin to revert to an archetype more characteristic of their feral ancestors.

Volyova closed the airlock and was gratified to feel the shuttle warming to readiness as soon as it sensed her. She tugged herself along to the cabin, already aglow with navigation readouts, already reconfiguring itself to match the kind of interface she preferred: surfaces flowing liquidly towards a new ideal.

Now all she had to do was get out.

'Did you just feel that?' Khouri asked from the metal and plush opulence of the spider-room. 'The whole ship just shuddered, like an earth tremor.'

'You think it was Ilia?'

'She said we should cast loose when we got a signal. And she said it'd be obvious as hell. That was pretty obvious, wasn't it?'

She knew if she waited any longer she would begin to doubt the evidence of her own senses; start wondering if there really had been a shudder, and then it would be too late, because if Volyova had been clear about anything it was that when the signal came, Khouri had to move quickly. There would not be very much time, she said.

So she cast off.

She twisted two of the matched brass controls to their extremities; not as she had seen Volyova do, but in the simple hope that something so drastic, random, and quite possibly stupid must surely result in something as normally undesirable as the spider-room losing its purchase on the hull, which was now all that she wanted.

The spider-room fell away from the hull.

'In the next few seconds,' Khouri said, stomach squirming in the sudden transition to freefall, 'we either live or die. If that was the signal Ilia meant to give, it's safe to leave the hull. But if it wasn't, we're going to be in range of the ship's own weapons in a few seconds.'

Khouri watched the ship recede, slowly falling up and away, until she had to squint to avoid the glare of the Conjoiner engines; barely ticking over, yet still sun-bright. Somewhere in the spider-room there was a way to close the shutters on its windows, but that was one detail Khouri had not committed to memory.

'Why won't it shoot us immediately?'

'Too much risk of damaging itself. Ilia said those limits were hardwired – nothing Sun Stealer can do about it except live with them. Guess we're about coming up on the mark now.'

'What do you think it was, that signal?' It seemed that Pascale preferred to talk.

'A program,' Khouri said. 'Buried deep in the ship, where Sun Stealer would never find it. Wired up to thousands of circuit breaks all around the ship. When she ran it – if she ran it – it would have killed thousands of systems simultaneously. One big crunch. That was the shudder, I think.'

'And it takes out the weapons?'

'No . . . not exactly. Not if I remember what she told me. Some of the sensors, and maybe some of the targeting systems, but the gunnery isn't affected; I remember that much. But I think the rest of the ship is so screwed up it'll take Sun Stealer a while to put himself back together again; a while to coordinate himself and get his bearings. Then he can start shooting again.'

'But the weapons could be online any time soon?'

'That's why we have to hurry.'

'We seem to be still having a conversation. Does that mean . . . ?'

'I think so.' Khouri forced a manic grin. 'I think I interpreted the signal right, and I think we're safe – for the time being, at least.'

Pascale let out a loud sigh. 'What now?'

'We have to find Ilia.'

'It shouldn't be hard. She said there wasn't anything we'd have to do; just wait for that signal. Then she'd be right . . .' Khouri trailed off. She was looking back at the lighthugger, hanging over them like a levitating cathedral spire. And something was wrong with it.

Something was disturbing its symmetry.

Something was breaking out of it.

It had begun with the smallest of excisions; as a chick might force the tip of its mandible through the shell of its egg. White light, and then a series of explosions. Shards of disrupted hull mushroomed away, quickly seized by the hand of gravity, so that the veil of destruction was whipped away to reveal the underlying damage. It was a tiny hole punched through the hull. Tiny, but because the ship was so large, the hole must really have been the best part of a hundred metres across.

And now Volyova's shuttle burst through the aperture she had opened, loitering momentarily next to the great trunk of the ship before pirouetting and diving towards the spider-room.

THIRTY-FOUR

Cerberus/Hades Orbit, 2566

Khouri let Volyova do all the hard work of getting the spider-room safely ensconced in the *Melancholia*. The operation was trickier than it seemed; not because the body of the spider-room was too large to fit the available volume, but because the room's dangling legs refused to fold themselves neatly away, inhibiting closure of the cargo doors. In the end – and it could not have been more than a minute or so after the operation had commenced – Volyova had to send out a squad of servitors to wrestle the legs into position. To an external observer – not that there was one, of course, except the brooding, semi-paralysed mass of the lighthugger – the procedure must have resembled a team of pixies trying to cram an insect into a jewel-box.

Finally, Volyova was able to close the doors, blocking out the last narrowing rectangle of twisting starfield from view. Interior lights came on, followed by the rapid, loudening howl of pressurisation, transmitted through the spider-room's metallic hull. The servitors reappeared, quickly clamping the room against drift, and then, not more than a minute later, Volyova showed up, unsuited.

'Follow me,' she shouted, her voice ringing. 'The sooner we're out of weapons range the better.'

'How far, exactly, is weapons range?' Khouri said.

'I'm not sure.'

'You hit him with your program,' Khouri said, as the three of them pulled themselves hand-over-hand up to the shuttle's cabin. 'Good work, Ilia. We felt it out there – one mother of a shutdown.'

'I think it hurt him,' she said. 'After my experience with the cache-weapon, I put Palsy back into place with a few additional interrupts. This time the paralysis would have reached much more than skin-deep. But I wish I'd installed destructive devices around the Conjoiner drives. Then we could torch the ship and run.'

'Wouldn't that make it a bit difficult to get home?'

'Very probably. But it would certainly put an end to Sun Stealer.' As an afterthought she added, 'More than that, too. Without the ship, the bridgehead would begin to fail, since there would be no more updates from the warchive. We'd have won.'

'Is that the most optimistic outcome you can think of?'

Volyova didn't answer.

They had reached the flightdeck, which Khouri saw was as gratifyingly modern as any she had seen: all white and sterile, like a dentist's operating room.

'Listen,' Volyova said, looking at Pascale. 'I don't know how much of this has sunk in yet, but if the bridgehead should fail now – which is what we want – it wouldn't necessarily be good for your husband.'

'Assuming he's reached it yet.'

'Oh, I think we can assume that.'

'On the other hand,' Khouri said, 'if he's already inside, having it fail now wouldn't change anything, except to prevent us reaching him.' She paused, added, 'That is what we're planning, isn't it? I mean, we have to at least try.'

'Somebody has to,' Volyova said, already buckling herself into one of the control chairs, reaching across to interface her fingers with the archaic touch-sensitive control board she affected. 'Now, I strongly suggest you find yourselves somewhere to sit. We're about to put a lot of space between ourselves and the lighthugger, in not a great deal of time.'

She had barely finished speaking when the engines came online, howling to readiness, and the previously indeterminately defined walls and floors and ceilings suddenly assumed very concrete reality.

When the shaft vanished and they were dropping through emptiness, the sense of vertical speed suddenly ceasing was so great that Sylveste felt his body tense in expectation of imaginary stress. But it was illusion: they were still falling, faster now than ever, but the points of reference were so much more distant that there was little impression of motion.

He was inside Cerberus.

'Well,' Calvin said, speaking for what seemed like the first time in days, 'is this all you expected?'

'This is nothing,' Sylveste said. 'Just a prelude.'

But it was still the strangest artificial structure he had ever seen; the oddest place in which he had ever been confined. The crust curved over him: a world-englobing roof pierced by the narrow end of the bridgehead. The place was aglow with its own wan luminescence, seemingly generated by the immense snakes which lay in coiled complexity across what he now thought of as the floor. The huge tree-trunk buttresses reached all the way to the ceiling, gnarled and organic. Now that the view was an improvement on that gained from the robotic probes, he could see that the buttresses looked more as if they had grown out of the ceiling into the floor than the other way around. Their roots blended into the floor. The firmament looked less alive; more crystalline. In a flash of insight he saw that the floor was older than the ceiling; that the ceiling had been constructed around the world after the floor was already finished. It was almost as if they stemmed from different phases of Amarantin science.

'Check your fall,' Sajaki said. 'We don't want to hit the floor too quickly. Nor do we want to stray into some defence system which the bridgehead hasn't neutralised.'

'You think there might still be hostile elements?'

'Perhaps not on this level,' the Triumvir said. 'But lower – I believe we can count on it. Such defences may not however have seen much use in the last million years, so they may be rather . . .' He seemed to have to search for the word. 'Rusty.'

'On the other hand, maybe we shouldn't count on that either.'

'No, perhaps not.'

Suit thrust increased, and with it the feeling of gravity. Only a quarter of a gee, yet the vaulted ceiling was still an artefact of terrifying size. There was a kilometre of it between him and open space; a kilometre he would have to get through again if he ever wanted to leave. Of course, there were another thousand kilometres of planet below his feet, but he had no idea how far into those depths he would have to tunnel before he found what he was looking for. He hoped it would not be far: the nominal five days he had allotted himself for the journey and return now seemed to be cutting it dangerously close to the mark. Seen from outside, it was easy to accept Volyova's equations of gain and loss and believe that they had some connection to reality. Here, when the forces represented by her equations had crystallised into vast and threatening structures, he had much less confidence in their predictive power.

'You're shit-scared, aren't you?' Calvin said.

'You can read my emotions now, is that it?'

'No. It's just that your emotions ought to mirror mine. We think very similarly, you and I. More so than ever now.' Calvin paused. 'And I don't mind admitting – I'm very, very scared. Probably more scared than a piece of software has any right to feel. Isn't that profound, Dan?'

'Save your profundities for later – I'm sure you'll get the opportunity.'

'I imagine you feel insignificant,' Sajaki said, almost as if he had been listening in on the conversation. 'Well; you're justified in feeling that way. You are insignificant. That's the majesty of this place. Would you choose it any other way?'

The ground was rushing towards him, strewn with geometric rubble. The suit's proximity alarm began to chime, indicating the nearness of the floor. Less than a kilometre now, though it looked close enough to touch. He felt the suit begin to adjust itself around him, remoulding itself for surface operation. One hundred metres. They were descending towards a flattish crystal slab: presumably some chunk of the ceiling which had fallen all this way. It was the size of a small ballroom. He could see the blinding glare of his suit thrusters in its marbled surface.

'Cut your thrust five seconds before impact,' Sajaki said. 'We don't want the heat to trigger a defensive reaction.'

'No,' Sylveste said. 'That's the last thing we want.'

He assumed the suit would protect him from the fall, though it took an effort of will to follow Sajaki's instructions, slipping into freefall five seconds before his feet were due to touch the crystal. The suit bulged slightly, projecting cushioning armour plates. The density of the gel-air rose and for a moment he almost blacked out. But when the impact came, it was almost too gentle to register.

He blinked, and realised he had fallen on his back. Great, he thought – very dignified. Then the suit righted itself and popped him back on his feet.

He was standing in Cerberus.

THIRTY-FIVE

Cerberus, Interior, 2567

'How long now?'

'We've been out a day.' Sajaki's voice sounded thin and distant, though his suit was only a few tens of metres away from Sylveste. 'We still have plenty of time; don't worry.'

'I believe you,' Sylveste said. 'At least, part of me does. The other part isn't so sure.'

'That other part might be me,' Calvin said quietly. 'And no, I don't believe we still have plenty of time. We might do, but I don't think we should count on it. Not when we know so little.'

'If that's meant to inspire confidence . . .'

'No, it wasn't.'

'Then shut up until you've got something constructive to say.'

They were kilometres into the second layer of Cerberus now; good progress by some yardsticks, since they had descended more vertical distance now than the tallest mountains on Earth – but it was still too slow. At this rate they would never make it back in time, if they even succeeded in reaching whatever destination they were striving towards. Before then, the bridgehead would surely have given in to the tireless expulsive energies being directed against it by the crustal defences, and it would be digested or spat away into space like an unwanted pip.

The second layer – the bedrock on which the snakes writhed, and into which the roof-supporting trees thrust their roots – had a crystalline topography, markedly different to the kind of quasi-organic look of the overlying structures. They had been forced to thread their way downwards in the narrow interstices between the densely packed crystal forms, like ants navigating between courses of brickwork. It was slow work, and it quickly depleted the suits' reaction reservoirs, since all the downward movement had to be constantly checked by thrust. At first Sylveste had suggested that they use the monofilament grapples which the suits could deploy (or grow, or extrude; he did not bother himself with the details), but Sajaki had argued him out of it: it would have conserved reaction mass, but it would also have greatly delayed their descent, since hundreds of kilometres still lay below them. Apart from that, it would also have limited them to strictly vertical motion, which would have made them easy targets for hypothetical counter-insurgent systems. So they flew most of the time, stopping when necessary to ablate small quantities of Cerberus material. So far, Cerberus had not objected to their vampiric activities, and the crystals contained enough heavy trace-elements to feed the thruster reservoirs.

'It's as if it doesn't know we're here,' Sylveste said.

Calvin answered him. 'Maybe it doesn't. Not much can have reached this far down in living memory. The systems designed to detect intruders and defend against them might have atrophied through disuse – assuming they ever existed in the first place.'

'Why do I have the impression you're suddenly trying to cheer me up?'

'I suppose I have your best interests at heart.' He imagined Calvin smiling, though there was no visual component to the simulation. 'In any case, I believe what I just said. I think the deeper we go, the less likelihood we'll have of being recognised as something unwanted. It's like the human body – the greatest density of pain receptors lies in the skin.'

Sylveste remembered a stomach cramp he had once experienced through drinking too much cold water during a surface hike out from Chasm City, and wondered if there was even a glint of truth in what Calvin had just said to him. It was reassuring though; of that there was no doubt. But did it also mean that everything deeper would be half-sleeping; as if the mighty defences of the crust were now meaningless, because what lay below no longer worked as the Amarantin had intended? Was Cerberus a treasure chest which, though firmly locked and burnished to a high polish, contained nothing but rusting junk – if that?

There was no sense thinking that way. If any of this meant anything, if the last fifty years of his life (and perhaps even more than that) had been anything other than delusional obsession, there had to be something worth finding. The feeling was nothing he could articulate, but he was more sure of it than he had ever before been sure of anything.

Another day of descent passed; during intervals Sylveste slept, being awakened by his suit only when something notable occurred, or the external scene changed beyond some inbuilt tolerance and the suit decided that he had better be awake to witness it. If Sajaki slept Sylveste was unaware of it, but he ascribed this to the generally odd physiology of the man; his blood thickened by medichines, constantly cleansing; his Juggler-configured mind able to do without the auditing hours of normal sleep. When the going was easiest, they descended at a maximum rate of one kilometre a minute, which usually happened when some deep abyssal shaft hove into view. The return would be quicker, of course, since the suits would know the way they had come, barring changes in the structure of Cerberus itself. Now it was not uncommon for them to descend for several kilometres before hitting a dead end, or a shaft too narrow for safety, at which point they would retreat to the last branch point and attempt another route. It was pure trial and error, since the suit sensors could not see more than a few hundred metres ahead at any point, blocked by the massive solidity of the crystal elements. But, kilometre by kilometre, they made slow progress, bathed always in sickly turquoise-green light spilling from the crystals.

Gradually the character of the formations had been altering; there were shards here many kilometres across, impassive and immobile as glaciers. All the crystals were attached to one another, but the vaultlike spaces and vertiginous rifts between them gave the impression that they were floating freely, as if in mute denial of the world's gravitational field. What were they, Sylveste wondered? Dead matter – literally, crystalline – or something stranger? Were they components; parts of some world-englobing mechanism which was too large to be glimpsed or even imagined? If they were machines, they must have been exploiting some hazy state of quantum reality, where concepts like heat and energy dissolved into uncertainty. Certainly, they were as cold as ice (the suit's thermal sensors told him this), and yet beneath their translucent faces he sometimes sensed tremendous subliminal motion, like the ticking guts of a clock glimpsed through a veil of lucite. But when he asked the suit to investigate with its senses, the results it sent back were too ambiguous to be much help.

After forty hours of rambling descent they made a significant and helpful discovery. The crystal matrix thinned out in a transitional zone only a kilometre deep, exposing shafts wider and deeper than any they had yet encountered; more deliberate in design. They were two kilometres in width, and each of the ten shafts they examined fell towards convergent nothingness for two hundred vertical kilometres. The walls of the shafts emitted the same slightly nauseating green radiance as the crystal elements, and they shivered with the same underlying sense of pent-up motion, suggesting that they were parts of the same mechanisms, though fulfilling some very different function. Sylveste remembered what he knew about the great pyramids in Egypt; how they were riddled with shafts which had been dictated by the construction technique; escape routes for the workers who sealed the tombs within. Perhaps something similar applied here, or perhaps the shafts had once served to radiate the heat of engines now quietened.

Discovering them was a godsend, since it enormously quickened their rate of descent, but that gift was not without its hazards. Constrained by the linear walls of the shaft, there would be nowhere to seek refuge if an attack came, and only two possible directions of escape. Yet if they delayed further, they would face imprisonment in Cerberus when the bridgehead collapsed; no more palatable a fate. So they risked using the shafts.

They could not simply fall. That had been possible before, when the vertical distance was no more than a kilometre or so, but here the very size of the shafts brought unanticipated problems. They found themselves drifting mysteriously towards the walls, and had to keep applying bursts of corrective thrust to stop themselves being dashed against the rushing precipice of sickly jade. It was Coriolis force, of course: the same fictitious force which curved wind vectors into cyclones on the surface of a rotating planet. Here, Coriolis force objected to a strictly linear descent, since Cerberus was rotating, and Sylveste and Sajaki had to shed excess angular momentum with each movement closer to the core. Yet compared to their earlier slow progress, it was gratifyingly rapid.

They had fallen a hundred kilometres when the attack began.

'It's moving,' Volyova said.

Ten hours had passed since leaving the lighthugger. She was

exhausted, despite having catnapped for odd hours, knowing that she would need the energy soon. But it had not really helped; she needed more than little intermissions of unconsciousness to begin to heal all the physiological and mental stress of recent days. Now, though, she was fully awake, as if at the limits of fatigue her body had grudgingly accessed some stagnant pool of reserve energy. Doubtless it would not last, and there would be an even heavier premium to pay when she had exhausted this stop-gap – but for now she was glad of the alertness, however transitory.

'What's moving?' Khouri asked.

Volyova nodded at the shuttle's glaringly white console, at the readout windows she had called into being across its horseshoe profile.

'What else but the damned ship?'

Pascale yawned awake. 'What's up?'

'What's up is we have trouble,' Volyova said, fingers dancing on the keyboard to call up other readouts, though she did not really need confirmation of this. Bad news carried its own certification. 'The lighthugger is on the move again. This means two things, neither of them good. Sun Stealer must have reinstated the major systems I disabled with Palsy.'

'Well, ten hours wasn't bad – at least it allowed us to get this far.' Pascale nodded at the nearest positional display, which showed the shuttle more than one third of the distance to Cerberus.

'What else?' Khouri asked.

'What it implies, which is that Sun Stealer must now have gained enough experience to manipulate the drive. Previously it was something he was only cautiously investigating, in case he harmed the ship.'

'Meaning what?'

Volyova indicated the same positional readout. 'Let's assume he now has total control of the drive and knows the tolerances. The ship's current vector puts it on an intercept trajectory with us. Sun Stealer's trying to reach us before we reach Dan, or even the bridgehead. We're too small a target at this range – beam weapons would disperse too much to hit us, and we could outmanoeuvre all the sub-relativistic projectiles just by executing a random flight path – but it won't be long before we're within kill-range.'

'Just how long is that?' Pascale frowned. It was not, Volyova thought, the woman's most endearing habit, but she endured it expressionlessly. 'Don't we already have a massive head-start?'

'We do, but now there's nothing to stop Sun Stealer ramping the lighthugger's thrust all the way up to multiple tens of gees – accelerations we simply can't match without pulping ourselves in the process. But that's not a problem for him. There's nothing left alive aboard that ship which doesn't run around on four legs and squeak and make a mess when you shoot it.'

'And maybe the Captain,' Khouri said. 'Except I don't think he'll be much of a consideration.'

'I asked how long,' Pascale said.

'If we're lucky, we might just reach Cerberus,' Volyova said. 'But it wouldn't give us much time to scout around and have second thoughts. We'd have to get inside just to avoid the ship's weapons. And even then we'd have to get pretty deep inside.' She dredged a clucking laugh from somewhere inside herself. 'Maybe your husband had the right idea all along. He might be in a much safer position than any of us. For the time being at least.'

Patterns resolved in the walls of the shaft, areas of crystal beginning to glow a little more intently than the rest. The patterns were so vast that Sylveste did not immediately recognise them for what they were: vast Amarantin graphicforms. It was not simply their size, in fact, but also the fact that they were rendered differently from any he had seen before; almost another language entirely. In an intuitive flash he realised that he was seeing the language used by the Banished; the flock which had followed Sun Stealer into exile, and eventually to the stars. Tens of thousands of years spaced this writing from any example he had ever seen, which made it even more of a miracle that he was able to tease any sense out of it at all.

'What are they telling us?' Calvin asked.

'That we're not welcome,' Sylveste said, half astonished that the graphicforms spoke to him. 'To put it mildly.'

Sajaki must have picked up his subvocalisation. 'What, exactly?'

'They're saying that they made this level,' Sylveste said. 'That they manufactured it.'

'I guess,' Calvin said, 'that you've finally been vindicated – this place really was the handiwork of the Amarantin.'

'In any other circumstances this would call for a drink,' Sylveste

515

said, but he was only paying half attention to the conversation now; fascinated by what he was reading; by the thoughts which were springing into his mind. More than once he had felt this feeling when deep into the process of translating Amarantin script, but never before with this fluency, or this sense of total certainty. It was enthralling, and not a little terrifying.

'Please go on,' Sajaki said.

'Well, it's what I said: a warning. It's saying we shouldn't progress any further.'

'That probably means we're not far from what we came for.'

Sylveste had that feeling as well, though he could not justify it. 'The warning says there's something below we shouldn't see,' he said.

'See? Is that what it says, literally?'

'Amarantin thought is very visual, Sajaki. Whatever it is, they don't want us anywhere near it.'

'Which suggests that whatever it is has value – don't you agree?'

'What if it really is a warning?' Calvin said. 'I don't mean a threat; I mean a genuine heart-felt plea to keep away. Can you tell from the context if that's the case?'

'If it was conventional Amarantin script, perhaps.' What Sylveste did not add was that he felt that the message was exactly what Calvin had implied, though there was no way he could rationalise that feeling. It did not deter him, though. Instead, he found himself wondering just what could have driven the Amarantin to this; what was so bad that it had to be encased in a facsimile of a world and defended by the most awesome weapons known to a civilisation? What was so unspeakable that it could not simply be destroyed? What kind of monster had they created?

Or found?

The thought jarred home, seeming to find a vacant hole in his mind where it fitted precisely. As if it belonged there. *They found something; Sun Stealer's flock. Far out on the edge of the system, they found something.*

He was still trying to deal with the certainty of that feeling when the closest of the graphicforms detached from the shaft, leaving a hollow recess where it had been a second earlier. Others followed; whole words, clauses and sentences unpeeled from the shaft and loomed around him, vast as buildings, circling Sajaki and Sylveste with raptorial patience. They floated free, suspended by some unguessable mechanism invisible to the suit defences; no gravitational or magnetic fluctuation. For a moment Sylveste was stunned at the sheer alienness behind the objects, but then he grasped that there was a kind of indisputable logic at play here. What made more sense than a warning message which, when transgressed, enforced itself?

But suddenly there was no time for detached consideration.

'Suit defences to automatic,' Sajaki said, voice rising an octave only above his routine implacable calm. 'I believe these things seek to crush us to death.'

As if he really needed telling.

The floating words had them spherically corralled now, and had commenced a ponderous spiralling-in. Sylveste let his suit do its thing, visual shields snicking down to guard against the retina-melting glare of plasma-bursts, all manual control modes temporarily suspended. It was for the best: the last thing his suit needed was a human being trying to do the job better than it could. Even with the dense shielding in place, Sylveste's vision was aflame with fireworks, photon events triggering his circuits, and he knew that there must have been fryingly intense multi-spectrum radiation just beyond the skin of his suit. He registered bucking surges of motion; episodes of up/down thrust (he assumed) so intense that he passed in and out of consciousness like a train threading a series of short mountain tunnels. He assumed that his suit was trying to cut and run, and with each crushing deceleration was being thwarted.

Finally he blacked out long and hard.

Volyova ramped up the *Melancholia*'s thrust, until it was nudging four gees of steady acceleration, with intermittent random-swerves programmed in for extra effect, in case the lighthugger launched any kinetics. It was the most they could withstand without protective suits or tabards; more than was comfortable, especially for Pascale, who was even less accustomed to this sort of thing than Khouri. It meant they could not leave their seats, and that movement of their arms had to be restricted to a minimum. But they could speak, after a fashion, and even hold something approximating a coherent discussion.

'You spoke to him, didn't you?' Khouri said. 'Sun Stealer. I could tell by the look on your face when you rescued us from the rats in the infirmary. I'm right, aren't I?'

Volyova's voice sounded slightly choked, as if she were in the process of slow strangulation.

'If I had any doubts about your story, they vanished the instant I looked into his face. There was never any question that I was confronting something alien. And I began to understand some of what Boris Nagorny must have gone through.'

'What drove him mad, you mean.'

'Believe me, I think I'd have suffered something similar if I'd had that in my head. What worries me, too, is that some of Boris might have corrupted Sun Stealer.'

'Then how do you think I feel?' Khouri asked. 'I have got that thing in my head.'

'No, you haven't.'

Volyova was shaking her head now, a gesture which verged on the reckless in the four-gee field. 'You had him in your head for a while, Khouri – just long enough for him to crush what remained of the Mademoiselle. But then he got out.'

'Got out when?'

'When Sajaki trawled you. It was my fault, I suppose. I should not have allowed him even to switch on the trawl.' For someone admitting guilt she sounded remarkably devoid of repentance. Perhaps for Volyova the act of admission was enough in itself. 'When your neural patterns were scanned, Sun Stealer embedded himself in them and reached the trawl, encoded in the data. From there it was only a short hop to every other system in the ship.'

They absorbed that in silence, until Khouri said, 'Letting Sajaki do that wasn't your smartest ever move, Ilia.'

'No,' she said, as if the thought had only just struck her. 'I don't think it was.'

When he came round – it might have been tens of seconds later, or tens of minutes – the visual shields had retracted and he was falling unimpeded down the shaft. He looked up, and though it was now kilometres overhead, he saw the residual glow of their skirmish, the shaft walls pocked and scarred by energy impacts. Some of the words were still circling, but parts of them had been chipped off so that they no longer made much sense. As if in recognition that their warning was now hopelessly corrupted, the words seemed to have given up being weapons. Even as he watched, they were returning to their hollows, like sullen rooks returning to the rookery.

But something was wrong.

Where was Sajaki?

'What the hell happened?' he asked, hoping that his suit would interpret the query successfully. 'Where's he gone?'

'There was an engagement against an autonomous defence system,' the suit informed him, as if commenting on the weather earlier that morning.

'Thank you, I realised that, but where's Sajaki?'

'His suit sustained critical damage during the evasive action. Crypted telemetry squirts indicate extensive and possibly irreparable damage to both primary and secondary thrust units.'

'I said where is he?'

'His suit would not have been able to restrict his rate of fall or counteract Coriolis drift towards the wall. Telemetry bursts indicate he is fifteen kilometres below and still falling, with a blueshift relative to your position of one point one kilometres a second and climbing.'

'Still falling?'

'It is likely that, owing to the non-functionality of his thruster units, and the inability to deploy a monofilament braking line at his current speed, he will fall until further descent is inhibited by the termination of the shaft.'

'You mean he's going to die?'

'At his predicted terminal velocity, survival is excluded in all models except as an extreme statistical outlier.'

'One chance in a million,' Calvin said.

Sylveste angled himself so that he was able to peer vertically down the shaft. Fifteen kilometres – more than seven times the shaft's echoless width. He looked and looked, all the while falling himself . . . and thought that perhaps he saw a flash, once or twice, at the extreme limit of his vision. He wondered if the flash had been the spark of friction, as Sajaki brushed against the walls in his unstoppable descent. If he had seen it at all, it was fainter each time, and soon he stopped seeing anything except the uninterrupted walls of the shaft.

THIRTY-SIX

Cerberus/Hades Orbit, 2567

'You learnt something,' Pascale said. 'Sun Stealer told you something. That's why you've been so desperate to stop him ever since.'

She was addressing Volyova, who had begun to feel slightly less vulnerable once the shuttle had passed turnover, midway between Cerberus and the point where she had increased the thrust to four gees. Now, with the drive flame pointing away from the pursuing lighthugger, they would make a far less conspicuous target. The downside of this, of course, was that the drive flame was now wafting towards Cerberus, and might be interpreted as a sign of hostility by the planet itself, if it had not already got the message that its recent human visitors did not necessarily have its best interests at heart.

But there was nothing any of them could do about that.

The lighthugger was sustaining a comfortable six gees now; enough to steadily whittle the distance down, bringing it within kill-range of the shuttle in five hours. Sun Stealer could have pushed the ship faster, which suggested to her that he was still cautiously exploring the limits of the drive. It was not, she thought, that he particularly cared about his own survival, but if the lighthugger was destroyed, the bridgehead would quickly follow. And although Sylveste was now inside, perhaps the alien needed to know that the objective had been achieved, which presumably required the prolonged opening of the crustal breach, so that some signal could return to outside space. She did not believe for one instant that Sylveste's safe return had any place in Sun Stealer's plans.

'Was it what the Mademoiselle showed me?' Khouri asked. After hours of sustained gee-load, her voice sounded like someone after a heavy drinking session. 'The thing I could never get quite right in my head – was it that?'

'I don't think we'll ever know for sure,' Volyova said. 'All I know is what he showed me. I believe it was the truth – but I doubt that we'll ever know for sure.'

'You could start by telling me what it was,' Pascale said. 'Seeing as I'm the one among us who definitely doesn't know. Then you can fight over the details between yourselves.'

The console chimed, as it had done once or twice in the last few hours, signifying that a radar beam had just swept across them from aft, directed from the lighthugger. For the moment, it was not especially valuable data, since light-travel delay between the ship and the shuttle was still in the order of seconds, long enough for the shuttle to displace itself from its radar-tagged position with a burst of lateral thrust. But it was unnerving, since it confirmed that the lighthugger was indeed chasing them, and that it was indeed attempting to get a sufficiently accurate positional fix to justify opening fire. It would be hours before that situation came to pass, but the machine's intent was grimly obvious.

'I'll start with what I know,' Volyova said, drawing in a generous inhalation of breath. 'Once, the galaxy was a lot more populous than it is now. Millions of cultures, though only a handful of big players. In fact, just the way all the predictive models say the galaxy ought to be today, based on the occurrence rates of G-type stars and terrestrial planets in the right orbits for liquid water.' She was digressing, but Pascale and Khouri decided not to fight it. 'That's always been a major paradox, you know. On paper, life looks a lot commoner than we find it to be. Theories for the developmental timescales for tool-using intelligence are a lot harder to quantify, but they suffer from much the same problem. They predict too many cultures.'

'Hence the Fermi paradox,' Pascale said.

'The what?' asked Khouri.

'The old dichotomy between the relative ease of interstellar flight, especially for robotic envoys – and the complete absence of any such envoys turning up from non-human cultures. The only logical conclusion was that no one else was around to send them, anywhere in the galaxy.'

'But the galaxy's a big place,' Khouri said. 'Couldn't there be cultures elsewhere, except that we just don't know about them yet?'

'Doesn't work,' Volyova said emphatically, Pascale nodding in agreement. 'The galaxy's big, but not that big – and it's also very old. Once a single culture decided to send out probes, everyone else in the galaxy would know about it within a few million years. And the galaxy happens to be several thousand times older than that. Granted, several generations of stars had to live and die before there were enough heavy elements to sustain life, but even if machine-building cultures only arise once every million years or so, they've had thousands of opportunities to dominate the entire galaxy.'

'To which there have always been two answers,' Pascale said. 'Firstly, that they are here, but we just haven't ever noticed them. Maybe that was conceivable a few hundred years ago, but no one takes it seriously now; not when every square inch of every asteroid belt in about a hundred systems has been mapped.'

'Then maybe they never existed in the first place?'

Pascale nodded at Khouri. 'Which was perfectly tenable until we knew more about the galaxy, which begins to look suspiciously accommodating of life, at least in the essentials; what Volyova just said – the right types of stars, and the right kind of planets in the right places. And the biological models were still arguing for a higher occurrence rate, right on up to intelligent cultures.'

'So the models were wrong,' Khouri said.

'Except they probably weren't.' Volyova was speaking now. 'Once we got into space, once we left the First System, we began to find dead cultures all over the place. None had survived until much more recently than a million years ago, and some had gone out a lot earlier than that. But they all pointed to one thing. The galaxy had been a lot more fecund in the past. So why not now? Why was it suddenly so lonely?'

'The war,' Khouri said, and for a moment no one spoke. The silence was only interrupted when Volyova began speaking, softly and reverently, as if they were discussing something sacred.

'Yes,' she said. 'The Dawn War – that was what they called it, wasn't it?'

'I remembered that much.'

'When was this?' Pascale asked, and for a moment Volyova sympathised with her, caught between two who had been vouch-safed glimpses of something extraordinary, and who were less interested in adumbrating the whole of it than in exploring each other's ignorances, shoring up each other's doubts and misconceptions. But Pascale knew none of it; not yet.

'It was a billion years ago,' Khouri said, and for a moment Volyova let her speak without interruption. 'And it sucked up all those cultures and spat them out in shapes and forms a lot different to the ones they'd had when they went in. I don't think we can really understand what it was about, or who or what exactly survived it – except that they were more like machines than living creatures, although as far beyond anything we can envisage as our machines are beyond stone tools. But they had a name, or they were given it – I don't really remember the details. But I do remember the name.'

'The Inhibitors,' Volyova said.

Khouri nodded. 'And they deserved it.'

'Why?'

'It was what they did afterwards,' Khouri said. 'Not during the war, but in its aftermath. It was like they subscribed to a creed; a rule of discipline. Intelligent, organic life had given rise to the Dawn War. What they were now was something different; post-intelligent, I guess. Anyway, it made what they did a lot easier.'

'Which was?'

'Inhibition. Literally: they inhibited the rise of intelligent cultures around the galaxy, so that nothing like the Dawn War could ever happen again.'

Volyova took over now. 'It wasn't just a case of annihilating any extant cultures which might have survived war. They also set about disturbing the conditions which could lead to intelligent life ever arising again. Not stellar engineering – I think that would have been too great an interference; too much an act which contradicted their own strictures – but inhibition on a lesser scale. They could have done it without tampering in the evolution of a single star, except in extreme cases – by altering cometary orbits, for instance, so that episodes of planetary bombardment lasted much longer than the norm. Life probably would have found niches in which to survive – deep underground, or around hydrothermal vents – but it would never have become very complex. Certainly nothing which would threaten the Inhibitors.'

'You said this was a billion years ago,' Pascale said. 'And yet we've come all that way since then – from single-celled creatures right up to *Homo sapiens*. Are you saying we slipped through the net?'

'Exactly that,' Volyova said. 'Because the net was falling apart.'

Khouri nodded. 'The Inhibitors seeded the galaxy with machines, designed to detect the emergence of life and then suppress it. For a long time it looked like they worked as planned – that's why the galaxy isn't teeming today, although all the preconditions look favourable.' She shook her head. 'I sound like I actually know this stuff.'

'Maybe you do,' Pascale said. 'In any case, I want to hear what you have to say. All of it.'

'All right, all right.' Khouri fidgeted in her acceleration couch, doubtless trying to do what Volyova had been doing for the last hour: avoiding putting pressure on the bruises she had already gained. 'Their machines worked fine for a few hundred million years,' she said. 'But then stuff started to go wrong. They started failing; not working as efficiently as intended. Intelligent cultures began to emerge which would have previously been suppressed at birth.'

There was a look on Pascale's face which showed that she had just made a connection. 'Like the Amarantin . . .'

'Just like the Amarantin. They weren't the only culture to slip through the net, but they did happen to lie close to us in the galaxy, which is why what happened to them has had such an . . . impact on us.' Volyova was doing the talking now. 'Maybe there should have been an Inhibition device keeping a close watch on Resurgam, but that one either never existed or stopped working long before they emerged to intelligence. So they ascended to civilisation, and later budded off a starfaring sub-species – all without attracting the attention of the Inhibitors.'

'Sun Stealer.'

'Yes. He took the Banished with him into space – changed them biologically and mentally, until they had little but their ancestry and language in common with the Amarantin who had stayed at home. And of course they explored, reaching out into their solar system, and later to its periphery.'

'Where they found . . .' Pascale nodded at the image of Hades and Cerberus. 'This. Is that what you're saying?'

Khouri nodded in agreement, and then began to explain the rest; what little there was to relate.

*

Sylveste fell and fell, and in his falling he hardly bothered to note the passing of time. Finally there came a point where more than two hundred kilometres of the shaft reached above his head; barely a few kilometres lay below his feet. Twinkling lights shone below, arranged into constellation-like patterns, and for an instant he entertained the idea that he had travelled much further than seemed possible, and these lights were actually stars, and that he was on the point of leaving Cerberus completely. But the thought died as soon as it had come to mind. There was something just a little too regular about the way the lights were aligned, just a little too purposeful; a little too pregnant with intelligent design.

He dropped out of the shaft into emptiness as, much earlier, he had passed out of the bridgehead. As then, he found himself falling through a tremendous unoccupied volume, but this chamber seemed very much larger than the one immediately below the crust. No gnarled tree-trunks rose up from a crystal floor to support the ceiling over his head, and he doubted that any lay beyond the immediate curvature of the horizon. Yet there was a floor below him, and it must have been that the ceiling was unsupported, thrown around the entire volume of the world-within-a-world below, suspended only by the preposterous counter-balancing of its own gravitational infall, or something beyond Sylveste's imagination. Whatever; he was dropping now towards the starred floor tens of kilometres below.

It was not difficult, finding Sajaki's suit; not once Sylveste had begun that lonely descent. His own still-functioning suit did all that was required, locking onto the signature of its fallen companion (something of which must therefore have survived) and then directing Sylveste's fall towards it, bringing him down only tens of metres from the spot where Sajaki had fallen. The Triumvir had hit fast; that much was obvious. But then there were few other options if one had to accept an uncontrolled fall from two hundred kilometres up. He appeared to have partially buried himself in the metallic floor, before undergoing a bounce which had resulted in his final resting position being face down.

Sylveste had not been expecting to find Sajaki alive, but the mangled contours of his suit were still shocking; rather as if it were a china doll which had been subjected to some terrible temper tantrum by a malevolent child. The suit was gashed and scarred and discoloured, damage which had probably happened during the battle and Sajaki's subsequent grazing fall, as the Coriolis force knocked him repeatedly against the shaft walls.

Sylveste moved him onto his back, using his own suit's amplification to ease the process. He knew that what he would be confronted with would not be pleasant, but that it was nonetheless something he had to endure so he could press on; the closing of a mental chapter. He had seldom felt anything but antipathy towards Sajaki, alleviated by a forced respect for the man's cleverness and the sheer bloody-minded stubbornness with which he had sought Sylveste across all the decades. It was nothing remotely resembling friendship; merely the craftsmanlike appreciation for a piece of equipment which did its job exceptionally well. That was Sajaki, Sylveste thought: a well-honed tool; shaped admirably towards one end and one end only.

The suit's faceplate was riven by a thumb-wide crack. Something drew Sylveste forward, kneeling until his own head was next to that of the dead Triumvir.

'I'm sorry it had to end like this,' he said. 'I can't say we were ever friends, Yuuji – but I suppose in the end I wanted you to see what lay ahead as much as I did. I think you'd have appreciated it.'

And then he saw that the suit was empty; that all it had ever been was a shell.

This was what Khouri knew.

The Banished had reached the edge of the solar system, thousands of years after their exile from mainstream Amarantin culture. It was in the nature of things that they progressed slowly, since it was not simply technological limits against which they were pushing. They were also ramming against the constraints of their own psychology, barriers no less impervious.

The Banished, at first, still retained the flock instincts of their brethren. They had evolved into a society highly dependent on visual modes of communication; highly organised into large collectives, where the individual was of less importance than the whole. Displaced from its position in a flock, a single Amarantin underwent a kind of psychosis; the equivalent of massive sensory deprivation. Even small groupings were not enough to assuage that terror, which meant that Amarantin culture was extremely stable; extremely resilient against internal plots and treason. But it also meant that the Banished were, by their very isolation, consigned to a kind of insanity.

So they accepted this, and worked with it. They changed themselves; cultured sociopathy. In only a few hundred generations the Banished had stopped being a flock at all, but had fragmented into dozens of specialised clades, each tuned to a particular strain of madness. Or what would have been seen as madness by those who had stayed at home . . .

The ability to function in smaller groups enabled the Banished to probe further from Resurgam, out of the immediate volume of light-limited communication. The more psychotic individuals reached even further from the sun, until they found Hades and the odd, troubling planet which orbited it. By this time the Banished had gone through the same philosophical hoops which Volyova and Pascale had just summarised for Khouri's benefit. How the galaxy should have been a busier place than it really was, if their ideas were correct – which, as a consequence, was probably not the case. They had listened in the radio, optical, gravitational and neutrino bands for the voices of other cultures, others like them, but had heard nothing. Some of the more adventurous among them – or the more deranged, depending on one's point of view – had even left the system entirely, and had found nothing of great consequence to report back to home: a few ruins here and there (enigmatic) and a puzzling sludge-like organism which hinted at organisational sophistication, encountered on a handful of aquatic planets, as if it had been placed there.

But all of this became incidental when they found the thing around Hades.

It was, beyond any possible doubt, artefactual. It had been placed there by another civilisation, uncountable millions of years in the past. It seemed to actively invite them to enter its mysteries. So they began to explore it.

And that was when their problems began.

'It was an Inhibitor device,' Pascale said. 'That was what they found, wasn't it?'

'It had been waiting there for millions of years,' Khouri said. 'All the time they were evolving from what we'd think of as dinosaurs, or birds. All the time they spent reaching towards intelligence; learning to use tools; discovering fire . . .'

'Just waiting,' Volyova echoed. Behind her, the tactical display had been pulsing red for many minutes now, indicating that the shuttle had now fallen within the theoretical maximum range of the lighthugger's beam weapons. A kill at this distance would be difficult but not impossible, and neither would it be swift. She continued, 'Waiting for something recognisably intelligent to enter its vicinity – at which point it doesn't strike out mindlessly; doesn't destroy them. Because that would defeat the point. What it does is encourage them in, so it can learn as much about them as possible. Where they come from. What kind of technology they have, how they think, how they co-operate and communicate.'

'Gathering intelligence.'

'Yes.' Volyova's voice was as dolorous as a church bell. 'It's patient, you see. But sooner or later there comes a point when it decides that it has all the intelligence it needs. And then – only then – it acts.'

Now the three of them were on common ground. 'Which is why the Amarantin died out,' Pascale said, wonderingly. 'It did something to their sun; tampered with it, triggered something like a vast coronal mass ejection; just enough to scour Resurgam clean of life, and cause a phase of cometary-infall for a few hundred thousand years.'

'Ordinarily the Inhibitors wouldn't go to such drastic lengths,' Volyova said. 'But in this case they'd left it far too late for anything less. And even that wasn't sufficient, of course; the Banished were already spaceborn. They had to be hunted down; across tens of light-years, if necessary.'

Again there was a chime from the hull sensors, warning of a directed radar scan. Another chime followed soon after; evidence that the pursuing ship was narrowing its focus.

'The Inhibitor device around Hades must have alerted others, elsewhere,' Khouri said, trying to ignore the mechanised prophecies of imminent doom. 'Transmitted the intelligence it had gathered, warning them to be on the lookout for the Banished.'

'It can't have simply been a case of sitting around waiting for them to show up,' Volyova said. 'The machines must have switched over from passivity to something more active – replicating hunting machines, for instance, programmed with the templates of the Banished. No matter which direction the Banished turned to flee, light would have outraced them, and Inhibitor systems would always be one step ahead, alert and waiting.'

'They wouldn't have stood a chance.'

'But it can't have been instantaneous extinction,' Pascale said. 'The Banished had time to return to Resurgam; time to preserve what they could of the old culture. Even if they knew they were being hunted down, and that the sun was in the process of destroying their homeworld.'

'Maybe it took ten years; maybe a century.' The way Volyova spoke, it was obvious she didn't think it made a great deal of difference. 'All we know is that some managed to get further than others.'

'But none survived,' Pascale said. 'Did they?'

'Some did,' Khouri said. 'In a manner of speaking.'

Behind Volyova, the tactical display began to shriek.

THIRTY-SEVEN

Cerberus Interior, 2567

The final shell was hollow.

It had taken him three days to reach it; a day since he had left Sajaki's bodyless suit on the floor of the third shell, more than five hundred kilometres above him now. If he stopped to think about those distances, he knew, he would go quietly mad, so he carefully quarantined them from his thoughts. Simply being in an entirely alien environment was troubling enough; he did not wish to compound his fear with an additional dose of claustrophobia. Yet his quarantining was not complete, so that behind every thought there was a nagging background of crushing fright, the thought that at any instant some action he did would cause the delicate equilibria of this place to shift catastrophically, bringing down that vast, impossible ceiling.

With each inward layer he seemed to pass through a subtly different phase of Amarantin construction methodology. History, too, he supposed – but nothing was ever that simple. The levels did not seem to get systematically more or less advanced as he penetrated deeper, but rather evinced different philosophies; different approaches. It was as if the first Amarantin to arrive here had found something (what, he had not yet begun to guess) and had taken the decision to englobe it in an artificial shell armoured and capable of defending itself. Then another group must have arrived and elected to englobe that, perhaps because they believed their fortifications were more secure. The last of all had taken the process one logical step further, by camouflaging their fortifications so that they did not resemble anything artificial at all. It was impossible to guess over what timescales this layering had taken place, so he studiously avoided doing so. Maybe the different layers had been emplaced almost simultaneously – or perhaps the process had been drawn out over the thousands of years between Sun Stealer's departure with the Banished Ones, and his godlike return.

Naturally, he had been less than comforted by what he found in Sajaki's suit.

'He was never there,' Calvin said, filling in his thoughts. 'All the while you thought he was in the suit, he wasn't. The suit was empty. No wonder he never let you get too close.'

'Sneaky bastard.'

'I'll say. But it wasn't actually Sajaki being a sneaky bastard, was it?'

Sylveste was desperately trying to find another way to explain this paradox, but was failing at every attempt. 'But if not Sajaki . . .' He trailed off, remembering how he had not actually seen the Triumvir in person before they departed the ship. Sajaki had called him from the clinic, but he had no reason to believe that had really been Sajaki.

'Listen, something was driving that suit until it crashed.' Calvin was doing his favourite trick of sounding absurdly calm, despite the situation. But he lacked the usual bravado. 'I'd say there's only one logical culprit.'

'Sun Stealer.' Sylveste said the words experimentally, testing the idea for its repulsiveness. It was no less bitter than he had imagined it would be. 'It was him, wasn't it? Khouri had it right all along.'

'I'd say that at this juncture we'd be staggeringly foolish to reject that hypothesis. Do you want me to continue?'

'No,' Sylveste said. 'Not just yet. Give me a moment to think things through, then you can inflict all the pious wisdom on me you see fit.'

'What's there to think through?'

'I'd have thought it was obvious. Whether we go on or not.'

The decision had not been one of the simpler ones in his life. Now he knew that, for all or part of this, he had been manipulated. How deep had that manipulation gone? Had it extended to his very powers of reason? Had his thought processes been subjugated towards this one end for most of his life in fact, since returning from Lascaille's Shroud? Had he really died out there, and returned to Yellowstone as some kind of automaton, acting and feeling like his old self, but really directed towards one goal only, which was now on the point of being achieved? And did it honestly matter?

After all, no matter which way he cut it, no matter how false these feelings were, no matter how irrational the logic, this was the place he had always wanted to be.

He could not go back; not yet.

Not until he knew.

'*Svinoi* pig-dog,' Volyova said.

The first graser burst had hit the nose of the shuttle thirty seconds after the tactical attack siren had begun to shriek; barely enough time to throw off a cloud of ablative chaff, designed to dissipate the initial energies of the incoming gamma-ray photons. Just before the flightdeck windows rendered themselves opaque, Volyova saw a silver flash, as sacrificial hull armour vanished in a gasp of excited metal ions. The structural shock rammed through the fuselage like a concussion charge. More sirens joined in the threnody, and a vast acreage of the tactical display switched over to offensive mode, graphing up weapons readiness data.

Useless; all of it useless. The *Melancholia*'s defences were simply too small-scale, too short-range, to have any chance against the pursuing megatonnage of the lighthugger. Hardly surprising; some of the *Infinity*'s guns were larger than the shuttle, and those were probably the ones that it had not yet bothered deploying.

Cerberus was a grey immensity, filling a third of the sky from the shuttle's perspective. By now they should be decelerating, yet they were busy wasting precious seconds being fried. Even if they fought off the attack, they would be moving uncomfortably fast . . .

More of the hull vaporised.

She let her fingers do the talking, typing in a programmed evasive pattern that would undoubtedly get them out of the immediate focus of the graser onslaught. The only trouble was, it depended on sustaining thrust at ten gees.

She executed the routine, and almost immediately blacked out.

The chamber was hollow, but not empty.

Three hundred kilometres wide, Sylveste guessed it to be, though that was sheer guesswork, because his suit radar stubbornly refused to come up with a consistent distance for the diameter of the chamber, no matter how many readings he asked it to make. No doubt what was in the middle of the chamber was causing his suit difficulty. He could understand that. The thing was causing him difficulty as well, though in perhaps not quite the same way. It was giving him a headache.

In fact, there were two of them, and he wasn't sure which was the stranger. They were moving, or rather one of them was, locked in orbit around the other. The one that moved was like a gem, but it was a gem so complicated, and so constantly in flux, that it was impossible to describe its shape, or even its colour and lustre from moment to moment. All he knew was that it was large – tens of kilometres wide, it seemed – but again, when he asked the suit to confirm this, it was unable to give him a coherent reply. He might as well have asked the suit to comment on the subtext of a piece of free-form haiku, for all the sense it gave him.

He tried to enlarge it with his eyes' zoom faculty, but it seemed to defy enlargement, if anything growing smaller when he examined it under magnification. Something seriously strange had happened to spacetime in the vicinity of that jewel.

Next, he tried to record a snapshot of it using his eyes' image capture facility, but that failed as well, and what the image showed was something paradoxically more blurred than what he appeared to see in realtime, as if the object were changing more rapidly on small timescales – more thoroughly – than on timescales of seconds or longer. He tried to hold this concept in his head and for a moment thought he might have succeeded, but the illusion of understanding was only fleeting.

And the other thing . . .

The other thing, the stationary thing . . . if anything, this was worse.

It was like a gash in reality, a gaping hole from which erupted white light from the mouth of infinity. The light was intense, more intense and pure than any he had known or dreamt of – like the light which the near-dead spoke of, beckoning them to the afterlife. He too felt the light was beckoning. It was so bright he should have been blinded. But the more he looked into its fulgent depths, the less it seemed to glare; the more it became only a tranquil, fathomless whiteness.

The light refracted through the orbiting gem, casting varicoloured, constantly shifting slabs of illumination on the chamber walls. It was beautiful; intense and ever-shifting, beguiling.

'At this point,' Calvin said, 'I think a little humility may be in order. You're impressed, aren't you?'

'Of course.' If he spoke, he did not hear his own words. But Calvin seemed to understand.

'And this is enough, isn't it? I mean, now you know what it was they had to conceal from us. Something so strange . . . God only knows what it is . . .'

'Perhaps that's just what it is. God.'

'Staring into that light, I almost believe you.'

'You feel it too, is that what you're saying?'

'I'm not sure what I feel. I'm not sure I like it, either.'

Sylveste said, 'Do you think they made this, or was it something they happened to find?'

'This is a first – you asking my opinion.' Calvin seemed to deliberate, but his answer was hardly surprising when it came. 'They never made this, Dan. They were clever – maybe even cleverer than us. But the Amarantin were never gods.'

'Someone else, then.'

'Someone I hope we never meet.'

'Then hold your breath, because for all I know, we're about to.'

Weightless, he jetted the suit into the chamber, towards the dancing jewel and the source of searingly beautiful light.

When Volyova came around, it was to the sound of the radar warning siren, which meant that the *Infinity* was preparing to re-aim its grasers. It would not take it more than a few seconds to do so, even allowing for her random-walk evasive manoeuvre. She glanced at the hull health indicator and saw that they were down to only a few remaining millimetres of sacrificial metal, that the chaff throwers were depleted, and that – realistically – they could withstand no more than one or two additional bursts of graser-strike.

'Are we still here?' Khouri asked, seemingly astonished that she was even capable of framing the question.

One more strike and the hull would start outgassing in a dozen places, if it did not spontaneously vaporise. It was hot now;

noticeably. The heat of the first few sweeps had been efficiently dissipated, but the last one had not been so easily parried, and its lethal warming energies had seeped inwards.

'Get to the spider-room,' Volyova shouted, momentarily throttling down the thrust to permit locomotion around the ship. 'The insulation will enable you to survive another few strikes.'

'No!' Khouri was shouting now. 'We can't! At least here we've got a chance!'

'She's right,' Pascale said.

'You'll still have one in the spider-room,' Volyova said. 'Better, in fact. It's a smaller target, for one. I'm guessing the ship will direct its weapons against the shuttle in preference, or it may not even realise that the spider-room is anything but wreckage.'

'But what about you?'

She was angry now. 'Do you think I'm the type to indulge in heroics, Khouri? I'm coming too; with or without you. But I have to program a flight pattern into the shuttle first – unless you think you can do it.'

Khouri hesitated, as if the idea was not totally absurd. Then she unbuckled from her couch, jabbed a thumb towards Pascale and began moving, as if her life depended on it.

Which, rationally, it probably did.

Volyova did what she had promised she would do, inputting the most hair-raising evasive pattern she could imagine, one that she was not even sure she or her companions would be capable of surviving, with peak bursts exceeding fifteen gees for whole seconds. But did it really matter now? Somehow, the idea of dying while already unconscious, in the warm, muggy torpor of gee-induced blackout, was preferable to being burned alive, in vacuum, in the invisible heat of gamma-rays.

Grabbing the helmet she had worn when she boarded the shuttle, she prepared to join the others, mentally counting down until the initiation of the evasive pattern.

Khouri was halfway across to the waiting spider-room when she felt the wave of heat slap across her face, followed by the dreadful sound of the hull giving up its final ghost. The illumination in the cargo bay was gone now, as the *Melancholia*'s energy grid collapsed under the onslaught of the attack. But the spider-room's interior was still powered up, its implausibly plush décor visible through the observation windows.

'Get in!' she shouted to Pascale, and although the noise of the ship's death-throes was now tremendous, like a concerto played on scrap metal, somehow Sylveste's wife heard what she said and clambered into the spider-room, just as a tremendous shock wave slammed through the hull (or what remained of it), and the spider-room exploded free of the moorings in which it had been locked by Volyova's servitors.

Now there was a terrible howl of escaping air from elsewhere in the shuttle, and suddenly Khouri felt it tug against her, resisting her forward progress. The spider-room twisted and turned, its legs thrashing wildly, randomly. She could see Pascale now, in the observation window, but there was nothing the woman could do to help; she understood the room's controls even less comprehensively than Khouri.

She looked behind, hoping and praying that she would see Volyova there, having followed them, and that she would know what to do, but there was nothing except empty access corridor, and that awful sucking stream of escaping air.

'Ilia . . .'

The damned fool had done just what they'd feared; stayed behind, for all that she had denied that she would.

With what little light remained, she saw the hull quiver, like a sounding-board. And then suddenly the gale that was pulling her away from the spider-room lost its strength; counter-balanced by an equally fierce decompression halfway across the cargo bay. She looked towards it, eyes already veiling over as the cold hit them, and then she was falling towards the gap where only a second earlier there had been metal—

'Where the—'

But almost as soon as she had opened her mouth, Khouri knew where she was, which was inside the spider-room. There was no mistaking the place; not after all the time she had spent in it. And it felt comfortable; warm and safe and silent; a universe away from where she had been up to the point when she could not remember anything more. Her hands hurt; hurt rather a lot, in fact – but apart from that, she felt better than she imagined she had any right to feel; not when her last memory had been of falling towards naked space, from the womb of a dying ship . . .

'We made it,' Pascale said, although something in her voice sounded anything but triumphant. 'Don't try to move; not just yet – you've burnt your hands rather badly.'

'Burnt them?' Khouri was lying on one of the velvet couches which stretched along either wall of the room, head against the curved cushioned-brass end-piece. 'What happened?'

'You hit the spider-room; the draught pulled you towards it. I don't know how, but you managed to climb around the outside to the airlock. You were breathing vacuum for five or six seconds at least. The metal cooled so quickly that you got frost-burns where your hands touched it.'

'I don't remember any of that.' But she only had to look at the evidence of her palms to see that it must have been true.

'You blacked out as soon as you came aboard. I don't blame you.'

There was still that utterly uncelebratory tone in her voice, as if all that Khouri had done had been pointless. And Khouri thought she was probably right. The best that could happen to them was that they would somehow find a way to land the spider-room on Cerberus, and then see how long they could take their chances against the crustal defences. It would be interesting, if nothing else. And if not that, she supposed, then a slow wait until either the lighthugger found them and picked them off, or they died of cold or asphyxia, when their reserves expired. She racked her memory, trying to recall how long Volyova had said the spider-room was capable of surviving on its own.

'Ilia . . .'

'She didn't make it in time,' Pascale said. 'She died. I saw it happen. The second you were aboard, the shuttle just exploded.'

'You think Volyova made it happen deliberately, so that we'd at least have a chance? So we'd be mistaken for wreckage, as she said?'

'If so, I suppose we owe her thanks.'

Khouri slipped off her jacket, removed her shirt, slipped her jacket back on again and then tore the shirt into narrow strips with which she then bound her black, blistered palms. They hurt like hell, but it was nothing worse than the kind of pain she had known during training, from rope burns or carrying heavy artillery. She gritted her teeth and, while acknowledging it, put the pain somewhere beyond her immediate concerns.

Which, now she had to focus on them, made the prospect of submerging herself in the pain somewhat more tempting. But she resisted. She had to at least acknowledge her predicament, even if there was nothing obvious she could do about it. She had to know how it was going to happen, as it surely would.

'We're going to die, aren't we?'

Pascale Sylveste nodded. 'But not the way you're thinking, I'm willing to bet.'

'You mean we don't land on Cerberus?'

'No; not even if we knew how to operate this thing. We're not going to hit it either, and I think our velocity's too high for us to go into any kind of orbit around it.'

Now that Pascale mentioned it, the hemisphere of Cerberus through the observation windows looked further away than it had appeared prior to the attack against the shuttle. They must have slammed past the world with the velocity which had not been negated from the shuttle's approach pattern, hundreds of kilometres a second.

'So what happens now?'

'I'm only guessing,' Pascale said, 'but I think we're falling towards Hades.' She nodded at the forward observation window, at the pinprick of red light ahead of them. 'It seems to be in roughly the right direction, doesn't it?'

Khouri did not need to be told that Hades was a neutron star, any more than she needed to be told that there was no such thing as a safe close encounter with one. You either kept well away or you died; those were the rules, and there was no force in the universe capable of negating them. Gravity ruled, and gravity did not take into account circumstances, or the unfairness of things, or listen to eleventh-hour petitions before reluctantly repealing its laws. Gravity crushed, and near the surface of a neutron star gravity crushed absolutely, until diamond flowed like water; until a mountain collapsed into a millionth of its height. It was not even necessary to get close to suffer those crushing forces.

A few hundred thousand kilometres would be more than sufficient.

'Yes,' Khouri said. 'I think you're right. And that's not good.'

'No,' Pascale said. 'I rather imagined it wasn't.'

THIRTY-EIGHT

Cerberus Interior, 2567

Sylveste thought of it as the chamber of miracles.

It seemed appropriate: he had been here less than an hour (he assumed, though he had long since ceased paying much attention to time) and in that period he had seen nothing that was less than miraculous, and much for which the term itself seemed mildly insufficient. Somehow he knew that a lifetime would not be sufficient to encompass a fraction of what this place contained; what it was. He had felt like this before, on glimpsing some vista of tremendous potential knowledge not yet learnt, not yet codified and shaped into theory. But he knew that those previous occasions had been pale foreshadowings of what he felt now.

He had no more than hours here, before any chance of return was dashed. What could he do in a matter of hours? Very little, rationally, but he did have the recording systems of the suit, and his eyes, and he knew he had to try. History would not forgive him if he did anything less. More importantly, he would never forgive himself.

He jetted his suit towards the centre of the chamber, towards the two objects which snared his attention; the gash of transcendent light and the jewel-like thing which rotated around it. As he approached, the walls of the chamber began to move, as if he were being sucked into the rotational frame of the objects; as if space itself were being drawn into an eddy; as if the nature of space were in flux. His suit told him as much, chirruping with detailed analyses of the way the substrate was altering; quantum indices ticking towards unexplored new realms. He remembered something similar on the way in to Lascaille's Shroud. As then, he felt normal enough, as if his whole being were in the process of being transcribed, transliterated, the closer he came to the jewel and its radiant partner.

It took hours to reach it, and he began to doubt that his initial estimate of the diameter of the chamber had been accurate. But, inexorably, the apparent rate of revolution of the jewel dropped to zero, until the chamber walls were spinning dizzily. He knew then that he had to be close, although the jewel did not seem very much larger than when he had first glimpsed it. Still it was in constant motion, reminding him of a child's kaleidoscope, the ever-shifting symmetric patterns revealed by coloured glints of light, but extended to three (and possibly more) dimensions. Occasionally the thing threw out spires or spikes which reached threateningly towards him, causing him to flinch, but he held his ground and even allowed himself to drift closer in the moments when it seemed to shift into a phase of relatively low-level transformation. He sensed that his survival did not depend on closely watching the readouts of his suit. He was beyond such simplicities.

'What do you think it is?' Calvin asked, his voice so low that it almost merged with Sylveste's own thoughts, almost *was* one of Sylveste's own thoughts.

'I was hoping you'd have some suggestions.'

'Sorry; all out of shattering insights. Too many for one lifetime.'

Volyova drifted in space.

She had not died when the *Melancholia* went up, though she had not managed to make it to the spider-room in time. What she had done was don her helmet just before the hull whispered away, like a moth's wing against a candle. Falling away from the wreckage, she had not been targeted by the lighthugger. It had ignored her; just as it ignored the spider-room.

She could not simply die. That was emphatically not her style. And though she knew that her chances of survival were statistically negligible, and that what she was doing was entirely bereft of logic, she had to prolong the hours she had left. She scanned her air and power reserves and saw that they were not good; not good at all. She had taken the suit hastily, thinking that the only use she would have for it was to reach the shuttle across the hangar. She had not even had the presence of mind to hook it up to one of the recharging modules aboard the shuttle during their flight. That at least would have bought her a few days, rather than the fraction of a day she now faced. Yet, perversely, she did not simply arrange to end things immediately. She knew she could make the reserves last longer if she slept when consciousness was not required (assuming, of course, that she ever had any further use for it).

So she programmed the suit to drift, telling it to alert her only if something interesting – or, more probably, threatening – happened. And now, because she had woken, something evidently had.

She asked the suit what it was.

The suit told her.

'Shit,' Ilia Volyova said.

The *Infinity*'s radar had just swept across her; the same radar which it had used against the shuttle, just before deploying its gamma-ray weapon. And it had done so with an intensity which suggested that the ship was in her immediate neighbourhood; no more than a few tens of thousands of kilometres away; not even spitting distance when it came to picking off a target as large, defenceless, static and conspicuous as she now was.

She hoped the ship would have the good grace to finish her off with something swift. After all, there was a very high likelihood that whatever it chose to use against her would be a system she had designed herself.

Not for the first time, she cursed her ingenuity.

Volyova enabled the suit's binocular overlay and began sweeping the starfield from which the targeting radar had projected. At first she saw only blackness and stars – and then the ship, tiny as a chip of coal, but edging closer with every second.

'It's not Amarantin, is it? We agree on that.'

'The jewel, you mean?'

'Whatever it is. And I don't think they were responsible for the light, whatever that is.'

'No. That's not their handiwork either.' Sylveste realised now that he was deeply grateful for Calvin's presence, no matter how illusory it was; no matter how much it was a deception. 'Whatever these things are – whatever their relationship to each other – the Amarantin just found them.'

'I think you're right.'

'Maybe they didn't even understand what they had found – not properly, anyway. But for one reason or another they had to enclose it; had to hide it from the rest of the universe.'

'Jealousy?'

'Perhaps. But that wouldn't explain the warnings we got coming here. Perhaps they enclosed them as a favour to the rest of Creation, because they couldn't destroy them, or move them elsewhere.'

Sylveste thought. 'Whoever put them here originally – around a neutron star – must have meant for them to attract someone's attention. Don't you think?'

'Like a lure?'

'Neutron stars are common enough, but they're still exotic; especially from the point of view of a culture just achieving the capability for starflight. It was guaranteed that the Amarantin would be drawn here through sheer curiosity.'

'They weren't the last, were they?'

'No, I don't suppose they were.' Sylveste drew a breath. 'Do you think we should go back, while we still can?'

'Rationally, yes. Is that enough of an answer for you?'

They pushed forward.

'Take us towards the light first,' Calvin said, minutes later. 'I want to see it closer. It seems – this is going to sound stupid – but it seems somehow stranger than the other thing. If there's one thing I'd choose to die having seen up close, I think it's that light.'

'That's how I feel,' Sylveste said. He was already doing what Calvin had suggested, as if the intention had sprung from his own will. What Calvin said was right; there was indeed something deeper about the strangeness of the light; something more profound, older. He had not been able to put that feeling into words, or even properly acknowledge it, but now it was out in the open, and it felt right. The light was where they had to go.

It was silvery in texture; a diamond gash in the fabric of reality, simultaneously intense and calm. Approaching it, the orbiting jewel (stationary now, in this frame) seemed to dwindle. Smooth pearly radiance surrounded the suit. He felt that the light should hurt his eyes, but there was nothing except a feeling of warmth, and a kind of slowly magnifying knowing. Gradually he lost sight of the rest of the chamber and the jewel, until he seemed to be enveloped in a blizzard of silver and whiteness. He felt no danger; no threat; only resignation – and it was a joyous resignation, bursting with immanence. Slowly, magically, the suit itself seemed to turn transparent, the silver luminance bursting through until it reached his skin, and then pushed deeper, into his flesh and bones.

It was not quite what he had been expecting.

Afterwards, when he came to consciousness (or descended to it, since it seemed that in the hiatus he had been somewhere above it), there was only understanding.

He was back in the chamber again, some distance from the white light, still within the rotating frame of the jewel.

And he knew.

'Well,' Calvin said, his voice as unexpected and out-of-place in the tranquillity that followed as a trumpet blast. 'That was some trip, wasn't it?'

'Did you . . . experience all that?'

'Put it this way. That was weirdest damned thing I've ever felt. Does that answer you?'

It was. There was no need to push beyond that; no need to convince himself further that Calvin had shared all that he had felt, or that for a moment their thoughts – and more – had liquefied and flowed indivisibly, along with a trillion others. And that he understood perfectly what had happened, because in the moment of shared wisdom, all his questions had been answered.

'We were *read*, weren't we? That light is a scanning device; a machine for retrieving information.' The words sounded perfectly reasonable before he said them, but in the saying of them he felt he was expressing himself poorly, debasing the thing of which he spoke by the crudity of language. But for all the insights he had felt in that place, his vocabulary had not been enlarged enough to encompass them. And even now they seemed to be fading; the way a dream's magical qualities seemed to wither in the first few seconds of waking. But he had to say it, to at least crystallise what he felt; get it recorded by the suit's memory for posterity, if nothing else. 'For a moment I think we were turned into information, and that in that instant we were linked to every other piece of information ever known; every thought ever thought, or at least ever captured by the light.'

'That's how it felt to me,' Calvin said.

Sylveste wondered if Calvin shared the increasing amnesia he felt; the slow fading of the knowing.

'We were in Hades, weren't we?' Sylveste felt his thoughts

stampeding at the gates of expression, desperate to be vocalised before they evaporated. 'That thing isn't a neutron star at all. Maybe it was once, but it isn't now. It's been transformed; turned into a . . .'

'A computer,' Calvin said, finishing the sentence for him. 'That's what Hades is. A computer made out of nuclear matter, the mass of a star devoted to processing information, storing it. And this light is an aperture into it; a way to enter the computational matrix. I think for a moment we were actually in it.'

But it was much stranger than that.

Once, a star with a mass thirty or forty times heavier than Earth's sun had reached the end of its nuclear-burning lifetime. After several million years of profligate energy-expenditure the star had exploded as a supernova, and in its heart, tremendous gravitational pressure had smashed a lump of matter within its own Schwarzschild radius, until a black hole had been formed. The black hole was so named because nothing, not even light, could escape from its critical radius. Matter and light could only fall into the black hole, thereby engorging it towards greater mass and greater attractive force; a vicious circle.

A culture arose that had use for such an object. They knew a technique whereby a black hole could be transformed into something far more exotic, far more paradoxical. First, they waited until the universe was considerably older than when the black hole had been formed; until the predominant stellar population consisted of very old red-dwarf stars, stars which were barely massive enough to ignite their own fusion fires. Next, they shepherded a dozen of these dwarves into an accretion disk around the black hole and slowly allowed the disk to feed the hole, raining starstuff onto its light-swallowing event horizon.

This much Sylveste understood, or could at least deceive himself into thinking that he understood. But the next part – the core of it – was much harder to hold in his mind, like a self-contradictory koan. What he grasped was that, once within the event horizon, particles continued to fall along particular trajectories, particular orbits which swung them around the kernel of infinite density which was the singularity at the black hole's heart. Falling along these lines, time and space began to blend into one another, until they were no longer properly separable. And – crucially – there was one set of trajectories in which they swapped places completely;

where a trajectory in space became one in time. And one subset of this bunch of paths actually allowed matter to tunnel into the past, earlier into the black hole's history.

'I'm accessing texts from the twentieth century,' Calvin murmured, seemingly able to follow his thoughts. 'This effect was known – predicted – even then. It seemed to follow from the mathematics describing black holes. But no one knew how seriously to take it.'

'Whoever engineered Hades had no such qualms.'

'So it would seem.'

What happened was that light, energy, particle-flux, wormed along these special trajectories, burrowing ever deeper into the past with each orbit around the singularity. None of this was 'evident' to the outside universe since it was confined behind the impenetrable barrier of the event horizon, and so there was no overt violation of causality. According to the mathematics which Calvin had accessed, there could be none, since these trajectories could never pass back into the external universe. Yet they did. What the mathematics had overlooked was the special case of the tiny subset-of-a-subset-of-a-subset of trajectories which actually carried quanta back to the birth of the black hole, when it collapsed in the supernova detonation of its progenitor star.

At that instant, the minute outward pressure exerted by the particles arriving from the future served to delay the gravitational infall.

The delay was not even measurable; it was barely longer than the smallest theoretical subdivision of quantised time. But it existed. And, small though it was, it was sufficient to send ripples of causal shock propagating back into the future.

These ripples of causal shock met the incoming particles and established a grid of causal interference, a standing wave extending symmetrically into the past and the future.

Enmeshed in this grid, the collapsed object was no longer sure that it was meant to be a black hole. The initial conditions had always been borderline, and perhaps these entanglements could be avoided if it remained poised above its Schwarzschild radius; if it collapsed down to a stable configuration of strange quarks and degenerate neutrons instead.

It flickered indeterminately between the two states. The indeterminacy crystallised, and what remained behind was something unique in the universe – except that elsewhere, similar transformations were being wrought on other black holes, similar causal paradoxes coming into being.

The object settled on a stable configuration whereby its paradoxical nature was not immediately obvious to the outside universe. Externally, it resembled a neutron star – for the first few centimetres of its crust, at least. Below, the nuclear matter had been catalysed into intricate forms capable of lightning-swift computation, a self-organisation which had emerged spontaneously from the resolution of its two opposed states. The crust seethed and processed, containing information at the theoretical maximum density of storage of matter, anywhere in the universe.

And it thought.

Below, the crust blended seamlessly with a flickering storm of unresolved possibility, as the interior of the collapsed object danced to the music of acausality. While the crust ran endless simulations, endless computations, the core bridged the future and the past, allowing information to channel effortlessly between them. The crust, in effect, had become one element of a massive parallel-processor, except that the other elements in its array were the future and past versions of itself.

And it knew.

It knew that, even with this totality of processing power strewn across the aeons, it was only part of something much larger.

And it had a name.

Sylveste had to let his mind rest for a moment. The immensity of it was dwindling now, leaving only the ringing aftertones, like the last echoes of the final chord of the greatest symphony ever played. In a few moments, he doubted that he would remember much at all. There was simply insufficient room in his head for it all. And, strangely, he did not feel the slightest sorrow at its passing. For those few moments, it had been wonderful to taste that transhuman knowledge, but it was simply too much for one man to know. It was better to live; better to carry a memory of a memory, than suffer the vast burden of knowing.

He was not meant to think like a god.

After many minutes, he checked his suit clock, and was only mildly surprised to find that he had lost several hours, assuming his last check on the time had been correct. There was still time to get out, he thought; still time to make it to the surface before the bridgehead closed.

He looked at the jewel; no less enigmatic for all that he had now experienced. It had not ceased its constant fluxing, and he still felt its beguiling attraction. He felt that he knew more about it now; that his time in the porthole to the Hades matrix had taught him something – but for a moment the memories were too thickly integrated into the other experiences he had gained, and he could not quite bring them to conscious examination.

All he knew was that he felt a foreboding which had not been there before.

Still, he moved towards it.

The agonised red eye of Hades was noticeably larger now, but the neutron star at the heart of that burning point would never amount to more than a glint; it was only a few tens of kilometres across, and they would be dead long before they were close enough to resolve it properly, shredded by the intense differential force of gravity.

'I feel I should tell you,' Pascale Sylveste said, 'I don't think it will be fast, what's going to happen to us. Not unless we're very lucky.'

Khouri tried her best not to sound irritated at the woman's tone of superior understanding, admitting to herself that Pascale was probably quite justified in adopting that manner.

'How do you know so much? You're no astrophysicist.'

'No, but I remember Dan telling me about how the tidal forces would limit the close approach of any of the probes he wanted to send here.'

'You're talking as if he's dead already.'

'I don't think he is,' Pascale said. 'I think he might even survive. But we're not going to. I'm sorry, but it amounts to the same thing.'

'You still love that bastard, don't you?'

'He loved me too, believe it or not. I know from the way he acted – what he did – the way he seemed so driven, it must have been hard for outsiders to see. But he did care. More than anyone will ever know.'

'Maybe people won't be so hard on him when they find out the way he was manipulated.'

'You think anyone's going to find out? We're the only ones who know, Khouri. As far as the rest of the universe is concerned, he was just a monomaniac. They don't understand that he used people because he had no choice. Because something bigger than any of us was driving him forward.'

Khouri nodded. 'I wanted to kill him once – but only because it was a way to get back to Fazil. There was never any hatred in it. Matter of fact, I can't say I honestly disliked him. I admired anyone who could carry around that much arrogance, like it was his birthright, or something. Most people, they don't carry it off. But he wore it like a king. It stopped being arrogance, then – became something else. Something you could admire.'

Pascale elected not to reply, but Khouri could tell that she was not in complete disagreement. Maybe she was just not quite ready to come out and say it aloud. That she had loved Sylveste because he was such a self-important bastard and made something noble of being a self-important bastard, did it with such utter aplomb that it became a kind of virtue, like the wearing of sackcloth.

'Listen,' Khouri said, eventually. 'I've got an idea. When those tides begin to bite, do you want to be fully conscious, or would you rather approach the matter with a little fortification?'

'What do you mean?'

'Ilia always told me this place was built to show clients around the outside of the ship; the kind of clients you wanted to impress if you wanted to keep the contract. So I'm thinking, somewhere on board there has to be a drinks cabinet. Probably well-stocked, assuming it hasn't been drunk dry over the last few centuries. And then again, it might even be self-replenishing. Are you with me?'

Pascale said nothing, during which time the gravitational sinkhole of Hades crept closer. Finally, just when Khouri assumed that the other woman had elected not to hear her proposition, Pascale released herself from her seat and headed rearwards, to the unexplored realms of plush and brass behind them.

THIRTY-NINE

Cerberus Interior, Final Chamber, 2567

The jewel shone with a noticeable bluish radiance now, as if his proximity had stilled its spectral transformations; forced it towards some temporary quiescence. Sylveste still felt that it was wrong to approach it, but now his own curiosity – and a sense of predestiny – was impelling him forwards. Maybe it was something springing from the basal parts of his mind; a need to confront the dangerous and thereby tame it. It was an instinct which must have driven the first touching of fire, the first flinch of pain and the wisdom that came with that pain.

The jewel unfolded before him, undergoing geometric transformations to which he did not dare devote too much attention, for fear that understanding them would cleave his mind open along similar fault lines.

'Are you sure this is wise?' Calvin asked, his utterances now more than ever forming part of the normal background of Sylveste's inner dialogue.

'It's too late to return now,' said a voice.

A voice which belonged neither to Calvin nor Sylveste, but which seemed deeply familiar, as if it had long been a part of him, merely silent.

'Sun Stealer, isn't it?'

'He's been with us all along,' Calvin said. 'Haven't you?'

'Longer than you imagine. Since you returned from Lascaille's Shroud, Dan.'

'Then everything Khouri said was right,' he said, while already knowing the truth of it. If Sajaki's empty suit had not confirmed it, then the revelations he had shared in the white light had ended his doubts, completely.

'What do you want of me?'

'Only that you enter the – jewel – as you call it.' The creature's

549

voice, and its voice was the only thing that he heard, was sibilant; chillingly so. 'You have nothing to fear. You will not be harmed by it, nor will you be prevented from leaving.'

'You would say that, wouldn't you?'

'Except that it is the truth.'

'What about the bridgehead?'

'The device is still operational. It will remain so until you have left Cerberus.'

'There's no way of knowing,' Calvin said. 'Whatever he – it – says, could well be a lie. He's deceived and manipulated us at every step; all to bring you here. Why should he suddenly start telling the truth now?'

'Because it is of no consequence,' Sun Stealer said. 'Now that you have reached this far, your own desires play no further part in the matter.'

And Sylveste felt the suit surge forward, directly into the opened jewel, along a brilliantly faceted, ever-flickering corridor which extended into the structure.

'What—' Calvin began.

'I'm not doing anything,' Sylveste said. 'The bastard must have control of my suit!'

'Stands to reason. He could control Sajaki's, after all. Must have preferred to sit back and let you do all the work until now. Lazy bastard.'

'At this point,' Sylveste said, 'I don't think insulting him's going to make a great deal of difference.'

'Do you have a better idea?'

'As a matter of fact—'

The corridor surrounded him completely now, a glowing tracheal tunnel which twisted and turned until it seemed impossible that he could still be inside the jewel. But then, he told himself, he had never come to a clear conclusion as to its true size – it might have been anywhere between a few hundred metres across or tens of kilometres. Its fluctuating shape made it impossible to know, and perhaps meant that there was no meaningful answer; in the same way that one could not specify the volume of a fractal solid.

'Uh, you were saying?'

'I was saying . . .' Sylveste trailed off. 'Sun Stealer, are you listening to me?'

'As always.'

'I don't understand why I had to come here. If you managed to animate Sajaki's suit – and you had conscious control of mine all this time – why did I have to come along in the first place? If there's something you want inside this thing, something you want to bring out, you could do it without me being here at all.'

'The device will only respond to organic life. An empty suit would be interpreted as machine sentience.'

'This – thing – is a device? Is that what you're saying?'

'It is an Inhibitor device.'

For a moment the words seemed meaningless, but only for a moment. Then – fuzzily – the words attached to some of the memories he retained from his time in the white light; the portal to the Hades matrix. Those memories attached to others; an endless braid of association.

And he came to a kind of understanding.

More than ever, he knew that he should not continue; that if he reached the inner realm of the jewel – of the Inhibitor device, as he now knew it to be – things would be very, very bad. In fact, it would be difficult to imagine how things could be worse.

'We can't go on,' Calvin said. 'I understand now what this is.'

'Me too, belatedly.'

The device had been left here by the Inhibitors. They had placed it in orbit around Hades, next to the glimmering white portal; something older even than the Inhibitors. It did not bother them that they did not properly understand its function, or have any real inkling of who had placed it there, next to the neutron star which – according to some puzzling indications they had allowed to linger unexplored – was not quite as it should be. But, the enigma of its origin aside, it entirely suited their plans. Their own devices were constructed to lure the sentient, and by placing one of them next to an entity even more perplexing, they were guaranteed visitors. It was a strategy they followed across the galaxy, in fact: leaving Inhibitor devices in close proximity to objects of astrophysical interest, or near the ruins of extinct cultures. Anywhere where they were likely to draw attention.

And the Amarantin had come, and tinkered, and made themselves known to the device. It had studied them, and learned their weaknesses.

And it had wiped them out – all except for a handful of descendants of the Banished, who found two means to escape the ruthless predation of the Inhibitors. Some had used the portal itself, mapping themselves into the crustal matrix, where they continued to run as simulations, preserved in the impervious amber of nuclear matter enslaved for computational purposes.

It was hardly living, Sylveste thought, but at least something of them had been preserved.

And then there were the others: the others who had found the other way to escape the Inhibitors. Their mode of escape had been no less drastic, no less irreversible . . .

'They became the Shrouders, didn't they?' Calvin was speaking now – or was it Sylveste, voicing his own thoughts, the way he sometimes did, in the heat of concentration? He could barely tell, much less care. 'This was in the last days; when Resurgam was already gone, and most of the spaceborn had already been tracked down and annihilated. One faction went into the Hades matrix. Another learned what they could about manipulating spacetime, probably from the transformations near the portal. And they found a solution; a way to barricade themselves against the Inhibitor weapons. They found a way to wrap spacetime around themselves; a way to curdle and solidify it, until it formed an impervious shell. And they retreated behind those shells and sealed them for eternity.

'But at least it was better than dying.'

Everything, for an instant, was clear in his head. How those behind the Shrouds had waited, and waited, barely cognisant of the outside universe; barely able to communicate with it, so secure were the walls they had wrapped around themselves.

And they had waited.

They had known, even at the time of enclosure, that the systems left behind by the Inhibitors were slowly failing; slowly losing their ability to suppress intelligence. Not soon enough, for them – but after a million years of waiting, trapped in their bubble of spacetime, they began to wonder if the threat had now diminished . . .

They could not simply dismantle the Shrouds and look around – far too hazardous; especially as the Inhibitor machines were nothing if not patient. Their apparent silence might only be part of the trap, a waiting game designed to entice the Amarantin – who were now the Shrouders – out of their shells, into the open arena of naked space, where they could be destroyed with ease, terminating the million-year purge against their kind.

Yet, in time, others came.

Perhaps there was something about this region of space which favoured the evolution of vertebrate life, or perhaps it was only coincidence, but in the newly starfaring humans, the Shrouders saw echoes of what they had once been. Something of the same psychosis, almost: the simultaneous craving for solitude and companionship; the need for the comfort of society and the open steppes of space; a schism which drove them onwards, outwards.

Philip Lascaille had been the first to meet them, around the Shroud which now bore his name.

The tortured spacetime around the Shroud had ripped his mind open, twisted it and reassembled it, into a drooling travesty of what it had once been. But it was a travesty shot with brilliance. They had put something in him; the knowledge that was needed for someone else to get much closer ... and the lie that would make him do it.

Just before he died, Lascaille had communicated this to the young Dan Sylveste.

Go to the Jugglers, he had said.

Because the Amarantin had once visited them; once imprinted their neural patterns into the Juggler ocean. Those patterns stabilised the spacetime around the Shroud; enabled one to penetrate deeper into its thickening folds without being torn asunder by the stresses. It was how Sylveste, having accepted the Juggler transform, was able to ride the storms into the depths of the Shroud itself.

He came out alive.

But changed.

Something had come back with him; something which called itself Sun Stealer, though he knew now that this was no more than a myth-name; that the thing which had lived within him ever since was better thought of as an assemblage; an artificial personality woven into the shell of the Shroud, put there by those within who wanted Sylveste to act as their emissary; to extend their influence beyond the curtain of impassable spacetime.

What they wanted him to do was very simple, in hindsight.

Travel to Resurgam, where the bones of their corporeal ancestors were buried.

Find the Inhibitor device.

Place himself in a position where, if the device was still functioning, it would activate and identify him as a member of a newly uprisen intelligent culture.

If the Inhibitors were still around, humanity would be identified as the next species to be put to the slaughter.

If not, the Shrouders could emerge into safety.

Now the bluish light which surrounded him seemed evil; unspeakably so. He knew that simply by entering this place he might have already done too much; already exhibited enough apparent intelligence to convince the Inhibitor device that he represented a breed worthy of extinction.

He hated what the Amarantin had become; hated himself for devoting so much of his life to their study. But what could he do now? It was far too late for second thoughts.

The tunnel had widened, and where he found himself – still without any conscious control of the suit – was in a faceted chamber, bathed in the same putrid blue glow. The chamber was filled with odd hanging shapes, reminding him of reconstructions he had seen of the inside of a human cell. The shapes were all rectilinear, complexly interconnected rectangles and squares and rhomboids, forming hanging sculptures which subscribed to no recognisable aesthetic tendency.

'What are they?' he breathed.

'Think of them as puzzles,' Sun Stealer said. 'The idea is that, as an intelligent explorer, you feel a curious urge to complete them, to move the shapes into the geometric configurations which are implied in the pieces.'

He could see what Sun Stealer meant. The nearest assemblage, for instance. It was obvious that with a few manipulations he could make the shapes into a tesseract ... almost tempting ...

'I won't do it,' he said.

'You won't have to.' And in demonstration, Sun Stealer made the limbs of his suit reach out towards the assemblage, which was much closer than he had first guessed. The suit fingers grasped for the first piece, swinging it effortlessly into place. 'There will be other tests, other chambers,' the alien said. 'Your mental processes will be subjected to rigid scrutiny, and – later – your biology. I do not expect that the latter procedure will be especially pleasant. But neither will it be fatal. That would deter others, from which a broader picture of the enemy could be assembled.' There was something almost like humour in the thing's voice now; as if he had been long enough in human company to glean some of their manners. 'You, alas, will be the only human representative to enter this device. But rest assured you will prove an excellent specimen.'

'That's where you're wrong,' Sylveste said.

The first hint of alarm entered Sun Stealer's implacable, noiseless voice. 'Please explain.'

For a moment Sylveste did not oblige. 'Calvin,' he said. 'There's something I have to say.' Even as he spoke, he was not really sure why he was doing so, not really sure who he was addressing. 'When we were in the white light – when we shared everything, in the Hades matrix – there was something I found out; something I should have known years ago.'

'About you, that is.'

'About me, yes. About what I am.' Sylveste wanted to cry, now, knowing that this would be his last chance, but his eyes did not allow that; they never had. 'About why I can't hate you, unless I want to turn that hatred against myself. If I ever really hated you in the first place.'

'It didn't really work, did it? What I made of you. It wasn't the way I planned it. But I can't say I'm disappointed with the way you turned out.' Calvin corrected himself. 'The way I turned out.'

'I'm glad I found out, even if it has to be now.'

'What are you going to do?'

'You already know. We shared everything, didn't we?' Sylveste found himself laughing. 'Now you know my secrets, as well.'

'Ah. You're talking about that little secret, aren't you?'

'What?' hissed Sun Stealer; voice like the radio crackle of distant quasars.

'I guess you were privy to the conversations I had on the ship,' he said, addressing the alien again. 'When I let them think I'd been bluffing.'

'Bluffing?' it asked. 'About what?'

'About the hot-dust in my eyes,' Sylveste said.

He laughed, louder this time. And then executed the series of neural triggers, long committed to memory, which initiated a cascade of events in the circuitry of his eyes, and – finally – in the tiny motes of contained antimatter embedded within them.

There was a light purer than any he had known, even in the portal which led to Hades.

And then there was nothing.

Volyova saw it first.

She was waiting for the *Infinity* to finish her off; watching the vast conic form of the vessel, dark as night, visible only because it blocked starlight, edging closer towards her with sharklike deliberation. Doubtless somewhere in its hugeness, systems were pondering over the matter of how to expedite her death in the most interesting manner. That was the only explanation for why it had not already killed her, since she was within strike-range of every one of its weapons. Perhaps Sun Stealer's presence aboard the ship had given it a kind of sick sense of humour; a desire to put her to death with sadistic slowness; a process that commenced with this deathly wait for something to happen. Her imagination was now her worst enemy, efficiently reminding her of all the systems which might suit Sun Stealer's purpose; the defences which could boil her over hours, or dismember her without killing her immediately (lasers which were tuned to cauterise flesh, for instance), or crush her (a squad of external servitors, for instance). Oh, the processes of her mind were a glorious thing. And it was, by and large, that same fertility which had given rise to so many possible modes of execution.

But then she saw it.

The flash, sparking from the surface of Cerberus, briefly marking the spot where the bridgehead was installed. It was as if, for a split second, a tremendous light had ignited within the world, only to be immediately dimmed.

Or a tremendous explosion.

She watched entrails of rock and scalded machinery puff into space.

Khouri took a moment to come to terms with the fact that she was not actually dead, despite the certainty she had felt that this would come to pass. At the very least, she had expected to wake transiently to pain, her last moments of consciousness before Hades pulled her apart; body and soul flensed by the monstrous talons of gravity around the neutron star. She had also expected to wake to the worst headache since the Mademoiselle had invoked her buried memories of the Dawn War. But this time it would be a headache of purely chemical origin.

They had found the drinks cabinet in the spider-room.

And they had drunk it empty.

But her head felt achingly clear of any intoxication, like a freshly scrubbed window. She had come to consciousness swiftly as well, with no groggy transition, as if there had been no existence in the instant before her eyes opened. But it was not in the spider-room. Now that she thought about it, she remembered waking; remembered the terrible onset of those tides; how she and Pascale had crawled to the midpoint of the room to lessen the differential stresses. But it had surely failed; they had known at that point there was no possible way to survive; that the only thing they could do was to somehow lessen the pain—

Where in hell's name was she?

She had awakened with her back against a hard surface, unyielding as concrete. Above, the stars cartwheeled with insane speed through the sky, and there was something wrong with the way they moved; as if seen through a thick lens which stretched from horizon to horizon. She found she could move and struggled to her feet, almost toppling back as she did so.

She was wearing a suit.

She had not been wearing one in the spider-room. It was the same kind that she had used during her surface activities on Resurgam; the same kind that Sylveste would have taken with him into Cerberus. How could this be? If this experience was a dream, then it was unlike any she had known, because she could consciously question its contradictions without the whole edifice crumbling around her.

She was on a plain. It was the colour of cooling metal; almost but not quite bright enough to hurt the eye. It was as flat as a beach after the tide had retreated. The plain, now that she looked at it more closely, was patterned; not randomly, but in the intricately ordered manner of a Persian carpet. Between each level of patterning was another, until the ordering teetered on the edge of the microscopic and probably plunged down to even smaller realms, towards the subnuclear and the quantum. And it was shifting; blurring in and out of focus, never the same from moment to moment. Eventually it started to make her feel vaguely unwell, so she snapped her attention away to the horizon.

It seemed very close indeed.

She started walking. Her feet crunched into the flickering ground. The patterns rearranged themselves to create smooth stepping stones where she could plant her feet.

Something lay ahead.

It rose above the close curve of the horizon: a slight mound, a raised plinth stark against the tumbling starscape. She approached it, and as she neared it she saw movement. The raised part was like the entrance to a subway, three low walls enclosing a series of descending steps, burrowing into the world.

The movement was a figure emerging from the depths; a woman. She heaved herself up the steps with strength and patience, as if she were taking the morning air for the first time. Unlike Khouri, she wore no spacesuit. In fact, she was dressed in exactly the way Khouri remembered her from the last time they were together.

It was Pascale Sylveste.

'I've been waiting a long time,' she said, her voice carrying across the airless black space between them.

'Pascale?'

'Yes,' she said, and then qualified herself. 'In a manner of speaking. Oh dear; this isn't going to be easy to explain – and I've had so long to rehearse it . . .'

'What happened, Pascale?' It seemed impudent to ask her why she wasn't wearing a suit; why she wasn't dead. 'Where is this?'

'Haven't you guessed yet?'

'Sorry to disappoint you.'

Pascale smiled sympathetically. 'You're on Hades. Remember that? The neutron star; the one which was pulling us in. Well, it wasn't. A neutron star, I mean.'

'On it?'

'On it, yes. I don't think you were expecting that.'

'No; you could say that.'

'I've been here as long as you have,' Pascale said. 'Which is only a few hours. But I've spent the time beneath the crust, where things happen a bit quicker. So it seems like considerably more than a few hours to me.'

'How much more?'

'Try a few decades . . . although time really doesn't pass at all here, in some respects.'

Khouri nodded, as if all this made perfect sense. 'Pascale . . . I think you need to explain . . .'

'Good idea. I'll do it on the way down.'

'The way down where?'

She beckoned Khouri towards the stairs which descended into the cherry-red plain, as if she were inviting a neighbour indoors for cocktails.

'Inside,' Pascale said. 'Into the matrix.'

Death had still not come.

Over the next hour, using the suit's image-zoom overlay, Volyova watched the bridgehead slowly lose its form, like a piece of pottery being inexpertly shaped. Gradually it began to dissolve into the crust. It was being digested, having finally lost the battle against Cerberus.

Too soon; too soon.

The wrongness of it gnawed into her. She might be about to die, but she did not like seeing one of her creations fail, and – dammit – fail so prematurely.

Finally, unable to take any more, she turned towards the ship, pointing towards her with daggerlike intent, and spread her arms wide. She had no idea if the ship was capable of reading her vocal transmissions.

'Come on then, *svinoi*. Finish me off. I've had enough. I don't want to see any more. Get it over with.'

A hatch opened somewhere down the ship's conic flank, briefly aglow with orange interior lighting. She half expected some nasty and dimly remembered weapon to cruise out; perhaps something she had knocked together in a spasm of drunken creativity.

Instead a shuttle emerged, and powered slowly towards her.

The way Pascale told it to Khouri, the neutron star was in fact nothing of the sort. Or at least it had been once, or would have been – had it not been for interference by some third party Pascale declined to talk about in any great detail. But the gist was simple. They had converted the neutron star into a giant, blindingly fast computer – one that, in some bizarre manner, was able to communicate with its own past and future selves.

'What am I doing here?' Khouri asked, as they descended the

stairway. 'No, better question: what are *we* doing here? And how do you know so much more than me all of a sudden?'

'I told you; I was in the matrix for longer.' Pascale paused on one of the steps. 'Listen, Khouri – you might not like what I'm about to tell you. Namely, that you're dead – for now, at least.'

Khouri was less surprised by this than she had expected. It seemed almost predictable.

'We died in the gravitational tides,' Pascale said matter-of-factly. 'We got too close to Hades, and the tides pulled us apart. It wasn't very pleasant, either – but most of your memories of it were never captured, so you don't recall them now.'

'Captured?'

'According to all the normal laws, we should have been crushed to atoms. And in a sense we were. But the information which described us was preserved in the flow of gravitons between what remained of us and Hades. The force that killed us also recorded us, transmitted that information to the crust . . .'

'Right,' Khouri said slowly, prepared to take this as given for the time being. 'And once we were transmitted into the crust?'

'We were – um – simulated back to life. Of course, computation in the crust happens much faster than realtime – which is why I've spent several decades of subjective time in it.'

She sounded almost apologetic.

'I don't remember spending several decades anywhere.'

'That's because you didn't. You were brought to life, but you didn't want to stay here. You don't remember any of that; you chose not to, in fact. There was nothing to keep you here.'

'Implying there was something to keep *you* here?'

'Oh yes,' Pascale said, with wonder. 'Oh yes. We'll come to that.'

The stairwell reached its foot now, leading into a lanterned corridor, bright with randomly strewn fairytale lights. The walls, when she looked at them, were alive with the same computational shimmer she had seen on the surface. An impression of intense busyness; of unguessably complex machine algebra constantly churning just beyond her reach.

'What am I?' Khouri said. 'What are you? You said I was dead. I don't feel it. And I don't feel like I'm being simulated in any matrix. I was out on the surface, wasn't I?'

'You're flesh and blood,' Pascale said. 'You died, and you were recreated. Your body was reconstructed from the chemical elements already present in the matrix's outer crust, and then you were reanimated, and quickened to consciousness. The suit you're wearing – that came from the matrix as well.'

'You mean someone wearing a suit got close enough to be killed by the tides?'

'No . . .' Pascale said carefully. 'No; there's another way into the matrix. A much easier way – or at least it once was.'

'I should still be dead. Nothing can live on a neutron star. Or in it, for that matter.'

'I told you; it isn't one.' And then she explained how it was possible; how the matrix itself was generating a pocket of tolerable gravity in which she could live; how it was achieved by the circulation deeper in the crust of awesome quantities of degenerate matter; perhaps as a computational by-product; perhaps not. But like a diverging lens, the flow focused gravity away from her, while equally ferocious forces kept the walls from crushing in at only fractionally less than the speed of light.

'What about you?'

'I'm not like you,' Pascale said. 'This body I'm wearing – that's all it is, something to puppet; something in which to meet you. It's formed from the same nuclear material as the crust. The neutrons are bound together by strange quarks, so I don't fly apart under my own quantum pressure.' She touched her forehead. 'But I'm not doing any thinking. That's going on all around you, in the matrix itself. You'll excuse me – and this is going to sound terribly rude – but I'd find it mind-numbingly boring if I was forced into doing nothing except talk to you. As I said, our computational rates are highly divergent. You're not offended, are you? I mean, it's nothing personal, I hope you understand.'

'Forget it,' Khouri said. 'I'm sure I'd feel the same.'

The corridor widened out now, into what seemed to be a well-appointed scientific study, from any time in the last five or six centuries. The room's predominant colour was brown, the brown of age: on the wooden shelves which ran along its walls, on the browning spines of the ancient paper books arrayed along those shelves, the lustrous brown of the mahogany desk, and the golden-brown metal of the antique scientific tools placed around the desk's periphery for effect. Wooden cabinets buttressed the walls which did not carry shelves, and in them hung yellowing bones;

alien bones which at first glance might be mistaken for the fossils of dinosaurs or large, extinct flightless birds, provided one did not pay undue attention to the capaciousness of the alien skull, the roominess of the mind it had surely once entrapped.

There were examples of modern apparatus too: scanning devices, advanced cutting instruments, racks of eidetics and holographic storage wafers. A servitor of intermediate modernity waited inertly in one corner, head slightly bowed, like a trusty retainer taking a well-earned snooze while still on his feet.

In one wall, slatted windows overlooked an arid, windswept terrain of mesas and precarious rock formations, bathed in the reddish light of a setting sun, already disappearing behind the chaotic horizon.

And at the desk – rising from it as they entered the room, as if disturbed from concentration – was Sylveste.

She looked into his eyes – human eyes – for the first time, in what passed for the flesh.

For a moment he looked annoyed by their intrusion, but his expression softened until half a smile played across his features. 'I'm glad you took the time to visit us,' he said. 'And I hope Pascale has explained all that you asked of her.'

'Most of it,' Khouri said, stepping further into the study, marvelling at the fastidiousness of its recreation. It was as good as any simulation she had ever experienced. Yet – and the thought was as impressive as it was frightening – every single object in this room was moulded from nuclear matter, at densities so large that, ordinarily, the smallest paperweight on his desk would have exerted a fatal gravitational pull, even from halfway across the room. 'But not all of it. How did you get here?'

'Pascale probably mentioned that there was another way into the matrix.' He offered her the palms of his hands. 'I found it, that's all. Passed through it.'

'And what happened to your . . .'

'My real self?' The smile had a quality of self-amusement now, as if he were enjoying some private joke too subtle to share. 'I doubt that he survived. And frankly, it doesn't really concern me. I'm the real me now. I'm all that I ever was.'

'What happened in Cerberus?'

'That's a very long story, Khouri.'

But he told her anyway. How he had travelled into the world;

how Sajaki's suit had turned out to be an empty shell; how that realisation had done nothing but strengthen his resolve to push on further, and what, finally, he had found, in the final chamber. How he had passed into the matrix – at which point, his memories diverged from his other self. But when he told her he was sure that his other self was dead, he did so with such conviction that Khouri wondered if there was not another way of knowing; if some other, less tangible bond had linked them, right until the end.

There were things even Sylveste did not really understand; that much she sensed. He had not achieved godhead – or at least, not for more than an instant, when he bathed in the portal. Had that been a choice he had made subsequently? she wondered. If the matrix was simulating him; and if the matrix was essentially infinite in its computational capacity ... what limits had been imposed on him, other than those he had consciously selected?

What she learnt was this: Carine Lefevre had been kept alive by part of the Shroud, but there had been nothing accidental about it.

'It's as if there were two factions,' Sylveste said, toying with one of the brass microscopes on his desk, angling its little mirror this way and that, as if trying to catch the last rays of the setting sun. 'One that wanted to use me to find out if the Inhibitors were still around, still capable of posing a threat to the Shrouders. And the other faction, which I don't think cared for humanity any more than the first. But they were more cautious. They thought there had to be a better way, other than goading the Inhibitor device to see if it still generated a response.'

'But what happens to us now? Who actually won? Was it Sun Stealer or the Mademoiselle?'

'Neither,' Sylveste said, placing the microscope back down again, its velvet base softly bumping against the desk. 'At least, that's my instinctual feeling. I think we – I – came close to triggering the device, close to giving it the stimulus it needed to alert the remaining devices and begin the war against humanity.' He laughed. 'Calling it a war implied it might have been a two-sided thing. But I don't think it would have been like that at all.'

'But you don't think it got that far?'

'I hope and I pray, that's all.' He shrugged. 'Of course, I could be wrong. I used to say I was never wrong about anything, but that's one lesson I have learnt.'

'And what about the Amarantin, the Shrouders?'

'Only time will tell.'

'That's all?'

'I don't have all the answers, Khouri.' He looked around the room, as if appraising the volumes on the shelves, reassuring himself that they were still present. 'Not even here.'

'It's time to go,' Pascale said, suddenly. She had appeared at her husband's side with a glass of something clear; vodka, maybe. She placed it on the desk, next to a polished skull the colour of parchment.

'Where?'

'Back into space, Khouri. Isn't that what you want? You surely don't want to spend the rest of eternity here.'

'There's nowhere to go,' Khouri said. 'You should know that, Pascale. The ship was against us; the spider-room destroyed; Ilia killed—'

'She made it, Khouri. She wasn't killed when the shuttle was destroyed.'

So she had managed to get into a suit – but what good did that do her? Khouri was about to question Pascale further, when she realised that whatever the woman told her was very likely to be true, no matter how unbelievable it seemed – and no matter how useless the truth, no matter how little difference it could possibly make.

'What are you two going to do?'

Sylveste reached for the vodka glass and took a discreet sip. 'Haven't you guessed yet? This room isn't just for your benefit. We inhabit it as well, except that we inhabit a simulated version in the matrix. And not just this room, but the rest of the base; just as it always was – except now we have it all to ourselves.'

'Is that all?'

'No . . . not quite.'

And then Pascale moved to his side and he put an arm around her waist and the two of them turned towards the slatted window; towards the red-drenched alien sunset, the arid landscape of Resurgam stretching away, lifeless.

And then it changed.

It began at the horizon; a sweeping wave of transformation which raced towards them with the speed of an oncoming day. Clouds burst into the sky, vast as empires; now the sky was bluer, even though the sun was still sinking towards dusk. And the landscape was no longer arid, but erupting into tumultuous greenery, a verdant tidal wave. She could see lakes, and trees, alien trees, and now roads, winding between egglike houses, clustered into hamlets and, on the horizon, a larger community, rising towards a single slender spire. She stared into the distance, and stared, struck dumb by the immensity of what she was seeing, which was an entire world returned to life, and – perhaps it was a trick of the eye; she would never know – she thought she saw them moving between the houses, moving with the speed of birds, but never leaving the ground; never reaching the air.

'Everything that they ever were,' Pascale said, 'or most of it, at any rate, is stored in the matrix. This isn't some archaeological reconstruction, Khouri. This *is* Resurgam, as they inhabit it now. Brought into being by sheer force of will, by those who survived. It's a whole world, down to the smallest detail.'

Khouri looked around the room, and now she understood. 'And you're going to study it, aren't you?'

'Not just study it,' Sylveste said, draining a little more of his vodka. 'But live in it. Until it bores us, which – I suspect – won't be any time now.'

And then she left them, in their study, to resume whatever deep and meaningful conversation they had put in abeyance while they entertained her.

She finished climbing the stairwell, stepping once more onto the surface of Hades. The crust was still aglow with red fire, still alive with computation. Now that she had been here for long enough to attune her senses, she realised that, all along, the crust had been drumming beneath her feet, as if a titanic engine were roaring in a basement. That, she supposed, was not far from the truth. It was an engine of simulation.

She thought of Sylveste and Pascale, commencing another day's exploration of their fabulous new world. In the time since she had left them, years might have passed for them. That seemed to matter very little. She had the suspicion that they would only choose death when all else had ceased to hold their fascination. Which, as Sylveste had said, was not going to happen any time soon.

She turned on the suit communicator.

'Ilia . . . can you hear me? Shit; this is stupid, but they said you might still be alive.'

There was nothing but static. Hopes crushed, she looked around at the searing plain and wondered what she was meant to do next.

Then: 'Khouri, is that you? What business have you got still being alive?'

There was something very odd about her voice. It kept speeding up and slowing down, like she was drunk, but too ominously regular for that.

'I could ask you the same thing. Last thing I remember is the shuttle going belly-up. You telling me you're still out there, drifting?'

'Better than that,' Volyova said, voice whooshing up and down the spectrum. 'I'm aboard a shuttle; do you hear that? I'm aboard a shuttle.'

'How the—'

'The ship sent it. The *Infinity*.' For once, Volyova sounded breathless with excitement; as if this was something she had been desperately anxious to tell someone. 'I thought it was going to kill me. That's all I was waiting for; that final attack. But it didn't come. Instead, the ship sent out a shuttle for me.'

'This doesn't make any sense. Sun Stealer should still be running it; should still be trying to finish us off . . .'

'No,' Volyova said, still with the same tone of childish delight, 'no; it makes perfect sense – provided what I did worked, which I think it must have—'

'What did you do, Ilia?'

'I – um – let the Captain warm.'

'You did *what*?'

'Yes; it was rather a terminal approach to the problem. But I thought if one parasite was trying to gain control of the ship, the surest way to fight it was by unleashing an even more potent one.' Volyova paused, as if awaiting Khouri's confirmation that this had indeed been a sensible thing to do. When none came, she continued, 'This was barely a day ago – do you know what that means? The plague must have transformed a substantial mass of the ship in only a few hours! The speed of the transformation must have been incredible; centimetres a second!'

'Are you sure it was wise?'

'Khouri, it's probably the least wise thing I've ever done in my life. But it does seem to have worked. At the very least, we've swapped one megalomaniac for another – but this one doesn't seem quite so dedicated to our destruction.'

'I guess that's a step in the right direction. Where are you now? Have you been back aboard yet?'

'Hardly. No, I've spent the last few hours searching for you. Where the hell are you, Khouri? I can't seem to get a meaningful fix on your location.'

'You don't really want to know.'

'Well, we'll see. But I want you aboard this ship as soon as possible. I'm not going back into the lighthugger alone, in case you had any doubts. I don't think it's going to look quite the way we remembered it. You – uh – can reach me, can't you?'

'Yes, I think so.'

Khouri did what she had been told she should do, when she wanted to leave the surface of Hades. It made very little sense, but Pascale had been quite insistent – she had said it was a message that the matrix would understand; one that would cause it to project its bubble of low-field gravity into space; a bottle in which she could ride to safety.

She spread arms wide, as if she had wings; as if she could fly.

The red ground – fluctuating, shimmering as ever – dropped smoothly away.